CRIME BY DESIGN
OMNIBUS 1

Books 1-3 in one volume

JANE THORNLEY

Riverflow Press

CRIME BY DESIGN, THE PREQUEL

ROGUE WAVE

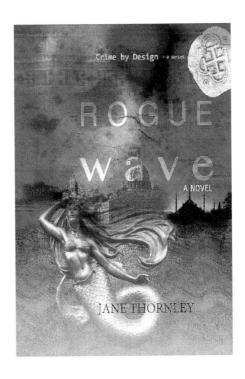

ROGUE WAVE

I

The bitter Nor'easter shoved me downhill. Once the package slipped from my fingers and slid two feet down, forcing me to stop long enough to retrieve it. Only then did I risk checking behind me: nobody following except freezing office workers dashing for cover.

I kept moving through the icy wind until I reached my Jeep. Popping the lock, I tossed the box along with my bag onto the passenger seat and leapt inside just as the squall whipped up a fury. For a moment, I sat suspended in the center of a snowy vortex. Turning on the ignition with the heater blasting, I blew onto my fingers while the adrenalin percolated through my bloodstream like jolts of espresso.

Little did I know it at the time, but I had just made my first foray into a life of crime. Me, the half-baked lawyer with a degree in art history and a heart filled with noble intentions had just let myself down, way down.

The whiteout continued while I stared out towards Halifax Harbor, everything beyond the windshield bleached and bitter. Seeking relief, I gazed at the rich reds of my battered Turkish carpet bag, well-padded by my latest knitting project, before plunging my hand into its innards seeking my cell phone. With the phone to my ear, I pressed my friend's number and waited.

"Nancy Mahoney, Attorney at Law. Sorry I missed your call. Please leave a message—"

I stabbed a key and jumped to voice mail. "Nancy, it's Phoebe. Please call me as soon as you get a chance. I just committed a misdemeanor. I—"

She picked up before I made it to the next sentence. "What misdemeanor?"

"Petty theft, I guess, only I'm not sure who was pettier, me or Julie. She's divorcing Bob and closing Global Threads, but forgot to mention it until today. I've been amputated like a spare limb. No warning, no heads-up, just a 'get-out-of-my-face-I'm-upset' attitude." I slowed myself down with a deep breath. "So, being the adult I am, I took it badly and, in the end, just took it." I sighed. "Am I making sense?"

"Yes and no. The 'it' being *Tide Weaver*, I presume?" said my friend in a voice of melodious calm.

"Exactly."

Nancy, always my anchor and source of reason, replied. "Put your emotions aside for the moment and think. So, you've been laid off, hit the rage button, and reacted without thinking. You're human. Rise above it. Remember that Julie's in chaos herself. Divorce can do that to anyone. Go back to her, apologize, and return the tapestry. I understand it's important to you, but we can go after it through legal means just as efficiently."

"But not as quickly." Waves of calm emanated from the phone, but my energy stormed with rage and grief. "Time is running out for Dad. That doesn't make a shred of difference to Julie. She's all about money. No, I'm taking the hanging back to Dad today. He needs to see all that color, a little piece of Toby and Mom, to keep his spirits buoyed, especially now. He needs it to ease his pain, Nancy."

"And maybe you need it to ease yours?"

"So? My bloodline's embedded in those fibers. She could have offered it to me in lieu of severance pay but refused."

Nancy took a deep breath. "Severance pay? You're not thinking clearly. You were only working part-time, remember? We'll get that tapestry for you, just not like this. Take it back. It's stolen property. You know the law as well as I do."

That might have been true once but since I walked out in the middle of my bar exam, it no longer applied. Still, a thief was still a thief. "Thanks for listening," I said. "I just needed to confess my sins. Otherwise, I'll live with my decision."

"That's not a decision, that's an impulse." Nancy had grown accustomed to providing me with advice I rarely followed. "Ask yourself what you really want out of life and whether this act brings you closer."

Sometimes Nancy sounded like a cross between Oprah and Mother Teresa, the only cross-denominational, deeply spiritual working lawyer in existence, as far as I knew.

I gazed out at a seagull pecking at an upturned carton of fries in the parking lot. What did I really want out of life? Once I could answer that absolutely, though in mundane terms: an exciting career, love, maybe a great place to live. Now, though I still craved all of those things, I wanted them with a hundred caveats like maybe excitement, a sense of purpose, a chance to live in the world of art and history. I watched the gull gulp a whole fry, his white neck undulating with effort.

"I want a new life," I said, finally.

"If the Universe registers that, you're in for a ride," Nancy said.

And then my phone vibrated, announcing an in-coming call from FAIRY GODFATHER. "Nancy, it's Max on the other line. Finally."

"You'd better get it, then. Talk later."

I pressed END and then TALK. "Max? Why haven't you returned my messages? Where are you, anyway?"

The familiar Australian accent rumbled into my ear. "Phoebe, love, sorry I couldn't get to you sooner but I've been tied up. You all right?"

I leaned back against the seat, my cell phone pressed against my ear. Outside, the squall had diminished to a swirl of ice crystals. "It's not like you not to respond right away. I thought something was wrong." Anxiety had become my constant companion.

"I've been tracking down Toby, like I promised."

My breath caught. "And?"

"And I've found something ."

I leaned forward, resting my head against the steering wheel. I couldn't believe it. At last, at last. "Is he all right?"

He paused. "No details over the phone. It's complicated. We'll need to meet. I'll set something up."

"Is he in some kind of trouble again?" Just like my brother to get snarled in something murky. Still, I'd like to wring his neck for putting Dad and me through all this crap. It had been 10 weeks with no word. He rarely fell off-grid for more than a week at a time. "Are you here in Nova Scotia?"

"No, but I'll bring you to me. Meanwhile, got to know if you'll do what it takes to help find your brother."

I stilled, gazing at the dashboard in disbelief. "What kind of question is that? Of course, I will."

"Had to ask. So, do as I say?"

"I don't do what anybody says without information. Is Toby into something?"

"No questions asked, I said. It has to be that way. You'll understand better once we talk in person."

"Where is he? Surely you can tell me that much?"

"Listen carefully. Go to your father's cottage and look for something Toby may have hidden there. I have no idea what exactly but you'll know it's important when you see it. I have reason to believe it could be a clue to his disappearance."

"Are you kidding me? Toby hasn't been back to see Dad for months."

"He made a surprise visit weeks before he disappeared. I know, I didn't realize that, either, until a few days ago. Go there now and poke around. Don't tell your father what you're up to. Don't even mention my name, understand?"

As if I would. My godfather's name had become a no-fly zone in the McCabe household and I had no idea why. He was supposedly part of the family but now I couldn't speak his name. How I hated secrets. They throttled the life out of you and left you hanging in the wind. "What happened between you two? "

"Phoebe—"

"Okay, so I go down and look for some unidentified hidden object that may connect to my missing brother in some unexplained way but can't tell Dad because you two aren't talking. I'm on my way."

"You knew Toby as well as anyone. Use that to search, okay?"

My heart caught in my throat. "You said 'knew,' not 'know'."

"Just a slip of the tongue, darling. No worries. I'll call later."

2

A bleak wash of sea and sky came along for the ride that afternoon as I followed the St. Margaret's Bay road along the ragged Nova Scotian coastline. A grey pall had settled in behind the snow, leaving the world a seamless blur of white and grey melting into the water's churlish blue. Both the highway and my thoughts ran parallel, twisting in and out of the icy fog.

All the places where I grieved or fretted lay along that route—the little church tucked into a hillside above the cove where we'd held Mom's funeral, the stretches of beach I walked after Toby disappeared, plus this road that I'd driven countless times back and forth delivering both parents to city hospitals. Funny thing, my life to that point had really been more joy than sorrow but these days I only remembered the fog.

The sun sagged in cloud by the time I rounded the bend to the little beach community where I grew up. My family home perched on a low rise across the one-lane highway, facing a curve of stony beach. Once a clapboard cottage painted a bright blue, it had so many extensions added over the years that it now looked like like a small hotel.

I parked the Jeep beside Dad's old Dodge truck, tucked the carton under one arm, and climbed the path, my boots crunching clumps of melting slush. A round woman in a maroon puffer coat emerged from the front door and waited on the steps, a laundry basket in her hands.

"Mrs. Hugli, hi," I greeted. "How's Dad today?"

Dad's housekeeper and sometime caregiver smiled. "One of his better days, overall. You're timing's perfect. I just made a big casserole, so help yourself. He's settling in with the evening news." Her face briefly bloomed into a smile.

"Not too curmudgeonly?"

"I didn't say that," she said with a laugh. "Some things never change." As my father's next-door neighbor, she had known the family for over 30 years and I was endlessly grateful that she kept an eye on him considering the pittance Toby and I paid.

"Thanks for everything, Mrs. Hugli, for always and forever," I slapped one hand over my heart and put one foot on the step.

"Phoebe, wait."

I froze.

"I wanted to talk to you about the always and forever part. It's just that I don't know how much longer I can keep doing this. I'm not getting any younger, either. It's not the money, you know. I don't care about that."

I sighed. "Yes, of course. Dad's getting on your last nerve."

"Have you thought about having him come live in the city with you, maybe go into a home?"

"Yes, the way one considers establishing world peace and ending hunger. In other words, I do what I can but don't expect miracles. He refuses to leave."

"Right," she said, shaking her head. "When pigs fly."

"Exactly."

"But he's soon going to need someone with him 24/7. You know that. Keep trying, that's all I ask. As long as you're working on it, I'll do the best I can." She gave me a heartening pat on the arm as she pushed past. I watched her trudge down the path, the sleeve of one of Dad's flannel shirts dangling from the basket in a limp wave.

Dad would never leave this place, at least not willingly. Removing him from his home would be like prying a barnacle from a rock only to find it fixed even tighter two seconds later. Could I bear to return to take care of him? How much courage did it take to face a past with no future, anyway?

Pushing the door open, I entered the little vestibule and kicked off my boots, hung up my coat, and stepped into the kitchen. The endless clash of colors from my mother's folk art-meets-department-store decorating scheme warmed my heart while the wood stove toasted everything else.

My mother had loved color and, though her works involved carefully planned and executed compositions, here the decor ran riot. FiestaWare sat stacked on organic earth mugs; jubilant floral curtains danced across the windows; a hooked rug tossed little boats among waves of cobalt blue. No cohesion, just joyous color. "Kitchens are where the house lives," she had said, "and shouldn't be designed so much as celebrated."

I smiled and stepped towards the stove, hands extended to the warmth. Despite all the modern appliances like an electric stove and a heat pump, my family always kept an old-fashioned wood stove to ward away the winter freeze. It was like a point of honor with my parents.

How many times had my brother and I devoured cookies and milk after school in this very room, chattering while Mom bustled around the kitchen? We had once been so close, two siblings clinging to one another by virtue of our existence on the fringes of school life, oddballs in the adolescent game. Then four years between us stretched into empty air. After my brother moved away, traveling around the world as a talented dilettante delving into computer gaming, graphics, and who knows what else, our lives occasionally intersected but seldom merged.

I could hear the television droning away in the den. I sat the package down on the freshly-wiped pine table while scanning the kitchen, taking in dishes drying in the rack, fresh-baked cookies cooling on the counter, and the underlying scent of possible lasagna. If I closed my eyes, I could almost believe that Mom still lived, Toby only an email away, and life remained captured in the amber of perfect memory, my family intact forever. Only, reality always waited to ambush me.

Now supper called, my stomach rumbling as I located the casserole cooling under tin foil on the counter. Slipping a chunk of lasagna onto my plate, I sat down to eat. I would have gobbled shoelaces coated in plastic right then, since I hadn't eaten since breakfast, but Bertha Hugli happened to be a fabulous cook like my mother, the two having traded recipes years ago.

"Dad?" I called out as I picked up my fork.

"Phoebe, is that you?" There was nothing wrong with his hearing. He shuffled into the kitchen and stopped, feigning shock. "What? You're going to stuff your face before giving your old man a hug?"

"Sorry." I got to my feet and gave him a big one, the kind the McCabes bestowed upon each other since the beginning of time. Dad always gave the best , in this case scrunching my face deep into the scratchy wool of the Aran sweater Mom knit decades ago.

"You must have ESP. Been thinking about you all day. Lord, it's good to see you. It's been so long. Why is my own daughter a stranger these days?" he said, giving me another fierce squeeze for good measure.

I pulled away, laughing. "I was here only last weekend, which happens to be only four days ago."

"What? Seems longer. So, you want tea with that?"

"Sure, but I'll make it." I moved towards the stove.

"You will not. Do you think I can't make my own daughter damn tea when she visits? That Bertha comes in here all the time cooking, cleaning, banging around here as if I can't take care of myself. Sit down and finish your supper. I'll make the tea."

I returned to my seat, trying not to watch his every move while I gobbled up the last of the casserole. He moved slowly but with traces of the old energy still visible in the way he plucked a mug off the hook or banged the stainless kettle down on the stovetop. Dad making a point communicated "I can still do any damn thing I did before and don't you forget it, little girl." Klunk. Despite a heart attack he'd suffered the year Mom died and the stroke after Toby disappeared plus all the troubles in between, he still looked younger than 85 with his gray beard trimmed neatly around a sturdy chin and blue eyes sparkling with feisty humor or just plain bad temper, take your pick.

Once he had been so witty, handsome, and sexy in that man-at-the-helm-of-a-ship way. Mom said that he'd swept her art student self off her feet and lured her to his sea shanty home—the siren myth reversed. She claimed she'd been smitten beyond reason.

The wall phone shook my reverie. Dad swung around, sugar bowl in hand, eyes alert and eager. "Toby?"

I reached for the phone, heart twisting with his. How many times had hope struck with the ring of a phone? Desperation and hope had conjoined in the McCabe family.

"Hi, Phoebe," Mrs. Hugli said into my ear, "I forgot to mention that your Dad's upped and locked the door of Toby's room."

My heart fell. "I'll take care of it, thanks, Mrs. Hugli."

I replaced the receiver. "Not Toby. Sorry, Dad."

He, turned his back to me. "That Bertha again?" he asked, banging a tin on the counter where he proceeded to scoop sugar into a bowl. "What does that meddling woman want this time?"

"She says you've locked Toby's room."

"Sure, I did. She has no business sneaking around in there."

"That's called cleaning," I pointed out.

"Same thing for her. I don't want her in there and that's that. You want cookies with your tea?"

When Dad locked the door on a topic, it would take heaven and the seven seas to pry it open. He'd close in on himself, boiling with emotional currents and dark thoughts he'd never share. The only one who could ever pry him open was Mom.

I swallowed hard and shook my head.

"How's your boyfriend, whatshisname?" Dad asked, moving about the kitchen tidying.

"Christian. We're done." This wasn't the first time he'd been told that. I ended the Christian thing months ago.

"Oh, good. Never liked him. Had too high an opinion of himself. What else is new?"

"As of today, I'm no longer working at Global Threads," I said. "Julie and I parted company earlier, rather dramatically."

Dad swung around. "Well, hell's bells, it's about time. I never did like her or that Mr. Big husband of hers. You should have left long ago. Did you quit?"

"Ex Mr. Big husband. They're getting a divorce. I got laid off." Axed, more like it. Blindsided. Forget all the promises for work-in-kind compensation.

"Those two deserved each other like two crabs at a tea party. You stayed too long, anyway. I'm glad you left."

"But staying all that time was easy." Everything else took too much effort, too much risk. After I'd given up on being an international lawyer specializing in stolen art, what else was there?

"You can do much better."

"I know that," I said with a sigh, "but I loved that job for a while. It was the perfect reprieve from years of studying." In a better economy, Julie and Bob had brought in some of the most luscious yarn and fabrics from all over the world —Chinese silks, Italian blends. Mom used to buy all her stuff from them. With my urging, they had begun adding textile art, even antique tribal rugs Max had help me source. In fact, the Fairy Godfather had magically sent a few impressive customers our way to purchase the very pieces he supplied. Four years ago, surrounded by beautiful textiles and yarn, Global Threads had been my sweet spot. After things began unraveling, I had no idea what else to do.

Dad poured boiling water into the pot and shoved one of Mom's knitted tea cozies over all. "Don't you worry, dear. With your skills and qualifications, you'll find something better."

A half-baked lawyer with a Masters' in Art History who'd just dawdled away years selling yarn and old rugs didn't exactly attract headhunters. "Sure."

"You want one of them cookies with that?" He slid some of the chocolate chip goodies onto a plate and sat it down on the table across from me.

I shook my head. "First, I want to show you something. I brought you a present."

Dad's gaze swung from my face to the box and back again. "That?" he asked.

I nodded, clearing the plates and cutlery to the counter. "Hang on a minute. This needs room to breathe."

Dad had the carton open and removed the folded piece without a clue as to its contents.

"Allow me."

He passed me folded cloth, perplexed. I stepped back and carefully unfurled the tapestry across the table.

A sudden, inexplicable surge of joy stirred me, the same impact I experienced time after time. The 6'x3' piece flowed across our table in a swirl of blue-green blending with captured light. Rolling waves worked in silk and wool leaped and curled before the eye, the sea swallowing all but the top one-third where eight inches of sky melded from dawn to moonlight, left to right, burnished gold to deep silver-haloed ultramarine. Light streaming through the inner curve of the wave tops shimmered in turquoise and green silk, the threads so expertly worked, they glowed.

As the eye traveled below, the wonders only intensified. The sea of life, teaming with fish, mammals, coral reefs, and two gilded merpeople hovering over a treasure chest glinting with riches, were all fashioned in a smaller thread count with surface embroidery adding richness to the tiniest detail. And the colors! Delicate yet vibrant, we had hand-dyed most of the shades ourselves, and the gilded thread came all the way from England. Nothing but the perfect nuance would do.

The *Tide Weaver* wove together strands of the McCabe family's inner world and our collective imaginations. Toby and I were the merpeople based on a fairytale Mom read to us as kids. We embraced the image of creatures at home at sea yet craving another dimension to which they could never belong. We made it our own. Toby and I had designed the scene, Toby sketching the drawing, me painting it, and my mother, a master weaver, working it into being right here in this very house.

As a journey of life and art, it had taken five years with me running back and forth from university in town and Toby flying in from wherever whenever. We should never have sold it. Why had we? Because Mom had so wanted the endorsement the piece would bring hanging in a gallery and I could survive parting with it as long as it hung over my head in the place where I worked. I fingered the golden mermaid charm hanging from my neck, lost in a sea of memories.

A snuffling noise pulled me from my reverie. Dad stood wiping his eyes on the back of his sleeve.

"Oh, Dad, I'm sorry!" I ran to hug him. "I forgot how it might hurt you to see this again but—"

"Put it away," he growled, pain turning to anger or some other emotion I couldn't identify. "I don't want to see that thing again. Put it away."

I stopped steps away from him, bewildered. "What?"

"Get rid of it," he told me, shoving the carton at me.

"Get rid of it? Dad, this is Mom's work, Toby's, and my design—your family!"

"I don't care. Just get rid of it. Hide it if you have to." And with that, he swung around and lumbered back into the den, leaving me stupefied.

EVEN DAD'S NOTORIOUS TEMPER DID NOT EXPLAIN THIS OUTBURST. Tears I could understand, not fury. I expected joy or maybe relief, solace— something, anything but rage. It had to be his illness and, again, the impact of loss punched me in the gut.

Once he'd calmed down, I joined him in the den, knitting while he watched the news, my brain churning. I'd packed the tapestry away in Mom's studio until I could figure out what to do next and along the way, tried Toby's door—locked, just as Bertha said, secured by a clunky industrial padlock of questionable vintage. Bewildering. I decided then and there to stay the night, holed up on my narrow bed in my old room next door until I could get to the bottom of this, or at least, search the cottage for whatever Max sought.

I sat, deep into my memories, knitting long drop stitches into free-form waves that had begun turquoise but now brooded into a deep, moody blue. These days, I saw the irregular rise and fall of wave-like stitches as a metaphor for my life: erratic but with some mysterious rhythm I had yet to grasp. If the piece grew into a wrap or a scarf or a something else, I'd be fine with that, just as long as it kept moving forward. That's all that mattered.

"Dad," I ventured. "I hope you don't plan on keeping me out of Toby's room along with Bertha Hugli?"

Without taking his eyes from the History Channel where he was watching reruns, he said, "Why do you want to go in there, anyway?"

"Why would you ever want to keep me out? I miss him, too," I said over the moderator's voice describing an ancient Etruscan tomb.

When he didn't respond, I studied him. Yes, my father had gone under again but his face registered something I couldn't identify. Fear? That made sense since fear had garroted our emotions since Toby disappeared, but something else brewed there, too. I just didn't understand what. Confusion from his deteriorating health? My poor, dear father. "Dad?"

"I love you, you know that," he muttered, still not looking at me.

"And I love you, too, but what's that got to do with it?"

"I just want that room kept locked for now. It's trouble. Stay out if it."

"What? I don't understand."

"Stay out of it, I said. Maybe I lost one child but I won't be losing another one."

Damn it. That family secret again. How long would my life be held hostage by that? I stabbed my needle into my wrap to anchor my stitches, struck again by how quickly things were changing . It felt as though my hands were struggling to hold onto a sandy beach while the tide hauled me further into the deep. "What are you hiding from me, Dad? In fact, what have you been hiding for the last two decades? I'm an adult, remember? I have a right to know."

"I'm not hiding anything."

"Then tell me why won't you talk to Uncle Max anymore?"

"He's not your uncle and don't you forget it. Your mother and I should never have agreed to let him be your godfather, either. Now, don't go mentioning his name in this house again."

I soldiered on. "Dad, a pall of secrecy has dominated this house since I was a kid. It began the day I came home from school to find a strange man in the kitchen." Max Baker, a tall Australian with a sense of foreign climes hanging off him like exotic aftershave, no more fit our little kitchen back then than the new stainless steel dishwasher that arrived shortly afterwards.

"I don't want to talk about that, I said."

"Dad, I need to know. It's important. Just tell me what an urbane Australian really wanted with the fisherman and why the two of you would stay up all night whispering while we kids had to stay in our rooms? Tell me what Max really wanted with a smelly workhorse lobster boat and why you eventually sold her, complete with coveted license, to buy some sleek new cabin cruiser?"

"What are you talking about?" he turned towards me, face flushed and eyes puzzled. "You know why I bought *The Merry Day.*"

"The Merry Dance. Right, to take tourists on supposed joyrides up and down the coast—like I believed that. There was more to it, Dad, and I need to know what."

My father just stared at me as if struggling to remember. I watched the expression in his eyes alter as if he had found something tucked deep in his memory that surfaced long enough to startle him and disappeared again. He looked away. "Did I tell you that there's a new cafe in Hubbards? One of those yuppie places looking to serve gourmet hamburgers?"

I sank back into my seat. Whether Dad had lost certain details of our past life or chose not to remember them, the results were the same. He wouldn't or couldn't tell me, leaving a huge vacuum in my family history I might never be able to fill. With Toby missing, the chasm yawned deeper.

As the night wore on, Dad and I bided the time making small-talk during commercials as the news ran into a sitcom followed by a string of his favorite television shows. We discussed possible job options for me, the escalating price of electricity, and the new cafe Sheldon MacDonald had opened in Hubbards . No mention of Max, Toby, or the family secret crossed my lips again.

At ten o'clock sharp, he shuffled to his feet. "I'm off to bed, Sweet-heart. You'll turn off the lights, won't you?"

"I will," I said, rising to give him a hug.

"Good to have you here with me, you know. I get lonely without your mother."

That's the way it was with him: growling one minute, hugging the next.

"I know, Dad."

I sat knitting for a while with the television turned off and nothing but the subtle sound of the sea beyond. At times like these, I felt the ocean flowing in my veins, connecting me to the great beyond, the sense of being a single molecule amid a zillion, bringing the illusion of cohesion to my fractured life.

With yarns the colors of the chill Atlantic, I made long freeform drop stitches across my rows, the yarns suspended in some kind of life-line I wished reality would provide. Something rhythmic in working with fiber always soothed me in some profound way as if my hands reached deep inside the ocean and dropped an anchor of calm. I'd forget pain, loss, and survival, surrendering to a moment where only yarn and I existed in our own perfect world.

Dad's snoring began disturbing the peace at around ten thirty. It occurred to me somewhere between a yarn change, that soon enough even my father would be gone. What had begun as a bright, vibrant, turquoise began muting down into deep, moody blue. It was as though my life was slowly being drained of everyone I loved, all the threads unraveling, all colors blurring from joy to sorrow.

At around quarter to eleven, I reluctantly set my half-born wrap aside in a jumble of wavy patterns and plucked my cell phone from my bag. Four missed calls and many more text messages leapt on the little screen. I girded my loins and began scanning:

JULIE: missed call.

JULIE: missed call.

JULIE: Phoebe, tell me you didn't just do what I think you did? Call me.

JULIE: Phoebe, bring it back now and I promise to forget you ever took it. CALL ME!

JULIE: Phoebe, please. Let's talk. Bring it back and we'll work something out, I promise. Look, I sold it, okay? The Bank of Montreal offered a nice price so we let it go. It's supposed to be delivered later today. CALL ME, WILL YOU?

JULIE: Are you out of your —— mind?? That's theft and you can bet your ass I won't let you get away with it. Call me before I call the police!

JULIE: missed call.

I took a deep breath and let my gaze sail up to the whitewashed ceiling. She sold it. She sold my mother's tapestry and lied about that along with everything else. Could I trust anyone? I returned to my scanning.

NANCY: Are you okay, my friend? I sense darkness around you.

I texted a brief reply: You sense right but I will prevail. I'll phone today (your today. You'll be sleeping now) I'm at Dad's. XXX Phoebe

FAIRY GODFATHER: Any luck in your hunt?

FAIRY GODFATHER: Are you at the cottage now?

I messaged back: Max, yes, I'm at Dad's. Will text as soon as I finish searching. What am I looking for?

Slipping the phone in my pocket, the ringer still set on mute, I stood listening to my father's sonorous breathing while attempting to climb inside my brother's mind. If he tried to hide something in the cottage, that is, if he would ever do such a thing, where? And, perhaps the more fitting question would be why? What kind of trouble could my brother get into, anyway? Though an artist by nature and a computer graphics genius by profession, his inclination swerved to living on the edge mostly through imagination. The games he created, the ones that lined his pockets, featured warriors plunging into fantasy worlds populated by monsters and bizarre creatures. I could only pray the dangers remained imaginary.

And where would he hide something worth hiding? Certainly not anywhere my father regularly inhabited. Maybe his bedroom room or Mom's studio.

I left the den and entered the next room, the door creaking open into a shadowy world where a huge loom half-lit by the deck light held court. The wall on one side held bins of yarn and tools, the other three nothing but broad windows with more storage shelves against the floor. The unheated space stood chill and still, its warmth having left with its queen years ago.

Much like all the other once-owned rooms under this roof, Dad never infringed on the spaces of those dead or elsewhere. He kept every room intact as a way to keep us close. Every time I visited, I'd enter this room as a kind of homage to my mom. I'd sit and mourn, remembering the days when mother and daughter conjured some textile feat in our creative togetherness. "Phoebe , dear, what do you think of this idea?" or "Let's make a dye as rich and red as all the carpets in the Ottoman Empire!"

Dad built this studio for her. He used to joke that he'd made his biggest catch on his wedding day. At first glance, the pairing of an art student and a lobster fisherman may have seemed peculiar but Ariadne Bracket had a long-standing romance with the sea and, Dad, in his youth, had been passionate, inquisitive, charming, and worthy of sweeping any woman off her land-locked pins.

I stood in the darkness smiling, running down the inner corridors of a happier life. Enough. I had work to do, but even before I began rummaging half-heartedly through the drawers and yarn bins, I knew absolutely that Toby would never hide anything here. He would see it as an affront to our mother. I left the bins and shelves and backed away.

Dad's snoring rumbled through the house as I began hunting for the padlock key. He used to keep keys and change in a jar by the wood stove but no such jar existed now. I dove into the pockets of his jackets hanging in the hall, fingering nails, rubber bands, and candy so old, they'd gummed to the wrappers. No key. I rifled through the kitchen in every drawer, box, bottle, and jar I could lay my hands on with no luck. I concluded he must have stashed the key somewhere in his room, which I absolutely would not penetrate.

Weary now, I wandered into the kitchen to make a cup of tea. Dad must have tidied up while I was off stashing the tapestry because the dishes had been put away. I stood leaning against the counter, wondering again what Max thought Toby might hide, here of all places, while the tea steeped and I ruminated.

I opened the cupboard and found all the dirty mugs shelved among the clean, went to the fridge to grab the milk and found the sugar bowl instead. A few seconds later, I retrieved the milk carton from another cupboard and fished a single key from the sugar bowl.

It was the padlock key. I broke down and cried.

IN TOBY'S ROOM LATER, I SAT MY MUG ON HIS DRESSER AND FLICKED ON the overhead light. My brother's teenage world jumped into high relief in posters and paintings, all his early work, many pieces of which Mom had framed. Sweeping canvases where painted sunsets sent shots of color across our local beachfront rose above many smaller vistas, some traditional, some abstract, some outright whimsical, all drawing me back into what had once been our shared world.

His talent circa age 19 hinted of all my brother would become. Even here he revealed a strong, energetic exploration of many mediums —oil, watercolor, acrylic, and mixed media—which would eventually morph into computer animations. Though his strokes were bold, he could also work with amazing delicacy and tenderness, a tenderness that left him vulnerable on the schoolyard where boys measure their worth in bravado and testosterone rather than art and design.

My gaze landed on the merman, *his* merman, a three-foot high he-fish with a brawny torso, long red hair, and a blue-green tail, a merry caricature self-portrait of Toby the artist. The companion piece, the mermaid, hung in my room, my fifteenth birthday present, painted gold, ultra-female in shape, with long hair and a seashell bra. I still imagined myself that way: the queen of her own domain, free to follow her heart wherever it may lead.

Those two images became symbolic for how we once saw ourselves as brother and sister in our early years: two fish out of water, afloat in our own imaginative worlds surrounded by the treacherous nets of secrecy. Just standing there almost broke my heart. *Toby, where are you?*

I began searching in all the usual places, in drawers and under the bed. My mother had packed many of Toby's things in boxes stashed in the closet so I unpacked all of those, finding nothing but old clothes. I looked behind the paintings, feeling around for taped keys or messages or something, anything. How did I know what to look for? I thought perhaps a key or maybe a letter might be significant, but nothing like that remained anywhere in Toby's domain.

The only thing I came across was Toby's sketch for *Tide Weaver* stored in a roll of painted white poster paper, which had once hung behind Mom's loom to serve as the "cartoon" design guide. For some reason, the piece had been stuffed in a mailing tube and wedged high over the bed in a narrow slot formed between the cottage's original rafter roof and the newer ceiling. As far as I knew, I was the only one who knew of the hidey-hole's existence, Toby having long ago made me swear never to reveal his secret place.

I pulled the tightly rolled paper from the tube and spread its stiff, watercolor-painted surface across the bed. It was an exact duplicate of the weaving and, as such, struck me anew with its vibrancy, even though the painting had suffered over the years. Despite being tucked away in a tube, it had been torn and cracked. Toby seemed to have attempted to strengthen the flimsy paper by backing it with a few additional layers, which he sealed to the original by taping the edges.

By then, I was so tired, I just replaced the cartoon in its tube and took it with me as I headed for bed.

That night, I dreamt our cottage rocked and rolled far out to sea. Huge waves crashed against the walls, sloshing through the open windows and running icy currents across the floors. I struggled out of bed, sinking up to my ankles in running water sluicing back and forth across the floor. I knew I had to find something of value but wasn't sure where to begin. I needed fins, I realized. I needed a magic tail that would propel me deeper and farther than I could otherwise travel.

When my eyes opened, I sat blinking into the dark. Home, I realized, as in childhood home, and I was sitting in bed, not standing in water. My phone's light illuminated my room. Throwing off the covers, I padded over to my dresser and plucked up the phone. Max had texted me: "Check your email. I just sent you a ticket to Bermuda. Meet me there tomorrow night."

I texted back: "I'll come providing you promise to answer every question I ask."

The response came the next morning. "A deal."

※ 3 ※

I stood in the living room of the Astwood Cove cottage taking in the
Colonial tropical tourist decor. Rattan and bamboo accessorized by
potted palms and lots of polished mahogany created a cosy "Eng-
lishman in the tropics" ambience. I missed home already. Though I appreciated the bowls of hibiscus and the fire burning in the hearth, after six
hours snow-stayed at the Toronto airport followed by another four in the
air, I missed authentic more. The one consolation was that, somewhere
beyond those walls, I sensed a warmer sea.

I lowered my carpet bag now seconding as a knitting bag-cum-carryall
onto an ottoman and sighed.

"Is everything to your satisfaction?" asked Ted, the Astwood Cove
service elf who had picked me up from the airport to deliver me into this
lush nest.

"Perfectly," I said, taking in his pink windbreaker and white chinos, the
resort's uniform, I gathered.

"Any questions?" he beamed, all friendliness and white teeth as he
stood there holding my battered suitcase and vintage carry-on . "Mr. Baker
instructed me to cater to your every comfort."

That would be just like my godfather, still trying to sprinkle fairy dust
after all these years. "How much does all of this cost per night, anyway?"

Ted laughed, as if anyone staying in a place like this had to ask. The depth of Max's pockets had always piqued my curiosity. "The bedroom's on the second floor. Here, I'll take your bags up," he said with another grin.

"Okay," I murmured, following behind him long enough to glimpse the four-poster bed, candlewick bedspread, and continuation of applied ambience in all the right places. I acknowledged the luxury of the en suite spa bath room with a nod, my eyes glazing over downstairs halfway through the tour of the well-appointed kitchen with its stock of gourmet edibles, the sunroom with cove views, and patio with built-in barbecue/fireplace. Just in case an ocean didn't offer water enough, the cottage even had a small pool. By the time Ted finished the sweeping parade of amenities, I couldn't stop yawning.

"If you want anything at all, just call the front office. Someone's on duty 24 hours a day to answer to your every need," Ted told me after adding more wood to the fire. I thanked him and finally he exited.

Alone at last, I sank into the cushy chair by the fire and closed my eyes. Long ago I'd dubbed Max Baker 'fairy godfather' for good reason. He always came bearing gifts, treats big and small, rare and expensive, the kind that rural Nova Scotian kids rarely saw let alone owned.

Why had I come? Why did I allow Max to keep pulling my strings? I should have insisted he tell me what he knew over the phone, but it's like I allowed him to spread a magic carpet at my feet to dull all the rough edges of the world. As if he could. Yet, I needed answers, I reminded myself, and I knew I'd never find them by staying home.

My eyes opened. What did Bermuda have to do with Toby's disappearance? My fairy godfather had some explaining to do and I couldn't wait to grill him until his wings dropped off. Where was he?

Fishing my phone from my pocket, I released the airplane mode and waited until the cell signal engaged. Minutes later, a text message slipped into view: HI, PHOEBE. WELCOME TO BERMUDA. SEE YOU AT 10:00. MAX

I checked the time: 9:29. That left half an hour before facing my summoner. I strolled into the kitchen, plucked an apple from the fruit bowl, and headed out the front door.

I'd researched the island online before I left, slipping across page upon page of tourist spiel. Bermuda was served up as the epitome of British culture encapsulated in a semitropical climate. Tea and shorts, mopeds, and cottages the color of breath mints were all portrayed against a brilliant turquoise sea. Charming but why would Toby come here? He preferred his travel straight-up exotic. And he would never miss Dad's birthday.

I pondered this while following the sounds of the sea. Even on this moonless night, the well-lit paths crisscrossing the grounds found the beach in any direction. Still, I figured I could find water even without a guide. All I needed to do was keen my ears and follow the siren's song.

The scent of flowers spiced the air, their velvet faces brushing my hands as I jogged down the path towards the beach. I lurched into a full run downhill. Breaking through the oleander hedges and crossing the sand, I headed straight for the water's edge. A trio of spotlights fixed on one of the fringing palms illuminated the surf's low boil.

I stood staring out to sea, the wind whipping my hair. How I longed to dive deep and far, as if that watery void might somehow soothe all my aching parts. I tugged off my sneakers, peeled away my socks, and rolled up my jeans, wading up to my calves in the salty bite. The chill invigorated me like a zap of body caffeine.

Thus began the old game of feint and parry between the sea and me. I always played; I always lost. Seeing an oncoming roller, I'd turn, scrambling back to shore, vying for safety before a wave grabbed my knees. It may as well be a metaphor for my life.

I made five successful dash and scrambles before one biggie flung a mass of icy tide against my back and force me neck-deep into the absurdity of it all. Beware the rogue wave, Dad always said. That unexpected swell of invisible currents and tidal pull will bring you to your knees every time. You won't even see it coming. I never did. I'd keep making the same mistakes again and again. In fact, I was about to make another one, by far the worst.

I laughed at my folly and struggled to my feet. Shivering, I trudged back to dry land and ground my wet feet into my sneakers, wadding my socks up and pocketing them. With sand chafing my feet, I followed a stone pathway up to headland overlooking the sea. I'd scan the topography and then return to the cottage for a shower and change.

A viewing area carved into the rock formed a prime scenic spot. Two low stone benches braced a round gate that framed the dark sea heaving beyond. If I stood under that arch of that moon gate, I could see the lights winking from other cottages nestled about the property across the cove. If I leaned forward far enough, I could glimpse tropical fish shooting jolts of color in the underwater spotlights nestled into the cliffs. I squelched a sudden craving to dive in with the fishes. Maybe another time. And then my cell phone rang.

Turning my back to the wind, I plucked the phone from my pocket and hit TALK.

"Phoebe? It's me."

"Dad! What are you doing calling?'

"What d'you mean, 'what am I doing calling'? I'm your father and it's my God-given right to call my daughter. Besides, I've been worried sick. Why haven't you called? You're breaking up."

I moved to the other side of the lookout to fix a better signal. "Dad, I spoke to you only a few hours ago. Is everything all right?"

"Sure, everything's all right with me. It's you I'm worried about."

I closed my eyes. It had to be because Toby was missing or maybe it had to do with the disease. Anxiety hit him over my absences, no matter how brief. Even though, to his knowledge, I was still in Halifax, beneath it all, he sensed something. "Everything's fine, Dad. I'm just out for a walk. I'd better get back home, though. It's getting late."

"You shouldn't be walking the city streets alone. It's not safe."

I hated lying to him but his anxiety was too fever-pitched to know the truth. "It's fine, Dad. I'm fine. Stop worrying. Besides, I can take care of myself. "

"Like Toby?"

Damn. "Dad, I'd better go."

"If you're worried about money, I can lend you some. I got a little put by."

Dad always thought himself well-off if he had more than a month's grocery money stashed. He didn't realize Toby and I supplemented his pension after the sudden wealth we'd once experienced dried up. "Thanks, Dad, really but I'm fine for money." I wasn't but he didn't need to know that.

A flashlight flickered up the path towards me. "Look, I'd better go, my battery's giving out. I'll call soon, I promise. In the meantime, mind your ticker and don't go overdoing it."

Pressing END, I dropped the phone back into my pocket and watched the figure approach.

HE ARRIVED AT THE TOP OF THE BLUFF. WINDBLOWN, A TALL, TANNED man with a lean, rangy, body, he struck me as lithe like a panther. Though I couldn't see his features in the dark, I had the sense of a sharp angled face and deep-set eyes. He could have been another Astwood service elf or maybe a fellow resort resident except this man didn't wear pink or dress in typical tourist garb. Dark jeans, a turtleneck, and leather jacket struck me as more biker dude than resort wear, even off-season .

"Hi," I greeted him.

"You're Phoebe."

"Thanks for telling me. And you are?"

"Noel Halloren. I work for Max." The accent was undeniably Australian. Another Aussie.

Well, of course, I knew Max had employees but, other than his girlfriend who acted like my aunt, I'd never met any of them before. "Really? What do you do for him?"

Halloran grinned, an unsettling flash of white in the shadows. "Anything he wants me to."

"Anything? Does that make you sort of an all-purpose dogsbody? No job description, just a blank page where he fills in the job?" For some reason, the man's presence provoked my smart-ass side.

He laughed. "Fits. In this economy, an employee's got to diversify, even a hound."

"'Dogsbody,'" I mused, uncomfortable under this stranger's scrutiny. "That's a naval term referring to a gofer, in case you didn't know."

"Hails from the early nineteenth century, and gofer is fitting enough, too, since I was sent here to fetch you. Max is waiting in the cottage."

"Oh, good." I slipped past him and made my way down the path, the dogsbody at my heels.

I burst through the door of the cottage into the lounge where Max

Baker stood helping himself to the house Scotch dressed in a navy turtle-neck, jeans, and his signature crocodile boots. "Phoebe!" he exclaimed.

"Max!"

He laughed, spreading his arms for the kind of embrace we'd exchanged since he officially became my godfather some 20 years earlier, but mine was more guarded. He squeezed me tight, regardless, as if trying to press away the years that separated us, this tall man who always smelled of sandalwood laced with foreign shores. I squelched the bittersweet memories along with an inexplicable urge to cry. "I miss those days when you'd call me your 'fairy godfather' though maybe we could ditch the fairy part," he said into my hair, his voice muffling laughter.

I stepped away. "We all have to grow and change, Max. Anyway, I'd say that Dad's been asking after you, but you're persona non grata these days. Why's that?"

He shook his head. "No clue. He's been mad at me since Toby disappeared."

"Oh, it started long before that but, I admit, he seems to blame you for Toby's disappearance."

"What kind of fool thinking is that? I'd do anything for Toby and your family, he knows that. Every time I call, he hangs up, and after the heart bonker, he wouldn't let me in the hospital to visit him. What's up with him, Phoebe?"

I shook my head. "I found the milk in the cupboard and the sugar bowl in the fridge, if that helps answer your question,. The doctors say it's the onset of dementia but there's something else going on. Whatever Dad's hiding or can't remember, concerns Toby, which is why I'm here."

"I'm sorry, love. I truly am. If you need money for special care or anything, just ask."

I never would and sensed he knew it. I'd thrown up a speed bump along the highway of endless gifts long ago. "Thanks. How's Maggie?" Maggie being Max's longtime secretary/assistant/partner and otherwise undefined companion, considered herself my aunt by default.

"Great. You'll see her tomorrow."

Like that made me happier. "The last time I saw you both was the night Toby didn't show for Dad's birthday bash. He fell apart that night and I've never been able to mention your name since. I tried again last night but he's clammed shut. I just don't know how much of it is due to stroke damage, the dementia, or to something else but the time for getting answers is running out. The doc says he suffered a series of minor strokes that night. Did I tell you that already?"

"You did, honey."

I wrapped my arms around myself and stepped towards the fire. "I didn't even know it at first. For weeks, I put his behavior down to Toby's disappearance."

"You aren't a doctor, Phoeb. Don't blame yourself for what you couldn't have known."

I turned around to face him again, finding him standing tense, hands flexing at his sides. He ran one hand through his thick silver hair and tried to smile.

"I've got you covered in sand." I pointed to his sweater.

He looked down at the grit-sprinkled chest. "No worries. You go swimming with your clothes on or something?" He stepped towards me until his outstretched arms touched my shoulders. With the fireplace at my back, I stayed put. "You're soaked."

"She was cavorting in the waves," I heard Noel comment behind me. So he'd been watching. I wished he'd leave so I could talk to Max in private.

I shrugged. "Water and I go way back. "

Max grinned, still a handsome, powerful, presence at nearly 72. He stood six feet tall, the permanently tanned skin below the silver mane suggesting either a life outdoors or months prone on a tanning bed. The latter didn't fit. "Always the mermaid. I remember you playing on the beach when you were a kid. Your mum said she couldn't keep you dry during summer hols. You always headed straight for water."

"Speaking of which, I'm damp. I'm going up to change," I said, stepping past him towards the stairs.

"I'll be waiting."

I nodded, heading up without another word, my emotions boiling. It wasn't just seeing Max again that had unsettled me or the sudden transport to this otherworld island, but the whole brew of anxiety, fear, and grief I'd been living under for years. Seeing Max triggered everything all over again.

Hot water washed away the sand and salt, offering a little pulse-motion shower message between my shoulder blades in the process. After I'd wiped myself down with towels more plush and pink than I thought possible, I finger-curled my shoulder-length red hair while rooting through the carry-on bag for something to wear.

I loved clothes but couldn't afford much, preferring to squander my expendable income on art and yarn . Occasionally, I'd make my own or upcycle some of Julie's cast-offs into my own perverse sense of style—boho meets yahoo with a dash of historical reference. I particularly favored velvet, no matter how moth-eaten.

But all I brought this trip was a hastily plucked assortment of jeans, tops, and knitwear, leaving an undue amount of space for yarn and Toby's *Tide Weaver* cartoon that just fit crosswise into the bottom of my suitcase. I ended hiding the tapestry up in Toby's old hidey-hole and bringing the drawing, instead. I figured it must signify something.

I selected a green turtleneck and a fresh pair of jeans. Moments later, I investigated the damp redhead in the mirror and, keeping with the dog metaphor, decided I looked like a cross between an Irish setter and a wet beagle after a romp in the waves.

Downstairs I found Max standing in the living room with the curtains open staring out to sea, a Scotch glass in hand. Noel occupied a chair by the hearth, long legs stretched out before him in an insouciant man-spread. They had been heatedly discussing something. Conversation stopped abruptly when I entered.

"There you are," Max greeted, gazing at me fondly for several long moments. "That's much better. So, do you like the place?" he indicated the cottage with a wave of his glass. "Comfortable?"

"It's beautiful, thanks, but I would have been just as happy with something less grand."

"You've got to get over that. You deserve the best of everything."

"Why, if I haven't earned it or can't afford it? You forget that I'm over-educated and underemployed—unemployed, actually—underachiever who lives in a lovely but cheap little flat in Halifax."

"No goddaughter of mine's going to hole up someplace shabby, if I can help it. And with all that education of yours, you could do anything you wanted. Weren't you going to be a lawyer specializing in art crimes?"

"Yes, but you've missed the latest chapter where I take a few years off to do nothing but make fiber art and work for somebody else."

"Global Threads. But that was just a passing thing, right?"

"Passing as in gone. They're closing the shop."

He shook his head and took another sip from his glass. "No wonder. That pair didn't know a dog's ass about running a business. You should have let me buy it out for you long ago before they ran it into the ground."

"The economy ran it into the ground, not them." Not that I believed that, but there was no way I'd allow my godfather's largess to extend to buying me a business. Enough was enough. "A lot has changed."

"Not that, not you. Well, you have changed, obviously, grown into a lovely young woman , but you'll always be a daughter to me. I'd give you the world if you'd let me."

Okay, so maybe that was the liquor talking but he probably meant every word. " I know and thanks, but right now all I want is my brother back plus answers to this secret you and dad concocted years ago. Ever since I was a kid, certain topics were always off-limits. I'd always accept that and back off, but no more. I'm not stopping now until I get the answers I came for."

"You may not like the answers, Phoebe."

"What the hell is that supposed to mean? Look," I said, raising my hands and letting them drop again. "It's like this: I have nothing left to lose so start talking. Where's Toby?"

"It's a long story, Phoebe."

"Then give me the short version. Have you found him, yes or no?"

"No, I haven't found him but I know where he was the week before he vanished."

"Here in Bermuda?"

"Right on. Why not join me in a drink while I fill you in on the details?"

"No, thanks."

"Tea, then."

I sighed in frustration. "Look, all I really want is answers but, if it will make you happy, I'll drink tea while you explain every detail. Come into the kitchen with me while I make it so you can get started." I turned towards the kitchen.

"No worries. Noel will make it for you, won't you boy?"

Boy? I turned to Noel, finding him lounged deep in his chair studying me with a morose expression. Not tanned, I realized. His skin was a naturally deep caramel color and his face a fierce combo of angles Mom would have dubbed "swarthy". Striking, not handsome, but no boy. He had to be at least 35.

Noel's lips quirked into a smile as he unfolded himself from the chair. Tall, maybe six foot four, he towered over Max by at least two inches. In two steps he was before me, bending his waist in a mock bow. "The dogsbody at your service. Milk with that, ma'am?" he said in a passably British accent.

"Yes, please, but no sugar. Look, I'm particular. I like my tea the old-fashioned way in a warmed pot rather than just a bag dumped into a pot and boiled to within an inch of its life. I better do it."

He looked over at me from his still-bent position, eyes sparkling. "No worries. I live to serve. Anything else?'

"Bikkies," Max interjected. "Or crackers and cheese. She must be starving."

"As you wish." He straightened, cast me a long look, and strode into the kitchen.

I turned to Max. "Who is he?"

"My second in command. I need someone to help run my businesses. No worries about him."

Businesses. I only knew about the antiques shop in London, at least officially. "Okay. Now, back to Toby."

Max poured himself another inch of whiskey, replacing the nearly empty bottle on the side table. "I've got a lead, like I said," he said, tossing back a draw of liquor.

"But he didn't mention making a detour to Bermuda in his emails. He made it seem like he was flying in directly from LA via New York."

"No doubt wanted you to think that."

"But why?"

"You know Toby, always chasing down something. You didn't find any clues at your dad's?"

"Nothing new or different."

Max went over to a briefcase sitting on the couch and removed a folder of papers. "Look here." He passed me an eight by eleven black-and-white photo of two men on a wharf. The picture was of poor quality, taken from a distance, and obviously enlarged. "Taken by a security camera at Smith's Cove up coast one week before Toby disappeared. Notice anything?"

I brought the photo under a lamp and studied it hard. One man had his arm raised in discussion while the other faced him, hands on hips. The figure on the right could be anyone. In a long dark greatcoat, his body was turned away from the camera, he had his collar up around his ears.

"Who wears a greatcoat in Bermuda?" I asked.

"Someone with a theatrical bent. Look at the other one."

I stared. The second man with his hand pointing skyward could be Toby. He had Toby's lithe build, though it was difficult to identify much conclusively since he wore a baseball hat and sunglasses. I could just see the outline of his face, all similar to my brother's jawline.

"My brother hates baseball caps."

"Which makes it the perfect disguise. Look again." Max pointed to the upraised hand before slipping another photo on top the first, this one an enlargement of the hand. I nodded. Toby's tattoo was clearly visible on the fleshy part just beneath the thumb. "Who else you think would have a tat of a bloody mermaid on his hand?"

"Merman," I corrected. I had the mermaid but in a less public place. Toby, that had to be Toby. I turned to Max. "Who's the other guy?"

"Name's Adrian Wyndridge. Ring any bells?"

I shook my head. "Sounds familiar."

"Author, wrote all kinds of high seas historical novels, romantic stuff."

"*Thunder on the Seas* and *Brethren of the Coast* ? I read a couple of those years ago." My eyes fell to the picture again, a tremor coursing through me as though some great force had just plucked my spinal cord. "He came here to meet Adrian Wyndridge? But why?" Then I turned to search Max's face. "What else do you know?"

"Wyndridge denies ever having seen him, denies even knowing who he is."

"You asked?"

"In a roundabout way. Bastard's hiding something. He saw Toby and this proves it."

"So, why not confront him with this photo and demand an explanation?"

"Do you think he'd tell me if he didn't tell the police? Besides, he's a bloody recluse. Only makes appearances for the occasional book signing or an auction or two. Used to collect rare manuscripts. Has a few screws loose, if you ask me." Max tugged the photos from my hands and led me over to the couch, indicating that we sit. "We need subtler methods."

Noel entered at that moment bearing a tray clinking with tea things that he put on the ottoman. Keeping his eyes averted, he carefully placed a mug on the table beside me and poured milk from a crystal jug. "Say when."

"When."

With aplomb, he whisked up the botanical teapot and poured the brew into my mug, twisting his wrist at the perfect moment to avoid drips. "Biscuit with that, ma'am?"

I plucked a shortbread from the proffered plate. "I'm impressed." I smiled up at him. "You're an excellent dogsbody."

"Trained in England," he remarked with a quirky grin.

"A corgi, then."

"Corgi's a purebred. I'm too much of a bitzer for that."

"Bitzer?"

"Bits of this, bits of that."

"Cut it out, you two," Max said.

"Right, so, Max," I said, turning back to my godfather, "Define your version of subtle."

"The kind that pretends to be something he or she is not. We need to get inside Wyndridge's and hunt for clues."

My eyes widened. I bit into a cookie. "Which is where I come in."

"You're perfect."

I chewed less enthusiastically. "Because?"

"Because you know Toby better than anyone. You'll know a clue when you see it. We'll get you in there for a couple of days only and then pull you out. It's safer that way."

I placed the half-eaten cookie on the edge of my plate and laced my fingers in my lap, noting that Noel now sat across from me, eyes scrutinizing my face. "Just how do you propose to get me in there?"

"Wyndridge placed in an advert for someone to organize his library a couple of weeks ago," Max said with a grin. "Perfect timing. He wants someone to plough through a bunch of manuscripts he's collected—cataloguing, classification, that sort of thing. Think he plans to sell his collection. It's just so damn perfect, I couldn't believe our luck. He put the ad out incognito-style using a box number but I have informants."

"Of course you do." I shrugged, the sense of unreality intensifying. "What qualifications is he looking for?"

"A Masters of Librarianship or an archivist preferred."

"Perfect. My degree in Art History plus all my stale law courses and work experience as a gallery slog ought to make me the star applicant."

"Phoebe," Max spoke with exaggerated patience. "You wouldn't be applying as yourself. I took the liberty of submitting an application in your name."

"Not her name," Noel corrected.

"Right, not your name. Look."

He passed me a file folder. I flipped it open only long enough to scan the name SUSAN WAVERLEY neatly printed on the top page along with a list of degrees and work experiences definitely not my own. I let the folder drop to my lap to rub my temples. "Are you suggesting I assume a false identity with fabricated credentials to enter a famous author's employ on a ruse?"

"You say you're not backing down on finding Toby or unlocking your dad's secrets. I promise you, this will do both."

I looked at him. "Wyndridge and my father are connected?"

"Look, it's complicated. If you say no, Maggie would take it on in a heartbeat, but she wouldn't be half as good as you would be at this."

"You're trying to coerce me into doing something illegal and certainly unethical when I came here for answers!"

"And you'll get them but I can't hand everything to you on a plate 'cause I don't have all the details. Find out what Toby was doing with Wyndridge first. Susan Waverley's been short-listed. Now we're just waiting for an interview time."

Just when I thought the prize might be in reach, he'd jerked the damn string again. "Is this for real?"

"Do you want to find your brother or not?" Max asked.

I held up my hand. "Stop with the emotional blackmail. I said I'll do what it takes, but I didn't expect it to be this." Admittedly, I was roiling in confusion and probably not thinking straight but that still didn't excuse going forward with any of this. Yet, in truth, it seemed like going forward was the only avenue I had.

"Fair enough," Noel remarked.

"Glad you approve," I said without looking at him.

"Sorry, honey. I didn't want to involve you but this is just too damn good to pass up. Only you can make full use of the op. We had a man in there for a while who had all the finesse of a front-end loader. Stupid drop-kick left me in the lurch." Max drained the last of his glass and stared out into space. "We need you, darlin'."

"What's with the old 'I have a man in there now' kind of thing that just rolled off your tongue like you're a godfather of another kind?"

"I do whatever it takes when seeking something important, Phoebe," he told me, eyes a little unfocused.

"And do you seek important things often, Max?" I'd often wondered. Actually, deep-down I knew the answer but this was the first time I'd voiced anything about my godfather's alternative career.

"Often enough, and right now it's your brother. What we need to do isn't strictly legal, if that's what's worrying you."

"Everything's worrying me, Max, and let's get something straight: I know your business is somewhere south of legal. You sell antiques and objets d'art, but I always wondered how you source them and how you make so much money doing it. Do you think I haven't figured out what must be behind acquiring fifteenth century Ottoman rugs and genuine Roman statues when countries have laws forbidding their sale?"

"You used to call me 'Uncle Max'". The blue eyes turned on me were blurry and reproachful.

"Don't change the subject."

"With money, that's how. Anything can be bought for the right price and somewhere, somebody else is ready to buy it for a higher one. Sometimes objects arrive at my door with uncertain provenance but the world is an unstable place, darlin'. Plenty of Roman artifacts are emerging from Afghanistan, for example."

"As in stolen, looted, or just purchased from the war-torn and desperate?"

Max passed his empty glass to Noel, who reached over and slid it onto the coffee table minus a refill.

"I source art and artifacts for wealthy clients, mostly private collectors and museums, and—Noel, fill that bloody glass!—but sometimes I don't know the exact provenance for every item." He shrugged. "I just do what I do."

"And what did you do with my father all those years ago?"

"Noel, get me another drink!"

"No." Noel scowled. "You're over limit."

"Who the hell limits me?"

"Get me one, then," I said. "I'm the one who needs a stiff drink right now."

Noel shook his head, a little smile on his lips. Attractive lips, I thought, full and sensual. Like I needed to drift down that canal.

Max turned to me, face as red as a boiled crustacean, fingers drumming on the chair arm. "I liked your dad, feisty old bugger."

"Yeah, so what does the feisty old bugger and the arts and artifacts dealer really have in common?"

Max took a deep breath. "I promised your father that I'd never tell you. He made me swear and I'm damn well going to honor that one if it kills me, but I can't help it if you find out on your own. God knows you have a right to the truth."

"Then tell me."

"Go in there and you'll probably find out. That's all I'm saying."

I stared at him in disgust, climbing to my feet. "Give me a break, Max; soon my father won't remember what day it is. If it concerns my family, I have a right to know and from your lips, since you dragged him into this, whatever it is. We've all been affected by this secret. It's been throttling my family for years and now may have harmed my brother. Tell me."

"Your dad believed it was too dangerous to get you involved."

"It's my right as an adult to measure my own risks."

"And your father's right to protect his daughter as long as he wants. If you were my daughter, I wouldn't tell you, either!"

Noel let out a grunt of derision. We both shot him a quick glance but he kept his gaze fixed on the floor.

"Did Mom know?"

"Yes."

"But she didn't like it, did she?"

"No, she didn't like it. Or me."

"How can you even face me again and still remain silent?" I was standing now, fists clenched at my side.

"I'm protecting you, like your dad wants. It's bad enough that—" His words faded away.

I went cold. "It's bad enough what?" I swallowed hard. "Bad enough that Toby found out?"

"I was going to say it's bad enough that I brought you here when your father told me never to contact you again."

4

"N ancy?"

"Phoebe? Where are you?"

"I'm standing in the upstairs room of a little vacation condo in Bermuda, here at Max's request. I've come to find Toby."

My friend sighed deeply as if to steady her voice. "You'd better tell me everything."

When I explained how I ended up there, along with a few salient details, she listened without saying a word. "If you go into Wyndridge's under an assumed identity you'll be breaking a more serious law than just stealing what we might argue belongs to you and yours," she said, finally. "But you already know that."

"I do, but, Nancy, I've backed down from too many things in my life. I just don't want finding Toby to be one of them. And now I'm afraid Dad might know more about this than he's letting on, or can remember. And Max has a lead that looks as though I may be in the best position to follow, plus I'm right where I need to be to unlock everything that's been kept hidden from me for far too long. I know it sounds crazy but what do I have to lose that hasn't gone already?"

"I can think of several responses to that but so can you. Your dad's protecting you, so why not let him do it?"

"Because he lost that right long ago and maybe it's time I do the protecting, which is impossible without all the information."

"I have court in 20 minutes but I'm going to set a little research in motion on this Wyndridge character. In the meantime, stay in touch and try not to do anything too impulsive or dangerous, as if my saying that will make a shred of difference."

After the call ended, I stood by the window watching sunshine billow through the lacy curtains of the open casement. Nancy would enter a situation only after she'd studied all the facts and lined up the pros and cons for an educated, reasoned decision. Not me. I'd dive headlong into a situation and try swimming my way to the surface. If that failed, I'd just tread water while the world spun around me. So how had that worked for me so far?

The glinting turquoise sea surged beyond the casements. This island, I realized, was like a rough-cut jewel. Turn it one way and the polished surface sparkled with brilliance; turn it another, and the sharp primordial layers of ancient stone eclipsed the luster.

I removed my cell from the charger realizing that the scent of bacon and coffee rode the morning air and that someone was rattling around downstairs. Donning the regulation-issue pink robe, I dropped the phone into my pocket and padded down to find a woman in the kitchen, dressed in a pink apron setting a table on the patio.

"Morning, miss. I'm Dora James, your housekeeper. Are you hungry this fine day?"

"Yes, I am, Dora, and whatever you're cooking smells delish."

"Eggs, any way you like them, with bacon, ham, French toast, home fries, the works."

"What's the occasion?" I indicated the white tablecloth, the table set for three on the adjoining patio overlooking the cove.

"Mr. Max sent me over to prepare breakfast. He and the missus will be here in a few minutes."

He and the missus? In a few minutes? Crud. I turned and dashed back upstairs, nabbing a coffee along the way. Twenty minutes later, I arrived at the bottom of the stairs just in time to open the door for Max and Maggie, who was definitely not Max's missus, much to her chagrin.

"Phoebe, hon!" The tall blonde of indeterminate age swept down upon me, wrapped in perfume and some linen designer ensemble the color of fevered coral. "Oh, it's so good to see you again," she said, air-kissing either side of my head. "I'm just so excited that we're all down here together. Last time was so upsetting with Toby missing and all."

"He's still missing, Maggie."

"Sure he is, honey, but we're so much closer to finding him. Come on, let me look at you." She stood back, one long painted nail on her chin. "You look a bit pale."

"I'm tired but fine. Besides, pale is my default position."

"Still, you need some color in your cheeks. What do you think, Max?"

"I think she looks bloody lovely, as usual," Max commented, passing me with a squeeze of my shoulder. "Come on, let's have brekkie. My head's killing me."

She rolled her eyes. "Baby's got a brain-pain today. Wonder why?"

"Over-imbibed."

"Over-imbibed — love it!"

"So, where's Noel this morning?"

Maggie waved a hand. "Off on business. Come along. Let's have break-fast and get down to work." Maggie linked arms with me as we strolled towards the patio. "I know this Toby thing has been hard on you, but we can't have you going in to Wyndridge's unprepared now, can we? You nervous?"

"About what?"

"About your role?"

"Role?" I slipped into a chair on the patio and studied her. Damn, but the woman never aged. She still pulled off the same blonde bombshell look she carried 20 years back, including the gravity-defying cleavage. The legs, I noted with a pang of envy, remained sleek, toned, and incredibly long. With the aqua sea backdrop and the intense coral of her jacket, squinting was in order.

"Hon, you all right?" she leaned towards me while Dora poured coffee into our mugs.

"I'm fine," I said, waiting for the maid to get out of earshot. Once Dora retreated, I returned to our conversation. "Are you referring to this research assistant ruse as a 'role'?"

"Sure I am. I mean, that's what you'll be doing, isn't it? Acting? I'd love a job like that. Still, our casting director here," she thumbed towards Max, "didn't think I looked the type, even though I would have gone in if you refused. Maybe I'm not scholarly looking enough, anyway." She shrugged, grinning with her laminate teeth. "I could have worn a bad wig. Still, I get to help you get ready. I'm in charge of wardrobe, too."

I stirred milk into my coffee with more care than it deserved. Max, I noted, had zoned out, sipping his brew and gazing out at to sea. "Maggie, I know you used to act once upon a time, but I hardly think pretending to be a librarian requires a wardrobe mistress."

"Oh, you're so wrong," Maggie said, sprinkling artificial sweetener into her coffee. "And, I didn't just used to act, I had supporting roles in a couple of near-hits. I almost got to star beside Julia Roberts."

I'd heard that many times before. "You were legit."

"Very legit. The thing is, you have to look the part. It so won't do to have you looking like your present state of," she paused, trawling for a word, "whatever. Toby understood that clothes matter."

"Toby can afford to satisfy his tastes, I can't. Please get to the point."

"The point is Adrian Wyndridge is filthy rich, like, as in a collector and connoisseur, and unmarried, too. He appreciates beautiful things. Like any man, he'll choose a pretty woman over not so much any day."

"So, a woman is the same as a thing."

"You know what I mean."

"No points for brains, in other words."

"Oh, please. Do you think he wanted me for my brain." She nodded towards Max. "He doesn't know I have one half the time."

I decided to leave that untouched. "Personally, I prefer to think of myself as interesting or arresting, and possibly intelligent, at least some of the time, but not pretty. Maybe attractive on a good day," I added. "And I think I could pull off amusing."

"Interesting doesn't cut it, hon, and neither does all the rest. Appearances count, and let's face it: you need work. Try not to be yourself, for once. We've got to outdo the competition."

"Ah," I said with a nod, "the competition. Of course, others must be vying for underpaid librarian to the famous reclusive author."

"They wouldn't know who placed the ad unless they have the inside track . Wyndridge gave a box number."

"Still, these things have a way of getting out, especially with the Internet. Anyway, surely no mere mortal can compete against that stellar, platinum-plated resumé you guys concocted. I mean, the bogus Susan Waverley not only has every degree possible for an A-type librarian, but has done several stints in noted institutions and published, too. She's some kind of wunderkind bibliophile. Aren't you afraid Wyndridge will question why she'd want his little job?"

"Did you read the script I left you or not? She's taking time off, staying with her aunt here in Bermuda — that's me—and this job seems the perfect little break for a big career girl. People are complicated. They don't do the expected stuff all the time. Look at me: former actress now taking a detour in the arts and antiquities business. Who knew?" She shot a quick glance at Max. "But there are fringe benefits."

"What about reference checks?"

"*If* he does a reference check, and that's a big if, the phone numbers I gave will connect with somebody ready with a rehearsed story. Wyndridge doesn't get out much, that helps. Don't worry," Maggie flicked her right hand, sending the diamond ring on her middle finger into a sparkle-fest, "we've done this kind of thing before. Besides, those citations are real. Susan Waverley was a real person. She just happens to be a real dead person."

I lowered my mug to the table. "I'm assuming a dead person's identity?"

"Sort of. That's just in case he does an Internet search, which he probably won't. He doesn't even have a web page. Can you believe that? Imagine an author without a website? His publisher's doesn't count."

"I've assumed the identity of a dead person?"

"You'd have to really dig to find her obituary. Wyndridge isn't much for doing thorough background checks. He's stuck in his fictional world like most writers. Anyway, let us worry about that stuff. You just ace the interview and get in and find clues on Toby."

Dora reappeared distributing bowls of fresh fruit. For a few minutes we suspended conversation while placing our breakfast orders. I decided on eggs, bacon, toast, and more fruit, while Max settled for toast with a side of Tylenol. He did appear rather yellow around the gills. Maggie, on the other hand, ordered a green smoothie and a fruit plate.

Despite the big breakfast order, I still hadn't recovered from the dead-

Susan information. "How did she die?" I asked during our next inter-
mission.

"Who?" Maggie asked, sipping her brew.

"The real Susan Waverley."

"Are you still on about that? I don't remember. I don't think the obit
said. Forget that. Let's talk about the interview."

"Do I even have one yet?"

"No, but you will. We've given the cottage here as a contact number.
It's all in the background sheets I prepared." Maggie dissected her fruit
into tiny pieces.

"After I set Noel and Max packing last night, I went through everything—all the sheets on Wyndridge, the background info on Susan Waverley, may she rest in peace, everything. I also reviewed your character profile
for the bogus Susan, if that's the right term. You have a bit of a flair for
writing fiction yourself, Mags, not that any of it seems even slightly based
on reality. Anyway, I've got the particulars committed to memory and will
ad-lib the rest." In theory, it sounded like fun. I doubted reality would be.

Maggie paused, her knife suspended over a wedge of cantaloupe. "You
liked my writing?"

"I appreciate comedy."

"I think that's the nicest thing you've ever said to me."

I turned to her, momentarily speechless. "Mags, please don't miss my
note of irony. Besides, I'm sure I've said other nice things to you over the
years."

"I choose to ignore the irony and I can't remember a single other nice
thing you've said since you were a kid. Toby was much nicer. You always
acted like I'm stupid or something," she continued. "Your mother didn't
like me so you automatically didn't, either. She thought I was a tart."

"Mom was being protective and, considering my family's shenanigans, I
needed it."

Maggie lowered her knife. "Look, hon, I always adored you. You were
always such a plucky little snot even as a kid, always so smart-mouthed.
You were like the daughter I never had, which is why I bought you all
those presents. Yeah, maybe Chanel at a school prom was a little over the
top but you looked like dynamite in those heels. Blew those junior
achievers right out of the water."

"And they hated me even more afterwards."

"Yeah, jealousy. So what? Where are they now, anyway — stuck in the backwoods somewhere with a lout for a husband and twenty kids? Look at you."

"Unemployed, you mean?"

Maggie sighed. "Look, my point is you never even thanked me for any of the presents for all these years."

I stared at her dumbstruck. "But I thought they were from Max."

She laughed. "Yeah, sure. Just picture Max on Fifth Avenue picking out a Chanel dress. He could pick out car, a surfboard, and maybe a rare antique something or other, but never that. The only thing he gave you himself was that smelly old carpet bag you love so much. It figures that something so old and beat up would be such a hit."

"It's made from an original antique textile."

She picked up her knife and began slicing the fruit again. "Yeah, yeah, yeah. And Chanel is made from old potato sacks. The point is, try showing me some respect, okay?"

I was about to respond when Max interrupted. "Mags will play the aunt, if you need her." He was rousing himself from detox, not that he had been listening. "Anything you need, any back up at all, we've got you covered."

"We're not taking any chances," Maggie said. "You got to get that position and that's that." She speared a melon chunk with her fork and placed it delicately in her mouth where she proceeded to roll it around with her tongue as if she might suck it to death.

"Supposing I'm quickly revealed as a fraud the moment I try to tackle real archival work, classification, that kind of thing? I can fake it only up to a point," I said, relieved to be out of the Maggie mire.

"Yeah," Maggie said, finally swallowing, "but you won't be in there long enough to really do anything but snoop. You always start really strong and then end up a mess, so we're pulling you out after a couple of days."

"I thought I was to be pulled out, as you call it, for my own safety?"

"Same thing. Either way, I'm betting you'll waver, spill the beans to Wyndridge, or muck it up some other way." She shot me a quick look. "Don't take it personally, hon. Nobody's perfect."

"I presume you think that because I quit law at the final hour it therefore follows that I can't stick to anything? That's a faulty assumption since many young people embark on false starts." I was rationalizing but it helped somehow. "I decided law wasn't for me and hit the eject button before I ended up working in an environment that didn't suit me. It's art, history, and textiles that really impassions me." Actually, I liked the idea of being a lawyer more than the reality of the actual career.

"Yeah, yeah, and then you took four more years of—what was it now, painting 101?"

"Art history," I said, fighting the desire to throw food at her. "And I stayed at it until I graduated with a master's."

"Big whoop. All that education so you could play Cinderella for Mrs. Snotty Pants in some museum somewhere. Great move. Just don't mess this up, okay? Anyway, I figure you can play librarian easy enough for a few days. Just look reasonably intelligent and tidy the shelves. How hard can it be?"

I stabbed a banana chunk. Listening to Max's mistress bate me worked every single time even though I knew what she was doing. "A proper librarian knows his or her stuff. It's not like organizing papers by small, medium, and large. Skill and training are involved. That's why people take degrees. And I don't waver so much as see all the pros and cons to the point until I can't choose just one."

"Exactly. You see gray when there's ever only black and white." Maggie speared a cube of pineapple. "Anyway, it's easy to fake anything with a lot of confidence and a little information. You'll have me on speed-dial. The moment you need me to dig up information, say the word."

"Susan Waverley was an accomplished scholar. I doubt having you on speed-dial is going to compensate."

Max, looking slightly fortified after coffee and pain killers, looked over at me. "Look, Phoeb, you've been around libraries long enough to pull off a little confidence trick for a few days. With two degrees under your belt, you must have solid library experience."

I sighed. "Well, I dated an archivist for a few months. Does that count?"

Maggie grinned. "You bet! You must have learned a thing or two from him."

"Probably not what you need. Christian and I stayed mostly in the closed stacks for the full four months of our relationship, wedged between rare books and the conservation room. Classification never came up. Actually, neither did conversation." I popped a mouthful of fruit and smiled.

Maggie grinned back. Max scraped back his chair and disappeared into the cottage with a grunt, apparently looking for a coffee refill. "He doesn't like thinking of his goddaughter getting it on with a guy. So, was this guy good?"

"He had solid expertise, which I appreciated, but he took up with a freshman, or should I say, fresh woman, so I dropped him. Those rare book men can be real Lothsarios."

"Really? Who'd have thought. I always figured they'd be kind of stuffy. Is he why you're still not with anyone?"

How I hated this question. Why did woman past puberty still need a male accessory? "I've never found a man interesting enough to make it worth sitting through episodes of Hockey Night in Canada." Not that Christian was much of an athlete beyond our exertions in the stacks but it seemed like every other heterosexual man needed a tribal game fix. His just came in the board game variety.

Maggie snorted. "For me it's been the World Cup soccer matches. Yuck."

"Mags," Max interrupted, returning. "Stop bumping your gums and tell her about Edna Smith."

Maggie nodded. "She's the one you've got to beat. We've gone through the applications. Lots qualify but she's worked for him before and she's local so we have to assume she's a serious contender. Works in the Public Library in Hamilton. Not very good-looking but she is a professional librarian. Oh, and has local history listed as an interest."

"You accessed the applications? " Would I ever get used to the way these two worked?

"Yeah, sure. Wyndridge collected them by mail, so Frank only had to get into his den and scan the particulars. No computer hacking or anything."

"Frank, I presume, is your inside guy?" I sliced a loquat in two, trying to stay cool.

"Ex-inside guy."

Dora entered carrying a tray of eggs and sides. After our breakfasts were distributed, we ate in silence for a few minutes.

"Why ex?" I ventured after a bit.

Max replied between gulps of coffee. "Useless dropkick left a few days ago. Said he wanted more money but I paid through my teeth for him in the first place. Nothing but a bludger. I wasn't paying him more. Wyndridge hired a replacement before we even knew Frank had gone, some jack-of-all-trades named Bert, but that's not his real name. Probably works for a competitor. We've got a few plans in the works."

I paused, a forkful of egg en route to my mouth. "Like what?"

"Wyndridge has had some staff turnover recently. He's looking out for a head housekeeper but has had trouble finding someone mommy likes," Max said.

Maggie sighed. "I so want that role."

Max barked out a laugh. "That's like trying to make a Ferrari look like a truck!"

Maggie scowled and sipped her smoothie. "Give me some credit. I could do it."

"Hey, that sounds like a compliment to me," I pointed out. "I'd probably be compared to some little economy number."

But Max wasn't listening to me. "You don't even know how to clean," he said to Maggie.

"Well, how hard is that?"

My cue to change the topic. "What else do you know about Edna Smith?"

"Not much," Maggie muttered, casting baleful glances at Max. "What else do you need to know except you've got to beat her for that job?"

"What if I don't get that job, then what?"

"We have a contingency plan." Maggie dabbed her lips with a napkin. "There are always contingencies."

"Like what?"

"You don't need to know the details."

"I like details. Try me."

She dismissed that with a wave of her hand.

"At least give me the gist."

"Look, hon, if you must know, we're prepared to offer her more money to take another job."

"Stop calling me 'hon', will you? I hate it."

Maggie stared at me. "Really? Okay, so forget about her, *Phoebe*. She's our problem."

After that, I let conversation drop and answered questions only when asked. Of course, I wondered what I'd gotten myself into and, of course, I knew that whatever the definition it was fundamentally stupid, stupid, stupid. But I was desperate. And young. Besides, stupidity has nothing to do with intelligence. That much I had learned a long time ago.

My instructions that day were simple: I was to search out some kind of virtual librarian crib sheet online while waiting for the interview call. If no call came through by 2:00, I was to contact the Wyndridge estate and request a status update. Apparently, Max's vacated informant had told him that Wyndridge was fast-tracking the assignment and wanted someone in place as soon as possible.

The moment everyone exited, I checked my phone and found two text messages, one from Nancy requesting I call back and one from Julie: PHOEBE, I'M SORRY. I'VE BEEN SUCH AN ASS. DECIDED TO REOPEN GLOBAL THREADS AS A WEBSTORE. PLEASE BE MY MANAGER. WE'LL TALK ABOUT THE TAPESTRY.

For a tiny instant, a lilt of joy danced in my heart. I had a job, if I wanted it; Julie was finally taking my recommendation to broaden her reach via the web! Then, I quashed it all. No more going backward for me, only ahead. I left the call unanswered.

But I did call Nancy. "Phoebe, my researcher mined some interesting facts about Adrian Wyndridge this morning. An estate agency has been making enquiries on his behalf to purchase property in the Maldives."

"The Maldives? You mean Adrian Wyndridge is going to jump ship?"

"Possibly. The interesting point is that his finances don't appear to support the purchase of an island anywhere. Despite the relative success of his fiction ventures, he's more or less broke with all his assets tied up in his Bermudan house, which, by the way, is quite a pile. Are you still going through with the library ruse?"

"Of course I am," I said quickly. "Nancy, am I quitter?"

"Whoa," said my friend. "Back up here. I think you're a little lost at the moment but I know you have more stick-with-it-ness then most. What's this about?"

"Maggie provided me with a character assessment over breakfast today. She claimed me to be a wavering quitter who can't be trusted to go the distance."

"We are all on our own journey, Phoebe. Yours is just a bit haphazard at the moment. Rather than paying attention to her, start listening to yourself. Have to go now. Talk later." And then she hung up.

I sighed, gazing around at the cozy cottage for answers and finding none. I called Dad. Besides the usual complaints about Bertha Hugli, all seemed well on that front or, at least, well enough.

Next, I paced the patio rehearsing myself as Susan Waverley, a professional information organizer, a published scholar, and the exact opposite of law school dropout, aspiring artist, and collector-of -fiber-bits, me. Susan had a stellar career once, had slowly risen in her profession of choice, to arrive at the apex of success. I rarely finished anything, more certain of what I didn't want to do than what I did. Maturity was purely physical, after all.

And assuming a dead person's identity struck me as creepy, not to mention illegal. She was dead, I was not. I was borrowing all she had accomplished for dubious ends. Maybe, if the dead did see beyond the grave, she'd forgive me, knowing that I was only seeking my brother. Or some life other than my own.

Maggie had printed out a few pages on Susan's accomplishments, including a list of her publications, such as the obscure title Managing Rare Documents in the Modern World. Crud, she had written an entire book about that?

The more I considered the impersonation, the more nervous I became. By eleven-thirty or so, I was frantic. Could I be somebody else for an extended period? Wasn't pretense only a lie playing dress up? And who the hell was I, anyway? Shouldn't I get that much straight first?

Finally, I grabbed my tranquilizer of choice and sat by the pool, knitting my way to calm. Deep in the quiet world of alternating knit and purl, I breathed and loosened. I could do this. I *had* to do this.

I held up my wrap, forming now like an amoeba in the throes of a hurricane, all long dropped stitches and waves of undulating fiber going in no fixed direction—another life metaphor —and yet it pleased me. Regularity was merely a yawn waiting to happen, whereas sudden surprises and detours were the stuff of discovery and transformation. Or, so I told myself.

In the meantime, nobody called the cottage to arrange an appointment. At 2:00, I set my knitting aside and called the number Max had left for the Wyndridge estate. A woman with a British accent answered. "Good afternoon, the Wyndridge's residence. Mrs. Wyndridge speaking."

Since he wasn't married, I presumed I was addressing his mother. "Hi, Mrs. Wyndridge. My name is Susan Waverley, and I'm calling in regard to the status of the research position that I've been short-listed for." Would Susan sound so hesitant or end her sentence in a preposition? I needed to be more assertive, polished. "I understand that interviews are to commence shortly. Please inform me as to the time and place so I can arrange my time accordingly," I added. Now, I sounded as though I was choking on a carrot.

Silence followed. I thought for a moment she'd hung up. Or expired. "Mrs. Wyndridge?"

"Yes, Miss Waverley. I regret to inform you that the position has been filled."

"Filled?" I blurted out. "How can that be after I'd been told I'd been short-listed? That's highly unprofessional, probably against Bermudan labor laws or something. I could have you cited for faulty hiring practices."

"Very sorry to have inconvenienced you. Good afternoon." The line went dead.

I stood staring out the patio door, across the table, towards the brilliant sea. Damn. Wyndridge must have offered the job to Edna Smith and she accepted. I pulled out my IPhone and texted Max: HE'S BYPASSED THE INTERVIEWS AND HIRED SOMEONE ELSE, PRESUMABLY E.S.

⚜ 5 ⚜

I bounded along a flower-lined path thinking what I would do if I couldn't get into the estate. Would that mean never finding Toby? I jogged past stone benches, moon gates, hidden fountains, and two swimming pools artfully hidden in foliage, all very lovely but my mind was elsewhere.

The Astwood office stood storybook perfect, a white-roofed pink cottage with shutters and a mass of fiery red bougainvillea rioting across one wall. Besides a few guys packing a golf cart and two speed-walking women, the property seemed deserted.

Ted, the service elf, sat behind the desk studying a computer screen. At the sight of me, his face split into a wide grin. "Well, how may I help you this fine day?"

"I need transportation. Can I rent a car somewhere near?"

Ted spread his hands, his grin wide and white. The world had become a much brighter place since teeth whiteners. "I have just the thing."

I followed him out the door and across the lawn to where a line of mopeds sat shining in the parking lot.

"Surely I'd break my neck on one of those. No car rentals?"

"Car rentals are not allowed—too small an island, so visitors use mopeds. Only residents may own a car. Care must be taken but that's the only way to get around effectively. It's what most of us ever drive. We keep a few on hand just for the convenience of our residents. Come, I'll give you a quick lesson."

He selected one from a row of identical shiny blue clones, each complete with a helmet, a lock, and a prayer. He rolled one out for my inspection. After a rundown of preliminary safety tips, he urged me to drive around the parking area under his supervision. Straddling the bike, I considered the gears briefly, tested the brakes, and practiced turning. It didn't feel half bad.

"Is this it?" I asked, pulling up beside him. "Am I now licensed to be killed?"

He laughed. "You won't be killed. Just be careful. Wear your helmet; it's the law. If a big lorry comes bearing down on you, pull over to the side but never stop in the middle of the road, no matter how beautiful the scenery. Go slow, but not too slow. Those things won't get much faster than 50 miles per hour anyway. Take your time and enjoy yourself. Oh, one more thing," he added with a snap of his fingers. "Take the tribe roads across the center of the island to avoid the traffic. Use them as shortcuts. Here, I'll show you."

Ted unfolded a tiny, pocket-sized map and spread it across the handle-bars. "Most of them cross perpendicular to the main coastal routes and cut up through the island's suburbs, like there and there." He traced the tiny lines shooting across the island. "Take those if you'd prefer to avoid the scenic routes. They can be distracting and, I won't kid you, the coral cliffs around here are deadly." He noticed my carpet bag slung over my shoulder. "And that won't do."

"You don't like my style?"

He flashed a grin. "I like your style just fine but lock that bag of yours in the rear compartment so it doesn't go falling off on the road or knock you off-balance."

"Oh, right." I unlocked the compartment, shoved my bag in, and turned to him with a salute.

Thanking him, I scooted off, the breeze blowing in my face amid the intoxicating scent of growing things. For the next 30 minutes, I focused on the simple task of staying alive but soon morphed to staying alive at top legal speed in a glorious setting.

Astwood Properties occupied prime real estate on the south coast of Bermuda, the land of picture postcard beaches and stretches of parkland. The vistas of turquoise sea and pink sand off to my left offered endless distraction with hardly a piece of shoreline I didn't long to explore. Instead, I gripped the handlebars and kept my eyes on the road. This wasn't a vacation. At least I didn't have to fight tootling tourists, just the constant whizz of the locals passing me with what seemed like a death wish.

I travelled at a good clip, searching for a tribe road jutting off into the hills until, finally, I spied a tiny lane nested between a restaurant and a banana grove. I peeled the brakes ever so slightly when I made the turn. The moped sputtered and bit the ground up a steep incline. A thick canopy of trees shaded the road. Only when I reached the crest of the hill did I relax, letting the bike coast down into the leafy shadows towards another stunning vista before shooting out onto the highway.

By the time I reached Hamilton, the moped and I had bonded. Traffic congested the narrow streets as I wound through the town looking for a parking area with bike designations. Glancing at the other bikes for direction, I parked, locking the helmet onto the seat, and grabbed my bag. While standing in the parking lot, I checked my phone, seeing a roll of text messages and missed calls all from Max. Dropping the phone in my pocket, I slung my bag over my shoulder and strode across the street. Most of them demanded I call him back, which I would, after I completed my mission.

I walked past the Front Street shops soaking in the town's colors and bustle. A stiff harbor breeze blew against my back as I strolled uphill toward the library, which nestled on a steep street running perpendicular to the water. A renovated building of creamy stucco, it lacked the impact of the earlier British Colonial version I'd glimpsed online, but as a library, any manifestation was fine by me.

Inside, I breathed deeply the familiar scent of books and photocopiers which brought back memories of Christian and the heady stew of lust I once called love. Man, that guy knew his stuff.

I marched to the information desk on the second floor to ask for Edna Smith. When the clerk indicated a sturdy black woman in a denim suit accessorized by a pair of biker boots assisting an elderly client with pink hair, I hesitated. Now what? It's not like I had a plan. I waited until the elderly lady shuffled off to the borrower's desk with a clutch of books under arm before stepping forward. "Ms. Smith?"

The librarian turned with a smile, one of the genuine varieties that reach the eyes as well as the mouth. "Yes, how can I help?"

"Hi, I'm looking for information on Adrian Wyndridge and someone suggested you'd be the one to ask."

"You could ask anybody here and they could steer you in the direction of our local celebrity, but I'm as good as any," she grinned. "What kind of information? Maybe one of his novels? We have them all. We're expecting the final volume in his Bermudian trilogy soon but I'm afraid you'll have to wait for that one."

The elderly lady approached again, saw us talking, and settled down at the nearest table to wait.

"I don't want information, or at least, not that kind. I just need to talk to you. Could we go somewhere private? There's something I need to ask or, maybe I should say, tell you, about Adrian Wyndridge."

Edna didn't hide her amazement. "You want to speak to me in private about Adrian Wyndridge? Are you a reporter or something?"

"No way. This is personal, very personal."

"And you think I can help you with that?"

"Yes, but in confidence. This really isn't the place to get into it."

Edna put her hands on her hips, eyeing me for a few seconds, shaking her head. "Are you some kind of nutter?"

I smiled at that. "I guess that depends on who you ask. I'm joking; I'm perfectly sane. I just need to tell you something."

"Then tell me here."

"I can't. It's private but I know you'll want to hear it. This is very important. Please."

Maybe she read something in my face, something like desperation mixed with sincerity. "Well, this is a first. I have a book talk starting in twenty minute —P.D.James, *An Unsuitable Job for a Woman*, in case you want to sit in—and then I head right home after that. I have kids to take care of and dinner to prepare."

"Could I meet you somewhere on the way, someplace private? I have a bike. I won't take too much time."

I saw her hesitate. "Against my better judgment, all right. I'll meet you at the Old Devonshire Church. Do you know where that is?"

"I'll find it."

"If you want, meet me outside the library at 5:00—I park around the rear. You can follow me there. I live in Flatts Village and the church is about halfway. You'll find it interesting. What's your name, by the way?"

"Susan Waverley."

"Okay, Susan. See you later."

I thanked her and exited the building, not wanting to sit in for a book talk nor anything else, for that matter.

Clouds scudded in from the ocean as I perched in a little city park by a huge banyan tree and called Max. The phone rang directly to his messages. Relieved that I didn't have to explain anything in person, I told him I'd just taken a trip to Hamilton for the afternoon. If all went according to plan, by the time we made voice contact, I'd have the Wyndridge job.

I bided the next half-hour in a little corner book store purchasing tourist-issue local interest books with titles like *Bermuda Triangle: Unexplained Shipwrecks* and Wyndridge's recent *Brethren of the Coast*, which I began reading on the spot.

The man favored high-seas adventures set in the seventeenth century with dashing naval officers wresting booty from pirates while upholding Britain's mandate to go forth and conquer. Women appeared as the occasional spoils of war but rarely made an appearance on Wyndridge's brigantines and frigates, other than as a figurehead strapped to a prow.

Not my reading tastes, perhaps, but I knew Toby once enjoyed them. One of the Wyndridge novels had been made into a big action film with the starring role played masterfully by one of his boyhood crushes.

At the appointed time, I stuffed the books into my bag and waited, saddled on the moped in the rear parking area as Edna emerged from the library. She pointed at the glowering sky, making a face before beckoning me to follow. In a moment, I was merging into the traffic at her tail. Bikes and cars surrounded us in a steady stream of vehicles heading home after the day's work. Keeping Edna in sight demanded all my faculties.

She drove like a biker chick, legs straddled, skirt hitched up exposing those funky boots. In comparison, I gripped the handlebars like Pollyanna on a joyride through hell. The darkening skies, the threat of rain, an increasing sense of urgency, all forced me to hang on tight, gunning the engine at the first sign of clear road. Sometimes I lost her only to catch sight of her moments later three or four vehicles ahead.

We followed Middle Road along the island's backbone while banana groves, botanical gardens and cottages whizzed by. The January darkness fell hard, thickening like glue amidst the shrubbery. I shivered as the cool wind bit through my hoodie. In my haste, I hadn't brought a jacket or anything but my carpet bag squashed in the seat compartment along with my new books.

Gradually the traffic thinned, peeling off to the tribe roads and the cozy cottages lining our route and, when Edna finally indicated to turn, I couldn't wait to get off the road. I followed her into a parking lot, propping my bike beside hers near a path leading to a low white church.

I stood for a moment, stretching my legs, gazing around at what I knew to be a landmark. The Old Devonshire Church, a one-story cottage-like building, sat in a copse of palms on a low rise surrounded by whitewashed sarcophagi and above-ground tombs glowing ghostly in the gloom. The structure had the simple lines of seventeenth century design, practical and unfussy.

"Built by the first settlers?"

"Originally, but this is a reconstruction. The first church blew down in a hurricane in 1715, with the next rebuilt version burned to the ground by an arsonist in 1975. Who knows why? Lots of theories going around on that one. Come on, let's get inside before the heavens open up. Like I said, I don't have much time."

"Thanks for meeting me like this. I wouldn't have asked if it weren't important. The place is certainly private enough," I remarked as we walked up the path.

"Only the dead eavesdrop here, and they're not talking."

"Good thing. The living make enough noise."

"Got that right. Come on in. I've got a key."

I studied the rounded coffin-shaped, mounds as Edna unlocked the door. "These are family plots, aren't they?" Cemeteries fascinated me in a morbid way but my interest preferred to flex its wings in the daylight hours.

"Yes. An island this small gets crowded below ground." Edna glanced over her shoulder across the graveyard. "Every one of these tombs are stacked six to seven coffins deep, since there just isn't enough space to do it any other way. These are all family plots. Mine's on the other side. It's kind of comforting," Edna shrugged. "Together in death as in life, though I had an aunt once who always fought with her husband, my uncle Sam, so badly, she said they'd be scrapping down there, too."

I shivered despite myself. "Do you believe in ghosts?"

"I do, and you?"

"Undecided. Right now, I'd rather stay that way. This place has a sense of foreboding."

"Sure it does. It's called 'death,'" and she laughed. "Everybody ends up that way, one way or the other," she said as the key clicked into the lock. The thick cedar door swung open and she went in ahead of me to switch on the lights. "My cousin, the deacon, made me honorary assistant charged with replenishing the flowers and performing a few other custodial tasks. I kind of enjoy it. The place is so peaceful when a service isn't on and the tourists are gone."

"Do you mind the tourists?"

"Oh, they're all right as long as they're well-fed and the sun's shining. When it rains, it's like we locals are responsible. I'm sorry for the weather, you know, but it's not my fault."

"It still beats Nova Scotia this time of year." I stepped into a lovely wooden church, completely unexpected given the exterior. Old cedar beams overhead took the shape of ship's knees, a construction technique used for boat building that I recognized from the old buildings back home.

"Is that where you're from?"

"It is." Since Susan Waverley hailed from Baltimore, I figured I'd better change the subject. "Wow."

"Nice, isn't it? I like that it's not pretentious. Just those rows of pews made in the days when the island still had plenty of natural cedar. Some pieces survived the fire but you can still see the scorch marks. Over there's the altar, our pride and joy, you might say. That and our candlesticks, which date from the sixteen hundreds, are about all that's left with any value. All right, Susan, tell me what you have to say but make it quick."

Edna strolled up the aisle towards the altar, me trailing behind while rehearsing my words over and over again. Everything seemed silly, overwrought, or just plain lies, especially the truth. Damned if the truth didn't sound the worst of the lot but that's what came out of me in the end.

"My brother is missing and his last known destination was here in Bermuda. As far as I can tell, the last person to see him alive was Adrian Wyndridge, only he denies it."

Edna stopped, swinging around to face me. "Are you kidding me?"

"No way."

"How do you know that?"

"I have a picture of him standing with my brother out at Smith's Cove. It's a long story as to how I got the photo. Let's just say for simplicity's sake that I have a private investigator on the case."

"And has this investigator spoken to Wyndridge?"

"How can he even get to him? From what I understand, the man avoids contact with the outside world."

"That he does," Edna said, nodding. "He suffers from agoraphobia and a few other afflictions. He's a bit odd to some people's thinking."

"So," I said picking up the story, "I applied to Wyndridge's research job hoping to get in to find out what's going on. I was even short-listed, but today I discovered the position had been filled. No interview required."

"And somehow this investigator found out I was the lucky applicant," Edna was gazing at me, hands on hips. "Wow, he or she must be some crackerjack."

"I have to find my brother, Edna. I don't care how reckless or crazy it sounds, but I need to get into Wyndridge's and find out what he's hiding."

"And your brother's name?"

"Tobias McCabe. You probably don't know of him since he goes by the pseudonym Tobias Thomas, but he designs high-tech computer games with award-winning graphics. but he's an artist. He's tall, slim yet muscular, and has bright red hair, which he often wears long in deference to his latest Viking or high-seas animated characters. He—"

"Shit!" Edna slapped her hand to her mouth, dropped it to add: "Sorry, God. Tobias Thomas?"

"You've heard of him?"

"Hell, I saw him!" And she almost slapped her hand over her mouth again but rolled her eyes up heavenward and mouthed *Sorry, God*, instead.

"I saw him," she repeated, dropping her hand. "I saw him at Mr. Wyndridge's."

I stared at her in hopeful disbelief. "When?"

"The last time I worked for him, about two months ago."

"Two months ago?" I did a quick calculation. "That was long before he went missing."

"He was a house guest. I didn't see him around much but bumped into him one day by Wyndridge's dock when I was out for some air. Alistair didn't introduce me or anything, which I thought odd, but Toby introduced himself. Really charming guy. Said he was there on a diving holiday but I can't say I believed that. Alistair dives but he's a pretty solitary character."

Suddenly, I felt weak in the knees and plunked down on one of the pews. "Why would Wyndridge lie? Something's going on in there and I have to find out what."

"And you're thinking to get in there as a librarian to snoop? Are you even a librarian?"

"No, but I have to get in somehow. What else can I do? He's my brother."

Edna held up her hand. "Look, I like Alistair. We get along just fine but I just go in there and do my job knowing he's fiercely private. I don't snoop. I don't ask awkward questions. I just put my head down and work. He called me yesterday to press me to take the job after I convinced him to post for a proper archivist in the first place —you should see the manuscripts and artifacts he's collected, way beyond my skills— only he chickened out. Told me he'd had a change of heart and just wanted someone he knew and trusted. That's why I said I'd take the job. Now you're thinking of going in and digging around? Bad move, bad move."

I opened my mouth to speak but she hushed me with an upheld finger. "Let me finish. Maybe he's hiding more than just knowing your brother. Something's up with him and I don't know what. I don't want to know. Well," she amended, "I do but I sense it's better that I don't. The Wyndridges go way back on this island and there's always been rumors. The more I worked in there, the more I sensed all the stuff he might be hiding. Stay out of it."

I shook my head. "But I can't just go away without knowing. The police aren't pursuing this seriously. Wyndridge is probably the only one who may have the answers. How can I stay out of it?"

"I don't know and I don't know what I'd do if it were my brother but that's my advice. You just convinced me there's no way I'm taking this job, after all. I'm going to call and say I'm not taking it. If he asks you next and you're fool enough to say yes, that's up to you."

"You sound scared."

"Let's just say that I like to read my mysteries, not live them."

"Well, how cryptic is that? Are you afraid of him?"

"Not really, though he is eccentric. I think I'm more afraid of what he might be hiding. Enough said."

"Oh, hell, I don't believe this. You saw Toby! You can testify to his being with Adrian Wyndridge. Don't you see what this means? He denied ever seeing him."

"That's probably not enough to get the police back on the case, if that's what you're thinking."

I dug my hands into my lap. "I don't know what I'm thinking except to confirm I'm on the right track."

Edna plopped herself down beside me. "God help you, but I think you're doing this all wrong."

"What aren't you telling me?"

She jumped to her feet. "I've got to get going. It's getting late." She reached inside her leather jacket. "I just hope you know what you're doing."

A Blackberry emerged from her right pocket, along with a packet of tissues and a mini-bottle of contact cleaner. Scanning the digital screen briefly, she pressed a button and waited in silence as the phone rang while stuffing the other objects back in her pocket.

"Yes, Mrs. Wyndridge. This is Edna Smith. Yes, that one. Sorry for calling at dinner time but is Mr. Wyndridge there? It's important." A pause, then, "Yes, of course. I understand. Would you please pass the message on that I'm withdrawing my name from the position. Yes, yes, I know, but I'd rather not get into specifics on the phone. Something's come up. Yes. Thank you." And she clicked off. "There, done. Now, I have to go. Keep in touch, okay?"

I followed her to the door. "I will, one way or the other. Thanks for everything."

At the entrance, she paused, listening. "Hear that rain?"

It was hard not to since it pelted the building in a torrent of wind and water. I couldn't hide my alarm. Like, I was ready to drive in that?

Edna peered out the door. "Typical. When it pours here in January, it's like it rains sideways." And then her phone rang. She had it pressed to her ear in an instant. "I'm here," was her form of hello. "What? Are you kidding me? I thought I told you to come home right after school? Southampton? But I told you not to. Wait by the entrance then." She shrugged, dropping the phone back into her pocket. "My eldest kid. With all the wisdom of a 14-year-old, he decides to play cricket this afternoon with his mates. Now he's stranded on the other side of the island in this rain and guess who gets to pick him up?"

"Oh, I'm sorry. It's wild out there."

"Which way are you headed?"

"Near Astwood Cove."

"You've a drive ahead of you, too. Maybe you should head for a cafe and wait it out. I'm used to driving in bad weather here. There's one just down the road."

"No, thanks. I have to get back, too."

"We may as well travel in convoy, then. We're heading in the same direction for part of the way. You don't have a raincoat, do you?"

"No, but I'll be fine."

She pulled out a little blue plastic pouch from her left pocket. "Here, take this. It's like wearing a trash bag but it will do. I have another under my bike seat. Drop it off at the library someday when you're in town."

"Thanks." I pulled the sheath of crinkly blue over my head gratefully.

"You need to get better prepared for this island. She's full of surprises," Edna remarked, opening the door wide. "Carry rain gear wherever you go, even if the sun's shining. So, follow me up until the junction. Be careful."

Outside the wind whipped the words from our lips as we dashed for our bikes, rain stinging our faces. Edna didn't bother putting on her second rain jacket, if she even had one, just jumped on her bike and eased her way onto the road, waiting for me to catch up.

I'd planned to call Max to say that Edna had withdrawn her application, but I couldn't keep her waiting in this. I had no alternative but to clutch the handlebars and steer the bike onto the slick road.

With the helmet fastened and the visor down, I couldn't see more than a few yards ahead of me, enough to fix Edna's taillights in my gaze.

THE OCCASIONAL BUS, TAXI, AND MOPED, WHIZZED PAST ON THE opposite side, stirring up a water whirl to further drench my skin. Rain jacket or not, my jeans were soaked, my hands red with cold. Plunging through the dark on that motorized hunk of metal was miserable enough, but trying to keep up with Edna took everything I had.

And once on the open road, Edna drove like a banshee. We cut across the center of the island until we reached the long stretch following the south coast, me struggling to keep her in sight. Not many bikes kept us company by then, most of them smart enough to stay off the road. A few cars passed while a few skilled bikers darted between Edna and me with crazy confidence. I thought I'd lose sight of her completely but managed to keep my eyes one her.

Soon we were alone on the South Road, the glory of that scenic coast now consumed by wind and rain, the postcard views obliterated by an upstart tempest. I tried not to think about the waves crashing against the cliffs to my left. Though I had grown up with the sea, it never stopped terrifying me in bad weather. We'd had too many deaths by ocean in my family history: an uncle who fell overboard on a fishing trawler plus many more going back down our salty family tree. Dad had regaled us with plenty of stories over the years.

After about ten minutes, I saw the lights of a solitary rider in my rearview mirror. At first, I almost welcomed the company, since Edna wove in and out of sight by then, disappearing at every bend. At least here was another human being out in this crazy night. I had slowed way down, fear of hydroplaning consuming my earlier need to keep up. The bike remained at a polite distance behind me as the thick coastal shrubbery of Warwick Long Bay hedged away to the left. I remembered this stretch from my earlier drive when I could actually see. An abrupt turn ahead would lift the road away from this mostly uninhabited range and on towards the South Shore resorts and small properties. Soon I would be at Astwood Cove.

The rear rider suddenly moved up to my tailpipe as if wanting to pass. Great. All I needed was another brave or crazy Bermudian driver. I saw no oncoming traffic so slowed down, edging to one side to let him by. But he didn't take the offer. Instead, he matched his speed with mine so that we were both crawling along.

Which was all wrong. Panic hit hard. I clutched the handles. Who was this? Why was he crowding me? And then another bike came into view behind us, this one gunning quickly as if to overtake us both. Before I could form a plan or devise a response, this bike whipped past us, accelerating around the bend.

Edna! It wasn't so much a thought as a stab in my head. Something bad about to happen. I knew it, I just didn't know how. I hit the gas, picking up speed, terrified of what I'd find ahead. When the crash came, I was rounding the corner. I couldn't see anything, just heard the scream. And the driver who passed me didn't stop. The taillights were a mere prick of red far ahead.

Edna had disappeared. An awful cry followed by crashing metal, and then nothing.

Nothing at all.

I brought the bike to a skidding halt. The wheels spun gravel while I ran to where tire tracks drove into the abyss. I called Edna's name, called and called until my throat rasped raw. I stumbled along through the darkness crying out until I was standing on the edge of a precipice. Only the broken foliage of sea grapes and aloes separated me from what I feared most.

"Edna! Edna!"

Hands grasped my shoulders, drawing me back from the edge.

I shook him away. "She's down there! Help her, not me."

"Wait here," he ordered. "Call 911."

I already had my phone out, numb fingers tapping the numbers.

He disappeared, climbing over the rocks to the shore below. "Can't see anything," he shouted up.

"Find her!" I cried, blinded by rain. I screamed into the phone: "There's an accident on the South Road near Warwick Long Bay. Hurry!" And then

I tried following after him, the stones slippery, visibility nothing. With one hand grasping the shrubs, the other the rocks, I tried shimmying down the steep slope along a narrow path eked out between the rocks.

He clambered up, pushing me back. "It's too late. The bike, the crash— no one could survive that."

"No!" I screamed at him. "No, no, no! Someone killed her! The man who passed me drove her off the road!"

Soon there were other lights, a police car, an ambulance, someone asking questions. Did I know victim? "Yes, we had just met. A man was following us. He passed her and then this happened. He killed her."

"Accidents happen," the officer said. "Bad weather, greasy tarmac. I assure you that we'll investigate it. Can you give me a description of the driver or the bike he was driving?"

But how could I? "It was dark. He was wearing a helmet and a visor. His bike was like all the others on this island. He may even have been a she, for all I know."

"Right. A policeman will take you back to your accommodation, miss, and ask you a few more questions. Perhaps you should see a doctor for shock."

I just shrank into my shivering self. I craved an antidote for death, not some pill to lull the pain.

Peering through the faces in the crowd, I found him, the man who had looked for Edna first. A few strands of dark hair lay plastered against his forehead under the black hood of his slicker. Noel.

6

I eyed the glass in Noel's hand, my teeth chattering. "I don't do Scotch."

"Drink it, I said."

"Bully." But I slugged back the contents, wincing as it burned its way down. Damned if burn didn't suit my mood. I was angry enough to ignite the world. "Edna's dead," I said, holding out the glass for more. "You and Max will pay for this."

Damp towels lay heaped in piles about the floor of the little cottage. Noel's jacket hung over a chair drying before the fire while the man himself stood dark and ragged, his black hair plastered against his head.

"We didn't kill her, I said. I came along behind you, remember? I even gave my statement to the police. I was tailing you, not her. When you didn't return to the cottage, I took off to find you." He poured another inch of liquid into my glass. "That's your limit."

"Maggie said they had a contingency plan if I didn't get the job." I tossed back the scotch. "I didn't get the job, and who made you the liquor police, anyway?"

"Max may be many things but a killer isn't bloody one of them. The plan was to offer her a better-paying job. Had she arrived home tonight, she would have found a message on her answering machine." He took my glass and slipped it onto the side table. "And I deputized myself."

"Somebody ran her off the road,. If not you, then who?" I got to my feet, tried pacing, but wobbly legs swerved me dangerously close to the glass coffee table. He caught my arm and steered me back into sitting. I sat there for a moment, my emotions twisting. Edna had died at the scene. I couldn't believe it; I couldn't bear it, and what was worse, I couldn't stop thinking I was somehow responsible.

"Have you considered it might have been just an accident?" Noel remarked. "It's not like road accidents don't happen on this island."

"That bike passed me and gunned it around the bend. Maybe I didn't see anything, but I know he ran her off the road."

"You don't know anything, that's the point."

I shot him a foul look. "It's an informed conjecture. The best kinds of murders look like accidents. Don't you read?"

"Not murder mysteries, if that's what you're implying. And why would anyone want to kill her?" He tugged a throw from off the back of a chair and wrapped it around my quaking shoulders. Crouching down in front of me, he added, "Go have a shower and get out of those wet clothes." He remained too close, his face all sharp angles and inscrutable green eyes. "Now."

I stared at him. "Why would anybody want to kill Edna, you ask? How about why would anyone want to kill Toby?"

I wished I could claw back the words as soon as they escaped my lips.

"Don't talk like that. Toby's still alive."

"All these months, I refused to believe the possibility. How could anything or anyone harm my brother? He's brilliant, an illustrator, an athlete, an artist! He took risks every day of his life but not stupid ones. He always said to follow your heart, even if it steered you into the deep end because that's where the juice of life exists, in risk, in passion! I was the safe one. I was the one who stayed home, went to school, studied a conservative vocation, and then backed out. It was me who didn't have the guts to grab life by the throat. How could he die?" Oh, God, I was swerving right over the edge, coming totally undone. I'd soon be blubbering, wailing with grief and fury. It wasn't fair, wasn't right!

"You don't know what happened to Toby. Stop thinking the worst," Noel said gently. "You're here to find out. Focus on that."

"How can I focus on anything? Edna was frightened of something, Noel. Do you understand? Scared to death of something but wouldn't say what."

"Look, for all we know, tonight was a tragic accident. The librarian —"

"Edna, her name was *Edna*!"

"Edna was driving too fast. You said so yourself.”

“Maybe, but she also knew things she wouldn't talk about, some secret surrounding Adrian Wyndridge. She was going to step down from the job. She called Wyndridge's place while we were together at the church, not because I needed to find out about Toby, but because she was frightened and whatever I said spooked her.”

Noel went still. “What did you say?"

"I told her about Toby, said that I needed to get in there to find out what happened to him."

"Jesus, Phoebe."

"She'd seen Toby at Wyndridges two months ago. She saw him!"

“What if she had gone straight to the police?”

I lifted my head, streaming tears. “As it was, she went straight to her death.”

He swore again, getting to his feet. "We did not kill her, get that? I spoke to Max. He's at the other end of the island on a yacht. He's going to dock and catch a cab to get here as soon as he can."

"Great." I said through rattling teeth as I launched to my wobbly feet. He tried to steady me but I slapped his hand away. "I'll be ready for him. I'll just take a shower."

I didn't wait to see if he left. All I wanted was solitude with lots of hot water pounding down on my head, and yet all the hot water in the world wouldn't blast away my bleakness. To make matters worse, I was loopy from alcohol on an empty stomach and lurched around the bathroom trying to find my sea legs. In the shower, I leaned my forehead against the marble tiles, crying for Edna and my lost brother until tears and shower blurred into one torrential wash.

Finally, exhausted and spent, I turned off the water taps and toweled down . Under the whine of the hairdryer, I tried to review the whole messy business but my brain stalled. Pulling on one of the sweaters I knit long ago, I climbed into my worn corduroy pants, letting my hair curl wildly in its own wayward energy. Tonight it could go to hell with the rest of me.

When had I eaten last? Breakfast. Hunger chewed my gut. Downstairs, the fire still crackled in the hearth but the damp towels had disappeared. Hushed thumping could be heard from the laundry closet, with clinking china emanating from the kitchen. A kettle whistled. Wavering between annoyance and fury, I stepped into the kitchen.

Noel stood with his back towards me dressed in an Astwood Cove pink bathrobe, long hairy legs sticking out beneath, pouring boiling water into a hibiscus-painted teapot. The table had been set for two in cheery flowered placemats and blue linen napkins with a tray of sandwiches and fruit in the center, everything a little glow of cozy in a sea of gloom.

"Hungry?" he asked without turning. "Thought you'd better soak up that Scotch with grub, though you're probably already buggered. I found enough in the fridge to feed an army of two." Turning, he set the teapot on the table and tugged a cotton Bermudan cottage-shaped cozy down over it without looking at me.

I averted my eyes from the triangle of chest hair curling above the robe's pink collar.

"I availed myself of the downstairs shower and am in the process of drying my clothes. Do you mind?" he asked.

"Would it matter if I did?"

"Not a bit since I'm hanging around until Max gets here. Besides, I'm currently minus clothes."

"Your cottage is, what, a couple of twists and turns to the right? Did you think you couldn't walk that far?"

"I'd just get wet all over again. You wouldn't want that. How about tea? Made to your specs, I might add. I am definitely a tea man myself, but I prefer mine milky with two teaspoons of sugar."

"You're babbling now."

He stopped, turning towards me, a wry smile playing on his lips. "I'm standing in the kitchen of a glowering woman wearing nothing but a bubble-gum pink bathrobe after having just tugged a small cottage-shaped something-or-other over a teapot. Wouldn't you babble?"

I smiled despite myself. "You look ridiculous."

"I'm chronically aware of that fact. Here, sit."

Nodding, I slumped into the chair, resting my chin in my hands as he moved about the kitchen. I didn't mean to stare. At first my gaze was unfocused, landing on anything that moved, which happened to be him. Only a few moments later when I looked, I mean really looked, did I notice the tattoo curving down his right leg.

I leaned over, arms on knees, for a closer look as he poured the tea into my mug. The design was intriguing, a distinctive Aboriginal sand or dot painting rich with ochers and rusts, the execution surprisingly intricate. "A snake?"

"Pardon?" he stepped back as if shocked to find my face so close to his person. He caught the line of my gaze.

"Your tat, is it of a snake?"

"Kangaroo," he said. "You're looking at the tail."

"I think of you as more of a snake."

"Ah, but you don't know me."

"Snake still seems more apt. Is it kangaroo dreaming?"

He met my eyes. "What do you know about the dreaming?"

"Just what I've read. Unlike you, my reading tastes are eclectic and Max kindly gave me plenty of Australian reading material as a child. He seemed very interested in the Aboriginals."

"He would."

"Which tribe are you from?"

"Walpiri."

"But one of your parents is white?'

"How observant."

I just continued, hoping to ride out awkwardness. "I've always been fascinated by the Aboriginals, their art especially. Art connecting with the culture is kind of my thing. That tat looks like a work of art. Is it from where you were born?"

"It is."

He didn't want to pursue this line of questioning. On the other hand, I didn't want to drop it. "Must have taken a long time. It looks large."

The corners of his mouth melted into a slow, lazy smile. "It covers two-thirds of my body and, yes, it took three days. Should I be flattered by your interest?" He placed a flowered pitcher of milk on the table, his brows arched in amusement.

"In your tat? Definitely not. I'm only interested from an aesthetic and cultural perspective."

"It's a very beautifully rendered piece of artwork. I'd offer to show it to you in all its glory but most women are interested in the whole package."

"Whereas I definitely am not. All-over body tats are a bit of a turnoff." Which was a lie I wished were true. In fact, I admit they emanated an irresistible bad-boy attraction, especially on this bad boy. Blame the Scotch. Pulling my gaze away, I stirred my tea.

"Too bad. I think you'd appreciate the details."

He had me wondering, though. A kangaroo? So, if the tail wound around his leg, where did it begin? What part of his anatomy did it cross? "When is Max supposed to arrive?"

"Soon. He texted me that he's hired a cab and is on his way. "Here, eat, mate. I believe the one in the middle is rock lobster salad, and the wheat versions are cheese with something green inside, not mold, I hope." He passed the tray.

"Watercress." I plucked a lobster and a wheat each onto my plate, my voice shaky. "Pink isn't your color, by the way. You're more a black leather man."

He smiled. "There, I've gone and ruined my style manifesto. Luckily, my clothes should be dry soon."

We ate in silence, me devouring two lobster and two watercress and cucumber sandwiches washed down with mugs of tea, my eyes fixed on my plate. I checked the wall clock. Nine p.m.

"Mind if I help myself to a beer?" he asked.

"I can't believe you asked."

"Habit."

"You really were trained in England. What were you doing there, anyway?"

"Studying history and archaeology. I went to Cambridge and the University of Queensland back home, just in case you pegged me for a complete loser."

"I pegged you for a dogsbody, not a loser."

"Same thing."

When he sauntered past on the way to the living room bar, I swung around to check out that tattoo again. How long were Kangaroo tails, anyway?

He returned moments later with a bottle of Heineken.

"Why are you working for Max? He treats you like dirt."

Sitting down, he popped the cap off the beer and took a couple of deep swallows while I fixed on his Adam's apple. "The pay is good and the work's interesting. The rest is just surface noise. Besides, it suits my present needs." He held the bottle out and made a face. "I miss Foster's. Now there's a beer."

"Where are you living now?"

"I have a flat in London near Max's shop. You should come visit," he said with a slow smile. "I could show you around."

"What an offer."

"Ever been to London?"

"Yes, once, before Max opened a shop there. How did you and Max meet, anyhow?"

"You might say I looked him up." He took two more very large gulps. "So, do you like the Australian wines?"

I got it: He did not want to discuss Max or his Aboriginal roots. "Are we going to make small talk from here on in? Because I'm no good at it, just so you know."

"Small talk lubricates the social wheels."

"Mine just might fall off my axle from boredom."

And he laughed at that, a full-throated howl of mirth which, I've got to admit, completely transformed his face into something bright and devastatingly sexy. Damn.

"All right then, I'll try a more substantial topic: Why did you quit law?"

I studied the palm frond on my tea cup. "I was only interested in criminal law, had this idealistic notion I could make the world a safer place by championing justice. By the time I decided to switch to art crime, it was too late, to my way of thinking anyway."

"Ah, an idealist. So, what did all that idealism get you?"

"Conflict. I soon realized that our legal system requires even rapists and murders to be defended, and that someday I had might have to defend the guilty. Didn't think I could stomach that so I returned to my default position of underemployed art and textile lover going nowhere."

"Soul-satisfying but economically disastrous."

I sighed, toying with my mug. "Exactly. I'm perpetually broke."

He leaned forward, his sharp-angled face suddenly serious. "Does your definition of justice fall on the side of ethics or the law?"

I thought of the tapestry I'd absconded and made a face. "Some might argue the two are synonymous, but not me, not any more. I define ethics more broadly these days. What is legal may not always be just, what is criminal may be morally necessary. In other words, don't ask that question. And that doesn't mean I agree with what you and Max are up to."

He grinned. "I expected you'd say that."

The phone rang. We both turned to stare at the wall phone at my elbow.

"Answer it."

"Why me?"

"You're the one staying here."

"Right." I plucked the receiver from its cradle. "Hello?"

"Miss Waverley?"

"Yes."

"This is Mrs. Wyndridge."

"Right."

"My son has requested that I call to see if you are still interested in accepting the position as researcher, which has opened unexpectedly. If you consent, you are to start as soon as possible." The tone clipped into my ear, abrupt and imperious.

I swallowed. "What, no interview?"

"You have the necessary qualifications. He finds an interview unnecessary. Will you accept the position or not?"

"Yes. When do I begin?"

"Tomorrow afternoon. Mr. Wyndridge requires intensive research within a tight timeframe and requests that you accept room and board on the estate. This is part of your salary, of course. We will send the driver to the Astwood Properties at promptly 4:30 p.m."

"Fine but I—"The line went dead. That woman had a thing about long goodbyes. I laid the cordless phone on the table and turned to Noel. "Just like that, Wyndridge has moved on to his second choice without even waiting for Edna's funeral. I start tomorrow." Despair washed over me. "I need air."

I strode to the living room and flung open the French doors to the main patio where I circumvented the pool. Scents of salt and damp leaves mingled after the rain. The sea pounded against the cliffs below as my feet scrunched over the wet flagstones to the far side of the patio.

Leaning against the stone wall, I stared out at the night scape. Below, a dark fringe of palms, ahead, the heaving darkness of the sea. A lighthouse pulsed its steady heartbeat across the night.

An impenetrable sense of loss swallowed me whole. People died. Time eroded lives and objects, both. I leaned against the stone, resisting the pull of despair. We were all so utterly alone in the end. I closed my eyes.

Tomorrow it would begin.

I didn't hear him approach.

"Are you all right?"

"What do you think?"

"I think you're in way over your head, little mermaid."

I smiled. "But mermaids are born way over their heads. Don't you get that, dogsbody? So, guess we'll have to see which one of us underestimates me the most." Turning towards him, it startled me to find he'd changed back into his own clothes, the black on black completely erasing the accessibility of minutes earlier.

He plunged his hands deep into his pockets. "I've called Max and told him you've got the job. He'll be here soon."

I pushed past him. "I want another drink" .

"Bad idea," he called after me.

7

By the time Max arrived, I'd discovered the joys of Bourbon poured over ice and slurped back like toxic honey. I sat in the chair by the fire calming my nerves with alcohol-laced knitting to the point where I'd lost the ability to tell a dropped-on-purpose stitch from a long yarn-over. Everything looked the same and I was fine with that. Noel lounged in the chair opposite, legs stretched out in front of him, looking grim, his gaze fixed on the carpet. We'd stopped speaking after he'd failed to prevent me from foraging in the liquor cabinet.

The door swung open. We were on our feet in an instant.

"Phoebe, are you all right?" Max asked, tossing his drenched jacket over the chair and heading for me, arms wide. I sidestepped his embrace , almost toppling into the coffee table. Righting myself, I shoved back a lock of hair, untangled the yarn from my leg and glared. "Did you kill her?"

He stood stunned. "Kill who?"

"Edna Smith. She was run off the road tonight. Deliberately, as in murder."

Max shot a quick look at Noel. "Wasn't that an accident?"

"She doesn't think so," Noel answered. "She thinks someone ran her off the road on purpose, someone like maybe you or me."

Max looked aghast. "Why would we do that?"

"So I could get in the Wyndridge estate according to plan. Killing her was the contingency."

"Phoebe, get a grip. We were not responsible for that accident. I would never have someone killed. "

Then Maggie came breezing through the door enveloped in couture rainwear and some scent that grabbed me by the throat. "A man's bringing up the luggage. Thanks for helping, Maxi. Jeez, so I'm there standing in the rain and you just take off. I—"Then she caught sight of me. "Phoebe, hon, how are you doing?" She swept towards me as if to bestow kisses into my air space but I backed away, putting a chair between me and her.

"What luggage?" I asked.

"Clothes for your role. You start tomorrow, right?"

"Screw the clothes," said I.

"Mags, sit down, for God's sake," Max growled.

She glanced at him. "I got, like, maybe only a few hours to do hair, makeup and wardrobe."

"Sit down, I said."

Maggie huffed over to the couch and flopped down with a sullen stare, while I resumed my attack. I leaned forward, pointing my finger at Max. "I know you're looking for more than just Toby. Edna was scared witless. She told me that the author is sitting on a secret, a big secret, and I think you're sending me in to find it just like you did Toby."

Max's face paled. "Phoebe, I—"

"Skip it. I don't want to hear any more of your invasive tactics. I mean, evasive tactics." I spun around looking for my drink, seeing it halfway across the world on the side table beside my knitting. Turning back, I eyed my godfather. "You and Dad were up to something all those years ago, something to do with money. You think I'm going to wait patiently while you throw me crumbs? I remember the time you two took off in the boat one night when we were all supposed to be in bed. Toby and I sneaked into the kitchen and found that nautical map spread over the table under the coffee mugs, so we followed you in our dinghy."

"Bloody hell! And you two ended up clinging to a buoy after your boat capsized, and your dad and I only found you the next morning. Two little drowned rats crying your eyes out. How could I forget that? You almost bloody drowned!"

"You wouldn't tell us where you were going!"

We were shouting now.

"You were bloody kids!"

"Not anymore!" I made a dive for my drink, stumbling only once on my way to the table. I took several deep sips before wiping my mouth with the back of my hand. "I'm not a kid anymore."

"Then stop acting like one." Noel had somehow emerged at my elbow.

I glanced up at him. "What are you doing?"

"Keeping you from crashing into the furniture," he said mildly. "We don't want to lose our deposit."

"Back off. I don't need you as a bumper."

"You're drunk," Max said.

"And you're a liar! Toby came here to meet Wyndridge because of you, didn't he? And Dad found out and told you never to come near him again. That's what you were arguing about the night he disappeared and why you're all puckered in guilt now. You think keeping me in the dark will absolve you and grant me some kind of immunity while you risk my neck, too, right?"

He looked like I'd slapped him.

"Bingo," I said, waving my drink at him. "Nailed it, didn't I?"

He looked stricken. "I never want anything to happen to you," he said hoarsely. "Or Toby."

"Tell her, Max. She has a right to know," Noel said.

"Damn right I do. What were you, Dad, and now Toby, after, Max? What was Toby hunting down when he went AWOL? And what does Wyndridge have to do with it? Oh, wait. Let me guess: you're all after the Oak Island treasure, right? We saw the chart that night." I said it half-joking but, with a jolt, realized I'd nailed that, too. "Holy shit." Noel caught my glass seconds before I dropped it. I stood, wobbly and stunned, everything roiling. "You couldn't possibly join the legions of idiots who have sunk millions of dollars and lost countless lives trying to dig up the Oak Island treasure?"

Max took a deep breath, his eyes never leaving my face. "I came to Nova Scotia all those years ago on a hunch. A friend of mine had scrounged up new research on Oak Island which indicated that it might be connected to a group of well-connected British naval officers in the sixteen hundreds."

"Sixteen eighty-seven, specifically. Lord Mordaunt, The Duke of Albemarle, Sir John Narbrough and Sir William Phips," Noel added.

"I needed someone who knew that coastline inside and out so I asked around, which brought me to your dad. Sheldon McCabe was up for the challenge. He knew the stories about Oak Island better than anybody and wanted in on the adventure. I was one of the financial backers of the latest dig, so I added him to my contingent. We found enough to know we were onto something, and then important new research hit publication."

"Researchers discovered that the conspirators found the remains of the Spanish galleon, the *Concepcion*, under the initial auspices of no less a personage than the then-king of England, William of Orange," Noel continued. "Only Sir William Phips, a noted royal scavenger, managed to squirrel away a significant portion of the hoard for himself. With his ship *Good Luck* and the *Boy Huzzar* in attendance, they detoured to a remote corner of what is now Nova Scotia and engineered an ingenious flood chamber to preserve the loot."

"I know all that," I snapped. "There isn't a kid in Nova Scotia who doesn't know about the Money Pit or that millions have been invested in trying to out-manoeuvre that flood shaft including the most recent brothers." Suddenly, my stomach felt distinctly unstable. "What does all that have to do with Bermuda?"

"The Money Pit's flood chamber was partly a ruse, "Noel continued, sounding more the academic and less the dogsbody by the minute. "The large portion of the treasure was entrusted by Phips to his chief engineer and captain, John Wyndridge, who sailed it to Bermuda and buried it in another tidal shaft, where we believe it remains to this day."

I swung around to face them, first Noel, then Max. "Adrian Wyndridge is sitting on part of the Oak Island treasure?"

"Technically, the Bermuda treasure, since this portion never ended up inside Oak Island's Money Pit in the first place," Noel said. "John Ashley Wyndridge may have used some of the loot to finance his business dealings in the Bermudan colony and stashed the rest, or hid the whole lot. We surmise that he may have melted down the coins but kept the jewels. Either way, there is literally millions of dollars' worth in today's currency missing, the bulk of which is in precious artifacts and jewels. William of Orange appeared to have received only silver, but that galleon carried far more than that."

"Heaps of treasure were reportedly stacked on the *Concepcion* with chests of more than four million pesos, including booty unearthed from the mines of Central America, Aztec, and Mayan artifacts, jewels reportedly absconded from pirates and the like, literally a bloody fortune by any century's standards," Max said. "That's what I do, Phoebe, that's my business: I source antiquities for museums and collectors."

"By stealing?"

"Who says this belongs to Wyndridge? It was stolen in the first place!" Noel interrupted.

"That doesn't make it in the public domain. Legally, he owns it."

"Frig the law," Noel asserted. "Wyndridge has no right. His family have sat on millions for centuries while watching men lose their lives trying to unearth what isn't there!"

I shook my head, pressing my index finger between my eyes as if to push a reset button. "Is he trying to keep it for himself, trying to extract it, or what?"

"We're not sure. Can't literally get to the bottom of it. That dropkick, Frank, couldn't find anything, but he says Wyndridge seems more fixed on writing his damn book than anything else. But he has no right to hoard it!" Max said, punctuating the air with his index finger. "The treasure is stolen goods, first from the Spanish who, in turn, pillaged it from all the lands they conquered, then from William of Orange, then from Phips himself. It belongs in museums, maybe, spread among the countries as history and art. Toby went to meet him ages ago, and if he's harmed him, I'll make him pay!"

I lowered my hand, tightening my gut against another lurch. "Toby wouldn't have gone in there to steal, surely?" I said. "He'd only be interested in uncovering the mystery and the challenge of it all, but you source artifacts, Max, so you actually want all that shiny stuff, don't you? You are a treasure hunter, you and the dogsbody here—thieves."

"I want what's fair. I want that stuff uncovered. Nobody has a right to sit on that much wealth and beauty forever."

"So ironic. Dad used to say treasure hunters were the craziest, badassed loonies in the world. Couldn't let go of the dream of gold, would keep hunting even if it killed them." I looked up. "That's you, and maybe Toby for different reasons, and now my father, too? When did Dad pull himself away?"

"When it got real," Max replied. "At first it was just a game I was paying him well to play. Years passed where not much happened. I got on with my business and your dad carried on with the boat tours. Then Toby got wind of the Bermuda connection and your dad started bucking his involvement." He took a step towards me. "Phoebe, I made a mistake with Toby. I should never have let it go this far. I'm not making the same mistake with you. You're not going in there. I've changed my mind. You phone Wyndridge right now, say you're refusing the job."

I laughed, stepping back. "Like hell. It's too late for that." And then my stomach heaved. I spun away, heading for the bathroom, only Noel got in the way.

8

A bruised sky loomed overhead as I waited outside the Astwood gatehouse late the next afternoon. Yesterday had been a nightmare and today an audition for another. All day Maggie had clipped and groomed me like some show poodle while I sat glued to my tablet researching everything I could find on Wyndridge, the *Concepcion*, and current Oak Island research. A combination of hangover and heartache poisoned my mood a deep shade of foul. It was as if I put one foot in front of the other even though I knew a cliff lay ahead.

The new luggage stacked beside me coordinated with the cream trench coat and linen suit. Everything pinched, jabbed, and squeezed. I wiggled my toes in the tan leather pumps and glowered down at my feet. Pumps, hell. Despite my family legacy, almost because of my family legacy, I always erred on the side of honesty but now stood dressed for deceit. Only my battered carpet bag leaning against my ankles like a cowering puppy looked remotely mine. I took comfort in studying the rich kilim reds and ochre in its design. I practically clawed Maggie when she tried replacing it with one of those designer bags.

I looked up. Noel bounded over the damp grass towards me in black jeans and a grey t-shirt under his black leather jacket. The damned man looked good enough to eat.

"You look very professional," he remarked, drawing closer, hair in his eyes. "A true Susan Waverley."

"If Susan were heading for a banking job in downtown Manhattan, maybe."

"You still look good."

Spoken like a man who hadn't quite figured out how to compliment a woman properly. "What a relief. Except for the headache, I'm feeling much better today, thanks for asking."

His mouth quirked. "I told you to lay off that bourbon. And I managed to launder my jeans after you up-chucked all over them, thanks for asking. Anyway, I didn't come to discuss wardrobes. I have news."

I held up my hand. "What could be worse than what I already know?"

"It's not too late to back out, Phoebe. You can turn on your sleek new heels and march right back to Nova Scotia."

"Do these shoes look made for walking? I'm going to find my brother and, like I've said before, it's information I'm seeking, not treasure. Now, say what you've come for."

His expression was guarded. "It's about the driver Wyndridge is sending, Bert."

I scanned the empty driveway. "You mean the one picking me up?"

He shoved his hands into his pockets. "Right. Wyndridge hired him after Frank pulled a cropper suddenly. He's going by Bert, but his real handle is Hector Bolt and he's done time in England for an assortment of criminal activities."

My mouth went dry. "Max mentioned him. It seems Wyndridge doesn't check his references too carefully."

"References are easily forged."

"Don't I know it."

"My point is, be careful."

"Oh, my God!" I slapped a hand against my forehead. "I'm in danger! Why hadn't I noticed earlier?" I crossed my arms. "A bit late for that, isn't it? I suppose it hasn't occurred to you that there might be more than one treasure hunter after this loot? All of you are dangerous, no exceptions."

"Of course, we're dangerous, but I'm not the one apt to hurt your pretty little neck."

"Can't you come up with a better phrase than that?"

"Sorry. Archaic-speak belied my more expansive vocabulary. Let me simplify: Be careful. Don't try anything rash. Is that better? Just get in, get what we need, and get out. Max wants you out of there within three days, at the latest."

"Get what *we* need, you said. I'm going in to get what *I* need and to hell with what Max wants or you. I'm looking for my brother, remember?"

"That's what I meant. Avoid using your cell phone to call either Max or me. We'll contact you."

"How?"

"We'll find a way. Max will be on a yacht nearby and I'll be staying close to Wyndridge's. When I send you a signal, meet me down at the base of Wyndridge's jetty. If you run into trouble and have to contact me, I took the liberty of entering a speed-dial number on your iPhone. Let the phone ring once then hang up. I'll know you need me. The title for the contact is Yarn Maven."

"Yarn Maven. You're joking?"

"It sounded suitably innocuous. You're a knitter aren't you?" He pointed to my carpet bag.

"You have no idea, do you?"

"That's an authentic piece of antique carpet from the Ottoman empire."

I shot him a quick look. "I meant you know nothing about my knitting. You're probably imagining I make doilies or socks or something. As for the bag, Max gave it to me."

"I know. He covered a seat in his London townhouse with the same fabric after finding much of it destroyed at the bottom of a trunk at an estate sale. You'd love the work he does, you know. Many of our clients seek rare and beautiful textiles, among other objets d'art. Imagine spending your days sourcing those?"

"Gee, another job offer. It's either feast or famine these days." I sensed he had more to say but the sight of a car slipping up the drive stopped him.

"Here he comes. I'd better disappear. Take care of yourself." He turned and dashed into the shrubbery like some kind of leather-glad gazelle.

I shivered as a dark green Jaguar purred up the drive. The car whispered to a stop. A thickset uniformed man climbed out, aiming the key fob at the trunk. Tall, dark and hefty, with a brush of short dark hair streaked with grey, he reminded me of a football player melting into flabby retirement. "Morning ma'am. Susan Waverley, I presume?"

"Correct and you must be the driver from Mr. Wyndridge's."

"Just so. Bert's the name." He nodded while reaching for the two suitcases, clutching the handles with sausage fingers and striding over to toss them into the trunk. When he returned moments later for my carpet bag, I had it safely slung over my shoulder.

He doffed his cap and stretched his lips back, revealing a march of perfect teeth. The distinct scent of menthol competed with his aftershave, a war that made me sneeze. "Always nice to meet a new colleague. Care to take a seat in the car?" Cockney accent. I avoided his proffered hand and slid into the back seat, the door slamming shut while I dug around my bag for a tissue. The sounds of sea and wind instantly ceased as if we'd been vacuum-sealed. I pushed down the electric window button for breeze control.

Bert climbed into the driver's seat and power-controlled my window back up. Soon the car was slipping down the drive through the gardens and candy-colored buildings towards the South Shore Road. My Google search had identified our destination as somewhere near Stonehole Bay. Wyndridge apparently lived along the length of an otherwise uninhabited national park, something he'd probably managed through an uninterrupted and influential family presence. Old money, in other words.

I leaned back in the seat trying to relax. Mopeds, motorcycles, and the occasional car whizzed past. The ocean behind the landscape brewed deep teal under the brooding sky.

"So, how long have you been working for Mr. Wyndridge?" I asked.

"Three days. His driver took off unexpectedly." He popped a mint into his mouth, refreshing his menthol reek. "You know these young punks. Can't trust them. As soon as a better offer comes, pouf! They're gone."

"Strange how that happens," I remarked.

"Ah yes, just so. Look at that poor library lady you're replacing. Here yesterday, gone today. And Wyndridge arrives from a two-day sail only to find out that his jackass-of-all-trades has left him stranded. Staff turnover is big at his place. So, I just came along with my perfect curriculum minutiae packaged with a little gardening experience and a whole pile of serious chauffeuring shit, and Wyndridge snapped me up. He knew a bargain when he saw one."

"Must be fate."

He grinned. "That's what I thought."

Rounding the corner near Warwick Long Cove, I recognized the spot where Edna met her death. I couldn't look away.

"This is where the library lady died," the driver remarked. My eyes slid to his in the rearview mirror.

"How do you know that?"

He shrugged. "Small island. Everybody knows everything. Tragic, I thought, but here you are to fill her shoes. Just proves that nobody's expendable , Sue. Mind if I call you Sue?"

"Susan, please."

"How about 'Suzy'?"

"Worse."

"Right, Suzy it is."

I sank back into the seat, shivering in the air conditioning. The exterior temperature didn't warrant the extreme temperature. "Could you please turn the air con down?"

So he turned it up.

"You're going to love the Wyndridge digs—something else, if I do say myself," Bert said, glancing at me in the mirror. "The place has been here for over 250 years. Very nice, if you like old places. Lots of little nooks and crannies, good for rendezvousing with cute little redheads. You enjoying the ride, Suzy?"

"Go to hell, Bertie."

His doughy grin stretched wide.

The estate lay about four miles down the South Shore Road, well-hidden from the highway, as expected. I must have passed the entry twice yesterday without knowing, thinking that stretch of coast consisted of only parkland and hidden beaches. A gap between boulders marked the driveway, which plunged in switchback turns down the hill towards the shore.

The early winter twilight thickened the darkness amid the trees as the Jag nosed along the drive. Halfway down, Bert stopped the car, jumped out, and unlocked a gated barricade. Minutes later, we drove into a clearing. On a crest of a cliff bounded by low stone walls and occupied by a single freestanding garage, Bert stopped the car.

I could only stare.

Wyndridge Estate rose like a cottage-castle from the other side of a leaping span of bridge. Perched in the center of a tiny island promontory, the structure looked like an overblown cottage organism that had sprouted wings vertically and horizontally. Each section carried the typical Bermudan features of white stepped roofs, pink coral stone walls, shutters, and casement windows, everything, that is, but the single stone tower rising from its midst like a transplant from another era.

"Old watchtower," Bert said. "First thing the original Wyndridge built. Gives a full view of the ocean ahead and the mainland behind. Think he had something to guard, little Suzy?"

I climbed out, too absorbed to spar. It reminded me of a blenderized sugar-pink fortress, a contradiction in every aspect.

Bert unloaded the luggage onto a buggy. "I can't drive you over. The bridge is just for people and bikes, so you just walk across and I'll bring the bags along."

But for minor repairs, the old stone bridge couldn't have changed much in centuries. Two buggy tracks grooved ridges into the cobbles with low stone walls on either side. I strode across the span with the wind whipping my hair and the crash of waves in my ears. Halfway across, I leaned over the chest-high wall. At least 50 feet below, foam boiled over rocks in a narrow channel separating the island from the mainland. Edna's death flashed into my mind before I pulled back.

"High, isn't it?" shouted Bert, the baggage buggy rattling behind him. "Treacherous for a place so lovely."

I continued without comment. Once across the channel, I followed a natural stone path curving from the bridge onto a terraced patio where a small wall hunkered against the wind. Beyond that, a tiny kitchen garden nurtured herbs spotted through with rain-battered flowers next to the house's casement windows.

The first drop of rain hit my face the exact moment I saw Adrian Wyndridge framed in the light of a doorway. In a white poet's shirt and moleskin breeches, he looked like a specter from another age, a magnificent paragon of manly beauty who just missed the mark by a few centuries. "Mr. Wyndridge, hello. I'm Susan Waverley."

"Obviously," he said with a flip of his hand. "I apologize for not being more welcoming, but I'm most distressed over Edna Smith's death. You have heard of the accident?"

"Of course. Actually, I was kind of a witness. She was showing me the Old Devonshire Church and I was following her home. I'll never get over it as long as I live. We were just driving along and then—and then she was gone." My voice hitched.

His gray eyes were searching but then he sighed, stepping back from the door. "Too many accidents is all rather unsettling. Do come in."

Wyndridge stepped aside to let me to pass. Inside, I glimpsed white stucco walls punctuated by dark wooden ceiling beams, wide-planked cedar floorboards, and a hallway stretching deep to the rest of the house. Lemon furniture polish assaulted my nostrils, waxy and pungent.

An old woman stood like a sentry beside a potted palm. Surgical stockings bound her swollen legs and the knobby hands resting on broad hips twisted with arthritis.

Wyndridge turned to her. "May I introduce my mother, Mrs. Wyndridge, and Mother, meet Ms. Waverley." And to me, "My mother will take good care of you. Consider her your main contact when I'm unavailable."

I smiled over at the woman. "Nice to meet you."

She gave me a sharp-eyed once-over. "Good day to you."

"Um, we spoke on the phone, I think."

Wyndridge held up his hand. "Mother, do take good care of her. See to it that she has what she needs. Why don't you show her to her room so she'll have a chance to freshen before dinner?"

The woman nodded. "You'll be dining at seven, son?"

"Tonight, yes. I must explain the work to Ms. Waverley and then return to my own," he said. "I expect matters to get rather hectic over the next few days and I'm eager to expedite the matter."

"I'll show her to the Bottle room, then," she said.

"Excellent. I'll look forward to speaking with you both later." And he took off down the hall. I almost tried to curtsy until I remembered I didn't know how.

I turned to the old woman, whose shrewd gaze never left my person. She had to be at least my dad's age. "I understand that Bert is bringing my baggage in."

"Well, I certainly won't be doing it, but that Bert is a useless sod if ever there was, a big sack of no-good-intent. And now you. There's just too many strangers entering our lives for my liking. Too many people gone missing or dying, like that poor Edna Smith, and no one will work for us anymore. Not that I blame them. The Wyndridges just aren't what they used to be. Well then, follow me. Bert will probably be along soon. He must be good for something."

"I doubt that."

"Mind that you tell me if he steps out of line. I'll have him out on his ear the moment we find a replacement."

I followed behind the woman's shuffling footsteps down a hall hung with painted seascapes and plenty of little mullioned windows designed to frame the real thing beyond. To be in a house where people named rooms other than "bathroom" and "kitchen" was novel enough, let alone walking corridors where every second object could be a museum piece.

"I don't believe in accidents myself," Mrs Wyndridge muttered. "Things happen for a reason, if you ask me, not that anyone does, of course." She flashed a pointed look over her shoulder, catching me inspecting a French seventeenth century burled wood console. "Plenty of nice art and antiques in this house. I keep an inventory in my head."

"I won't steal the silverware, if that's what you're thinking." I grinned at her. "And I certainly won't be spiriting away a commode in the night."

She sniffed, turning away.

Short stairways linked different levels throughout the house as if every wing had been another generation's afterthought. I'd need to go through every room taking photos and then sketch my own navigational blueprint to find my way.

"Where does Bert stay?"

"Not in the house, I can tell you that. We give the grounds man use of a little cottage at the end of the garden. Used to be Frank's before he disappeared. That's the young man Bert's supposedly replacing." She stopped to switch on a pair of brass wall sconces where bulbs had replaced candles long ago.

"What happened to Frank?"

"I wouldn't mind knowing myself. He left suddenly with no explanation besides a note saying that he had a better job offer. We're very short-staffed at the moment, so keep that in mind. Come along."

Signs of age increased by the tip of the hallways, the slight skew in the doorjambs. Three stairs down, we made a left turn and ended in a long corridor where four doors opened, two per side.

"This is the bedroom wing. I'm going to put you right beside me, young lady. That way I can keep an eye on you. My son won't, you can be sure of that. He spends most of the time locked up in his study or on his yacht. Writers don't pay much attention to the real world. He needs me to make sure things go right around here."

"Is his room in this wing, too?"

"He stays in the old part, near the tower and the library, on the other side of the house. My son's a very private man. Remember that. Here, this one's yours."

The woman pushed open a door and ushered me through. Old bottles in myriad shades of blue lined the upper sills of casement windows, promising color puddles in the sunlight. A sleigh bed, its chintz spread abloom in pink roses, dominated the space between two carved side tables. Otherwise, a desk, bureau, and wingback chair were the only furnishings clustered around a Persian scatter rug.

"It's charming," I said.

"Of course it's charming. Do you think we'd go putting you in some little hole-in-the-wall? You'd be hard-pressed to find anything but a nice room in this place, anyway, even if the place is falling apart." She pointed to a door leading off to the right. "There's a private bathroom right over there —saves us from sharing. Young women like you and old ones like me spend a long time in the washrooms for different reasons."

She indicated an embroidered bell cord hung discretely near the bed. "That's not for calling servants, mind. We don't have any of those in this household these days, so don't be expecting anyone to wait on you. It's just me, Bert, the cook, and a girl who comes in to help me a couple of times a month. You'll have to make your own bed and reuse your towels until the end of the week. Nobody's going to wait on you here."

"Nobody ever has before so why would I expect it now?"

The woman studied me from over the tops of her bifocals. "Yes, well, things aren't like they were back when the whole family came over from England on holidays. That was when my other son, George, was still alive. Then we needed full staff. Now, George is gone along with my husband and nobody comes here anymore. Now, you go do your freshening up, then knock on my door across the hall at ten to seven and I'll deliver you to the dining room. No sooner, no later, understand? Ten to seven."

"Wait. Please."

The woman turned.

"When will I get a tour of the house?"

Mrs. Wyndridge's eyes narrowed. "This is a private home not a resort. You'll be shown where you need to go and the places you're granted access to, nothing else. Consider the rest of the house off-bounds. Now, I'm going to take me a little lie-down. Remain in your room." She shuffled painfully to the door, shutting it behind her.

Remain in my room? Right. This whole place felt like somebody else's dream, perhaps some Gothic-infused preamble to a nightmare. But, all that aside, I loved the room and, strangely enough, the house. Anything with a patina of age, anything layered in history or softened by the touch of human lives, suited me fine. Preferably not under these circumstances, though.

Toby would appreciate this, too, the way he appreciated places that might serve as a setting for his electronic worlds. Had he stayed in this room? I scanned the space as if half-expecting some sign of his presence, something, anything, that had once been his. Crazy.

Suddenly awash with loss, I sat down in the wing chair and pulled out my knitting for a dose of solace. The feel of yarn flowing across my fingers soothed me. I could almost convince myself that everything would be all right in the end; I'd find Toby, pick up all my loose ends, and we'd all live happily ever after.

Several minutes passed before , jolting alert, I found Bert standing only yards from the chair, heavy and still, his beefy hands gripping my luggage.

"Is knocking too much to ask?"

"Weren't you expecting me, Suzy?" He dropped the bags to the floor. "What do you think of Old Ironsides?"

"Keep your voice down. She's next door."

"And as deaf as a rock. Takes her hearing aid out when she naps."

I got to my feet, carefully replacing my knitting on the chair arm.

"What are you making, Suzy?"

"Nothing you'd be interested in, Bert."

He stepped closer and peered down at the piece. "My mum used to knit when she wasn't poking me with her needles. She had those metal ones, you know? Multipurpose, like. Still, she could make things without those big holes all over the place."

"These holes are deliberate." Damn, why was explaining myself to him? "Would you mind putting my bags on the bed?"

"Surely." He threw the two bags onto the bedspread. "Expensive luggage. I'm impressed a library scholar type like you can afford such niceties."

"What's it to you?" And then I caught sight of the little brass locks dangling open on my bags. I gaped in disbelief. "You pried open my bags?"

"Just took a little peek, that's all. Nothing much in it but clothes anyway," he shrugged. "Nice undies though. I took a pair as a memento. Hope you don't mind. The green silk, very nice."

"What were you looking for besides silk panties to wear with your navy serge uniform?"

He shrugged again. "Don't know, exactly. Mr. Wyndridge said that I'm to keep my eyes peeled for everything about you, Suzy. Why don't you let me see inside that tapestry bag you keep so close, as a sign of good faith and all?"

"Just get out of here before I forget what good buds we've become and start screaming harassment. That might get Mr Wyndridge's attention, don't you think?"

"You don't want to be doing that now, little Suzy. Harassment is so overused these days. We both got things to hide, don't we? Best that we work together rather than apart."

"Get out of my room. Now. Oh, and before you leave, give me back my underwear."

He stared at my outstretched hand. "You know, it would make it easier for you if you just resigned yourself to being nice to me. I'd accept those panties as a token of your affection and we could be that much closer to becoming friends."

"Sorry, I'm just not there yet. Guess I need more courtship. Give me back my underwear. The color's all wrong for you. Try something black and blue."

He reached into his pocket and pulled out the little clutch of lime silk. "I usually get what I want in the end," he said, dropping the bikinis on the floor. "And ends are exactly what I want. For me, it's ladies bottoms. I love nothing more than to give a good spanking on a nice bare backside. I think I'd like yours very much, little Suzy. I'll be waiting."

Slamming the door shut behind him, I stared down at the puddle of lime green silk. God help me.

$$\text{❀ } 9 \text{ ❀}$$

"**P**hoebe, why haven't you called?"

"Dad, I'm sorry. I've just been busy job hunting." I paced the floor, crossing and recrossing the Persian scatter rug in the bedroom, telling myself that there were worst things than lying to my father. "How are you doing?"

"Fine. Why shouldn't I be?"

"Just wondering." I braked beside the bed, inches away from where my knitting flowed textured color across the counterpane. I'd stolen an hour to knit, even working in one of the purple silk yarns I'd found in Mom's studio. The color sang with luminous magic across the piece, prompting a stir of giddy pleasure. I traced the drop-stitch undulations across the row. "Has Julie called again?"

"Not talking to her. Told Bertha to say I wasn't home. When are you coming down home again?"

"Not for a few weeks. I was only there a couple of days ago, remember?"

He exploded. "Of course I remember! Why wouldn't I remember that?"

"No problem, Dad. It's just a figure of speech, that's all. What did you do today?"

"Nothing, as usual. Read a little and Bertha came by with one of her casseroles and a bag of cookies."

"She cleaned up a little, too, though, right?"

"Right, as if I can't take care of my own business. Enough about me. I'm sick to death of myself, anyways. How are you doing?"

"I'm fine. I'm reading a novel by Adrian Wyndridge. Do you know him? He writes those high-sea romance stories set in the seventeenth and eighteenth centuries—you know, romantic versions of Horatio Hornblower."

"Toby gave me one of those books once."

I stopped, stunned. "He did?"

"Yeah, last Christmas. Said he'd like to develop one of those computer games based on the story line."

"He did?"

"Why do you keep saying that? Yes, he did, I said."

"Last Christmas?"

"Yes, last Christmas. It was called *Brethren of the Coast.*"

And Dad remembered that. That's the way it was these days: He'd do instant recall one minute and falter on the edge of oblivion the next. How long would it be before he forgot everything?

"Did you enjoy it?"

"Well enough. I got it out last night and tried to read it but couldn't concentrate. I mostly just sat and looked at the inscription like a blubbering fool."

Picturing Dad alone in the cottage staring down at the loving signature of his missing son squeezed the heart out of me. I shoved hair from my forehead while navigating around the wing chair. I could not break it to him, absolutely could not share the doctor's latest assessment of his mental lapses. He'd lost so much already—his wife, his son. To know his mind was on the way out, too...

"Phoebe, you still there?"

"I'm still here, Dad. What did the inscription say?"

"Don't remember it all now, but he made a little drawing of starfish holding a sword. Cracked me up."

I grinned. Pausing by the bed, I crooked the phone between neck and shoulder and picked up my needles. I could multi-task with the best of them. Knit and talk on the phone? No problem. I bent down to better support my emerging wild wave shawl on the bed. "I'm glad that made you laugh. Were there any pirates in the story?"

"Pirates, why would there be pirates?"

"Well, high-sea adventures often involve pirates, don't they?" An unnerving silence followed. Did Dad catch the bait I'd dangled or was something else amiss? "Dad?"

Then I dropped a stitch. "Damn! Are you still there?"

"Yeah, but I'm thinking I should be finding my son instead of hoisted on dry dock like a catch of rotting fish."

"Dad, stop. Besides, your son's—"

"Don't say it."

My fingers froze on the needles. A pall of ache and grief filled the silence between us.

I took a deep breath. "But Dad, you know —"

The dropped stitch released, laddering down several rows.

"I know nothing and neither do you! Toby's still alive until we know otherwise. How many times do I have to tell you that?"

I swallowed hard. "Right."

"So, when are you coming home?"

"Soon, Dad." I knelt beside the bed, prayer-style, to better catch the runaway stitch with the work flattened on top of the bedspread. Armed with a cable needle, I sent the point deep within the stitches to capture the errant stitch.

"When's soon?"

"Soon, as in a couple of weeks. I have to concentrate on job hunting." If I could just slip the cable tip through the escapee stitch and anchor it until I could fix things.

"You be careful out there in the city and make it sooner."

"I'm always careful."

"You are not. Hell, girl, can't I raise one sensible child? One gets himself lost somewhere and the other does God-knows what and thinks she can fool her old man."

The phone slipped from the crook of my neck and hit the floor. I picked it up in an instant.

"Phoebe?"

"Sorry, Dad," I said. "I'd better go. I'm going out for supper with friends and I'm not even dressed yet."

"You seeing that library guy still?'

"No, we broke up."

"Good thing. He was a stuff-shirt, if I ever saw one."

I tried to laugh but couldn't. I knew he was only trying to keep me on the line. "I'll phone soon, honest."

"You'd better. Love you."

"Love you, too."

Tossing the phone on the bed, I studied my dropped stitch through a blurring of tears. No time to fix that mess now, since I was about to wade into the deep end of another.

❦

AT 6:50 SHARP, I KNOCKED AT MRS.WYNDRIDGE'S DOOR WEARING A green velvet dress, the most subdued of Maggie's wardrobe choices. She had left nothing of my own clothes but a pair of jeans and sneakers. I should have paid more attention to what she was up to in my room yesterday but preoccupation ruled. Here I stood sheathed in velvet, tottering on impossibly high heels. Beneath it all, those foreign silk panties —blue, since I'd washed out the ones Bert fondled—felt as wanton as a thong in a convent.

Mrs. Wyndridge studied me as I stood unsteadily before her. "This isn't a date, remember. He wouldn't be interested in the likes of you."

I couldn't have said it better myself. "I'm sure that's true. Look, I can find my way to the dining room if you'd rather rest."

"You'd lose your way and only keep him waiting which he wouldn't approve of at all. I'll deliver you, as I said I would. Follow me."

I obeyed, keeping pace behind the woman's labored shuffle in an effort to practice indentured servitude.

Sconces cast amber pools across walls and antiques, plunging the atmosphere into shadow and glow. I committed to memory each turn of the maze-like route, taking pictures with my phone at every clandestine opportunity until the double doors of the dining room came into view.

"Here we are. Knock first." She began shuffling down the hall in the opposite direction.

"Aren't you joining us?"

The woman snorted. "Hardly. I prefer my meals in the kitchen, as you will after tonight."

I sighed, knocking before opening the heavy wooden doors.

Positioned by the mantle of a crackling hearth stood my employer, donned in an elaborately embroidered fawn waistcoat, breeches, and silk hose, his hair flowing long over his shoulders. With one hand holding a brandy snifter and the other resting against the mantle, he awaited in what had to be a piece of brilliant staging.

How would Susan handle this one?

"Mr. Wyndridge, you do look dashing."

"Dashing? How very Regency of you but thank you, nonetheless. Do come in, Ms. Waverley."

"Susan, please."

"Susan. Do come in and try not to look so surprised, if I read your expression truly. Is it my garb you find so alarming as to cast a shadow across your countenance? May I remind you that I am a writer of historical novels and, like an actor, assume the garb and setting of my characters in a similar spirit. Tonight I shall write and thus assume the skin of my protagonist."

"Like method acting?" I stepped forward.

"Rather. I immerse my environment according to the period of my novels, in this case the late seventeenth century."

I stepped closer, fixed on the intricate silk crewel work of his jacket . It looked hand-done, all silk and a little worn in places. With a shock, I realized it could be the real thing which meant that he stood wearing a museum-quality period costume. I forced my attention back into role. "Which would be roughly when your ancestor was establishing himself on this island, correct?"

Wyndridge's smile held little warmth. "So, you have done your homework. May I offer you brandy?"

"No thanks."

The room, an area about the size of my entire apartment, glowed in candlelight, everything reflecting against polished wood and brass. Not a single electrical anything made an appearance. Against a far wall, flanked by a waterfall of blue velvet, stood a richly inlaid harpsichord. A collection of sailing artifacts hung along the single walnut paneled wall to the right, with a particularly fine sextant holding center stage over the fireplace.

My host followed my gaze. "A lovely specimen, isn't it?"

Only a few sentences into our evening and already he'd allowed a modern contraction to slip into his speech. Not so methodical a method author, after all.

Wyndridge's spicy cologne teased my nostrils. "Am I right in saying that it is one of the original sextants created in 1757 by Captain John Campbell?"

He shot me a quick, appreciative, look. "And how would you know that?"

Because I studied the list of pieces you won at a Christie's auction and took a guess. "I'm interested in maritime sailing antiques." I sank uninvited into one of the two brocade wingback chairs beside the fire.

Wyndridge crossed one white-hosed ankle over the other while continuing to lean against the mantle. "You are, indeed, well-qualified. In fact, you may wonder why you weren't my first choice, given your academic background?"

"I realize Edna Smith had worked for you before."

"You knew her?"

"We'd met briefly only yesterday."

"Yes, well, she had worked for me, and admirably so. She agreed to again after initial resistance, insisting that I required a more erudite assistant for the nature of my collection. I convinced her otherwise, deciding that I would rather remain with a known entity. Then she met with a tragic accident . Forced back to our list, we viewed your resume and, yes, you are undoubtedly well-qualified, possibly overly so, and, since I have not the time or patience to spend too long on the search, and based on your stellar qualifications, your proximity, and my need for haste, you are here."

"And I'm very happy to be. This looks like interesting work."

"I trust you will proceed quickly with little interruption. It is my intention, you see, to itemize my manuscript collection for sale."

I feigned surprise. "Sale?

"If all goes according to my desire, I will be living elsewhere within the year, after having relinquished my manuscripts and artifacts to auction and sold the house."

"You mean you're going to sell the property, too?" On the run, in other words.

"His gaze remained fixed on some distant point across the room. "With much regret, yes. Though painful, it is imperative that I move forward. A man cannot live forever in the past, though I've done better than most in that regard. But first, I must finish the final novel of my Bermuda trilogy and organize the vast collection housed in the tower library. Your task, Ms. Waverley—pardon me, Susan—is to ready that collection for auction. Ms. Smith informed me at great length what that would involve, but I wish the task completed as soon as is humanly possible, though perhaps not with all the care she recommended."

"Of course. I'll begin first thing tomorrow."

"I will also put you under certain restrictions. Pray do not be dismayed by my cautionary rules. However, a series of distressing and unaccountable accidents have occurred of late, beginning with the sudden disappearance of my groundsman, which compels me to take certain precautions."

"Such as?"

"Such as, I neither encourage nor facilitate extraneous investigations within or beyond the material I have assigned, all of which is articulated in the contract which I have provided for your signature. In addition, you must sign a confidentiality agreement forbidding you to share or use the content of the manuscripts or disclose anything you see in this house in any form without my written permission, which I assure you, I will never grant. Is this clear?"

Legality was the least of my concerns, though it held more than a passing interest. "I'd like to see the contracts in advance."

"If you wish. They will be awaiting you on your desk in the tower tomorrow morning. If you choose not to sign them, pray bid my driver to deliver you off-premises to the destination of your choice. I will be unavailable from this point on. Your tasks have been itemized for you in written form in the tower library. Do you accept the terms thus far?"

"Yes, so far."

"Excellent. On the morrow you will begin. Mrs. Wyndridge will deliver you to my tower library, where you will work for seven hours per day with a one-hour lunch period to be determined in advance. All necessary documentation will be contained in that room and under no circumstances are you to roam the estate without my permission. I am not, however, some ogre from a Gothic romance. On your free time, you will have access to the beach, the garden, and the patios, plus the lounge areas reserved for staff."

"What lounge areas would they be?"

"The kitchen or anything unlocked, obviously," he said with asperity.

If I harbored ideas that I might be treated as a guest rather than an employee, that squelched it. "I presume I'm allowed to leave the estate on my off-hours and not be chained to my desk?"

If there was a flash of amusement in his face, it was brief. "Most certainly. You are not at a boarding school. Now, I'd like nothing more than to dally over aperitifs, but I fear time presses heavily on me tonight. You will find me very exacting, given to flourishes, and providing extraneous details only at my choosing."

"Will we have regular meetings where I update my progress?"

"Unnecessary. I will contact you upon occasion so you can apprise me of your progress, but I will be deeply ensconced in my writing and do not wish to be disturbed. Please keep a journal of your day's work, in longhand, not on computer."

"Wait." I raised my hand, traffic-cop style. "Please. I mean, presumably you have computers? You must. Don't you write your manuscripts on one? I'd much prefer to write my summary and notes by email and I can save them to a flash drive, if needed. In the interest of time, of course."

Wyndridge slipped the empty snifter onto the mantle and straightened, hands behind his back, after which he proceeded to lift himself up and down on the balls of his leather-shoed, high-heeled feet. "I anticipated you might make such a request. Would it surprise you to learn that I write all my manuscripts in longhand and have a secretary type them into a word-processing program afterwards?"

"Well, yes and no. I mean, given what I've seen so far, no surprises at all, yet when I think of how much easier editing is on the computer—"

"All of which I've heard before in great, tedious, detail. However, I prefer to write in the dying art of longhand. Our ancestors managed communication rather admirably without technology and in this house we do the same, except where absolutely necessary or where the staff have beseeched me otherwise."

"So, no WiFi?"

"No WiFi. I have one hard-wired connection—I am not a complete Luddite—in my security office, which we use for ordering supplies offshore and occasionally to post manuscripts to New York. Any further questions?"

How would I survive without the Internet? My cell phone data bills would be astronomical even if Max covered them. "Not at the moment. Your wish is my command."

That provoked a genuine smile. "Oh, I doubt that. Now, let us dine. I will, quite rudely, I admit, leave you to enjoy dessert without my company."

He led me through yet another set of double doors to a small dining room graced by a rather long table dressed in candelabra and formal china. The overwhelming sense of being dropped bodily into some period movie intensified.

"Please, be seated."

And I was supposed to flirt with this one? Maggie had him all wrong. On a sliding scale of sexual tension, I'd place ours 40 near a polar vortex.

I took the seat he drew, lowering myself down before the bleached and starched damask tablecloth, gazing at glistening crystal, gold-limned china, and silver, everything gleaming intensely. On either side of my charger, a line of cutlery stood at attention like glossy little soldiers. I may as well have saluted them since all but the obvious ones were totally foreign.

Soup arrived first, delivered by an employee I'd yet to meet, a slender graceful woman with hair piled into a cascade of tiny braids and skin like warm coffee. Wyndridge didn't offer introductions, of course, but she flashed me a quick smile.

"Her name is Joquita," Wyndridge said once the woman had exited.

"I'm not used to such formality," I confessed.

"No doubt. I do run a formal household but that's mostly for my own pleasure. This is the manner in which my protagonist would have dined."

Joquita returned with a basket of rolls. Wyndridge watched as she scooped a thick, spicy mixture into a paper-thin china bowl. "I do hope you find the tower more atmospheric than uncomfortable," he said.

Joquita caught my eye before disappearing through the side door, presumably to the kitchen. I tasted the soup—chowder, I realized. Delicious. "That's in the oldest part of the house, isn't it?" I tried not to slurp.

"Exactly." Wyndridge sipped his soup in small elegant gestures, something I couldn't master. "My ancestors were merchants, as you know. John Ashley built a lucrative trading empire between the colonies, and it is he who built this house. The full story will unfold in my new book."

"He was associated with Sir William Phips, right?'

Slowly he raised his gaze to me. "Why do you ask that?"

I put down my spoon. "It's a matter of public record, isn't it?"

"No, it is not."

Damn.

"I did do some preliminary research before coming because I thought that might be useful in better understanding your collection."

"It will not."

"Did I say something wrong?"

Wyndridge's expression hardened. "I expected you to comprehend the nature of your position here. I do want you to organize my collection, nothing more. Is that understood?"

"Of course."

He stood up, shoving back his chair. "I require a cataloguer, not a speculator. Here, you are expected to play by my rules."

"Sorry."

He flung his napkin on the chair. "I want the job completely quickly and you gone with equal haste. You'll find your first instructions on your tower desk tomorrow morning. Dine without me. I have work to do."

The cedar doors thudded behind him as he stormed out. What was up with that? I propped my elbows on the table and sighed into my hands.

"What did you say to him to get him so pissed?" a voice whispered.

I looked up at Joquita peeking through the opposite doorway. "I chanced to mention the esteemed ancestor. "

Joquita slipped into the room. "Okay, so it's like this: the guy's high-strung. Well, probably neurotic." She stirred her finger in the air near her head. "The arty-farty artiste is really quite sweet in his way but he's got boundaries. If I had a chance, I could have prepared you for His Almighty but Mrs. W likes to rule the roost and would be much happier if you got fired early. Anyway, eat your salad. Somebody may as well have the benefit of all the food." Joquita scooped leafy greens onto a Wedgwood plate, whipping away the soup bowl with her other hand.

"What's your advice?"

"Say as little as possible. All the stuff going on around here is making him paranoid. We've been told not to talk to outsiders about anything concerning the estate. Here's the dressing—honey mustard, which is perfect with the avocado and rock crab, in case you're interested."

"Looks delicious."

"My special recipe."

I took a bite, savoring the flavors and textures. "Delish."

"Good. I've got to get back to the kitchen. Enjoy."

"Jocquita, thanks, but I'm going back to my room after this. No main or second or whatever comes next, but coffee to take with me would be great."

The woman laughed. "Do you want me to fix some camomile tea instead of coffee?"

"No thanks. I'll take the hard stuff. Sorry if the food's going to waste."

"Don't worry, nothing will go to waste here, not with Shrek parked in the kitchen devouring everything in sight."

"Shrek was a good guy. Bert is not."

"Got that right. Sit here and enjoy your salad. I'll put on some fresh coffee." Backing through the door, her hands stacked with bowls and used cutlery, Joquita exited.

I ate quietly, attempting to Zen myself into inner calm but playing with bunch of treasure hunters was like swimming with sharks. Now I had the uncomfortable sense that I may have been born into a school of them without even knowing.

I'd return to my lovely room, set the phone alarm, knit for an hour or two, and sleep. I absolutely would not panic, refused to panic.

But the storm brewing inside my gut felt exactly like panic.

🕊 10 🕊

The floor of my room was awash in ocean, the currents streaming past, rocking my bed violently while I clung to the sheets. Water splashed against the sides, tossing bits of flotsam and sea creatures onto the covers.

First a glimmering fish, then a squid, then a starfish. I risked peering over the side, gazing down, deep down, through schools of silver fish, to the bottom of the ocean where a merman beckoned for me to join him. A merman, red-haired and smiling, wearing a gold coin suspended on his chest, and a tail the color of emeralds embroidered with turquoise silk. Toby, I'm coming. Hold on. I jumped overboard and kicked my way downward, only seemed unable to make progress, as if suspended in the currents. Toby, Toby!

Something beeped inside that oceanic dark, dragging me back. I swam up from the bottom of a fretful and exhausted sleep, breaking the surface knowing I was dreaming yet so wanting it to be real. I just stared into the darkness, fumbling for a coherent thought, tears rolling down my face. Something throbbed green. Brain cells connected. I recognized my iPhone alarm.

It was 2:30 a.m. and I had to get up.

Shivering, I plunged my bare feet onto the cold floor. Switching on the bedside lamp, I quickly pulled on my stealth gear of couture black leather jeans and a black cashmere turtleneck, compliments of my wardrobe mistress. That was the only dark-colored thing in my suitcase suitable for evening missions. I cursed Mags for not leaving me a pair of black jeans.

After a few swigs of cold coffee, I felt fortified enough to open the bedroom door and step into the hall, my iPhone acting as flashlight.

The house breathed around me and, though it felt atmospheric, I knew wind, not ghosts, rattled the windows and blew drafty breaths into the hall. Wood creaked and the casements thumped as gusts hit from the sea. I shivered, considered returning to my room for an extra sweater, but nixed the idea in the interests of time.

My mission was simple: explore, fix my bearings, take photos—a reconnaissance only. I'd use my phone camera to help commit navigational details to virtual memory and assess the layout of the house for future reference. In the morning when I began work in the tower, I'd gain a daylight view to add to my repository. This much I thought I could do and, just maybe, I'd find something regarding Toby in the process. I resolutely would not look for anything regarding missing treasure. Not my concern., or so I hoped.

Past the kitchen, down the little hall with its window facing a fringe of palms, take a right-hand turn by the grandfather clock, go down two stairs and to the dining room and then onto the oldest part of the house. Once past the dining room, another set of stairs would lead down to the oldest wing. After that, I'd play it by ear.

The kitchen linked to the patio which, in turn connected to the path leading to the bridge. Tonight, the ornate wrought iron lamps gleamed across the deserted garden. I checked for signs of life. An eddy of leaves swirled over the flagstones between the low walls while a lone date palm swayed a frantic dance. Otherwise, no living thing moved.

The grandfather clock ticked away the seconds as I fumbled my way down the stairway and into another hall. Using my light by the windows was too risky, so I shoved it into my pocket until past the kitchen, where the house once again tunneled through interior corridors.

Making a right-hand turn, I maneuvered by a spindly-legged Louis XIV-style table, past walls of seascapes, and a single tapestry hanging in dusty solitude along one side. Flashing the light across the threads, I realized that textile couldn't be more than 75 years old yet it was fraying from neglect. I moved on.

Thickening walls and lower doorjambs signified I'd arrived at the older part of the house. I stopped outside a doorway embedded with a hand-hewed cedar beam, flashing my light up and over the lintel, admiring the axe marks. At my feet, the floorboards widened, each plank grown in an age when Bermudan cedars expanded like redwoods amid aromatic forests.

Wyndridge's private quarters and the tower lay ahead. My heart thumped at the thought of penetrating his private domain. I had no right, but then, I reasoned, if this man had anything to do with Toby's disappearance, Wyndridge's rights were waived.

Once through that door, I'd have no good explanation for being there. I crossed the threshold, praying that Wyndridge didn't take to night strolling or nocturnal snack attacks. A small casement window set deep into the wall offered a square of pale illumination. I could hear waves crashing on the rocks but heard no other sounds nor detected signs of movement.

I stilled, craning my ears. How could I go through with this? More important, what if I got caught?

A subtle shift in atmosphere weighed down around me as if the weight of ages had settled over my shoulders. I tried to shrug it off, fixing my attention down the hallway and the rooms I must investigate. A door lay at the end of the passageway flanked by two others. Wyndridge's room with maybe a den? And where was the staircase to the tower?

I cringed at every creaky floorboard as I approached the first door on the left, which I fully expected to find locked but wasn't. It would be so much easier to believe I had no recourse but to scuttle back to my room and pretend I'd never left my bed.

Instead, I stepped into a small study walled in books. To the right, a table and chair flanked a double casement window facing seaward. I took a deep breath and scanned the light across the bookcases, four floor-to-ceiling shelves liberally stacked with books and boxed sets of magazines.

It would take a whole evening or more to explore these. I stood waffling in indecision. Searching every book was impossible, not to mention probably useless. Then again, what better place to hide a clue than in a needle-in-a haystack bookshelf or four? On the other hand, since I had only a couple of days to find something on Toby, wouldn't it be better to focus on a more fruitful strategy? What was I looking for, anyway?

In lieu of a better idea, I began taking pictures with my iPhone camera and was just about to focus in on shelf number two when a hand slapped over my mouth. The phone fell to the floor as an arm squeezed my waist, the reek of peppermint jabbing my nostrils.

"What's little Suzy doing slinking through the house at night without telling Bert, eh?" The hand tightened and I kicked backwards hard. He yelped as heel met shin. The mitt dropped from my mouth, the arm slackened, and I tumbled against a shelf. He blazed the flashlight right in my eyes.

"Bitch." He stood rubbing his shin with one hand, flashlight still aimed for my eyes with the other.

"Bastard."

"Why are you doing skulking through the house? Did you think I wouldn't know? I know everything."

"Take that thing out of my eyes," I said through my hand shield.

"What are you doing?" he asked, dropping the light.

"Same as you, obviously." I glanced out into the hall but nothing stirred. I picked up my phone before he could snatch it.

"He's not home."

"He isn't?"

"Think I'd be talking out loud if he were around?"

"Where'd he go?"

"Dunno. Saw him sail away on his yacht. Left after supper and said he wouldn't be back tonight. Told me to look after the ladies. It's just me, you, and the old woman. What do you mean, 'same as me'?"

"You know what I mean. You're looking for something, too." It was an act of desperation, my stab at strategy.

"Why do you think that?"

"Because you said as much earlier. Anyway, the question is do we work together or against each other?" I was in a gambling mood.

"I'd much rather have you working against me, naked as a jaybird." He chuckled at his little joke. "I figured you weren't no real library lady, anyway. Too cute for that. Who are you working for?"

"I can't say. What about you?"

"Can't say, either. Why wouldn't I just kill you now and say it was an accident?"

"Because you don't need any more unexplained accidents going on, do you, Bertie? Wyndridge is spooked enough as it is."

"Peter Pan hired me as his bodyguard."

"Cute. Don't you just love irony? So," I said, turning back to the room with more bravado than I felt. "How about you holding that light up while I just finish photographing?"

"What are you looking for in here? Nothing but magazines and stuff. He hardly ever uses this room."

"I work on the principle that the more information, the better." That actually sounded impressive. I went back to work, trying to forget his leering presence while he cooperatively held his flashlight. Every time I bent down, I did my best to keep my bottom inaccessible.

"So, somebody hired you to come here and pretend to be a library lady?"

"How do you know I'm not a library lady?"

"Don't look the type but you don't look like much of a snoop, either. Just wondering what that really makes you."

I focused on a set of mariner encyclopedias, taking several shots in groups of five. "Think of it this way: how many actual librarians would be willing to do this kind of work?"

"Right, so you're not a librarian or much of anything else, either. If you want, and ask real nice, I might help you out for a while. It would make things easier for you, I promise you that." He thumbed over his shoulder. "Wyndridge's bedroom's at the end of the hall. The opening to the tower is right across from that."

I stood up. "Show me."

I followed him out into the corridor, almost enjoying my doubly duplicitous role.

Bert tromped to the end of the hall and thumbed at the door. "Keeps it locked."

"Have you been inside?"

"What do you think, sweetheart? Getting into places is my specialty. What's yours?"

"Research. I'm the scholarly type. I have degrees."

"Big whoop. That's not helping you here, is it?"

"Once I'm in the tower it will."

That seemed to pacify him. "This lock's pretty uncomplicated, might even say unimaginative. I can pick it and presto! We're in."

"Pick away. Would he know it's been tampered with?"

"Not a chance. He doesn't believe in security systems except for the tower. Spoils the mood or some such shit. He's got me, instead. You want in or not?'

"Absolutely. Pull a presto."

Bert donned gloves, pulled out a leather wallet of picking tools from his jacket pocket, and had the door unlocked in minutes. He pushed it open with his shoulder and stood aside for me to pass.

Inside, the eighteenth century had been preserved to the nth detail. I roamed my phone light around the spacious room lined searching for a light switch.

"No lights."

"He takes this historical accuracy seriously, doesn't he?"

"A pain in the ass. He only goes by candle power in this wing. Man's got a screw loose."

"Does he have a girlfriend? Not that the two are related."

"None that I've seen but he takes that boat of his out all the time, so who knows what or who he gets into there? If I were him, I would have stayed here and done the library lady."

"You're assuming the library lady would let herself be done."

Floor-to-ceiling bookcases lined one wall. Bert shone his flashlight across oil lamps and candelabras, brushing across a harpsichord, past the four-poster, heavily-canopied bed, and rested on a closed rolled-top desk. He must have concluded the desk to be the only place worth investigation since he didn't bother lighting anything else.

I took a step forward. "Is the desk locked?"

"Sure it is but I can open it for you. Here, hold this."

I held the flashlight while he deftly selected the right pick.

"Wow, you're good at that."

"I'm a professional."

The mechanism clicked with ease, and he rolled the walnut slats up to reveal a brass desk set complete with ink pot and quill. Other than a leather book, the wooden surface was empty.

When I reached for the book, he grabbed my arm. "Think like a thief instead of a scholar, or whatever the hell you are. Leather shows finger-prints . You need gloves."

I withdrew my hand. "I forgot to bring them."

"No thief comes into a place looking for something without gloves. What kind are you?" He stared at me.

"This is the first time, okay? Someone with my specific skill set combined with thieving is hard to find so, yeah, I'm in training. Will you help me do better?"

He pulled out a couple sets of surgical gloves. "Do I look like a bloody babysitter? Here, use these." And he held out a pair of plastic surgical gloves.

"Why thanks, Bertie."

"In this line of work, always use gloves, and be very careful to put everything back exactly as you found it."

I nodded, snapping on the gloves and carefully opening the journal.

"Nothing much in there," he said, leaning over me.

"I need to be sure."

The initials WMT appeared on the current date but nothing else.

"Think that means anything?" Bert asked.

"It means something. We just don't know what." A chill shot down my spine. I needed to study this further. "Could you hold the pages flat for me while I take photos of every entry?"

"What's that going to tell you?"

"How do I know until I read it?"

He did as I asked, flattening the pages with surprising care while I used my phone to photograph every double-page spread that contained an entry.

Not many did. The weekly two-year journal began the previous year, each page divided into seven days, with some entries more detailed than others. I didn't waste time reading, but remained focused on taking the shots. Once finished, Bert returned the diary to its spot. Conscious of the time, I quickly checked the drawers, noting stationery supplies, address books, calendars, and the usual desk plethora, but nothing striking.

"Did you check the room for a safe?" I asked.

"Natch, but the place is clean."

I began photographing the room while Bert closed the desk. "So," I asked, keeping my voice neutral, "did you kill Edna Smith?"

"I consider that an unfortunate accident. If she hadn't died, I wouldn't have gone back and finished her off or anything."

"Very big of you but why harm her in the first place?"

"Why'd you think, little Suzy? For someone trying to be a criminal, you're kind of clueless. Obviously, she knew too much. It was only a matter of time before she bleated to someone about all she saw in here. Couldn't have that, now could we?"

"No way." Seemed like I might be destined for the same fate.

"Why are you doing that?" he wanted to know.

I had my response ready. "I'm getting an organizational snapshot of every room taken sequentially. It means photographing one wall completely, top to bottom, followed by the others, missing no square foot of space. It might take 20 individual shots to photograph every wall but it provides a visual reference I can use later on." I delivered that little spiel with enough self-importance to nearly impress myself and maybe him, too. Maybe now he'd actually believe I had a skill set.

"Do you know what we're looking for?"

He shrugged. "It's best not to ask too many questions in this business."

I shot him a quick look. "You really don't know?"

"I work on a need-to-know basis. My employer gives me just enough info for me to get a job done. The main thing is he's real generous when things go right and not so much when things go wrong. Do you know the particulars?"

"This is a big one. I know that much."

"Stinking big."

"Does your boss have a lot of people working for him?"

"How the hell do I know? You think we've got ourselves a staff room?"

"Just wondering."

"If you're real nice, I'll put in a good word for you," he laughed. "Maybe you can get a job with him once we're through."

"Sweet. How about showing me the secret door?" I said, returning to the hall as he relocked the door.

"Behind there." He pointed his light to the tapestry in the hall.

Pulling back the fraying fabric revealed a solid-looking cedar door with a modern control panel set into the wall nearby.

"I thought Wyndridge didn't do electronics?"

"Made an exception for the tower. What does that tell you?"

"He's inconsistent."

"I'm thinking he's got something worth protecting up there."

"Do you have the key code?"

Bert grimaced. "No, and it pisses me right off. I have keys to every door in this house except there, even to your room, little Suzy. I'm the caretaker, after all, and I take very good care. "

"I'm impressed."

"You should be. I can tell you that the old bag keeps her dentures in a teacup in the bathroom and wears the biggest, ugliest old-lady drawers I've ever seen. Hangs them up over the tub to dry, probably because she thinks it immodest to fly those flags on the line. Not worth adding to my collection, even if I had the room. The pretty little cook, now, she doesn't sleep here but she does do her wash sometimes. I—"

"Stop. I'm done. I don't need all the perverted details of your tiny life. Can you get me an extra set of all those keys?"

"Now, why would I do that?"

I backed away. "Obviously because we're on our way to being close friends."

"Not close enough."

"We are supposedly cooperating."

"Only because it suits me to play cat and mouse with a cute piece of pussy like you. Besides, I can unlock any room for you any time you want."

"You can't be with me 24 hours a day."

"Yes, I could."

The persistent smell of mint turned my stomach.

"Thank you but no thank you. We could work strategically: I could check out some areas while you're checking out others."

"So nice of you but, no. Bert goes everywhere you go, no exceptions. You want to work with me, you play by my rules, starting tomorrow when you gain access to the tower here. You'll share the code with me."

"Why would I do that?"

"Because you fancy staying alive ."

"Seems an unfair balance of power."

"Get something straight, little Suzy: I've got power, you've got the will to stay alive. End of story."

I checked my phone for time: 4:32. I had to get some sleep. "That's it for tonight. I'm going back to my room."

He clutched my arm before I could move, leaning into my air space. "I said it would make it much easier if you were nice to me, Suzy. I'm just saying."

"And I am being nice to you, Bertie. I haven't kicked your shins a second time or anything, have I?"

"Don't forget about what happened to the real library lady." His fingers bit into my flesh. "You'll want us to be real close friends when the time comes."

I shoved him hard with my other arm until he released me, and then half-ran back to my room.

11

The sun poured through the bottles lining my window, splashing blue puddles across the rug. Outside, the sea sparkled turquoise upon the waves, inviting me out to play, but I remained trapped and earthbound. Never had I been so isolated in such a glorious a hell.

I'd been reviewing the photos I'd taken on my phone the night before, studying every little detail of the house, including each entry in Adrian Wyndridge's journal. Nothing made an impact except one tiny doodle penciled in the margin of one of Wyndridge's datebook entries. Someone else might have passed it by as a random jotting, much like others I'd found scattered about the journal, but this was different. A merman, anatomically correct despite the diminutive size, was the exact copy of Toby's thumb tattoo and affected me like a stab in the gut.

I stared out to sea. Toby had not only been here but had been so familiar with Wyndridge that he'd doodled in the man's datebook. What did that mean?

Backing away, I went to the bed, lifted the mattress, and carefully pulled out the cartoon tube from its hiding place. Spreading the stiff, crackling paper flat on the bed, I stared down at Toby's brilliant goldfish-colored merman in one corner before sweeping my gaze across to its counterbalancing mermaid on the opposite side. The treasure chest wrapped in the merman's tail took on a weighted meaning as did the doubloon dangling on his brawny chest. Even here, Toby had hinted at treasure.

I recalled how he had insisted Mom and I embroider the treasure chest onto the tapestry after its completion. A joke, I thought, since he just bantered away until we capitulated. "What's an underwater dream scene without sunken treasure?" Toby had asked.

"You think *Tide Weaver* should be some kind of image from the bottom of a kid's aquarium or something?" Mom countered, not as amused as I would have expected.

Thinking back, she'd seemed annoyed. An argument had followed. I recalled the angry whispers, though I didn't pay much attention to them at the time. Toby pushing for his own way was common enough in our household, and one of my parents usually capitulated. Once his charisma, wit, and charm were activated, Toby was a hard man to refuse. I would be the one to give up, not him.

Did Mom, unhappy with Dad's focus on the Oak Island treasure, fear that her son might be getting involved? Was that embroidered treasure chest a sign that Toby had plunged deep into my father's obsession years ago?

I stared down at the drawing, willing it to speak, answer all my questions, preferably in my brother's own voice. Dad might know, whether he'd remember hardly being as significant as his refusal to tell me.

I quickly refolded the drawing and tucked it back in the center of the mattress, more angry now than I'd ever been. That settled it. I'd speak to Wyndridge now, back him into a corner, and demand he tell me why my brother doodled on his journal, why he lied to the police.

But first, I owed to Max a call.

I paced the room, trying to fix a signal. Despite the clear weather, my phone flat-lined. I was unable to get calls through to anyone. Instead, I tapped in a brief message to Max, expecting it to be delivered when I hit a good signal: BERT PREVIOUSLY EMPLOYED. He'd know what that meant. The rest I'd rather say in person.

Then I pocketed the phone in disgust, ready to track down Wyndridge, only a sudden thought ambushed me en route to the door. I stopped, balanced on the balls of my feet. Why would Wyndridge tell me anything? If he really had something to hide, and clearly he had, what incentive did he have to reveal all to the woman who'd just sneaked into his house? And if he had harmed my brother, why not me, too?

No, Max was right about one thing: I needed subtlety. Two more days under this roof and, if I didn't find anything, I'd decide on next steps. I turned around and readied myself for a day in the tower.

Wearing my jeans jeans and a cashmere sweater, the only items in my new wardrobe suitable for work rather than seduction, I packed my bag for the day. I'd take my notebook, pen, and iPad. Though I imagined knitting a few rows in the tower as a possible soothing strategy, in the end, I reluctantly left my knitting behind.

I followed the scent of coffee through the halls to join Mrs. Wyndridge at a round table beside a window overlooking the garden. Joquita worked at the Aga stove at the far wall while Mrs. Wyndridge sat sipping her tea. "You are 10 minutes tardy."

"Do you have a stopwatch or something?" I asked while I pouring myself a mug from the urn. I took my seat across from her. Really, the situation was impossible.

She pointed to the wall clock. "The employees at the Wyndridge estate are always are mindful of the hour."

"You mean the only two employees left?"

She looked shocked.

"I'm sorry, " I said, realizing how bratty that sounded. "I know that was rude but I'm just upset. I tried to get a call to my Dad this morning, but couldn't. That always worries him and me. Anyway, I'll try to be on time from now on, though I don't see what difference it makes as long as I get the job done. Maybe if I could speak to your son, I could explain? Is he home?"

Joquita slid a plate of scrambled eggs before me, caught my eye, and made a warning grimace, her back blocking Mrs. Wyndridge. I nodded my understanding and picked up my fork.

"My son's whereabouts is no business of yours."

"I have to ask him something."

"Did he or did he not give you instructions?"

"He did, yes."

"Well, you've missed your opportunity, haven't you? Now, you will just have to wait." She sat across from me, watching as I shoved scrambled eggs around my plate. "Aren't our eggs good enough?"

I kept my eyes on the food. "The eggs are delicious, thanks. I'm just not that hungry. I don't usually sleep well my first night in a strange bed."

"Perhaps if you didn't drink coffee after supper, you'd sleep better," she remarked.

I glanced up at her, surprised. She spied on my dining habits? "Sorry if I caused too much bother."

"It was no bother," Joquita said, stopping near the sink. "I didn't mind at all."

"We don't usually drink coffee in this household, that's the point," Mrs. Wyndridge added.

Baffled, I smiled at Joquita. "Well, thanks for going to the trouble."

"Like I said, no problem."

I plucked a slab of toast chilling on the silver toast rack and gnawed away at it, wondering if son had spoken to mother after last night's dinner fracas and if I were now on even thinner ground. "Where's Bert this morning?" I asked, hoping to change the topic.

"He ate earlier," Mrs. W remarked, sipping her tea. "I refuse to dine with him. Quite unpleasant. Now, I'm going to deliver you to the tower room this morning and lock you in," the older woman announced, stirring her tea while glancing at the wall clock. "But I'll be back to release you at 12:00."

I dropped my toast onto the plate. "Nobody's going to lock me in anywhere."

Mrs. Wyndridge sat back in her chair, hands resting on the table. "Those are my instructions, for security reasons."

"That's not a term of my employment I would ever agree to and your son certainly didn't mention anything about locking me in anywhere last night."

"Nevertheless, I insist."

I got to my feet. "I'm claustrophobic. I won't do it." Based on this, maybe I could leave today, go back to Max, and forget about finding Toby, maybe leave it to somebody else? Only there was nobody else.

"You have not been given free access to this house," Mrs. Wyndridge said, climbing laboriously to her feet.

Could they know about my nocturnal snooping last night? "Leave me the key or whatever, or I'm not going inside the tower."

We faced one another across the table while I sensed Joquita tense and listening. The old woman dropped her gaze first. "I don't blame you," she said, finally, as she carried her plate to the counter. "If it were me, I wouldn't be locked up in there for anything in the world. I told him as much. I'll just leave you the key, then, and the code, though I warn you, I change it daily. Don't let Bert inside."

I stared in disbelief. I actually won that round? "I won't let Bert inside, I promise you that." If I had my way, he would stay in the garden all day chained to a fence.

I watched as the older woman paused by the bay window, stopped, and just stared beyond with unfocused eyes.

"Is everything all right, Mrs. Wyndridge?" I asked.

"Just tired is all, nothing for you to worry about, Missy. Come on. It's nearly nine o'clock. Time for work."

I left my half-eaten breakfast, picked up my bag, and followed her down the stairs, almost bumping into her when she stopped suddenly to stare out a side window.

"Look at that useless piece of work," she said, pointing. Bert dug around the poinsettias lining the path, ripping out green leaves with yellowed ones, snapping off the occasional healthy flower head and tossing it to the side.

"He doesn't know a blessed thing about gardening. I won't let him take four steps near my rosebushes," Mrs. Wyndridge said.

"I think he hates plants."

She moved painfully to the window and rolled open the casement. "Hey, you there, Mr. Stone."

The man looked up. "Yes, ma'am?"

"I need you to fix the tap in my bathroom and be quick about it. It's leaking again."

Bert hesitated before getting to his feet. "Yes, ma'am. Right away, ma'am." He lumbered toward the house, hands covered in dirt.

"Well, don't be doing anything before going down to the shed and washing up first!" She called after him. "Are you daft?"

He stopped. "The kitchen sink is closer."

"I don't care how close it is. I won't be having you tracking in mud all over the house."

Bert glared briefly before loping down the path out of view. Whether by deliberation or happy coincidence, he would now be nowhere near the tower when I entered. Relief loosened the knots in my shoulders.

"That man has no more sense than God gave geese. Come with me, young woman."

She led me in the same direction I'd taken the night before, along the main corridor and into the long hall, stopping before the tower door with its impressive key code panel. "Go through there and take the staircase straight up. The library's on the top floor with nothing much along the way. That upper door's locked, too, but the older key will open that. You'll need a code for this one, however."

She reached into her pocket and passed over a brass ring clinking with two keys, one modern , one an ornate antique.

"I have the other set on my key fob here." She dangled a clutch of keys on a tacky keychain fashioned like a pair of glittery flip-flops. "The code is 1923, the year my Henry was born, Henry being Adrian's father and a fine man who knew better than I how to manage his sons. I swap between five codes. I'll give you the new one tomorrow. First you tap in the numbers, then use the key. Open it while I watch. The thing can be tricky sometimes."

I complied, first punching in the code, and then inserting the key. It took four attempts before something clicked and the door swung open.

"There's a light switch on the left. Best turn it on before you shut the door behind you or you'll be stuck in the dark. It locks by itself. The first window is a ways up the steps. Mind those, too. They're as narrow as the day they were built and just as steep. You can thank Edna Smith for the lamps up there. He didn't want the place wired but she insisted. She was a good woman." The emphasis implied that I wasn't, which, under the circumstances, I thought fair.

She turned to shuffle back the way she had come.

"Wait. Please."

She turned.

"When does he return?"

"Why do you need to know?"

"Because I'm working for him and have questions."

"Do as you're told and wait until he comes to you. When he's writing, this world and everybody in it ceases to exist. Lunch will be ready at twelve o'clock. Find your way back to the kitchen a few minutes before."

"Yes, of course." Suddenly I didn't want to enter that tower for anything in the world. "What's it like inside? Have you been?"

"Of course, but long ago when my legs still carried me. Henry first took me here when I arrived as a young bride so long ago. It seemed so romantic then, but now it's old and dreary, like you'd expect. Henry would never have allowed things to fall apart. He'd do what had to be done, make no mistake about it. These days we can't even keep the place clean. Is that what you wanted to hear? Get to work now. I'll be taking a lie-down. Mind that you be in the kitchen at twelve sharp for lunch or there'll be nothing else until tea."

I watched her slow progress down the hall before pushing open the door and stepping inside. An assault of musty odors trapped in shadows hit my sinuses. I braced the door ajar long enough to find the light switch which, thankfully, was only a hand span away. A single bulb dangling from a cable illuminated a low-ceiling square room with a set of stairs marching upward into the dark. I heard the lock slide into place as the door banged shut behind me.

I knew I wasn't going to like this place. Maybe a rug and a couple of paintings might elevate the stark stone interior, but the wash of white paint didn't help a thing. A small door sat tucked beneath the stairwell straight ahead. I walked over, ducked my head, and stepped under the curving stairs, uneasy to be wedged inside what felt like a pocket of shadow. Though locked, the door rattled easily in my hand as though it saw plenty of use. I guessed it must go down to a basement somewhere.

Backing away, I studied the tower landing again, recognizing similarities between this structure and the British-built military forts back in Halifax—the same regimented chunks of stone stacked one atop the other, utilizing whatever natural resources lay nearby, granite for Halifax, coral stone here. The mark of Sir John Ashley Wyndridge, the naval engineer, was in full evidence. This entrance had probably originally served for storage, with the living quarters upstairs.

The stairs. I eyed them curving up and out of sight, a structure designed to hug the outside wall, with a steep drop straight to the floor, the floor of the second landing acting as ceiling to the first. Some earlier Wyndridge had had the foresight to construct a wire-rope railing on one side for a little support en route to the first landing ,after which the walls appeared to close in around the stairs.

I flung my bag midway over my back for balance and took the first step. Wouldn't constructing a tower like this indicate that someone had something to defend? But back then, I reasoned, times were hard, pirates abundant, making a tower structure more commonplace, especially as a watchtower. I doubted I'd find any clue to Toby's whereabouts up here but figured there might be plenty of interesting material for a treasure seeker.

Not that I was there to find treasure. But didn't I need to go through the motions as Wyndridge's hireling for appearances sake? Snooping around the house after hours seemed much more promising, providing I could ditch Bert and avoid detection.

The stone steps were steep but regular with the exception of the tenth tread from the bottom, which had been cut twice as high as the rest. I was forced to hoist myself up. Two steps more and I reached the first landing.

Daylight washed bleary light through a narrow glass mullioned window set deep into the stone. I leaned against the sill, catching my breath, trying to peer through the salt-scummed glass. Impossible, and the latch had rusted shut, too. Forget that. Turning, I forced myself to move. I still had a long way to go.

One hundred and fifty-five more steps followed before I arrived at the top. I sank to my haunches against a thick wooden door while fumbling for the key, which slid easily into the mechanism, allowing me to shove the door open with my shoulder. Rather than have the weighted door slam shut behind me, I propped it open with my carpet bag after removing my iPad.

I entered a gloomy stone room with a high ceiling hidden in shadows overhead. Books, boxes, and folders lined three walls, from the floor to within a few feet of the ceiling beams with a large wooden map cabinet centering the space. A single desk had been positioned below the double casement windows on the opposite side, the only wall minus shelves and the sole source of natural light.

The space reeked of mildew as if a million microorganisms were partying among the piles. Someone, probably Edna, had begun the monumental job of cataloguing but had stopped, leaving a few shelves marching upright and orderly while most lounged in disarray. Other shelves seemed arranged by size, maybe date, and possibly color, with an entire wall of boxes and Princeton files. One look overwhelmed me. This was more storage heap than library.

Setting my iPad on the map cabinet, I tried to fix a cell signal with my phone. No luck. The walls were too thick. Pocketing the phone, I navigated around to the desk and leaned over it to study the view. One casement had been replaced and seemed relatively new, while the other retained its original blurry glass. From the tower's good 'eye', I could see past the cove and straight out to sea, the vantage commanding a breathtaking view of Bermuda coastline.

I glanced down to the desk, where a fresh pad of lined paper sat in the middle of a green blotter with a list neatly written in a flourishing hand. I switched on the desk lamp and studied the pen and ink script. His instructions were clear. I was to continue classifying the shelf labeled "A" indicated by a sticky note, weed the pile to the left of the desk, which a quick glance revealed to be a box of papers in various states of decay, and classify the jumble of mixed papers sitting in another box on the right. These instructions accompanied a report hand-printed and signed by Edna, which outlined her efforts to date, plus endless recommendations in point form.

Below the pad lay both my contract and confidentiality agreement, printed and described in legal terms with a Hamilton Law Firm's letterhead. I scanned the documents to check the legal terminology before setting them down with the list. I had no plans on doing anything so named and, since Wyndridge wasn't standing over me insisting, I wouldn't sign anything, either.

I had a day to pass up here before I could resume exploring in the house that night. How much of value might Wyndridge hide in this paper jungle? Clues to the supposedly buried treasure? It struck me as far too obvious. Still, it wouldn't hurt to give a sample of those boxes a spot-check while I was there. If nothing else, it would satisfy my curiosity and fill in time. Maybe I'd even make it look like I was doing organizational work before the day was done.

Back at the map cabinet, I switched on the room's only other light and pulled out each drawer, finding nautical charts and old maps, including a few old specimens dating from the seventeen hundreds. In the top drawer, a large diagram of the tower had been executed in pen and ink on parchment thick enough to survive the assault of time and humidity, since it appeared to be in excellent condition.

Pulling the drawer out fully, I scrutinized the drawing under the light of my iPhone. It looked to be an old blueprint. Lifting the corner, I found several others of similar vintage, each by the same hand, signed JAW. One, which looked to be a master schematic, indicated an extensive tunnel and cave system extending below the tower, possibly linking up to that little door I'd seen below.

This would interest Max and Noel, not that I planned on showing it to them any time soon. On the other hand, supposing Toby had gone down there? He would have investigated those cave warrens if he was on the hunt for something and maybe even if he wasn't, since he loved anything secretive and potentially dangerous. Using the scanning application on my iPad, I committed them all into virtual memory for closer study later.

I leaned against the cabinet, fighting the tremors. I had a bad feeling. Toby had been here; Toby had found something or knew something or did something. I just knew that without knowing how.

My brother had been deeply interested in this house, this place, and the secret Wyndridge reportedly sequestered here, but I didn't understand why. Not to steal, surely. My brother wasn't a thief. He'd find all this interesting as a mystery, a kind of real-life game; but picturing him involved in a theft of this magnitude? No way. Maybe he tailed along with Max and company on a lark and maybe discovered something he shouldn't have. I shoved the hair from my eyes. Hell, what was I going to do?

A geriatric library stair sagged against the far wall. I swung it onto its wheels and into position over one shelf, more as a way to work off nervous energy than anything else. After giving the ladder a good shake, I climbed the creaking steps into the gloom. The contraption only took me about six feet up, leaving at least six more out of reach overhead. My head spun as I gazed up at boxes stacked one on top of the other, looking as though they hadn't been disturbed in years.

The first box I dropped onto the cabinet below consisted of old

Bermudan newspapers, circa 1856-1900, so fragile and yellowed that they were all but illegible. Touching them would only hasten their demise, so I set them aside. The next four boxes contained mismatched jumbles of clippings from magazines and periodicals in no particular order with no connecting theme. At least five wads wrapped in ribbons were recipes for everything from hog hock stews to biscuits written by past Wyndridge cooks. Wiping my hands in disgust, I returned the boxes to their spaces while sneezing repeatedly.

One volume of botanical drawings, circa 1600, and a leather-covered compendium of all known chemical substances, dated 1714, had been wedged between the boxes. Edna would have eventually found these and added them to the list of items worth cataloguing and, hence, selling. I set them on top of the map cabinet, reluctant to return them to that mess.

Two hours later, I stood tired, smeared with dust, and disgusted. Some of the things I encountered were already too far gone to hold value. Though not a document expert, I did hold a passing interest in protecting the old and rotting.

But the mold nailed my lungs. Wheezing, I checked my watch: eleven o'clock. Only one hour left before lunch. I doubted I could remain up here much longer, but if I had to, I might as well stay busy.

Intending to make only one final foray into the gloom, I rolled the ladder a few degrees west and began climbing, the wooden slats groaning beneath my feet. Overhead, I could just see the edge of something sticking out from the very top of the shelving. It was a box unlike all the others, a container made of wood. People might store something of value more readily in wood than cardboard, which required further investigation. Only I couldn't reach it even when balanced on the ladder's uppermost rung.

On the other hand, if I used the ruler—a nice, long, old-fashioned yard-stick with metal edges I'd found on the floor—to lever the thing forward, I could pull it into my hands as long as I kept my body weight braced against the stacks. It seemed so simple.

I took one more step up, as far as I could go without losing the stair's handgrip, and stretched up and out to slip the edge of the stick under the box, my left hand gripping the handrail. No luck. The box remained jammed. I grew more aggressive by propping one leg over the side of the ladder until I could apply my other foot to the edge of the shelf for leverage. The shelf lurched away from the wall, the whole thing falling backward, with me flailing my arms trying to rebalance everything.

I had time enough to imagine death by shelving and being found by Wyndridge in a hideous tangle, when the bottom end of the ladder banged into the map cabinet and catapulted me over the top. I landed on my back amid a bundle of newspapers as the shelf rained books, papers, and storage boxes down over me.

I lay in a winded heap. The light had gone out and my brain registered pain but I couldn't tell from where. I heaved breath back into my lungs and propped myself up on my elbows. After a fit of sneezing, I tested a few body parts, finding my leg bruised, not broken. Overhead, the shelf remained propped over the cabinet, angling over my body in an ominous mass of wood. I crawled out from under the mess and managed to stand. Ouch. Damn.

What a disaster. The map cabinet lay buried under heaps of paper with the shelf leaning against it in an unstable angle. In the thin light, I saw that the shelf's one bottom edge had collapsed with most of the weight resting on a stump of splintered wood. Leaning my shoulder into it, I managed to shove it back against the wall where it rested as if ready to pivot at the slightest nudge. As a precautionary measure, I stacked a few books in front of it for stabilization.

I wiped the hair from my eyes and moaned. Definitely a violation of Wyndridge's snooping rules. He'd probably fire me on the spot. He'd eject me soon enough if I asked about Toby, which I might risk as soon as he returned. What did I have to lose that I hadn't already lost?

I picked up a few random pieces unloosed in the deluge, including a list of weights and measures, circa 1662. Odd pieces emerged such as notes to a servant requesting certain dishes for dinner, a recipe for pickled hog hocks, a ship's supplies list. The rest of the tower contents appeared to be nothing more than family sediment accumulated across the ages with a few interesting artifacts in between.

I rooted through the debris for the box, finding it crushed under a hefty unabridged dictionary. Carrying the pieces over to the window, I loosely reconstructed an old lap desk about two feet wide and six inches deep with a warped lid. Inside, two inkwells flanked a narrow trough that still held a single quill pen and a yellowed wad of deteriorating paper stuffed in the cavity. I gently explored under the paper and lifted the trough until I found a clump of sealing wax solidified on the edge of a single piece of paper. A note, I realized. No, a list.

Holding the fragile paper by the glob of sealing wax, I felt the distinctive energy of the script emerging through the blotches and blurred ink. John Ashley Wyndridge signed the page after describing the contents of a hold, mostly illegible but for the words "10 chests of igote...." The script trailed away into mildew feasts, blackened splotches, and smeared ink. I dropped the thing as if it burned my fingers—proof of treasure I wanted no part of.

I leaned against the window, fighting panic. Everything I'd discovered today was weighty with significance for treasure seekers but not for me. I would love nothing more than to view something that rare with my own eyes, but this quest was tainted with loss, my loss. I wanted no part of any of it. I just wanted Toby back. To take or photograph any of these documents, to assist Max in any way, would only make me complicit in his theft. I was not here for that.

On the other hand, perhaps something might serve as leverage. Supposing I needed a bargaining chip to find the truth or even to save my neck? I sat my Ipad on the desk, replaced the carpet bag with a large book to prop open the door, and headed for the stairs, resigned to return that afternoon to tidy the mess, take pictures, never to return again.

❧ 12 ❧

I reached the kitchen just as Mrs. Wyndridge was heading to her room, a cup of tea grasped in her fingers. "What happened to you?" She looked me up and down. "I waited until just 15 minutes past the hour but you were tardy, as usual," she said. "You look as though disaster befell you."

"Sorry." I had made some attempt to tidy myself but knew I wasn't much improved. "I had a little accident in the tower. A shelf toppled down on top of me. That place is like a train wreck. You should see it: piles moldering away, heaps of litter everywhere, and though Edna made a monumental effort to restore order, it's a huge job. And a fire hazard," I added, "Both unhealthy and unsafe," the latter phrase included just a touch of righteous indignation.

She studied me for a moment before nodding. "I keep telling him the whole lot should be carted out and dealt with somewhere else. I left you a sandwich. Tuna. We don't eat fancy these days. I'm just going to watch the telly for a while and maybe take a nap. I'll leave you to it then. Mind that you work extra time to make up for your lateness." She made for the door, her green cotton frock still wrapped by an apron.

"Is Mr. Wyndridge back yet?"

"No, he is not," she scolded. "He probably wouldn't return until tomorrow. He's writing. Now, eat your lunch."

In an instant, I was at her side, taking the cup out of her hand. "Here, let me just carry this to your room for you—your sweater too." I lifted the green cardigan from over her arm.

"I don't need your help, Missy."

"That's what my Dad keeps saying." Presumably Susan Waverley had a father, too. "But we can all use a hand once in a while."

"How old is your father?"

"Eighty-two."

"Well, I'm older than him by a few years but still have all my faculties and don't you forget it."

I thought of how Dad was losing his. It broke my heart, but I shoved those thoughts along with the anxiety of not speaking with him this morning. He'd be so worried. Meanwhile, I helped her to her room, a spacious master suite with an uninhibited sea view, resolved to call him before I did anything more. Setting the teacup by her chair, I turned on the television at her direction.

"Is Bert around?" I asked before leaving.

"He is not. I sent him to town to fill my grocery list. He should be gone for most of the afternoon. You can thank me for that."

I smiled and shut the door, leaving her tuned into *Coronation Street* reruns.

Back in the kitchen, I scooped up the tuna sandwich from the plate, downed a full glass of water, and headed outside, letting the wind play with my hair. It took several attempts to fix a signal but finally I succeeded. The phone rang in my ear as I followed the path.

The garden was a series of small areas sheltered behind either low walls or hedges which, in combination, formed a long winding greenbelt following the side of house towards the oceanfront. Date palms, frangipani, and ornamental shrubbery wove into a lush green ribbon sprinkled with spots of color between the house and the cliff edge. The sea-facing front garden opened up to a swathe of lawn with marble benches and the occasional table-and-sun-umbrella combo.

I could just see the step-roofed gardener's cottage buried in bougainvillea over to the right. The phone rang unanswered in my ear. Dad didn't do answering machines but I vaguely remembered today was a doctor's appointment to which Bertha had kindly agreed to escort him. Devouring the rest of the sandwich, I brushed the crumbs from my sweater and approached Bert's cottage. While the cat's away...

The cottage reminded me of the gatehouse at Astwood Cottages with the same white stepped roof and candy pink exterior. A casement window had been rolled open to let in the air.

I pushed back the hibiscus blocking the window and peered inside. No one home. Next, I tried the door, which opened easily in my hand. I cautiously stepped inside, ready with an excuse should Bert suddenly come roaring out of the closet. He didn't.

Thus I entered a tiny lounge with a television, a couch and a chair. Magazines and newspapers fanned across the low coffee table, positioned like displays in a hotel lobby, if hotels offered Playboy, Hustler, and the London Times. A single coffee mug sat on its coaster with an empty bag of chips folded neatly into quarters nearby.

The tiny kitchen continued the neatnik theme with stacks of drying dishes and a fry pan soaking in the sink. The bathroom, still faintly damp from a shower earlier that morning, revealed towels neatly hanging and a single leather shaving kit on the counter.

In the bedroom, I stepped through the reek of industrial-strength men's cologne riding heavily over a note of mint. I headed for a suitcase on the bed—standard vintage hard-sided version. It yawned open on the made bed as if the owner had been searching for something in a hurry.

I stepped forward, noting the laundered boxing shorts stacked to one side on the bedcover—checked and striped patterns—with five packaged white shirts on the other. Bert must have been looking for something, too rushed to replace shirts and shorts back into the case. Clearly he stayed packed when he traveled rather than depositing his clothes in drawers or closets, which meant what? That he was prepared for a hasty retreat?

The thought of touching anything of his turned my stomach but I had to find out who he worked for. I slipped my hand into the case and felt around the tidy folds, not sure what I was looking for. Maybe a notebook or a letter from a boss? Everything incriminating probably resided on a laptop or cell phone, neither of which he left lying around.

At the very bottom of the suitcase, flush against the side pocket, my fingers touched something hard. I tried lifting it out, but it felt as if it had been strapped to the inside. I tugged and pulled, nearly yanking the case right off the bed. But with the final tug, I ended up holding up a holstered gun, the belt straps dangling over my hand.

I felt faint. A gun. I stood holding my arm outstretched as if it might bite me. I had to put it back, but had Bert packed it with the belt wrapped around the holster right to left or left to right? He was so methodical and he'd also know who to blame for anything out of place. In my agitation, I must have nudged the case with my thigh because it slipped sideways off the bed to the floor, dumping the contents everywhere.

Now what? I'd never get everything back in order. Maybe he'd think the suitcase fell on its own but what about the damn gun? Wouldn't leaving it be like: "Here I just rifled through your belongings so just shoot me."

I made for the door, the gun wedged under my arm, straps dangling. Outside, I jogged past a hibiscus hedge and across a patch of grass to where a moon gate opened onto the cliff and the cove below. A steep stairway carved into the natural rock plunged down. Beyond the little cove, the crash of waves on reef outlined the natural barrier between the Atlantic and the house.

All I needed was to get get midway down so I could toss the gun into the surf. More steps, oh how I hated steps! These were unnervingly treacherous despite the iron railing bracing one side.

I began climbing down carefully, one hand clutching the rail, trying to keep the gun from slipping from under my arm, until it occurred to me that fastening the thing to my body with the holster belt made more sense. Perched on a step, I buckled the thing over one shoulder, leaving both hands free, and continued my descent.

Waves rolled against the cliffs below and seabirds wheeled overhead as the wind whipped my hair and the sun bore into my eyes. If I peered down over the stairs far enough, I could just see the edge of a jetty but not much else.

Not a good place for tossing firearms so I continued down. Then a jingling sound disrupted my concentration. My phone alert. Lowering myself to sitting, I plucked my phone from my pocket, and blinked at the text YARN MAVEN DOWN. Shielding my eyes with one hand, I scanned the horizon. Noel had to be watching me.

I almost leapt down the rest of the stairs, arriving at a wooden jetty designed as both dock and swimming platform. I peered over the edge. The water wasn't deep enough for gun disposal here, either. A small boathouse sat on one end with metal stairs descending into the water at the other. No Noel. The cliffs formed a stark vertical wall overhead . Nobody could see me from the house; nobody could see me from the water. Where the hell was he?

The boathouse sat with its wide double doors thrown open to the sea. I unlatched the side door and stepped into a relatively new shed. A wooden dinghy rocked in its berth with room for maybe three more. No pungent scent of either motor oil or gasoline I associated with boathouses. Paddles and life vests lined one wall with wetsuits, tanks, masks, regulators, and other diving accessories, on racks behind me.

I inspected the diving gear. Everything looked in good condition, if a bit dated. There were tanks well-maintained, even full of oxygen, as if in wait for the next diver. Wetsuits in all sizes. Why so many suits for one, maybe two people? I stroked the sleeve of one newer green neoprene suit as if my brother's arm had just been there. He loved that color. I felt his presence so intensely at that moment, it brought me dangerously close to tears.

"My God, you're armed!"

I swung around. "Noel." He stood on the other side of the berth, dripping in a black wetsuit, hair slicked back, the imprint of a mask still visible on his cheeks. He must have entered through the sea door.

"You look almost dangerous," he remarked.

"Not as much as you. You're actually diving?"

"You're actually packing a gun?"

I glanced down at the holster. "I found it hidden in Bert's cottage and, on impulse, decided to dispose of it in case he plans to shoot someone— me, for instance. I was thinking of throwing into the sea."

He shook his head. "Wouldn't it be smarter to hang on to it in case you need it?" He seemed more amused than concerned.

"I don't know how to use a gun but I suppose I could Google it." I patted the gun.

"Or you could give it to me and I'll take care of it for you."

"No thanks. What are you looking for?"

He walked around the edge towards me, holding flippers in one hand, mask apparatus in the other. I couldn't see tanks. "Exploring. That's what I'm here for, same as you."

"Only you know specifics, which I don't. Do you expect to find sunken treasure in the cove?"

"You know the treasure's elsewhere."

"The only things I know, or even trust, are what I find out on my own. Everything and everybody are suspect."

"Now you're learning."

"Thanks for the patronizing compliment. Try answering a question for once: What are you diving for?" I turned away, shoved the hair from my eyes, and turned back to him, stabbing my finger in the air between us. "Tell me what you know or suspect so I can help you properly. Aren't we supposed to be on the same team?"

"Yes and no. You're on the legal side, remember? And as soon as you know everything, you can't play innocent if we get tangled up with the law. You've already figured out that we're planning a treasure heist. Do you really want to be on our team?"

"If it means finding Toby."

"You can't play it both ways. Toby's involved in this. Haven't you figured that out yet?"

I shook my head. "That's not the Toby I know."

He stepped closer until he was towering over me. "Maybe you know even less than you think. Love is blind and all that. Max and I are protecting you as much as we can but the less you know, the better it is."

"For whom?"

He turned away in disgust. "Just find something useful and we'll take it from there. This is far too dangerous for you. You're not prepared."

I wanted to both kiss him and kick him. "Then make me better prepared. Tell me exactly what you want me to find? Be specific."

"A diagram or a sketch of the Wyndridge estate would be helpful. John Ashley was a naval engineer and it follows that he'd keep meticulous notes, blueprints, and diagrams. They've got to be somewhere."

"And how would this help to find Toby?"

"Maybe Toby went exploring on his own, playing it solo instead of working with us. Maybe he had an accident, or maybe Wyndridge found out what he was up to and did something to him. Either way, we need full access to the property to find out. Did you find anything in the tower?"

"Nothing but old recipes and plenty of mold."

"Keep looking. I'm going back to the water." He swung around and padded back to the sea door to pull on his flippers. I followed behind him.

"What do you expect to find out there?"

He sat on the edge, pulling on his flippers, after which he pulled his mask down, shrugged on the tanks he'd hooked on the edge of the jetty, and began tightening the belt at his waist, all without speaking. In a second, he had checked his regulator, waved, and flipped backward into the water. He remained visible a few minutes longer before disappearing into the depths.

I scrambled back into the boathouse and nabbed a set of binoculars I'd seen hanging inside. Moments later, I had them focused on the cove. Minutes passed with nothing showing until I spied a bob of a head and flash of a tank at the far end of the cove.

Bastard.

13

In seconds, I was back inside the boathouse, pawing through the wetsuits looking for one sized small to medium. Finally, I found an aged black long-sleeved jacket that fit. Peeling off my sweater and jeans, socks and shoes, I tried it on, managing to zip it up over my bra. The leggings all looked far too long and I didn't have time to try them all on. That left me no option but to dive with nothing but my silk bikinis on my bottom half.

A full set of double oxygen tanks and a regulator completed my assemble. Maggie might not care, but I preferred to round out my accessories with primary and secondary demand valves, a submersible pressure gauge, and low-pressure hose.

Nevertheless, I was about to break every rule ever learned about diving: never dive alone; always use your own equipment (or at least that which had been checked by a PADI regulation diving office) and; never dive alone. That last one bore repeating. In my defense, I wasn't planning a deep sea dive or a long one so, therefore, I reasoned, I'd be fine.

I tucked my socks and sneakers against the wall, shoving my phone into the toe of one shoe for safekeeping, and piling my clothes on top. Next, I took a pair of flippers in my size, tried on a face mask, and a belt weight from the shelf, tossing everything to the bottom of the boat, with the gun placed under the boat seat.

By the time I had punted out of the boathouse, the sun burned high and bright, making me visible should anyone glance out the window above. Only, I figured, with Bert off shopping for the afternoon and Mrs. Wyndridge sleeping, I had maybe three or four hours in which to spy on Noel. Of course, I'd lost sight of him by then but knew the direction to take: straight for the far cliffs on the other side of the cove.

On the water again brought joy, joy as if I'd returned to my element after a long, cold hiatus. The water granted me strength and confidence again. Though I hadn't oiled my rowing muscles for a few months, they woke up under the familiar activity and powered me through the rising chop. Blissfully happy for even a few seconds was more than I'd expected that day or any time soon.

The surrounding cliffs formed a near-perfect arc around the Wyndridge promontory, with only a narrow opening to the sea between the headlands. All around, translucent turquoise shone while, seaward, the ocean brewed a deep moody teal flecked with foam.

Foam boils indicated reefs, of which plenty encircled the cove and hugged the coastline. Half way across the cove, I paused, checked the house for signs of observation, and slipped the gun overboard. Looking up after watching it sink like a sluggish octopus, belts trailing behind, I saw a deep gap in the encroaching cliff—a cave, a very large cave. Pushing harder against the oars, I powered myself forward.

As I approached the cliffs, reefs broke the surface in jagged piles of coral, the sea barely covering the brilliant colonies. Low tide. My muscles struggled against the broken surf as I aimed the boat closer to the cave ahead. A channel between two reefs offered enough depth to accommodate a small boat like mine.

The outgoing tide rushed between the reef ledges, funneling through the rock spars and pushing me diagonally towards the cliff. Though the sea breathed out, I wanted in. I needed to ride the next wave through the channel by keeping the boat straight and nosed forward, avoiding scraping against the reefs. I'd done it countless times before, though usually heading for a beach rather than towards a cave, and not with so much living coral to protect in the process.

Shoulders complaining now, I rode the bronco sea on its next forward wash until it propelled me into the cave. The roof rose thirty or more feet overhead and had to be twenty feet wide, while the walls magnified the sound of wave slapping stone. Seaweed stranded down from the ceiling festooned with barnacles and starfish. I peered ahead into the deep, narrowing throat, sure that I caught the flash of a light back there.

I used my thighs to stabilize myself and the oars to shove the boat away from the walls as the boat rode the sea deeper into the cave. Ahead, I saw the back wall looming, awash with foam with the next big tidal exhale bound to fling me right against it. I powered the oars hard down to keep riding the surf rather than be ruled by it all the while scanning the area for Noel.

I saw that light but where was he? I'd have to turn the boat around somehow or punt myself backward to exit but then I spied a large opening to my left. A secondary cave! I punted the boat inside, the oars levering me forward until the boat slid around a corner and into calmer waters. I just sat for a moment catching my breath. A pale wash of light illuminated a small area, maybe twelve feet wide and eight feet tall, rimmed with two deep, seaweed-strewn ledges.

An inflatable boat rocked from its mooring on one side. On the ledge beside it, an extra set of oxygen tanks and a black bag had been deposited. I maneuvered the dinghy to the wall opposite the Zodiac, hooked the rope around a rock, and leaped onto a ledge about a foot wide. Damn. I needed a lamp. Why hadn't I thought of that? I surveyed the equipment on the opposite wall. No lamp. At my feet, a ribbon of bubbles broke surface. I traced them, moving along one side as if looking for something.

Back in the dinghy, my legs braced against the rocking, I shrugged on the tanks, donned my mask, and checked the regulator. Next, I added the weight belt, removing two weights to better adjust to my body mass, and pulled on my flippers. Perching on the dinghy's side and holding the mouthpiece firmly to my face, I tipped backward into the water.

Blessed, blessed ocean. It embraced me as I twisted my body around and kicked deeper down. The cave floor rose up to meet me with coral-covered stone and enough light so that I could see parrot fish pecking away at the walls and glimpse darting purple wrasses on the cave floor. A thin beam shone like a pilot light in the darkness to my right. Noel must be wearing a mask lamp. I kicked towards him, keeping him in my sights until the light unexpectedly disappeared . I kicked faster.

The cave floor deepened. Daylight receded completely after about twenty feet. If Noel knew I was behind him, he didn't let on. His light revealed enough for me to navigate by, paddling steadily on until a black bite of darkness opened in the cliff wall ahead. A tunnel. He powered into it without hesitation, making me think he must have known of its existence.

I followed him in, pushing back my fear of dark, enclosed spaces. Soon he'd know someone followed him, since my air bubbles were about to mingle with his. I decided to announce my presence.

At first, the opening was wide enough for two to swim side by side, so I tried moving up beside him. He powered himself faster forward, leaving me behind. Now the tunnel narrowed with room for only single file.

Then I remembered why I hated cave diving—the oppression of water and stone pressing in from all directions. Swimming blind with the light mostly blocked by Noel's body, I fought panic yet remained fixed on the pale illumination until suddenly the tunnel widened into a much larger space. Noel kicked upward and I followed.

We broke surface inside a large chamber, a kind of natural well with a steep wall of rock encircling a pool about 25 feet in diameter. Overhead , a ceiling covered in barnacles indicated it would fill with tide.

"What the hell are you doing following me?" he asked, removing his mouthpiece.

I pulled out mine. "Because if you won't tell me what's going on, I damn well have to find out on my own. You knew about this cave!"

"I had a hunch."

"Like hell! Maybe Toby's been here."

Noel turned full circle, using his mask light to scope out the space. A small recess jumped into view in the light.

"Wait here, " he called.

"I'm not waiting anywhere!"

"Only for a second!"

But he swam to the edge and hauled himself up in one fluid movement and ducked inside the opening, his light bopping up and down before vanishing completely. That left me in total darkness. I hated this. It was blacker than black and freezing. I felt like a child locked in a closet with lurking monsters. Only, this was the sea, I reminded myself, and the monsters were mine. The question was whether I had the guts to face them.

After what felt like ages, his light flickered out of the opening and he beckoned me over.

"Take off your flippers. We'll leave them here with the tanks," he called.

In a minute, I had yanked off my flippers to clamber up beside him. Crouching on a cramped ledge with teeth rattling, I removed my tanks. Noel took them and wedged both cylinders into a barnacle-crusted opening along with the flippers. "That should hold until the tide rises."

"That won't be long. It's turning now."

"Better hurry, then."

"How deep does it go?"

"Up to another cavern, " he said, pointing behind him. "There's a tide pool in the tunnel, so we know the sea comes at least that far. Come on."

I cursed myself for the lack of wetsuit leggings when we descended the tunnel. After scraping along on hands and knees for about three feet, we finally had enough room to stand up, but only long enough to slide ankle-deep into a slimy pool. The tunnel snaked around tide-smoothed rocks but luckily extended no more than 20 feet before widening into a huge chamber.

Noel gripped my arm to keep me from tumbling forward and hung on to me as he removed his mask. Swinging the light back and forth revealed a forest of stalactites and stalagmites stretching out of sight. Deep pools glimmered still and crystalline, with one large basin curving away into the darkness at my feet.

"Wow!" I exclaimed.

"Aptly put."

Glinting pools and pink-amber stalagmites transfixed me until I caught the glimpse of something red flash in the passing light. "Wait." I caught his wrist, aiming the mask lamp on the opposite wall. We stood in silence, gazing at an arrow-like mark painted in red across the pool.

"A sign," Noel remarked.

"A bit obvious, isn't it? Almost like 'X marks the spot'?"

"Not unusual for the time period."

"Even so."

"There must be a way down here from the house. John Ashley would require easy access to his loot over the decades. I figured he'd been using it as his own little bank."

I thought of the diagrams. "Let's get back. The tide's rising. Lead the way."

I ducked back into the tunnel behind him, stumbling through the pool more carelessly now that the sea was already streaming in.

"Hurry up!" he called over his shoulder.

"I'm hurrying!"

When the water reached my hips, Noel grabbed my hand and tugged me along. I was about protest when his light went out. Fear stabbed my gut.

Noel cursed.

"Didn't you bring a spare?" I asked.

"In my boat. Come on. If we hurry, we should still be able to find our way out."

"We'd have better luck in the cavern," I called.

"Doubt that. We're going to the boat. Hold your breath!"

Ahead, the tunnel narrowed into the main pool. I tried arguing that there'd be less risk of drowning back in the caverns but Noel had already shoved me onto my hands and knees ahead of him and was pushing me into the incoming tide. Holding my breath, I kicked forward, using my arms as leverage against the water's force. My heart banged violently in my chest. I blocked out thoughts of drowning, my only thought being to reach air.

We broke into dark space in the main pool. I kicked up through the rush of water, breaking the surface before my lungs exploded. Black, black, everywhere. I reached out and caught a flipper that nudged my face. "Noel?" I called out. "This one's already flooded!"

I listened in the sloshing darkness for the sound of him breaking the surface. It took far too long.

"Phoebe?"

"Here!"

"Get the tanks!"

Everything churned in darkness. I could hear, not see, metal banging against the cave walls. Swimming toward the sound, I reached one set of floating canisters at the same time as Noel. His hand squeezed mine in the darkness. "I'll help you put it on," he said.

"What about yours?"

"I'll get it."

"Get your own tanks and take this flipper. It's not mine." He didn't answer, being too intent on fastening the tanks to my back, a tricky business in the water. I could hear metal still clanging against the cave wall. "Get the other set! We don't have time!"

"You go on ahead and I'll join you. Just push against the current."

"I'll wait."

"Don't be an ass," he called. "I'll be right behind you!"

The cave roof was no more than a foot away by then, with no time to look for flippers. I dove down, kicking awkwardly with one flipper, pushing against the streaming current, my eyes closed against darkness, sea, and panic.

Adrenalin fueled me. I didn't think about the abyss, the surging water, or the narrow tunnel. I thought about life and how I wanted to stay a part of it. I thought about Dad sitting home in Nova Scotia and how I could not have him lose another child.

My tanks scraped against the rock while the water pushed against me, trying to force me backward. The screaming in my head could be a battle cry. Damned if I would die like this! The tide fought me hard and I fought back, grasping the sides of the tunnel at its narrowest point and pushing myself on.

Minutes felt like hours before I broke into the sea cave. Daylight at last! Up I swam until my head whacked against the dinghy, which rocked violently no more than three feet from the cave roof. Paddling backward, I flipped up the mask and searched for Noel. Nowhere. I'd go back for him, take the extra tanks in case he didn't nab his set in time.

Turning back to the boat, I was reaching up to unhook the rope when a wave slapped me hard against the rock. Briefly blinded, I spat out sea, coughing and sputtering, and then his head popped up beside me.

"You all right?" he called.

"Fabulous," I cried, so glad to see him. "You?"

"Bloody marvelous! Get in the dinghy," he called. "I'll push, you row."

"What about the Zodiac?"

"I'll tie it to the back."

I hoisted myself up, Noel shoving me from behind, until I flopped into the dinghy like sluggish tuna. In an instant, I'd unfastened my tanks and nabbed the oars while he shoved the boat around until the prow faced seaward.

The whole thing was crazy: coming into a sea cave during rising tide in this wicked brew of surf and rock. Crazy and exhilarating. I kept the boat as level as possible while the space between ceiling and sea closed in and Noel shoved the boats toward the opening. A wave flung the boat against the cave roof when we'd almost reached the entrance, scraping my back and knocking one of the oars from my hand.

Noel held the prow, using his weight to dip us down and out under the cave roof, rescuing the oar at the same time. Once outside, I rowed with a furious energy, while he kicked alongside until we were safely away from the reefs. Only then did he hoist himself into the boat, the Zodiac rocking on its tether behind us.

In the center of the cove, we stared at one another for a moment, knees touching, grinning inanely like two kids who'd just raided the cookie jar.

"I see you have a taste for danger," he said.

"It's the exhilaration factor."

And then he leaned over, framed my head in his hands and kissed me. I tried pulling away but he held me firm, his lips cool and salty, his fingers tangling in my hair. Then he pulled away and I recovered long enough to start working the oars again. "Mmm, tasty, though I prefer a little less salt," I remarked. "What was that for?"

"I believe people should always kiss following a near-death situation." He scraped his hair back from his face, arms braced on his legs and grinned.

"Really? Had many of those?" I kept my gaze focused on the boathouse far ahead.

"A few. Meanwhile, I'm an opportunist and you're a lot more than I expected," he called over the waves. "Full of surprises. I would never have expected you to follow me in."

"You don't know me." More like I didn't know myself.

"I'm learning."

"Remember that I'm not here to be seduced but to find my brother."

"And you'll never give up, will you?"

"Never."

"One of the many things I admire about you." He leaned forward. "So I'll help you find Toby, like I promised, but help me, too. I need those cave diagrams, Phoebe. They have to exist and you have to find them."

So that was it. I rowed harder, biting down on a string of curses. They had to think me stupid as well as gullible: just go into the estate and find your brother. Oh, and while you're at it, how about helping us steal a fortune? Did he think kissing me would turn me into putty? I'd return to the tower all right, but it wouldn't be for Noel and Max.

I'd do it for Toby.

I acted as though rowing took all my concentration. He didn't offer to take over and I proved he didn't need to.

"You know how to handle those oars, my lady. I'll leave you to it, then."

He was leaving? "Where are you going?"

"Back the way I came," he said, untying the Zodiac. "I'll be in touch. Oh, and before I forget, I love your mermaid. She's a corker." With a salute, he tipped backwards into the water and swam towards the inflatable.

Hell. I uttered every expletive I knew, adding a few cobbled on the spot. I'd forgotten I was practically naked under the wetsuit jacket. He must have got quite an eyeful when he pushed my rear into the boat. Despite the dim light, the little tat on my upper rear thigh must have made an impact.

Drenched, bone-weary and seething, I rowed against the tide all the way to the boathouse. By the time I had the boat secured inside, the sea had risen to the edge of the jetty. The air blew chill and the sun disappeared behind a scud of clouds. It had to be close to four o'clock.

I stood shivering, wondering if my legs would even carry me up those stairs. And what about explaining my appearance to Mrs. Wyndridge this time? Say I'd gone diving in my undies? On a seriously extended lunch break?

I sank to the floor to pull on my sneakers and socks when I realized my clothes were gone. I'd piled them on top of my shoes. Standing up, I looked around, thinking maybe they'd been knocked over in my haste to get seaborne, but no, they had totally disappeared. Panic hit. Who would have taken my stuff and why? I sat back down to put on my sneakers, determined to get upstairs as soon as possible.

Shaking my left shoe with my palm outstretched, I waited for the weight of my phone to land. It didn't. I shook both shoes again and again before clambering to my feet scanning the shed. I checked every shelf, between, under, and inside every compartment in case I'd shoved it some-place without thinking. But my clothes were gone and so was my phone.

Gone!

My clothes weren't nearly as important as the phone. Oh, my God, someone took my phone! Not Wyndridge, since he wasn't home, and not his mother, obviously. That left only one possibility. I pulled a strand of seaweed from my hair and swallowed hard, pulled on my sneakers, and readied myself to climb those damn stairs all the way to the top.

14

Dad was at the end of that phone, along with Nancy, Max, *everyone who mattered,* plus all my personal information, including email, notes, and photographs. A survival pack for modern civilization lay stored in that little device. Open the apps and expose my life: how much I weighed, my grocery list, a favorite stitch pattern, what movies I watched or books I read, all my photos of everyone I loved and lost, my addresses and emails. My limb had been amputated and who ever took it would pay.

I arrived at the top of the stairs totally spent. I could only perch on a marble seat and stare blankly into the nearest hibiscus for a few minutes. Bert took my phone and I took his gun. Did that make us even? No way, no damn way. Only my goose-puckered flesh prompted me to stand and stumble into the house.

I slipped inside the kitchen door, my legs trembling, teeth chattering, readying for a sprint to my room when Joquita appeared. "Good lord, woman, what happened to you?"

"Joquita, oh, hi." I gave a little wave, wiped the hair from my eyes, and lowered myself onto a wooden chair.

"You look like you were hit by a ferry boat. Stop dripping on the floor." She untied a dishcloth from her waist and threw it at me.

"Oh, sorry," I stood, wiping down my legs with the cloth. "May as well have. I thought I'd go for a swim, only I forgot my suit," I indicated my abbreviated dive wear with a shrug. "So I borrowed a wetsuit top and went anyway. Only I ran into a bit of trouble." It sounded like the lie it was. All I could do was wrap my arms around myself and keep from shivering.

Joquita stared. Hard.

"What time is it?" I asked.

She glanced at her watch. "Nearly four-thirty. I'm just getting supper ready. Mrs. W isn't feeling well and may not join us and the mister is still away, so it might just be you and Bert for supper tonight. We'll make it early, say six o'clock, in the kitchen."

"Is Bert around?"

She rolled her eyes. "Somewhere. I haven't seen him for the last hour, thank heavens. You'd better clean up in case the missus arouses. See you later." And she strolled back into the kitchen, her demeanor three degrees cooler than at breakfast. At the door she paused. "Oh, I almost forgot. A lady called here about an hour ago. Said she was your aunt and wants you to call her back." She fished a recipe card from her apron pocket and held it out.

I snatched it eagerly. Flipping the card over, I silently read "Aunt Margaret. Call Astwood Cottages" with the number. "Do you have a phone I can use? My cell isn't working."

Her eyes narrowed. "Having all kinds of trouble today, aren't you? There's a phone in the hall." She indicated the direction with a jerk of her head.

In an instant, I was in the long front corridor. I located the Georgian map-press serving as a phone table and leaned against the paneling while I dialed on a very retro-looking phone. Soon the ornate receiver buzzed in my ear. Maggie picked up immediately. "Hello?"

"Aunt Margaret. Susan here. I understand you called?"

"Susan, how delightful to hear from you! How are you, darling?" Crud, it was going to be like this, was it? Maggie had assumed a mangled upper-crust New England-meets-the-deep-south accent. "How is your position progressing? Are you all enjoying the new wardrobe I gifted you? I do miss you so."

"Yes, I do miss you so, too, so much, in fact, that I can't begin to put it into words with enough vigor. I'd love to see you again soon. How about right after supper, say 7:30? We can discuss my wardrobe malfunctions then."

"Perfect! I'll pick you up. Be on the other side of the footbridge at 7:30."

"Wonderful."

"Perfect."

I dropped the receiver back in its cradle. Just this once, I really did want to see her. Needed to, in fact. No sign of Bert yet. I dialed my Dad next, only the phone rang and rang. Damn. Maybe Bertha had lured him over to her place for supper.

Taking a deep breath, I proceeded down the hall, itching with anxiety, praying for minimum interference en route to the bedroom. First, change, then go into disaster management. I had just reached the bedroom wing, unzipping my neoprene jacket along the way, when out stepped Bert. Up went the zipper.

"Well, well. Don't ruin the view, Suzy, or should I say Phoebe? Let Bert take a better peak at those two beauties of yours."

"Go to hell, Bert, or should I say Hector? And give me back my damn phone."

He stepped toward me, rolling a mint in his mouth, hands clenched at his sides. "Give me my gun first, bitch. Where'd you hide it?"

"Some place safe. Let me pass."

He shoved me back against the wall, one hand cupping a breast. "First, get my gun and then we have business to attend, in that order."

"I threw it in the sea." Try as I may, I couldn't keep my teeth from chattering.

"What the hell did you do that for?" His hand tightened on my breast.

"So you wouldn't shoot me with it?"

"Girlie, surely you don't think shooting is the only way I could kill you? I can think of maybe twenty others, most right here, all made to look accidental. And you were even dumb-assed enough to rummage through my stuff, too. Shit, if I didn't know better, I'd think you had a death wish." Now both hands began squeezing my breasts.

I kicked out at him, tried shoving him away. "Get away from me and give me my phone back!"

"I have needs too, Phoebe. Feel one pressing against you now? "He was back on me in seconds, his full body pinning me to the wall.

"No! I'll scream. Joquita will hear me. She'll call the police!"

He stepped back an inch, still keeping me pinned. "You do that and I'll kill you here and now."

"And ruin your chances of getting rich?"

He seemed to consider that. "Yeah, best to have my cake and eat you, too, eh? Here's what's going to happen, little Phoebe: You're going to keep Bert informed from now on in because you'll be working for me." He dropped his hands.

I tugged the jacket taut over my hips. "You mean, I'm to keep Hector informed. I know all about you, too."

"My reputation exceeds me. I suppose Noel told you."

I hesitated. How well did Hector know Noel? "Of course. He said you two were such great buds."

"Yeah, brothers-in-arms, you might say."

"Charming. So, where does stealing my phone fit in?"

He plucked my cell from his pocket, holding it from my reach. "After I saw you two in the boat and realized you were looking elsewhere without telling me. Poor choice, sweetie, 'cause that puts you on the losing team. No way he's going to nab a heist this big."

Did the "he" mean Noel or Max? Maybe he didn't know about Max, since he hadn't mentioned him. Could it be that this godfather played that far in the background? "Then is this officially a heist?"

He shrugged. "Call it what you want. Point is, I'm going to get it and he's not, which puts you in a very bad spot." He loomed down over me now, one hand now fingering the zip of my suit, the other holding my phone behind his back. "If you play nice, I'll give you back your phone. I might even forgive you tossing my gun and maybe offer you a job myself when this is over."

"Define 'play nice'." Buying time seemed my immediate option. Besides, he made no reference to my assignation with Maggie, which gave me a brief lilt of hope.

"I want access into the tower. Now."

"And, in return, all I get is my phone back and maybe improve my job prospects?"

"No, sweetheart." His hand moved to my throat where he squeezed gently. "In return, you get to stay alive and daddy doesn't have some nasty accident back in Nova Scotia."

I felt the blood drain from my face. "You hurt my father and, my God, I swear I'll kill you."

Bert smiled his over-bright grin. "Yeah, yeah. And aren't you in just the best position to be making threats? The little ex-gallery worker over-educated knitter pretending to be a fancified library lady who doesn't know her ass from a hole in the ground? I'm just quivering in my boots. Oh, yes, I've found all kinds of things about Phoebe McCabe, thanks to your phone. Handy little things, aren't they? I even spoke to Daddy."

"What?" I went rigid, hating the squeak in my voice. "What did you say to him?"

"Just that I was your new boyfriend and was phoning to make myself acquainted. Said you and I were going for a date tonight. He sounded all upset, kept asking to speak to you and asking why you hadn't called. I said you were too busy."

Damn him all to hell. I was trembling now, tears spilling down my face, helpless and afraid. Which I hated. Somewhere in that millisecond of terror, I swore to myself that I was going to get tough fast and beat these bastards at their own game. But right then I was too frightened to think. "Let me call him now. Please. He'll be worried. He has a bad heart."

"Aw, bad hearts can be so tricky, can't they? Better not mess things up then, hey, little Phoebe. Wouldn't want him to die from shock now, would we?" His hand moved from my throat to my cheek, stroking it as if calming a terrified animal. "First the tower. Then, if you're good, you can have the phone back. And, like I said, if you're really good, I mean, really, really, good, Hector will keep you alive." The hand slipped from my cheek to my breast, pinching it hard. "Understood?"

"Understood."

He stepped away. "Now, get changed. We'll go to the tower now."

"No," I said, between chattering teeth, almost doubling over. "Please, I mean not now. Look at me, I'm freezing. I have to change, and then, if we don't appear for supper at six, Joquita will know something's up. Do you want to blow the whole thing? Why not meet me outside the tower tonight at 9:30 after Joquita leaves? That makes more sense, doesn't it?

And what's a couple more hours? I'll be there, I promise. I just need a chance to catch my breath, get something to eat."

And then I started crying, as in full heart-felt bawl, nothing feigned. I felt so weak and idiotic, so helpless and vulnerable. I hated myself right then but I hated him more. Those tears were real.

He grabbed my wrist, twisting viciously, eyes hard. "Stop blubbering. I hate blubbering women. Go make yourself all pretty again. We'll make like normal over supper and meet at the tower at 9:30 but don't mess with me, Suzy-Phoebe. If you try, I'll have the old codger back home done in and have it filmed for your pleasure, just for starts. I've got friends who'd love nothing better than pick up a few grand for an easy kill. Get it?"

"Got it."

He grinned. "You be a good girl now and make Hector happy." Then he swung me around, patting me on the bottom before giving me a push towards my room. I heard his footsteps lumbering down the hall as I flung open the door and stepped in.

And stopped dead. The place had been ransacked. Clothes lay strewn across the floor, the contents of the drawers tipped out on the floor. In two strides, I was at the bed, gazing down in anguish. My carpet bag had been upended, my knitting ripped from the needles and tossed into a tangled mass. Another metaphor for my life.

✤ 15 ✤

As if the threads holding me together had unraveled, I could not stop crying. Like my beautiful knitting which now lay like a pile of tangled entrails, I had been ripped off my supports and lay in a heap. All I could do was wail, bent over like some plush toy with the stuffing kicked out of me. *He's threatening Dad! He knows where we live, who I am, everything about me! He ruined my knitting!*

And then I smartened up and straightened up. I'd had enough, really had enough. I could not, would not, lose anything more.

I straightened, took several deep, steadying breaths, and tried to pull myself together. First, I assessed the damage with my head, not my emotions.

All my papers had been rifled through, but my notes contained mostly generic information on Oak Island, which wouldn't have offered Hector anything new. He had also tipped over the mattress but missed Toby's drawing between the mattress cover and the box spring, not like that would have told him much, either. In fact, the bully boy would have learned nothing new from his search.

My clothes had been tossed over the room, with one green silk bra slung over the lampshade for added effect. The pink version with matching panties were gone, no doubt taken as a trophy. So, I reasoned, Bertie-

Hector had probably ripped my knitting out of spite because he hadn't found anything worth taking. He'd still think me here to find the treasure.

And my iPad was still safe in the tower. All was not lost. I took another deep breath. I would survive this. I would pick up my stitches and go on.

I stripped down and climbed into the shower. This late in the day, all I got was a cold, fitful trickle that sluiced me clean but did nothing to warm me up. I shivered just as hard getting out as I did getting in. Wrapping myself in a towel, I administered to my cuts and bruises with a makeshift first-aid kit found in the cupboard under the sink while struggling to pull myself together.

That bastard threatened my father! And Hector's employer would kill anyone who knows the truth about the treasure, no matter what Hector says. I'm as good as dead! A surge of panic threatened to swallow my newfound calm but I shoved it way back. Hector the hatchet man would kill anybody who got in his way, of that I was sure, so my usefulness would probably expire right after he had those diagrams, *if* he got those diagrams, unless of course, I offered special benefits. The thought of me giving Hector special benefits turned my stomach.

I stared at myself in the bathroom mirror. Hector thought me an inexperienced, weak little ninny in way over her head; and in some respects, he was right. But there was another truth that might shock him, might shock me, in fact. Something was happening at my core, something I couldn't define but knew to be made of strong, tensile stuff.

I tore through Maggie's wardrobe offerings looking for something suitable. Did those leather pants and a vintage Yves Saint Laurent silk gypsy blouse qualify? Did I care? Nothing remained but dresses and gowns, anyway, so on went the luxury wear.

I scraped my hair into a ponytail, applied a bit of the makeup Maggie had provided and surveyed the result. God, I looked like a trespasser at a costume ball. I cursed Maggie's sense of irony for packing this nod to pirate couture, while tucking the voluminous blouse into the pants. Though skintight, they offered just enough pocket space to shove in the room and tower keys.

I spent a few moments mourning my ruined wrap, lifting it by the wing like a wounded bird. Somewhere deep in those ravaged stitches, I glimpsed a thread of hope. If I could unravel back to the few remaining inches, I could begin again, perhaps even making the next version more beauteous than the first. But not now. I tucked the tangled mess lovingly into my bag, tossed my old companion over my shoulder, and left the room.

On my way to the kitchen, I knocked on Mrs. Wyndridge's door.

"Who is it?"

"Susan."

"Come in."

I entered, expecting to find her still propped in her chair watching reruns, but, instead, she lay on the bed with an afghan pulled up to her chin, her pallor alarming.

"Are you all right?" I noticed a pot of tea and a half-full teacup on her side table along with a plate of nibbled sandwiches.

"Just tired, that's all. When you're old, weariness hits out of the blue." Then her sharp eyes roamed up and down my person. "What in heaven's name are you wearing?" She pointed a finger at my overflowing silk blouse and leather pants.

I tried a nonchalant shrug. "I thought the blouse sort of goes with the house."

She smiled grimly. "More like you thought you'd impress my son, isn't that so? Well, you're wasting your time there, my girl. Mind my words, he won't be attracted to the likes of you. All young people do is think of mating. Best focus on your job, instead. How are things going in the tower?" Her tone sounded more sad than cutting.

"Fine," I lied. "I did a lot of rearranging up there and plan to go back up after supper to work some more."

She nodded. "Good. You must make up for all your tardiness. Now, let me rest."

"Can I get you anything?"

"Joquita will bring me my supper a little later."

I exited, closing the door softly behind me.

Supper was a dreary affair. Joquita said little while serving Hector and me generous helpings of grilled vegetables and baked chicken, casting sharp glances at us both. I ate in silence, trying to deflect Hector's occasional leer while he shoveled food into his mouth and chewed noisily. The man nearly put me off my fodder. Everything tasted the same to me, anyway.

"Mrs. Wyndridge isn't looking well at all," I commented. "Do you think we should call Mr. Wyndridge?"

"She wouldn't appreciate me doing that and neither would he unless it was an emergency," Joquita responded. "She has off days like this once in a while and just needs to rest. Besides, I wouldn't know how to contact him even if I thought it a good idea."

Joquita slipped a bowl of ice cream in front of us after clearing the plates. "But the weather might send him back. Report says we're getting the tail end of that storm that hit Jamaica. Mrs. Wyndridge says you must bring in the lawn furniture and latch the shutters, Mr. Stone. That means the tables and umbrellas around back, plus anything that might fly around has to be secured. We usually bring in the flower pots, too."

Hector stopped chewing, considering the request. I could almost read his thoughts: *Should I bother doing that grunt work when I have other fish to fry?* He weighed on the side of caution. "Sure thing. I'll get right on it. How long are you staying around for tonight, Joey?"

"Don't call me anything but Jocquita, Mr. Stone." Joquita slapped a dishtowel against her apron before draping it over a rack by the sink. "As soon as I make the missus her supper and clean up a bit, I'm out of here. If the weather's bad, I won't be coming in tomorrow, either, so I'll just prepare a few meals in advance. Expect cold food tomorrow. Salads. In the meantime, Mrs. W asked me to show you what needs to be done, Mr. Stone. As soon as you're finished, I'll do that. My boyfriend's picking me up at 9:00 and I have lots to do in between, if you don't mind."

"As soon as I've devoured this delectable feast, we'll just tally-ho and all that," Hector said, obviously enjoying the night's prospects, presumably the episodes that included me.

"Is the storm supposed to be bad?" I asked. It was a stupid question, as all island dwellers know.

"They're all bad this time of year, plus the electricity usually cuts out. High winds and rain is what they're saying—the usual stuff." She turned her back on us and began chopping vegetables.

I glanced at Hector and caught him looking back. Sly bastard. He beamed. "Worried about big waves, Susan? I'd have thought you' like them nice and big."

I rolled my eyes.

"There are lots of flashlights and batteries in the drawer there." Joquita pointed to a cabinet next to the door. "Now, excuse me while I take some supper to Mrs. W. I'll be right back."

The moment she exited, Hector leaned over and squeezed my knee. "You look a right dish in that getup, little Phoebe. I like a tight ass encased in leather. Did you dress up just for me?"

I fixed him with a look. "Sure thing, Hector. I dressed just for you."

He smirked. "I'll enjoy it when you undress just for me after we finished our little business. All part of your new working conditions."

Joquita entered the kitchen seconds after Hector had snatched back his hand. "Mrs. W isn't looking great but she ate a little."

"I'll check on her later on," I said.

Joquita nodded and went back to food preparation.

I dawdled over the ice cream until Joquita lead Hector out to the garden. The moment they disappeared, I dashed to the drawer and wrapped the two flashlights and three packages of batteries into a dish-cloth and I tucked the lot under my arm.

Hiding places were bountiful in places like this but I needed someplace Hector wouldn't look. My room was definitely out. In the end, I settled for the salon where I'd met Alistair Wyndridge and tucked the bundle inside the harpsichord, wincing when the strings twanged in complaint. That done, I had exactly 15 minutes left to get across the bridge to meet Maggie.

❦

NIGHT GLOMMED ONTO THE SHADOWS AS I DASHED OVER THE BRIDGE TO the parking area. Though Hector and Joquita were nowhere in sight, the green shutters at the front of the house had all been levered down. I could only hope the other tasks would keep him occupied while he imagined me cowering in my room waiting for the clock to chime 9:30.

I couldn't see Maggie at first, but the moment I headed up the drive, a car engine roared into life as headlights blazed. I ran towards the car, climbing breathless into the back seat.

"Hello, Susan, darling. Driver, take us to the Henry the Eighth Pub."

I was in a cab heading for a pub? I turned to Maggie, shrouded in darkness next to me, her perfume so strong, it socked me in the temples. "I thought we'd go someplace a little more private."

"Noisy is best, sweetheart, if we girls are going to share."

We girls. Share. Crud. I clasped my hands together and stared out into the night.

The Henry the Eighth Pub & Restaurant embodied every element of an old English pub except location and authenticity. As Maggie paid the driver, I plowed into the crowd, a waiter steering me through the mock Tudor decor to an empty booth. He slipped a couple of menus in the waiting spots as music launched from somewhere—an Irish singing group designed to work the crowd into a hand-clapping, beer-swilling mood.

Damn. I needed a phone. I leapt to my feet, ready to seek one out, when Maggie arrived in her pink cashmere twinset and Bermuda shorts.

"Where you going?"

"I need to borrow your cell."

"Please."

"Please."

"Who are you calling?"

"Dad. I'll explain everything in a sec." I plucked her Blackberry out of her hands and pushed through the throng, searching out an eddy of calm. The closest I came was the bathroom, where I dialed Dad's number with my back against the stall door.

He picked up immediately and I almost yelped in relief.

"Dad!"

"Phoebe? Is that you? What the hell's going on? I've been worrying myself to knots!"

"Dad, I'm so sorry. If you received a call today from someone saying he's my boyfriend, it's a lie."

"He didn't sound your type. You go for those overeducated, stuck-up sorts. This one had an English accent, but not the kind you like. What's going on? And don't try hiding anything."

I couldn't lie to him anymore. There had been too many lies for too long and the time to solder our family together with the truth was running out. "Dad, I'm tracking down Toby and I need you to stay calm."

Maggie scowled at me as I approached the booth minutes later. Two deep blue colored drinks with drunken-looking parrots perched on their rims sat on the table. "You look like shit. Guess my grooming tips didn't take. So, like, I get the ponytail thing but those sneakers kill the look. That's Yves Saint Laurent. Show some respect. Here, I ordered you a martini. You look like you could use it." She shoved the drink towards me.

"I'll share my opinions about your wardrobe choices some other time." I clutched her pink-nailed hand as it reached for the martini glass and tugged her forwards. "Listen, Maggie. Hector knows I'm not Susan Waverley. He thinks I work for Max and is blackmailing me to help him find the treasure. He's threatening Dad, not to mention me."

Maggie, froze. "Shit."

"Exactly. So, I need to contact Max. Can he can send somebody to the cottage to watch Dad unobtrusively? Hector stole my cell phone. He knows everything about me, everything."

Maggie twisted her hand around and gripped mine instead, giving it a hard squeeze. "How'd he get your phone?"

"Let's just say I left it by the wharf when I went for a dive earlier today."

"You went diving?"

"With Noel. He can fill you in with the details later."

"You went diving with Noel? I didn't know you two had hit it off so well. Find anything?"

I pulled my hand away. "Just let me speak to Max. Noel said I wasn't to try calling anyone in the usual fashion but, since my phone's dead, that's not an option."

She snatched her phone from the table and typed a quick message. "I'll contact him for you, but it's Noel you need to speak to, not Max."

"I want to speak to Max."

"It doesn't work that way. He's on the boat on the other side of the cove. So, I text a number, which contacts another number, and so on about five times until Max gets the message. Then, he texts me back with an address that I go to, usually a phone booth or something, and wait for his call." Catching my look of exasperation, she added, "Look, cells are open season in this business. Anybody can listen in, and ditto with landlines. We don't take chances."

I shook my head, grappling yet again with my godfather's business. "It's so cloak and dagger."

A waiter appeared at the table. "May I take your orders?"

Maggie beamed at him. "I'll have a Caesar salad with the dressing on the side, no bread. What about you, Susan, dear?"

"Nothing for me, thanks, Auntie Margaret." I smiled brightly.

The moment the guy slipped away, Maggie leaned forward. "I haven't spoken to Noel today. He's not responding to our agreed signal."

I leaned forward, too, pitching my whisper above the rising noise. "I don't care about your HR issues, Mags. Focus on the problem here, okay? I need help."

"Yeah, I get it but *this* is the issue. You need to speak to Noel, not Max. Obviously you can't go back to the house now."

"I have to go back. I have no choice."

"That's nuts. You need to get in touch with Noel first. He's the one handling Hector. Hector's a mean bastard unless he's kept in line."

I stared at her. "What do you mean by *handling Hector*? I thought he worked for a rival sleaze-bag."

She sipped her martini. "He does—sort of. Max has affiliates, too. The guy who Hector works fore runs an operation out of Britain. He and Max are associates—kind of. Depends on the day, even the hour. They're always squabbling."

"God, Maggie. This is insane. Who works for whom when is hardly a minor point in situations like this."

"It's complicated, okay? Everybody knows everybody in this business, I mean. The important thing is that Noel knows how to handle Hector. He's dangerous."

"Tell me about it. Does this associate he's working for have a name?"

She shrugged. "Not important. Focus on the task at hand."

I sank back in my seat, thinking ahead to my night locked in the tower with Hector. "How do I contact Noel without a cell phone?"

"I'll keep trying." Maggie continued between sips. In memory of bourbon past, I left mine untouched. "But look, hon, it's just that things have gotten way too dangerous with that brute on the loose. You've got to see that. Maybe you should get out now. Your three days are almost up, anyways."

"Forget it, Mags. Things have just become interesting. I'm not going anywhere until I find what I've come for."

Maggie paused mid-sip. "You mean Toby?"

"Of course I mean Toby."

"Maybe you won't like what you find; maybe it's better that you stay far away from this shit. We should never have involved you. That was a big mistake. I told Max that but he wouldn't listen."

I studied her, knowing that my pseudo aunt might act brainless but was far from it. She was up to something. "Forget it, I said. I'm seeing this through."

"Look, I didn't want to say anything so soon, and I know Max would rather tell you himself but we could offer you a job someplace safe. In London. Running the rare carpet gallery Max owns. You'd like that, wouldn't you—all that old fabric and ethnographic stuff?"

I was almost too stunned to speak. "Another job offer? That's the second I've had today."

"Think of it as long-range planning."

"More like poor timing. Besides, if Max wants to offer me a job, I'd rather he do it himself. No offense."

Maggie sipped the dregs of her aperitif and moved on to mine. "The dish ran away with the spoon."

"I beg your pardon?"

"Means don't be a snot. Max isn't the only one with a brain, though he thinks he is. I'm trying to help you here."

"The only help I need right now is protection for Dad and a way to get out of tonight alive. Do you have something for either of those?"

Maggie leaned towards me, lowering her voice. "Yeah. I'll get to work on the first and I have just the thing for the second." She patted her bag. "My gun."

My eyes widened. "I just tossed one of those into the ocean today."

"A bit short-sighted of you, wasn't it?"

I was beginning to see her point. "Maybe, but I still don't know how to use one of those."

"It's easy like a camera: just point and shoot."

"I'm not comfortable with guns."

"More comfortable with getting killed, then? You can hide it easily enough in that sack you drag everywhere. Take it."

I leaned forward again. "I try to use brains over bullets. Hector thinks I'm stupid, so I'll use that to my advantage."

Maggie nodded. "That would work for me until I tried to stop a killer at 20 feet. Look, once I get hold of Noel, he'll take care of Hector."

"But what about Max?"

"What about him? Noel's the man on the ground. Forget Max."

Forget Max? I checked my watch: 8:15. Maggie's salad had arrived, and after the perfunctory thank yous and no thanks to the waiter, I began again. "How can I contact Noel? How do you contact him?"

"Same way as for Max."

"What good is that convoluted business in emergencies?"

"That's what guns are for. They're real good in emergencies and keep your voice down." She picked up her fork.

I watched her pluck the choicest leaves from her salad while the minutes ticked by. "I have to go," I said, finally.

"I'm still eating."

That did it. I got to my feet. "And I'm still breathing—so far. I plan to keep it that way."

"Wait!"

She didn't stop haranguing me even while we waited for the cab outside the restaurant. When we finally parted company, me heading in one cab, she in another, she gave me such a fierce hug, I practically had to wrestle myself free.

"You need the gun, sister," she hissed in my ear.

"No, I don't," and I as I shoved her off and scrambled into the cab.

🕊 16 🕊

Hector ambushed me halfway between the bridge and the house.
"Where have you been, little Suzy?" He twisted my arm behind my back and steered me up the path.

"Let go. I went to meet my associate. If I didn't, she would have been suspicious, wouldn't she?"

"What did you tell Mags, then?" He yanked my wrist so hard, tears sprang to my eyes.

So he knew. Of course, he knew. "Not that I'm planning to jump ship, if that's what you're thinking. Let me go!"

He released me, sending me stumbling into the pontisettas, my carpet bag all that saved me from cracking my shins on a marble bench. "When I set a time, I expect you to be there, not when you feel like it. You're 10 bloody minutes late."

I stood there rubbing my wrist. "Big deal. You sound like Mrs. Wyndridge with added profanities. Look, I'm trying to keep my current employer from suspecting anything."

"Wouldn't want old Maxie to get twitchy, is that it?"

"Yeah."

He laughed. "You do that, little Suzy, but just remember what it takes to be on the winning team."

"Pleasing you or your boss?"

"Same thing."

"From what I understand, you're actually working for more than one employer at the moment. Must be confusing."

"Naw—I can handle it."

"And what was ruining my knitting about?"

"Consider it a warning and be glad that holey mess wasn't you. Now let's just proceed to the tower and get the job done."

I nodded, hoisting my carpet bag more securely on my shoulder and making for the kitchen door. His paw landed on my butt the moment I turned.

"Stop it!" I swatted his hand away.

"Ah, Phoebe, don't you like a little male appreciation? I bet Noel appreciated you a whole pile this afternoon dressed the way you were—or weren't, I should say. Nothing like a little wet silk to get a man's attention. Besides," he added, leaning closer, "I'm just getting a little taste of what I'll be enjoying later."

"Just keep your hands to yourself and let me concentrate." I sprinted up the path.

"What are you going to do about it?" he hissed after me. "Charge me for sexual harassment. Haha. Hey, do you know there's an 'ass' in harassment. Bloody brilliant!"

The house felt too quiet. Though Joquita had left the kitchen light on, something heavy and dark had descended on the atmosphere. My own fear, probably. I scanned the neatly stacked dishes, the notes left on the fridge and counter, and commented absently. "Funny, very funny. Let me check on Mrs. Wyndridge first, okay?"

"Not okay. The old bag is sleeping soundly. I drugged her tea."

"What?" I turned to face him. "You can't do that! She's on other medication. Who knows how the drugs might conflict with her existing meds?"

He mimed a violin, his arm sliding a bow across imaginary strings. "You're breaking my heart, little Phoebe. If you want to succeed in this business, it doesn't pay to be too soft-hearted. Now, move."

Anxiety flooded every nerve as I walked through the corridors. As if I climbed a moving stairway up a steep precipice with no way off, I strode through the too-quiet house towards the tower, unable to figure out how to avoid calamity. Clutching my carpet bag more closely to my chest, I realized how desperately I wanted to survive.

When we reached the darkened corridors of the old wing, Hector flicked on his flashlight and jangled a set of keys before my eyes.

"Those are Mrs. Wyndridge's," I said.

"Very observant. I just borrowed them from her seeing as she won't be needing them for a while."

I swallowed. "Did you hurt her?"

"I drugged her, I said." He shoved me aside and inserted the key. "Now enter the code, slow-like, so I can watch." He beamed the light on the key panel.

"Fine, but you're not going to find much up there."

"Is that why you were sent in pretending to be a librarian?"

I sighed, realizing I had no choice but to reveal the code under his piggy eyes. I tapped in the numbers and the door swung open, Hector singing a merry little tune under his breath.

As soon as the door slammed behind us, the darkness swallowed us whole. "The light's burned out. You'll have to use the flashlight," I lied.

He flashed his light around the stone walls, muttering. "I didn't expect him to have electricity in here except for the lock. I'm almost impressed."

I pointed to the stairs. "There's no elevator, obviously. I counted one hundred and ninety-six steps."

That launched a string of invectives and, while he studied the bottom landing to the sound of his own voice, I bolted for the steps as fast as my bruised legs could carry me. He heaved after me seconds later.

"Wait! Slow down, damn it!" he panted.

I hoisted myself over the weird irregular step, calling back, "What's the matter, Heck? Not keeping up with your gym dates?"

Several times I paused, bent over catching my breath while listening to him gasping below. He had a light, I didn't, and I was too aware of the wire rope forming a thin barrier between me and the drop below.

Once I reached the top, I plunged into the room, still propped open by my book jamb. Fumbling towards the window, I made for the desk lamp that had toppled over earlier. I found it in seconds and soon had it righted and the bulb tightened, sighing relief as it bloomed light.

I placed it on top of the desk and dashed back to wedge my carpet bag behind the door, careful not to dislodge my makeshift doorstopper in the process. Retrieving my iPad on the way back, I was soon at the map cabinet carefully placing the key letters I'd found back onto the debris pile, leaving them with what I hoped was a just-fallen look.

When Hector arrived panting minutes later , I was standing by the cabinet studying an aged parchment under the light of my iPad. "Not going to go all cardiac on me, are you, Heck? I'm not much good at CPR, especially if it means putting my lips on yours," I said without looking up.

He didn't have the breath to do more than growl. I thought he might really have a heart attack but that was only wishful thinking. He stepped into the room. "What the hell happened in here?"

"I was rooting around on the ladder when the shelf toppled over."

"Shit. Is this what you academics call methodical? You're a bloody disaster."

"Who said I'm methodical? Can you help set things to rights here?"

"What do you take me for, a house boy?"

"No, I take you for a house thug. Everybody needs one, apparently. Do you want to find what Wyndridge has been hiding or not?"

"Got your smart mouth back, I see. I prefer you servile but what does it matter since you'll look the same naked, either way."

I watched him maneuvering over the mounds to stand opposite me with the map cabinet between us. He glanced at the broken shelf behind me and then down at the tumble at his feet.

"You made a right mess, all right. Shit, couldn't have done better myself."

"Thank you." I pointed at the pile. "I went through some of that stuff earlier and found some letters but haven't had the chance to go through all of them yet."

He bent over and picked up one I had deposited, holding it under his flashlight before letting it fall again. I'd hoped he'd study it more closely, but instead he began pawing through the pile like a foraging bear.

"Be careful. Those are old and fragile. Hey, look, here's something you might be interested in. I read aloud from one of the pages I'd left on the cabinet. *"The Boy Huzzar* sailed..."

"Sailed where?" he asked, standing up.

He tried to snatch it from my fingers but I held it away. "Careful. It's delicate, almost completely illegible. I can't make out what the rest of it says, see?" I passed it towards him. "Take care. That's it. You hold it for me and I'll take a photo."

"Why the hell would I do that?"

"So we can magnify it later to scrutinize more carefully."

"You know anything about old writing?"

"Cursive script? Sure I do. Do you know anything about the *Boy Huzzar*?"

"Never heard of it."

"Liar."

Still, he did as I asked while trying to squint down at the faded script. I held my tablet up and took the shot.

"I got a proper camera in me pocket. Here, you hold it now and I'll take a picture." Which I did, watching him snap away with a tiny but powerful spy-worthy tool. If I had doubts about what he was after, they ended there . He recognized the name Boy Huzzar.

"Can you read anything else it says?" he asked.

"Not in this light. Maybe later. Anyway, where there's one, there may be others," I remarked, pointing to the pile. "Should we divide up the work? I'll start looking in that pile and you take the map cabinet?"

"Not bloody likely. I'll start looking right here and you do the map cabinet."

I wiped my forehead against the back of my silk sleeve, which was filthy already. "Suit yourself."

Hector snorted. "I intend to, little Phoebe, and don't try giving me orders, see? If you want to start working for me, prove yourself useful."

"I will. Two of us can sort through this stuff independently faster than in tandem, don't you think? "

He nodded, lowering himself to his knees with a grunt. "That works as long as you don't try anything stupid. Time's running out and I'm losing patience." Soon, he was rooting around for more letters, his heavy breathing filling the space.

I began pulling out drawers, careful not to knock against the broken shelf leaning tipsily against the wall behind me. When I had the diagrams in full view, I also pulled out a wad of nautical maps to slide over the top for shielding purposes. I began taking shots of each diagram with the tablet camera, trying to get in every quadrant clearly with one eye fixed on Hector. The iPad registered a red low-battery alert. Like I needed that right then.

"Why'd he give you that thing for a camera?" Hector asked, catching sight of lining up a shot.

"Why not? It works."

"If you'd worked for me, you'd use real tools."

I looked over at him. "I thought you work for somebody else?"

He smirked. "Used to. Not anymore. Hector's going solo as of today. What have you found, anyway?" he asked while photographing something on his side, a letter, possibly.

"Just some old maps."

"What kind of maps?" He huffed to his feet to take a look.

I slipped the nautical maps across the diagrams and pointed to a seventeenth century map of Jamaica. He peered over, studying the parchment with his flashlight.

"What good's that?"

"Aren't we looking for something buried or sunken like a shipwreck?"

"Is that what Noel told you he's doing, looking for shipwrecks?"

Noel, why Noel? "Maybe." My breath caught as his stubby fingers flicked through the sheaf, the diagrams flashing past without interest.

I took a deep breath. "What are you looking for?"

"Said I don't know."

"Find anything interesting in that pile?"

"Maybe. Found a couple of letters from a certain captain to the king of England," he chuckled, knowing damn well the significance of those. He was finding all the stuff a true treasure hunter craved, original tertiary documents. I doubted I'd ever see them, but why would I want to? I wasn't there for treasure.

"What kind of shape are they in?" I asked.

"Not bad considering the dates are between 1687 and 1688."

"What do they say?"

"How the hell do I know?" he growled. "All kids of curlicues and stuff. Those dudes wrote like a bunch of faggots."

That made me hate him even more.

I finished photographing the diagrams, paying specific attention to one showing the tower above a mass of arterial lines leading to the sea. Tiny script labeled various tunnels and chambers; a main access point clearly noted running from the base of the tower to the underground system. My blood pounded in my ears. It was exactly what everyone wanted and the very thing I couldn't let anyone see. It had to go with me.

While the lug was preoccupied with the letters, I folded the parchment into quarters, breaking every conservationist's rule plus a few of my own, and slipped it under my blouse.

The windows thumped fitfully in the wind. The single banker's lamp cast nothing but a greenish glow into the shadows punctuated by Hector's flashlight and my iPad's ambient light. My companion breathed heavily, oblivious to either time or tide. He was studying something beside the failing flashlight he had propped on the edge of the cabinet. I picked my way over to stand by the leaning shelf.

"Looks like your flashlight's giving out," I said. "Don't you have spare batteries?"

"Eh? Yeah, sure. Damn torch. Should have brought a better one." He plucked the flashlight off the counter, giving it a slap with his fist before heaving to his feet to dig around his jacket pocket.

He climbed over the pile to lean towards the desk lamp, angling for light. I watched as he opened the battery compartment, counting the seconds until he stood up again and headed back towards his spot. When he reached midway between the desk and the cabinet, I gave the broken shelf a furious sideways shove, sending the cracked wood hurling down right on top of him. He fell to his knees with a curse.

I estimated mere seconds before he'd be on his feet, time enough to leap over the shelf and mounds of books, and yank the desk lamp cord from the socket while holding my iPad ahead for light.

Hector was still groaning in the dark when I grabbed my carpet bag and kicked the book from the door. The heavy portal clanged shut behind me as I hurled downstairs, the adrenalin pounding in my ears, aiming my pad light towards the well of darkness.

I fixed on keeping away from the edge; I fixed on the rhythm of the steps; I fixed on what I would do once I got to the bottom. I fixed on everything except that one wonky step. When I jettisoned into the darkness, I flung my carpet bag ahead of me like an offering to the gods.

❧ 17 ❧

Impossible to know how long I lay at the bottom of the stairs. Probably only seconds though it could have been a lifetime. When I came to, darkness suffocated me and I couldn't breathe.

"Goddam bitch. I'll kill you for this!"

I shoved myself upwards, pushing air into my lungs, energy into my legs, staggering upright. My carpet bag lay directly below me and probably cushioned my fall, but my right knee had hit hard.

He was coming! I bent down, grabbed my bag by the strap, and stumbled just far enough to the left to slam into the wall. I stood stunned in agony as my knee stabbed vicious pain all the way up my spine while Hector huffed downwards like a fury in the dark . I couldn't move, couldn't see. *Couldn't think!*

A brute cry preceded a thump-thump of a mass tumbling downstairs. Turning around, I stood shivering, my back pressed against the wall, as a large shape landed only inches away. I held my breath, listening. Nothing. I fumbled for the wall switch behind me and blazed light into the space.

Hector lay face-down on the stone floor, an immobile mass of flesh. I prodded him with my foot, wanting him dead. He lay with one arm bent beneath him at an unnatural angle, the other flung out where he tried to buffer his fall. Crouching, I felt for a pulse, finding it strong. Damn brute should be dead, not just knocked senseless. I needed to finish him off.

I picked up my cracked iPad lying a foot away and considered whacking him over the head with it but slid the damaged tablet into my bag instead. Maybe he'd be badly enough concussed to stay put but I couldn't be the one to send him into oblivion. Instead, I fumbled in his pockets for Mrs. Wyndridge's keys, plus his wallet and my phone, dropping everything into my bag.

Getting unsteadily to my feet, I resolved to come back with a rope to bind his feet and hands. Then I caught sight of my poet's shirt, splattered with blood, thinking how pissed Maggie would be. Stupid thought, maybe, but it gave some satisfaction.

I identified the metallic taste rolling around my mouth as blood but couldn't figure out where it was coming from. No time to think. Had to move, had to go, but felt so damn dizzy. I opened the door, flicked off the light, and exited the tower, the door slamming shut behind me.

In the hall, I stood trembling and disoriented. My body felt fracked. It was so dark and I needed a light. Did I even have a light?

I fumbled inside my bag until I grasped my iPhone, clutching the thing as if it were a lifeline. I brought it to eye-level but when pressed, all I got was a feeble red low battery alert. Damn it! I flung it back into the satchel in disgust. Which way to my room? The world tilted, my legs buckled, and down I went, the shock of knee hitting floor so brutal, I yelped.

Dragging myself up again, I stumbled forward, cursing every stab of pain. I must have twisted something and bruised something else. Dizzy and knocking into furniture, I made my laborious way to the bedroom wing, lugging my carpet bag behind me.

Wind rattled the shutters and howled beyond the walls, mournful and threatening all at once. Somehow, I made it through the house in a blur of pain, noting that there were lights on that shouldn't be, including the one in my bedroom.

I leaned against the wall in the corridor staring at my half-opened door. I knew I'd shut it before meeting Maggie. Hobbling forward, I lurched in. Lamplight pooled on the walls, silhouetting the dark figure of a man rifling through my bureau drawers.

"Noel?"

He swung around. "Phoebe! What the hell happened? I've been looking all over for you!"

"In the drawer?"

He was before me in an instant, his concerned gaze taking in my wounded person.

"You look a mess." I swatted his hand away when he tried to touched my face. His hands dropped to his side. "You need bandaging. You're bleeding. What happened?"

I looked down at my blood-splatterred, once-snowy silk shirt. "I fell," but for a moment I couldn't recall when or where.

"Mags said you were in trouble, something about Hector stealing your phone? I came immediately. The kitchen door was unlocked so I walked right in, searched the house far enough to find Mrs. Wyndridge sleeping next door, and your room deserted. What do you mean, you fell? You look like you were hit by a truck."

I touched my mouth where something small and bulbous had fastened to my bottom lip.

He lifted his hands in a kind of shrug. "You cut your lip. Let me fix you up. Where's Hector?"

I pushed past him, heading for the bed, struggling to remember the sequence of events. "Bottom of the tower stairs. He tripped ." I eased myself to sitting on the bed and tried pulling up my pant leg, but skinny leather pants don't scrunch. "I had a crash bag and he didn't."

"Crash bag?"

I pointed to the carpet bag on the floor where I'd dropped it. "Yarn saved me. Always said it would." I rolled my tongue inside my mouth and winced. Puffy and sore.

He knelt beside me. "You're hurt and confused," he said, his voice as mellow and soothing as a narcotic. Maybe I could slip away to another world inside a voice like that.

"Stop trying to talk . I'll clean you up."

"Is Mrs. Wyndridge all right?"

"She's sleeping next door."

"Hector drugged her."

"Bastard."

"Tie him up," I mumbled. Mumble was all I could do.

He checked his watch. "Leave Hector to me. First, I'm going to ice your lip and bandage you up. Let me look at that leg."

He passed over a bottle of water pulled from a leather pack worn slung across one shoulder. I took it and drank deeply, dribbling lots down my shirt in the process, while he bolted into the bathroom.

I stared down at my ruined blouse, watching the blood dilute to pale . What color was that? Pink? Light red? The sound of Noel in the bathroom prodded my stunned brain cells. I had forgotten something critical but the details wouldn't come. Fainting seemed a galling possibility.

He called out. "I found bandages." A moment later, he was trying to ease me to standing. "Come into the bathroom where the light's better."

He overruled my protests and picked me up in his arms, a sensation I found half-pleasant, thinking that must be what it feels like to be carried away by y

He deposited me gently on the toilet seat, which ruined the effect. There I sat enthroned while he knelt before me like some knave of first aid, dabbing my lip and bandaging my forehead.

"How gallant," I said. He looked so damned sexy in the overhead light, something that penetrated my foggy senses despite pain and dizziness. In any state, he got to me, but, I reminded my battered self sternly, I could not afford to be got. Or had.

"That's me, Sir Dogsbody. Now, let me look at that leg. Take off your pants."

I would have laughed if I could. "Hell, no," said I.

He looked amused. "I'm not trying to seduce you but I've got to see that leg."

"I can't imagine pulling these things down. I'll never get them back up. Don't have anything else."

"Is it your right leg?"

I nodded.

And he pulled out a knife from his shoulder pack and sliced the bottom half of my leather jeans clean off, revealing an ugly blue-black bruise the color of a storm at sea puffing as mightily as my lip. He glanced up at me. "My God, woman, you're lucky you didn't break this or worse. As it is, I think it's just sprained. I'm going to bandage it. Here, hold on while I get ice. Take this for now."

I took the wet washcloth he proffered and sat with it pressed against my mouth, feeling as though I was about to be swallowed alive by fog. I could not, would not, faint. I leaned over, head between my knees and waited.

Noel disappeared for a few moments, maybe years, returning with a mug of cold coffee, two baggies of ice, and a couple of Advil. "I found the cold coffee still in the pot and the pills in that rug thing you carry around. Take two."

"Went through my stuff, again," I muttered as I swallowed coffee and painkillers and waited for the world to refocus. "Did you find what you wanted?" I asked after a bit.

"You know I didn't." He was just finishing bandaging my leg in a layer of flex bandage while I sat wincing when the next question came. "Where'd you hide them?"

"Hide what?"

"Don't play with me, Phoebe. The diagrams."

My left leg shot out and caught him in the thigh.

"What was that for?"

"Reflex. Always happens when I smell a rat."

He jumped to his feet while I got unsteadily to mine, hanging on to the sink for support. My brain toggled images of the diagram folded inside my blouse. I could feel the parchment where it had slipped under my arm to hang in a sling of ruined silk. It was all I could do not to glance down.

"I need those diagrams, Phoebe."

I threw the ice bag into sink. "That's what you're here for, isn't it? The diagrams? Did you think I'd stick them in the drawers for you to find?"

"But you did find them?"

My eyes met his. "I didn't say that."

"You're a terrible liar. Where are they? And, thank you for coming through for me."

"Nothing I do is for you."

He shot me a wry smile, turned, and strode back into the bedroom. I leaned against the door frame long enough to see him shake the contents of my carpet bag onto the bed in a mass of tangled yarn before I slammed the bathroom door, and secured the feeble hook into the catch. I pulled the folded parchment from my blouse seconds later , finding it just as damaged as expected, splotched in blood and bleeding ink. No time to study it.

The door rattled dangerously. "Let me in!"

"I have to use the bathroom!"

"I'll find the bloody thing!"

I desperately scanned the tiny area for a hiding place before turning the taps on full and letting the rushing water mask the sound of me lifting the toilet back cover. Everybody in every drug heist movie I ever saw hid things in toilets, making it a bad idea but the only one I had. Under the bath mat hardly made a good alternative.

I emptied the ice from one baggie into the sink, wiped it dry, and refolded the parchment into eights before squeezing it into the bag and wedging it by one corner on the edge of the tank. When I flushed seconds later, the plastic would touch water but hopefully the document would stay dry.

When Noel kicked the door in moments later, I had just finished washing my hands. I turned to him. "You didn't need to break the door down. I only took a few minutes."

"Where is it?"

"Where 's what?" I leaned against the sink, struck by the dangerous glitter in his eyes.

"Don't waste my time, Phoebe. You found the diagrams. You know I'm going to see this through."

"And you know I'm not going to help you."

"Even when you know that finding the treasure connects to Toby?"

"Don't use that on me. Finding Toby and stealing the treasure are not synonymous. Start telling the truth for once."

"You don't know the half of it. Toby's not quite the noble one you take him for. He came here looking for it, too. What you don't know is that he found a copy of the diagram, information that he texted to Max days before he disappeared. Max hasn't told you everything."

Like that surprised me. "What else?"

"Toby has been working off and on with Max for the past five years. Max sent Toby here to infiltrate the Wyndridge estate, which he did very successfully. He found something, Phoebe, something important. He alluded to charts and diagrams, but wouldn't give specifics. Instead, he returned home to tell your dad and presumably hide a clue relating to the treasure."

Dad was in on this, too. I knew it. I shook my head. I'd been so clueless.

"Toby planned one more trip back here before joining you at your father's birthday party for the big reveal. He told Max to meet him there, only Toby never returned. Are you going to help me or not?"

"No. You can just go to hell with the rest of them. Get out of here and leave me alone."

"Phoebe," his voice dropped , "treasure hunters never stop until the treasure is found, you know that. Toby didn't stop and neither did Max. You can be damn sure I won't."

"Even if it kills you or me?"

"That's the risk you take when the stakes are this high."

Toby would have said something stupid like that. I swallowed hard. "Toby wouldn't steal anything. He might track it down—God knows he loved nothing better than solving a good mystery—but he'd never steal."

"Don't be so bloody naive. People change. He had the information that leads right to it. He was working with us, Phoebe. He did dive that cave we were in today and followed the signs to the shaft. I was just checking to see how good an escape it might make if I have to exit in a hurry. What I need is the diagram."

"But Toby wouldn't steal. He wouldn't run off without seeing Dad. Something happened to him."

"I'll find you answers."

"Tell me what you know now."

"Sure but are you going to listen or keep believing the fairytales? We were friends. We shared a lot on our dive trips. He told me all about you, even the story about why you got that mermaid tattoo."

Toby told him that? I held my breath, staring at him, transfixed in pained disbelief. "Are you...?"

"No, of course not, but we were friends, I said. He told me how much he loved you and appreciated your support for encouraging him to be himself, no matter what. The merpeople tats were—"

"Stop!" That did it. *Toby, Toby.*

"Phoebe..." He stepped towards me.

"Don't touch me," I said without looking up. "Go to hell." Salt rolled down my cheeks, searing everything it touched.

"First, the treasure, then maybe hell, preferably in that order. I'm going down there with or without a diagram."

"Do you even know how to get there from the here?"

"Toby said there's a hidden door right outside the base of the tower."

I squeezed my eyes shut. It was true, then. *Toby, why? Dad needs you; I need you.* The sound of the toilet tank cover being lifted jarred me from my pain. I watched Noel remove the baggie and made no move to stop him.

"There was only one place you could hide anything in here," he commented as he unfolded the parchment. "And you bled all over this."

"Good."

"But I can still make out enough to confirm my theory: another tidal shaft built right into the natural stone and probably rigged to flood with the tide as in Oak Island."

"A trap just like the Money Pit."

"Maybe. If it's a trap, it's a simplistic one. The Wyndridges used this one as a bank so you can be sure they enabled an easier withdrawal than the Money Pit."

"Why keep the loot buried for two centuries? That's crazy."

He turned to me then, lean face tense, eyes sparking fiercely. "Because the Wyndridges were a family of collectors. They couldn't bear to destroy precious jewels like Queen Isabella's pectoral cross or Aztec ceremonial gold. They melted down the coins but kept the main pieces intact."

"How do you know that?"

"Toby."

"Toby would never do that."

"Believe what you will. I have to go. This shaft isn't an exact duplicate of the Money Pit. I'm confident I can work out the specifics. Everything depends on the tide." He glanced at his watch. "And it will be fully turned within the hour. Got to go."

"What about Max?"

"He's waiting on the boat offshore."

"You go out that door and I'll call the police."

He strode from the bathroom, me hobbling behind him. "Right. Knock yourself out trying. The landlines have been cut and your cell phone is drained. Oh, and your iPad is smashed, too. I'd say you're incommunica-do." He pointed at my devices tangled amid the yarn pile on the bed. "Wait until morning and then make a run for the shore, but until then, stay here and, for God's sake, keep the gun close in case Wyndridge returns."

"What gun?"

He plucked a pearl-handled pistol from the yarn nest and slid open the chamber. "How many do you have?"

I stared ."Maggie."

"She's even loaded it for you. Do you know how to use this thing?"

"No."

"Listen up."

I tried taking in the details of which mechanism did what and when but befuddlement ruled. All I could think of was death and betrayal on multiple fronts. How could I be so blind-sided? Why at my age couldn't I at least be smart? Why did Toby get into this mess and why did I track him into the vortex? Question upon question screamed inside my head.

"I'm going now." He replaced the gun on the bed and in two strides was beside me, looking down like he wanted to kiss me but couldn't find a suit-able place. His hands hovered over my arms, barely touching my skin though I could feel the heat. "Phoebe, I want you to know that I—"

"Get out."

He stepped away, taking a deep breath. "Right. I'll find a way to come back for you. Be careful in here in the meantime. If we're alone in this house now, we won't be for long, and you could be in danger still. Use the gun if you have to."

Then he swung around and reached the door in three long strides.

18

I hobbled forward as the key turned in the lock. And he thought he could lock me in, too? Even if I had to drag myself out bone by bone, I was leaving that night. I'd tell the police, unravel the whole ugly story, and the hell with the consequences.

Toby was in this absolutely and my fury over what he had done burned holes in my heart. He had been involved in this plot—and Dad, too, not to mention Max and Noel—each one of those stupid men risking their lives for this idiot quest. Why did men have to be such idiots? Was there a hack for that?

Back at the bed, I gazed down at the tangled mess, my grief and anger writhing. The gun glinted menacingly from atop the mass of blue fiber. The yarn below it tangled around the disparate objects like fibrous seaweed, slipping around the iPhone, snagging my charger, and catching in amongst all my stuff.

After a quick inventory, I realized Noel had claimed Mrs. Wyndridge's chatelaine of keys but appeared to have left everything else. How kind. I'd just take my belongings and go: my unraveled knitting, dead cell phone, smashed iPad, a bottle of pain killers and cram them back into my carpet bag amidst the jumbled artifacts from my ruined life. That left the gun. I buried it deep within my bag, only adding to its mounting weight.

But before leaving, I had to retrieve Toby's drawing from deep in the boxspring hiding place, something I could have done with ease a few hours ago but which now seemed monumental.

I dumped the carpet bag by the door. Then, with my bum leg stretched stiff in front of me, I lowered myself to the floor, my back against the bed. With my operable leg levered against the wing chair which, in turn, pressed against the wall, I applied all the pressure I could. After several agonizing moments, the mattress budged, slipping far enough off the frame for me to reach in and pluck the tube from the hole. It took several moments of recovery mode before I could conceive of moving again.

Which gave me time to think. So, Toby's reason for coming here involved this damn treasure. Maybe I'd never hear his voice again, never see his face, or find out why he had risked his life for this, of all things. And we think we know someone...And to think he participated in some criminal act with Dad only infuriated further. Who would I rail against now—my demented father or my missing brother? And, in the end, the only one who had been left out of the loop was me.

I thought I'd break in two, as if grief and fury ripped a jagged line right through my core. Nothing left but mementos, memories, and this twisting, bitter rage threatening to tear me apart. I wanted to slap my brother, yell at him, and hug him all at once. Only maybe I'd never get the chance.

Slowly, I pulled the cartoon from the tube and spread it out across my thighs, wanting to see something in Toby's hand. Maybe my elevated emotions combined with caffeine and pain killers had left me strangely focused but for some reason the crinkling paper suddenly struck me as too thick. We had painted the original on a sheet of white poster paper bought at an artist's supply store. Though thicker than the regular stuff, this felt unnaturally so, double, maybe triple. And then it hit me. *This* was what Toby had hidden and Max sought. *This!*

I held the paper up to the light. The outline of a third sheet silhouetted a shadowy square. Three sheets of paper, not two! All I had to do was peel away the two sheets that had been glued along the edges to reveal the secret third sandwiched between. It took a few fumbling moments, a little impatient tearing on one corner but finally I had pulled out the secret sheet, holding it up in triumph.

A drawing so totally Toby, my heart swelled. It could have been a fanciful, stylized, felt-tipped mock-up of one of his computer games or maybe a board game like some underwater snakes-and-ladders merged with Monopoly-does-Atlantis. Sinuous snake-like forms undulated in a submerged world peopled by upside down mermen, skull and crossbones, and starfish wearing tricornered hats, arms brandishing swords.

The largest snake, a very ominous thickly drawn creature, twisted like a mutant intestine, dominating center page and curving downward before straightening into an exploding head, swirling skulls and, exclamation points. Oh my god! Not a snake, but a tunnel!

I leaned over, absorbing every detail, slipping into Toby's imagination, thinking in my brother's symbolic whimsical style. The snake's tail in the upper right-hand corner represented the cave entrance; the little house above it, the tower, and the reptile's tortured body twisting below was, clear to me now, the treasure tunnel. And it ended in destruction, no doubt about it, all those crossbones and signs of alarm, but how? Why?

I swallowed hard, not grasping every nuance, not getting what this portrayed or why Toby had hidden it but understanding the warnings clearly. I could almost feel my brother then, as if he'd dropped down around me enveloping me in a sense of imminent danger confirming my own. STAY AWAY! And, whatever it was, Noel was walking right into it.

I hoisted myself to standing, rolled the sheets back up, and inserted them back into the tube. Let it not be said that I was a total idiot. Bad enough I came here against my instincts, but now I had to leave fueled by intellect and raw self-preservation alone. I would contact the authorities so a team could descend into the caves and save Noel. And, yes, he'd be arrested and, maybe Max, too, and, no, that would never bring my brother home, but would Noel listen to me if I tracked him down with a drawing of exploding snakes and parrying starfish? Not likely. I had to think of me, of Dad. I had to get the hell out of there. I jotted a quick note to leave on Mrs. Wyndridge's night table: HAVE GONE FOR THE POLICE. SUSAN

My leg had stiffened now made bending it impossible, even if it weren't for the bandage. Hobble was all I could do and that not very well, considering I had to simultaneously drag a textile albatross on the floor behind me. Nevertheless, I made it to the door, where I bent down to insert the tube into the bag without falling over. I felt in my leather pants for my room key, which I had fortuitously stuck deep into the pocket. Ha! In went the key, I flung open the door, relieved to find the hall lights burning.

I made to hop my way out, only the weight of my carpet bag anchored to the floor, nearly knocking me off-balance. Hell and damnation! I would not leave that bag behind. Hopping back, I bent over with the bad leg stretched off to the side and reluctantly pulled out the iPad. That would just have to stay.

Propping the wounded tablet against the hall table, I tried again, this time getting two feet before sagging against the table in exhaustion. I gazed around. Why was the house so bright? Only my room light had been on an hour ago. Now a bar of light beamed from under Mrs. Wyndridge's door and the table lamp opposite her room glowed. In fact, it seemed as though every lamp along the way shone brightly. Noel wouldn't have turned those on. And then, as if the house caught my thoughts, everything went out all at once.

Afraid to breathe, I strained to listen. Except for the wind beating against the shutters, everything was silent. Didn't Joquita say the power often went out in high winds? Taking a deep breath, I shuffled towards Mrs. Wyndridge's room, planning to check on her and deposit the note. Fumbling along the wall and navigating by memory, I pushed her door open and hopped forward, letting momentum propel me until my thighs hit the bed.

"Mrs. Wyndridge, are you awake?" I felt the bedspread, sweeping my hands back and forth searching for her sleeping form. "Mrs. Wyndridge? Wake up!"

The bed felt strangely flat. The wind shook the shutters, blocking out subtler sounds. Could I hear breathing? "Mrs. Wyndridge?" I sensed another presence in the room.

"Stop where you stand, or by God, I will slice you asunder!"

I SWUNG AROUND, LOST MY BALANCE, AND TIPPED BACKWARD AGAINST the bed, arms flailing. "Wyndridge?"

Light flared, shooting the haggard face of Adrian Wyndridge into focus as he stepped out from behind the door, a lantern in one hand, a sword in the other.

"Thank God!" I said. "I'd given up—"

"Silence!" His face sealed in a mask of fury, his usually perfect garb shredded and soaking wet. He looked like he'd been in a shipwreck three centuries ago.

"But I've been waiting—"

"Do not speak! I've had enough of your lies! Did you think I would permit you to harm my mother as well as steal me blind?" He bore down on me, sword glinting silver.

I pressed my back against the bed with no place to go, staring at the sword with a sickening sense that he knew how to wield it. "I would never hurt your mother,"

"Indeed not, for I have transported her to safety, the better to deal with your gang unencumbered. Ms. Waverley, or whoever the hell you are—a detestable little thief, by any definition. Get to your feet!"

"Let me explain."

"I am disinterested in your lies, madam! Do not deny that you conspire with my enemies, murderers and cutthroats all. Get to your feet!"

"I-I can't get up without help."

He held the lantern over my head, swiftly assessing my condition. "Met some measure of your just rewards, I see." Satisfied that I was suitably helpless, he sheathed his sword and hoisted me to standing by practically wrenching one arm from its socket.

"Take it easy!"

He yanked me up until my face leveled with his: "You, ma'am, are not worthy of my consideration. I will not hear your lies," he said between his teeth. "How many times need I say it? Now move!"

He shoved me towards the door. I couldn't balance in time and hurled forward into the hall, crashing into a table. The lamp shattered on the floor as I gripped the wood to steady myself. He was on me in seconds, grabbing my arm and dragging me down the corridor.

"Wait!" I cried. "My bag. Back there." I let my full weight drop towards the floor. "Can't leave it behind and there's Bert to deal with."

He released me like a sack of potatoes. I fell in a heap as he marched back down the way we'd come. "Where?" he called over his shoulder.

I lay on the floor squeezing back the pain. "By. the. door."

He returned in seconds, the bag slung over one shoulder, and hauled me upright again. After that, I stopped trying to speak. It was enough just to keep from crying as he dragged me stumbling through the house.

I had no idea where we were heading. Everything sunk into agony blurred by twisting hallways and leaping shadows, surreal images stabbing me with sharp edges and glinting surfaces. Shadows jumped out at me then slunk back into darkness after the lantern swept past. Nothing slowed him down. The man's fury burned into the air around us and I was in too much pain to fight. Besides, all I could think was guilty, guilty, guilty as charged. I was here under false pretenses. My family had conspired to steal from his. *Guilty*.

I squeezed my eyes closed, gritting my teeth. I was close to fainting by the time he finally jerked to a halt. We had arrived. Somewhere.

I hung limp, all my weight borne on the arm he gripped while he fumbled for a key. The latch caught and he kicked the door open, pitching me forward into a room. The momentum propelled me across the floor until I banged into a piece of furniture, a bedpost, I realized. I clung to the carved wood, realizing we were in his bedroom. What was he going to do to me here? I thought of the gun in my bag. Maybe I could get to it somehow but what then—distract him, reach in and what, *shoot*? Hell, the man had every right to be angry, even unhinged, and I *had* entered his house under a ruse. Besides, I couldn't shoot him, even if I figured out how to work the damn gun.

He strode over to the bookcase lining one wall. A latch or a lever clicked and the wall of books slid back, revealing a secret room. Just like the movies, I thought, resting my forehead on the wood. Would I ever wake up from this nightmare?

"You did not discover this on your little night ambles through my property, did you? No, you did not. And that brute, Bert, could not detect my house's secrets no matter how many times he clumsily searched, being far too bovine for that. You, on the other hand, just might have but, fortuitously, did not."

I lifted my head. "I'm not too swift when all's said and done. You knew?"

"I knew!" He wrested my grip from the bedpost and shoved me into the secret room, forcing me down into a chair. There I slumped, watching him hook the lantern on one wall and lighting others from a long taper— two more lanterns, a candelabra and four wall sconces, including a cluster of pillar candles inside the craw of a huge, empty fireplace.

Gradually, a large, cluttered space came into view dominated by heavy dark wooden tables flush against the walls, display cases everywhere, and two seventeenth century carved chairs angled companionably with a small table between. A grandfather clock standing at attention in the far corner tick-tocked away. No windows.

Wyndridge unbuckled his sword belt, letting scabbard and belt thump to the floor along with my bag, now forgotten. The door creaked shut behind us in a wall of books.

"But how?" In retrospect, that probably wasn't the line I should have taken just then.

He swung towards me. "From the moment you entered the house, I knew you were part of the plot to steal from me!"

The fact that theft wasn't my intent hardly mattered now. Wasn't I guilty by association, guilt embedded in my very DNA? Since my brother and father had been involved, my true motivation seemed too weak a point to mention. "Why didn't you stop us?"

Placing hands on hips, he took a deep breath as if struggling for composure. His eyes swept the ceiling, fixing on the cedar beams for a count of seconds. When he refocused on me, he seemed slightly calmer. "Because I was awaiting my trap to spring, and spring it did. I was on my ship until a few hours ago watching my plan unfold."

"Watching how?"

He held up his hand to silence me and shot me a tense, triumphant smile before turning and moving about the room. I watched him shuffling papers before he took a brief swig of some deep ruby liquid from a decanter and goblet.

The details of the room began distracting me in an impressionistic blur of candlelit antique tapestries on stone walls, heavy dark wood tables, and carved cabinets everywhere. Along with the furniture, I took in lots of sparkling and gleaming objects inside glass interiors. A small oval case at my right elbow held a huge mounted necklace encrusted with pearls and gems. I leaned towards it, slack-jawed as the clock chimed once.

"Yes, indeed, Ms. Waverley, do look." Wyndridge appeared beside me. "By all means, retrieve it from its perch. Try it on, do, for wearing a piece of history will be the only reward you will ever gain for your efforts in this matter, regardless of what you were promised."

I shook my head, only half-listening. I couldn't believe the glory in my line of vision.

"Oh, now, do not be timorous. You have come all this way, after all." He leaned over, flicked the latch and lifted the gleaming rope of pearls from its stand to drop over my head. I caught the lower length in both hands, struck by the cool, smooth weight of pearls the size of gooseberries, lifting the lower end into the light to better see its dangling gold cross. Rubies, emeralds, and sapphires sparked brilliantly in the light, each piercing me in some unexpected way. I had never seen anything so gorgeous. The piece hung heavy and lustrous, the gold cool against my skin as I let it drop to my chest.

"Amazing!" I said, totally gem-struck. "Is it a pectoral cross, fifteenth century—Spanish, maybe?"

"Indeed. I believe this piece was once worn by Queen Isabella herself. I would pose the worth to be millions in today's market, should it ever see the light of day, which sadly, it will not. Ask yourself, beauteous as it is, is it worth dying for?"

My eyes met his. "That's a question I usually ask."

But he wasn't listening. "Feast your eyes on the rest, Ms. Waverley—" He spread his arms to encompass the room.

"My name is Phoebe." Why that mattered to me then, I'll never know.

"Phoebe? Not Phoebe! The irony that you should be named after an object of light when, in truth, you are an agent of corruption, is more than I can bear. You introduced yourself as Susan Waverley, the late Susan Waverley, I understand, and so you shall remain."

I didn't try to protest further. That he'd keep calling me after a deceased person seemed all that I deserved.

Arms still spread, he stepped back. "Precious artifacts from pirate hoards, the famed treasure my ancestor, Sir John Ashley Wyndridge, did abscond at the request of Sir William Phips, who would never return to claim his prize, lie herein. Mounted in every case, an artifact of great worth. Yes, a fortune lies encompassed here, a fortune gleaned across many centuries and civilizations, a fortune drenched in the blood of the conquered and the misfortune of multitudes—the shipwrecked, the plundered, the murdered! It has become the quest of many to wrest it from me at any expense, regardless of the wash of bloodshed and mishap that ensues. Death and beauty are my legacy. For, by the blood of my ancestors, I am Ward of the Tides."

Ward of the Tides, from one of his novels? Was fact and fiction mingled in his brain? I leaned forward. "I'm sorry for—"

"Silence!" He lifted one hand, raking his hair with the other, which only served to drag wet strands from his queue. His anxiety had begun to rise again as he began pacing the room, gaze fixed downwards. "Apologies hold no merit under the circumstances. You came to steal, madam. You sought out dear Ms. Smith and drove her to her death."

"I did not!"

"Do not deny it! You were even in the company of that brute when you entered my bedroom and pawed through my personal effects. I have you on film!"

"Film?"

He waved his hand. "Digital—whatever it is called. I know not the name. Suffice to say that I saw you with my own eyes."

"By camera?"

"Of course by camera and on film!" He ripped the ribbon from his queue, letting his hair fall across his shoulders in damp straggles while flinging the sodden silk to the floor. "You thought me a Luddite, did you not, for I convinced you of such easily enough; but in truth I have ensured that this entire estate is wired, as they say. At the urging of a dear friend of mine, I —" He stopped suddenly, pressing his hand to his lips, "I—warded my—my *home* against trespassers and thieves. Here."

He snatched papers from the sideboard and flung them at me. A series of black-and-white photos rained over me, most sliding to the floor. I picked one up, then another, all still shots of me searching Wyndridge's desk and one of me foraging through his map cabinet with Hector looking on. Guilty.

"The others tell a similar tale, "he remarked. "I have hidden cameras all over the house and, in testament to your arrogant stupidity, you believed me when I stated I did not use technology." He gave a grim little laugh.

"That should have been your first inkling that I was dissembling. Technology is a tool I could not afford to ignore, given my circumstances."

A sudden jolt of vertigo sent my head reeling. "I—"

"Silence!" he shouted. "One after the other, a stream of brutes and criminals have dogged this bounty for decades, nay centuries, with this being only the latest insufferable attempt on the treasure. Only," and he stared straight ahead, fixing at some point on the far wall and took a deep breath. "Only, it will end here, now. Tonight. It must."

I looked up as he strode towards me, index finger stabbing the air. "You thought me a fool you could play, but it is you and yours who are the fools, not I. You have befallen my trap, not I yours."

I tried to straighten in my chair. "Then call the police," I said.

"Too late for that by far! And yet, if I do not make this stop, more will die here and beyond. This is my legacy, and I must man up to the task." He shot a quick look at the clock. "The bell has chimed once. I must begin preparations but I will return. Pray, do not expend your energy trying to escape, for I will secure this room so you cannot leave. My ancestor's design is brilliant in all respects." Picking up his sword, he made for the wall.

"Wait, what are you going to do?"

With his back to me, he flicked something and bookcase-cum-door began sliding jerkily open. "Set the stage for the ultimate finale, the grand denouement, of course, whilst simultaneously writing the epilogue."

What the hell? I heaved myself from the chair to hobble towards him, but a wall of books slid shut before I even made it partway.

❧ 19 ❧

A rusty lever was clearly visible in the opening between two embossed books, yet no amount of twisting or lifting or pulling activated the mechanism. He had locked me in. Not the first time that night a man had thought to keep me caged. Fine. I'd take his advice and wouldn't waste energy trying to break out, since I didn't have much energy to squander.

I turned, hobbled over to where my bag lay dumped on the floor and hefted it up to the chair, cursing my leg as I went. I needed painkillers. Badly.

I set Toby's tube on the chair before fumbling around inside for my phone and pills. My hand encountered the gun. That damn gun! I pulled it out, glared at it, and finally shoved it under the needlepoint cushion for safekeeping. Back inside my bag, my fingers tangled in yarn as I dug around for phone and Advil bottle. I pulled out first one and then the other, staring in exasperation at my now dead cell phone. Even the red line had gone. I threw the phone on top of the bag in disgust and hopped around the room, blocking out the come-hither gleam of precious objects glinting from the cabinets.

At first, I was only looking for a power source, thinking maybe he had this room wired, too, but I could see nothing as obvious as a plug outlet. I doubted Wyndridge could bear having electronics in this sanctum, anyway. Probably surveillance cameras focused on the exterior of the room only. So, forget the phone. Besides, the walls were so thick and windowless, I doubted I could fix a signal even with a charged cell phone. No, this secret retreat of Adrian Wyndridge remained thoroughly ensconced in the seventeenth century and me along with it.

I slipped a candle holder from the table to study the contents of the display cases next, taking in what looked to be an Aztec ceremonial mask keeping company with other ancient artifacts, all incredibly rare and valuable. If Max, Toby, and Dad understood even a fraction of its worth, I could almost understand their compulsion. Almost. Max claimed he'd see it go to museums, if possible, though he hadn't ruled out private collectors' higher bids.

Who knew who really owned this cache under international law—Spain or the ancient civilizations she plundered? Wyndridge's lawyers would claim three centuries of possession holding sway for the family, but the other nations would argue ownership, too. Either way, sorting out rights in court would result in a battle that could tie up this loot for years, if not decades.

That didn't excuse my family's involvement or "Uncle Max" for leading them into it. Wrong thinking. No one leads anyone into anything. Each person makes his or her own choices, including me.

I swallowed hard, moving on to a case of jeweled earrings and gem-encrusted bracelets, all probably the same vintage as the pectoral cross. Another case held religious objects and still another, gold buckles. I leaned against the buckle case, pushing back a headache building behind my temples. God, the worth of this treasure must surpass anything except King Tutankhamen's tomb. Since most treasure is found encrusted in barnacles on some sea bottom or picked away in underground tombs, I couldn't imagine what a cache of pristine artifacts might fetch. Since no doubloons or pieces of eight were included, I surmised the family must have melted down coins to finance their dealings across the centuries.

Leaving the display cases, I hobbled towards the sideboard, one of those sixteenth century carved monstrosities where Wyndridge kept a decanter of red liquor with a silver tray and two matching goblets. Why two, I wondered? Two chairs, two goblets. Did he regularly entertain a guest in this little museum-cum-treasure nest? I tried picturing his mother sitting in one of those chairs sipping wine but couldn't do it. A tea set, maybe, but not liquor.

I poured a small amount of the deep crimson liquid into one of the goblets and downed two pills. Being no connoisseur of fine liqueurs, I couldn't identify the stuff but liked the taste enough to pour myself another.

With the goblet in one hand, I shuffled along the waist-high sideboard, investigating the papers spread across its surface. The first pile consisted of more security stills of either me or Hector each about some nefarious-looking task, including rifling drawers or prowling rooms we had no right to be in. Most had been taken with a night-vision camera, testifying to Wyndridge's sophisticated equipment, wherever he had it stashed. Several revealed me in the tower digging through the map cabinet.

I held one photo up to candlelight. By the angle of the shot, I figured the camera must have been positioned somewhere on the shelf that crashed, which explained why no evidence of me ambushing Hector lurked in the pile. Said camera must have already toppled with the shelf. Like that would prove my innocence. Wyndridge had at least seven clear shots of me folding his diagrams and stuffing them in my shirt, enough evidence to lock me away for a long time.

I let the photos slide back to the surface and studied the room again. Wyndridge must have a bank of monitoring equipment somewhere, including printers and possibly WiFi, though walls this thick required a router per room, and hiding a router wouldn't be easy. Hard-wiring made a better choice. Cameras, on the other hand, were used by the police for covert operations with many small enough to fit into a peephole. Who knew what Wyndridge had seen?

I turned back to the sideboard to focus on a large diagram anchored flat by four paperweights, one per corner. I set down the goblet and stared. It was a duplicate of the one I found in the tower, yet somehow different. The paper seemed older, for one thing, the ink legible yet faded. It almost looked as if this were an original and the tower version a copy.

I leaned over, studying the drawing in the flickering candlelight, my mouth gone dry. The tunnel, the cave, the tidal shaft, I followed the trail with my finger down from the tower all the way to an opening at the cliff face marked "Entrance to Cavern 1", which I recognized as the sea cave Noel and I had penetrated. Though the opening had been rendered much smaller here, the shape was unmistakable, as was the tunnel and pool that followed. Had we gone further, we would have been led along a convoluted tangle of corridors and tunnels, caves and pools, all conveniently marked by periodic red arrows such as the one I'd seen on the cave wall until we reached a large space labeled "Cavern 2 :Amber Lagoon". The Amber Lagoon linked, in turn, with an even larger natural cavern labeled "Cavern 3" shaped like a bowl. Lengthy entries had been penned in tiny script all over this area with the words FLOOD CHAMBER in block letters accompanied by an arrow pointing into what looked to be a hole in the cavern floor.

A small boxed drawing of what looked to be flood gate or some kind of mechanism had been inked in a careful hand on one side, an addition I knew hadn't been on the tower version. This mechanism appeared to be a bit of engineering designed to be lifted or closed to allow in more water—a floodgate. Should the gate be lifted, water would rush through the tunnel along with the tide, rendering the shaft inescapable. But even more startling were the wavy lines running counter to one another with notations indicating "Tidal pull" and "Extreme Current" and the ominous "Tidal Spout" accompanied by a tiny set of skull and crossbones spewing from the center of the hole like a geyser or an undersea volcano.

Hobbling back to the chair, I pulled Toby's sketch from the tube and hopped back to spread the drawing next to the diagram. I anchored the corners with goblets, a decanter, and my hand, and stared hard. Toby had sketched a version of the flood chamber, his whimsical diagrams belying the horror should a diver penetrate the treasure pool. Divers like Noel.

It all played out like a rolling video game: diver enters a hole in a cave floor expecting to find treasure at the bottom, only to be sucked down by a combination of tidal pull and diabolical engineering and later spit out again by a furious force. That last part boggled me. Did it imply an explosion? And then, in a touch of poetic justice, my split lip reopened, and a drop of blood splattered on the diagram. I dabbed my lip with my once-white sleeve as the clock struck two.

Noel could be heading for death that very moment.

I made my way back to the chair, fished out the gun, and lowered myself down to wait, a full goblet of liquor at my elbow. When Wyndridge entered a few minutes later, he found me sitting with my bum leg propped on a display case and a gun pointed at his chest.

HE PAID ME NO NOTICE AT FIRST, SO INTENT WAS HE IN LOWERING A leather satchel carefully to the floor before making certain the door closed properly behind him. When he lifted his head and saw me, his expression was almost comical.

"A gun?" he asked, agape.

"Yes, a gun. You know, I've been almost on your side from the moment I entered this house, under false pretenses, I admit, but still not intent on thieving or causing you harm once I got my answers."

"How dare you!"

"Shut up." I waved the gun at him.

"I have no time for this."

"Too bad. Sit down. We're going to have a back-and-forth dialogue, as in conversation. If anyone yells "silence!", it will be me, though "shut up" works just fine. Now, I'll ask the questions, you'll answer them, got that?"

He hesitated, gaze swinging to the clock and back to the gun. "I doubt you even know how to use a firearm."

"Oh, please. Modern guns are like cameras: you just point and shoot. Sit down, I said." I nodded towards the second chair.

He did as I asked, keeping one eye on the gun. "You drank my port," he said in an irritated and accusatory tone.

"Was that port? I like it. Okay, so as I was saying, I had been feeling sorry for you, guilty even, thinking poor Wyndridge, boohoo, everyone's intent on stealing your plundered fortune, including, apparently, my family. Everyone's breaking into your house, harming your staff—though that would be Hector-cum-Bert doing the harming, by the way, in case you hadn't figured that out—and I was sucked in by it right up until I realized that your family are the real murderers and the thieves here. It's all in how you look at it. First John Ashley partakes in a devious plot to plunder from the plunderers and steals the Spanish loot and designs an ingenious flood chamber in Nova Scotia."

"I beseech you to hear me out, for I—"

"Shut up and speak like you know what century you're in. Where was I? Oh, yeah: how many treasure seekers did that kill10 or 11, last count? And then self-same ancestor slips away to Bermuda and constructs an equally deadly device to further kill anyone trying to unearth said treasure here. So, more people die, either directly or indirectly, such as Edna Smith. Then you, Adriam Wyndridge," I leveled the gun at him, using both hands. "Damn, but these things are heavy. So, you planted a bogus diagram in the tower to lead seekers down into the caves to meet their end. Nasty and murderous, any way you look at it. That's when I'd had enough."

He leapt to his feet, one finger stabbing the air. "All the documents in the tower are either fraudulent or copies! Do you think me fool enough to leave something potentially dangerous or valuable available to prying idiots? I care not who found or acted upon what. And you, madam, are as conniving as the rest, insinuating yourself into my home, poisoning my mother, and rifling through my private belongings! Did you think I would just stand by? No, for I deliberately led you here once I realized the devious intent was afoot and, furthermore, anything that befalls you and your kind is all that you deserve. Any persons descending those tunnels has no right to be there, and thus , if they die, 'tis by their own greed!"

"Don't talk about greed to me. Look at this stuff! Your family have set up their own private art museum, paving the walls with precious artifacts for their own damn pleasure while others die trying to find it! For centuries!"

"It is our legacy!"

"Bullshit! Sit back down!"

Wyndridge collapsed back into the chair, burying his face in his hands, as I hoisted myself to standing and hobbled over to hold the gun inches from his head.

"Tell me what you did to my brother," I said in a small, tight voice.

He glanced up. "Noel is your brother? My god, but Max Baker has made this a family affair."

"Not Noel, Toby, Tobias McCabe, my brother. He came here and you lied about it to the police. That's why I'm really here, to find Toby. What happened to him?" My voice caught in my throat. I swallowed hard. I didn't need my bravado sinking into in a swamp of grief.

Wyndridge's face registered shock. "It cannot be." I stepped back as he rose to his feet, his eyes studying my face like a hungry man, oblivious to the gun. "Can this be true? Yes, there are similarities about the eye and chin and the hair color, certainly, but I hadn't seen it earlier. Toby mentioned a younger sister but I—"

"But you didn't expect her to track him here, is that it? What did you do to him?"

"Nothing! I would never harm Tobias, for I loved him!"

"Loved him?" I asked, almost losing my balance.

"Love him! Toby is —was— my partner."

❦ 20 ❦

I stared.

"Toby, dear Toby, my friend, my lover, my dear merman. We have been involved for months, a relationship that would have continued forever, had I my way, until this! We were true soul mates." Wyndridge sank back into the chair, staring straight ahead. "I loved him, *love* him, oh how I *love* him, and now he's gone, gone, I know not where."

"You *love* him?" I stood wavering, unsteady on my feet, trembling equally inside and out.

Wyndridge looked up with moist eyes. "You knew of his predilection, I presume? Toby claimed that his sister had always been his lifeline and biggest support."

"Of course I knew he was gay, if that's what you mean; I just didn't know about you. Why didn't I know about you? Surely he'd share something that important? You'd be like my brother-in-law or something."

"He planned to disclose all and to you first. It was his intent to reveal our relationship at your father's birthday gala, to make his declaration and to simultaneously prevent the move on the treasure. I was to join him at the cottage a day later."

I shook my head, not getting it but trying so hard to grapple with the shock. Of course Toby wasn't a crook. Of course he'd be on the side of the good guy. "My father's had trouble enough accepting Toby's homosexuality let alone meeting his partner under his own roof. He'd storm into a rage every time Toby alluded to it, as if yelling at him would somehow make him less gay. Toby said Dad would have a heart attack just from blustering at him, and you say he was going to introduce you?"

"That's what he promised me. I insisted. I was most certain that our father would react much as did mine when I disclosed the truth over a decade ago. I vowed from that point forth to hide my predilection rather than suffer ridicule by the public and my family, both. My father even vowed to disinherit me should I reveal my true nature broadly. Therefore, I assumed this garb," he indicated his costume with a flick of his hand, "by way of camouflage. Prior centuries granted men more freedom of expression by way of clothing, did they not? One could aspire to be both manly and gay, like Toby, like me. Behind this I chose to hide. I left England for Bermuda and have lived here as a recluse ever since, both writing and living in an earlier time. I assumed a life of solitude with none but my mother and a host of imaginary characters chattering around in my head, thinking this would always be the way, until Toby. Toby changed my world, my life."

I could see it all now, Toby and Adrian. My brother would be so drawn to this flamboyant and deeply passionate man, revel in his creativity, ache for his plunge into solitude, plus the measures he had taken to survive. "He was the one who urged you to wire the estate."

"Just so."

"And yet, you were planning to carry on the death and destruction tonight?"

Adrian sobbed into his hands. "I did not wish to but I have lost so much because of this already."

"Where is he?"

"He disappeared!" he cried. "He received a phone call and disappeared! I am afraid he descended the tunnels!"

I limped over to his chair, touching his shoulder both to steady myself and him. "Adrian , it seems as though we both love him, which should make us allies, don't you think? I could use an ally right now and maybe you could, too. What were you and Toby planning?"

He wrestled down his emotions and took a deep breath. "We had contrived a plan that would free us from this house. I would donate the treasure to four major museums in four countries, an act designed to coincide with the publication of my final novel in the Bermudan trilogy, *Ward of the Tides*, which tells the true story of John Ashley Wyndridge. The writs are drawn up and ready to mail, along with communications through other media destined for the appropriate authorities. But then he disappeared."

I shook my head. "You would really give up the treasure?"

"I would, truly, for how else can I be free? Toby convinced me of such and finally I saw the wisdom. His idea was brilliant: protect the treasure until it officially passed into safekeeping, the gist of which primarily involved technology, of which I had no previous comprehension. After the treasure was safe and my novel released to the world, I would sell the house and accompany him to a tropical island where we would design our own home and live a new life together. It was to be my ultimate happily ever after, a fitting denouement to this appalling legacy of grief and greed. And now it is ruined! I cannot go on without him!"

I stared down at him, gun hanging forgotten in my hand. "Then what happened ?"

"I know not what and that is the God's truth! One day he left to fly home and that is the last I heard of him. I was to wait for his call and then take the next flight to Halifax. No word since, absolutely nothing! I have been frantic and twisting with anxiety ever since. I thought perhaps he had abandoned me, but no, no, Tobias would never do so, not with all we had awaiting in our future and everything between us. I hid nothing from him. We were partners, our fates explicably entwined."

His sobbing intensified until he spoke between gasping heaves. "I love him and he is gone!"

Not knowing how to console him, I refilled his glass and set it on the table. "I love him, too. Adrian, we have to stay strong, both of us. Let's try to save the grieving until later."

He glanced from the glass to my face. "This treasure is accursed, I am accursed! Someone must have deduced our intent, though not from me, for I have disclosed this room to no one, nor has anyone in my family for centuries, the secret having gone from lip to ear only within my immediate circle and then but to a chosen few."

"Who in your immediate circle, what chosen few?"

"My mother is the only one remaining and she has long thought the treasure cursed and beseeched me to be rid of it. My brother is deceased which leaves me to struggle with whom to pass on the burden now that the male bloodline dwindles."

"Oh, right, the male bloodline dwindles but no females are worthy, is that it?"

"No, that is not it! I have no female relatives but untrustworthy second cousins—flighty socialites more interested in partying in London than assuming a burden like mine. My brother died childless; his wife divorced him before he could sire children."

"How do you know your mother didn't tell somebody?"

"If possible, she is more reclusive than I. Besides which, she knows nothing of Toby's plan, only that I have the details of the treasure's location sealed in a London safe with instructions for it to be opened only upon my death."

I slid the gun on top of the table. "Well, something went wrong, didn't it? Somewhere between Toby leaving you to fly back home, something or someone intervened, but who?"

"Could Tobias have disclosed our plan before the appointed time? Did he entrust the secret to someone he believed trustworthy? "

"He wouldn't be so foolish." I certainly hoped that were true but there was Max. Good old 'uncle' Max and his mysterious dogsbody.

"He planned to demand that Max cease his search, intended to record the discussion secretly on some device, and then threaten to release it to the media should the Baker clan not comply. He had no intention of revealing the treasure's true location. That would be foolhardy. My merman thought of every contingency. He was a brilliant strategist!"

"Gamers are master strategists," I remarked sadly, reaching for my goblet and taking a big gulp. "Only sometimes even they miss the endgame."

"Surely, as his sister, you would know whom he would tell?"

Wiping my mouth on my sleeve, I set the glass down. "Maybe he didn't tell anyone. I mean, the treasure's still here, isn't it? Aren't they looking in the wrong place, thinking the treasure's stashed in that tidal shaft in the cave? But I'm betting one of the bastards crawling through your house right now knows something—Max, Hector, or Noel. Those are the ones who can give us the answers."

"Yes," Adrian nodded. "I stake my bets on Noel as most likely, for he masterminded this whole plot."

"What?"

"Toby assured me that Noel exerts power behind Max's throne. He visited the pair of them at Baker's London office numerous times, always returning with tales of Noel's ambitions. He envisioned Baker & Associates as a major player in the ancient artifacts and antiquities market, serving primarily wealthy clients willing to place exorbitant bids on stolen goods."

"The black market?"

"Exactly, the black market. Before Noel became involved, Max was naught but a middling antiquities dealer, flipping through Christie's catalogues and attending auctions, successful enough, albeit small-time. Then matters took a more deadly turn."

"But Max treats Noel like a dog."

"Dog and master have been known to play out a complex relationship, much like father and son."

"Alpha dog in sheep's clothing, you mean?"

Adrian smiled grimly. "Indeed."

"I didn't trust that man from first."

"And yet you are attracted to him."

I shot him a sharp glance. "What do you mean by that?"

"One of the multitudinous benefits of watching this drama unfold through secret cameras is that a wealth of context emerges. I observed from my laptop and upon the many monitors Toby installed, a myriad of subtle details regarding the players in this nefarious game. One such insight I gleaned as Noel descended on a battered Hector sprawled on the bottom of the tower steps not but a couple of hours ago. He was fiercely furious that Hector threatened you but equally incensed by the fact that Hector had disobeyed his orders."

"Hector works for Max?"

"Hector works for Noel but originally he was employed by a man named Sir Rupert Fox, a London kingpin in the antiquities trade. I remain unsure as to where Baker fits in any of this."

"Only, now Hector is going solo. Damn it!" I slapped the table, dribbling port in the process. "Oh, sorry. Crud, I have been so blindsided! Noel warned me to be careful of Hector but implied he worked for someone else. Even Max said as much. What else did you see?"

"I ceased my observations after Noel forced Hector to his feet and down into the caves."

"Hector's still mobile? When I left him he was unconscious, and I'd hoped he broken a few important parts."

"I suspect a broken arm and possible leg, but he was still able to stand at Noel's prodding."

"I should have smashed my iPad over his head. So both of them are in the caves now?"

"I presume so, since I sealed the door to the house at that point and then proceeded to turn off the power to the house and thus the cameras. Their only way out now is through the sea tunnel which, in high seas is most treacherous, if not impassable. They are trapped down there. What is your relationship to Noel?" He added suddenly.

I turned away to study the clock. "Nothing. It's getting late. We should do something."

"He seemed rather too solicitous of your well-being considering the circumstances. Did he not take time from his machinations to attend to your wounds? Are you not romantically involved?"

I turned back to face him. "If you're concerned that my loyalties are divided, don't be. I accompanied Noel on a dive to the outer cave entrance. Oh, and he kissed me. Is that what you saw? I didn't ask for that, though I admit I didn't fight too hard, either. Blame hormones for drowning defenseless brain cells—an old story. Biology can be such a bitch. Anyway, we are not an item. Wait, if you saw the kiss, you must have external security cameras, too."

"Several are installed about the property, compliments of your brother, who urged me to heighten all my defenses. He installed everything himself. So masterful is Toby at all he undertakes. He taught me so much and beseeched me to be rigorous in reviewing all those saved security files, though I admit much remains to scrutinize."

"You don't buy into brevity, do you?" I hobbled back to the chair and collapsed. "So, Toby 's plan has fallen apart for some unknown reason; the enemy is crawling around under our feet looking for treasure that's not even there; and Noel is the true ringleader, though presumably Max is involved somewhere, too. What were you planning to do about all this when you dragged me in here?"

Wyndridge sighed. "I have staged a secondary trap, albeit a clumsy one next to Toby's machinations, but the best I could do on my own. I vowed to end this tonight once and for all. Everyone associated with this treasure suffers death or calamity. At one time, we successfully limited the mayhem by keeping the treasure locked away here, but that will work no more. Once those damnable researchers published *The Money Trap: the Greatest Web of Intrigue,* all was lost and 'twill be only a matter of time before the treasure's true location is disclosed. So I lured you and the others to my estate and devised an abrupt but calamitous end."

"Could we just cut the verbiage in the interests of time? What calamitous end?" I leaned forward. "What are you talking about?"

He jumped to his feet, dabbed his tears with a handkerchief pulled from his waistcoat, and began pacing circles around the room. "I should never have believed my life could be any different from what it has always been. All this," he waved at the photos still spread on the floor, "is just a feeble attempt to stop the inevitable. Nothing is worth the price my lineage pays to keep this monstrous secret. Yet, my dear merman would not allow me to remain shackled for the rest of my life. He intended to liberate me, set me free in heart and mind, so that I, too, could claim happiness. He would not betray me!" He swung back to me, pausing to fix me with his gaze, his face wrought with pain. "He would not, correct?"

"I thought I knew my brother better than anyone but I don't know anymore. I thought he was," I took a deep breath, "I thought he *is* a kind and good person as well as being a brilliant one but maybe not. How well do we know another really? What calamitous end? Are you planning for Noel to die trying to dive for the treasure, is that it?"

"Do you care?" he asked sharply.

"I care if someone else gets killed, yes, and so should you. The treasure has enough blood spilled over it. Noel took the diagram I found in the tower and is using it to locate what he believes is the treasure shaft. Is his death by drowning the calamitous end?"

"No, for I could not guarantee that end. Besides which that floodgate fell into disrepair centuries ago, though the cave, and that pool in particular, has natural perils enough. Furthermore, just to clarify, that bogus diagram you discovered was the design of a previous Wyndridge four generations ago. Everything in the tower is a red herring, so to speak." His face ragged with pain, he pointed to the satchel by the bookcase. "No, my concept is more definitive."

"Definitive how? A one-phrase answer, please."

"I planned an explosion."

I looked from him to the satchel. "You're kidding me. Blow up the caves?"

"No, the house—everything, treasure and all."

I held up my hands. "Wait, wait. You can't be serious. How would that help? You say there's a plan in place to donate the treasure to museums? Then, follow through on that. Forget explosives. We need answers and justice, not big kabooms. We need to find out what happened to Toby and the only ones who know the answers are likely crawling below our feet. Let's bring *them* down, not the house."

Adrian regarded me in silence for a moment. "You truly are Toby's sister," he said finally. "The same resolution, the same focus."

"Is that a yes?" I pulled myself up, retrieved the gun, and stuffed it back into my bag. "Okay, let's think." I took a slurp of port and slumped back into the chair for a moment's rest, bad leg stuck out before me in some male bus lounger pose. "We've got to get our proverbial ducks in a row and come up with a plan."

I t's like I couldn't stop myself.

"For that, we shall need a steady mind and hand, thus must forgo the port." Adrian whisked away my goblet. About to turn away, something caught his eye and left him staring down at the sideboard.

"I never even liked alcohol until I came to Bermuda, and here I am turning into an overnight guzzler," I remarked to his back.

But Adrian wasn't listening. "What is this?" He slid away my makeshift paperweights and lifted Toby's drawing up to eyelevel. "My God, I thought I would never see this again!"

"You know it?"

"Know it? Toby sketched this in this very room! What a night that was, so full of dreams and plans! Where did you find it?"

"Hidden in Toby's old room back home."

Alistair stepped towards me. "But why, why would he hide it? Why would he even take it with him?"

"I don't know. It looks like a sketch for a game based on a treasure hunt in the caves but I can't figure out its significance."

"It is a sketch for a game, for, in truth, he fully planned to continue creating his technological fiction even after we had launched our new life together. Yet, why hide it?"

"I don't know, " I repeated. In fact, the whole thing made me a little sick, as if a snake twisted itself in my gut, tying the world and me in knots. I knew my brother, understood him, didn't I? So why didn't anything he supposedly did make sense? I reached inside my bag and fished out my pills, taking two with the last inch of water in Noel's bottle. "Okay, back to the ducks," I said after a moment.

"Ducks? Oh, yes, ducks." He strode back to sit across from me, rolling up the drawing as he went. "How do you propose to align aforementioned ducks?"

"You switched off the power? Let's switch it back on and see what they're up to down there on your monitors. Where is the best viewing?"

"We must traverse to a secret location just off the kitchen. Can you manage that?"

"Sure."

He strode about the room, dousing the candles, leaving a single lantern burning, which he held in the crook of a finger. "Toby insisted I have the main monitoring depot here inside the house, whereas I used my laptop via satellite on the yacht. We shall proceed to the kitchen."

"Does anyone else know about it?"

"No. It was installed during one of my mother's forays to England and nobody but Toby and I were involved in its design or implementation. He insisted we even keep it from Frank, my previous driver." After refastening his scabbard, Adrian offered me his hand. "Let us proceed."

I realized he carried his satchel as well as my carpet bag. "What are you doing with that?"

"It contains both tools and my laptop."

"And explosives?"

"And dynamite."

"Why do you need dynamite if you're not going to blow up the house?"

"A precaution only."

"Adrian, there is nothing remotely practical about using dynamite as a defense unless you still plan to blow something up."

"That is no longer my intention."

"Relieved to hear it."

"Nevertheless, I think it wisest to carry it on my person. Toby once explained the underlying principles behind standard gaming strategy: bring all the tools in case it may prove useful some unforeseen way."

I nodded. "Okay, point made, but dynamite hardly seems the most practical weapon. But then, to my view, neither does the sword. Now, a gun is another story."

I took his arm and heaved myself to my feet, clinging to him while he hefted both bags over his shoulders. He was strong, lithe, dashing, creative, and tortured, the perfect romantic hero. How could Toby not have fallen for him, even hoped to rescue him? "So," I said, "Just to be clear: we're going out after a pack of thieves with a sword, a gun, and a pack of dynamite?"

"Indeed, not to mention my far more detailed knowledge of this property."

"Right." I watched him twist the lever so that the bookcase slid open. "Not run by electricity, I presume?"

"Powered by ingenuity," he said. "This is the same mechanical design John Ashley engineered three centuries ago and has required naught but a touch of oil to keep it in working order ever since."

The door slid into position behind us, leaving what appeared to be a seamless library wall as we made our way across the bedroom. In the hall, the darkness hung heavy, the sky obscured by shutters with nothing but the lamp gilding the gloom. Wind rattled the slats less ferociously now. That the storm might be abating did nothing to ease my nerves. Treacherous currents flowed through the hallways that night, eddying up against the walls. I could feel what I couldn't see. The mermaid was in way over her head again.

"We must be quick about it," Adrian said. "Who knows what mischief those brigands are about."

A man burdened by baggage, a sword strapped to his waist, and a wounded woman hanging onto his arm does not make easy progress down narrow corridors. Once my bag brushed against a vase, flinging it to the floor in shards.

"Damn," Adrian muttered, picking up his pace. "1710 Meissen."

"May it rest in pieces."

"How very amusing."

We had just reached the junction between the new extension and the old when he lurched to a halt. Damp, fresh air blew down the hall. "Someone has entered the house," he whispered. "The front door must be secured lest it blows open in the least wind. Come."

"Who would enter the front door? Why not a side door?" I asked.

"Hush!" he cautioned.

He tugged me down the stairs into the kitchen where we could still hear the door banging in the wind.

"Aren't you going to shut that?" I asked while furiously hopping beside him trying to keep up

"No."

By the time we crossed the floor, he was half-dragging me into a narrow space where coats hung from a brace of hooks. I would never have taken it for more than what it looked like: a kitchen corner near the far wall where boots, coats, and gloves were deposited.

He dropped one of the bags to better reach behind the umbrella stand, and soon the wall shimmied open wide enough to allow a person to squeeze through. He pushed me inside first and followed after.

"You have more hidey-holes than a Jacobean manor." I dropped onto a stool, gazing around an area no bigger than a closet where a monitor had been installed on every inch of wall space with a keyboard, a compact printer, and assorted remotes, cluttering a single long shelf on one side. Alistair set the lantern on the shelf before sitting down on the other stool with his long legs crammed between the narrow walls.

He sighed, rubbing his temples. "First, the central power controls." In an instant, he had flicked a couple of switches, turning on the power and closing the secret door simultaneously. He began pointing a remote control at each monitor. "There are but five controls, each manipulating five cameras."

"Toby didn't rig a universal remote?"

"That was his ultimate intention but it did not arrive from America in time. This is the captain's seat of all Toby's surveillance efforts. It disquieted me at first, but I soon appreciated the power behind the twinkling lights and of knowing what and who prowls one's domain. Watching him design and install the system was, well, thrilling."

"Technology can be such a turn-on."

I watched as the monitors lit up, one by one, counting fifteen all together. At first, I couldn't tell which camera focused on what except for the obvious scenes: the hall in the old wing, the den, the upper library room, the kitchen, the boathouse, Alistair's room, his mother's, and mine —not the bathroom, thankfully.

Almost every scene appeared illuminated by infrared, and a few showed lights burning, but nothing or no one moved in a single frame. I leaned forward, quickly scanning them again. "This can't be," I said. "There are at least two people, maybe three, in this house, yet everything seems empty. Look," I pointed to the tower's bottom landing where I had fallen hours before. The door leading to the caves yawned open.

Alistair rubbed his temples. "That is not as it should be. I secured that door."

"Can you remotely move the cameras?"

"I have never been able to manage such."

I recognized the pool where Noel and I had surfaced from the cove what seemed like eons ago. It foamed and boiled like a witch's cauldron, leaving the camera lens filmed in salt. "Which monitor features the bogus money shaft?"

He pointed to one on my left. By craning my neck, I could see a black-and-white scene of a large dark space dominated by what looked to be a tipsy tripod with a floodlight attached. The tripod appeared to have all but fallen over, leaning at a 90 degree angle braced by a pile of equipment which might be pulleys and ropes. The light still blazed, but upward towards the cave ceiling rather than down at the bubbling hole mid-center. I guessed that someone had rigged the tripod to lower a pulley system into the shaft, but something or someone had knocked it askew.

"The floodlight's not your style, I presume?"

"Indeed, not."

"So someone's in there or down there or both."

"So it seems." His calm unsettled me. It was as if all energy had expended itself and he was subsiding into his own denouement. "They may already be gone."

"Gone where?"

"Into the pool, the shaft, the sea."

"That shaft?" I pointed.

"Just so. All signs point to that pool by my ancestor's design, but there is no escape from there, nor treasure to find. One can exit only by the sea cave entrance, which, as you can see, is now impassable, or the door from the tower."

"Which is hanging open as we speak."

"It is, but it appears as though someone has attempted to dive the treasure pool this night. The sea has its own wards, does it not? The endless cycle of the tide, the force of storms that batters against the fluid edge of time?"

"What are you talking about? Adrian, don't go all weird on me. Hand me the camera remote." I held out my hand.

He passed me a device without a word, watching as I pressed various buttons, trying to bring the camera to life to no avail. The thing stayed resolutely fixed on the same location.

I turned to him in frustration. "Maybe Toby's down there," I said, pushing all the buttons once again. "We've got to go down and find out."

"No. I have traversed every inch of that cave but he is nowhere to be found. He is gone, they are gone. The curse continues."

I shoved the hair from my eyes and hitched myself to standing. "Listen, Adrian, whoever is down there knows what happened to Toby, remember? And maybe they need help. Where's your fire?"

"Despite all I've said and done, I pity the fool that tries to dive that shaft. My ancestor used it as a decoy with which to lead on the unwary. Only the outer lip is manmade; Nature has designed her own blowhole to erupt in certain weather conditions, which this time of year is often enough. Tonight, the spout has been most active. Anyone who goes down will certainly not survive."

As if on cue, the camera caught a blast of water bursting from the hole, spewing at least eight feet into the air in a horrific force, spraying water across the cave and hurling the tripod and the lamp into the boil.

For a moment the cave whirled in sea, surreally illuminated by a waterproof lamp bouncing around in the foam before even that went dark. The infrared camera kept rolling as the renegade spout retained its vertical deluge for seconds more before a powerful force sucked it back down in a gulp of foam. I watched transfixed, Toby's sketch exploding in my head. "My God."

"Precisely."

In my shock, I had unknowingly pressed two buttons simultaneously, and the camera jerked alive. One eye on the screen, I maneuvered the up and down buttons until the camera could sweep the perimeter of the cave. Besides a flotsam of beached equipment, somebody's jacket bunched in a sodden heap, a sneaker, and an oxygen tank could be seen. I pressed the button further until the camera finally landed on a set of legs jutting into view with the upper half caught in the blind side.

"Someone's hurt!" As we watched, one leg lifted before falling back limply. Those legs were long but not thin, wearing what looked like jeans and crocodile boots. "It's Max and he's hurt! Get up. We've got to help him!"

"Certainly not," he said from that faraway numb place he now inhabited. "The area is fraught with danger. That man entered knowing the risks. He has no one to blame but himself."

I tossed down the remote. "Don't say that! Don't you dare say that! He's my godfather and I am not, I repeat, *not* going to lose another family member! We're a team, remember? Get up and help me or I'm going without you!" I tugged on his arm, trying to force him to stand, which he did but only just long enough to push me back to sitting. At that moment, with the two of us braced in a will-wrestle, the power went out. Again.

"What just happened?" I whispered.

"I believe someone just cut the main power line."

🦢 22 🦢

"How to you know it wasn't just the storm?" I asked.

"Listen."

We stood clutching one another, senses keening. Not more than a foot away, on the other side of the wall came the unmistakable sound of scraping as if someone were sliding a heavy object against the door. The wall rattled briefly and then stilled. Someone had barricaded us in.

I threw myself against the wall, rattling the lever as if I could make it slide open by will alone. "Let us out! Who are you? Come back! Don't you dare leave us here! If you hurt Max, so help me I'll kill you!" I banged, knocked, and shook the wall until Adrian stilled me with a hand on my shoulder.

"He is gone."

"Who? Who locked us in? Not Max! God, I have to get to Max! He's hurt. And Noel's down there trying to dive that shaft! Open up!" I cried, resuming my assault.

Adrian grabbed me by the shoulders and twisted me around to face him. "Calm yourself!"

I breathed deeply, pushing down my panic with every exhale. "Okay," I said, holding up my hands. "Good now, thanks." I stood still, bracing myself on the shelf as Adrian lit the lantern.

"The door is not operated by electricity for Toby duplicated John Ashley's mechanism exactly. We need only break the —" He stopped abruptly, staring in horror at his feet.

"What?" I looked down at my crumpled bag.

"My satchel! I must have left it outside when we entered."

"Oh, hell, Adrian. Are you saying whoever locked us in is now running around with a bag of dynamite?"

"That appears to be the case."

I bent down and hoisted my bag up to drop it onto the chair. "Well, I've still got a gun and you a sword. Let's move to the offensive." I felt around for the gun, touching its cool surface with trembling fingers. Good, still there. "How do we get out of here?"

"We need only break the lever and push against whatever has been shoved before it. Or, so I hope." With that, he lifted one booted foot and began kicking at the brass lever.

I joined in by shoving a shoulder in time with his kick. After several minutes of battering, the latch remained intact. "How does this thing work?" I asked.

"The door is operated by a lever-and-pulley system but my guess is that the brass lock, which slid into the housing when I closed the door, is now jammed by whatever barricades said door."

I dove back into my bag and pulled out the gun, clutching the grip with both hands, aiming for the lever.

"Surely you do not think you can blast it apart?"

"Watch me." But first I had to figure out how to unlock the safety catch, which required slightly more dexterity than I expected. When finally I figured it out and pulled the trigger, the shot reverberated through my arms and knocked me backward into Adrian's arms.

Pushing me back to standing, he held the lantern over the hole in the door, revealing how badly I missed. I shattered the wood in parts but not much else.

"Guess I need practice."

"Stand back." Adrian drew his sword.

"Surely you don't plan to impale it?"

"Perhaps I can slice the wood until we can get a hand through."

"Let me try to shoot it again."

"Then aim for the indentation below the latch and this time, shoot to kill."

"Very funny." I braced my legs, tensed my arms with the gun in both hands, aimed the barrel straight for the defined spot, and fired. The blast exploded the wood, pinged against something metallic and sent a flurry of sparks into the air.

"Better," I claimed.

"Step away," Adrian ordered. Bracing himself against the shelf, he lifted both feet together and hurled his boots at the damaged latch. The door splintered as bits of metal and wood dropped to the floor. With both of us shoving at the damaged door, we managed to push the chair positioned on the outside away from the opening and send it clattering.

Once free, we scanned the empty room. "I don't suppose you have a secure phone line anywhere or even a cell? We need to call the police."

"I detest cell phones, and though Toby did insist I have one, I left it on the yacht."

"Great." My only thought was to help Max and Noel but we needed light, lots of reliable light. "To the dining room," I said. "I stuffed batteries and flashlights in the harpsichord when Joquita said that storms often cut the power.",

"You places objects inside that delicate instrument?"

"Why do you care? You wanted to blow up everything a few minutes ago."

"Point taken."

"Whatever possessed you not to take these torches with you?" Adrian whispered as we plundered my stash from the harpsichord accompanied by a ping of random chords. He set the lantern on top of a table and doused the flame.

"I forgot about them after all that happened." I handed him a flashlight and a handful of batteries, taking one for myself and tossing the rest in my bag slung over his shoulder. Thankfully, no intruder had yet appeared.

The front door no longer banged in the wind, a worrying point as we proceeded down the corridors towards the old wing. Adrian's flashlight picked up wet footprints tracking ahead of us. I still gripped the gun in one hand and, though the thing felt unbearably heavy, I couldn't let it go. He kept his sword drawn, too, holding it out in front of us ready to spear the first interloper to cross our path.

"What do you think they're going to do with the dynamite?"

"Hush." He urged me towards the outer tower door, which stood propped open with a chair. Still nobody in sight. We stepped through into the tower base where I flashed my light across the bottom steps, wincing at the sight of dried blood, either mine or Hector's, it didn't matter. My beam hit a black duffle bag positioned against the wall as if in readiness for a speedy exit. Adrian rifled through it, pulling out a coil of wet rope, a spotlight, and a watch, casting me a questioning gaze.

I shrugged back my answer.

Straightening, he looped my arm in his and led me tentatively to the threshold of the cavern stairs where we stood gazing down the curving rough-hewn steps to where a light shone somewhere far below.

"It is most steep and a log way down," Adrian stated the obvious.

"And I can't bend my knee." The logistics of a lame woman climbing down those slabs of stone hit me hard. Could I do this? Did I have the strength or even the courage?

The same thing must have occurred to Adrian. "I shall proceed first," he whispered, releasing my arm and dropping my bag. "If the way is safe, I shall return."

"No, wait! I'll go with you!" But he dashed down the stairs and out of sight without another word. The damn man was going to play hero armed with nothing but a sword! How could I follow him? The stairs may as well have been a straight drop to hell for all my stiff leg could manage.

Struck numb by indecision, I stood wavering. I couldn't do this and yet, I had to. Maybe I didn't have to topple head-first down those steps to make progress, after all. Maybe I could butt-shuffle.

Butt-shuffling is best done when you're a toddler, I decided, because mine felt inadequate for the job. Still, not for the first time that night did I thank Maggie's leather pants as I hoisted my way downward over rough stone, arms levering me down. I focused on speed and stealth, relieved to discover my passage surprisingly quiet. No scraping or thumping. Reluctantly, I left my carpet bag on the landing, confident that no one else would find the contents valuable. The gun stayed with me, caught in my back waistband, the safety catch secured.

When I approached the bottom landing where the light beamed, I stilled, listening. Detecting no movement, I proceeded cautiously, rounding the corner and making my way down the remaining two steps until I reached the stone floor.

Two duffle bags sat heaped one on top of the other against the wall above a modern lantern hanging on an iron hook. A set of double oxygen tanks and a pair of flippers had been tossed mid-floor, still wet. I scanned around looking for a safe place to hide but with only the tunnel ahead and the stairs at my back, the only way was forward.

Hitching myself up, braced against one wall, I hopped to the tunnel entrance and balked. The shaft dropped like a stone ramp into the darkness. The occasional lantern only revealed the steepness of the pitch. I visualized Toby's diagram, knowing this would be a long slant deep into the earth, followed by caves and pools, and who knew what else, maybe monsters of the human kind—Hector, for sure, and now some unknown person. Maybe they were armed, certainly they were dangerous.

Prior to this, I never pushed too far outside of my comfort zone but here I was shoving myself over a cliff. If I thought too hard or long, I'd never do it.

I stretched my arm on either side until my fingers touched the tunnel walls, a flashlight gripped in one hand, hopped into position and readied myself. I thought of Toby, my dad, Max, and now Adrian—where was Adrian?— took comfort in the gun, and pitched forward.

My hopping leg fought furiously to keep me upright as I hurled on a downward trajectory, more than once landing my full weight on the wounded side, and yelping. Sweat broke out on my forehead, I panted with effort and whammed into a turn before lunging around and pitching downward again. The flashlight fell with a clang, leaving me in the dark for part of the way only to dash into the light from a hanging lantern around the next corner.

And just when I thought it would never end, the bottom arrived abruptly, dumping me up to my thighs into an icy pool. A wild arm dance followed until I regained my balance, catching images of a large well-lit stalagmite-forested cavern. I grabbed a stalagmite and hoisted myself up to the cave floor, wincing as salt water seeped through my bandages.

Ahead, a black figure bent over a bag, unaware of my presence—not Adrian, not Noel or Max but some shapely female encased in a black leather catsuit. I tottered forward , dumbstruck. "Maggie?" I slipped one hand behind me and tugged my shirt down over the pistol. "Where's Noel? We've got to get to Max. He's hurt! Did Noel try diving the shaft?"

She swung around. "Oh, shit. How'd you get here?"

"What's going on?"

"What's it look like? I'm helping the guys." She straightened and stepped towards me, looking uncharacteristically competent and menacing in her leather suit with the thigh-high boots. All she needed was a whip. "You look like hell. I told Max not to bring you into this but once again, he didn't listen. Look at you, the poor little mermaid with half your tail scraped off. And you ruined that blouse."

"You're not answering my questions."

"Because you ask too damn many of them. No, Noel didn't dive the hole, and, yes, Max is a bit shook up but fine."

"He didn't look fine. I was afraid they tried to dive the shaft, but the whole thing is just another decoy. That's what I want to tell them. There is no treasure." My gaze shifted from Maggie to the equipment piled behind her. Was that Adrian's satchel?

"Yeah. Thanks for the dynamite," she said, catching my gaze. "Noel's found a use for it."

"Like what?"

"It will work into our plan nicely." She studied me for a few seconds. "It's not too late, you know. You can still join us and get rich beyond your wildest dreams."

"Gee, thanks but I'll pass. Besides, there's no treasure, I said."

"Oh, give it up."

"What?"

"I said, stop pretending there's no treasure. You never could lie."

"You locked us in the control room, didn't you?" I took one hop back, latching on to the nearest stalagmite.

"Yeah, I did, and that's where you should have stayed . It's safer. Do you still have the gun I gave you?"

"Lost it. Sorry."

"How could you lose a gun?"

"Because I didn't want it in the first place."

"Incompetent little snot. You never could go the distance, though I'm shocked you got this far. I suppose you blabbed everything to Wyndridge?"

"I told him everything."

"Which explains why he's running around acting like Errol Flynn. And here I thought I could make something out of you."

"Guess I'm just cut from another cloth."

"Some ratty old rug, you mean. Why couldn't you do what you were told instead of trying to mess things up? And getting all cozy with Wyndridge is a waste of time. He's gay."

"And I couldn't possibly relate to a man unless sex was in the picture, of course. Where is he?"

"Have no idea. Scrambled into the tunnels after Hector, but Noel decided he had better things to do than chase after the two of them. With luck, they'll both stay lost forever or do each other in. Now, Noel, there's a real man. He's got guts and vision. You should have nabbed him while you had the chance. He likes you."

"And I actually thought I might save him from walking into a trap."

"He's been one step ahead of you all along, hon. Sucks, doesn't it?"

"But the treasure is gone." I tried for a more compelling tone. "The Wyndridge family disposed of it all. I keep telling you that but you're not listening."

"You're talking a pile of shit so just shut up."

Why did she seem so damned unconcerned? I tried again. "If you all leave the house tonight, Adrian just might not press charges. It's worth a try. I mean, why end up in jail trying to steal something that doesn't even exist?"

She laughed and paused to adjust her chignon, tucking an escaped lock back under her chic beret. "Oh, Phoebe, I don't know whether you think I'm stupid or you're just denser than I thought. We've already got the treasure and we *are* leaving tonight, as in 38 minutes. We have a rendezvous with a boat in the cove, followed by an express pickup by helicopter at sea so, like, I don't have time to stand around chatting, you know? "

I shook my head. "What? Max planned all that?"

"Max didn't plan shit. He doesn't have the guts."

"Mags, what's happening? Is Max still lying in Cavern 3 or not?"

"It's all under control. Don't you worry." She stood smiling only inches away from me now, and I knew absolutely that I should worry with every inch of my being. "You know, hon, you should have been nicer to me when you had the chance. I never wanted anything to happen to you."

"Is something going to happen to me now?" Surely she wouldn't hurt me, and yet, what did I know about the people in my life?

"It's just getting messy, that's all. After tonight, we'll probably never see you again. That's sad."

"Then let me say goodbye to Max. He looked hurt when I saw him in the monitor a while ago. I want to make sure he's all right."

She glanced over her shoulder towards a large opening on the far side of the cave. "It's rough going here. You won't make it by yourself. I'll help you but you've got to hurry, okay?"

"Okay." I reached up and knocked off a long, skinny stalagmite .

Maggie lifted her perfectly groomed eyebrows at me.

"Serves as a cane," I explained.

"Right, so take my arm and let's go." She positioned me on her left, the side opposite her holstered pistol.

"I see you carry a spare," I pointed to the gun.

"Always come prepared."

I hopped beside her across a slippery surface where shallow pools reflected the stationed spotlights, using my new cane as leverage when needed and her arm the rest of the time.

"Does Hector work for Max?"

"He worked for another guy but then Noel, convinced him to work for us. Now Heck, that big a no-good piece of shit, tried going solo. And, yeah, he killed your library friend 'cause he gets off on killing people. Max would never put him on the payroll, but Noel had to. We were running out of hired hands in the end." Maggie spoke with so much nonchalance, she could have been referring to inconvenient weather.

"We?" I hesitated by a narrow ledge of stone edging the lagoon.

"Me and Noel. Hurry, will you?" She tugged me forward , forcing me to hop-jump more quickly. Realization jarred my skull with every hop: Hector worked for Noel; Noel didn't work for Max; Max was out of the picture. What were they going to do with him—us? Hell. Damn.

"Maggie," I said, suddenly holding her back. "You shafted Max?"

"Yeah, okay? He thinks too small and never lets me in on the game. There, satisfied? Here we are, on the brink of one of the biggest finds this decade has ever seen, bigger than even the Cheapside Hoard, and Maxie gets all hesitant, like, "Oh, we can't do this or that'", she mimicked his accent. "Like hell we can't. I'll adorn myself like Schliemann's wife. Remember those photos of her wearing the golden headdress?"

"The golden diadem presumably held in Russia?" I nearly slipped into a pool until she yanked me back. "Yes, sure, I remember it: solid gold, a priceless ancient artifact."

"Right on. I always wanted to be Sophia Schliemann at that moment. I'd even have designed a silk robe to get the look. I so get that photo."

"Wow," I said, forcing enthusiasm. "How will you pose for your cache?"

"I was thinking one of those velvet boleros that Penelope Cruz wore in a Vogue shoot a couple of years ago—black lace, sexy lace-up boots, the Spanish thing, you know? I'd get Noel to dress as a dashing bullfighter. Can't you just picture it?"

"Sure, only there'd be more bull than bullfighter under the circumstances, wouldn't it?"

She gave me a little shove. "Very funny."

"What about Toby," I said suddenly, desperately.

"No can tell. He's insisted on telling that story himself."

He is insisted, He's still alive but involved in this?

We had arrived at the entrance of the next cavern. I stood staring into a large still body of water the size of an Olympic pool rimmed by a forest of stalactites and stalagmites rising like stone branches, top and bottom. Two high-powered lamps had been fastened onto a couple of stalactites rising from the depths, casting the cavern into an eerie amber glow.

"Tell me about Toby!"

"Shut up. This is the Amber Lagoon. Watch yourself here," Maggie said. "We had a boat to ferry us when we were carrying stuff across, but Noel's using that elsewhere now."

"What stuff? Thought you said you didn't go diving?"

"I didn't say that. We didn't dive for the treasure, but Noel still needed his props."

"Props? What aren't I getting?"

"Stop the third degree, already. Keep moving and watch your step. We broke a path through here."

We began to weave single file through the stone forest, me clutching anything I could hold onto to keep from slipping into that dark expanse.

"Is Toby all right?"

"He's fine. Big brother has just set his course for a better life. The less you know the better. Now, move!"

Finally, we almost reached Cavern 3. Maggie shoved me up to the natural threshold and held me fast. "Watch it. There's a piss-hole of a chasm at your feet that I nearly fell into earlier. Noel's fixed a board on the left to make it easier to cross. See?"

She aimed her flashlight straight down the crevice, revealing a deep, stony gouge with water at the bottom. I nodded, remembering Toby's drawing. We shuffled across the planks , one after the other, me holding the wall for support, focused towards the pale light ahead. When we reached the threshold to the next cave, I stood trying to take it all in, the infamous Cavern 3.

Just as the diagrams indicated, it was larger than all the rest, and sunken like a wide, deep bowl with three tunnels veering off in different directions. A sea hole bubbled in the center illuminated by a single spot-light propped on the floor by the broken tripod. A mess of objects and equipment lay beached around the perimeter, including Max, splayed face-up against one wall.

I gasped, so focused on him that I didn't feel Maggie release my arm or anticipate her shoving me forward into the bowl. I trip-stumbled down-ward at full hurl until I caught myself on the tripod and stood steadying myself , anchored by my cane. Maggie now pointed the gun at me.

❧ 23 ❧

"**B**ut why?" I asked, turning to the woman I thought I knew.

"Because I'm not spending my life as somebody's assistant or somebody's not quite anything important. Did you see how he treats me? Like he treats Noel, like always the servant and never the partner. I'm so done with it."

I pulled the gun out of my waistband and tried to hold it steady.

"You don't seriously intend to shoot that, do you?" Maggie said, pausing three yards away from me.

"If I have to." I glanced at Max, still and deathly pale against the far wall. "What happened?"

She checked her watch and then me, as if not quite sure which concerned her more. "I don't have time for this."

"What happened?" I shouted.

"Max wasn't supposed to follow Noel in here. He was supposed to wait on the boat while Noel dived the hole, though there wasn't going to be any diving. This is all for Max's benefit, like a set, see? Max was supposed to wait on the boat while we took off with our ride. Noel sent him pics of the shaft and said he found something but to meet him in the cove, only the stupid ass followed him in, worried about *you!*"

I glanced quickly at Max, who was trying to lift himself on his elbows.

A livid gash dribbled blood from his forehead and his face was bleached pale. Drenched to the bone and quaking, he could barely hold himself up. "Get—away, Phoeb'!" He fell back down with a moan.

"Max!" I wanted to go to him but couldn't take my gun off Maggie. "Why not leave him? Why cheat him, why hurt him?"

"Oh, please. I didn't hurt him, Hector did. And why would I leave empty-handed? I'm grabbing a piece of the action. You could have gone in with us and shared the stash, but you can't even figure out what you want to be when you grow up. I'm just so done. Put down the gun. You know you don't have the guts to shoot it. Besides, that spout's going to blow any minute and you'd better be away from here when it does."

"No," I said gripping the gun with both hands while bracing myself against the tripod for balance. "You're going to tell me about Toby or we'll both get thrown in the wash!"

"Setup," Max mumbled. "Go."

"Do as he says, Phoebe," Mags said. "You don't want poor Uncle Max to be defenseless when the spout blows again."

The gun was shaking so badly, I thought I'd drop it. "The dish runs away with the spoon? This is preposterous! You're the dish and Noel is the spoon. That's disgusting!"

"It's not like that. Noel and I aren't lovers, we're partners. I'm done with lovers. Now, get away from that hole before you get hurt."

And then Adrian sprang into the cavern, his sword held high. He spun around and caught sight of us. "Phoebe!"

"Hold steady, Errol," Maggie warned him. "I won't hesitate to shoot you."

Adrian scanned the scene, shifting from one of us to the other. "Phoebe, move to the safety of the wall."

"Max is hurt," I told him, fixed on Maggie. "I'm not letting her leave."

"Like you're going to stop me. I've got a gun, too, only I know how to use it."

"Hector is raging around in the tunnels armed," Adrian said, inching closer to me. "I gave him chase to lead him astray but he may yet find his way back. Where is Noel?"

"Good question. Maggie?" I tried lifting the gun higher.

"Look, I'd love to chat but the bridge is going to blow any minute and

I'd like to be on the other side before it does. I'm not the diving kind. So you two stay here and take care of Maxie while I make a run for it."

"What kind of man leaves his father to die?" Adrian demanded, sweeping in behind me to lay a steadying hand on my back.

"Father?" I said, turning to him. Another sucker punch. "What do you mean *father*?"

"I believed you knew. Noel is Max's son."

"I didn't know. Again. Is that true, Maggie?" But when I turned back, she had ducked back towards the lagoon and disappeared.

"Come," Adrian said. "Let her go. We must leave here before the spout blows again. I know a secret route."

"I can't leave him," I said, running to Max. "I'm so mad right now I want to shake him until his teeth drop out, but I won't just leave him to die. After Dad, he's all I have left." A shock to realize the truth. Where did these emotions come from?

"We will move him to a safer location," he insisted.

I caught his eye. "But, Adrian, what was so damn important about Noel being his son that Max couldn't tell me?"

"Because I told him not to," came a voice at our backs.

Noel had entered from the lagoon wearing a wetsuit and carrying two duffle bags, which he dropped at his feet.

"Bastard!" I spat at him. "Lies, everything about you is a lie!"

"Not everything. Hear me out, Phoebe." He took one step into the bowl.

"Nothing you say can ever justify what you are doing to me, to Adrian, and your own father! Your *father!*"

"Biology alone does not a parent make. I have my reasons for doing what I do."

"I didn't know she was pregnant," Max came a weak voice from the floor.

"Would it have made a difference? You knocked her up and then went on your merry way, Pops. She was foolish enough to believe a handsome white bludger like you might actually return and pluck the Abo girl and her half-breed kid away to a better life. It never happened in her lifetime, did it?"

"Stop," Max moaned.

"There's no stopping me now. Now, I'm taking something for myself."

Max lurched to his elbows and rasped, "I love you! I gave you everything," before slumping back.

"Save it, Max. Mags and I are starting our own enterprise, sourcing the rare and precious all over the world, financed by the biggest find this century has ever seen. Thanks for that, Wyndridge. And, yeah, *father*, I learned the business from you. For that you have my thanks."

"What are you referring to? What find? There is nothing here!" Wyndridge said, waving his sword at the surrounding cave.

Noel flashed his smile. "Right you are, mate. Nothing here. Nice trick, by the way, but we've had the inside track all along, thanks to Toby. Must bid our adieus now." He checked his watch. "Our ride will be here soon." His eyes found mine. "Phoebe, come. You'll learn everything you need to about Toby if you come, I promise."

"You're crazy if you think I'd go anywhere with you. And what about Toby? You knew about Toby all along?"

His face, sharp-angled at the best of times, now seemed sliced in pain and exhaustion. "Come and let him tell you himself."

"Tell me now!"

"It has to be this way. I have no choice."

"Do you actually think I would go anywhere with you after this? You're despicable!"

"Sadly, I'm afraid your opinion of me is about to get worse, but I can't linger any longer to explain."

"You will go nowhere!" Adrian called out, falling into the classic en garde position, dancing his way towards Noel with his sword extended.

Noel glanced at him with disbelief and pulled a pistol from his belt. "Back off, mate. I don't want to hurt you."

And then Hector stumbled into the cavern from one of the other tunnels, a raging bull, head down, bloody and holding a gun aimed at Noel. "You're not going anywhere, kid." He stood wavering, one arm hanging limp at his side. "You bloody cheated me, damn you, and you," he swerved the gun in my direction, "bloody tried to kill me! You're all dead!"

"Shoot me, I shoot you," Noel warned. "Again, only this time I'll finish it, believe it."

Adrian slipped to the perimeter to approach Noel from behind while I swung my gun towards Hector. Noel's gun went off the same time as mine, only my bullet went pinging against the cave, or maybe it didn't since, at that moment, the blowhole erupted like a pressure cooker gone mad, knocking everyone off their feet, flinging the spotlight into the boil and the cave into a dark, frothing maelstrom.

I grappled for a handhold, thinking only of Max helpless against the far wall. My hands slid away from everything, and everything slid away from me. The swirling mass of darkness and water disoriented me until I couldn't tell up from down. Grunts and cries perforated the roaring water. Somebody called for help, maybe me.

I heard cries and shouts and somebody calling my name. I felt the water sucking me backward headfirst toward the hole. Scrabbling for a handhold, blind and dizzy in the darkness, acting in some kind of mindless survival mode, I somehow turned myself around. My flailing hand found another's but the fingers weren't friendly. They grabbed mine viciously, intent to haul me with him into the hole, the combined weight a sure thing. Hector.

And damn it if the bastard didn't have enough strength left in him to pull us both away, him dragging me up towards the lip of the bowl, his good arm hooked around my neck. I fought to get my bearings. A prick of light. The lagoon ahead. I couldn't breathe, and then he jerked backwards as somebody kicked him hard. The arm dropped away from my neck.

"Oh, no you don't. You're done, mate."

I sat slumped in the threshold between the two caves, dazed, as Noel shoved Hector into the chasm. I heard the man cry out then go silent. I thought to myself, I should push Noel in, too. So easy, as he stood there staring down into the crevice, maybe two seconds too long. But I couldn't do it, didn't want to do it. Only when he crouched before me seconds later, did I notice black oozing from his shoulder.

"You're shot," I said weakly.

"Thanks for that. Practice your aim, will you? Now I have to try diving out of here with this bad wing." He touched my face. "You'll be all right, no worries there. Father's safe with Wyndridge. Dear old Dad called the cops just before Mags tossed his phone into the lagoon so help is on its way. Sorry I can't hang by until they arrive. Can't miss my ride. Toby's waiting for us on the other side. He wants you to know that he loves you and that he's sorry but he's chosen this adventure and now he's committed to it. He hoped you'd join us. Surprised he didn't know you better."

My teeth chattered like machine-gun fire. "Don't do this, Noel. Don't let him do this."

"It's already done."

Yet he still held me while I gagged up water, stroking my face with unbearable gentleness. "What about your precious treasure?" I asked, once I caught my breath.

"Safe. It's been safely hidden down here for months. Tonight we removed it. Everything in that secret room is a fake—a good fake but a fake, none the less. I see you're wearing a memento." He pulled the pectoral cross from my shredded blouse and held it for a moment before letting it drop. I'd forgotten about it. "You'll understand soon enough." He got to his feet. "Goodbye, Phoebe. I wish circumstances had been different, I really do."

I gazed up at him, this black figure faintly backlit yet consumed by shadows. I barely had energy left to move. "I'll find you," my voice rasped. "I'll find Toby, too, and you'll both pay for this."

He managed a smile. "Good. We'll be waiting." He turned to leave.

"Tell me more!"

"I can't," he said with regret.

"Why?"

"Because it's not my story to tell." And with that, he left.

Leaning against the cave wall, weak and dizzy, I pulled at the necklace around my neck. It felt like lead, though I'd been dragging around for hours. What did he mean, I'd understand soon enough? Frustrated, I tugged at the relic, only the cross split into two, scattering pearls across the cavern floor.

EPILOGUE

I sat trying to cast on stitches in the chair beside the hospital bed as the Bermudan sun streamed through the windows. Despite the controlled environment, I managed to crack the window open an inch to let in a whiff of salt air. The nurse would probably close it on his next rounds.

With my leg propped on the bed frame, satisfied that today the bandage would finally come off, I tried recasting stitches for my Rogue Wave wrap. Surely I could do that much? Every physical inch of me seemed determined to heal while inside I remained a battered mess. It shocked me that I couldn't see signs of my festering heart when I looked in the mirror.

Adrian had been in several times during the past weeks and we had sat holding hands blubbering together in our mutual heartbreak. My brother had cheated him of his family treasure, broken his heart, and, in my case, shattered everything I believed I knew about my family, Toby, and maybe humanity itself. We were both among the walking wounded. In my case, the limping wounded.

"We must find it in our hearts to forgive him somehow," he told me on one visit as he sat stiff in a linen jacket that he wore like someone else's clothes. Some men wear the garb of another century far better than the current fashion.

"How can you say that after he cheated and used you?" I asked.

He buried his head in his hands. "Because I believe he loves me as I love him, despite it all and, more importantly, I see now that, in truth, he is a sick man. Do we forsake the mentally ill?"

I leaned forward. "Sick how?"

"I have seen him partake of recreational drugs on more than one occasion and his need of such appeared to be intensifying when last I saw him. I fear that oftimes he is not in his right mind even then."

I leaned back and closed my eyes. "I think you're making excuses for him. I can't justify anything he did, no matter what his state of mind. Look what he's done to my father, to me and you? Some things are unforgivable. The whole thing sickens me. *He* sickens me."

"But he is your brother and you love him still and, God help me but I still love him, too, no matter what. Whatever crimes he has committed against me, he is still my soul mate."

Sometimes there is just nothing left to say. "Adrian, I'm so sorry. What will you do now?"

He raised his head and gazed at me. "I will tend my mother here for as long as necessary and then sell the house and leave this place forever more."

After that last visit, we kept in touch through occasional phone calls while I continued to outwardly heal. After two weeks of convalescence punctuated by police statements and multiple visits from the authorities plus long-distance conversations with Nancy, my father, and even Julie, I'd finally managed to find time to get my stitches back on the needles. That day marked the first time I really felt like moving forward.

"Don't understand how you can knit at a time like this," Max murmured from the bed. He lay propped up on pillows, gazing at the ceiling, still in traction for his fractured spine. He'd been wallowing in his own misery since they brought him in.

"This is the best time to knit," I said, concentrating on my work. The yarn had suffered on its travels, slubbed in parts and knotted in others. I'd cut off the badly tangled entrails to wind back into balls, each color now secured in baggies. "Along with every other kind of time, except maybe while bathing. I haven't figured that one out yet."

"I'm bloody pathetic, aren't I? A man who gets shafted by his own son and the woman he's lived with for 20 years. I never saw it coming; I never knew they were cooking this against me. How could I be so blind?"

"There's a few of us holding memberships in that particular club. You should speak to Adrian."

"I'm a damn bloody fool." He began making snuffling sounds, a man unused to crying ."I'm chicken shit. I didn't treat them well enough, never made myself dad enough for my son. He thought I was ashamed of him but I wasn't. I was ashamed of myself. His mom was a beaut, a real artist. I met her when I went bush in the Top End buying Aboriginal art for my shop and, yeah, it was a fling, but I didn't know she got pregnant until Noel showed up at my door."

Thinking of Noel now delivered a punch of emotions I had yet to sort through. Why did the one man I thought I could fall for have to be a crook? I had never thought of myself as susceptible to bad-boy types.

"But Maggie, she was my girl," Max continued, sobbing now. "I always loved her. Gave her my credit cards, let her handle the stuff that interested her, but I should have married her. I'm a damn bludger."

"A dropkick, I think you called yourself yesterday. That fits. And, for the record, you were a rotten father, and an inadequate boyfriend. Oh, and a crummy godfather, who couldn't tell his goddaughter the truth about anything and led his godson into a life of corruption. Did I miss anything? Anyways, there it is. Now what?" I knit my first row back along the rescued stitches, reveling in the deep satisfaction of recreating those tiny knots. "Welcome to the human race. We're famous for our imperfections. The fact that you weren't the perfect father or the best man doesn't mean you deserved what they did to you. They're chicken shit, not you. You don't deserve it; I don't deserve it; and neither does Adrian."

"Do you forgive me, honey? I'll make it up to you, I promise."

"You're forgiven, and I'll settle for honesty over gifts any day." I plucked out a ball of turquoise silk from my carpet bag and held it up to the light. That much was truly perfect. I'd invite Bermuda blue to play along my next row.

"Can't believe Wyndridge won't have us prosecuted after all this. I expected him to, thought he should. Maybe not you, but certainly me."

The turquoise stitches settled in beside the dark blue, alleviating the somber mood with luminescent currents. "But he won't. He's a rare kind of guy, one who doesn't see good and evil quite the way we do. Still, he knows that hiding that treasure was illegal and he went along with it for decades, centuries even, considering his ancestors started the concealment. How much can he say about what was really in that room without incriminating his family?"

"I didn't think of that. Does that mean that Toby, Mags, and Noel will get away with it?"

"Crud, I hope not but they haven't caught them yet, have they? Meanwhile, you're as much a victim as he is. Adrian's a good man. Toby doesn't realize it yet but he sacrificed the greatest treasure if all" My gaze fixed on my needles. "He is too good for what that bastard did to him. And me. And Dad. And you."

"Are we talking about Toby or Noel?"

"Toby, the mastermind." Damn. I worked the last 4 stitches so tightly, I could hardly move them off the needle. Taking a deep breath, I lowered the project back into my lap and turned to Max.

"Do really believe that, Phoebe?"

"How else do you explain that the jewels in Adrian's secret room turned out to be replicas? Who but Toby knew about or had access to that room, let alone the skills necessary to strategically pull off a stunt like that? My brother, the master strategist and artist did a brilliant job of orchestrating this one."

"I can't believe it," Max muttered. "Noel, yes—that boy's got a chip on his shoulder the size of Uluru—but Toby?"

"Toby's the rogue wave. He came up behind us all and knocked us all to our knees. Love, apparently, doesn't matter. Only winning does."

"Toby loves you and your dad."

"Maybe, just not enough. He stabbed the man who loved him by using that love to snake into his sanctum. That's unforgiveable. And everything Noel said or hinted at implied Toby's involvement. 'Not my story to tell', he said. My own brother abandoned our father, used his lover, you, and me

—everyone who loved him—to mechanize the heist of the century. What kind of person does that?"

In my agitation, my knitting slipped to the floor, forcing me to bend over, grunting, to fetch it. Once back in my lap, I stroked it apologetically. "What kind of person would do that?" I repeated, forcing back tears. I would never forgive him; I'd hold rage in my heart until the seas dried up.

"The same kind who robs his father and conspires with his father's girl-friend." Max began snuffling again. "Two peas in a pod. Three peas," he corrected.

"Right. So what are we going to do about it, Max?" I thought of Noel, wondering if he'd made it through the sea caves with a bullet wound and trying not to care one way or the other.

"Do about it? What can we do about it? They're gone. The police haven't tracked them down, so how can we? Noel knows a ton of tricks on how to fence precious goods on the world market, and you can bloody believe he'll use every one of them. And if it's true that Toby's in on this, which I'm not buying yet, we're buggered. That boy's too bloody brilliant for his own good. They got away with it. End of story."

A mirthless laugh caught in my throat. "Like hell it's 'end of story', Max. The story's just beginning. Do you think I'm going to let them get away with this?" I hoisted myself to standing, letting my knitting fall to the floor once again. "We're going after them, Max—you and me."

He looked up at me, startled, gaze fixed on me as if seeing me fully for the first time: "You've changed, sweetheart."

"Damn right I have and my heart's no longer sweet, if you haven't noticed. Did you hear what I said? We're going after them."

"How?"

"We'll work together, use your shop in London as the base."

"But I was going to close the business, Phoebe, honey; I haven't the heart for it now."

"I'll give you emotional CPR, but you're not closing Baker & Associates. We need your contacts and that operation to track down Adri-an's treasure and our family of criminals. We owe it to our DNA. Besides, I think I'd love the work you do, providing I do it my way, as in legally."

"But what about your dad?"

I hobbled back to the chair and sat down. "I was going to say, but first I have to take care of Dad. I'll go home for as long as it takes. Nancy's with him now for a few days. She says he's confused and keeps crying. When I talk to him, he just tells me over and over again to come home. He blames himself, but the blessing is, he'll soon forget the details, or I think so. I'm just hoping he doesn't keep harboring the pain without knowledge of why he's feeling it. Anyway, I'll comfort him. He's my dad."

"Whatever you want, Phoebe. You're my only family now."

I stared unfocused on the floor, caught in the currents of love and loss, awash in grief and some powerful force I couldn't quite define. Eventually, the coil of blue yarn at my feet begged for attention. I leaned over, plucked up my needles, and began steadying my tension until the stitches realigned once more.

When all your stitches align, life can move forward again but who knows what shape it will take in the end?

The End

AFTERWORD

Oak Island really exists. It's a tiny island off the coast of Nova Scotia which continues to be a magnet for treasure-hunters to this very day, most recently by the Lagina brothers. The History Channel has been following their discoveries for years now but for me, Oak Island exists as part of my heritage as a Nova Scotian. I grew up with the tales of pirates and buried treasure and this story caught my imagination almost to the day it caught theirs.

However, though I've threaded real historical documentation through *Rogue Wave* it is entirely a work of fiction. Strangely, the one thing readers cite to me as being the most unbelievable is the water spout in the sea cave. Actually such phenomena are documented and not that unusual in rocky ocean coastlines. I make no apologies for giving the sea a leading role in *Rogue Wave*!

Jane

WARP IN THE WEAVE

WARP IN THE WEAVE

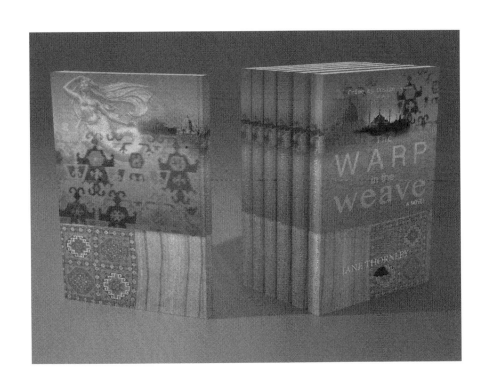

.

VOLUME TWO

WARP IN THE WEAVE

Crime by Design Book Two

❦ I ❦

Max and I huddled together under the awning as a sudden October downpour sluiced the Knightsbridge streets. Upstart rivulets streamed the curbs, causing pedestrians to pop their umbrellas and dive for cover.

Despite the deluge, getting wet didn't worry me as much as getting burned. We were there to pick up a trail gone cold, determined to track down a trio of friends and family who had shafted us so badly, it had left our belief in humanity shaken. This was our only lead.

I stared at the gallery across the road, a little broad-windowed shop with gilt lettering scripting *Carpe Diem Fine Antiques* above a sentry of ornamental greenery.

"Very posh."

"Don't let that fool you. Foxy thinks because his late wife was related to an earl or something, he's king of the hill. He's as crooked as the rest of them, just does it in better tailoring."

I stepped back against the wall as a bus whooshed around the corner in a blur of double-decker red. "Maybe I should go in alone."

"It's me he'll want to see."

"Is that why it's taken him four months to answer your call?"

"None of my old friends talk to me these days, Phoebe. I'm a has-been in this business. I just rang and rang until he agreed to see me. Probably wants me off his back."

"All the more reason why I should go in by myself."

"You don't know these criminal types."

"Nonsense, it's in my DNA, remember? Let me do this alone."

My godfather and I still had to acclimatize to our new working arrangement which was getting off to a rocky start. "Okay, so we'll go in together. Just promise me you won't lose your temper. I know you've been drinking already today."

"Just a nip." He sighed. "Do you have the goods?"

I fingered the pouch in my pocket. "Sure."

"That'll make old Foxy twitch. Well, my dear, it's 4:30 and the appointment time. Take my arm and let's go."

I linked my arm through his as we splashed across the zebra crossing that carved safe passage between three converging streets. A black cab hooted at us seconds before we reached the opposite sidewalk.

"Look left," Max said.

"I've been crossing streets for over three decades. I know how to do it."

"I just don't want anything happening to you."

"A little late for that, isn't it?"

He wiped his mouth with his sleeve and looked away.

"You look so dapper today, almost like your old self," I said as a peace offering.

"You look a right corker, too."

My godfather had applied the sartorial splendor at my insistence. Rather than slumping around in his usual dressed-to-depress blue jeans and tattered sweaters, today he sported gray flannel trousers, a heather-hued cashmere turtleneck, and his black leather jacket, the sum of which added to more money than most citizens earned in a month.

Only the crocodile boots suggested that the tall man with the silver mane was not minted in some rich British enclave but the product of a far wilder frontier. I, on the other hand, had styled my curly red hair into some semblance of sleek in an effort to pass as an urban sophisticate, which clearly wasn't working. Perhaps I'd become too comfortable with fraud in general.

"Expect to be escorted into one of his little client salons and plied with tea and cakes. I'd prefer a good shot of Scotch myself but don't worry, I won't ask." He patted my hand.

"Good. Beer is already competing with your aftershave."

"Stop worrying."

"Worrying is all I do. I'm good at it."

"Here we are."

Carpe Diem Rare Antiques' strategically placed topiary all but obscured the interior view. It was the kind of place one visits by appointment only or, at the very least, rings the bell and waits for admittance based on assessment of one's net worth.

"Here the book is judged by its cover, I see."

"And the book better have wads of cash for pages, or no one's getting past the title." Max stabbed the bell with his index finger. "Bloody nuisance," he muttered. "Does he want business or not?"

"So he caters to a wealthy clientele?"

"The kind with silver spoons up their butts."

A man opened the door, a security guard. His blue serge uniform bore the badge of an elite company. "Mr. Baker, madam." The man greeted Max and nodded at me. "You have an appointment, I understand."

"Good day, Rutgers. How's the wife and new pup? Still chewing up the furniture? That would be the dog I'm referring to, not your wife, unless she's long in the tooth, too." Max bellowed out a laugh.

But Rutgers didn't share the joke. He stepped back to let us enter, his face expressionless. "Follow me, please."

We entered a narrow gallery stretching ahead of us in a hush of subdued lighting. At regular intervals, display pedestals rose from the floor, haloed in light pools illuminating rare objects encased in glass. In passing, I glimpsed a Russian icon triptych, what looked to be an ancient Greek gold necklace in remarkable condition, and even a collection of emerald snuff-boxes that might be Persian. Closer investigation was not allowed. Rutgers ushered us along like a border collie herding sheep, yapping at us with a battery of "this way, this way" every few seconds.

At one point, Max veered towards a door to the left but the guard hailed him back.

"This way, Mr. Baker." Rutgers pointed towards the back of the gallery.

"But that's not the way to the salon."

"Mr. Fox prefers to meet you back here. Follow me, please."

"In the bloody storeroom? What are we, delivery boys?"

But the storeroom it was. We stepped through a steel door into a large but meticulously tidy utility room stacked in cartons and hanging shelves.

"Have a seat, please." The guard indicated a long steel packing table where three chairs had been arranged. The only decoration appeared to be a stack of brown envelopes beside a spool of tape on one end. No tea and cakes.

"I'll stand," Max said.

"Me, too."

"Suit yourselves." Rutgers turned his back to buzz an intercom announcing our arrival while I stared around at the crates, safes, and shelves. I'd have given anything for x-ray vision just then. What secret treasures were kept in reserve in the back recesses of Carpe Diem?

"One step up from the back door," Max muttered.

"Literally," I remarked, pointing to the steel version set into the back wall.

"Just shows how far I've fallen in the arts and antiquities business."

"In the black market, you mean," I whispered. "Which, given the circumstances, means you've actually come up in the world."

"Ssh. Don't say that too loudly around here. Foxy's probably listening in." He pointed to a camera following our every move from its ceiling recess. "He's got an ex MI6 man working for him."

Before I could say anything further, the door opened and in walked a short middle-aged man encased in a fine grey suit sporting a bright yellow silk tie. The bizarre impression of a bulldog-schnauzer mix swathed in silk gabardine struck me hard. Even the tufts of gray hair sticking out above his ears added to the effect.

The man extended a hand first to Max. "Maxwell. It's been a long time."

"Through no bloody fault of mine."

And then to me. "This must be your lovely partner, Ms. McCabe, I presume?" He took my hand firmly in his, squeezing it as if testing an orange for ripeness. "I am Rupert Fox, Sir Rupert Fox."

"Pleased to meet you, Sir Rupert," I said, smiling. I gripped his hand firmly and met his eyes. "You may call me Phoebe minus the 'ms'. You have a gorgeous shop and a brilliant editorial eye. I couldn't help but appreciate the range and exquisite nature of the objects while race-walking down your gallery. Most look museum-worthy."

"Indeed they are, Phoebe. As you know, museums often pass on many exquisite works due to the lack of funds, at which point, the private collector steps in." He smiled, pulling away his hand after administering one last squeeze. "I do try to gather the most unique and valuable of specimens to bring pleasure to my clients worldwide. Perhaps I could provide a personal tour of my exhibits sometime?"

"Not bloody likely," Max said, glowering. "We didn't come here for a tour, did we, Phoebe?"

I still held Mr. Fox's small blue eyes with mine. "Nevertheless, I'd love to see your collection. Perhaps we can arrange another time?"

"Certainly, and I'm most sorry Rutgers rushed you along."

"Which brings us to why we're here," Max interjected. "Phoebe, show him the goods."

Max ignored my pointed glance. Turning towards the table, I pulled the fold of velvet from my pocket and spread it across the surface with a subdued flourish. I positioned a pectoral cross mid-center of the deep blue background while coiling the length of its pearl necklace around the gilded centerpiece like a lustrous serpent. "The original belonged to Queen Isabella of Spain, circa 1561. The pivotal emerald is estimated to be approximately 22.5 carats and the rope is compiled of 325 pearls mixed with sapphires."

Max slipped a color photograph of a painting beside the necklace. A striking woman, swathed in elaborate velvet robes the color of bleeding rubies, her long neck framed in a high ruffed collar, stared out with the kind of regal bearing that commanded time itself. "A portrait of the queen painted in 1561 shows her wearing the exact piece, proving its provenance."

Mr. Fox's eyes widened. He cleared his throat and reached trembling fingers towards the piece, lifting it carefully from the velvet. He weighed it in his hand briefly before letting the necklace flop to the table in a clatter of ceramic on oak. "This is a fake."

"It's a copy, of course. Do you think we'd carry about a priceless object like that around town if we had it?" Max countered.

"But we don't have it. That's why we're here," I added smoothly. "It's a replica, albeit a clever one, don't you think?" My brother knew his stuff.

"Where is the original?" Mr. Fox asked.

"That, Foxy, is what we hope you'll tell us," Max said. "Phoebe and I have visited all my old dealer friends to see if anyone has heard if the original-or maybe one of the companion pieces—is circulating. You're the biggest fish by far, if you know what I mean. You cater to clients with a taste for such rare and priceless objects with pockets deep enough to land them. I hoped that you might have—"

Mr. Fox flexed the fingers of his right hand, his eyes hooded. "You hoped I'd implicate myself in an illegal sale? That sounds more your style than mine, Baker. I have no interest in black market dealings."

"Since when? You sure as hell looked interested enough a second ago."

"Mr. Fox," I interjected, "We only want information. We'd hoped you might have heard something which might help us locate my brother and his friends. Of course we're not implying you'd deal in black market goods."

"I bloody am. You and every damn dealer in the city have probably heard of what happened in Bermuda last January," Max added. "You know about the Oak Island heist, don't deny it. We're just trying to track them down, our family members, I mean. I don't care a damn about the treasure, but there were copies made of all the missing pieces and this is the only one we have in hand. Have you heard of anything like this—Spanish, possibly Aztec—being fleeced in London or on the international black market? Spit it out, Foxy. I know you have eyes and ears everywhere."

"Of course I know about your fumbled heist. You were double-crossed by your own bastard son, as I understand, not to mention your former girlfriend, both of whom took off with the hoard, leaving you empty-handed. Such a sorry tale of greed and the pitifully double-crossed. Indeed, you have my deepest sympathy on both counts. To be both duped and cuckolded is enough to send any man to drink. Is it true that that devilish handsome half-breed son of yours took up with your mistress, the delectable Miss Maggie? Well, well, a very sorry tale indeed. Yet, I assure you, I have no pertinent knowledge to aid your search."

I could feel Max go still beside me.

"Look, Mr. Fox," I began. "Coming here was a mistake, but there's no need for verbal sucker punches. Sorry you wasted our time. We'll just leave. Come on, Max."

But Max stood frozen to the spot, fixing Foxy with fierce blue eyes. "You know something, Foxhole. Spit it out or Interpol just might learn something you'd rather keep hidden."

I placed a warning hand on Max's arm.

Rupert Fox withdrew his hands to his sides, his shoulders stiffening. "Leave my premises immediately so as not to further waste my time or yours." He shot a quick glance to Rutgers, who jerked upright from his leaning post.

Max caught his glance. "After all these years that we've done business together and you can't even throw me a scrap of information? Do you think so little of me?"

My fingers dug deeper. "Max, let's get out of here."

"What I think of you has always been and remains irrelevant, Baker, but let us be clear on one thing: we were never 'in business together.'"

"I'm only looking for my son, can't you understand that? I don't care about the treasure." Max splayed his hands on the desk and leaned towards Mr. Fox. "We don't know where the hell it is, get that? But if you know something and are keeping it from me, I—"

"You'll what?" Fox snapped his fingers and Rutgers was at his side in seconds. "You'll growl and threaten to bite me with your toothless jaws? Don't be so pitiful. Rutgers, escort Mr. Baker out. We are finished here."

"I'm not finished with you, Foxy, not until I say we are. I know things about you that you wouldn't want New Scotland Yard hearing about. I—"

I pulled Max away from the table, grabbing the necklace in passing, and headed in the direction the guard pointed, straight towards the back door. I called over my shoulder. "Too bad you couldn't deign to help us. It would have been in your best interest."

Fox nodded towards Rutgers, a gesture I caught but didn't understand. The guard responded with a flick of his hand while Mr. Fox stood motionless, watching the eviction.

What happened next occurred so quickly, I had no time to react. Suddenly, Rutgers shoved Max into the back alley while simultaneously pulling me back into the room.

2

I swung around to face Rupert Fox. "What do you think you're doing?"

"Please don't be alarmed, but we truly must speak privately, away from your combustible godfather. I assure you, I mean no harm, Phoebe. I'll just ask a few questions and answer a few of yours in reciprocation. We both have information the other needs. I believe we can help each other."

"Why couldn't you be more collaborative a few minutes ago?"

"In truth, Maxwell quite rankles me. My apologies for being rude."

"So you do know something?"

"I believe I can help, yes."

I took a deep breath, expelling it slowly. "Rutgers can't harm Max."

"No harm will befall Maxwell, at least none for which I am responsible. Rutgers will merely escort him to the end of the street, where he will no doubt lumber off the nearest pub in which to drown his sorrows. You may phone him to ease your mind. In fact, it's best you do in case he takes it upon himself to call the police."

Pulling my cell phone from my pocket, I pressed the speed dial. Max picked up in seconds. "Phoebe, are you all right? What's that bludger doing to you?"

"Nothing. Calm down. He says he wants to talk privately and I'm all right with that. Is Rutgers still with you?"

"The mongrel left, presumably scurrying back to his master. I don't like you alone with that slippery bastard. Tell him to let you go immediately or I'll just call the coppers sooner than later."

"No, I said. Wait for me somewhere I can find you when I'm finished here. No police unless I give the word, got that?"

"I'll wait for you at the pub at the end of the street. Call the moment you're out."

I pressed END and deposited the phone back in my pocket. Turning to Mr. Fox, I said, "So, talk."

"First, let us retire to my salon where we'll be more comfortable and hold a civilized conversation. Allow me to dispel your unfortunate first impressions of me."

Down the length of the hushed gallery we went until he ushered me into a dark green-walled room furnished in tobacco-brown leather chairs and hung with illuminated hunting pictures. The effect reminded me of some swanky gentlemen's club fragranced with lingering cigars, only the no smoking signs proved the ambiance served as staging only.

A tea tray sat on a marble table beside a fireplace where a low-burning fire glowed. I wondered idly whether Rutgers had dashed back in time to play serving maid. I amused myself picturing the guard trussed up in a frilly apron setting out a paper-thin Nippon tea set, yet I saw no sign of him or anyone else.

"Ah, the salon," I remarked, taking a seat beside the cushion, a richly colored knitted piece of fruits and flowers. I proceeded to stroke the pillow as if comforting a lap dog.

"My late wife's piece. Lovely, isn't it?"

"Yes, but you need more color in here, maybe a few richly colored rugs. I have the perfect solution in my shop."

Sir Rupert beamed. "Oh, my. You are in the trade, aren't you? I shall take your advice. Perhaps I may drop by?"

"If you're interested in purchasing something, certainly. Is this where Max thought you'd be meeting us today?"

"Indeed. Forgive my bad manners, but I did not want Maxwell to have chummy notions."

"But you want me to have chummy notions?"

"You and I have a better chance for a mutually beneficial relationship and, besides, I find Maxwell rather tiresome these days. Tea, Phoebe?"

"Yes, please, Rupert." I watched him pour the steaming liquid into the delicate Japanese cups. "I hope you aren't suggesting more than just an exchange of information?"

"No, my dear, I assure you I am no aging Don Juan hoping to snare a lovely young woman. Even though my dear wife has passed, that would be most inappropriate. My interest is respectfully professional."

"In other words, you're hoping I can lead you to the pot of gold at the end of the proverbial rainbow." I poured milk into my cup, stirring the liquid into a cloudy caramel with a tiny spoon, the very same kind of silver suppository Max believed Foxy attracted. "Sorry to disappoint you but I know nothing."

"I understand that both your brother and your boyfriend were involved in the Bermuda heist."

"First of all—and I'm just going to say this once, so please pay attention—Noel Halloran is not and has never been my boyfriend. How did that rumor start? Never mind. The important thing is it's not true. If you think befriending me will somehow lead you closer to the Treacherous Trio, you're wrong."

He arched his eyebrows, two caterpillar growths that perfectly complemented the ear tufts. "And yet, a few pieces of the hoard have been trickling into the market of late, meaning your Treacherous Trio is on the move." I paused, lips on the rim of my cup. He read my surprise. "Yes, I have word from my network that a small collection of Aztec gold has been acquired by a Mexican museum."

"But museums don't buy illicit pieces without legal provenance."

"Some are unscrupulous enough to do exactly that, especially if it means acquiring something of great cultural value for considerably less than it's worth and, may I remind you, provenance can be faked just like everything else. Public coffers are not always deep. My contacts say they have attempted to purchase the pieces at a much higher price, but the seller seemed determined to have the gold returned to the country of its origin and to a museum, at that. A rather altruistic touch, don't you think?"

"Seller, not sellers? There was there only one?"

"Only one initiating the transaction, yes."

"Male or female?"

"Male, I believe."

"Red hair or dark?"

"My understanding is that the transaction was performed by an intermediary, which is often the case, so no direct contact transpired. The museum's buyer met the agent in an undisclosed European city, and the seller offered an impressive, though completely bogus, provenance trail with enough details to satisfy all but the most expert scrutiny."

"Forgeries."

"Yes. I understand your brother is a master forger. His skill, I presume, extends to sketches and maps?"

"Sketches, maps, artifacts, you name it." I lowered the tea cup to my lap untouched. "Is that why you think these pieces were part of the Bermuda heist?"

"No, there is more compelling evidence. The pieces match the description Adrian Wyndridge published two months ago in his autobiography, and because the style of the transaction—accepting a below-market price without the benefit of an auction—smacks of Dr. Noel Halloran."

"Why?" The tea was growing cold. I couldn't bring that cup to my lips without risking spillage.

"I believe Miss Maggie is far cleverer than Max ever gave her credit for. I confess to knowing little about your elusive brother but I have had dealings with Dr. Halloran in the past. He is an archaeologist first, criminal second. Many are the times he's chastised me with passionate diatribes regarding obtaining pieces for private collectors when he believed they should be in the hands of the public domain, preferably museums and art galleries. He's what I consider a crusader. Tedious though he can be, I rather admire him for that. The world is a better place with convictions, don't you think?"

"A crusader?" I said, nearly snorting. "Well, why not? Crusaders stormed off to foreign lands to raze temples to the ground in the name of conviction."

"Do I detect a note of sarcasm? Oh, indeed I do. My point is that sale has Halloran's mark all over it," Rupert continued. "Dr. Noel Halloran is on the move."

Noel's face flashed across my mind: the honey-skinned, exotic beauty of mixed racial parentage—Australian Aborigine combined with Max's Celtic bog of a gene pool. "Why, because he may have chosen to fleece the stolen goods at a lower price? Couldn't he have done that for expediency sake just to get quick cash?"

"There was nothing expedient about this. In all ways, it was carefully planned and executed."

I took a deep breath. "Okay, but why are you telling me this?"

"For your safety and information: Halloran's having you followed."

"What?"

"My dear, you have become the target of increased scrutiny over the past few weeks. Several competing interests are keeping you in their sights but one in particular has been identified as a friend of Noel Halloran's."

My hand jerked. I caught the cup just as it tipped tea and milk over my lap. "Sorry."

"Please, do take this napkin to mop that up. There now. Much better. There is a lavatory just around the corner if you'd like to use cold water."

I waved away the offer. The last thing I cared about was a pair of soggy thighs. "Why would Noel have me followed? I can understand the black market types but why him? He knows I don't have the loot. That doesn't make sense."

"Think, my dear. Noel Halloran is an impassioned archaeologist fixated on securing artifacts no matter what the cost. Just because he has successfully wrested away a fortune from your hapless godfather and that Bermudian author chap doesn't mean he's finished. My no, for there is a world filled with undiscovered treasures and artifacts waiting for the talented extractor, and you can believe Noel Halloran is keeping his eye on them all."

"You mean, he's already onto something new?"

"Of course. The Bermuda venture only served to finance future operations. Whatever and whenever he finds something of interest, he will be looking to unearth them, and those objects will require storage, and, eventually a market. Naturally, I am most interested in helping him with the latter but you, my dear, can certainly be of assistance in the storage department. What better place to secure stolen artifacts than the gallery he already knows intimately, having worked there himself for several years? My dear, he used you once and plans to do so again."

"Over my dead body." My Irish roots always prevented me from uttering those words but that didn't stop me now. "He wouldn't dare come back to London. It's too risky."

"Maybe he doesn't have to."

"Which means?"

"All he need do is send a package or shipment, something which looks legitimate and which you might hide without even knowing."

"I get the feeling you know more about this than you're saying."

"Should you accept my help, my knowledge will be at your disposal. Naturally, until such time as we are in a cooperative partnership, I must keep some key matters to myself. What I have told you thus far should serve as a taster."

"And I should trust you because?"

"Because you must trust somebody. Your godfather is totally unreliable at the moment; your family is either dead or crossed over to the dark side, shall we say, and; black market cutthroats are closing in on you by the minute. Who better to help you navigate than one with my vast experience, not only as a fellow gallery owner, but as one who has many contacts, many ears and eyes, plus considerable protective muscle? I will place my expertise and resources at your disposal. Let me help. You want to find the trio as do I, but for different reasons. No, I am not interested in having them arrested but I am interested in their past and future operations. Doesn't that make ours the perfect collaborative relationship?"

"An illegal relationship, as you well know. We've been cooperating with the police all along. Why should that change?"

"Do you really believe the international police protect stolen artifacts, let alone those threatened by their absconding? Their goal is to return such items to the registered owners but supposing that individual or institution came by the item illegally or, at the very least, through devious means? Priceless antiquities have long complicated histories."

"I've heard that line before. I didn't buy it then and I don't now."

"The short story is the police needn't know. I will merely enter the scene as your consultant assisting you with gallery management while Maxwell is indisposed. More importantly, I'm offering you protection,

Phoebe, something the police won't. I have the resources to keep you safe against the multiple interests trailing you, protection of which you have every need."

"Nobody's made a move. Why would they?"

"The London underworld finds you most interesting—sister and probable lover of the thieves, how enticing, perhaps useful as a hostage? You make the perfect mark. Do you realize that Max has been babbling into his cups all over London, blubbering on about how he was hoodwinked out of a fortune, until every two-bit crook in the boroughs knows about it, including your affiliation with the thieves? One will make a move someday soon, Phoebe. You are the most vulnerable. Make sure you're not also the most defenseless. I'll provide you with a bodyguard. All you need do in return is to keep me informed should anything suspicious happen on your gallery premises or beyond. We are not at cross-purposes with one another. Most importantly, I mean no harm to anyone you care about. My interests lay only in objets d'art"

I carefully replaced the cup on the table and got to my feet. "I'm not interested. Thank you for the offer but I have to go now. Max will be worried." I stepped towards the salon door.

"Wait. Please."

I paused.

"My offer stands. You may need my help some day or, at the very least, my advice. Take my card. Don't hesitate to call if you need anything."

Pocketing the card, I strode from the salon and down the length of the darkened gallery. Only when Rutgers appeared from the shadows to unlock the door, did the dealer speak again. "Do give thought to my offer but don't wait until it's too late. Matters will only grow more treacherous in the coming weeks."

Rutgers held the door as I stepped out onto the early evening. "Mr. Baker's at the Cock and Bull at the end of the road. Shall I walk you there, miss?"

"No, thanks." I shrugged my carpet bag more comfortably over my shoulder and headed off down the rain-slicked street.

3

Pubs in London merge from the lights and traffic like beacons of comfort, only these days Max couldn't seem to find comfort anywhere else. When he didn't answer his phone, I proceeded directly to the Cock and Bull. I slipped through the throng of natty suits and stylish work attire to find him hunched over a beer at the bar. I touched his arm.

"Phoebe! I was getting bloody worried about you." By his bleary eyes, I knew he was also getting bloody drunk. "What did he say?"

"Nothing. He thinks I know more than I do. What else is new?"

"He's the last one. We've come up empty. No place left to turn."

"What kind of talk is that? We have the gallery, don't we? Let's go home."

"No, I'm just going to have a little drink."

"Max, you've had enough. Come with me. We promised Rena we'd close the gallery for her today, remember? She's got a date with Marco. Come on, I'll buy you supper after we lock up. How about Asian fusion at the Paper Tiger?"

He dropped his gaze. "You go, sweetheart. I'll catch up with you later."

"Max, don't do this, please."

"Don't do what? Be the adult I am and do what I damn well please? Don't nag. I'll be home when I get there, maybe in an hour."

"Fine." But I knew I wouldn't see him in an hour, maybe even not that evening. For some reason, I always tried to keep up the fantasy, as if that helped. He was all that was left of my supposed family and I had to cling to something.

I plowed my way to the exit, elbowed along the way by the socializing business folk lubricating with a pint or two. Alcohol, companionship, and merriment—was I really missing something? All of it just made me lonelier.

All it takes is getting shafted by your brother, lied to by your late father, and finding out that your entire family is involved in an international art heisting ring to set your mood on grim. The fact that I had an art history degree and was a half-baked lawyer besides was an irony not lost on me.

Flipping up my collar, I darted down the road, intent on taking a shortcut to our shop. The streets were packed by harried workers dashing home, the traffic lights slicking the wet streets with color. As much as I loved London's energy, that rhythm and punchy creativity mixed with tradition, that night all I craved was a return to a smaller world where layers of memory gilded every street and home lay just around the corner.

Only home would never be that close for me again.

The faces passing me only intensified my alienation. *The apparition of these faces in the crowd; petals on a wet, black bough.* Poetry helped. Color helped. Knitting sustained me. When lost at sea, cling to whatever moves you. The gallery and my little top floor flat had become my sanctuary.

The underground to the Earl's Court Road was a relatively short hop but I'd rather cross the Antarctic in bedroom slippers than pack myself in with all the evening commuters so I strode right past the Knightsbridge Station. Catching a cab was next to impossible this time of night so I chose to walk. At least it had stopped raining.

I swerved out of the pedestrian stream and into a fast-food restaurant to pick up supper. Tonight I'd feast on an avocado and shrimp salad, a lemonade, and just because I could, a gooey chocolate brownie. Chocolate offered comfort more reliably than humans. Chocolate betrayed nobody, hurt nothing, except maybe a waistline or two. On impulse, I added a carton of stew for Max in case he returned to the office in time, though I knew he wouldn't. Fooling myself again.

Taking my bounty to the register line, I mused over my meeting with Rupert Fox, niggled by his offer for protection. Nothing about Sir Rupert inspired confidence, especially his trumped-up story of Noel having me followed. More likely I'd follow him; that is, if I could ever find enough information to begin tracking him down.

Fox would have done a better job at convincing me with a city or a contact name, something, anything concrete I could use to find the bastard. As it was, he had nothing to offer but thinly veiled intimidation and an offer which was no offer at all. I'd stay the course, go home and spend an evening the way I always did: Eat while studying tomes on antique carpets and then retire upstairs to my flat for an hour of knitting before bed. Though lonely in many ways, I'd nested out a little niche of my own in the big city, a way of shrinking the unwieldy urban world down to size.

The familiar tingle began spidering down my spine just before I reached the cashier. Turning quickly, I scanned the faces around me. Everyone stood with British patience awaiting their turn. If someone found me particularly interesting, they kept it well-shielded. All the tables lining the walls were filled with heads-down diners grabbing a quick bite. No one even looked at me, yet I knew I was being watched. Why didn't they leave me alone? Turning back to the queue, I paid the cashier, stuffed my dinner packages into my carpet bag, and bolted.

With the October darkness falling heavily down across the streets, all illusions of safety scuttled into the shadows. Harrods loomed ahead on the opposite side, beckoning me in with the golden glow of a luxury cruise ship afloat on an ink-black sea.

I dashed across the road and dove into the department store. Glass cases of shiny objects, a display of Hermes scarves, and a kiosk of Paddington-like bears blurred past. I accidentally bumped into a willowy sales associate, apologized, and ran on. I wasn't so much panicked as annoyed, but I wasn't going to make stalking me easy for anyone.

I took the escalator to the second floor and then dashed straight for the elevators at the rear wall. Moments later, I was back on the escalators heading down to the first floor, rushing towards the nearest exit. I never looked over my shoulder or paused for so much as a nanosecond, but by now I'd attracted the attention of the security troop patrolling the floors like stealthy operatives. I only smiled at the polite "May I be of assistance?" and slipped out the Basil Street exit just as a woman disembarked from a cab. Nabbing the ride in her wake, I gave the driver the address, and sank back into the seat.

Rupert Fox only confirmed what I already knew. I'd been followed almost the moment I arrived in London two m months ago. It began as a prickle between my shoulder blades while strolling through Covent Garden just weeks after I arrived and intensified the day I spent in the Victorian and Albert Museum roaming the textile gallery. Someone had entered one of the exhibit rooms behind me and, since I had been alone just seconds before, I sensed his presence. The moment I turned towards him, he scurried away as if caught pilfering the crown jewels. All I grasped was an impression of an elderly man in a tweed suit.

That marked one of those connective seconds when I realized this wasn't the first time. After that, I'd often catch a figure staring at me from a street corner only to dart down a side road as I approached. By height and build, I knew it wasn't always the same person, sometimes not even the same sex. Sometimes, my stalker was young and sometimes much older, sometimes dressed in a suit, and sometimes in jeans, but always intensely interested in me.

As if I knew anything. Did they really think that following me would reveal the Tricky Trio's hideout? My pseudo aunt Maggie, my brother Toby, and Max's bastard son, Noel, had to be long gone by now. They'd stolen a fortune worth of rare jewels and artifacts so it hardly made sense for them to make themselves visible, especially to me. Those three had to be holed down somewhere far away from London. Not one of them had ever been in contact with either Max or I since. My own brother hadn't even returned home to Nova Scotia for our father's funeral.

All I had to go on was the sense of being watched in a city where a million strangers accompanied my every step. Who would listen? I gazed out the window. Traffic hemmed in the cab on either side as we wove through the congested tributaries. I'd have been back at the shop had I walked. Fishing in my bag for my phone, I dialed Serena, our gallery assistant, who picked up in one ring. "Rena, I'm running late. Sorry. I wanted to get back early so you could leave. I don't suppose Max called to let you know?"

"No Max, Phoebe, but relax. Everything is all right, yes? Marco canceled."

"Again?"

"Again. When his love life cooks, mama gets shoved to the back of the stove. Jennifer forgives again."

"All the women forgive him." Marco Fogarty, Serena's son and an aspiring actor, ground girls' hearts under his booted heels like candy wafers, but Mom stuck to him like mothers should.

"Marco is being Marco and mothers are made to be all-suffering, yes? But girlfriends, what is their excuse?"

I laughed. "Hormones! We're just approaching Sloane Square now. I should be there in a few minutes. See you soon."

Only it took 15 minutes before the cab finally slid in front of Baker & Mermaid Art and Fine Antiques. I paid the driver, jumped out, and paused, temporarily transfixed by the site of our shop. Though not as prestigious as Carpe Diem, Baker & Mermaid had much more curb appeal. I had worked hard to eradicate all vestiges of Maggie, Max's former girlfriend and assistant, who had composed the gallery to look somewhere between a high-end dress shop and a Sears decorating store. Now it presented itself for what it was: a purveyor of fine textiles and antiques, many of which fell into the (legal) artifact category.

A gilded mermaid suspended on scrolled wrought iron hinges, curved her magnificent tail around the shop sign as if hugging it close. My symbol since childhood, she was my soul's pilot light, my reminder to keep swimming no matter how rough the seas. Both the sign and the partnership were an extravagantly generous gift from Max in honor of my arrival in London. Part apology, part heart-felt offering, and possibly also an act of consolation for our mutual losses, it still touched me in all my deepest places.

"I know she is magnifico, Phoebe, but will you crick your neck staring like that?"

My gaze shot down to Serena framed in the doorway, her head cocked to one side. Crud, how long had I been standing exposed on the street? "She gets me every time."

Serena grinned. A striking presence with hair colored a deep pink and shaped into a smooth bob, today she wore a long black tunic over leggings, her attire accessorized with clusters of vintage necklaces looped one over the other. I knew she'd be wearing attar of roses in honor of all things rose but tomorrow might choose another color theme and be scented accordingly. She swore that colors had scents. I only hoped I looked and smelled that good in my sixties.

"My only complaint is the bra, oh, the bra!" Serena continued, mock-cupping her bosom. "Ouch. Can she not find a more comfortable bra than that? Marks and Spencer has a sale this week."

I stepped towards the door grinning. "I think in mermaid terms, clam shells are the ultimate in shape-wear, kind of like Spanx on the half shell."

Rena laughed and clapped her hands. "I'm sure you are right."

She'd already closed the shop for the day. The back gallery space hung in darkness with just the two Ushak carpets in the window illuminated in a glory of golds and reds. It would break my heart the day one or both went home with someone else, though we desperately needed a big sale.

"I'm sorry I didn't get here sooner. I took a cab."

"I see." Rena stepped aside as I entered, locking the door behind me. "Would not the tube be faster?"

"Probably." I breathed deeply her rose fragrance and lowered my carpet bag to the floor. "Only I can't quite adjust to traveling in a cylinder."

I resisted the urge to double-check the deadbolt and scan the street through the glass for possible pursuers. What difference would that make? Everybody knew where I lived by now.

"In another year or two, you will be proper Londoner. I am almost glad that Marco stood me up tonight so that we can speak alone. I must say something."

Surely she wasn't going to hand in her notice? Serena Fogarty had been my right hand since I assumed part ownership of the gallery. She had once owned a gallery herself with her husband in Bath but following his sudden death a decade ago, she came to London with a teenage son and a bag-load of debt. She'd been working the booths at Portobello Road and other shop jobs until the day six months ago when she arrived at Baker & Mermaid and Max hired her on. He said that her application felt like a stroke of divine intervention.

"Is everything all right?" I asked.

"So I hope." She studied my face, her hands clasped before her like a supplicant. "Phoebe, maybe this is not my business and so I overstep my place, but I think you must know, yes? Your name is on the door, too." Her English, though excellent, couldn't quite eradicate her Italian imprint.

"I should know," I nodded. "Know what?"

"It is about Max."

I stared at her for a moment. My loyalty to my godfather remained unshaken no matter what. Discussing him with an employee didn't feel right, and yet, Serena verged on a friend and would never broach something unless it was important. "Right, so how about sharing supper with me first? I picked up some fodder on the way home."

"I couldn't possibly carve into what surely must be a banquet in a bag."

"Stew, salad, and a brownie the size of a truck—are you kidding me? I'm surprised I haven't gained half a pound just saying *brownie* out loud. You can't leave me to tackle it alone. That thing is huge."

"Chocolate?"

"Completely."

"Then I will be there for you tonight but you must promise to let me cook for you soon, something truly magnificent like squash ravioli, my specialty, yes?"

"From one of your family recipes? Absolutely." I picked up my bag and strode halfway down the gallery towards the glass staircase. That staircase was one of the few things of Maggie's renovation that remained after Max tried abolishing her memory from his existence. Extravagantly engineered in Plexiglas, it slipped upward to a kind of observatory-cum-workspace landing that seemed to float over the center of the gallery like my own stairway to heaven. I claimed it as my office and arranged for the assistant's desk to be located near the back on the main floor. The idea of sailing over art and textiles was too perfect to resist.

One more level up and hidden from view lay Max's third-story office with my flat tucked around the corner and down the hall. When Max had first acquired the building decades ago, he gutted the first and second floors to make a lofty display area suitable for hanging impressive objects like antique rugs. In those days, Maggie strove to hone the area with a modernistic edge. Just thinking of her now made my teeth ache. Physical responses to Noel and my missing brother, though similar, were far more painful and hovered about my gut. My response to Maggie's duplicity was simpler: a seething anger that provided an easier target for venom. Devious, conniving, and superficial pretty much summed up my adjectives for her.

In my suspended office above, I cleared a corner of my desk, spread a pashmina for a tablecloth, and set out the knives and forks we kept in the tea alcove. Rena and I ate in companionable silence interspersed with Marco tales and anecdotes. Some unspoken agreement passed between us that we'd avoid unpleasant topics until suitably fed and watered. As it turned out, my takeout dinner accommodated us both. Though a bit of stew remained, the brownie didn't stand a chance.

"Well, I guess it's time to get to the crux of it," I said, shaking crumbs into the wastebasket.

Rena sighed. "Maybe we could have a cup of tea first?"

"You know, for an Italian-born, you certainly have adopted British mores. I mean, you ask for tea like you mean it."

She brightened. "You have wine?"

I laughed. "No, sadly. I downed the last of my Chablis last night."

Rena shrugged. "Wine is always best but, after twenty-five years, I adapt."

"Right, so I'll plug in the kettle."

Rena followed me downstairs to the back room where a tea-making stand and water cooler sat just inside the door. Boxes, crates, and mailing tubes cluttered the rest of the space surrounding a long oak table.

Max had collected rare objects for years, storing them in every available corner until such time as they either took their turn on the gallery floor or faded into oblivion. Most of the really valuable objects were gone now but in a space the size of a single garage, it looked more like the Old Curiosity Shop than a business storeroom. Still, I'd know if something else were hidden there, wouldn't I?

"Someday I want the luxury of organizing this properly," I remarked.

"But why not now?"

I flicked on the electric kettle. "First I have to scale the mountainous learning curve that comes with being a gallery owner. I'd like to have been a textile expert by last month. There's so much to learn."

"You work too hard. You study all the time—study, study, study. What about love?"

"Love?" I made a face. "Please. I've given up on men." I almost gave up on people, too. My faith in the human race had taken a nosedive. "Okay," I said turning around. "About Max."

Rena sighed. "Right. The check you signed for me last week?"

"Your salary? Of course."

"My bank called to say it had not cleared."

I stared at her. "As in bounced?"

"Like a rubber ball-boing-de-boing," she made bouncing motions with her hand. "The one two weeks ago, same."

"That's impossible. Maybe I messed up the date or forgot to sign it?"

"You never mess up dates, Phoebe, and am I not careful to get either one or both of your signatures? There is more. Please wait here."

She slipped from the room and returned moments later to lay a stack of envelopes snapped together with an elastic band on the table. "I don't know what to do with them. I place them on Max's desk every morning, and every day I see them in the same place. The pile mounts."

My icy fingers pulled the stack from the rubber band, quickly flicking through the unopened letters, requests, invitations, and two envelopes stamped FINAL NOTICE. I opened one, staring at a collection notice referencing one of our suppliers.

I tossed them on the desk. Collection agencies? Bounced checks? Had our bank account bottomed out? "It can't be." Max was rich. Evidence of his wealth greeted me every morning in this very building, followed me around in gifts, had, in fact, enveloped me since my father died and I left Nova Scotia to join him in London. What was happening?

"Phoebe, I am so sorry. I had hoped this would all just go away." Rena flapped her arms like an escaping bird.

I pressed my index finger between my temples to reset my brain, then dropped my hand, straightened my shoulders, and faced her. "You did right to tell me. Let's just handle this one step at a time. First, you need your salary. I'll transfer money from my personal account into the company and provide you with another check that you can cash tomorrow. Next, please leave me all the information you have regarding the accounts—ledgers, books, passwords, whatever. Does Max keep everything upstairs?"

Serena nodded. "There is an automated bookkeeping program which I try to keep up to date but Max doesn't provide me current information. He jots things down in a ledger in his desk, I think, but," she shrugged, "I am unsure."

"I haven't paid any attention to the accounts. I've just assumed too much."

The kettle began to boil. I moved to pour water into the nearby pot but Rena laid her hand on mine. "Forget the tea, yes? You have much on your mind. I will gather what I have and leave you now. I am certain you will get everything sorted out. Anything you need from me, anything at all, you ask."

4

ours later, I remained in Max's upstairs office poring over the ledgers. It didn't take an accountant to see how more money had been siphoned out of Baker & Mermaid than had been going in. The list of sales over the prior months had been small, something Max attributed to a poor economy as well as his sudden jettison into the legal trade, which he claimed cost him many high-ticket customers. Meanwhile, I'd spent far too long caught in the illusion that we were rich while he went far too long letting me believe it. Why hadn't I paid attention? Why didn't I ask questions, insist he go over the books with me?

I logged onto my bank account, still based in Halifax where my father's estate had yet to close, and checked my balances. The bottom line of my checking account delivered another shock. Almost twenty thousand dollars had been mysteriously deposited two days ago. I stared in disbelief. What was happening? With my brother and co-heir of my father's diminutive estate missing, I had yet to receive anything from Dad's will or even put the cottage up for sale. I lived on the ample salary Max paid, which I deposited into a British bank, but this? I now had over fifty thousand dollars that wasn't mine.

I checked the time: eleven o'clock in London meant seven o'clock back in Nova Scotia. My friend, Nancy, a lawyer, would still be at her office closing things down for the day. I sat staring unfocused at Max's collection of antique inkwells lining the wall before pushing back the chair, padding downstairs to my glass landing, and dialing my home province. She picked up on the first ring. "Nancy?"

"Phoebe, is everything okay?"

"I just discovered Baker & Mermaid is broke."

"How serious is it?"

"Serious enough, but that's not my only worry. I told you that someone deposited money in my account two weeks ago? So far, the bank hasn't been able to determine the source, but another deposit came through yesterday, a big one. It shows up online as 'Undisclosed Transfer'."

Nancy paused for a moment. "Toby."

"Of course it's Toby, who else? The bank said it was a wire transfer and gave the name of a bank in Switzerland but couldn't identify the owner."

"They wouldn't or couldn't. It's not illegal to give someone money, and bank transfers and money wires happen all the time, often anonymously. Switzerland specializes in anonymous wealth."

"Yes, but surely I have the right to accept or refuse the gift?" I stared into the empty air over the balcony. Saying that aloud sounded plain foolish.

"The right to refuse large infusions of money? I doubt banks have that request often enough to require stipulations."

"If he's trying to appease his conscience or otherwise make up for what he's done to me and Dad, he can forget it. But, look, what if he's using me to launder money?"

"Do you really believe Toby would do that?"

"Ask me if I thought any of the things he's done were possible a year ago."

"Point taken. Here's another thing: Someone's been infusing your dad's account with money, too. Remember when I told you how the bank statements showed an aberration from one month to the next? Typically in probate cases, the bank account pays outstanding bills, fees, and such, which means the assets should be going down until we finally close it out, except for the premium savings accounts, of course. But, and this is a big but, your dad's checking account has been increasing incrementally, first by hundreds, now by thousands, and what's more, it's been going on since long before your dad died. We were impressed by how much we thought he saved in his lifetime, but after studying his accounts, I've reached the conclusion that someone, presumably Toby, has been augmenting your father's account all along."

I pressed a finger against my forehead. "Okay, so Toby took care of Dad's expenses—good for him. That's what we kids are supposed to do for our ailing parents if we can—but to continue after he's gone means he has no compunction about using me to further his own ends. How little I knew my brother."

"He's still your brother and loves you, regardless of what compulsions rule him. Maybe he sees padding your father's assets as one way of taking care of you down the road? In six more years, he'll be declared legally dead and all of that inheritance goes to you."

"Unless I expose him first, which I will. And how do we know he isn't just hiding it from the government? It's tainted money. I don't want his apologies or his belated brotherly love, and certainly not his money, except--"

"Except you've decided to use it."

Sometimes she just knew me too damn well. "Except I need it to pay Serena's salary and keep Baker & Mermaid afloat. If I don't, we'll go under. I can't let that happen. This gallery means more to me than I ever expected. It's like all I have left."

"You have far more left than the gallery, but I understand how you're clinging to it right now. Still, technically what you're doing is illegal, which you know already."

"Sure, I know that but I'm not stealing anything, just borrowing something already stolen. Anyway, I've sent the request to the bank to transfer the funds into the company until I can repay it. That will give me time to get the gallery where it needs to be while I go after the Treacherous Trio."

Nancy laughed a melodious rumble. "That's why you left the law. You just can't do black and white. You always get snarled in the gray zone."

"Maggie said something like that once. Besides, I like blended colors."

"Which can get pretty muddy."

"At the time I quit law school, they called it a 'rebellious refusal to accept rules unconditionally'."

"Sounds about right. You know I'll have to share my suspicions to investigators, should they start poking around your father's estate?"

"Of course, but you wouldn't volunteer the information, would you?"

"I should."

I squeezed my eyes shut. Of course she should. What was I thinking? "Don't hold anything back, please. I don't want you mired in any of this or have your firm associated with obstructing justice. Once I track down the three of them, I'll pass their heads over to the law on a plate and that will look mighty fine in the eyes of the law."

"Just try to stay alive while you're doing it, will you? This is the black market we're talking about."

"Don't I know it. We visited one of Max's old comrades in crime today, a Sir Rupert Fox, and he's definitely dealing in stolen goods, though he wouldn't admit that. He says he has information that Noel has already begun fencing the goods to a Mexican museum while making on that he was more interested in returning the plunder to their rightful countries than money. He called Noel 'altruistic'. How's that for a joke? He claimed the duplicitous criminal treasure hunter might try using the gallery to hide stolen artifacts."

"Do you think that's a possibility?"

"Nothing that bastard does would surprise me but I don't see how he could have hidden anything here since the heist. Nobody's seen a hair of him. Anyway, for months I've just been keeping my head down trying to build a life for myself but all that poison keeps seeping back and tainting everything. I'll never be free until those three are in jail."

"But you don't need to be the one to put them there. This is dangerous stuff. Maybe you do need a bodyguard."

"Another person dodging my heels, you mean? Somehow that doesn't sound comforting. Besides, he's probably already having me followed apparently."

"Tell the police."

"No. I need flexibility. If the trio have begun fencing the loot, some-where, somehow, they'll trip up, leave a trail, and I'll be on it. I don't need the police following me on that adventure."

"Phoebe, what are you saying? Leave it to the authorities. It's their job to find the thieves, not yours."

"But this is personal and I'm taking it very personally. It's my brother and my—hell, I don't know what Maggie was   and even Noel has made this personal."

"Could you just think with your head instead of your heart for once? Don't act impulsively."

"Sure."

"Wish your 'sure' meant something."

"I'll try."

"Try really hard."

Speaking with Nancy left me feeling fortified, like taking a tonic for my resolve. Too bad such boosts lasted only until the next stray thought sent me off on a tangent. We hung up promising to talk soon.

Shoving myself away from the desk, I padded down the glass steps to the gallery. It was almost midnight and darkness had sunk the space in a subterranean glow. The street lamps cast long bars of illumination across the floor, brushing against the cases and artifacts that centered the space.

The family of Asian celadon incense burners on the long oak table now swam in a ghostly gloom and all the carpets and textiles lining the walls had withdrawn their brilliance. And yet, if I closed my eyes, I could imagine every detail of every piece—the wild Shekarlu Persian rug with its mellowed ocher and rusted reds, the trio of folk kilims dancing in pattern and color, the Greek 18th century bridal embroidery with its precise stitchery, and even the circular motifs that centered the deep green background of the Zoroastrian shawl.

We had forty-five pieces of textile art displayed here with another ten upstairs in my apartment to be brought down as pieces sold. Tonight, these expressions of humanity sat hushed in the dark yet I swear could hear them speaking a thousand languages in my heart.

These were my favorite moments, alone in the gallery surrounded by textiles and glorious objects. Rarely a night passed when I didn't descend from my aerie to stroll the gallery like some spirit on the prowl. Mostly, I counted my blessings, marveling over being right there, alone amid all this majesty.

I thought of my mother from whom I learned my love of textiles; I thought of my dad, gone now these seven months, who had once regarded his womenfolk's love for color and fiber an honor that had enlightened his life; thought of my brilliant, twisted, missing brother, and then quickly swerved away.

But, more importantly, why did it feel as if though I was being watched every step I took? Even here in my sanctum, something watched.

                           ꙅ   5   ꙅ

My apartment had originally been Max's storeroom attic tucked
under the dormers of the Georgian building and, before that,
probably servants' quarters for some elegant family. With the
cramped spaces and odd-angled walls, it needed plenty of refurbishment to
make habitable.

Down came walls to open up the rooms, wooden floors were buffed and
polished, bright new windows installed, plus Max added a bathroom and
mini kitchen. Into this lovely new world that had become my land of new
beginnings, I marched a collection of Art Nouveau tiles along the mantle,
hung framed stained glass windows, graced the available hanging areas with
antique rugs, and focused shots of color and pattern everywhere. My mother's loom occupied the center of the sitting area, leaving the rest of the
furniture—a chair, two side tables, and a carved bookcase—hugging the
walls like second-rate citizens. Stuffed with yarn as well as books, my well-
padded bookcase made a particularly dazzling accent along with the pieces
of knitting I draped everywhere.

Over the mantle hung *Tide Weaver*, the tapestry I'd created with Mom
and Toby years ago. Sometimes it still hurt to look at it but mostly I'd
come to take comfort in its presence. The energy from my mother's

creative spirit lay embedded in those threads along with some aspect of all I once believed my family represented.

Admiring my apartment that morning, I wondered why I hadn't asked how much that renovation cost. Actually, I had, only Max had refused to answer.

Gulping down a kale smoothie, I grabbed my jacket. Our shop hours ran from ten a.m. to seven p.m. on Wednesdays and, because I lived upstairs, I always opened the gallery in the mornings and ran it solo until Serena arrived at eleven o'clock. Today I wished I'd arranged for her early arrival so I could dash around the corner to Max's townhouse. I knew he wouldn't arrive until much later and what I had to say needed saying immediately and preferably in private. Since he wasn't answering the phone, I'd just have to wait.

I deactivated the security system and strolled around the gallery flicking on the lights, including the brace of halogens focused on the magnificent carpets lining the walls. Each textile deserved a personal greeting.

Each carpet was special, rare and inspiring. My loomed divas required acknowledgment of their incredible beauty and will to survive. Some had been smuggled out of conquered castles as war trophies; others had made their way across steppes and plains as part of a family's most treasured possessions; and all represented the human need to enrich our world in color and pattern. I was honored to be in their presence every single day and vowed never to forget it. I had been known to refuse a sale based on my assumed unworthiness of the buyer. Did they really plan to let their puppy pee on a work of art?

Down the center aisle ran our series of oak tables placed end to end over which we hung green Tiffany turtle-back glass lamps. Captured in each light pool lay clusters of tribal jewelry, carved celadon incense burners, and collections of small, rare objects grouped amid pots of African violets and miniature palms—Serena's and my idea, which we thought brilliant. The violets and greenery added an air of living grace over the inanimate objects like finding artifacts in a jungle garden.

I had just finished switching on the Tiffanies and testing the plants for water when the doorbell rang. I looked up, startled, watering can in hand.

Rarely did customers arrive this early and yet the outline of a man stood silhouetted against the sun.

I checked the time on my phone: one minute after ten o'clock. Okay, so I was a minute late. Then I had a thought: Supposing this was one of my stalkers come to check me out? Oh, hell. They would have done the checking out long before now, wouldn't they? But what did I know? I was new at the crook business. Besides, I couldn't very well refuse to answer the door. I had a business to run.

I strode forward in my best store manager mode, thinking that, if I had to, I could trip the emergency alarm located under the long table. As an added precaution, I kept one hand on the phone in case I had to speed-dial the cops.

Unlocking the door, I smiled up at the tall man in a greatcoat with the dark hair curling out from under a broad-brimmed hat and a long mustache that could have come straight out of Dr. Zhivago. His eyes were deep-set and silky brown like a stallion's glossy flank and for a moment I fell into their light.

"Hello, Phoebe."

My throat constricted. "Noel?"

"Back up," he said in a low voice. "Make on like I'm a customer. Say you have something put aside for me and walk towards the back to the camera's blind spot where we can talk."

I stepped back. "You're crazy coming here."

"Is that like 'hello'? I have to talk to you and this is the only way. Give me a minute."

To have him show up now set me in a tailspin. I wasn't prepared. I could hardly breathe. But I badly needed answers so I turned, half in shock, and began walking toward the back, gripping my phone in one hand and sliding the watering can onto the table in passing. How dare the bastard just show up like this. Was he crazy?

"Sorry to arrive so early," he said in a loud voice, the Australian jaunt replaced by a clipped British affectation. "I would have phoned but my blasted cell isn't on the ball today. Bloody nuisance! I had to come into the city anyway, so I thought I'd just swing around."

"I'm so glad you did, mister, ah, Drummond? I have the item you requested put aside for you right back here," I said, my voice a little too chirpy.

"Oh, jolly good."

Jolly good? I led him right into the far corner behind Rena's desk. The moment we were out of camera range, I dropped my phone on the desk, swung around and whispered: "You murderous, thieving bastard! What in hell did you come here for? Do you think I won't phone the police and have you locked up on the never-never plan? I want to see all three of you in jail as soon as possible. I think if I had a gun, I'd shoot it right now."

"You shot me a few months ago."

"That was different. I wasn't aiming for you."

He reached out to bring me to him but I pushed him away.

"Don't touch me. Don't you ever touch me."

He dropped his hands, those fine long-fingered, pilfering, criminal hands. "Okay, so I deserved that. Much worse, probably, but I—"

"Probably? Definitely, you sleazy, criminal, low-life, art-thieving bastard!"

"Will you cut the inspired adjectives and just listen for a moment?"

I wiped my eyes on the back of my sleeve and stepped towards him, so wired by pain and fury, I couldn't think straight. "How dare you come back here after all you've done to your father, to me. You don't care about anybody but yourself, you bastard!" I'd rehearsed this first meeting again and again, but my cache of spring-loaded barbs failed to launch. All I could do was repeat myself on auto-babble.

"I do care. Why do you think I'm here?"

"To steal something else, how the hell do I know? Are the Elgin Marbles taken yet?"

He suppressed a laugh but the eyes fixed on mine brewed something darker. "At least once by the British, but I suppose we could steal them back for Greece. How's Father?"

"What do you care?" God, why couldn't I say something intelligent?

He spread his gloved hands. "I've always cared."

"Bullshit!"

"Phoebe, look, you're angry, I get that. You should be. How could I expect anything else? But I never stop thinking you. I can't bear that I put you in danger. Since Bermuda, I've had someone looking out for you and

Father on a constant basis. Now my man tells me you've got a batch of thugs, detectives, and even Interpol types tailing you. He says they're so thick on your heels, they practically form queues. I had to come see for myself, find out what the hell's going on, and screw the risk. What *is* going on?"

"Are you serious? Look around, Noel. I'm trying to rebuild my life while shaking everyone's conviction that I must be in some way involved with your heist, your mess-up. You and my own damn brother have sunk Max and me in so deep, we have to claw our way out, and you ask me what's going on?"

"Interpol's watching."

I tried to steady my breath, rein in my thunder, think. "And I assured them that the moment one of you appears, I'll tell them. I want nothing more than to see you all rot in jail."

He took a deep breath, his expression shooting glib one minute and silk-softened the next. "I'm not even going to try to apologize, because nothing I say will ever be enough, at least not now, not like this. It would take a hell of a lot longer than the time I've got today to fill you in with what really happened in Bermuda, let alone what's going on now."

"I have it on good authority that you've begun fencing the goods."

"Foxy told you, I suppose—yes, I know you and Father went to see him —but it's a hell of a lot more complicated. I just can't explain the details here and now. I'm leaving the country today but I had to see you. Toby wanted to but can't. God, you look so good, like I imagined only better. I love your hair." He looked as if he wanted to touch my face but thought better of it.

"It's the full story I want and I want it now. If you can't stick around long enough to tell it, maybe I'll just ring the alarm. You'll have plenty of time to talk in prison."

"It's about Toby."

"Toby? Do you mean my missing brother Toby? The one who hasn't bothered to contact me for a year Toby? Would that be the Toby who shafted his boyfriend and broke his heart?"

He nodded solemnly. "You do go on, don't you? Toby wants to see you, Phoebe, desperately, but can't. I've come to give you a message from us both, really. We're not the monsters you think." He took a deep breath, and in that instant I realized how sunken his cheeks were under the disguise, how his usual buoyancy had flat-lined into a tightrope of anxiety and pain. I should have felt deliriously happy over his suffering but didn't. "Toby wants you to know that—" He paused.

"That what?"

"That he loves you."

"Give me a break. Love would have kept him beside while Dad was dying; love wouldn't have plunged his sister into such danger. And where the hell is he, anyway?"

Noel's dark eyes fixed on my face, his mouth twisted down. "Hell pretty much describes it."

"No details, eh? I'm supposed to just wait for answers on your god time?" I pushed past and sprang for the display table. In an instant, I had flicked the switch, turning to face him triumphantly as the siren ripped through the air.

"Oh, bloody hell, Phoebe! I haven't even told you about the Goddess with Vultures kilim yet, and now you're just going to have to figure it out by yourself." He lurched for the door, hat pulled low over his face. "When it arrives, leave it alone for God sakes!" He paused by the door. "And I meant what I said, all of it."

"What Goddess with Vultures kilim?" I called out after him but he slipped into the street and was gone.

❧ 6 ❧

Giving my statement to the metro police was a waste of time. Try explaining why you rang the alarm on someone who made no attempts to threaten or harm you physically, let alone steal anything. He didn't even break in. Technically, no crime had been committed.

"He's a known criminal. Contact Interpol," I told them. "They know the background and, in the meantime, an international art thief may be already escaping the country. Why are you just standing there?" I mentioned nothing about Noel's personal comments or the remark about a goddess-with-vultures kilim. I mean, one was personal and the other simply inscrutable—a goddess with vultures? After an hour of senseless questioning, they finally left. I turned to find Serena watching me.

"That handsome criminal really returned?" she asked, her face alight.

"Did I say he was handsome?'

"Swarthy, you said."

"Swarthy is not necessarily handsome and this is no potential lover, so enough already. He kissed me once, that was it. Maybe twice. The point is, he's a snake, the linchpin in the crime mechanism that ran the whole Bermudian heist operation, an archaeologist shit-head, in other words." Admittedly, I needed to work on my descriptors.

"But the archaeologist shit-head is very handsome, yes?"

"What does that have to do with anything?" I rubbed a hand over my eyes, smearing my mascara. I hated makeup. Why should a woman in tears be further humiliated? "He actually had the nerve to come back here and talk to me, said he wanted to tell me he wasn't the monster I thought he was. Can you believe it? Like he'd risk capture for that? He came for another purpose, the bastard." I didn't mention the kilim, either.

"He must care about you very much."

"Care about me?" I stared at her in disbelief. "You call that caring? Did he really think I wouldn't pull the alarm on him, that I wouldn't alert the police after everything he's done?"

"He told you about your brother?"

"He said Toby couldn't come to me in person—must have been too busy planning the next heist or something—but wanted me to know he loved me." I laughed. "I mean, give me a break. I know love when I see it."

"Did he try to kiss you again?" Serena asked.

"Serena, stop thinking life is like an Audrey Hepburn movie. It's not. It's more like a horror flick spliced together with a bad sitcom where everybody flubs the punch lines. No, he didn't try to kiss me. He tried to touch my face. God, I hate that man. And the most galling thing is that I burst into tears. Where is Max, anyway? He should have been here an hour ago. God, I hope Noel didn't visit him, too. That would really mess him up. He's not answering his damn phone!"

"Phoebe, Max does not come in early any more. Some days, never, and you know how he hates phones. He probably turned it off, yes?" Serena answered gently. "Try to calm yourself. I will make tea, yes?"

"No tea." I couldn't bear to see her watching me with those large eyes luminous with sympathy or some hope that my life story would somehow end with happily ever after. I took a deep breath. "I have to see Max. Cover for me, please."

"Of course, Phoebe, always."

I grabbed my carpet bag and left, relieved to be on the move, my fury lessening once my boots hit the sidewalk. I needed strength, not adrenalin. The police might catch Noel yet. After all, how long could a tall man dressed like an escapee from the Russian front go without attracting notice?

Halfway down the street, my phone rang. I answered it without even checking the caller's identity.

"Phoebe? Rupert Fox here. I understand you rang the alarm on a visitor this morning."

I veered out of the pedestrian traffic to stand against a brick wall. "How the hell do you know that? Are you having my gallery watched?"

"Part of the time, yes. What did he say, if you don't mind me asking?"

"I do mind you asking, so leave me alone." I pressed END and pocketed the phone. Damn him and everyone else to hell.

Continuing to Max's townhouse, I dropped into Costa for takeaway coffee and pastries, his eye-openers of choice. Holding the bag, I continued along the busy street. Noel claimed he would be leaving that night but for where? Why hadn't I asked him any real questions, and what did he mean about a goddess kilim? More damn mysteries and innuendos. Maybe Foxy knew something. Maybe I shouldn't have been so quick to hang up on him?

Horns honked, cars and motorcycles whizzed by, leaving me breathing the fumy air sharpened by the late autumn chill. Turning the corner, I arrived on Bedford Gardens, a residential street of mostly brick and stucco townhouses with manicured lawns and tiny gardens abloom with fall roses. Approaching Max's white corner property with its three stories and five bedrooms, I was struck anew by the signs of neglect.

Maggie, once his mistress of external appearances, had kept the window boxes filled with seasonal delights arranged through a pricey subscription florist. Now, the greenery stuffing the lacquered black boxes so obviously hailed from Christmas past that they could be harboring ghosts. The building cried out for a brightening of white paint and the small patch of grass out front had already lost the war to weeds.

I mounted the stairs and rang the bell, checking behind me for possible stalkers. I half expected to see Noel but knew in my heart that he was long gone, damn him. Hopefully he'd left his father alone.

After several moments of no response, I unlocked the door with my key, dropped my carpet bag onto the foyer chair, and stepped into the hall. I stopped dead staring ahead at the empty wall opposite. That spot had once held Max's prized Ersari-Bashir carpet from central Asia, an intricately patterned masterpiece, a design improvised by the weaver in a rare illustration of creative independence. Gone. I felt a cry build at the back of my throat.

"Max?" I called out.

"Phoebe? Back here."

Back here meant the kitchen, a light-washed room overlooking the narrow topiary garden. Those topiaries, once shaped like chess pieces, now resembled a gathering of mangy gnomes stumbling towards the back door.

My godfather, disheveled and unshaven in his bathrobe, sat at the kitchen table, a piece of gnawed toast minus a plate.

"Morning, Phoebe, dear. Come to drag me to work, have you?" He didn't meet my eyes.

I placed the coffee and croissant on the table. "Not exactly. Anything new?"

"Nothing," he said in a flat voice. No Noel then, thank God. He'd tell me that much.

"I came to talk. When were you planning to tell me?"

He half turned to look at me without meeting my eyes. "Tell you what?"

"That Baker & Mermaid is broke."

His anguished expression nearly cracked my heart. He studied his toast while I flipped the lid on my coffee cup, willing myself to stay strong. I couldn't tell him everything would be fine; I couldn't operate on denial one moment longer.

"How'd you find out?"

"Serena's payroll check bounced like Indian rubber. Twice."

He rubbed his bloodshot eyes. "I meant to have enough ackers in there to cover the checks but fell short. I thought I could fix this, Phoebe. I tried."

"So you sold the Bashir? That must have fetched a bundle."

"Not as much as you'd think but I needed to turn it quick to get the cash."

"Why didn't you say something? I could have saved you from selling the Bashir. You loved that carpet."

He shook his head, his hair looking particularly leonine that morning. "It's just an object, Phoebe, not a person. I thought I could get the money right into the gallery account but the taxes needed paying first plus a pile of other bills." He rubbed his eyes again. "Phoebe, love, I can't shore things up any longer. I can't do it. There's so much I didn't tell you. She drained my accounts. She siphoned all the money in my checking account, dinged my savings, and piled so much debt on my credit cards, I've had to pay it off in installments."

I lowered myself into the chair opposite him, my gaze skimming the stacks of dirty dishes lining the marble counter top. "Maggie," I said, while taking a sip of my latte. Just saying her name left a bitter taste no Italian roast could wash away.

"Maggie."

"Didn't you cancel the cards months ago?" I sounded so calm.

"I should have, but I put a dick on her and he said he could track her more easily if I left them open."

"Dick?"

"Dick Tracy, private eye."

"You hired a private eye and didn't tell me that, either?"

"Sorry, love, but you had a lot on your hands settling into the gallery so I thought I'd just do this on my own. The cops aren't doing anything."

I swallowed a mouthful of brew and took a deep breath. "So, you hired this dick and he told you to keep your credit cards open even though they were in the hands of a woman who had just stolen millions worth of treasure and kicked you in the nuts? Good advice."

"She's being tailed by Interpol. What was she thinking?"

"How about that she needs money? I know that's a bit obvious but, what the hell, some fool's bound to fall for it. Boy, has she got your number. Where did your private investigator say she'd been last?" These were all questions I should have had the presence of mind to ask Noel, not that he'd tell me the truth.

"Paris. She racked up over 5,000 pounds at Chanel last month."

"Wouldn't want to miss out on the new fall line even on the run. Hell, Max. Did you finally cancel the cards?"

"A couple of weeks ago but I can't even afford to keep the dick going any longer now. I'm broke, Phoebe. I'm done."

"You're not done; we're not done. Has Noel been involved in stealing your personal assets, too?" Even saying his name aloud hurt. Seeing his damn sexy face this morning hurt worse, but I needed to exorcise all my devils any way I could.

He shook his head. "I don't know. Don't think so. Maggie handled our personal accounts. Noel was more keen on getting the artifacts and sourcing the art." He let out a groan. "We can't make it, Phoeb. We don't have the cash flow or the clients. The moment I went legal, all my connections dried up."

"So we'll build the gallery back up, this time with clients not willing to stash ancient stolen ethnography. We'll establish a new reputation and rise to the top of the antique carpet and textile world. We will not, I repeat, will not, go simpering into the twilight because a bunch of thieving bastards we thought loved us picked our pockets and smashed our hearts."

He gazed at me startled. "But—"

"No buts! I'm siphoning a little of my own savings into Baker & Mermaid. I'll cover Serena's salary, pay our creditors, and begin establishing a new reputation. We're not the same company, so of course we need different clientele." I took a few more gulps of coffee.

"Whatever cash you have in your savings isn't going to get us out of this mess."

"Maybe not right away but it will help in the short term. At least it's a plan, a way to keep moving forward. What else can we do?"

"Sell the gallery."

For a moment I couldn't speak, and when I did, it came out in an explosion. "Like hell! Never, ever, ever, will we sell Baker & Mermaid."

"I know it hurts, sweetheart, but we have to do what we have to do. I gave you half the gallery so we could run it together but we're about to go tits up. I may have a buyer. Bloke kind of just showed up when I needed him most, though he's a crafty bludger, maybe, but he offered cash. Bought the carpets, too. Cuts a hard deal. Says he's interested in our stock and will take over the gallery, as either an investor or a buyer. Jason Young's his name."

I placed my hands palms down on the table. "Ever think this buyer could be working for Sir Foxy? He'd buy us out in a nanosecond. Ever wonder why? Wonder what they're all after? Tell this Jason Young to take a frosty leap. Better yet, give me his number and let me tell him."

He shot me a quick, startled glance. "Phoebe, he's offering us a way out."

"Into what? No future? A life of half-assed jobs doing something you hate?" I flipped the lid to his coffee and passed it over. "Drink up and listen carefully, Max: We are not selling the gallery, not as in ever. You'd need my signature to authorize a sale and you're not getting it, understand?"

"If we sell, we can start fresh, get out from under this debt."

"Max, this gallery is my fresh start and I'm not letting it go. Thank you from the bottom of my heart for giving me half but we're partners now. I'll buy you out if I have to first."

"With what?"

"I'll find a way and my Max would never go down without a fight or let a few bills, a bastard son, and a tricky ex keep him down."

"Don't call Noel a bastard. I would have married his mom if I knew."

"I'm not referring to his parentage but to his behavior. And don't change the subject. The point is, we're going to get back on top and get our lives back."

His stricken eyes said it all. "I'm stonkered. I have nothing left."

"You've got me and I've got you. All you need is to get off the booze so we can get our business back on its feet. Don't go off doing fool things with your broken heart instead of your head."

"Sweetheart—"

"Don't sweetheart me! Look at yourself. You're so consumed by self-pity, you can't find your way out of a paper bag. You're vulnerable in heart and mind and circumstance, and drinking is making it worse. You need help, Max. Face it, you have an alcohol problem."

"I don't!" he slapped his fist against the table hard enough to send the knife skittering off the table edge. "I just like a drink once in a while."

I caught the knife in my hand before jumping up and flinging open the cupboards. "Like morning, noon, and night? What's this?" I pulled out a bottle of Scotch wedged in among the tomato and Worcester sauces. "Good for eggs, maybe? And what's this?" I opened up the cabinets over the sink to find a jumble of half-opened liquor bottles. "I suppose this is a food group, now?"

"Everybody's got liquor in their cupboards in case of company, Phoeb."

"In your case, liquor is the company." I began opening the bottles one by one and pouring the contents down the drain.

Max heaved himself out of his chair and stood by, watching as if I'd slit his wrist to let him bleed to death. I didn't look at him, couldn't look at him. What had he become? They did this to him.

"Where's the rest?" I asked when I finished the last mickey of gin.

"Don't have any more," came the muffled reply.

"Don't lie to me. It's bad enough you're hiding things, which you swore you'd never do again, but lying is more than I can take."

I heard a snorting noise and looked up to find him collapsed over the table, crying into his arms, my big, strong, brave, flamboyant, deteriorating godfather crying like a child. I wanted to join him, bawl my eyes out and rage against the cruelty of the human heart but, right then, fury drove me on.

I'd get Maggie for this. I didn't care whether I had to tear the universe apart molecule by molecule, she'd pay for the damage done to him. Bad enough to make a fool out of a man but to keep twisting the knife? Noel might have been his son but he never promised him what Maggie had. My brother's masterful forgeries and strategic planning, Noel's duplicitous thievery and underhanded charm—they'd pay, too, each individually in different ways, but Maggie infuriated me the most just then. She wanted Max destroyed even after the mai.

Why hadn't I drilled Noel for information while I had the chance? He might have let something slip. Maybe, at that very moment, an Interpol team was intercepting him at Heathrow, shackling him with handcuffs, and dragging him into custody. Maybe I'd get to spit in his face after all.

It took me almost an hour to comb the house, nabbing bottles from hiding places under beds, in drawers, in wastebaskets. I emptied them all while wincing at every dust-limned vacancy I encountered on the walls. Each one had once held a personal treasure. Max must have been selling off his possessions for months while I traipsed along thinking the world ran on magically lubricated hinges.

In his study, I found so many bottles, I needed a laundry basket to carry them to the bathroom sink. Once I finished draining the alcohol, I took the card for a cleaning service I found on his desk and made an appointment for a full house-cleaning. Just as I hung up from the cleaners, my glance caught a second business card slipped under a dirty coffee mug. I picked it up: Jason Young. *Rare Ethnographic Art. New York, New York.* Pocketing the card, I began gathering up the dirty clothes strewn over the upstairs floor and stuffing them into pillowcases, dragging them down to the foyer to be picked up by the linen service.

When I entered the kitchen over an hour later, I found Max still sitting at the table staring into space. "You know I can buy more juice, Phoebe," he said without meeting my eyes.

"I know that, Max, but I'm desperately hoping you won't. I'm praying you care enough about me to start pulling yourself together because I need you. You promised that you'd be my family, that you'd never let me down, and just once I want someone I care about to keep their damn promises. You can start by booking yourself into a detox facility until you regain your equilibrium. Do it for me. I need you back. I just don't want to do this alone."

Max said nothing, just sat there staring at his clasped hands. Suddenly weary, I made for the door. Stopping just on the kitchen threshold, I turned. "Max, do you know anything about a goddess-with-vultures kilim?"

"A goddess what?"

"That's what I thought."

❧ 7 ❧

"**M**r. Young, this is Phoebe McCabe." I sat in Max's office glued to the phone after spending most of the afternoon going through more piles of unattended paperwork. How many major auctions had we missed, how many prime opportunities to network with potential clients? We could never rebuild our reputation unless we got to these events, but attending international exhibitions and conferences took capital we didn't have.

I set all the invitations to art and textile auctions aside, topping the pile with a postcard invitation to the major exhibition of the year in Istanbul taking place that same week. I couldn't make voice contact with Jason Young no matter how many times I tried. Finally, I left a message on his answering machine.

"Whatever agreement you think you have with my partner, Max Baker, is null and void considering that a) you do not have my signature on whatever he signed—it was probably a napkin, anyway—and b) my godfather was probably inebriated at the time, making any quasi-contract void. Cease and desist from pursuing either me, Max Baker, or this gallery, or I will take legal measures." I hung up the phone and stared at the wall. Well, that sounded officious. It was frightening how quickly my old legalese kicked in.

284

I pulled Sir Rupert's card from my pocket and stared at it. He had jotted his private cell number in fountain pen across his gallery's thick creamy bond. Well, damn. I keyed in the number and waited.

"Sir Rupert Fox speaking."

"Phoebe McCabe here. Do you know of a Jason Young?"

He cleared his throat. "Possibly. Why do you ask?"

"You know why I'm asking, Rupert. If you want us to cooperate, start by telling me who he is and what he wants."

"In the spirit of reciprocation, isn't it time that you also shared information?"

I sighed. "Fine. My visitor assured me that he is not a monster and that he's worried about me. Touching, don't you think? He didn't get to say much else before I pulled the alarm."

"Are you certain?"

"Of course."

"And I am certain you are not being forthcoming with me, Phoebe. Nevertheless, in the spirit of cooperation, I will say that Jason Young is an alias. He goes by other names and identities but is most definitely connected to antiquities business. Use extreme caution when engaging with him. He will have ulterior motives."

"Who doesn't?"

He chuckled. "Very true. What are your dealings with him?"

"Not my dealings, but Max's. He purchased many of Max's prized carpets at bargain basement prices and even made an offer on the gallery."

"Which pieces?"

"Why does that matter?"

"I'm a collector. Naturally, I'm interested."

"You don't deal in textiles so I don't see why you would. Or," I paused, "are you now changing specialties?"

"No, I am still primarily interested in smaller items. In any case, I suggest you prevent Maxwell from engaging in any further dealings with Jason Young. If money is the issue, I will double any offer he makes, both on carpets and on the gallery itself. If you need a buyer or money, please give me first option. Has this Jason Young pretender been into the gallery?"

"Not to my knowledge, but since I don't know what he looks like, I really can't be certain."

"I know what he looks like. I will put a watch out for him."

"I didn't ask for that kind of help, just information."

I hung up shortly after, fearing I had just cracked the lid on Pandora's box. I couldn't squander time fretting over it, in any case. There were just too much completion for my anxiety just then.

After a few minutes of searching online for prime London detox facilities and jotting down numbers, I moved into researching goddesses with vultures, unearthing obscure references to Neolithic pagan beliefs. In the middle of skimming one of these entries, I looked up to see Serena at the door.

"Phoebe, there's a man in the gallery to see you, a Mr. Walker."

"I don't know a Mr. Walker. Is he interested in anything specific?"

"I don't think so. He just says he must speak with you. He looks a bit, let's say, shady. It's closing time but I wait until he leaves, yes?"

I turned to check the monitors but it seemed that my mysterious customer remained in the blind spot. He was either close to Rena's desk or on the opposite side by the storage room door.

I mustered a smile. "I'm sure it will be fine, Mama Serena. No need to babysit. Isn't Marco keeping his date with you tonight?"

"Yes. I meet him and girlfriend numero uno for an early supper and then see the dress rehearsal for his big play. This is all good. I will study what's between them, yes? See how long they'll stay together this time."

"Better not be late for that and you do look gorgeous."

"Because I'm wearing your gift, see?" She spun a little pirouette, flaunting the multihued, predominantly pink wrap I'd knit for her.

"Just tell this Mr. Walker I'll be down in a minute."

I checked the security monitor again but the man stayed out of view. Perhaps he understood exactly how these systems worked. Not a comforting thought. Still, the emergency switch was never far away.

Downstairs, moments later, I finally spied him turning one of the carved jade incense burners in his hands. First impression: medium height, muscular, fortyish, dressed in a navy pea jacket and jeans, with a bullet-bald head.

Serena hovered around the desk feigning random acts of tidying.

"It doesn't say Made in China, if that's what you're looking for," I said as I approached, keeping my tone light. "But since it's Ming dynasty, it could."

"Made in China for the collector types, then? I thought I saw one a lot like this in Camden market last week. Probably a knock-off. Fakes are getting increasingly clever."

"So are crooks. The real thing can be identified by certain features like the sculptor's initials inscribed on the bottom."

"Oh. Yes, I see that now. Still, I suppose even those can be fabricated, can't they?"

"They can, but that's the real deal. Are you looking for something in particular?"

The man carefully replaced the piece amid the violets and turned to face me. "I'm Agent Walker, Sam Walker, from the International Criminal Police Organization, commonly known as Interpol." He held up his badge —his photo plus the symbol of the globe over a gold sword and pair of scales.

"Interpol? Okay, I expected you sometime. Heard about my visitor, right?"

The man's face was arresting. A massive scar zipped across his shaven head from the right side of his forehead to his cheek, bisecting one eyebrow and hitching the eye into a perpetually half-shocked expression. Yet the sum total of the man wasn't unattractive as much as startling.

His mouth twisted into a wry right-side smile. "Old soccer injury," he remarked, pointing to the scar before holding out his hand. "You must be Ms. McCabe."

The East London accent enhanced the impression of a back-alley scrapper or retired rugby player rather than an international law agent. Soccer player, I reminded myself. I detected distinct musculature beneath the jacket. This was Interpol? He looked more like a bouncer from an East End club.

"Yes, that's me. All the Interpol agents I've met to date have worn dark suits, or at least the Canadian versions."

"What, as in *Men in Black*?"

"More like the *Matrix*."

He whistled between his teeth and smiled a twisted grin. "My boss wears a suit but I like your uniform idea better. Must put the request in at head office for full leather trench coats to enhance our sartorial reputation."

"That's the least you could do. You came to ask me about Noel Halloran, right?"

"I did, Ms. McCabe. I'm sure you are aware that both you and Max Baker have been persons of interest for some time regarding the disappearance of millions of pounds worth of stolen antiquities. We understand your relationship with the suspects so we weren't surprised when this one turned up, a former boyfriend, I understand?"

"You understand wrong. Halloran and I were never in a relationship. I hardly knew the man. And you must also be aware that Max Baker and I are cooperating fully with the authorities. After all, I did sound the alarm."

"That you did."

"I am hiding nothing."

"So I understand."

I plunged my hands into my pocket. "Good, because I witnessed the event under investigation but wasn't involved in it, as I've said to various authorities countless times. I was as duped as Adrian Wyndridge, maybe more so. I was there looking for my errant brother and now no one wants to bring those bastards to justice more than we do."

"I'm just wondering why Halloran paid you a visit today. What did he say to you?"

"A lot of personal nonsense like that he and my brother care about us and they're not the monsters I think they are, blah blah. Said he could explain everything but didn't have the time. Said my brother couldn't come to see me himself but they wanted to make sure I was all right."

"And what did you say?"

"I called him a bunch of names, none of them brilliant, by the way." For reasons I couldn't understand, I was loath to say anything about the enigmatic Goddess kilim. "I also ranted at him for putting me something that attracts all kinds of criminal types. Then I rang the alarm."

"I understand the impetus for that, certainly, but we really could have used more information."

"So, you'd rather I hadn't called the police but tried to sit him down and grill him for incriminatory details he'd never reveal? Maybe offer him a coffee? He's not stupid, Agent Walker. He wouldn't tell me anything."

"And yet, had you kept him talking while alerting us covertly, we may have apprehended him."

"Sorry. That didn't occur to me. I admit I'm rather new at this. Is there a course I could take or something? Have you apprehended him yet?"

"A tall man in a fake mustache and a broad hat? No. I'm sure he dispatched that disguise quickly and travels under an assumed name and false passport. He'd have to or he'd never get this far."

"But he's very tall, at least six feet four."

"That's not unusual."

"He also has a multiethnic genetic blend—part Australian Aboriginal, part European kaleidoscopic mix, which means he could adapt to nearly any nationality. Halloran is his paternal grandmother's maiden name, by the way. He refused to take Max's. Oh, I get your point." I shrugged. "I don't see what else I can tell you."

"Why didn't Halloran attempt to see his father, too?"

"My godfather's been drinking too much. Noel hinted that he didn't think reaching out to him was such a good idea under the circumstances and I'd say he was right."

"And your brother?"

"What do you mean?"

"Halloran didn't say anything more about him?"

"Only that he couldn't come see me himself but he didn't specify why."

"But you haven't heard from your brother since the incident?"

"No. I haven't heard from him in months."

He turned and began strolling around the gallery, studying each of our carpets and artifacts like a casual browser rather than an investigator on the prowl.

I caught Serena's eye and nodded for her to leave. She made a face, picked up her bag, and headed for the door.

"I want the three of them captured, too—no exceptions. Do you think I'm hiding one of them behind a carpet?" I followed after him.

"Not necessarily. If Halloran contacted you, maybe your brother will next."

"If he does, you'll be the first to know."

He peered down at the Kenyan beaded loin cloth we kept in a glass inset embedded in one of the tables. "I don't understand why Halloran would come for the sole reason of proclaiming his innocence to you. A bit risky, don't you think?"

"I thought that, too. Besides, he's not innocent no matter which way you look at it. Still, he was only here for a few minutes and never left my sight except when I rang the alarm."

I heard a click-click-click on the glass at the front door and turned to see Serena waving on the other side. Dusk had already fallen behind her and she was making little throat-slitting motions. *I'm fine. Go away.* I mouthed. Reluctantly, she turned and left. When I turned back to Walker, he was watching me.

"You were present when they escaped with the treasure, I understand."

"Yes. They left us in the cave half-dead. Toby was in the background somewhere playing mastermind but I hadn't had contact with him or seen him in over a year. He had been missing just before the heist. I had no idea he was behind this at first."

"And even though he's your brother, you want to see him in jail?"

Oh, I got it: this was a loyalty test. "Absolutely. My brilliant missing brother infiltrated his lover's estate long enough to arrange fabrication of reproductions for a fortune's worth of jewels and artifacts and stage it so that Adrian Wyndridge wouldn't be the wiser. He plotted with Maggie and Noel to escape with the real treasure the night Max and I almost died— Tobias McCabe, my brother, thief, mastermind, and monster, has to pay for what he's done."

Walker whistled between his teeth. "And you're pissed."

"He left my poor sick dad never knowing whether his son lived or died, which may have contributed to his death. His disappearance certainly caused his stroke so, yeah, I'm pissed, very, very pissed."

"And you feel the same way about Halloran?"

"Yes, minus the sibling love."

He smirked. "So, it's revenge you're after?"

"It's justice I'm after, Agent Walker. I want the three of them brought to their knees. I want them to go to jail, pay the price of deception, betrayal, and greed."

He held up his hands. "Okay, you're very convincing, Ms. McCabe. Just checking to see if you're still on the right team."

"I am, I assure you. Will you keep me informed about the investigation? Oh, and by the way, I've heard word that Halloran has fenced some of the gold to a Mexican museum."

"Did he tell you that or Sir Rupert Fox?"

I stared at him. "Are you following me, too?"

"Of course and Sir Rupert has always been on our radar."

"What is Interpol doing, anyway, besides waiting and watching and tailing innocent people? We've heard nothing from you guys in months. Max hired a private investigator who pegged Maggie's last known location somewhere in Paris, probably near a Chanel atelier. What have you done?"

"We're on the case, Ms. McCabe and, up until now, the trail has gone cold. Now the thieves are on the move and much more likely to leave a trail. Are you certain Halloran didn't say anything else or have time in the gallery alone?"

"Positive."

"And nothing else irregular has occurred to your knowledge?"

I thought of my magically refilling bank account. "No, nothing. But listen, I want to be there when you bring them in. This is personal for me. I need to be part of the operation in some way."

His mouth crooked into that diagonal grin, maybe just the tiniest bit patronizing. "Not possible, I'm afraid. Standard procedure. Best to stay out of that part of the operation, Ms. McCabe. It's dangerous on multiple fronts, the least of which is tracking a fortune of jewels and artifacts across Europe with a bunch of ruthless thugs on its heels. Besides, emotions as high as yours can throw a spanner in the works of any investigation. A cool head must prevail in these matters or somebody's going to end up dead."

"Are you trying to frighten me?"

"Hope so. You already know you're being followed, yet you're not anxious?"

His eyes were an unsettling bleached blue, like denim parched under the desert sun. "I'm uneasy, sure."

"Besides us, who are certainly no risk to you, do you have any idea who else might be keeping an eye on you?"

"Maybe every two-bit scumbag who thinks we can lead him to the missing treasure. I've seen four, maybe five, different people stalk me. How do I make them stop? I don't have the loot, have never had it."

"You've been showing a replica of a necklace around. That's a bit like waving a red flag, don't you think?"

Now the patronization was unmistakable. "That wasn't my idea. Max started making the rounds without me knowing, and when I found out how he'd been threatening every dealer along the way, I tried to intervene." I fingered the stitch markers in my pockets. For some reason, I also found a pair of thread snippers in there, too.

"Let's just say that wasn't wise. You're already on the radar."

Breathing out slowly, I nodded. "It seemed the only way I could alleviate a bad situation."

"By making it worse? I'll take that necklace replica, if you don't mind. It will help our investigation."

I shrugged. "Sure. It's in my desk drawer. I'll get it for you."

Moments later, I poured the phony jewels into Walker's hand, amazed at how much it hurt to relinquish that little memento.

Walker pocketed it without comment. "Thank you. Here's my cell number." He passed me a card. "Put it on speed-dial in case Halloran reappears. Don't sound the alarm, send me a message on the sly and we'll take it from there, if you can, but don't do anything that will jeopardize your safety. You don't know what these bastards are capable of."

"Oh, I do."

"We'll be in touch."

I followed him to the door, pocketing the card. "Wait, how can I help this investigation besides alerting Interpol?"

"Stay vigilant. Remain in close contact with me at all times. Don't go out after dark alone—that sort of thing. Common sense, really. If anything suspicious happens, contact me ASAP. Both you and your godfather are key to this investigation. Your presence is already drawing them out, making them careless."

"In the meantime, I'm supposed to stand around and look bait-like?"

He smiled. "That shouldn't be too hard. You seem good at attracting all the wrong kind of attention."

I secured the door behind him and watched as he strode out of sight. Don't take chances? Everything I did these days was one big roll of the dice. Exhausted, I shut off the gallery lights and retired upstairs for the night.

8

Too tired to think, I headed for bed but, before turning in, I opened the door to the hall and padded down to Max's office in my bare feet. Every night I checked the security panel before bed.

Max had expanded the system when I moved in so that motion sensors had been installed in key areas of my flat. By checking the panel, I could visually scan the monitors to ensure that the perimeter sensors were activated and that the alarms were set to alert the police station in case of a breach. This electronically tucked me in for the night. Living alone on top of thousands of pounds of ethnographic inventory had its perils, as if I didn't bring enough of my own into the mix.

Tonight the system lights all glowed green, happily activated against possible threats. The monitors revealed the gallery hanging dark and still. Even the sidewalk outside lay empty. I yawned.

On the way down the hall towards my flat, I paused by the stairs, staring down into the deep shadows pooling around my suspended office. A bit of street and display light limned the edges of the landing glass like a halo. Still, I'd forgo my usual solitary communion with the textiles that night. The darkness didn't seem quite so friendly.

I fell into bed wired, afraid I'd never still my mind. Noel. Max. Interpol. Sir Foxy. Damn, damn, damn. Just when I thought I'd never get to sleep, something woke me. I blinked into the darkness, befuddled. A red light pulsed from the other side of the room. Not my digital clock. That was green, so what was that blinking?

The motion detector! I jolted upright. That didn't make sense. Why wasn't the alarm ringing? Nobody could move around the premises without setting off a God-awful ruckus. It would arouse the neighborhood until manually switched off. So, whoever was moving around had to be familiar enough with the system to deactivate the alarm. Max, maybe Noel.

But why would Max enter the gallery in the middle of the night? I could think of two possibilities, neither of them likely: He decided to pilfer the inventory to pay bills or he was too drunk to make it home and decided to camp out in the office. Noel, on the other hand, was capable of anything, and if Foxy was right about his agenda, it made perfect sense. It had to be Noel. He knew how to enter the gallery after hours and override the codes. Maybe he was stashing jewels on the premises that very minute.

I stood up, keening my senses into the darkness. It was deathly silent. No sound, no footsteps, no creak of doors opening around my tiny flat. He had to be downstairs. I retrieved my iPhone from the bureau and crept out of my bedroom, crossing the sitting room to the hall door. I needed to see what he was up to before confronting him, maybe even catch him in the act. In any case, I needed to stick my nose outside the safety of my apartment and head for the office.

For once, I wished I had a gun. Sometimes Maggie's advice made sense.

I entertained myself with nonsense thoughts while zipping down the hall, dashing past the stairs and risking a quick glance down to the depths below. Reaching the office, I lowered myself into Max's chair without eliciting so much as a squeak and stared at the monitors. Something moved in the storeroom. I held my breath as the camera followed a dark figure raking a flashlight across the shelves. What was he up to down there? Either hiding something or seeking something and damn him all to hell either way.

I picked up Walker's card, which I'd left on the desk earlier and tapped in the number. After an excruciating number of rings, he picked up, his voice muffled. "Yes?"

"Phoebe McCabe here. I have an intruder in my storeroom. No alarm went off. I think it's Noel."

"Where are you?"

"In the office upstairs."

"Stay put. I'm on my way." He hung up.

As if I'd just sit there while Noel Halloran messed with my gallery the way he did with my life. Pocketing my cell, I crept silently down the stairs. Once on the gallery floor, I could see the flashlight beam sweeping the storeroom shelves. I'd surprise him, make him talk, explain whatever he had intended to say earlier, and catch it all on security camera. I wouldn't allow my emotions to rule my head this time.

I reached the storeroom door ready to call out his name and froze. The light had flicked off. Stilling my breathing, I listened into the darkness and sensed it listening back. "Noel?" I ventured.

No answer, just that full, tense silence. Somehow I knew the intruder wasn't him. I turned, thinking I'd spring for the safety of my apartment, but something hit me from behind and knocked me to the floor.

9

I stood with my kimono thrown over my nightshirt answering questions as the police and Walker combed the premises.

"We could call an ambulance," Officer Howell said again.

"I'm just winded," I repeated, rubbing my chin where it hit the floor. "He knocked me down and exited the building, I said."

"And you didn't get a good look at him?" the officer asked. Her tone remained courteous and professional with just the right touch of sternness.

"No."

"And yet you decided to confront him by yourself?" But she was no fool.

"I thought I knew him."

"You believed you knew a possible burglar?"

"I didn't think he was a burglar exactly but I thought that he might be a man who used to work here."

"Accosting an intruder under any circumstance is not advised," she told me, "even if you think you recognize the perpetrator." Something about her manner made me think she was a rookie on one of her first assignments but she planned to go places.

"The alarm wasn't tripped," I explained again. "And I called Agent Walker immediately."

"And you are certain nothing was taken?"

"As certain as I can be. My business partner, Max Baker, is on his way over now and he knows the storeroom inventory better than I."

No sooner had I uttered those words when in dashed Max, sleep-tousled and still in his bedroom slippers, dark circles smudging his eyes. I could just see his old Bentley illegally parked outside. A whiff of stale alcohol followed him around.

"Phoebe! Are you okay?" He hugged me against him before I could reply. "Officer, have you caught the suspect yet? What was taken?" he said over my head. "Phoebe?"

I pushed myself away. "I'm fine, Max, and we don't know if anything was taken. I can't tell—certainly nothing from the main floor. The intruder spent time in the storeroom. I thought it might be somebody we knew."

He looked at me, shocked. "Maggie? Noel?"

"Maybe."

"You sure it wasn't a faulty alarm like what went off yesterday?"

"That wasn't a faulty alarm, Max. That was me getting nervous because a suspicious-looking guy dropped by. A little trigger-happy, that's all. This is different."

Max turned to look towards the back of the gallery where two other officers and Walker still inspected the space. He gave my shoulder a quick squeeze before dashing towards them.

"Mr. Baker," Officer Howell called. "I'd like to ask you a few questions first."

As she briskly took after him, I sagged against the center table. It had been a damn long night. Rest ended seconds later when Agent Walker strode up to me, his scarred face so tense, it was as if leather had been stretched across bone. "I told you to stay put, Ms. McCabe."

I tested my chin again with my index finger. Probably bruised. "I thought it was Noel back again and that I could get him to talk."

"I didn't suggest that you risk your safety."

"I wasn't hurt, okay?

"No, it is not okay. Had you done as I requested, I could have spread a net around the gallery and caught the intruder on the premises."

I nodded. "Mea culpa and all that."

"I'll be back to continue this later. Excuse me a moment." With that, he turned towards the storeroom.

"Wait."

He paused.

"Whatever you do, please don't let Max know that Noel came here yesterday."

Walker cleared his throat. "Ms. McCabe, as a co-owner of this gallery, Mr. Baker is a key component in this investigation and—"

"I don't care. He's not well. Leave him alone."

Without a word, he turned and sauntered towards the storeroom, leaving me hanging around like a third shoe. I took that opportunity to dash upstairs to dress. Throwing on an art-knit sweater and jeans, I was back down in the gallery just as Howell finished tapping notes into her tablet. Her team was already exiting the gallery carrying bags of equipment.

"I believe we're done here for the moment, Ms. McCabe. I suggest you change the codes immediately. Officer Singh has received a list of staff from Mr. Baker and will be questioning them in due time, as well as reviewing a copy of your security footage. In the event that you discover something missing, by all means give us a call citing that incident number in the left-hand corner." She passed me a sheet of paper. "Illegal entries and thefts are still within our jurisdiction, Ms. McCabe. Please remember that." She left, her team traipsing after, one nodding his head as he passed.

Clearly she wasn't thrilled that Interpol infringed on her turf. Metro handled local crime and Interpol networked with all agencies for the international felonies. Art theft was almost always international, while break and entry would inevitably be local. Tricky.

After locking the door behind Metro, I joined Max and Walker out back. Thankfully, Sunday morning meant the gallery would stay closed that day. "Well?"

Max looked up from counting boxes and shook his head. "Nothing missing." He pointed to the safe gaping open. "I even checked in there—not that I keep anything of value there since Maggie fleeced me."

Walker poked his shiny head up from under the table. "Who operates your security system?"

"Diamond and Dew, a major firm, as you know," Max said, rubbing his eyes. He almost sounded like his old self, though definitely a short-tempered version.

"I know they're legitimate and bond their staff, but they also encrypt codes through their phone system. Every time the alarm trips, a message is sent to their server pinning the exact time of the break-in as well as who the code was attributed to. Do you each use unique codes?"

I looked at Max.

"I gave you Maggie's old code," he told me.

"Great." Codes were the last thing I thought about when I arrived at the gallery months ago.

"Was it the same system you had operating while your son worked here?" Walker asked.

"What kind of a fool question is that?" Max barked. "Of course it was. What are you getting at?"

"I'm covering all the bases, Mr. Baker. Some crackerjack who knows what he's doing might be able to break the system, but let's assume for now that someone used one of your codes. That usually means somebody who knows it."

"Maybe it was Serena," Max said. "She's as honest as they come but maybe she let hers slip to that twit of a son."

"No way," I said. "But why would anyone enter the gallery and take nothing? It doesn't make sense."

"Maybe they were staking the place out, planning on making a return visit," said Max.

Walker shook his head. "That wouldn't be clever, would it? May as well post their intentions on Twitter. You'll need to change the system. I can recommend a company that uses state-of-the-art technology. Even if the audible alarm isn't tripped, a silent warning gets posted to the depot. I'd like to look around further, if you don't mind."

"We do mind," Max growled. "And who the hell are you to sniff around our place, anyway? This isn't your jurisdiction! Metro is handling this. Get a warrant."

"Max!" I shot him a warning. "We're cooperating with Interpol, remember?" And to Walker I added. "Of course you may look around. Where do you want to start?"

"Your security system. Metro took a copy of your footage but I'd like to take a look myself."

"It's upstairs. I'll show you."

"Thanks for not telling him about Noel's visit. You see what I mean by his mood," I said on the way upstairs to the office. "He's finding everything a bit of a struggle lately and I don't want him getting hurt."

"Right. Interviewing him has been like dancing on hot coals. Sure he's not hiding something?"

"He's not, at least not in the way you mean," I assured him. "He's getting pangs of paternal remorse, that's all. Don't worry. I'll make sure he cooperates."

As if I could.

I left Walker in the office and rejoined Max in the storeroom.

"Max, why are you blocking Interpol's investigation? So what if he checks the premises or reviews our security records? We have nothing to hide do we?"

Max leaned over the table. "Look Phoebe, the fewer people we've got mucking around, the better."

"Why?"

"Just because."

"That's not an answer."

He straightened. "Supposing Noel or Toby do get in touch with one of us?"

I waited. "And?"

"And, do you really think we're going to turn in our own flesh and blood?"

"Damn right. Don't go turning to mush on me. They're criminals."

Max shrugged. "So was I a year ago, remember? Events changed me. Maybe they've changed, too."

"How does that matter? They stole from Adrian, stole from you."

"Look, Phoebe, Noel can take what he wants—he's my son. I owe him, and who says Toby's even involved in this? That's just conjecture. Nobody's seen him—but Maggie needs her pretty little neck throttled. Her, I can turn in, no problem."

"Okay," I threw up my hands. "Let's continue this discussion upstairs. I need coffee. I'm obviously suffering from auditory hallucinations."

I managed to steer him upstairs and into my kitchen, nodding at Walker perched in the office in passing. As I plugged in the kettle and filled the coffee basket, it occurred to me that Walker probably witnessed our discussion in the storeroom from the security cam. Damn.

"Max," I said carefully, keeping my voice calm. "You've got to get a grip. If they think you're hiding something, or might aid Noel in any way, you'll be culpable, could even go to jail as an accessory to a crime. You're damn lucky Adrian didn't press charges in Bermuda as it was."

He rubbed his eyes. "I don't care."

"Well, I do, damn it!" I banged the coffee tin on the counter. I leaned there, my fists clenched so tightly my knuckles whitened. "Since when did you cross Noel off our most wanted list?"

"Noel's my son," he muttered, not meeting my eyes. "Hell knows I've been a rotten father to him. I owe him."

"He's an adult responsible for his own actions. Your parenting has nothing to do with it."

"So, we're family, that's what I'm saying. We don't go after family."

I slapped one hand against my forehead. "How could you forget what happened less than a year ago when your son got away with a fortune's worth of treasure and left us flopping around that cave like a couple of beached tuna? And he can't 'take what he wants' if it isn't his."

"He's my boy," Max mumbled, choking up.

"Has he been to see you, is that it?"

"Hell, no, but I wish he would."

Turning back to the counter, I exhaled my relief while pouring water over the coffee press. "I'm going after the three of them and I don't care whose DNA is involved."

"Can't you forgive them?"

"No. Who else has a code to our security system?"

He didn't respond.

I placed the brew things onto the table, grabbed the sugar and milk, and sat down across from him, my eyes never leaving his face. "Max?"

He kept his gaze on the mug. "Me and you and Rena. That's it."

"Not Noel?"

Max's eyes met mine. "Noel and I shared a code. You don't think he broke in last night?"

"Of course not." I'd already told him that. Besides, tonight's intruder had been focused on finding something, shoving me to the ground the way you'd kick aside a rabid dog. Noel would never do that. "Noel would have said something or tried to seduce me or some nonsense."

"Yes, he would. He cares about you," Max said, staring down at his mug. "Anyway, if it's my code he used to get in last night, I'll just say it was me that came in and I was plastered or something."

"Max, *think*: The camera recorded last night's activities. They may not be able to identify the intruder from those tapes but they can tell height and body shape. Who knows the security system better than Noel? He's not going to get caught on camera. The police already have a copy of the security tape and Walker's reviewing it now. Did you hear me say it couldn't be Noel?"

"Well, then, that's a good thing," he said, brightening.

I shook my head. My godfather confused. How could I confess to him that his son had paid me a visit yesterday or about the magic refilling bank account? I'd never felt so alone in all my life.

I poured coffee into two mugs, slid one over to him, and attacked mine with a couple of scalding sips. "It's not a good thing," I said wearily. "Nothing's a good thing anymore."

"Don't help the cops, Phoebe," Max said. "Please."

"I know what side I'm on, Max. I thought you did, too."

A knock on the door down the hall interrupted us. "Come in," I called. When Walker entered moments later, I held my mug up. "Can I offer you a coffee, officer? Oh, wait. You're an agent, not an officer. Sorry. I forgot my law enforcement nomenclature."

"Sam is fine. 'Agent Walker' makes me sound a bit like one of those computer viruses making the rounds."

"Fits," Max said under his breath.

Walker ignored him. "Thanks for the offer but I'll catch one later. Just wanted to ask if you would call in to Diamond and Dew to request the entry and exit stats. I could get it from Metro only after a bit of paperwork. This would be faster."

"Sure."

Max refused to look at him.

I pulled my phone from my pocket and pressed the speed dial for the security depot number and waited. In a moment I had given my password and was speaking with a dispatcher. When I finished, I laid the phone on the table and announced. "No alarms, silent or otherwise, went to Diamond and Dew last night, but they have a report of activation and deactivation times being faxed over now. The report will show which employee number touched the system last night, but apparently only we have the names associated with the employee number." I turned to Agent Walker. "Make sense?"

"It does. Do you have a list of the code assignations?"

Max nodded. "I gave them to Metro. Why should you get one?"

"I saw a copy on top of the desk. The fax from the depot should come in momentarily, too," I told him.

He nodded. "Thanks. I'll return to the office, then." In a second he was gone.

"What's with that face of his, anyway?" Max remarked after he'd left.

"He said it was a soccer injury."

"Looks like someone tried to split his melon open with a hatchet."

"Does it matter?"

Suddenly Max reached across the table and clutched my hand. "Don't do this, Phoebe. Let the cops do what they do. Don't help them."

I wrenched away my hand. "When I came to London, it was with the understanding that we would track down the trio together. Don't waffle on me. Stay the course."

"This is our blood we're talking about," Max said. "That's got to account for something."

I looked up to find Walker standing in the doorway. "Give us some privacy, okay?"

"My apologies. The fax came in and I knew you'd find it interesting."

He passed me the page. A few seconds later, I looked up at Max. "Who is employee 33?"

"You," Max replied.

"We shared a code? Okay, so it was me who activated the alarm at the regular time last night but employee number 45 deactivated the system at 2:45. And employee 45 is?"

Max dug his fingers into his wild gray hair. I couldn't hear his mumbled response.

"Pardon?"

"Me and Noel."

"You kept the same code after he left? Okay, but neither you nor Noel were in here tonight so now we have to figure out who used that code. Maybe you let it slip to someone?"

"I'd never do that." Yet, by the way he buried his head in his arms, I knew even he didn't believe that.

"What are the next steps, Walker?" I said, looking at him. Inside I felt glued together with adhesive and fairy dust but there was no way I was going to come undone.

"I'll continue reviewing the security backups. I see you keep them for two weeks before they get overwritten—bad move—but at least that's a place to start. And I think I'll take you up on the coffee offer, if you don't mind."

"She does mind," Max grumbled through his hands. "Why don't you just bugger off and leave us in peace?"

"Right," I countered brightly. "I'll make a new batch and bring it to you."

"Much appreciated." The agent got the message and quickly exited again.

Meanwhile, Max remained sagged into his forearms, as if all the air had escaped him. I sprang from my chair and threw my arms around his shoulders. "Max, I love you, no matter how cantankerous and snarly you get. You're all I've got left. I'm asking you, begging you, to book into a facility and let me take over around here for a while. Serena can help. She used to run a gallery, remember? You've been making bad decisions, doing things under the influence, not thinking straight. Hell, you tried to sell the gallery to that Jason Young creep and practically gave away your favorite carpets. It has to stop. There's no shame in needing help. You've been stonkered, as you say. Give yourself time to heal. Do it for me."

20 minutes later, he still hadn't promised me a thing but he seemed shaken enough to give it some thought.

By the time I returned to the office down the hall, fresh coffee in hand,

I found Sam Walker still glued to the monitor. "Look at this," he said, not looking up.

I joined him on the edge of the desk. "What are you doing?"

"Replaying the security footage back to where the drive overwrote itself a couple of weeks ago. You should keep fresh drives on hand and store the old, at least until you review them all. I gather you haven't checked these in a while."

"I didn't think I had to," I said miserably. Since the alarm hadn't gone off, why would I? "What have you found?"

"Take a look."

I peered at the monitor as he rewound to a date marked two weeks earlier. A dark figure could be seen crossing the gallery to the storeroom. He spun the replay further back until that same figure was now inside the storeroom on the same night. I swallowed and straightened, unconsciously gripping my stomach. "Somebody's been in here before?"

"Same somebody, is my guess. At least once, maybe more, but I can't tell because the disk gets recorded over every two weeks. I'll review all the old reports from Diamond and Dew to see how many times this blighter's been entering the gallery."

While I slept upstairs, somebody had been prowling around downstairs. I felt like I'd swallowed an electric fan. "Yes, please."

"You request them and I'll get right on it. Otherwise, I'll need to go through New Scotland Yard to get clearance, which takes too much time."

I nodded.

"This guy look familiar to you?"

"No," I said in a small voice.

"Medium height—maybe five ten—dressed in a black track suit with a ski mask. Gloved. Yeah, he's probably not wearing his usual threads. Again, he doesn't take anything, just studies the place. A bit freakish that but since the cameras don't reach the far corners on either side of the door, you can't see everything he does. Otherwise, it's like he's casing the place. You should get on to changing those codes, ASAP, and get a locksmith over here to change anything with a keyed entry, too. Otherwise, I'd have said leave everything as is and we'll stake it out to catch the perp but it's too late now."

"Right."

"How are you holding up?"

"Fine," I lied. Some stranger had been crawling all over my gallery while I slept and my godfather was falling apart. How good does it get?

And then Walker's cell rang. He held it pressed to his ear, listening intently, before turning to me. "It's New Scotland Yard. A body matching our intruder's description has just been found in a dumpster behind Sheffield Terrace."

❧ 10 ❧

Imagining Noel or Toby dead in the morgue hit like I'd been sucker punched. It didn't need to make sense to leave me reeling. It could have been either one.

Later, I endured Scotland Yard's excruciatingly polite questions as Walker sat in. At times, it almost seemed as though they considered me a suspect. Maybe they sensed I was hiding something and who could blame them? So far, I'd failed to mention the Anatolian Vulture Goddess let alone my magic bank account. Then, in the midst of the interrogation, in came the identification of the dead man as Fred Haze, aka Jason Young. I stared dumbfounded when Walker told me the news.

"Do you know him?" he asked.

"A Jason Young tried to buy the gallery from Max a couple of days ago, and I tried to phone him since to tell him to bugger off but he never got back to me," I said. "I never met him."

"Looks like he was looking for something, since the same bloke's been sniffing around in the gallery more than once." Walker fixed his chill blue eyes on my face.

"I have no idea what he was looking for, I swear," I said, my voice quivering with exhaustion. It's like the last bit of news had ripped away all the scaffolding that had been propping me up for days. "Look, I'm exhausted. Can I just go home now? I have nothing left to say."

Walker gave me a lift home, and though he wanted to come in and probably grill me further, I practically shut the door in his face. After setting the security system, I trudged towards the stairs. My cell rang before I reached the landing.

"Hello, Phoebe. Rupert Fox here. Is this a secure line?"

I gripped the railing. "It's my cell number, Rupert. You know how secure those aren't."

"As I feared. May I drop by for a moment?"

I was so weary, I wanted to melt into the stairs. "Yes, but make it short."

"I'll be there directly."

A black car dropped him off moments later, as if he had been circling the gallery waiting to pounce. After locking the gallery door behind him, I led him upstairs to my flat. Yes, it felt like I was opening the cookie jar to a ravenous rat but I saw no other way to ensure privacy.

He studied my decor in open curiosity. "I do approve. Very colorful and eclectic. Ah, and you are a knitter, I see."

He picked a ball of yarn from a basket on the floor and studied the label. "Hand-dyed silk in a perfect shade of orchid. How exquisite. My late wife would have loved this. As for me, I find yellow to be the most heavenly hue with which to knit. And lime, I do adore lime."

I couldn't process that just then. "Please sit." I indicated one of my two tapestry upholstered chairs. *And take your hand off my balls.*

He carefully returned the yarn to its nest. "It may surprise you to learn that I knit also," he said, lowering himself among the green vining motifs. "Mostly jumpers, though I have been known to do the occasional pair of argyle socks. In fact," he lifted his gray gabardine pant leg a few inches to reveal a flash of sock knit in fine-gauge gray, blue, and yellow. "Quite a feat, even if I do say so myself. These are remarkably comfy. I prefer Fair Isle in a multitude of colors so diverse I am tempted to use crewel floss."

"Did you really come here to discuss the textile arts?" The topic might be a favorite of mine, but I preferred the discourse some other time with some other person.

"I'm merely establishing a bond."

"I'm not in the mood."

I'm sure his ear tufts wiggled when he sighed. "Very well, onto business. I understand you had a visitor last night and the chap wound up murdered."

"And you must know the identity of that visitor so don't play games." I sat down across from him and picked up my mindless knitting project, an unborn wrap I kept on hand as a pacifier—simply, mindless. Intarsia was out of the question at the moment. "So, did you kill Jason Young?"

"My dear, I am many things, but a murderer isn't one of them. What would be my motive? Oh, my, but watching you knit causes my fingers to itch so. I don't suppose you have a spare project I might work on for a few rows? Maybe a nice sock? I can follow any pattern, even work lace."

"I don't follow patterns and I don't do socks." I stabbed my needle into a seed stitch and glowered across at him. "How do I know you didn't kill him?"

"Why would I? I did have him followed, it's true, and knew the chap paid an unauthorized visit to your gallery in the wee hours more than once, but I am embarrassed to say that last night my hireling refused to wait outside the gallery until he emerged. Indomitable behavior, not in the least bit professional. Let us just say that I henceforth relieved him of his duties. As a result, I have only just heard—and by just, I mean 45 minutes ago—that this Jason ended up in the undignified position of being quite dead in a dumpster. Shot, I understand, which is vastly better than being strangled or garroted, though the end result is the same." HIs eyes rolled towards the ceiling. "May the final punctuation of my life's sentence be less ignoble. Nevertheless, his demise is alarming. Matters are accelerating, my dear, as I feared they would. I do hope you are taking this very seriously and are reconsidering my offer."

I picked up a length of thick crimson cashmere. "Who killed him if not you?"

"Ah, there's the rub. My informant told me that our Mr. Young—what a tiresome name; surely he could have envisioned a more interesting alias—was himself being tailed by an undisclosed interest."

I paused, the red yarn looping around my hand as if my fingers were slashed and bleeding.

"I would choose a different hue for that row, maybe something in the magenta line? I fear a subtle clash."

"A subtle clash is an oxymoron. Why would this pseudo-Jason Young infiltrate my gallery repeatedly?"

"I would hasten to say he was either looking for something or planting something."

"But what?"

"I suspect you may have a clue to that, my dear. Why not tell me so I can assist you properly?"

I knit furiously for several stitches. "Isn't the missing Bermuda treasure what they're all after?"

"No, in fact, which is what I am attempting to say, albeit with perhaps too gentle a hand. I have reason to believe they may be seeking another cache and, if you don't yet possess the clues as to what it is and where it's been hidden, you had best hasten to educate yourself."

My project fell to my lap.

"I am convinced the clue lies in this building. Let us comb the premises together this very minute," he continued.

"Absolutely not."

He rose, smoothing his trousers down over his beefy legs. Eye to eye, he wasn't much taller than I. "Very well then, I see this meeting is at an end. Such a shame. Now, finish your row and I will show myself out."

I got to my feet and hastened after him. "You will not show yourself out. I'll escort you to the door."

"Very well," he sighed.

At the front door, he turned to face me. "Phoebe, I know you don't trust me and, naturally, I do understand why, but let me repeat that I mean you no harm, nor Maxwell, for that matter. I simply have little patience with drunkards in general, hence my abrasive and unforgiving nature around the man. My father lapsed into drink in his later years and such behavior dredges up unfortunate memories."

"Max is going to get help."

"I do hope so." He glanced towards his shoes, old-fashioned brogues as black and shiny as a beetle's back. "If you do successfully convince him to enter a detox facility—detox is such an unfortunate word—may I recommend the Dayton Fields clinic? It has an excellent reputation on all counts and requires a full 28 days' residency commitment."

"Dayton Fields. I'll remember that."

"Good, good. Let me also offer another small piece of advice: Avoid saying anything of note over the phone. Your lines are tapped and I'm guessing by three or four interests."

"Including you, I suppose?"

"Of course. May I recommend that all conversations of a sensitive nature be initiated using this." He passed me a phone. "Naturally, I took the liberty of keying in my own number should you ever wish to chat."

I turned the Android over in my hand. "You actually expect me to give you the sole opportunity to eavesdrop on my private conversations?"

He smiled. "I assure you the phone is encrypted and nearly impossible to trace, not to mention top drawer in all respects. You could use it as our secure line."

"If it's not secure from you, it's not secure. Besides, I have a smart phone of my own."

"Phones are never as smart as you think. Good day to you." He nodded once and stepped out the door to stride across the sidewalk to a waiting black sedan.

Back in my flat, I ripped out the crimson rows I had slashed across my wrap and wound a ball of magenta to add in at some point. I fell asleep on the couch with the knitting curled on my chest like a fibery cat, dreaming of death and destruction with all the men I loved/hated playing starring roles.

I awoke with a jolt hours later. Daylight had bled from the room, leaving the lounge stained in shadows. I quickly flicked on the lamp, breathing easier once the color seeped back to the carpets, the weavings, the yarn. Hell, was I going to be afraid of the dark now? The locks had been changed, the security codes renewed, with everybody and everything on high alert. Surely I was safe?

My personal cell phone was ringing. That must have been what woke me. I snatched it off the table after picking up Foxy's version by mistake. "Hello?"

"Phoebe, are you all right?"

"Max!" I hadn't been able to contact him all afternoon. "Look, could you phone me back on my flat's land line?"

"Yeah, sure."

The house phone rang seconds later. "You think you're being tapped?"

"Probably. So, did they grill you like a planked salmon, too? I saw you down the hall at Scotland Yard but couldn't catch your eye before they took you in."

"I got drilled by those wowsers, all right. Acted like I was some kind of suspect. How could I be when that two-bit sleaze was murdered while we were with the cops?"

"Was he?"

"Damn right."

"I guess so." I lowered myself back to sitting. "I was so busy saying over and over again that I wasn't hiding anything that I must have missed that part."

"The man they identified as Jason Young—though that was only one of his aliases, apparently—died at 3:35 a.m. while we had Metro police and Interpol mucking around our gallery. How rich is that?"

***

I took a deep breath and lowered myself back to sitting, letting my eyes fall on my *Tide Weaver* tapestry for moral support. "So, that means what? That someone knocked him off just after he left the gallery last night? But what was he looking for? Why was he even there?"

"Damned if I know, but if I hadn't been with the police at the time, I would have been a prime suspect. The dead guy broke into our gallery, the same dude who bought my prized carpets while I was in my cups, or so the story goes. That could be some kind of motive, I guess. I knew what the coppers were thinking—bloody stodgers. I wanted that snipe-faced Walker to ask me: 'Where were you between the hours of 3:30 a.m. and 4:45?' just so I could say 'with you, idiot.'"

I smiled. He sounded so normal, so Max-like, the same old irascible, pugnacious Max. He'd probably already had a few drinks pumping him up. "But what was he doing in the gallery if not stealing something?"

"That part's got me stumped."

"And someone's been following me, besides the usual Interpol watch, I mean."

"Yeah, honey, I know. I hired a bloke to keep an eye out for you—a good head, straight-up. Worked as a bouncer in a couple of big-name clubs. He's scampered off somewhere since but I couldn't afford to keep him on longer, anyway. Before he went AWOL, he told me a couple of guys were staking out us both."

"What?" The word escaped me like a croak. "You hired a bodyguard *and* a private eye without telling me? I've had so many people tailing me, I'm surprised they didn't form a line."

"I didn't want to spook you too soon. I thought I'd wait until I could find out who they were before saying anything. I still don't know and it's left me buggered. Now the gallery's been broken into and that guy murdered. Maybe Noel knows we're targets so he's hired his mates to protect us but then someone knocked him off?"

I closed my eyes. "You're not back on this Noel as good guy theme, are you?"

"Look, my boy could be protecting us. Maybe he's hired people to keep us safe and didn't just leave us swinging in the wind."

"What difference does it make? We're still on the gallows, aren't we?

And we don't know who's following us. Agent Walker says it may be multiple interests."

"I want you to leave town for a couple of weeks, maybe go home to visit Nancy in Nova Scotia until things cool down."

"And what about you?"

"What about me?"

"Are you going into rehab or not?" Silence followed. "I'm not going anywhere unless you book into detox."

He gusted a sigh. "I'll go if you get out of town for a while."

We hung up agreeing to mutually consider our ultimatums. The last thing I wanted was to run away just as matters began heating up. Yet I desperately wanted Max in detox, too. Now what?

I logged onto my laptop to check my bank account again and stared at the bottom line. Another 10,000 pounds sterling had been deposited. I had the deep sense that Toby knew the gallery was in trouble and that I'd use the money to keep it afloat. He knew me that well.

Why did love come with so much pain? I thought back to Dad in those last weeks of his life. He'd been so confused and kept insisting that his son had been to see him, something I knew to be impossible. Weeks after the heist and his long lost son suddenly appears after visiting hours to see his father? The hospital staff insisted no one had signed in and that Dad's dementia had progressed to such an extent that whole swathes of memory had fallen away. No, my brother had a lot to answer for.

But I needed that money and he knew it.

I shuffled into the kitchen to make myself a cup of chamomile tea, which I took downstairs. The gallery hung still with just the street light shifting through the plate glass up front.

Nobody would take this away from me. Ever. Clutching my mug, I strolled into the storeroom and switched on the light, shutting the door behind me in case someone peering too deeply into the gallery mistook us for open. This would be my first time alone there since the late Jason Young entered and wound up dead.

What had he been looking for? He had entered this room multiple times while I slept upstairs yet took nothing. To be surrounded by thousands of dollars of rare ethnographic objects and to walk out empty-handed didn't make sense. He had to be seeking something specific but

***

what if not the stolen jewels? There was no place to hide something in these concrete walls except inside the boxes and crates that lined the shelves. Max had gone through everything.

We did have an inventory of sorts, one that Maggie had compiled over a year ago and that Max ignored the way he did everything his ex had touched. Though I'd plucked it from the files and handed it to him while the police were here, Max ran on memory. He claimed he knew every damn thing inside the storeroom so what was the big deal? I watched him open all the crates, check the boxes against the content lists taped on the front of each, and run a visual scan over, behind, and inside every object. Nothing was missing, he insisted.

I needed to check myself and use the inventory as a place to start. We had acquired only a few pieces since it had last been compiled so it would still be useful. Picking up the file, I began going over everything against the sales records for the last year. After an hour of tedium, I still was no further ahead. Everything had been accounted for, as far as I could see. I tossed the file on the table in disgust.

Staring unfocused at the shelves, I suddenly remembered the day Max first took me for a tour through the gallery. I had been so excited that I couldn't stop videoing the experience with my phone. Part enthusiastic record-keeping, part the need to capture places and spaces of personal importance, I had acquired a visual record of the gallery as it was on that first day nine months earlier, shelf by shelf. I'd even shot a selfie version of me mock-introducing one of the rugs.

I pulled my iPhone from my pocket and began scrolling through the photos and videos until I landed on the storeroom group. By holding the phone up, it was relatively easy to compare the before shots against the shelves. I recognized the same boxes with the same contents or slightly depleted, all duly recorded on the packing note and corresponding sales records. We'd sold two jade pieces and replaced the ones in the gallery with two more, leaving one remaining in storage. The crates containing the carved African masks hadn't moved because no one had yet bought the carvings still on the floor. We only had so much room and would often circulate our pieces in and out of storage.

The five rolled carpets still leaned against the wall, bundled in plastic and anti-humectant paper, some brown, some still in their white shipping

316

covers, waiting for the hanging beauties on the walls beyond to sell or to take a break. Only one major carpet had sold in the last nine months.

I paused. We had replaced the Kuba rug with the Cloud Head, meaning there should only be four carpets in waiting. Why did we have five?

Pulling the rolls away from the wall, I checked the stickers in the left-hand corner against the inventory records. Max always inspected each item when it arrived before rewrapping it, or at least he used to. Every carpet was accounted for except one.

My heart pounded as I hefted the roll up onto the table. I was about to slice the string and cut the wrapping when my gaze landed on the shipping label—not the usual computer print-out, not accompanied by the standard brokerage labels and custom stamps. The printing on the label affected me so violently, I dropped the knife.

I backed away like I'd been burned. I stood there, heart thundering, staring at the white, bubble-packed roll as if it contained a ticking bomb. It may as well have, since the moment I opened that thing, I knew the course of my life would explode in some crazy, uncontrollable way all over again.

After several moments, I approached, staring at the label warily. It was addressed to me. The writing matched my brother's art printing, the kind he used to label his artwork and iconic cartoons—almost runic, as if carved deep into ancient stone—unmistakably his.

The return address claimed it had been sent from an *Erdogan Sevgi Carpets and Kilims, Sultanahmet, Istanbul.* The customs label stated only CARPET and cited the worth at 2,000 pounds sterling, or about $3,700, not an unusual amount for a rug. Nothing about this package would attract attention unless someone recognize that printing, someone like me.

Call Walker, cried my more reasonable self, the part who had once studied law, tried to abide by the rules, attempted to remain steady and straight in a family of apparent criminals. This carpet or whatever it was didn't belong here, had been sent directly to me by a thief. But the thief was my brother and, for some reason, I called no one.

His printing delivered multiple levels of longing and pain that jettisoned me past anger into something else. He was my brother, my brother! What if I had misunderstood his actions and he really wasn't the monster I believed, as Noel insisted? What if he had been forced to steal the whole time, held by gunpoint while he forged a fortune's worth of jewels? What kind of sister was I not to at least hear him out? So, the other me, the one who couldn't abide rules, was susceptible to random acts of impulse and reacted without reason, continued tampering with evidence.

I severed the strings and slit the white laminated paper, cut through the layer of bubble wrap down to a brown papered core. Inside, lay a roll measuring about three feet wide by six feet long, tied in regular intervals with more string. Once I cut those last cords, the brown paper curled away to reveal a very old textile—old by virtue of the back's discoloration, the thinning patches, which was all that I could see at first. Certainly it was a flat-weave, an old kilim in brown, rusty red, blue, and ivory wool.

An old kilim. Why would Toby send me this? Because he knew I'd love it? Because he was using it as a message, or both? I trembled on the precipice, shivering in the chill air of the lonely adult orphan craving something lost—a family, a home. Bringing the police into it would rip me from this one connection and transfer all the responsibility to an impersonal agency. How could I let that happen?

I blew on my fingers to warm them before spreading the carpet out on the table, tossing the brown wrapping to the floor, and staring fixedly at the old kilim.

I forgot to breathe. It was so old, how old I had no idea, but the faded wool motifs marching across the yellowed surface skipped over worn patches as if the carpet had honored many centuries, many floors and walls. Its vivid energy arrested the eye, seized the heart.

Vaguely female anthropomorphic shapes repeated across the rows, each wearing a skirt, arms held upward with something in the hands, and all bearing odd curled headdresses. Startling, dramatic and powerful, the figures called out from some ancient place. Every figure bore a symbol over the torsos—either more hooked motifs or wiggly flame things—or were those birds on branches? Vultures, maybe? Yes, vultures! Goddesses with vultures! Lining the edge of the yellowed ivory field and expertly balanced amid the figures, more strange shapes cavorted in a stylized, geometric frolic.

My heart flipped and danced. My blood beat deep within my veins. I felt powerful and centered and connected to that carpet and everything else. For one instant, I knew the universe on multiple levels and believed myself part of some great dynamic.

I kicked off my shoes and climbed on top of the table to sit before it cross-legged like a supplicant. How many thousands of people had sat on or before this rug? This textile was so beautiful, so rare, so old, and so powerful that I temporarily forgot who I was. Those symbols impacted me beyond words, touching me in my deepest recesses, and I realized that here was the goddess-with-vultures kilim Noel referred to, the one I was not to touch but about which he didn't have a chance to explain.

This carpet connected me to my brother and possibly to Jason Young and to who knew what else besides. And all of them connected to Istanbul.

Minutes later, as if shaking myself out of a spell, I climbed back down and began tidying up the mess. First, I sliced off the return address and stuck it in my pocket before gathering up the wrappings to burn in the upstairs fireplace. I'd need to erase the security footage that witnessed me finding the carpet and all evidence that it had ever arrived.

If someone had asked me what the hell I was doing, I wouldn't have been able to find the words to explain.

�֍ 11 ֍

I had never been to Istanbul, never journeyed too far from my own culture, but all necessary details fell together quickly. Serena agreed to manage the gallery after I waved the invitation to the International Rare Textile and Ethnographic Exposition under her nose, explaining how I must attend.

The reception, in particular, interested me, I said, despite the hefty fee. Imagine the contacts I could establish?

"Yes, you must go," she agreed soberly. "Mermaid & Baker needs new clients and a good profile, yes? That cannot come by staying here."

Then Max booked himself into the Drayton Fields detox center because I assured him I was going home to Nova Scotia for a few weeks, a necessary lie. On that same day, I found a seat sale with a direct flight to Istanbul packaged with a room at a hotel in the old city, only a short walk away from both the exhibition site and the return address of the kilim. It was as if, as Nancy claimed, the Universe conspired to clear my path.

Only Agent Walker tried throwing up a speed bump.

"Am I under some kind of advisory not to leave the country, is that it?" I asked him over the phone. The last thing I wanted was those startling blue eyes and that hijacked eyebrow focused on me in person.

"As I stated before, you're not under suspicion but a person of interest, but why the sudden decision to leave town and to Istanbul, of all places? Is there something you're not telling us?"

"What, like someone just ended up dead around the corner and that I might be feeling the need to get out of Dodge?"

"I would think that experience would put you on high alert."

I cleared my throat. "Agent Walker--"

"Sam, please."

Serena was mimicking a Frankenstein-like man lumbering around in front of me. I turned my back on her.

"Agent Walker," I began again, "I am trying to run a business under volatile circumstances. And, yes, I am under high alert, believe me, which is why I'd like to get away for a few days. Somebody connected to my gallery in ways I don't understand has just been murdered. Am I supposed to be calm? I need a break. I'm hoping my sudden exit will throw my stalkers off my tail and give me a bit of vacation."

"Istanbul is a huge city. We can't protect you as easily as we can in London and it's challenging enough here. Your stalkers will note your sudden relocation and will be sure to track you down wherever you go."

"Are you trying to scare me again?"

"Is it working?"

"No. Do you really think I feel any safer in London after all that's happened? I'm going and that's that." I turned back to find Serena standing with her arms crossed, frowning.

"Fine," he said, his voice taut. "I'll alert my colleagues at our Istanbul office and set up an appointment. Which hotel are you staying at?"

"I haven't booked one yet. Look Walker, I'm assuming you'll still be keeping an eye on the gallery while I'm gone? I've told my assistant not to be alarmed should you show up suddenly and start poking around. We've also discontinued our evening hours for the time being and are hiring a student to assist Serena so she's not here alone. You already know that you can't interview Max while he's in rehab, so don't even try."

"His booking himself in there in the midst of what has become a murder investigation is very inconvenient. We--"

"Oops—customer just arrived. Got to go. I'll be in touch. Bye." I pressed END and placed the phone in its stand.

Serena stood studying me, today a vision in purple wafting the scent of crushed violets. "He is not happy that you are leaving?"

"No, but the show must go on and all that." I waved the expo invitation in the air again like a battle standard. "Have you ever been to one of these?"

"Not that one. My husband and I went to the Brussels event once long ago—very grand! Lots of champagne!—but never to Istanbul. It is very exotic, yes? I understand the show is very fabulous. All those beautiful carpets. You will make good connections and have a very good break. And be very careful?"

"I will be careful, of course," I said, hoping I appeared confident and upbeat instead of driven and percolating with tension. "Traveling in a strange city requires nothing but common sense—never go out alone after dark and that kind of thing."

"Yes, so true. And no worrying over things back here. Jennifer and I will take care of the gallery."

I'd agreed to hire Marco's current girlfriend to help Serena in my absence. "You must be careful, too. Are you nervous?"

"About dead bodies and big scar-faced men? Never. About spending all day with Jennifer who moons over Marco, oh so lovesick? Maybe." Rena fluttered her hands like flapping lips, or maybe she was miming a flight of lovebirds.

I knew she wanted to know where the money was coming from since the gallery had apparently gone from broke to moving at full speed in record time. Her salary had been paid and I'd hired Marco's Gwyneth Paltrow lookalike girlfriend to keep her company. Another new security system was being installed that afternoon and obviously I was paying for Max's expensive detox facility.

She had to know something was up but would say nothing to no one. If she noticed that the wrapping over the fifth carpet in the storeroom had changed, she didn't comment on that, either. I had removed one of my upstairs wall-mounted rugs and rolled it into brown paper to add to the inventory. If anybody had chanced to count five carpets in storage, I made certain five remained. Oh, and the flash drive containing the recent security footage had been mysteriously replaced by a brand new version, several, in fact. It seemed I was taking Walker's advice and keeping multiple backups on hand.

That afternoon, I dropped in to see an old colleague of Max's, this one still on friendly terms. Ivan ran a small newsagent shop on Kensington High Street that sold cell cards along with extra services, available to only those who knew how to ask. I waited until the tiny space emptied of customers before introducing myself.

"Phoebe! Yes, Max told me you come to London. Where is he? Still good?" A little guy with a wily junkyard look, I knew he'd immigrated from Bosnia as a political refugee years ago.

"Well, thanks. He's just feeling a bit under the weather today. Hey, look, Ivan, can you help me with this phone?" I passed him my Foxy cell. "Someone gave it to me as a gift and I want to make sure I can use it to do business without eavesdroppers."

He studied it for a moment, flipping it over in his hands as if he'd never seen one before. "One moment. I come right back." He winked and disappeared into a back room, emerging minutes later. "Someone put on tracking device. See, under cover? Very sophisticated. Never scene anything quite so cool outside of MI6 stuff. Very cool." He pointed to a tiny metal disk inserted under the phone's gel cover. "I removed it, so no one know where you go."

"Thank you." I pocketed the Foxy phone and pulled out my own iPhone. "This one I use all the time. How do I keep it from sending location signals on me?"

"You must keep the locator lock off and not use GPS but still possible to track through the number always. You want to stay private, best to use this." He pulled a phone from under the counter. "Not pretty. Number untraceable. Use SIM card I sell and no one finds you. Throw away afterwards."

"A burner phone? Perfect!" I left the shop as the proud owner of three cell phones to which I assigned each a different purpose. The Foxy phone I would keep as my information channel, since I was convinced that Rupert could be as useful to me as I to him; my own smart phone would be my map and location device should I ever need to be found; and my new burner phone was appointed my secure line for phoning home or whatever. I felt ridiculously pleased with myself.

As I marched towards my bank, I passed the tattoo shop I'd crossed a hundred times or more since moving to London. The proprietor always caught my eye since her entire body had been inked in a complex vining design of thorns and leaves. Sometimes she'd stand outside smoking and either wave or roll her eyes at me, depending on her mood.

The black-on-black-stud-and-leather goth vibe never really stroked my friendly gene but today she actually smiled. Despite the onyx lipstick, that smile dazzled me. I actually smiled back, then paused, and finally retraced my steps until I was standing in front of her, trying not to stare at the noose of thorns strangling her neck.

"Hi. I'm not really into tattoos but I have one." Stupid opener but I was short on verbal brilliance.

"And you're telling me this because?"

"Because I want another. I want you to tattoo me."

She grinned. "You're having me on, right? You're gonna tell me you want a skull swallowing a dagger or maybe one of my ultra-popular poison apple tats?"

"Both sound stunning in a toxic way, but no thanks. I'll show you what I want." I was such an impulse shopper.

Inside her tiny shop papered by sample designs, I perched at a table strung with drill pens and ink pots and showed her my phone's photo of my Goddess with Vulture kilim. "I want one of those motifs. Is that possible?"

"I can draw anything. What is it?"

"A goddess with vultures."

She studied the image intensely before her eyes met mine. "A goddess with vultures? You're bloody kidding! How cool is that? But if you want a proper goddess, I could draw her in black spandex with an eye-popping set of boobs with maybe bulging biceps and toned abs."

"And maybe a broadsword? No, thanks. My goddess is more spirit leader than ball-breaker. I want the image just as it appears in the photo— about two inches high and as wide." I pointed to a laminated paper of intricate thorns criss-crossing a Frida Kahlo portrait. "If you can do that, you can do delicate and intricate. I want your best work in full color."

"You'll get it. Where do you want her?"

"Someplace where the sun don't shine. I have a mermaid tat just below my left butt cheek so maybe on the other side?"

"What's the point of art if no one sees it, not even you? Are you ashamed of your goddess?"

That made me think. "Of course not. I just don't feel the need to advertise my icons. Put her someplace I can see but not the general public."

And that's how I ended up with a goddess motif just below my left breast. Yes, it was awkward as hell lying in the backroom with that ink drill buzzing into my delicate flesh and, just so you know, it hurt, but the results were spectacular. It almost made me wish I wore bikinis or had a lover who I could show her off to, but just knowing I bore a goddess with vultures on my person was enough.

My last task of the day was to extract 1000 euros in cash, which I stuffed in my shoulder wallet under my clothes.

By early the next morning, while the world still slept, I took a cab to Heathrow and boarded a plane to Istanbul, the folded Anatolian Goddess with Vultures kilim occupying every inch of my carry-on bag and the skin under my breast burning. That, my phones, and my knitting featured as my only critical in-flight necessities.

During the four-hour flight, I actually managed to lay the foundation of my intarsia design, a feat of logistics which involved taping my sketch to the upright tray and keeping my yarn tucked in tiny butterfly balls dangling from my needles. I refused flight hospitality to keep my workspace clear, but the moment I needed to change yarn colors, I put the project aside and returned to researching everything I could about Istanbul and Turkish culture over the in-flight Wi-Fi.

12

Istanbul engulfed me in a blur of vignettes. The cab drove past ancient walls, Roman aqueducts, aborted marble columns, all standing juxtaposed alongside modern glass and steel structures with swathes of the Miramar running a cool blue along the highway.

Three civilizations had risen and fallen here—Byzantine, Roman, Ottoman—and I glimpsed relics of all three standing side by side in a single glance. While the car inched through the traffic towards the hotel, I strained to see the minarets soaring cloudward, the market stalls and vendors, the textiles that blazed in shop windows and spilled into the sidewalks of nearly every street. Ancient, modern, traditional, and edgy-new, the city jostled a thousand contractions, defying visitors to pigeonhole it in a single one. Fifteen million people lived in this crossroad between Europe and Asia Minor, and I swear they were all cramming the streets that afternoon.

I booked into my hotel, relieved to find the Crown Plaza Old Town offering exactly the kind of anonymity I sought. The marble foyer with its glass and mirrored hall and grand, soaring ceiling sketched an impressionistic Ottoman ambiance with velvet chairs, silk drapes, and uniformed men rushing about doing somebody's bidding.

My room was on the third floor accessible by either a glass bullet-shaped elevator or stairs. Both led to an open balcony-style hall over-looking a marble subfoyer with more red cushioned chairs beside a dress shop. After depositing my passport and most of the cash along with my kilim in the room safe, I popped a piece of complimentary Turkish delight into my mouth and hit the streets.

The impact nearly knocked me over. If I thought London a bustle, I underestimated the effect of stirring in a few million more humans and cramming vehicles into ancient streets against a panorama of contrasting cultures and competing wares. I could have been dropped into a human sea where all I could do was move with the stream or be bowled over. Should I go uphill or down, cross the broad road with the tramway running down the center, or jump into a shop to regroup? I chose downward, following the route I'd memorized on my map, the one that would take me directly to my kilim's return address.

Men in jeans and leather jackets, women in head scarves wearing long trench coats over gowns, strode beside clusters of tourists and many young Turks of both sexes in the latest fashion. Passing faces looked Slavic, Asian, Caucasian, Indian, Mongolian, and any combination in between. Though humanity swarmed around me, I soon relaxed into the company of the multitude, thrilled by the energy rather than overwhelmed by its diversity. I was in Istanbul, Istanbul!

Soon the broad-faced office buildings and modern shops shrank away to be replaced by rows of tiny coffee houses, pomegranate juice vendors, trinket shops, and jewelry boutiques, with every imaginable item to lure the eye. Every fifth shop appeared to be a carpet or scarf merchant, all of which caused me to pause as I scanned the color-saturated windows. I soon learned that pausing before a store in Istanbul was never without consequence.

"Lady, I have a beautiful carpet to show you. Come see, please."

I shook my head and moved on.

"Lady, lady! Come see my carpets! Best in town. Very good price."

I recognized the mass-produced, possibly Chinese or Indian knock-offs in many windows and soon learned to feign indifference. The constant calls didn't annoy me so much as slow me down and never once did I feel threatened. I knew Turkey as an open, relatively free-thinking Muslim country but I had yet to see one female shopkeeper. Unsure of how to interpret the absence of my sisters in merchandising, I kept my head fixed straight ahead and forged on.

Once I paused against a wall long enough to check my map and when I looked up, a man had arrived at my elbow to offer directions. The friendliness and eagerness to help seemed genuine.

"The address is at the Arasta Bazaar," he told me. "You follow the tram line until you see the Blue Mosque and the street is just behind there."

The Blue Mosque—a monument named after a color—how exotic did that sound? I'd read its history and longed to visit, but I was here on business. And when I followed the human stream along the narrow sidewalk until the street fell away to my right in a wide expanse of flowers, fountains, and gilded minarets, it was all I could do not to gasp. But I had no time to explore. All I wanted was to find the return address and come that much closer to Toby. Would Noel and Maggie be here, too? This city made a perfect hiding place, an invitation to any person of any stripe to blend with the multitude. Maybe I was getting closer.

I couldn't help but stare at the Blue Mosque and wonder at the magnificent structure, both delicate and imposing all at once. Here in the plaza, pedestrians strolled, enjoying the autumn sunshine in the open spaces. Slowing my pace, I ambled along, stopping only long enough to purchase a stick of roasted corn from a sidewalk vendor. The scent had been tantalizing me. Nibbling on my spicy corn, it suddenly occurred to me that I didn't stand a chance of detecting stalkers here. In London, I just knew. Here, plunged into a foreign world, I wasn't certain my twitchy sixth sense would still function.

I purchased a bottle of water and carried on, enjoying the sunshine and stunning skyscape of gilded minarets and blue domes. Uniformed men mounted on upright motorized scooters zipped around the plaza and I recognized them as tourist police guarding visitors against pickpockets. One of them cheerfully pointed me in the direction of the bazaar.

Down a set of concrete stairs, past a busy outdoor cafe, through a throng of tourists threaded by young men delivering trays of tea, I arrived at last at the Arasta Bazaar. An outdoor pedestrian arcade lined with modern shops tucked into old gray stone walls, it displayed all that had made Turkey a trade crossroads for centuries.

My steps faltered. I was seeking Erdogan Sevgi Carpets, which I had yet to find, but to walk past the Isnik tile shops, the store selling silken robes and vests, the jewelry shop glittering with lapis and high-karat gold, the shop specializing in embroidered pillows, and, of course, all the other carpet stores, was nearly impossible.

Everything I loved and honored resided here, and the merchants knew how to display their offerings, how to jumble patterns and colors together so that each excited the other in a harmonious symphony. My eyes couldn't bear to pass them by without proper acknowledgment.

"Miss, I have more inside."

I looked up from where I stood transfixed before a window displaying a magnificent Ottoman-style carpet, not old but expertly crafted in brilliant hues and intricate patterns, probably at least 25 knots per inch. A young man wearing the Turkish street uniform of jeans and leather stood in the doorway smiling.

"Um, I'm only looking, thank you, but this is a gorgeous piece."

Before I knew, I was sitting in the shop, sipping the small glass cup of tea Erkan offered, appreciating the show as he rolled out carpet after carpet until the floor at my feet was an overlay of wool and weaves. Most were new, the products of either small households or the many carpet cooperatives that operated across Turkey. Though handmade, they were still commercial productions and not what interested me as a collector or dealer, though beautiful nonetheless. A few emerged that were clearly older, less regular, with discolorations in the hand-dyed wool. They were pleasing but not spectacular. I insisted to Erkan that I was only looking, which he ignored and proceeded to show me even more.

Without acknowledging my business interest in textiles, without even letting on that I knew anything about carpets whatsoever, I let him explain the difference between flat-weave kilims and the soumak, where colored yarns are wrapped around the warps. I did this mostly to confirm my own understanding and to check my knowledge of techniques against the seller's.

The minutes ticked away until I shook myself out of my stupor. I couldn't keep doing this. I came here for a reason. "As much as I love these carpets, I don't plan on buying anything quite so new." I made the mistake of adding: "I'm really more interested in antique carpets."

"Never a waste of time, Miss. I am honored that you enter my store and accept my hospitality, but my friend across the street specializes in antique carpets. I take you to him but finish your tea first. No rush."

By the time I'd drained the last of my apple tea, Mr. Kalecik had appeared from across the street, eager to escort me across the arcade to his shop. Did I miss a hand signal or maybe a discreet phone call while I was mooning over pattern and color?

I'd figured out how it worked: Erkan would receive a commission from Mr. Kalecik should I buy anything, commissions being the grease in the wheels of Turkish commerce. A customer's refusals would be politely and pleasantly left unacknowledged as these expert salesman maneuvered buyers into a state of relaxation and stimulation piqued by more gorgeous textiles and genuine hospitality. My slack-jaw expressions of wonder made me an easy mark.

"Thank you," I said, replacing my glass on the silver tray. "As much as I would enjoy visiting your shop, I must leave it for another day. I have business with Erdogan Sevgi's. Could you point me in the right direction?"

If Erkan was disappointed because I named another dealer, it didn't show. He smiled broadly. "I take you there. It is just down the street."

"That is not necessary," beamed Mr. Kalecik, an older man in a suit and tie. "I can show her on my way back to my store."

"That's all right, really. Thank you both," I assured them. "I'll find it." Darting from the shop, I headed further down the arcade.

Erkan jogged at my heels anyway and, since he had to be twenty years younger than Mr. Kalecik, could easily win the race. I hung a left-hand turn into a silk shop as a diversionary tactic but, even so, I caught Erkan nodding knowingly at the shopkeeper at the door. The deal had been struck.

I wove deeper inside, tucking myself behind racks hung with gorgeous wearables. Lost for a moment in a forest of silken sleeves and Ottoman-style embroidered tunics, I suddenly stopped caring who got what. Let percentages rule. I had more important things to do like explore all that luminous fabric. Something as pearly as the inside of an oyster shell caught my eye. Ensorcelled, I lifted out an embroidered tunic with vining green and blue embroidered tulips curling across the glossy space. It looked as though it would fit perfectly.

"That is pure silk, miss. Very fine. Made in Bursa in honor of similar robes once worn by Ottoman sultans. May I offer you coffee or tea?" the shop owner asked.

I smiled, resigned to my fate. "Yes, thank you. Apple would be lovely."

He signaled to a tea boy and helped me out of my jacket and into the tunic, which slipped over my tee shirt and hugged my body in a fall of pattern and luster. Embroidered by hand in colors so perfect for my skin and hair that I swore that I suddenly appeared younger, smarter, and more interesting than I had ever been before. Wouldn't it look splendid over leggings, worn to the exhibition gala, to all the cocktail parties I never went to? I had to have it, only it was more money than I had ever paid for a single item of clothing in my life.

I shifted gears and joined Mr. Caesar for tea. After chatting on about how much I loved Istanbul, I eventually informed him what I'd be willing to pay for my tunic plus another one in pink for my friend back home. After all, I pointed out, I sold fine textiles in London and displayed a genuine Ottoman robe in my shop. I passed him my card, which he scrutinized before proceeding to bring out a few genuine Ottoman textiles from his back room. A gold-embroidered black wool felt lady's jacket, circa 1900, caught my interest and we negotiated until I purchased two tunics and the jacket at a fair price.

Pleased with myself, I headed down the street. Shopping can be such a distraction. This time I made it as far as the carpet bag shop.

"You have very good taste, lady," said the man at the door, indicating my carpet bag. "But that one is very worn and I can show you many others in much better condition."

I smiled and patted my bag. "This one is an old friend. It even saved my life once."

"That is a special friend, then. Maybe you would like to find it a companion?"

These guys were good. Somehow I ended up inside once again, drinking yet more tea and chatting over antique carpets and the businesses that made bags and boots out of damaged textiles. The Turks certainly were a sociable people, I decided, and, after purchasing a pair of carpet slippers, I finally escaped.

What was I doing? I couldn't afford this. I was spending dirty money. Even for what I considered a justifiable cause, I couldn't go overboard.

Finally, I walked with determined purpose down the rest of the street, looking neither left nor right, my stomach sloshing tea as I went.

A man emerged from a shop near the end of the street and stepped directly in front of me so suddenly that I jumped back. Startled, I looked at his face, took in the hazel eyes studying me calmly, yet intensely, and took another step away. "Sorry. I guess I wasn't looking where I was going." Yet I swear, he bumped into me, not me into him. He bowed slightly without uttering a word. I hastily excused myself and hurried on. Fatigue must be affecting me more than I knew.

At last, I spied Erdogan Sevgi's Carpets, the most unassuming shop on the street and almost the last one before the stairs. A tiny window was piled with rugs and tribal textiles, with the best spot for sunset viewing claimed by a fat gray tabby. I knew at once this merchant was of a different breed. A small mustached man with long graying hair and kind eyes met me at the door.

"Do you like my cat? His name is Harput and he thinks himself the most honored of guests." He took a quick puff from the cigarette he held before quickly extinguishing it in a bowl by the door.

I grinned. "I can see that. All he has to do all day is lie around on gorgeous rugs. How lucky can you get, Harput?" I asked the cat who barely opened an eye in greeting. "Are you Erdogan Sevgi?"

"I am. Will you enter my shop? Excuse my smoking. Bad habit. My wife and daughter say to quit." He shrugged. "I try at home, but here I am weak. Come in. May I offer coffee or tea?"

"Oh, yes, thank you. Tea, please. Apple." I was grateful that the cups were small enough that I might find room for maybe one more. I wondered where the public loo was?

A young man nodded at me and then dashed off to fill the order at the cafe across the street while I sat down on a bench of a narrow room where rolled rugs, stacks of cushion covers, and layers of other small textiles padded every available inch. A visitor could sit on the bench by the door or maybe perch on a tower of cushion covers or even on one of the narrow steps heading upward but, otherwise, the shop couldn't entertain many at once, which added to its cozy charm. Thus I sat padded in color.

A call to prayer blared into the air with a force no Muslim could miss. Slightly buzzy and metallic-sounding, it had to be a recording emitting from the nearest mosque. In seconds, a string of them erupted all over the city, haunting, almost mesmerizing. It was 5:00 o'clock.

Mr. Sevgi did not unfold one of the multiple prayer rugs lining his shop and perform his devotions. Instead, he smiled and watched as my gaze landed on salt bags, ornamental horse trappings, and several long antique kilims hanging in the narrow spaces above the forest of rolled carpets. A few Turkmen pieces added to the mix, but mostly I recognized Anatolian. My pulse quickened.

"You like the older textiles?" he asked.

"I do," I said. "I collect tribal kilims and soumaks, but nothing commercially made."

"Good! I am so glad to hear this. Many visitors come to Turkey and go to the big carpet farms. I say, yes, those carpets are hand-made but they are not from the heart, do you know what I say? These rugs come to me from the villages where the women work their own designs, not the same for the carpet farms. The carpet farms tell them what to make but, in the villages, the women do their own. It is getting harder and harder to find these."

"It's happening everywhere in almost every artisan art. On one hand, I understand why the women want the financial guarantees from the cooperatives but, on the other, experimentation and creativity are being quashed."

"Yes, yes!" said Mr. Sevgi excitedly. "I could not say it so well in English. You understand."

I fished out my card and passed it over. "Already I see many pieces here I may be interested in purchasing, but could you tell me first if you've seen this kilim?" I showed him my phone photo of my Anatolian vulture goddess. "It was sent to me in London from your shop's address. I'm hoping you can tell me about the man who sent it."

He took my phone and stared down at the photo, his expression not registering surprise. "But this is very old, fine piece and very valuable. I have never had such a kilim in my shop. It is very special, like a museum would want. I would never forget it if I had seen it."

I stared at him in disbelief. "But the kilim arrived in London with your return address on it. Swipe over to the next photo and you'll see the label."

He flicked his finger over the screen and shook his head. "This is not mine, not my writing or my label. Who would send you this with my address? I do not understand."

"I don't either. The sender didn't identify himself, only gave your address. I need to find out why it was sent to me and your shop has to be a clue. Do you know anything about the kilim?"

"It is from East-Central Anatolia, that I can tell. It is much like the one my friend found on one of her travels around Cappadocia. She is very interested in these kinds of kilims and is a scholar but collects, also," Erdogan said. "She has written many books. Here, I show you."

While he rummaged in a stack of books sandwiched among multicolored cushion covers, I sat down to sip the tea cooling on the ottoman. Nothing quite reached the chill of my disappointment. Did I really think it would be that easy, that I could just walk into the shop, show the photo, and be handed a clue to Toby's whereabouts? That he had sent it to me as a message, I knew absolutely. I just didn't know how to read it. Again, I kicked myself for not listening to Noel.

Mr. Sevgi, who had insisted I call him Erdogan, returned with a book opened to the colored photo of another striking kilim. This one, labeled *Kilim Fragment East-Central Anatolia, 18th century*, featured a white background with two six-sided medallions populated by bird-like figures and hooked squiggles similar to my goddesses only more stylized and compressed. It appeared to be one end of a much longer piece.

"The Goddess with Vultures," I acknowledged.

"The Anatolian Goddess with Vultures. Very old, see," Erdogan said. "My friend found it in a mosque and a museum purchased it. I would be lucky to find such a piece. The collectors go all over looking, but I must wait here for carpets to come to me. Not so many fine ones come anymore."

"Do you see that goddess often?"

"Not this. The hooked symbol—what do you call it?"

"Motif."

"Motif, yes. The hooked motif has been a traditional image in Anatolian kilims but not like this goddess. Look." He pointed to several kilims and runners which contained simplified versions of the design, goddesses who had lost their skirts and headdresses, their energy compressed into punchy geometric shapes. "This is much earlier."

"Erdogan, I need to find everything I can about this kilim and that motif. I'm a little desperate. Who can I ask, what can I do?"

"My friend, she is from London, too, but is here for the big carpet expo. I saw her only this morning. I will give her your email and maybe she will know more. She is writing another book."

"Thank you," I said. "I'm just so curious."

"Of course, yes, and very lucky to have such a beautiful piece given to you."

Luck wasn't the word. I felt more like Toby and the kilim had forced me into yet another adventure not of my choosing. I gave Erdogan my email address and watched as he typed in a quick message to a Dr. Eva Friedrich.

That done, I proceeded to select the best of Erdogan's pieces—two soumak salt bags used to carry salt to grazing animals on the steppes, both richly colored and festooned with tassels; one saddle cloth of deep Turkish madder-reds brewed with indigo trims; and four tribal kilims obviously from a villager intent to make something beautiful for her home rather than sell at the markets.

I imagined all of them hanging in glory around the gallery rather than languishing in my shop's current economic reality. Maybe these would help change our fortunes. Maybe I could promote them somehow and find a way to catch collectors' attentions? Because, I reminded myself, I had to save Mermaid & Baker, not just find my brother and the source of his mysterious gift.

Right then, the scope of my multiple quests seemed monumental. Just before our deal ended, Erdogan handed me a ceramic disk with a bright blue eye mid-center. "For you, a gift, to protect you from evil."

I'd seen talismans like these all over Istanbul and understood them to be a ward against the evil eye. I smiled down at the piece and thanked Erdogan. "Do you think I need protection?"

"We all do, yes? In my country, we carry one of these to help keep the evil spirits away, a very old tradition."

And I needed all the protection I could get. I placed the disk on top of my purchases for Erdogan to ship back to London. Though he took the textiles, he passed the paper-weight sized ceramic back to me. "You keep with you." Nodding, I tucked it into my bag. Its weight couldn't add more burden to the baggage I already carried.

But I had no time wonder further since I badly needed to use the bathroom. Erdogan's assistant escorted me from the shop to the public washroom tucked against a wall two doors down.

Dusk was already falling and I had a long walk back to the hotel. Relieved to find a Western-model stall rather than the famed hole in the ground, I exited moments later, planning to say goodbye to Erdogan, arrange for the shipment of my purchases, and then bolt back to the hotel.

As I was stepping into the shop, I chanced to look over my shoulder and down the street, now thinning of pedestrians and shoppers. The man I'd bumped into stood outside the shop, smoking a cigarette. Though I couldn't see his face, I knew he was watching me.

❧ 13 ☙

Masses of people and traffic heaved in all directions, focused and deliberate. A dense stream swarmed uphill towards the Crown Plaza. All I need do was stay with the flow until I reached my destination.

I clutched my bag to my hip and dove in. Other than swerving to avoid a man barreling downhill with a wagon of bundled goods, I thought I was making good progress, only somehow I slipped into the tram-bound current dominating the sidewalk's right-hand side.

This human surge poured up the Darŭlŭnun road ready to leap onto the zooming vehicle the moment it paused for intake. I was staring straight ahead, gaze fixed on the woman in front of me, when I found myself boarding along with the tram crowd. I tried to bolt backward but the forward pressure held me fast.

Now I was squeezed in with the crowd speeding along the darkened street. I couldn't tell which stop to take. Nothing looked familiar and, to make matters worse, I didn't have a ticket. That sent me scrambling in my bag looking for change in an unfamiliar denomination, jabbing people with my elbows while the tram attendant looked sternly on. Yes, I researched Turkish lira, but try fumbling for alien coins when your fingers have no idea what they're seeking. I was so obviously a tourist, that at last the attendant abruptly signaled me to stop looking and continued on his way.

I had to be way past the Crown Plaza by now. Unfamiliar buildings zipped by. There was nothing to do but wade my way to the door and disembark at the next stop. I kept saying "excuse me" in English while following a man ahead obviously exit-bound, too.

Together we stepped from the tram into the street, only when he took off in one direction, I was left standing dumbfounded. Lights flashed everywhere, ringing bells sounded along with honking horns and shouting. Four trams were bearing down on me from two directions with me stuck dead center feeling like I'd been dropped into a psychedelic pinball machine. Someone yanked me to safety just as a tram peeled to a stop inches away.

He rattled away at me, managing the words "be careful" in English before taking off. I nodded, gazing over his shoulder at another man jumping from an incoming tram. I recognized the smoking man immediately.

I turned and fled, not down the street towards the hotel but deeper into the congestion pooling around the depot, thinking I could find a place to hide. Vendors formed a row of brightly lit shops ahead—juice stands, food stalls, a coffee shop. I had no idea where I was heading, but soon the shops funneled downhill away from the main road.

A quick check behind and there he was, hands in pockets, following a few yards away. The food stalls changed to shawl and carpet stores with many shopkeepers closing down for the night. I veered into one, planning to ask the vendor for help but when I turned to point out my stalker, he had disappeared.

"Yes, lady? You see my scarves. Beautiful scarves, yes?" The shopkeeper's arms were swathed with textiles. "Pashminas, miss. Pure cashmere."

"What's down the street?" I asked pointing outside.

"Grand Bazaar, Miss, but pashminas there all overpriced from China. Mine real Turkish."

I glanced down at his wares, recognizing the distinctive warp of Indian silks and patterning. I bought one anyway, wrapping it around my head as if preparing for a windstorm and exited the shop.

The Grand Bazaar might be busy enough to be safe, I reasoned. No one could accost me there, surely? And so I entered the oldest shopping mall on earth, instantly plunging into an overwhelming kaleidoscope of color, pattern, and gloss.

The tile work overhead alone would be enough to prompt wonder, but to stir into that heaps upon heaps of textiles, gold, and colored glass banked outside shops selling more of the same was overwhelming in my present state. I didn't know where to look, which way to turn.

Without thinking, I barreled down the long corridor, casting glances over my shoulder, taking abrupt turns into smaller tributaries, saying "no thanks" at every vendor. First left and then right followed by two rights and more lefts. Since the Bazaar formed a labyrinth of corridors and tiled boulevards, the smoking man had many places to hide.

I was still a damn good dodger. I ducked under hanging pashminas, wove my way through corridors of tiny antique shops, always hiding among clutches of tourists where possible. Once, I dove into a carpet shop and darted to the depths of the salon. "Please, do you have a back door?" I asked the vendor. "A man's stalking me."

"What does he look like?"

I described every second man in Istanbul—a dark-haired man of approximate height and average height wearing a leather jacket and jeans.

"Quick, this way." The young guy called something to his colleague while hastening me out a back door so narrow that we had to duck to pass.

"You call tourist police?" he asked.

"No time."

"I told my friend to keep customers in front until I return," he assured me. We emerged in a passageway lined with clothing. "Here not so busy. Go straight to outside street."

Straight? Nothing here was straight. He left me in what I assumed to be somewhere deep in the rear of the Bazaar. The ornate tiles and sleek shop windows melded into stalls of household goods crammed into narrow concrete corridors under canvas awnings. I could smell fresh air but saw no way out. After ten minutes of ambling, I finally stumbled upon a narrow cobbled street where all the shops had been shuttered by steel slats for the night. Except for the occasional car, the street was empty.

I took off downward towards what I assumed must be the main road, navigating by instinct alone. Every time a car passed, I'd turn, hoping to see a cab, yet all were private vehicles going way too fast to pay notice to the lone woman waving in the dark.

Finally, a car slowed down. I turned to see a sleek black limo inching along at the top of the hill, its lights raking the sidewalk. No roof light, nothing to distinguish it as friendly. As I picked up my pace, the car followed. Fear stabbed hard.

I fumbled in my bag for one of my three phones, thinking I'd call 911. Was that even the right help number for Istanbul? Then, abruptly, something dark dropped over my head and simultaneously dragged me backward. I screamed and dug my heels into the pavement.

My attacker threw me down face-first on the ground and wrenched my arms behind my back and began binding my hands. I kicked and squirmed and cried for help.

"Shut up or I hit you," he said, his knees digging into my back. As he pulled the ropes tighter, I heard pounding footsteps. Somebody shouted. For blind seconds I heard scuffling as I tried to flop myself over. Footsteps rapidly retreated amid more shouting. I felt someone standing over me.

"My dear, just lay still for a moment until I cut these bindings. It is I, Sir Rupert Fox, come to your rescue. Nothing to fear now, I assure you. You are quite safe."

I stilled in shock. The hood was pulled from my head and I was helped to a sitting position. I found myself in a dark alley with Sir Rupert crouching beside me. My attacker had disappeared. "Foxy?"

"I prefer Rupert. My man is giving chase. Come, come. Let us proceed to the car where we can talk in comfort. Are you all right? No injuries, I trust?" He helped me to standing and retrieved my carpet bag and phone. "How can you possibly carry this bag without causing bodily harm?"

He led me to a black limo parked curbside, the same one I had seen earlier. The driver's side was empty with the keys dangling in the ignition. I slid into the back seat with Sir Rupert beside me and leaned against the leather, closing my eyes. "How did you know where I was?"

"Quite easily, as it happens. If you were attempting discretion, I fear you failed miserably. I did say I was having you followed, did I not? No prevarication there. My man told me you had taken a flight to Istanbul and the rest was relatively easy. I have some tea on hand for just such emergencies. Do you take milk and sugar?"

I opened my eyes and watched him pour liquid from a thermos into a little glass mug which he passed to me.

"Actually, I ask from habit only since I'm afraid I take mine with liberal lashings of both sugar and milk and, as you can see, I am without the necessary hosting supplies to honor specific requests. Nevertheless, I believe my preferred blend should fortify you."

My hands trembled when I took the mug. "I meant how did you know where I was in Istanbul?" Though I'd planned to swear off tea for a decade, the brew tasted amazingly good.

"Oh, yes. I presume you ask because you unfortunately removed my tracking device from my gift—very short-sighted on your part, Phoebe. How can I adequately protect you without knowing exactly where you are? However, there are other means. Would you like a biscuit with that, perhaps a Hobnob or digestive?"

A little tin emerged, the lid pried off, and the contents offered, each cookie swathed in tissue.

"What you mean is how can you easily track me to Noel and the next presumable hoard?" I chose a Hobnob and savored its oaten crunch.

"Well, that too, of course, but I am truly concerned for your safety and trust that tonight's episode serves to strengthen my offer. I've been watching since you arrived in Istanbul and, no, there's no point in asking how I came to know which hotel you were staying at. Following you today was more challenging, I admit—the crowds in this city—but once you arrived at the Arasta Bazaar, logistics became more manageable. It was there that my man noticed your stalker. When he returns from giving chase, hopefully we will be further illuminated on who exactly attempted the kidnapping."

"Kidnapping?" I passed my empty mug back to Foxy, who deposited in a wooden chest at his feet.

"Yes, of course. He bagged you, my dear, much as one does an exotic bird bound for market or even a fish—an angel fish, perhaps, though one would hope such lovely creatures would require more expert care. If he planned to kill you outright, no doubt you'd be quite dead by now. Such brutal acts can be achieved very quickly, I believe, via firearms, knives, garroting, and an impressive range of dastardly implements. No, I fear your attacker planned to take you off somewhere, perhaps to question you more forcefully. Another treasure-seeker, no doubt. One of your many admirers. Ah, here he comes."

A man was approaching up the street, brushing himself off as he trudged along with something draped over one arm. Not Rutgers, I realized, but taller, dressed in dark jeans and a long coat, though equally well-muscled. He opened the driver's side door and poked his head inside. Brown wavy hair, not bad looking. "He got away, Sir Rupert," he said in an English accent. "Tackled him but he escaped my grip. Left behind his jacket, though."

"Pass it over, Evan. Are you harmed?"

"A bruised rib or two, nothing serious. He's in worse shape than I. I believe I broke some of his parts. Is the lady all right?"

"I'm fine, thanks. Were you tailing me in London, too?"

He grinned an amazingly white set of teeth, climbing in behind the wheel. "Sometimes. You can be very good at escaping trackers, ma'am."

"Practice."

I watched Foxy pat down the captured jacket, his gloved hands smoothing along creases and over pockets. "Ah, here we are." Out came a cell phone. "Aren't we lucky that he chose to keep his communication device so conveniently close?"

"Let me see it. He's my attacker." I held out my hand.

"But my quarry, my dear. Finders keepers."

I relinquished my claim to watch Foxy scan the smart phone. While he scrolled through the numbers, I explored the jacket more thoroughly.

"Not much of interest in here, I'm afraid," Foxy said. "A few Turkish numbers I will have you check, Evan, plus a photo of some houses that may prove interesting. This is not a personal phone, is my guess. He uses it for business only. The man was Turkish, I presume?" he asked his driver.

"Yes."

"Probably a hired chap, then. The question is, who employed him?"

My searching fingers landed on stiff paper slipped in an inside lining pocket. A business card. I eagerly held it to the ceiling light, blinking in disbelief.

"Well, what is it?" Sir Foxy asked.

"*Margaret E. Buckmaster. Dealer in Ethnographic Goods* followed by a phone number with an unfamiliar zip code. That's Maggie! She tried to have me kidnapped? But why? She knows I don't have the hoard."

Rupert tsk-tsked as he gently pried the card from my fingers. "Indeed, why does she wish to have a private word with you in such a remarkably unfriendly fashion?"

"We're not exactly on the best of terms, considering that the last time she tried to shoot me but, still. Why not just ask to meet me somewhere or approach me the way Noel did? I can't imagine Noel or Toby agreeing to such methods."

"I will find out more about this number, if this helps. No doubt she has ensured it can't be traced but I will see what I can do."

"Where to now, Sir Rupert?" Evan asked as the car began easing away from the curb.

"The Crown Plaza, please," I said.

"Miss Maggie will most likely try to nab you again, which is where I may be of service."

"You've already been very helpful but I'm still not planning on making you my best friend just yet. I'll let you know if I need anything but for now, I just want rest."

"Yes, of course you do. I shall call once I learn more about this number. In the meantime, be very cautious."

Outside the hotel, tour buses and taxis congested every spare inch of curb. I had no choice but to leap into traffic and run to the door.

Foxy called out something like "See you tomorrow," which I ignored.

14

The first adhan of the day awoke me at dawn the next morning. Ringing strong and clear from the old mosque directly across the street, it startled me from a brief, deep sleep. *Allahu Akbar* (God is Great), the prayer began. Staring up at the ceiling, I tried to recall what little I knew of the words. I'd crammed a lot of research into the hours before my flight. Somewhere in this day-breaking passage I knew a special phrase had been added: *As-salaatu khayrun min'n-nawm*, or "Prayer is better than sleep."

I struggled to sitting and sighed. Prayer probably was better than sleep, but right then I could use a little more of both. I got up and set the coffee machine working and gathered up my knitting for a spell of sleepy solitude.

Knitting was the closest I came to devotional practice. The rhythmic stitches helped ease me into a nearly meditative state, loosening the noose of stress while helping me believe I could survive anything, that I connected in some profound way to all things great and small. How could I ever explain knitting as a spiritual experience to the uninitiated? Yet, it was in some profound way. Each in our own manner, we pray, we commune with the Universe, sometimes with no more than peace, needles, and yarn.

By eight o'clock, I was in the hotel cafeteria, scrolling through my email while devouring samples of breakfast fare from multiple cultures.

344

Rice and eggs with a side of sweet halvah wasn't half bad. I was just forking a bit of a Japanese noodle mix into my mouth when a message from fried-doc@gmail.com popped up in my in-box.

Hello, Dr. Eva Friedrich here. I understand you are interested in the Goddess with Vultures kilim. How fortuitous that we are both in Istanbul. Meet me for lunch to discuss. The e-signature declared her to be PhD Archaeology, University of London; Assistant Director of the British Institute of Archaeology in Ankara (retired), and listed several published books.

I tapped out a quick response. *Lunch would be perfect. Where and when?* No more than three gulps of tea later and she responded, giving me the address for a restaurant she said was near the Blue Mosque. *Meet me at 1:00 sharp. I'll be waiting.* I asked how I'd recognize her but received no response.

After I drank the last of my tea, I plowed through the throngs to the lobby, where I claimed one of the few available empty seats and used my own iPhone to check in with Serena. Everyone knew I was registered on that device.

"Is everything good, Phoebe?"

"Everything's great," I effused while tucking my legs closer against my chair to avoid a rolling suitcase attached to some harried tourist. My descriptions of the shops and bazaar almost caused Serena to hyperventilate.

"What did you buy? Tell me!"

"Just a few items for the gallery but I did nab a fabulous robe." I described the tunic in detail while she emitted excited sounds but I didn't mention my gift. That would be a surprise. "I'll wear it tonight at the International Rare Textile and Ethnographic Exposition reception."

"You will look so beautiful. Take a selfie for me and post it on Facebook! When will you return?" Did I only imagine the anxiety in her voice?

"Maybe the day after tomorrow or maybe later. I have an open ticket but I won't be away too long. Are you sure everything is all right?"

"Everything is fine," she assured me. "But I miss you and Max, too. I would go visit him but I am not allowed, yes?"

"No visitors for two weeks. It's one of the conditions of his treatment."

"Oh, well. It must be good. Things are quiet, so quiet. Except for Jennifer. She talks on and on about Marco. You would think I'd be happy to listen, but no."

"And Agent Walker hasn't been around?"

"No. All is calm. You go and have a good time and forget about everything here."

If only I could.

"What will you do today?" Serena wanted to know before the call ended.

"More shopping, maybe some sight-seeing," I told her, though that wasn't strictly true. If I were really on vacation, I'd be settling in for a day at the Topkapi Palace, perhaps visit the Islamic Museum of Art, the Hagia Sophia, and any one of the other major attractions.

I tried checking in with Nancy next but could only talk to her answering machine. The message I left was a synopsis of all I told Serena only, in Nancy's case, what I didn't say would be more important than what I did.

As I dropped that phone into my bag, one of the others began ringing. After fumbling a bit, I retrieved my Foxy phone. "Phoebe, what are you up to today and how may I help?"

"And where are you, Rupert?"

"Sitting across from your hotel illegally parked. I traced Maggie's number but, alas, as expected, it is now a dead end. I suspect she uses a number of revolving phones to shield her location."

"But she must be in Istanbul somewhere."

"No doubt. Oh, dear. I do believe an officer is about to issue us a ticket. May I offer you a lift somewhere before we are accosted?"

"No thanks."

"It would be so much easier if you'd just share your agenda so I could help."

"Bye for now, Foxy."

I clicked off and checked the time, seeing I had about two hours left before lunch, enough time for a little couture browsing. Stepping outside to Darülünun, the curb attendant hailed me a cab. Before climbing in, I waved at Foxy and Evan as they were ordered on their way by a policeman and then passed the driver the address for Istanbul's foremost upscale designer shopping area, Nişantaşı. Foxy would be far ahead of me unable to turn around by the time we were under way.

Fifteen minutes later, the cab left me at a glass and concrete promenade, leaving old Istanbul so far behind it was as if it had never been. Gone were the bazaars and the mosques, the sense that the city had grown up around its heritage, proud of all it once was and planned to become. This nondescript arcade could be dropped anywhere in the world where the wealthy forage. Only the Turkish signs below the English on the restaurants and cafes betrayed the country.

Shoppers thronged the street, mostly western-dressed though a few stylish traditional Turkish women strolled by with chic shoes visible beneath their robes. I didn't belong to the chic category. Though there were enough women dressed down much like me, most carried a status bag far removed from my beloved battered satchel.

I found the Chanel store easily. As a minimalist glass and black-trimmed salon with glossy depths stretching back from the street, it claimed its real estate with typical panache. Fixing a smile on my face, I slipped inside, inhaled the rarefied air of wealth and couture, and headed directly to a lean young sales associate dressed in basic black. She flicked her eyes across my person before raising her gaze to my face.

"Hi," I said, giving her a little wave. "Can you help me with something? I want to surprise my aunt with a gift."

Her eyes narrowed. I estimated her to be around twenty and to have fully embraced the notion that working in a couture shop elevated her above mere mortals. She couldn't look further down on me had I dropped down a storm drain. "How can I help with that?" she asked, her accent I tagged as Balkan.

"Well," I said, warming up to my ruse. "My aunt's totally Chanel and I know she comes here all the time because she's told me. So, I want to surprise her with a present, you know?"

The woman thinned her lips into a smile. "You should try maybe flowers. Flowers make nice gift." *Which you might be able to afford.*

I grinned. "No, no. I'm looking for a bag. She loves bags, especially Chanel. I'm sure she shops here."

"What would be her name?"

Maggie had to be using an alias so I pretended I hadn't heard. "Wait, if you see her picture, perhaps you'll recognize her. Here, look."

I pulled out my phone, tapped the photo icon, and began scrolling through all my pictures until I reached those I'd scanned before leaving

London. One in particular was my collateral: me dressed in head-to-toe white Chanel lace, standing in the gymnasium on my high school graduation, the outfit compliments of my pseudo-aunt Maggie, who stood at my side beaming away. My excruciating embarrassment of wearing something that cost more than most families in my community earned in months was alleviated by my excitement at having my whole tribe there: Max, Mom, and Dad. Toby took the photo.

I had looked damned good, I now decided with the retrospect of maturity, but at the time, that dress represented all I never wanted to become. Maggie, always playing beneficent aunt was totally oblivious to both the social awkwardness and my feelings.

I passed the woman my phone. She stared down at the picture in total disbelief. The ragged little non-label creature before her was really the same young couture-clad swan in the photo? She didn't seem to recognize Maggie who also wore complete Chanel.

Then another, older associate who had been hovering nearby slipped up and peered over the younger woman's shoulder. "Ah, oui! Let me see." She took the phone from the woman's hands and studied the photo closely. "Yes, I know her, Madame St. Remis, oui? But her hair is not blond now but black." French accent. I guessed this woman was the salon manager and a Parisian import.

"Oui!" I said excitedly. "Ma tante! She always changes her hair color like Linda Evangelista!" I pulled that model's name out of my head in a desperate attempt to seem in tune, realizing in a flash I had to be a good two decades out of date. I began rattling away in my best school French, trying to impart more Parisian than Nova Scotian Acadian into my accent. "She goes from black to blond to red. I never know what color her hair will be on any day!"

The woman nodded and passed back my phone, continuing in French. "I know those pieces from the archive, yes? The first collection Monsieur Lagerfeld created for Chanel. Magnifique! Do you still have the dress?"

"Mais, non. I was much younger then, as you can see, but I am certain Auntie collects all her pieces forever and ever. She never changes dress sizes like her hair color. When did you see her last?"

"But two days ago. We are tailoring pieces from the new collection for her. Wait. I will check my book."

Leave it to ma tante to put visiting a Chanel store on top of her weekly to-do list even while being hunted by Interpol. My hunch paid off, big time. I watched the woman slip away to a back room, leaving the younger sales associate attempting belated friendliness. "You are not from here?" she asked.

"Obviously not," I said. Luckily, a group of Japanese shoppers flocked into the salon in a flurry of excitement, so the saleswoman left my side.

When the senior associate returned it was to inform me that Madame St. Remis was indeed planning to pick up her purchases, tomorrow actually. "We said that we can deliver them to her hotel but, non, she insists to come into the shop herself, for more choosing, perhaps?"

"Of course! Never miss an opportunity to shop, that's my auntie. I will surprise her when she comes and have her select her own present. You won't betray me, will you?"

The woman placed a lovely manicured hand over her silk bodice. "Mais, non! Your secret is safe in my heart. I shall call you when she arrives, yes?"

"Yes, please. I will wait outside and then surprise her." I gave the woman the number for the blind phone and left the salon in a delirium of self-congratulation. If Maggie was here, Toby and Noel couldn't be far away.

Then I sobered. What would I do if and when I found them?

❧ 15 ❧

Soon I was back in old Istanbul and the Sultanahmet area, the oldest part of one of the oldest cities on earth. The taxi slid to a stop outside a row of tall wooden houses crammed together on a narrow, cobbled street where the soaring golden minarets and blue domes of the famed mosque could just be seen above a tall stone wall.

I disembarked on the curving street that dipped down towards the Bosporus. The noon call to prayer erupted all over the city in an eerie yet beautiful cadence. I paid the driver and gazed around, expecting an obvious restaurant sign but here, away from the jarring cacophony of traffic and neon, everything had toned down. A sign for a boutique hotel swung lazily in the breeze.

"Phoebe McCabe, over here!"

A sturdy little woman beckoned to me from a doorstep of a narrow brown-shingled house.

"Dr. Friedrich?" I asked, approaching.

Wearing an army-green safari jacket with buttons straining across her ample chest and a pair of tan cargo pants with red socks tucked into sneakers, she appeared at odds with the old world surroundings. A brilliant red silk scarf wrapped around her neck multiple times added to the impression of an army officer gone tribal.

"I am she and you are Phoebe McCabe. Erdogan describes you to perfection: 'Lots of red hair,' he said." Her accent was posh British with a slight Germanic bite. She pumped my outstretched hand energetically.

"That's all he could say about me was my hair color?" I asked, trying to retrieve my hand. Her hair, by contrast, consisted of no more than a skim of iron gray strands plastering her scalp—efficient, practical, and to the point.

"To Turks, red hair is significant, though as to what it signifies depends entirely upon the beholder. Erdogan is a good chap and I consider him my friend. Doubtless, he pegged you accurately." The kyanite blue eyes twinkled with amusement.

"Pegged me how?"

"Follow me. We'll talk inside. I have a table reserved upstairs."

She mustered me up a narrow flight of stairs that led past two dimly lit floors. I glimpsed empty dining rooms set with white table cloths and silverware. Gas light sconces on the stairwell flickered over silk brocade walls hung with sepia photos among paintings depicting Ottoman life. A waiter dashed downstairs balancing a tray, greeting Dr. Friedrich in Turkish, smiling, and nodding while exchanging pleasantries.

At last we reached the top floor, where another gentleman threaded us through the busy dining area to a balcony overlooking the Blue Mosque. We maneuvered directly to a table tucked into a far corner flush against the railing.

Eva grinned. "Yes, yes, quite the tourist vista, I'd say, but I'd rather pay for a touch of privacy than be tossed into the milling throng of most Istanbul restaurants. This is a favorite. Be seated. Yes, right there. You are the guest and so claim the benefit of this most magnificent view."

I lowered myself down, watching as she unraveled the long patterned scarf from her neck and dropped her green canvas utility sack to the floor. I slipped my own carpet bag between my feet.

"There," she said, grinning over at me as she sat down with a thud. "Lovely piece you have there," she nodded towards my bag. "A fine old Ottoman textile—an early depiction of the traditional tulip design. The enterprising Turks are forever squeezing dollars out of their textile treasures, but who blames them but we motley scholars?" Her smile dimpled her cheeks with a deceptively cherubic sweetness. "So, Phoebe, let's dispense with both preliminaries and formalities. I understand you have acquired an Anatolian kilim of some note. Show me."

I opened my mouth but she silenced me with her hand as a waiter slipped up to our table. She gave him a battery of instructions in Turkish, only consulting me once. "Are you vegan?"

"Still a carnivore," I assured her.

"Good show," and she finished giving our orders, leaving me perplexed. The last time someone ordered for me in a restaurant, I was five years old.

After the waiter disappeared, Eva turned back to me. "Well?"

"Well what?"

"The kilim, Phoebe. Let me see it."

I passed her my phone opened to the photo, which she took without giving it a glance. "I mean the original. I need to see the original."

"I didn't bring it," I said.

"Not here, perhaps, but I am quite certain you brought it to Istanbul. Don't be disingenuous with me, Phoebe. Be honest. Ex veritas scientia."

"Which means?"

"In truth knowledge. Be truthful and I can assist you."

"I only want to ask your opinion on the kilim. I wouldn't call that help."

"Don't quibble."

I said nothing further as I watched her focus in on the photo. Her eyes flickered as she pinch-widened the shot and peered down at the screen in quarter segments. When she lifted her gaze, her cheeks were flushed. "How did you come by such a specimen?"

"It showed up unbidden in my London gallery with Erdogan's return address."

"How extraordinary. Do you know who sent it?"

"Yes and no. It's complicated."

"Of course it's complicated. Luckily we have all lunch for you to untangle the specifics. Begin."

"Presuming I want to explain, which I don't. I mean, I don't know you, Eva. I'd hoped you'd share some knowledge with me, that's all. If I presume too much, my apologies for wasting your time. I'll just be on my way." I grabbed my carpet bag and raised my butt inches off the chair.

"Touchy, touchy. Do sit back down, Phoebe. Please." She waved me back, her tone softening. "I've become far too excited about these matters and tend to run a little roughshod over everything and everyone. Bad habit. Let me make amends. A woman on a mission must be forgiven. I'll disclose first, as a show of good faith, then it's your turn. Sound fair?"

"I've been getting that offer a lot lately. Go ahead."

"To begin with, I presume you comprehend the preliminary importance of this kilim?"

I still clutched my carpet bag in my lap ready to bolt. "You mean that it's definitely rare and a possible museum piece? Yes, I got that. I sell kilims and old textiles in London but admit to being still very much in learning mode. Anything else about this kilim's provenance, other than it's Anatolian and probably at least three hundred years old, is pretty thin on the ground with me."

"But you do know about the Anatolian Goddess, since you called the kilim by name?"

"I know she predates the current world religions, going back, in one form or another, to the earliest fertility goddesses in Neolithic cultures."

Eva grinned. "You said 'She'—I like that—She being the Queen of Heaven and Earth, the Divine Feminine, the manifestation of the connecting force between feminine and masculine, mother and child, life and death, and the essence of transformative spirit that enlivens all things."

I nodded, startled to hear a spiritual stream pour from Dr. Friedrich. "I guess," I said, relaxing my grip on my bag.

"The Anatolian Goddess forms the crux of my research and also lies at the center of a significant academic and theological controversy."

"What kind of controversy?"

"One that cost me my career and forced me into early retirement, as if that would stop me."

The waiter reappeared, smiling pleasantly as he began pouring white wine into glass goblets. I tried protesting but Eva shooed away my refusal. "Certain Turkish wines are actually quite palatable, contrary to popular opinion. This is one of the better vintages and hails from a little vineyard outside of Izmir—and, yes, Turkey is a Muslim country but one espousing moderate views, at least so far as wine is concerned."

Several small plates began appearing next: dishes of hummus, dolmades, small bowls of rice topped with various purees and olive oils, along with a basket of hot flat bread. Everything enticed me at once and I accepted Eva's insistence that I try a bit of everything. "Please, continue disclosing. I'll just eat and listen. What kind of controversy costs a scholar her career?" I asked before taking a bite of delicious bread.

"One that is connected to a theory not adequately substantiated by a significant archaeological find, in the view of her peers, and that also has the misfortune of being wildly unpopular with any number of competing interests, including several major religions. In other words, one that may threaten the world order."

I stopped chewing. "Go on."

"I once held the esteemed position of Assistant Director of the British Institute of Archeology in Ankara."

"I saw that on your email signature."

"Which they'd rather I stop using but whatever our disagreements, they can't erase history. My book will redeem me in the eyes of my colleagues and tip the world on its end."

"Wow. But how does the kilim fit in with world-tipping?"

"Allow me to give a little background first. Feel free to stop me if I'm repeating things you already know. It's a bad habit left over from my lecturing days. Anyway, as you no doubt realize, traditional kilims serve as an expression of group identity, a way for a family within a clan to express how they are both unique and part of a larger community. Designs and motifs are passed down the centuries to modern times by generations of Anatolian women."

"Yes, got that. So far, you haven't disclosed anything enlightening. These dolmades are incredible."

"Try the wine."

I never could do boozy lunches with dignity, but I was in Istanbul looking out over the Blue Mosque. I took a sip, startled by a flash of sensory images of sun-ripened vines on my tongue, smiled, and swallowed more. Eva drank deeply, well into her second glass.

"As I was saying, these kilims are an ancient symbolic language as well as the unique creative manifestation of woman's art, since the men do not weave in Turkish culture."

"I know."

"At the heart of my research is the role of this visual language as it emerges across the centuries in Anatolia. When occasionally one finds motifs that predate even Mohammed in this ancient land, they denote a thread leading deep into the human heart, back before recorded history."

I paused. "Aren't all Anatolian motifs ancient?"

"Most are, but over time some have become diluted, corrupted, if you will, and may look little like the originals. The first images were more anthropomorphic."

"Like my vulture goddess."

"Exactly. Where once women honored their goddess by working her representation into their art for home and community, gradually this became more difficult as society changed around them."

"Religious beliefs, you mean?"

"Religion has altered every society the world over, for better and for worse, in unequal measure. As the churches, synagogues, and mosques arose vying for spiritual dominance, all headed by men, of course, the Divine Feminine was forced underground—suppressed, transmuted, and annihilated. Women, presumably the weaker sex, were diminished in kind. We were forced to adapt, to hide, to be subjugated, both societally and spiritually. To work an image of a recognizable primitive female deity into their art in some communities is very dangerous and could be seen as heretical even today. Eventually, they forgot the original meaning of the motifs."

I nodded. "A woman's role in 2400 BC must have been significantly different from now."

"Research has landed soundly on the prospects of a matrilineal culture at work in early humanity. We were not so quick to weigh down on the relative worth of one sex over the other back in the beginning. Some scholars remain convinced that early humanity revered the giver of life as being at least equal in worth to her protector, the warrior male, if not more so." Eva shook her head and refilled her glass. "Women might have come a long way, but in the wrong direction when you consider that God was once a she or, at least, not exclusively male."

"Imagine how the world would have evolved had our species not spent the last few thousand years in full warrior mode? What if motherhood and nurturing were heralded as the most desirable traits?" I said, sipping my wine. "How would it have looked? Where would we be today?"

"Perhaps we might not be teetering on the brink of annihilation at this very moment." Eva lifted her glass. "I propose a toast: to the Vulture Goddess. May She find her wings again for the sake of all humanity."

I clinked my glass to hers. "To the Vulture Goddess!" I took a deep drink of the crisp wine and sat back. "But where does the vulture come in?"

"Vultures were not always seen as the dirty, opportunistic scavengers we see them as today but rather as a revered and significant part of the cycle of life and death. They were the cleansers, the ultimate recyclers. The Goddess gave life knowing that death is inevitable, and one of her totems, the vulture—she was rather fond of big cats, too—helped in the transformation."

"Vultures and goddesses seem so incongruous."

"To our modern way of thinking, perhaps. The Anatolian Goddess speaks in a visual language predating mankind's development of the written word."

"Initially, men transcribed while women described."

"You could say that. Our ancestors communicated visually and read the natural world around them to impart meaning to the universe. They saw how life came into being and then died, how certain creatures like the vultures participated in the great recycling." Eva sipped her wine and gazed away, past the Blue Mosque, past all the mosques, all the churches, all the synagogues.

"And?"

"And when I find a kilim like yours with that ancient motif almost intact, that close to the original goddess image, so unusually anthropomorphic, I know it can lead me closer to the truth. Somewhere in Anatolia several hundred years ago, a handful of women kept that motif alive, despite whatever secular pressures might attempt to influence their art. Somewhere I believe they still do."

"Still, as in today?"

"Quite possibly. I have seen enough of these images in similar kilim fragments of varying dates to lead me to believe that a family somewhere is still holding true to the ancient goddess across multiple centuries."

I swallowed, blinking back visions of circling vultures as the main dishes began arriving—lamb and beef kebabs and salad.

"Speaking of vultures, do eat!" my hostess exclaimed.

The next twenty minutes were a continuation of our feast, minus conversation. There was too much to enjoy and maneuver with the speared meat and various sauces. When finally, I sat back in my seat my stomach had expanded so much I could hardly breathe. "Oh, that was wonderful," I sighed.

Eva smiled. "I do so love to share a good meal with a friend, old or new."

"So, am I your new friend?"

"We share a certain passion."

"For kilims, you mean?"

"At the very least but it's much deeper than that. We are on the Goddess's business and we are meant to help one another."

"Pardon me?" The wine blurred my thoughts. "Me, on the Goddess's business? I don't think so. Really, the Goddess and I have only recently become acquainted." I closed my eyes.

"So you think."

"My days have become so fraught. Nothing is easy."

"Think how boring easy really is and be grateful you don't live that life. You said the circumstances around the kilim's arrival was complicated. Explain what you think you know."

I opened my eyes. "No, I mean, not so fast," I said, leaning forward. "Other than to give me a retrospective of Turkish tribal kilims and discuss the Goddess culture, what have you really disclosed?"

"You need to listen better, Phoebe. I said: supposing that family of women still protects the ancient goddess for reasons yet to be determined?"

"So?"

"Look around you, really look. How easy do you think it is for a traditional Turkish woman in a Central Anatolian village to protect the image of a prehistoric fertility goddess? In some households, women are not even permitted to pray in the mosques with the men. Is keeping the goddess alive a question of faith, resistance, or something else?"

Though my thoughts were jumbled, excitement still stirred as if I'd glimpsed something grand from far away and longed for a closer look. Or maybe I was just drunk. Probably the latter. Either way, I didn't see how the kilim linked with my brother.

"Help me find the answer, Phoebe. Let me see your kilim. It was sent to you for a reason. You're part of this somehow."

Yes, I knew Toby had sent that kilim to me for a reason; the man calling himself Jason Young had died for a reason. Noel dropped in to see me for a reason. Maggie tried to kidnap me for a reason. Foxy was tailing me for a reason. What did thieves have to do with goddesses? Was I the only one who didn't understand?

"She is calling to you. Heed Her call. Work with me here. Let me see your kilim in person. By assessing the dyes and wools, I may be able to hone in on the exact village, which to date has eluded me. Most of the kilims I've inspected so far have not been so complete. I must see it."

"Coffee," I said, waving my hand like a downing woman. I knew I was in no condition to make decisions.

Eva lifted a finger and a waiter darted to her side. "Coffee for my friend, please, Anin."

As the man dashed away, I sat studying my companion.

"I'm your strongest ally. We are both in service to the Goddess, whether you know it or not. Together, we'll vanquish our enemies."

For an instant I imagined Eva dressed in armor brandishing a sword. "But you don't even know who my enemies are," I pointed out. "I'm not even sure I do. Besides, it's overwhelming how many people suddenly want to be my friend."

"Ah," she nodded. "Which means you must have enemies."

I sat in silence for a few moments, my thoughts skittering around like fish in a bucket while Anin poured thick black coffee into tiny cups. Me, in service to the Goddess? Who was I but a lowly carpet monger struggling to extricate herself from her brother's criminal entanglements? And this former esteemed archaeologist was beginning to seem a little unhinged.

"That's Turkish coffee. Try it," Eva urged.

I took a sip. The brew burned sweet and strong down my throat. If only it would jump-start my brain, I might stand a chance of extricating myself from this lunch intact.

"We will attend together the International Textile gala tonight," Eva said with a nod. She leaned forward with elbows on the table, holding her tiny cup in both hands.

I blinked at her. "We will?"

"Of course. I'm sure you don't want to attend alone."

"How do you know I'm even attending?"

"I have seen the attendance list."

"You have?"

"I will introduce you to the key players in the ethnographic art world here in Istanbul, or at least those who think they are."

I could use a few key introductions. And maybe a nap. I nodded, trying to rouse myself. "What time is it now?"

"Two minutes to three and don't concern yourself with the tab. Lunch is my treat."

I stifled a yawn. "Oh, thank you. That's very kind. I'm so tired. I need to get back to the hotel or I'll be in no condition for tonight."

"What, no baklava? You haven't tasted baklava until you try it here."

"I really have to go. It's the wine." I rubbed my eyes and suppressed another yawn.

"If you must, go on then. Meet me in the lobby of your hotel at 6:30 sharp."

❧ 16 ❧

O nce in my room, I was so relieved to find the kilim still tucked inside the safe that I hugged it to my chest. I spread it across the bedspread and hovered my hands reverently above the weave. So old, so incredible, so powerful. Did it really represent an underground spiritual movement running counter to social and religious norms for hundreds, maybe thousands, of years? Or Eva was just a slightly unhinged though fervent scholar? And, more importantly, did I have the right to cloister it away as if it were truly mine? Toby had entangled me in this enigma. At least he could have sent proper instructions.

I didn't want to attend the gala with the hyper-insistent Dr. Friedrich any more than I wanted to go alone. Carefully, I returned the kilim to the safe and flopped onto the bed. Before my head hit the pillow, I struggled to recall if I had even told Dr. Friedrich where I was staying. I didn't remember one way or the other and in seconds I was past caring.

My phone rang me awake in what seemed like minutes but was nearly an hour later. "Phoebe, Sir Rupert here. I understand you are going to the reception tonight. May I offer you a lift?"

I bolted upright. "No, thanks. Did you wheedle an invitation?"

"My dear, I do not wheedle. Unfortunately, not being a textile aficionado means I am not on the mailing list and I have not been successful in acquiring an invitation. Most disappointing. I had thought to go as a pasha."

"I can picture you in a nice blue silk."

"I was thinking jonquil but, really, beggars can't be choosers. You do realize that your admirers may be present at this event?"

"If you're referring to Maggie, I doubt she'll ambush me in such a public place. As for the other two, I can only hope they'll be there."

"Do try not to be naive, Phoebe. I understand the event is in full Turkish costume so a potential threat could come in a multitude of disguises."

"I'll be vigilant. I'd better hang up and get dressed now."

"Did you enjoy your lunch with Dr. Friedrich?"

I paused, half annoyed, half amused. Had he read my iPhone emails or had tailed? "It was delicious, thanks for asking."

"Do beware of the noted doctor, as certain events in her history may place her firmly the side of the enemy."

"Ah, you mean of the duplicitous, treasure-seeking kind?"

"Exactly."

"I have so many of those individuals to choose from."

"Indeed. It is best not to align yourself with those that cannot be trusted."

"So true. Good night, Sir Foxy." And I pressed END before turning the phone off.

Clutching my toiletry bag, I climbed into the shower, emerging twenty minutes later ready to force my coarse hair in line with miracle tonics and gels. Tackling my face next, I smoothed on a little foundation to de-emphasize my freckles and tried applying powder to contour my face, tricks I'd learned from Maggie eons ago. Chic never worked for me so I aimed for interesting.

Next, I dressed. The silk tunic fell across my body in a flow of pattern, dousing me with just enough confidence to believe I could make it through the night. When I finally emerged from the bathroom, my room message light was flashing. An automated voice informed me that an envelope awaited me at the front desk. I grabbed my satchel, took one more glance at myself in the mirror, and exited the room.

Downstairs, the lobby was swarming with incoming bus tours, the lineups at the reception desk straggling six to seven weary people deep. I waited in the queue impatiently, scanning the lobby for Dr. Friedrich. When I finally reached the desk, the agent passed me an envelope but couldn't tell me who delivered it and when.

I scuttled through the throng and into one of the little antefoyers that branched from the main reception area. They were almost always empty. Perching on a velvet ottoman, I ripped open the envelope and there, scribbled on the back of a postcard, I read the following handwritten message:

MEET ME AT THE GALA AND HEAR ME OUT—N

Flipping over the card, I stared down at a picture of the Bosporus taken from the Topkapi Palace gardens. Noel at last. Finally, I'd get some answers.

"There you are!"

I blinked up at a red gold-embroidered robe belted over white harem pants and nearly dropped the card. The person inside the costume was nearly invisible. "Dr. Friedrich?" I peered under a coin-spangled fez with an attached veil. "Is that you?"

She laughed, apparently delighted by my consternation. "Had you fooled, did I not? Good show! I was obliged to have it shortened and widened, of course, but, at one time, it actually belted properly across my middle. Behold the perils of too many baklavas! There's nothing a carefully placed safety pin can't rectify."

"Or packing tape for extreme measures." I stood up, admiring every detail. "It's an Anatolian wedding dress, right?"

"Correct."

"It's gorgeous. I love that red," I said, all the time remaining distracted by Noel's note. Before the night was out, I'd have another chance to ask the right questions and perhaps even hear the answers.

"Thank you and you look quite the vision in that silk tunic, Phoebe. From that shop at the Arasta Bazaar, right? Splendid!"

I turned her around to study the veil's lace crochet edging and to admire the embroidered slippers. The ensemble appeared lovingly cared-for despite the scent of camphor.

"You'll see many people in traditional costumes tonight. The textile experts like to strut their proverbial stuff and nobody's prouder of their textile art than the Turks. Those who associate their dignity with standard suits and high fashion will just saunter about trying to look officious. We'll ignore those unless they have something interesting to say, which most don't. What's that in your hand?"

"Just a postcard." I shoved the card into my satchel and forced a smile. "Shall we walk, take a cab, what?"

"We'll take a cab. If not, we'll be stopping every six feet for photo ops. Tourists adore folk costume. I've been accosted five times just passing through the lobby. Come along."

Eva posed twice with visitors before we even made it to the door. Tourists believed her to be Turkish, a misconception she made no attempt to correct as she regaled the photographers with detailed accounts of Anatolian wedding costumes. I declined the urges from the Texan couple to include me in their selfie and hung back against the wall. The last thing I needed was to end up on Facebook or be Instagrammed across the world.

I slid next to one of the lobby shops that sold textile-covered boots and bags, thinking my patterned tunic might blend with the display. There, with my back to the glass, I stared out at the throng, searching for Toby or Noel. Would they be at the gala, too? Would I even recognize any of them before they spied me? Wouldn't I love to have the upper hand just once.

By the time Eva retrieved me, it had just turned 6:45. "You look rattled, Phoebe. What's wrong?"

"Nothing," I smiled. "I'm just not one for crowds."

"And yet you live in London and came to Istanbul." She stood peering into my face, her expression masked under the veil.

"You're not the veil type," I remarked.

She laughed. "They do very well when women use them for their own purposes, as I will be tonight."

"Are you trying to stay under wraps?"

"Rather. We'd better go."

"Oh, yes," I checked my phone. "Aren't we late?"

"They will lock the doors in 25 minutes so, yes, we must make haste. I'd rather not arrive too early and thus be conspicuous. Nevertheless, we don't want to miss the hors d'oeuvres, do we? The Museum of Islamic Art is sponsoring the event this year and they always present an impressive spread."

"You can't possibly be thinking of food after that enormous lunch."

"Nonsense. I can always accommodate food. Move along, Phoebe. Don't dawdle. We must push ahead of that clutch in front to nab the next cab." She tugged me through the revolving doors towards the curb, rattling off something in Turkish to the bellman, which resulted in us butting ahead to snatch the next taxi.

"What did you say?" I asked, sliding into the seat.

"That we were meeting government officials and couldn't be late."

"And are we meeting government officials?"

"Of course! These events are infested with them." She leaned forward and barked instructions to the driver before sitting back in the seat and patting my hand. "Calm down, Phoebe. You'll be fine. I won't let anyone eat you up. You do look a bit out of sorts. Just stick with me and smile."

The International Rare Textile and Ethnographic Exposition gala was being held in a building on the Topkapi Palace grounds. The invitations cost a hefty $500 in equivalent US dollars and were issued only to two hundred people per year. How Max made it to such an esteemed list, I'd never know.

My thrill mounted as we climbed from the cab to join a gathering milling about in front of armed guards. The sight of so many glorious costumes, both women and men swathed in silks and embroidery, thrilled me. That is, until the sight of gun-bearing men shot down my glee. And Noel planned to meet me in this armed fortress? It seemed crazy. On the other hand, here was an event where disguise and costume were nearly synonymous, making it a brilliant plan.

"Semi-automatic weapon seem a bit of overkill, no pun intended," I whispered to my companion.

"We're about to enter a venerable palace housing a fortune worth of priceless historical and religious artifacts. Feather dusters and slingshots would hardly have the desired effect. Just don't try stealing anything."

The Topkapi palace, home of the Ottomans for 400 years, naturally had armed guards. I just wasn't expecting so many, all looking as though infractions would be dealt with swiftly and probably at the end of a gun.

"Above all else, we are not to leave the prescribed area allocated to the event," Eva informed me, reading from a brochure we'd been handed as we waited in line outside the gates. "Which happens to be the royal harem this year, with some exhibits situated in the Imperial Hall. Oh, very good. One year, they piled us all in the Grand Kiosk, lovely with its view of the Bosporus and Marmara Sea, but a bit cramped. Here we go. Have your invitation in hand."

I did, watching as a guard inspected the card, checked me off on his computer, and passed me a name tag embellished like an Isnik tile strung at the end of a silken cord. Dropping it over my head, I noted with satisfaction the play of pattern and color against my tunic. I fervently hoped I'd glimpse those famed tiles that very night.

When it came to Eva, the guard hesitated. "Dr. Yilmaz?"

"That's correct."

I looked at her in amazement as the guard studied his computer. "It says here that Dr. Yilmaz is deceased."

"Also correct. There were once two and now only one. I am the Dr. Eva Yilmaz component. As you can see, I am still among the living. You can check your database going back three decades or more and find that I have attended many such events with my late husband. We were both doctors of archaeology. Obviously your current information requires an update."

"I apologize, Dr. Yilmaz. Please proceed." He passed her a name tag, which she pocketed quickly. In a moment she had waded ahead of me in the line.

I caught up to her standing in the next queue. "Dr. Yilmaz?" I whispered.

"My married name. I use either one or the other as it suits me."

"I didn't realize you had been married."

"Why would you? He was a renown Turkish archaeologist and a great man but that point didn't arise in our conversation. I, however, have fallen out of favor in Turkey so prefer to flash his name wherever possible lest they block my entrance. Borek had a standing invitation; I do not. More later. Look ahead. We're entering the gates."

Questions took second place to my mounting excitement. Here I was about to visit the Topkapi Palace, or at least part of it, and not with thousands of visitors but as part of a small group of special guests. Feeling honored, I followed the other attendees through a double-turreted gatehouse that could have been the model for Disney's fairy castle, only authentic . Authentic struck me as far more enchanting. Spotlights illuminated the venerable stone overhead as we passed through.

"The Gate of Salutation. Be prepared for a pat-down," Eva told me. "Security here will make Heathrow seem like a walk in the mall."

I spread my arms as a woman guard ran a metal detector up and down my limbs, remaining comfortable and relaxed right up until a guard at the next checkpoint demanded I pass over my carpet bag for the evening.

"What, why? Can't you just x-ray it and pass it back?"

"No bags permitted inside the grounds," the man explained. "We keep here."

Eva sidled up to me. "It's all right, Phoebe. They stand over them all evening like pit bulls with guns for teeth. It will be perfectly secure. What do you have in there that you can't part with? Nothing too valuable, I hope."

"My knitting."

The guard, who was performing a manual inspection of the contents, paused to lift out my project, which I'd carefully bundled and secured with my bamboo needles. He held it aloft like a fibrous octopus, the little balls of colored yarn dangling around his hands in woolly tentacles. "Please be careful," I urged him.

He handled my project with the respect afforded to small furry animals and carefully tucked it back into my satchel. After placing the bag on a shelf behind him, he handed me a check tag.

"Impressive piece, from what I could see," Eva remarked. "I'm a hooker myself. Never could make good with those two sticks."

"I keep forgetting that knitting needles second as dangerous implements to security folks. I might try stealing a jewel-encrusted sword by wielding a bamboo stick. Anyway, what did you do that keeps you from using Dr. Friedrich tonight?"

"Long story, Phoebe. I'll explain all another time. We must stay with these last stragglers."

Along with about eighteen others, we formed the last group admitted into the grounds before the gates closed. After that, I guessed guests would be turned away whether they were ticket-holders or not. Nobody I saw could be either my brother or Noel, regardless of attire, both men being over six feet tall. As for Maggie, the three women in our group were definitely shorter and wider than she.

We proceeded into a courtyard where lights and lanterns glowed among the gardens as if the stars themselves had entangled in the foliage. Music and the scent of roses and night jasmine infused the air. I fell under the spell, thinking how this moment, this symphony of the senses, must have been similar to what an Ottoman courtier experienced hundreds of years ago. All I wanted was to still myself in the moment and capture the swish of perfumed silks.

"You can almost imagine the sultan taking his pick-of-the-night concubine for a stroll around the gardens, can't you?" Eva asked.

I catapulted back to earth. "Oh, I forgot about that—the harem. Yes, I can picture it perfectly: the sultan strolling arm-in-arm with one of his many beautiful concubines selected from his harem like the choicest chocolate from a box of delectables, all splendor amid roses and lamplight." I sighed loudly. "Only women as sexual slaves is a real mood spoiler for me. Being a member of the ruling gender in the Ottoman Empire must have seemed like a male fairy tale."

"Pardon me but I must interrupt. I see you completely misconstrue the sultan's responsibilities," a male voice interjected. Eva and I turned to find a man in a dark tuxedo walking beside us. Of middle height and age with closely cropped gray-streaked hair and matching mustache brushing his upper lip, he gazed across at me with a slight supercilious smile.

Though he had stood out as we entered the palace in the way of a black-clad crow amid a flock of extravagant tropical birds, I hadn't noticed him in the last 15 minutes. "Excuse my interruption but I couldn't help overhearing. I am Mr. Attar Demir, Director of Ottoman Studies and adviser to the Topkapi Palace historical review."

I extended my hand. "Please to meet your acquaintance." Before I could introduce myself, he continued. "Ottoman sultans actually lived quite a tedious life sequestered in their luxury. Sitting day after day, hour after hour, hearing the tedium of plaintiffs in his audience chamber without the freedom afforded the simpler man."

"Poor guy," I said with little conviction.

"Yes, and where is the glory in such?" Mr. Demir said. "As for the harem, it was a little-understood but necessary feature of a culture that must assure the sanctity of the royal lineage at all costs. Many sultans rotated among the harem to ensure that each woman be afforded the same opportunity to carry his seed, a great honor at the time. Therefore, not selected like 'choicest chocolate' at all."

Eva snorted behind her veil and positioned herself between me and Mr. Demir. "You mean it was more like a salmon fertilizing spawn."

"No so at all!" humphed Mr. Demir.

"No, of course not—my apologies. Salmon mass fertilize, whereas the sultan had to do it sequentially, night after night, that is, if he chose. How tedious, indeed."

Mr. Demir's face had assumed the hue of a ripening pomegranate. "My point is that women of the harem lived a far richer life than the poorer classes. Most considered it a step up in circumstances to be pressed into the Sultan's service."

"Slavery was considered better than being under the control of a poorer man or starving?" I asked, leaning towards Mr. Demir.

"Women were not totally powerless in the Ottoman world. The mother of the sultan, for instance, exercised considerable influence in politics whether she came from slavery or not. Concubines of the sultan rose in rank according to ability."

"Influence is not true power, Demir. It is pleading and whispering and wheedling and persuasion behind the scenes, manipulation being often the only power women have been afforded historically," Eva stated.

Mr. Demir leaned towards my companion. "Eva Yilmaz, is that you under there? How could I mistake the tone?"

"It is and it's still *Doctor* Eva Yilmaz, Demir."

"I am surprised to find you here, Eva. I thought you had retired and returned to London in a fitting resolution to the unfortunate incidents of the past."

Eva brushed aside her veil, revealing a reddened face with eyes sparking fiercely. "As much as I would enjoy revisiting old arguments on the inter-pretation of social and cultural mores in a historic context, my friend and I have come to have a jolly good time. Good night to you. Come along, Phoebe." She linked arms with me and steered me ahead of the group towards a long building ablaze with lights.

"An old sparring partner?"

"Indeed, but not one of the more pleasant ones. Never liked him but I wish I had kept my mouth shut instead of announcing my presence like that. Soon every officious little twit at this event will know I've returned."

"Returned to Istanbul, you mean?"

"To Turkey, the land of my passion."

"You prefer to go incognito?"

"As much as possible, indeed."

"Why's that?"

"Later, Phoebe. I promise to explain everything soon."

"I see you have a lot of water running under your bridge."

"In truth, a veritable storm drain. Come, let's join the melee."

We proceeded across the broad grounds surrounded by elegant buildings and tall trees, the uniformed guards replaced now by men dressed in the imperial uniform of former times—baggy white pants gathered into boots, long gold tunics, and tall, conical hats.

The men were positioned along a paved boulevard that led to a set of porticoes gracing a richly tiled exterior. My eyes flickered across tiles patterned in blue, white, and gold leaf as we stepped between the guards wearing yet another century's uniforms and on into a long room dazzling with more pattern and color. This country intoxicated my senses.

Past the glittering wonder, I sought Noel but saw no one with his height and bearing. Where would he expect to rendezvous?

"Here is the gilded cage wherein those lucky women lived out their lives," Eva remarked. "The building houses 400 rooms and apartments surrounding a central courtyard where women could dally away their days waiting to catch one man's eye."

"How delightful," I remarked, feasting on the colors. "And they'd be warded by eunuchs, I suppose?"

"Absolutely. All male slaves lucky enough to hold this trusted position were relieved of their genitalia."

"Seems like a fair trade." I gazed around, seeking tall men in costume. I would enjoy nothing better than the sight of Noel Halloran dressed as a eunuch but doubted even his sense of irony would prevail there. Since a sultan probably selected the tallest and the strongest male slaves from many lands, Noel could easily pass as a guard.

The guests had donned a stunning array of costumes from various centuries, all resplendent as they milled about the long hall, sipping drinks and chatting while a quartet played in one of the side niches. Only a handful wore suits and modern attire, while most appeared to have plunged into the spirit of the evening, a celebration of Turkish historical dress across the ages.

My eyes glossed over the glory, resting on several sultans and pashas dressed in big pillowy hats festooned with jewels and feathers. Many women wore long gowns, some with short jackets typical of the last days of the Ottoman Empire, while others donned veils or displayed their faces below tall, fez-like headgear.

Everything sparkled, shone, and glowed against the background of intricate tiles and fabulous fabrics. Color scrolled in patterns, entwined in images, and gleamed across tiles along with silk, wool, and velvet. Forget minimalist. Here, no white space prevailed, or so I thought.

At first, all I could do was stand and stare, trying to bear up under the sensual assault until I glimpsed a few men in long white robes sailing through the gathering. Some wore tall camel-colored hats, while others wore skull caps, but all appeared like snowy pages weaving through an illuminated manuscript.

"Eva, who are those men in white?"

"They are traditional Muslims who more closely follow the path of Mohammed while those in the shorter white robes with the tall felt hats are from the Mevlevi order, more commonly known as the Whirling Dervishes or Sufis."

"The Sufis as in Rumi? I have heard of them."

"I do wonder if they are here as costume or if the order will be giving us one of their mystic dances? Oh, I do hope so. The Mevlevi are quite wonderful. They embrace love in the way of Rumi, and their dancing closely aligns with the sacred feminine practices of ancient Greece and beyond where dancing awakens the sacred communion. Of all Islamic sects, Sufism above all focuses on love, tolerance, and the elimination of personal ego."

"Are there women Sufis?"

"Not in the true sense but many women practice in secret. Islam, like all the major religions, doesn't permit women access to the higher spiritual orders, since we apparently have inferior souls or no souls at all, much the same in other religious practices. I have had many engaging conversations with Sufis, and there is much agreement among them that women have been excluded, not by the word of God but by the dictates of man."

I found myself staring at one of the men in the tall tan hats as he wove through the gathering, his back to me still, nodding at the guests along the way. He towered over everyone in stature, but the addition of the foot-high hat only made him seem like a moving turret. Something about his slow ambling stride seemed familiar.

"Phoebe." Eva touched my sleeve, "Come, I'd like you to meet an old friend."

I was reluctant to tear my gaze away, but Eva urged me forward towards a woman standing by the wall fountain dressed in a dark blue velvet robe trimmed in what looked like real fur. She turned to Eva quizzically as if not recognizing her at first, her wide almond-shaped eyes searching and intelligent.

"Talya, it's so good to see you again. It's me, Eva."

"Eva, Eva Yilmaz? Is that really you?"

"It is," Eva exclaimed, throwing back her veil. "I'd like you to meet my friend, Phoebe McCabe, here for the exhibition. Phoebe, this is Dr. Talya Beren, Director of the Turkish Costume division of the Museum of Islamic Art."

We shook hands, Talya's smile genuine and warm. "So happy you could join us, Phoebe. But dear Eva, I thought we might never see you again. You have been so quiet and I have missed you."

"My work keeps me busy, Talya, but I have been coming to Turkey off and on across the years, just not on official business. I've been keeping low to the ground. You know I would never be kept away so easily."

She nodded. "I know it well and would have been very disappointed had it been otherwise. We need more scholars of your ilk. Did you know that we have an Anatolian Goddess kilim on display tonight?"

Eva grinned. "Of course. This is why I am here and to accompany Phoebe, of course. Where is the goddess?"

"I will show you. Follow me."

We left the crowded hall, bypassing the servants bearing trays of food and drinks, making our way through several rooms and down a hall guarded by men in more period uniforms until we reached a long corridor where the walls appeared paved by textiles under glass. Only a few guests stood admiring the exhibition.

"Oh," I gasped, drinking in the sight of antique rugs encased on either side. I yearned to soak up the detail of every textile, read every description, not rush a single moment, but Eva and Talya strode purposefully down the length of the corridor. I followed them to stop before a single kilim suspended as if in midair behind the glass.

"Behold, the best preserved of the Anatolian Goddess kilims to my knowledge," Talya announced. "I knew you'd want to see this one. If you hadn't come, I would have sent you a photograph."

Upon an indigo background, intersecting triangles with hooked extensions worked in rust, white, and cream wool, occupied the center field with banding flanks of hands-on-hips motifs in black and rust. Each motif mirrored the one below in double symmetry. Not as anthropomorphic as my kilim, the motifs only echoed my goddess without equaling her power, but it was still a stunning specimen.

I turned to Eva, finding her staring fixed at the kilim, hands pressed to her lips. "Eva?"

"There She is, Phoebe, my goddess, caught within the weave. Isn't She amazing?"

"She is," I agreed.

"I simply must inspect the back. Talya, please inform whomever is in charge that I must inspect the reverse of the kilim immediately."

My gaze caught Talya's, who turned away as if embarrassed or anxious or both. "That's not possible Eva, not tonight or probably at any other time, though I'd certainly be pleased to submit a request on your behalf."

"Why must I endure the tedium of a long wait when it would be easy to grant me this simple request in a timely manner? I am a scholar and deserving of such courtesy."

"Of course you are. It's just that it's a very rare piece—"

"Of course it's a very rare piece," Eva said, her voice rising. "Am I not partially responsible for assisting Turkey in recognizing the value of such kilims? Has my research been totally undermined; is that what you're implying?"

"I'm implying nothing of the sort. I'm only explaining that we have certain rules and regulations in place to protect our art and that immediately dismantling an exhibition on the spot at the request of one person, no matter how esteemed, is not practical. We keep it in a sealed environment for conservation reasons, you must understand that."

"But you must understand that somewhere in Anatolia at this very moment, unscrupulous thieves may be robbing a site connected to this kilim. All proof of the significance of this motif may be destroyed along with precious artifacts. It is imperative that I see the reverse now so that I can best assist the authorities to find this sacred site."

"Eva, you are no longer permitted to engage in archaeological activities in this country. You know this."

"You don't understand, Talya." Eva pressed her palm against the glass.

"Eva, don't! The sensors—"

A guard stepped forward, shouting: "Madam, stop!"

An alarm ripped the air just as I glanced down the hall and caught sight of the tall Sufi standing no more than 50 yards away—unmistakable face, arresting eyes, bone structure, and expression, watching me. I cried out and lunged down the hall, guards streaming past me in the opposite direction. Once at the door, he had disappeared.

The alarm blared relentlessly. Behind me, chaos erupted as Eva called out something in Turkish and both Talya's and the guards' voices joined the fracas.

I caught a glimpse of a white robe heading rapidly towards the harem main hall and bolted after him, eyes fixed on the tall hat bobbing above the heads of the guests.

He was exiting a side door to the grounds. Pushing my way through, I burst out into an unfamiliar lantern-lit courtyard and circled the fountain calling his name.

Turning in all directions looking for some sight of him, I finally caught a flash of white out of the corner of my eye. In seconds I was bounding across the garden towards the ghostly swirl of white robes, oblivious of the guard calling out behind me.

I didn't tackle him so much as reach out to slow him down. In so doing, I grabbed his arm, which caused him to stop so suddenly that I whammed into him. He lost his balance, the force pitching us both into the rose bushes, me on top. Everything blurred. I only recall the guards lifting me off the holy man, who lay on his back in a probable state of shock. As he unfolded himself and climbed to his feet, I found myself staring at a much shorter man, a man who was definitely not Noel.

Two guards pointed rifles at me.

"Don't shoot!" I held up my hands. "It was mistaken identity!"

❧ 17 ❧

Eva and I sat together in my hotel room, she in the only chair and me perching on the bed opposite. We had hardly spoken since being escorted off the Topkapi Palace premises and forbidden to return, our passes revoked, both unceremoniously bundled into a cab and banished from the gala.

"If it weren't for Talya, we'd be in jail right now. Or, in my case, probably shot," I said, breaking the silence. "I don't know what she told those guards in the end but I swear she took our necks out of the noose."

"Yes," Eva said in a flat voice. "She insisted we were both mentally unstable and petitioned our release accordingly. Why would anyone take a pair of crazy women seriously?"

"Well, really, what did we do that was such an act of insanity? You touched a glass case while demanding an exhibited item be inspected by you on the spot while I jumped a holy man and sent him flying into the rose bushes. In an unauthorized part of the grounds," I added before stifling a laugh. Eva's appearance soon sobered me.

She sat, hands between her knees, staring at the floor. Somehow her red dress had been ripped, leaving the headdress dangling down her back by its shredded veil. Though her knitted Turkish slippers remained intact, for the first time I noticed they had been pulled over sneakers. If mentally unstable were a look, I thought guiltily, she'd nailed it.

"Your dress is ripped. Maybe I can try to repair it? I have scissors and thread somewhere."

"It was once my wedding dress long ago, so long ago. Thank you for the offer but I will just retire it as it is."

I got up and untied the veil, unwinding it gently from her neck and laying the ruined hat in her lap. "Your wedding dress? Then it's too special to leave ruined. It's symbolic and laden with memories."

"Perhaps."

"Everybody believed we were crazy readily enough, didn't they? The wacky Canadian attacking a Sufi accompanied by the retired archaeologist demanding to inspect a museum display," I said, gazing down at the top of the gray hair.

"I'm not retired, whatever they may think. Passion and commitment do not get old. It is because I spoke in an authoritative manner that they assume I must be unhinged. A woman with authority—especially an older woman with authority—is a subject of suspicion, always. How dare I? You have faced sexism as a woman, Phoebe, but you are still too young to face sexism and agism together."

I shook my head and pushed back tears.

"If I still bore my previous title," she continued, "they might grant me some measure of respect but, once stripped of that, I became nothing more than a mere self-important old woman. Why must becoming older relegate women to irrelevance?" Her gaze remained fixed on the carpet, but her tone now bristled with its usual energy. "Why must passion be suspect?"

"A woman should be seen as a sum of everything she was and is rather than as diminishing according to our biology."

"Sexual attraction is the measure by which society weighs us. Once, long ago, the old were revered, not marginalized. Perhaps, if enough of us refuse to be devalued, you just might inhabit a different world thirty years from now, Phoebe."

"In the meantime, I'd rather be a free crazy female than an imprisoned sane one any day. Would you like tea or something else to drink?"

"Thank you, no."

"How about something from the mini bar? We have to re-establish our dignity somehow. Chocolate helps." I opened the refrigerator door to assess the contents. "No chocolate here. Not a Turkish thing, I guess. Ugh, potato chips just won't do—too flaky. We need something rich and nuanced with flavor, much like ourselves. Wait, how about Turkish delight?" When Eva didn't answer, I shook the tiny ornate tin appreciatively, flipped the lid, and offered her contents.

"They all think I'm crazy," she said finally, plucking a piece of paper-wrapped jelly from the tin. "Mad, totally mad. How dare I enter that event and stomp and puff and make demands?" She looked across at me. "They don't listen, refuse to understand, and yet it was me, not Borek, who revealed the significance of the goddess motifs all those years ago. He found the site but I provided the overlay of significance."

"Why don't they know that?"

Eva sighed deeply, gazing out to space. "We had an agreement, Borek and I, the details of which are too complicated to explain tonight. Even then, I was too vehement in my convictions. A scholar must be stripped of passion and speak only from the intellect while remaining well-buttressed by concrete facts and citations. My facts were always thin on the ground and I could not reveal the location, details the government demanded for other reasons. As a result, I fell into disgrace."

"Well," I said, returning to my perch and selecting a candy for myself. "We're safe now."

"Why did you jump the Sufi?"

"I didn't jump the Sufi, Eva. That sounds judgmental."

"My apologies. Judgment is not my intention, I assure you."

"I kind of fell into him, really, because I thought he was someone else."

"You thought you recognized him?" Eva's eyes fixed on me, suddenly alert.

"I saw a man dressed as a Sufi earlier and I recognized him at once as somebody I needed to speak with. Even in the disguise, he was unmistakable. I might have finally got the answers I needed but the alarm went off. Again." I studied the Turkish delight moments before taking the first bite. Pistachio and cherry. After chewing reflectively for a few seconds, I added: "Only, how did he get in? What's he up to in Istanbul, anyway, besides hiding, I mean?"

"Perhaps he also came to see the kilim at the exhibition?"

I turned, studying her as she studied me. "What is it about the kilim that is so interesting? Sure, I get the link to some anthropological marvel but there's something you're not telling me."

"The kilim will help us find something lost that must be regained at all costs."

"A tribe of women clinging to an ancient fertility sect?"

"That in itself would be enough."

"To an archaeologist, perhaps. The company this archaeologist keeps will be interested in something more marketable." I replaced the half-eaten piece of Turkish delight into its paper wrapper.

"Perhaps."

"When are you going to fill me in on all the details?"

"All will unfold as it should, regardless, for you are about the Goddess's business."

I shook my head vigorously. "I am not about the Goddess's business. Please stop saying that. I am here to purchase kilims for my shop and, yes, to find the person who sent me that kilim and his ... friends."

"The Goddess sent it to you."

Maybe she *was* crazy. "The Goddess did not send me that kilim. I'm sure it had more to do with low-life vices like greed and avarice than any higher power."

"We are all part of a greater plan, Phoebe, our lives intersecting and entangling far beyond our understanding or awareness. We think we act independently when, in fact, our lives are but threads in the Goddess's loom. If I said God instead of Goddess would my words make more sense to you?"

"I would better understand your religious fervor maybe."

"Then substitute 'God' for 'Goddess', if you must. Continue to live in the patriarchal view of the world, if you must. When you can take a broader vista, ask yourself how a Universal Spirit can be relegated to a gender which is totally animal in nature?"

I looked away, confused. These spiritual proclamations left me reeling. No wonder her colleagues had lost confidence in her capabilities—an archaeologist muttering about goddesses? At the same time, everything she said had a ring of truth like a clear bell chiming in the wilderness so far away I could barely hear.

"That candy was just way too sweet for me this late at night." I tossed the half-eaten piece into the wastebasket and yawned. "Anyways, it's late and I need to get to bed. Are you okay to get home by yourself? Where are you staying, by the way?"

"I'm staying with my brother-in-law and his family not far away. I'll take a cab but, Phoebe," she reached across the distance between us and grasped my arm, "first let me see the kilim. I know you brought it with you. She would not let you leave it behind."

"She? Oh, you mean the Goddess." I hesitated, worried that the kilim might ignite another rant but wanting to comfort her any way I could. What harm would it be to show her the kilim? "Wait here," I said.

I left her standing by the bed as I strode around the corner to the short hall leading up to the door. Opening the closet, I crouched, tapping in the numbers for the digital safe. Relieved to find everything just as I left it, I pulled out my kilim like a sleeping baby.

Eva stood directly behind me, gaze fixed on my bundle.

"I asked you to wait," I said over my shoulder.

"I have waited far too long." She held out both hands as if in readiness to receive a holy child.

I brushed past her, returning to the bed to carefully unfold the kilim across the cover, Eva following me like a puppy. "I have to say, this specimen is much more impressive than the one we saw tonight." I said as I spread the textile open. "Look at it. So beautiful!" It never failed to impress me.

"Oh," Eva fell to her knees, in prayer, I thought momentarily, but, no, instead she gently turned the piece over and bent her head to study the back. A monocle-style magnifying glass appeared from somewhere—she carried one in her pocket?—and now traveled the kilim's reverse pressed to one eye. "Yes!" she muttered amid strings of Turkish.

"Is it what you expected?"

"No, yes! More, much more." The monocle dropped from her eye as she turned her sharp blue eyes to me. "Phoebe, I think I know where this originated."

"Really?"

"I can identify the exact area in Anatolia where the kilim was woven. See this," she pointed to a tuft of rusty wool that sprouted around the frayed parts. "Turkish red was developed by using madder root mixed with sheep's blood. Typically, the yarn was steeped, mixed with dung and olive oil, and steeped again, usually finished off with gall nut solution, which has a high level of tannic acid. However, sometimes whole forests were wiped out in wildfires, resulting in dyers needing to source alternative mordants through experimentation."

Despite the sudden switch to lecture mode, she fingered the tuft lovingly. "One such fire whipped across the steppes of a certain region in Anatolia three hundred years ago, destroying grasslands, forests, and nearly the entire village. The weavers thereafter needed to source alternate mordants in a region devastated by fire, resulting in an inferior dye that turned rusty brown rather than remaining red in the ensuing years. Hence, this kilim's striking discoloration."

She could flick from fevered to scholarly in seconds. "Fascinating," I remarked and meant it, but weariness had taken hold and I just wanted to go to bed. "Do you want to take pictures of it or something before you go?"

Eva turned back to study the kilim for a long moment. Sighing, she climbed to her feet and retrieved the monocle from the floor. "I suppose it would be useless to implore you to let me take the kilim for safekeeping?"

"Totally."

"And yet you must recognize that its value far exceeds even its museum worth and should be under better protection than a hotel safe? Any employee could access that safe with a little finagling."

"I'm not letting it go. It was given to me for a reason."

"And so it was. The Goddess has entrusted you with its care. If you won't, in turn, entrust it to me, then I beseech you to come with me to Anatolia to find the village of its origin. Help me find what's lost."

"Explain exactly what you mean by *what's lost?*"

"It's a very long story, best told when we have much time, which is currently not the case. Come with me, Phoebe."

"No." I didn't mean to sound so abrupt but I was tired of her mystic references and just wanted answers, preferably served in block print. "I mean, thank you for the offer but I simply can't. I'm here to find what's

WARP IN THE WEAVE

lost, too, but I'm looking for something of the human variety, and when I find them, I plan to serve up some very ungoddess-like retribution. Besides, I have a few more errands to run here in Istanbul and then I must return to London. I have a gallery to manage and just too many loose ends to go on a road trip."

Eva sighed. "Very well, but don't be surprised if the Goddess sends you in unexpected directions. My cell number is at the bottom of the card I left on the bed. Call me when you change your mind."

"What do you mean by *when?* I won't change my mind," I said while holding the door.

She gathered up her ruined fez, stuffed the veil into her bag, and strode towards me. "The Goddess may change it for you."

18

"Serena?" I pressed my iPhone against my ear as I backed up against a low wall. Behind me lay a strange octagonal building the guide book didn't identify, and ahead, a lovely park. I'd already seen Sir Foxy's limo coasting along the streets. Luckily there'd been no place for him to pull over. Though I kept his phone off, I did wave a couple of times.

"Phoebe! I have been so worried—no call, no emails! Say you are too busy to phone me every hour but that everything is so fantastic."

"I'm too busy to call you every hour, maybe even every day, Serena. I just haven't had a moment to call. I have a few errands to run and then I'll be home soon. Everything is so fantastic as in impossible to believe. More on that when I get home. I'm supposed to leave the day after tomorrow, which isn't too far away. Is everything good at the shop?"

"Everything is fine. You must not worry about a thing."

"Oh, good." I kneaded my neck muscles with my free hand. "And Agent Walker?"

"Nothing—no shocked eyebrow, no shiny head."

"I expected him to be haunting you, pressing for details. I just don't get that guy."

"Be glad he is elsewhere chasing real criminals, yes? But the exhibition, tell me, was it is as magnificent as you hoped?"

"Oh, yes, the exhibition certainly exceeded every expectation." Thoughts of that fiasco hit me like a taser. "I'll tell you all about it once I'm home."

Then my burner phone began ringing. "Rena, I've got to go. I'm standing on a street and it's crazy here. I'll talk soon." I clicked off and tossed one phone into the bag while scrambling around for the other. Precious seconds were squandered finding the right one, and I ended up pressing TALK mere seconds before the call disconnected.

"Hello?"

"Mademoiselle? Il est Madame a la Chanel."

"Oui!" I turned my back on the street traffic to better hear.

She told me in hurried French that Madame St.Remis had just called to confirm that she would be picking up her order within the hour. Could I come over immediately?

"I'll be there waiting outside. Please don't give me away," I said in French. The prospects of finally cornering Maggie excited me so much, I could barely contain myself—the hunter closing in on prey. Usually the one stalked, finally I was the hunter.

Scrambling to the curb to hail a taxi, it suddenly occurred to me that I couldn't track Maggie with my red hair blazing or risk Foxy tagging along. Subterfuge was critical. Luckily, the perfect disguise was an easy find.

I slipped into a small shopping arcade wedged between two large buildings. After scouting a few shops, I located one catering to traditional Turkish working women and hastily purchased a headscarf, or hijab, and a long navy trench coat.

The shop attendant smiled but asked no questions when a western woman burst into her shop requesting traditional attire to wear over jeans. Her graciousness extended to assisting me with the proper application of the headscarf. She explained in excellent English how the wearing of the hijab had once been banned but now reinstated by the present government. I gathered that this arrangement satisfied her but I did nothing to encourage details. Precious minutes were ticking by. Supposing Maggie picked up her loot in minutes and went on her way?

Upon exiting the shop, I realized my biggest signature was slung over my shoulder. That bag offended Maggie as an affront to mandatory chicness. In desperation, I bought a large cheapo backpack from a street vendor and shoved my carpet bag inside. That done, I was ready for stalking.

I hailed a cab and explained to the driver that I needed him to wait outside a shopping arcade while I went into a store. His English was good but my explanation complex. He needed to wait but be ready to drive really fast once I came out. "Why you not call another cab when finished?" he asked. I assured him that wasn't possible but I'd pay him well. We struck a deal and I climbed into the car.

"Bad traffic always," he said as we pulled into the stream of cars and began weaving across town. No sign of Foxy's black limo followed.

"Yes, I can see that." I sank against the seat. What would I do when I finally tracked her down? I always did best thinking on my feet even if it meant breaking a limb along the way. I meant that literally since I still bore the scars on my leg from my last adventure.

"You married Turkish?" the driver asked.

"Pardon?" Oh, I realized, he referred to the hijab. "Yes. Engaged," I told him. "My soon-to-be husband is from Istanbul." I scrambled to embellish further. "I must keep the mother-in-law happy." I nodded and smiled.

He gazed at me in his rear view mirror, his expression puzzled. "You will be Muslim?"

"Ah, no. I don't know," I said, flustered. Why would a western woman wear a hijab if she wasn't converting to Islam?

"My wife wears hijab. I not force but her father, he say she must."

"But does she want to?" I asked, avoiding asking why either a husband or a father had the right to dictate a grown woman's choices.

"She wants to keep peace. She is good woman."

Did that mean she'd be a bad woman if she didn't please her father? This thinking was so foreign to me but, as a guest in another world, I sealed my lips.

I had to admit, the anonymity of the hijab and trench coat suited my purposes. If not for my pale complexion, I could have blended in with the Istanbul street population. Many women wore the hijab here. Those who didn't, brandished their individuality, relaxed and open, while others found artful ways to wear their hijab and still be fashionable. Despite my unease at wearing Muslim clothing, I preferred not to advertise myself as an obvious outsider, either.

When we reached the arcade, I paid him up to that point and explained again that I needed him to wait. By then, I knew him as Mr. Burek.

"But no stopping here," he pointed out. "No place to wait."

"Could you drive around the corner? I will be back, I promise. No, better still, I'll call you." He nodded his agreement and I took his phone number, entering it into my speed dial as he drove away.

I slipped into the shoppers strolling the arcade. With my head down, my backpack over my shoulders, I headed towards the Chanel shop. Nobody gave me a second glance.

I approached the shop, standing just outside the plate glass window, studying my cell phone while covertly glancing inside. I couldn't see a thing from that vantage, but I couldn't risk entering, either. My solution was to slip across the promenade and stand against a wall, watching, the cell phone as my ruse.

Humans fixed on a tiny screen was the new norm worldwide. I watched and waited, pretending to be texting. So many minutes passed that I was certain I had either missed Maggie or she was very late. Either way, I couldn't stand there all day. Eventually, even a forever-texting woman would look conspicuous.

Then a man in dark blue trousers, a white shirt, and tie, wearing a peaked hat, stepped from the shop and lit a cigarette. He leisurely paced outside the store, his gaze slipping across me without interest. A security guard taking a break?

I stood, flicking through my iPhone photos and re-reading email for what seemed ages while covertly watching. When his phone jangled, he ground out his cigarette under his shoe, and slipped back into the store, exiting moments later burdened with black boxes and Chanel shopping bags. Head down, he rapidly dashed off down the street.

Seconds later, out swept a shapely woman, coiffed with shiny black hair seemingly shellacked to her scalp. Her lips slicked brilliant red above a priestly white-collared black jacket belted over a pencil skirt. It was a startling juxtaposition of wanton severity and so Maggie— the fashion slave, paying homage to couture.

I watched her five-inch heels peck the ground like foraging fowl as she proceeded down the arcade in the direction of the man.

The sight erupted a fire storm in me so strong, I wanted to shove her to the ground, wipe that gash of lipstick from her mouth, and shake her until her eyes bulged. Instead, I fell in among the pedestrians behind her, clenching my teeth. She would not escape me this time.

We emerged onto another road, heavy with traffic, all one-way, but I couldn't see a street name anywhere. I pressed the speed dial and waited for the cab driver to answer while Maggie darted across the street to a limousine.

My call got snagged in a telecommunications loop. An automated voice fired away in Turkish. I hadn't done something necessary to connect with an international call. Blah blah. Several clicks followed in quick succession until a London operator asked how she could help.

Maggie's black car slipped away from the curb while I barked frenzied orders to the operator, who coolly informed me that I needed to add the Turkish country code to my number and, if I'd provide the number, she'd connect my call. Only, I didn't have the number, seeing as my phone was currently pressed against my ear and Maggie was getting away.

Then, incredibly, blessedly, I saw Mr. Burek on a sidewalk ahead, smoking outside his car while chatting to a minivan driver. I sprinted up to him and gesticulated towards the speck of black car stuck in traffic. "Follow that car!"

Startled, he stared where my finger pointed. "Like the movies?"

"Yes, hurry, please!"

He tossed away his cigarette and leaped into the driver's seat while I dispensed with formality and climbed in beside him. "I must catch that woman! She's my aunt but I haven't been able to call." I waved my phone. "No connection, you know?"

Mr. Burek, nodded, intent on keeping the black car in his sights as we merged into a four-lane road. We proceeded along a broad avenue graced by large white buildings, apartment complexes, and a lovely mosque. "Suleyman Seba Caddesi," he said.

I had no idea what he referred to, so fixed was I on keeping Maggie in view. We wove in and out of traffic, losing the limousine only to have it reappear moments later as a bus passed or a corner straightened into another boulevard. We entered a curving road that wove through a park.

"Yildiz Park," Mr. Burek told me.

"Okay."

Now we were on a divided highway running parallel to the Bosporus. Yachts and large pleasure craft bobbed on the blue water while parkland and grand houses occupied the opposite side. The limo took a left-hand turn, diving under an overpass and across the highway to the parkland.

We hit a traffic light and ground to a halt. Mr. Burek seemed unconcerned. "Slow traffic among houses," he remarked. "Your aunt must be very rich."

"Very." Pulling out my iPhone, I opened my Google map app and dropped a pin on our current location so I could follow our route on the map.

When finally we caught a glimpse of the limo slowing down on a tree-lined hill in front of us, I cautioned the driver to stay back and pull to the side.

"I can drive right up," he offered.

"No, it's okay. I want this to be a surprise." And it would be a big one. I saved the location on the map and pocketed the phone.

I hastily paid Mr. Burek, thanking him profusely and adding a generous tip. He pulled away, leaving me standing on a deeply shaded hill, the trees framing the Bosporus behind me and secluding grand houses all around.

I began to climb, keeping beside the tall manicured hedge. The limo had turned into a driveway ahead, and when I reached the spot, it was no shock to find an ornate gate locked against intruders. Peering through the iron bars, I saw a tiny guard house positioned beside a curving driveway that disappeared amid the foliage. Though the gatehouse appeared unoccupied, the camera beside the intercom didn't encourage lingering.

I left the gate and slipped along the hedge until I found a break wide enough for me to squeeze through. All that got me was a scraped cheek and a view through the fence at broad rolling lawn.

There had to be an alarm system rigged with all kinds of fancy burglar detection devices here, not to mention employees. I burrowed deeper into the hedge until I could better peek through the rails. A white three-story mansion with wraparound balconies, tall arched windows, and green lawns abloom with flowers indicated that Maggie, possibly the whole trio, had nabbed an impressive hideaway. But how was I supposed to get in?

I backed outside the hedge, surveying the quiet street, considering my options. I almost missed the sound of an approaching car before diving back undercover just as a white van pulled up to the gate. An exchange of Turkish followed over the intercom.

I could hear the gates creaking open and counted ten seconds before leaping out behind the van and scuttling through, the gates closing behind me. I ducked behind a berry bush, adrenalin racing.

After several minutes hearing no alarms, I crawled from bush to bush until I was deep inside the garden. There I found the perfect hidey-hole: a copse of ornamental palms surrounded by banks of glossy-leaved jasmine bordering a tinkling fountain. By scooting deep into the fragrant underbrush, I could rest my back against the fence in what turned out to be a leafy little tent.

I took a few minutes to allow my heart to return to normal before leaving my bag and crawling on my hands and knees to the edge of the shrubbery. There, I found a great view of the back patio. Large French doors opened to the garden. A maid was setting a table under a kind of arabesque-style loggia with a fireplace and big comfy chairs. A manservant dashed about in a fez and short jacket, adjusting a coffee urn and setting a bouquet of flowers in the center of a white tablecloth.

I waited and watched until, at last, Maggie slipped into view. Gone was chic Chanel along with the glossy wig. In its place she had donned a long pale blue silk robe patterned with stylized tulips, her blond hair loose over her shoulders. The manservant pulled out her chair as she lowered herself down, crossed her legs, and waited while he adjusted a napkin over her lap.

In minutes, the maid appeared carrying a coffee urn and a tray of snacks that seemed to be a variety of artfully constructed vegetables. Though not close enough to see the particulars, I guessed she had ordered some near calorie-free mid-afternoon repast that could be inhaled molecule by molecule. I nearly gagged. Maggie playing to the manor born on her stolen loot while Max drowned his broken heart?

Waiting and watching, I keened for a glimpse of Toby or Noel, but Maggie seemed alone but for her staff. She kept checking her phone for messages, looking tense because maybe someone somewhere didn't contact her when she expected.

Finally, she snapped an order to her man who leaped over to light a cigarette. Back to smoking? Bad nerves, maybe? Several minutes passed before I grew weary of watching Maggie flip from bored to frustrated while picking away at some carrot escargot or eggplant tartar. I couldn't make a move in daylight with so many people around, so my only option was to stay hidden until nightfall.

Scuttling backward, I returned to my jasmine bower, made myself comfy against the fence, and settled in to wait until nightfall. Knitting, my constant companion, kept boredom at bay.

Before resuming the ornamental stranded border which would frame my design, I positioned the project on the ground, added a sprig of jasmine, and took a photo with my iPhone—one more addition to my Knitting Exotica digital photo album. To date, I had knit in the Tower of London, on the London Eye, and in a beautiful little cove in Bermuda. Today, I would add Knitting in a Jasmine Hedge in Istanbul.

Content, I knit while working out some semblance of a plan. Something almost plausible began taking shape. With a little luck, it might actually work. Time slid by until all light drained from my bower. I checked the time at 7:45—still too early to penetrate the lair, yet too dark to continue knitting. I tucked my project back into my carpet bag, plumped the satchel behind my head, and allowed myself to drift into a doze.

When I awoke, it was cold and surprisingly dark. Sleep had left me chill and disorientated. Stiff from lying propped up with knees pressing against branches, I tried to shake myself awake by wiggling my limbs.

My iPhone registered the time as 8:45. I'd slept that long? On the other hand, the air wafted sweet jasmine and I could see lights twinkling through the foliage.

Though my stomach complained and my throat felt dry and scratchy, I had stores stashed deep in my bag. Finishing off the last of my water bottle, I dug around until I retrieved a cube of halva and an apple stashed from breakfast. By the time I'd finished eating, I was nearly alert.

I set my iPhone to the record app before shoving it into the inside breast pocket with the mute ready to deactivate. Next, I shifted the burner phone to the coat pocket and left Foxy's buried deep in my carpet bag next to the fence.

That done, I crawled on my hands and knees back to the edge of the lawn. Though the patio doors were still open with the fire burning low in the grate, the house sat blanketed in dark except for a few lights burning here and there. One by one I watched them click off as if someone were going about tucking the house in for the night. My suspicions were confirmed when I saw a maid shut an open casement on the bottom floor.

Springing from the foliage, I dashed across the lawn, diving for cover at the edge of the patio. I heard someone call out to another in Turkish, the tone along the *Did you lock the front door?* variety. I leapt from the bushes and kept low to the ground as I skirted the perimeter of the loggia and slipped inside the French doors.

It was a dining room with a long central table dressed in brocade and lined with a sentry of chairs. A single lamp burned on a sideboard against the wall.

Footsteps were tapping down the hall towards me. I scrambled between the forest of chair legs and overhanging tablecloth to press deep under the table. There I lowered my head to my hands and forced my breathing to still.

Somebody strode into the room, marching with efficiency towards the doors. I heard them click shut, the latch fastened, and the curtains slide across. The footsteps turned and started back the way they'd come but suddenly stopped. I couldn't bear to look, keeping my eyes squeezed shut and my breath shallow. Seconds ground by. I heard the maid fiddle with something, muttering under her breath. Seconds later, the light doused and I was alone.

My heart pounded in darkness so dense, I couldn't see my hands in front of me, but at least I was safe. All I had to do was wait until the staff retired for the night before proceeding with part three, or was it part four? For the most part, the house felt surprisingly empty and I sensed that Maggie occupied the residence alone but for servants.

Hopefully the motion sensors weren't engaged. Maybe Maggie was awake in her upstairs salon and wouldn't activate the security system until going to bed? Too many maybes drove me crazy.

Approximately twenty minutes later, I shuffled out from under the table and stood. I could hear nothing, see nothing. Fishing for my iPhone, I flicked it on and used the ambient screen to illuminate my way to a door which opened soundlessly onto a long hallway. Night lights positioned over wall sockets allowed me to proceed with ease.

Pocketing my phone, I carried on down the hall into a cavernous kitchen humming with electronics where various pilot lights glowed in red and amber—an espresso maker, a stove, and, a refrigerator.

The kitchen opened into another hallway, which led to a smaller dining room adjoining a lounge and a library, all grand spaces lit by tiny night lights at baseboard level. I had circumnavigated the house without finding a single stairway. On a hunch, I retraced my steps to the kitchen, where I tried yet another door, this one opening onto narrow steps heading upward, steps which I took two at a time until reaching the top.

My guess that this was a service route to the bedrooms proved right. A spacious landing overlooking a central curving staircase spanned ahead, the other side of which a bar of light glowed beneath a door.

A total of five rooms encircled the landing, all dark with the doors either ajar or closed except for one. That had to be hers. Targeting the room next door, I sprang, ducking across the hall and into the darkness, easing the door shut behind me.

Mounds of boxes and trunks loomed in the half-light gleaming from the windows. I flicked on my iPhone and beamed it across the piles. Luggage, I realized, lifting a lid and peering inside. Maggie had either just arrived or was planning a speedy getaway, probably both.

I tiptoed through the piles, my light brushing over clothes, shoes, a small carton of new cosmetics—a year's supply?—and finally halted by a map spread open over a Louis Vuitton steamer trunk. Bending in, I held the phone over its surface, following the geographical contours until I read the letters spelling ANATOLIA stretched across the terrain. I nearly dropped the damn phone.

Pocketing the phone, I crept to the adjoining door and pressed an ear against the wood. No sound. The door turned easily in my hand. A huge bedroom spread before me, all red silken pillows, quilted divans, and mirrored walls.

No Maggie in sight, but ahead two doors flanked the enormous silk tented bed; one door lay half opened revealing clothes and a vanity desk, and the other closed with a light beneath the door—the bathroom. Maggie would be immersed in her nightly bubble stew.

I padded across the wooden floor to the dressing room. Nothing but hanging clothes, stacked shoe boxes, and unopened Chanel packages, yet one dress appeared to have been freshly unsheathed and now hung on its padded hanger in a prominent position.

I unhooked the black silk from the mirrored wall and draped it over one arm before my gaze landed on exactly what I sought: Maggie's bag plunked gaping on the vanity table. I plunged my hand deep inside, fumbling until I gripped the little pistol I knew she carried everywhere the way most women carried lipstick. Pulling it out, I studied the pearl-handled Colt before hiding it under the dress.

Scanning the top of the vanity next, I spied the gold-plated antique scissors she used for snipping off tags. Pocketing those, I raced back out to the bedroom and dove for a corner chair.

There I sat, heart hammering, the dress draped over my lap, hiding gun, scissors, and phone, the latter ready to activate the recorder. I waited, counting the seconds to 32 before spying another bag, this one a fur-covered tote squeezed in between a lamp and a clock on the nightstand. Another bag meant another gun. No sooner had I lifted my butt to check it out, when the bathroom door flew open.

❧ 19 ❧

Maggie swept into the room in a long pink robe, hair wrapped in a towel. With her cheeks flushed and makeup-free, she seemed more vulnerable than I had ever seen her before. She plucked her phone from the bed, jabbed her thumb at the screen as if checking for messages, and then tossed it back on the silken spread.

I squeezed the gun handle beneath the couture. "Isn't it aggravating when people don't do what you expect?"

"Holy shit!" She backed up against the bureau, knocking a jar to the floor. Her eyes widened. "You!"

"Me," I agreed.

"How did you get here?"

"It wasn't all that difficult."

She crossed her arms. "How did you find me?"

"Also not difficult. You leave a Chanel trail wherever you go."

"So, what do you want?"

"What do you want? You sent that goon after me, remember. If you wanted to talk so badly, I'm sure we could have arranged something. Anyway, here I am."

She looked me over as if inspecting a cockroach infestation. I pulled the pistol out from under the dress and wiggled it, thinking that might increase the intimidation factor.

Her eyes flicked from the gun to my face and smiled. "Put that down before you hurt yourself."

My grip tightened. "I appreciate your concern but I'll just hang on to it for now."

She shrugged. "You'd never pull the trigger even if you knew how."

"Are you sure about that? Noel taught me the basics of gun usage in Bermuda. I particularly recall the release-the-catch- and-pull-the-trigger part. Oh, wait—I forgot. You didn't stick around long enough to see me fire those shots. You'd already scuttled off."

"Yeah, but I heard all about it. You nailed lover boy in the shoulder while aiming for Hector. That showed real expertise."

I remembered that moment too clearly. "He wasn't my lover." I stopped myself from launching into another diatribe. "Thing is, I'm bound to hit something at point-blank range and chances are it will be you."

"You'd likely just hit a wall and ding my security deposit."

"Want to risk it? Sit down and let's talk. I repeat, why did you send that goon after me?" It felt damn good to be in control for once, even though I sensed I was only fooling myself.

"I knew you were in town and just wanted to talk."

"So we'll talk now. I'd like answers and, since I've got the gun, you can give them to me."

"Think so? What kind of answers?"

"Like where are Toby and Noel?"

She pushed a damp tendril from her forehead. "Boggles me how you can be so smart yet do so many dumb-assed things. Must run in the family."

Walking across the room, wafting the scent of some exotic bath oil, she sat down in the chair opposite mine, crossed her legs, and proceeded to study me. "That napkin on your head suits you. Keeps that Raggedy Anne hair of yours in place. Couldn't have found a better style solution myself."

"It's called a hijab." I tried to appear cool and relaxed, desperately hoping she couldn't see my gun hand shaking. I tried propping my elbow on the chair arm.

"Why do you have my dress in your lap—trying for a bit of chic? Forget it, hon. I'm a size four and you're what, a twelve or fourteen?"

I smiled at that. "I don't want to wear your dress, Mags—not my style. No, I thought I'd rip it to shreds before your eyes just to see your face crumple."

"Bitch."

I laughed. "Don't worry, I'd rather shoot you than damage silk any day. Where are they?"

"I hear Max gave you half of Baker & Associates, like he ever did anything like that for me."

"It's Baker & Mermaid now and, yeah, imagine what it would be like if he'd named it Baker and Bitch after you? Nice alliteration, though. I'm going to resuscitate the business after you bled it and Max dry. Max gave you everything he had and then some. How could you do that to him after so many years?" That just slipped out.

"You mean, how could I last so long without doing it sooner? He totally took me for granted."

"You could have left him instead of kicking him in the nuts."

"Oh, poor baby. Is he all heartbroken?"

"Why wouldn't he be? His girlfriend of twenty years left him hanging and ran off with his money in the heist of the century."

Her face brightened. "Are they calling it the heist of the century?"

"The century's still young, Mags. Like I said, you stole millions of dollars' worth of priceless artifacts from Adrian Wyndridge." I needed her to admit it, hopefully embellish it, make a confession so the iPhone recorder would catch every word. I had the thing activated in my lap.

"It wasn't Wyndridge's. Like Noel said, it belonged to museums, the world, all that shit."

"Justify it any way you want, you stole it."

"Not me. I was only the assistant. Your brother and his buddy, Noel, were the real masterminds. That pissed me off. Like, here we go all over again with the man on top shit."

My mouth went dry. "Where are they?"

Maggie gazed over at me, her expression pained. "Poor Phoebe. They fooled you, too, didn't they? They plotted to steal Wyndridge's treasure while we women sort of hung on like women do. Yeah, I helped out a little here and there but I got screwed in the end, too."

"I presume you mean figuratively?" Stupid question.

"Maybe I do and maybe I don't. Your bro is gay but Noel is as virile as they come and I'm in pretty good shape." She licked her lips. "Figure it out yourself."

My hand tightened on the gun. This wasn't going the way I'd planned. "Where are they?"

"How the hell should I know?"

"Maggie, if you're lying to me again, I'll—"

"You'll what? Slice the hem off my dress? Shoot the wall? Give me a break. You don't have the guts to do anything like that. You're the type of wuss who takes spiders outside rather than squish them. Look, I lied about not knowing where Toby was back in Bermuda but I'm not lying now. I don't know where the hell either of them are. I know one thing, though: your brother's only half the man you remembered him to be."

"What in hell does that mean?"

She smiled. "Let's just say that he'll never forget how screwing with me doesn't pay."

I raised the gun a little higher. "What are you talking about? What did you do?"

"Chill, hon. I don't know where they are, I said. They dumped me."

"Dumped you?" Why is it that in time of stress I can't utter a coherent sentence?

She sighed. "It was supposed to be a three-way partnership with all of us equal, right? Only, the moment things started heating up, they cut me out. Noel said I was too big a risk. He wanted us to stay low, not fence the loot, though there were enough buyers ready to pounce at any minute. Wait? What the hell is the point of having millions worth of stuff if you're just going to sit on it? Meanwhile, we're on the run going from dive to dive —a farmhouse here, a shack there."

"No five-star hotels?"

"Yeah. Give me a break. If I wanted the simple life, I would have stayed with Max. I was in this for the money, you know what I mean? No delayed gratification for me, thank you very much. So, I contacted some of the collectors myself and took just one piece to sell, just one piece. Big whoop.

What's wrong with that? I deserved much more. The bastards got pissed and shafted me."

I breathed slowly out and in, trying to steady my heart. "Never were a team player, eh, Mags? So, they finally realized it's always been all about you."

"Listen up, hon. You're supposed to be some kind of a feminist, right? You fit the description—no boyfriend, dresses like shit—well, I said we three were supposed to be equal partners, which means that the men don't get to call the shots without my approval. I never agreed to not fencing the loot right away, see?"

"What happened next?"

"They just left me in some little shack in France and took off. All I had was the money from the necklace. God, it paid good but it won't keep me living like this forever. They've got the rest of it hidden somewhere and part of it is mine. I could kick their asses, the pair of them. If they think they can cut me out of their next heist, they got another thing coming. I've got things organized in ways they haven't." She fixed me with her chill blue eyes and breathed deeply. "See, we're like two peas in a pod, you and me—both of us kicked to shit by the men in our lives."

I nodded. "Sure. We could be twins only you're much, much older."

"Shut up. You always thought you were smarter than me—everybody makes that mistake—but being smart doesn't mean shit if you don't use the brains you've got."

"We're just motivated by different things," I said carefully. "I figure Noel and Toby are here in Istanbul which is why you're here, too."

"Yeah, maybe. After all, why else are you here along with Foxy and that dingbat professor you've been hanging out with? Yeah, I know things. Did you bring that old rug?"

"Look, who's holding the gun here? I'm asking the questions. What old rug?"

She wagged her finger at me. "Oh, Phoebe, don't pretend. You're so not good at it. Toby sent a rug to you for safekeeping, like that would work. That's why you're here, why we all are. Noel claimed there's a clue about the whereabouts of this next hoard embedded in that thing. I saw it but I don't get it. Besides, if it's that important, you're the last person to send it to. You never think, you just react. You brought it with you to Istanbul, didn't you?"

I had sunk back against the chair, brain spiking, heart hurting, the fever burning all over again. Foxy was right, they were hunting down another find, here in Turkey, related to the Anatolian Goddess kilim. Toby sent it to me for safe-keeping and risked my neck all over again. I suspected as much but now the pieces were falling together. Toby and Noel were hunting the Anatolian Goddess and Maggie was hunting Noel and Toby.

In my seconds of preoccupation, Maggie lunged across the space between us and snatched the gun out of my hand. Now she was standing over me with the gun pointing at my skull. "You're way out of your league again. You need to be ruthless for this game and you're a sheep in bad clothing. Listen up. I know Toby sent the rug to you in London thinking he could keep it away from me—silly bastard—and you brought it right back here because that's the kind of idiot thing you do. Never think it out, just knee-jerk your way into a shit-fest."

I gazed up at her, fearing she was right. I'd lost the upper hand, lost everything. "Was that Jason Young character working for the three of you?" I still hoped to get something out of this disastrous meeting.

"Hell, no. Jason worked for Noel and Toby. The guy who killed him works for me. Noel hired Jason to keep an eye out for you and Max after we parted company. He had Jason hide the kilim in the storeroom and I had my guy try to get it back, only when that didn't work out so well, I had him kill Young instead." My face must have crumpled. "Do you know what that kilim really means? Does it have some kind of map in it or something? Tell me." She pressed the gun closer to my skull.

"This is why you tried to kidnap me, so I could tell you something I don't know?"

Her eyes had narrowed. "Maybe Foxy knows or maybe Ava told you something?"

"It's Eva and nobody tells me anything. They just drag me around using me as bait for their own damn purposes." I sounded so petulant, I nearly convinced myself.

She considered that for a moment, rolling her tongue inside her mouth as if test-tasting a flavor. "Yeah, that's true enough. Poor little Phoebe.

Why would anybody tell you anything? I sure as hell wouldn't. They're just trying to get the kilim away from you, same as me. So, where is it?"

"I don't need the actual rug. I brought a photo, instead."

"You're lying but it doesn't matter. I've got a good idea where the kilim leads." She'd backed against the bed, gun still pointed at me but no longer quite as threatening.

"Can I go now?"

"Sure, but first, I want to show you something. Don't move." She kept the gun pointed at me as she turned to the dresser, but I took that opportunity to slip my iPhone back into my breast pocket. With a little luck, I had enough evidence to nail her.

She pulled out a drawer, returning moments later holding a framed photograph in her free hand. "See?"

I studied the photograph she held. Maggie in her slick black wig, bejeweled in a stunning pectoral cross encrusted with pearls and gems, stood wearing a long red gown. "That's the piece you fenced, Queen Isabella's?"

"That's the one. May as well go for the biggies, right? So, remember I told you how I wanted to have myself photographed the way Sophie Schliemann did wearing the diadem from Troy? What do you think?"

"You were trying to look like a Spanish Queen? Are you kidding me? You look more like some punk Cleopatra turned loose in a theme park."

"God, you're such a spoiler. Couldn't you just be happy for me for once?" She tossed the picture on the bed. "Next, I want a picture of me dressed like an ancient goddess."

"You could pull off ancient, Mags, but I doubt you'd nail the goddess part. So," I inched myself to standing. "On that note, I'll just leave."

Maggie wagged the gun at me. "Sit back down, Phoebe. I was lying when I said I'd let you go. I can't do that. Who knows you're here?"

"Interpol. I alerted them before I came."

"Stop taking me for a fool. Sit, I said."

I remained standing. "Look, Maggie, I know we never really got along, but I tried to be the surrogate daughter you always wanted, only I had parents of my own and my style and yours clashed."

"You were always jealous of me."

"Not true. I just didn't get you anymore than you got me. I didn't grasp why you craved so much stuff, why you always made Max buy you more and more expensive things."

"It doesn't matter now. It's all in the past."

"I don't care what you do. Let me go."

"You do care what I do, that's the problem. Now, stop wasting time. We're done." She picked up her cell from the bed and pressed a number. "Hi, Hali? Yeah. Come up to my room ASAP, only keep your pants on this time, okay?"

I inched my way towards the door. She tossed the phone onto the bed and fired once, the shot so close it zinged the table beside me. I froze.

"Unlike you, I do what has to be done, even if it means pulling the trigger on a girl I used to care for. Where's that stupid carpet bag you lug everywhere?"

"Back in my hotel room. Don't think I'd drag it here, do you?"

She held out her hand. "Pass me your phone."

I dug into my other pocket and handed her the burner.

"What the hell is this? Where's your iPhone?"

"I lost it, okay? I bought that one as a replacement."

"Can't you do anything right?"

"Guess not." I eyed the door, wondering if she'd shoot me in the back. Yeah, she would.

Then in walked the chauffeur, his eyes raking over Maggie's half-clad body like a panting puppy.

"Not this time, hon. We have to take care of her first." Maggie pointed to me.

Hali turned, his fine aquiline face rigid with surprise.

"Don't worry, she's not Muslim. That's her idea of a disguise." Maggie bent over and retrieved the dress and scissors from where they'd slid to the floor. "This little shit has to go."

"She got in?"

"Yeah, she got in but get her out, as in far away, you know? I don't want her getting in my way. Do something with her. I don't care what. Don't even tell me the details. Just arrange for her to get out of sight and out of mind for a long, long time. Make it permanent."

A slow smile spread across his handsome face, reminding me of Errol

Flynn in those old films, only Flynn played good guys and this man clearly had another role. "Yes, I comprehend. I have connections."

"So, go connect."

"I tie her up, okay?"

"Do it."

"I go get stuff."

"Good. We'll just wait, won't we Phoebe?"

Hali left to make arrangements for my disposal, the details of which I tried not to imagine. Maggie stood watch.

"Are you going to add kidnapping and murder to your list of accomplishments?"

"Don't worry, sweetheart, he won't murder you, or at least, not right away. I want to make sure you're going someplace where you won't be getting in my way this time."

Hali reappeared in moments, nodding to Maggie. "Arrangements made," he told her. "She go someplace far. No coming back."

Maggie nodded. "Good."

"They pay me to take her," Hali grinned, "She dangerous?"

Maggie laughed. "Her? More like a nuisance, the kind you don't want buzzing around your house or landing on your food. She always lands on shit. Have your connections keep her out of my face any way they want."

Hali grinned.

I turned to Maggie, my heart galloping wildly. "You're going to let them hurt me? I thought you said you had guts? You're just a coward who gets someone else to do your dirty work."

"Don't want to break a nail." To Hali she added: "How are you going to keep her quiet? She can scream like a stuck pig."

He held up a napkin and an ominous-looking bottle, the contents of which began dabbing into the cloth, smiling all the while. "She'll sleep." Then he put down the bottle and lunged at me while I scrambled away over the bed. Maggie blocked my path on the other side, wrenching me off the mattress by my arm onto the floor and throwing herself down on my back.

I lay winded, pinned to the spot with my face squashed into the rug.

"Never come into a place and wave a gun you can't or won't use. Should have shot me when you had the chance. Hurry, Hali!"

I bucked and raked my nails over her bare thigh.

"Ouch! You little bitch!" She whacked the back of my head.

Hali shoved Maggie off me, straddled me with his heftier weight, and wrenched my neck from the floor until I thought he'd snap it off.

"Now breathe, bitch," he said. He pressed the cloth over my mouth while I struggled to fight and not breathe at the same time. Impossible. Reflex took over. I inhaled.

In seconds, I gagged into blackness.

20

I was lying on my side. Ahead, a red light shed a bloody glow across mountains of crates in an otherwise shadowy realm. I tried to shift but couldn't—hands tied behind my back, feet bound—and the headache whamming against my skull threatened to black me out again.

The last thing I remembered was trying not to breathe. Hali must have tied me up and thrown me in a storeroom of some kind but where? Not at Maggie's. There was nothing residential about this place. It smelled faintly of diesel and I could hear swishing sounds accompanied by a steady drone.

I struggled to sit upright when the floor suddenly shifted, pitching me off a platform onto a metal surface stomach first. I managed not to retch as I heaved myself to my knees. The floor was rocking, a slow swaying back and forth. The hold of a ship!

Supported by the sacks, I struggled to my feet, knocking against boxes and tripping into a wooden crate. I leaned, trembling, my heart hammering. They were going to throw me into the Bosporus! No, wait. *Think.* Surely they'd have done that by now. No, they had something else in mind. They were transporting me somewhere.

I slid down to the floor and leaned forward, trying to free my hands. The bastard had tied me with some kind of nylon, which cut into my flesh and numbed my hands. I couldn't feel my fingers behind me let alone work myself free. I spent minutes, maybe hours, trying to loosen those knots to no avail.

Then lights flashed on overhead. I squinted around as men's voices approached. Two men arrived. I didn't register features at first but knew they were thickly built and strong.

I looked up. Maybe they didn't realize I was an unwitting stowaway? "Help me," I pleaded.

One laughed and motioned to his companion who stepped closer, hands in pockets. They spoke a battery of some language I didn't recognize, like Turkish but not Turkish. Russian, maybe. Both wore dark pants over matching shirts—a uniform of some kind. The man standing closest pulled out a switchblade, a wicked-looking thing that sliced the air as he waved it before my eyes.

"Wow. Such a big knife for a little tied-up woman. Aren't you mighty?"

No understanding flickered in his face. No English, then.

He grabbed my neck. Shoving my head down, he began slicing off the hijab, the blade close enough to my skin to nick me. I cried out and bucked against this onslaught until, finally, he vised my head between his knees and finished slicing without interruption, tearing away the last of the fabric in shreds. Then he yanked at the pins securing my hair until he'd freed a mass of unruly strands, which he grabbed by the fistful to haul me to my feet.

Both men now stood on either side of me. Each grabbed an arm and tipped me on my back over the sacks and proceeded to discuss my attributes while squeezing my breasts through my clothes. I didn't need Russian to get their drift.

One lifted my coat, unfastened my fly, and pulled down my jeans and panties while the other pinned me down by gripping my shoulders. Thus pinioned, I lay helpless squirming with humiliation. I tried squeezing my legs tight but the man in charge pried them open with his knees and began digging his dirty fingers into my flesh.

I screamed and spat and bucked. I couldn't stop struggling even though I knew my efforts probably excited them further. When I screamed at the top of my lungs, one of them whacked me across the cheek.

My head fell back on the sack. I thought I was going to faint. A whistle blew somewhere and both men sprung away, one returning seconds later to pull my jeans up and hastily rearrange my coat, kicking me over onto my stomach in the process.

I lay there stunned, churning with disgust and shame, feeling dirty as if I was somehow to blame for the violation. How could this be happening? My brain scrambled for a coherent thought.

If I was on the Bosporus Strait headed for the Black Sea, I could be easily sold into the sex trade. It was rampant all through the area, in Russia in particular. I was no more than a piece of meat.

Hunger, thirst, and despair darkened all the colors in my heart. I drifted in and out of consciousness, effected by the drug I had inhaled and the abuse I suffered.

At some point, my eyes opened as someone rolled me onto my back. Three men stood over me arguing—the two from before plus one other—a big meaty man built like a heifer. This new one wore a peaked cap with an insignia on his shirt. The captain? The captain!

"Help me, please," I gasped.

The captain glanced at me with little interest before returning to his discussion. With the impact of a fist to the gut, I saw myself from the outside in: a woman, worthless in of herself. Weak. A sexual toy to be enjoyed and traded like livestock but otherwise possessing no brain, no heart, and no soul, certainly not worthy of respect. To these men, I was less than an animal. I felt cheap and useless, a born victim.

Why had I ever come here? What made me think I could tackle this brutal world alone? I couldn't do it, I just couldn't. Or, if I did, I'd have to get tough fast.

I swam up from the bottom of despair long enough to try understanding what the men were saying. The two underlings seemed earnestly attempting to convince the captain of something. My worth on the black market?

The bastard who had roughed me up gesticulated wildly, pointing to me then towards the door. The captain cut him off—I heard the name Sergei —as he pointed at my bruised cheek. I guessed he didn't like the boys battering the merchandise. Leave that for the buyers.

He snapped an order which sent Sergei scrambling away while his buddy stood by silently. The captain approached me, looking me up and down as if inspecting a particularly troublesome bag of potatoes until

Sergei returned moments later with a bottle of water and a plate which he lowered to the floor beside me—a wedge of bread with something slimy that reeked of boiled cabbage.

The captain nudged me with his foot barking an order I deduced might be "EAT!" I shook my head and hunched my bound arms helplessly.

Sergei muttered angrily, lurching me to sitting, and pointing to the plate before slicing off the twine binding my wrists. I moaned, bringing my raw and swollen hands in front of my face. The men were already heading for the door.

The captain must have insisted they at least feed and water the cargo so it would stay in reasonably good condition. How much would I fetch half-dead? And I couldn't very well eat with my hands bound, could I? He couldn't spare a man to spoon-feed me on this working ship, either, so he must have ordered everyone back to their post, confident that with the door locked, I wouldn't be going anywhere.

Shaking the circulation back into my hands, I stared at my wrists through my tears, still feeling that man's disgusting grope. If only I had the time to retch and wail and cry. But that's for kids and I had to grow up fast. Instead, I fumbled for my iPhone with my numb fingers. The phone remained buried deep in my coat pocket where I'd managed to hide it. Maggie took my word that I had lost it, and then nobody bothered to search.

I plucked the sleek surface out with fumbling fingers, dropping it on the floor beside me. The battery was almost dead and the reception weak, but it might eke out enough juice to get a message out.

Agent Walker was on speed-dial so I pressed his name and waited. The call rang and rang, me cursing every wasted second. I kept my ears keened for the men's return.

When Walker's answering machine clicked in, I rasped into the phone. "Walker, it's me, Phoebe, in Istanbul. I've been kidnapped. I'm on a ship in the Bosporus—don't know the name, Russian, I think. I found Maggie. Help." Then I clicked off, switched to email and sent him a link to Maggie's Google map address, still open on my phone.

Whether that posted successfully, I had no idea, since my phone blacked out seconds after I hit SEND. I noted the time before it died— 12:45 a.m. local time.

A long shot is better than never pressing the trigger. I'd remember that the next time I saw Maggie.

Shoving my phone back in my pocket, I wrestled with the water bottle until the cap popped off, downing nearly the entire contents before reining myself in. Next, I tackled the cabbage thing and the bread, which snaked down my throat like a glutinous mass. I needed energy so didn't care.

Thus fortified, I tried untying the knots binding my ankles, but my hands, though gradually regaining circulation, were nearly useless. I fumbled, spending precious seconds picking the knot loose until finally I could shake my ankles free.

On my feet at last, I stumbled across the floor, banging into crates labeled in Turkish, making my way to the door. Metal like the floor and walls, the door stayed solidly shut. It probably locked automatically from the outside but still required a key. Not so modern a ship to go with digital locks, either. I turned away to begin exploring my world, shaking the blood back into my limbs as I went.

God, I so did not want to be a victim. Women suffered worse abuse than I just had again and again. Why had I never really grasped how half the female world survives? I'd been protected and cosseted all my life without realizing it.

Now I teetered on the edge. I would not go down without a fight. If I didn't do something, I'd end up living in the worst kind of subjugation.

My captors had switched off the overhead fluorescents before leaving but I flicked them back on. The room flooded intensely bright, revealing an industrial metal space stacked with crates and sacks. Some country brought cargo to Istanbul and filled the outgoing ship with goods for home, me being the bonus.

I scanned every shelf, up and down, until I found something useful: a utility knife sitting on a stack of papers along with a dirty coffee mug and a half-smoked cigarette. Thank you, Ivan, or whoever this careless sailor was. Maybe he'd just saved my life.

I returned to my sack, sat down, the knife concealed in my trench coat, and considered strategy. Every avenue was as risky as the next but none more so than doing nothing. I didn't yet know what I was made of, what I was capable of doing. I only knew that if I didn't take desperate action, I'd spend a life of the worst kind of subjugation. I'd rather die than be pawed and prodded by a bunch of brutes for the rest of my days. The sheep had to turn wolf fast.

The door opening roused me from a doze. I bolted upright into the still brightly lit space, every sinew tensing as footsteps approached—one set only.

Sergei slipped around the corner, eyeing me speculatively. Bastard probably sneaked from his berth thinking he'd have me to himself. Who would know if he raped me? Everyone but the bridge and night watch would be asleep and no one could hear me scream in here. Who even cared?

Play the game, I warned myself. Women had been playing the same one for thousands of years. I figured I could to do the same. I forced a shy smile, trying to appear submissive. "Please don't hurt me," I said aloud. "I'll do what you want."

Some communication went beyond words. I unbuttoned the top of my trench, smiling, patting the floor with my hand.

"Come join me," I whispered. "Just don't hurt me."

Sergei's face lit with eagerness. He must have known he'd get in big trouble if he bruised me, but if I was willing to offer myself freely...

On my knees, I smiled up at him as he unzipped his pants and let them drop. I did my best to appear eager, excited by the prospects of this wormy little man about to ravish me. Suppressing nausea, I smiled in anticipation.

He gestured for me to pleasure him. *Oh, hell, no.* Hurry. He ordered me in Russian.

I moved closer and, as he swiveled to check the door once more, I pulled out the utility knife, clutched it in both hands, and raked it deep and hard across his scrotum—such a vulnerable piece of the male anatomy —sending him screaming and toppling backward on the floor.

I sprung forward, blinded by fury as the slick knife fell from my hands and skittered away. Picking it up again, I came after him knife outstretched.

The pants bunched around his ankles kept him flopping helplessly on the floor like a beached tuna. I should stab him, realizing I couldn't just half do this thing, but blood slicked the knife and gummed my resolve.

Instead, I sliced the straps off the nearest crate and heaved it down on top of him. Hearing him cry out made me bellow in triumph like some warrior queen. With the crate pinning down his upper half, I could now pluck the keys from his pants pocket.

Shoving the gooey knife into my pocket, I ran for the door, trying multiple keys until the right one fit.

The corridor was empty as I eased the door shut behind me, hearing the lock catch at my back.

I just knifed a man. I was covered in blood. Who was I?

Lights bleared fluorescent inside wire cases as I slipped down the hall towards the stairs. I climbed up to the next deck and heaved open the door. Outside, the ship plied the strait under a starry sky, lights beaming from the headlands on either side. I could see other vessels to the left and behind us on this busy thoroughfare.

Since only a skeleton crew would be on duty this time of night and they'd be manning the bridge, a lone person scuttling along the lower deck could go undetected.

It was a small tanker, a bit rusty and probably old, which meant I couldn't expect new-model escape pods or maybe not even inflatable rafts. I looked for traditional lifeboats fastened to the sides on winches and found them straight ahead, two lifeboats suspended on ropes bound to the side.

They reminded me of the kind used on the fishing trawler where I'd worked my summers as a student. I'd spent my day filleting haddock for the freezer hold but had learned the basic abandon ship drills: break the glass, activate the pulley, and be prepared to leap. Since the written instructions were in Russian, I needed to apply memory with a touch of resourcefulness.

I wouldn't have much time after activating the pulleys before the alarm sounded. I removed the fire ax strapped to the ship's side, whacked the glass, pressed the pulley, and watched as the dinghy shook once and began lowering by winch.

The alarm shrilled immediately. Men shouted overhead. The lifeboat was taking too long to lower. They were going to recapture me, me who had just knifed their crewmate and robbed the captain of his bonus!

I leapt on top of the dinghy's canvas cover as the boat leveled with the deck. The winch snagged and jammed to a stop. There I crouched, suspended on a boat swaying at least thirty feet above the water, going nowhere.

Flat on my stomach, I inched to the edge and peered over. It was a long way down but I'd jump if I had to. Yet, something else was happening out there: a spotlight raked the darkness ahead.

I squinted into the blaze unable to see anything. A loudspeaker sounded off to my right, as if from another ship. The tanker bridge responded by megaphone and I could feel the ship slowing down. As the spotlight swept to the right, I watched a small craft approach with flashing red lights and uniformed men.

"Phoebe McCabe? Stay where you are. We're coming to get you down." Agent Sam Walker's voice blared over a loudspeaker.

I sunk back down on the canvas, dizzy with relief mixed with a different kind of fear.

21

I sipped apple tea and tried again to focus on the questions instead of my bandaged wrists. The world around me had taken on a surreal haze as if I played a starring role in someone else's nightmare. I may have been on a police boat sailing towards Istanbul, but nothing about the woman I now inhabited felt familiar.

Earlier above deck I asked, "Where is Sergei? Where is the man I knifed? Is he going to live?"

"I have no idea. Too early to say. They're rushing him to hospital. You can give us the rest of your statement below," Walker said. Not unkind, just brusque.

Back in the galley, I told my story to the Turkish police with Walker and his Istanbul colleague looking on. They requested I repeat several aspects, especially the part where I stabbed Sergei. My responses appeared to satisfy the local police, if not myself. "It was in self-defense," I said repeatedly.

"Of course," Agent Walker said. "We don't believe that you boarded a Russian tanker and knifed a sailor for entertainment."

I looked at him. "Right." So why did I have that sick pang in the pit of my stomach?

Russian kidnappers and human traffickers didn't have many rights

JANE THORNLEY

under Turkish law, apparently, so the police seemed more admiring of me than anything else.

Once the police captain had exited the galley, it was just Walker, the Turkish Interpol agent, Adalet Kapitz, and me sitting around the chrome table like we were sharing tea at the bazaar. My iPhone needed recharging so I couldn't check what the recorder had captured. I wanted to hear it first in private, anyway. "You followed me to Istanbul?"

"Your phone helped us pinpoint your exact location today. Did you really think I believed you were just coming here for a carpet sale?" Agent Walker asked.

"An Antique Carpet and Ethnographic Exhibition is hardly just a carpet sale," I countered, mustering energy. "I'm in the trade, remember?"

"And since you arrived, you've hardly been behaving like someone in the trade. You've been seen with Dr. Eva Friedrich and Sir Rupert Fox."

"Both are connected to ethnography."

"Both are on Interpol's radar."

"Dr. Friedrich is assisting me with the provenance of a carpet I purchased, and Sir Foxy is wooing me because he wants to buy the gallery." Oh, how truth can also shield a lie.

"We believe both may be interested in a secret archaeological site in Turkey."

"Really? Nobody tells me anything."

Walker leaned towards me, fixing me with his unsettling gaze. "And you tackled a holy man at the opening event."

"A Sufi," Agent Kapitz pointed out, hardly suppressing his pique.

"A case of mistaken identity," I stated.

"Who did you mistake him for, one of the Twelve Apostles?" Walker quipped. "He wore a white robe, as I understand."

"Most people attending were in some kind of costume so he could have been anybody."

"But you thought it was Noel Halloran, didn't you? You suspect he's in Istanbul."

"I don't know where he is," I said. "I only found Maggie by tracking her to a Chanel store on a hunch. Have the police arrested her yet?"

Walker turned to Kapitz who shrugged. A man of few words, I gathered.

"The police are on their way. We'll know more when we dock. Don't change the topic. You came here to find your brother and Halloran, admit it. Did they contact you?"

I sighed, looking down at my hands. I wondered if I could still knit now that I needed that consolation the most. Then my mind wandered to my carpet bag still stuffed under the jasmine hedge back at Maggie's. My attention refused to anchor.

"Answer my questions," Walker said. "Did your brother contact you or did Noel Halloren give you instructions when he visited you in London?"

"No and no," I said. "I haven't spoken to my brother in fourteen months. I told you that. I want to see him again, sure. Who wouldn't want to see their brother after all that's happened? But I swear I don't know where he is. I thought Maggie knew, but she insists they dropped her once she started fencing the jewels without their knowledge."

"How did you know Maggie was in Istanbul?"

"Someone attacked me near the Grand Bazaar, who I later discovered was working for Maggie. She has a penchant for Chanel so I went on a hunch." I added, "Anyway, she told me she'd fenced the Isabella necklace to finance her habits and insists the men had been planning to sit on the cache but she got impatient."

"Did she say to whom she fenced the necklace?"

"No, she didn't disclose that. She bragged how she stole the piece from Toby and Noel. She has access to all Max's old clientele—the wealthy private collectors that feed off the black market. It could be any of those."

I kept my gaze fixed on my hands.

Kapitz leaned forward. "Just understand, Ms. McCabe, if you are withholding anything, we will consider this aiding the fugitives, which is a serious offense in international law. You are already in big trouble."

I glanced at him. "So, I'm either with you or against you, is that it?"

"That is it exactly," the agent nodded. Kapitz's dark hair and penetrating eyes reminded me uncomfortably of Noel. The Turks were handsome men. He rose to his feet. "I will excuse myself and check the pilot house to see if there is word from the shore team."

That left me alone with Walker, who sat across from me gripping his mug while that scarred eyebrow jutted under his wool cap like a skid mark from a crash scene. I shifted in my seat.

413

"You're hiding something," he said flatly.

"Maybe you mistake shock for reticence. I've had a grueling night. What will happen to me?"

"I'll be escorting you on an 11:00 a.m. flight back to London in the morning. Charges will probably be laid, something which you could lessen the extent of by assisting me now."

"You have insufficient evidence to charge me with anything."

If possible, the ragged eyebrow peaked further. "I forgot you studied the law. Who are you protecting, Phoebe?"

"No one accept myself, Agent Walker. Look, I led you to Maggie's lair, didn't I? Sure, I admit to wanting to find her—all of them—but I've told you everything I know. I came for the carpet exposition and to purchase pieces for my shop. I located Maggie by luck, if you can call what just happened to me luck."

"How do you know Dr. Eva Friedrich?"

I turned the mug around in my cupped hands. "Her name was given to me by a carpet dealer at the Arasta Bazaar when I was inquiring about authenticating Anatolian kilims for the gallery. In my business, a carpet that comes with provenance is instantly made more valuable, making it necessary to bring in experts on occasion. Dr. Friedrich and I hit it off."

"Do you know she's had dealings with the police in the past?"

"I don't know much about her either way."

"Which kilim were you inquiring about?"

"I purchased several Anatolian tribal kilims of a certain type. That's my job. They are being shipped back to the gallery."

"I will need to inspect them all once they arrive in London."

"Of course." Nausea and desperation roiled over me. "Look, could you grill me some other time? I'm exhausted and I just knifed a man."

"In self-defense."

"It doesn't matter." I held up my hands. "These just committed an act of horrific violence and I can't just shrug it off, okay?"

"Of course. I understand. We can continue our dialog tomorrow en route to London." He got to his feet and exited the cabin, feet clattering on the metal stairs as he dashed above deck.

That left me alone in the small galley crowded by memories of leering men, Maggie's sneers, and the impact of knifing a man in what could be a fatal blow—terrifying acts inflicted on me and by me. My bandaged hands felt all wrong, as if still sticky with the blood I'd washed away countless times.

Fifteen minutes later, I felt the boat slowing down followed by the thrust of engines navigating a pier. Walker clattered downstairs to tell me to come above deck.

"I'll deliver you to your hotel, where you'll have a few hours to rest before we head for the airport."

"Wait, the police must have reached Maggie's address. Let me go with you to the site on the way back to the hotel. I need to retrieve the bag I stashed in the shrubbery and maybe I'll get to spit in her face. Surely, I deserve that much?"

He hesitated. "I thought you had enough for one night?"

"If she gets what she deserves, I'll get the best sleep I've had for ages."

He finally he allowed me to accompany him, and we wove through the darkened streets and up into Maggie's leafy neighborhood. I could barely contain myself. With Maggie finally apprehended, I might consider the night a partial success, or at least not a total disaster.

We pulled into the open gate, the driveway now crowded with police vehicles. It only took Walker a moment to inform me that Maggie had escaped. By the time the police arrived, she had already vacated the premises.

I stood on the lawn, reunited with my bag but awash with sick disbelief as the police continued fanning out across the grounds. But for the pre-existing furniture and stores laden with food, the place was empty.

"If you had informed me the moment you caught sight of her, she might be in custody now. As it is, she obviously had enough sense not to risk hanging around," Walker said, his authoritative voice banging against my skull.

Without saying much further, he delivered me to the hotel with strict instructions to pack and be ready for pickup at eight o'clock sharp.

I stepped into the hotel room, inserted my key card into the slot, and turned just as the light automatically flooded the room.

I stared. Everything had been ransacked. I swung towards the safe, saw it gaping open and fell to my knees, clawing the empty cavity. It couldn't be gone, it couldn't!

But it was.

My spare cash lay in a wad on the floor along with my passport. This was no ordinary thief. If Maggie took the kilim, she'd destroy it. I sobbed uncontrollably.

An hour later, I sat perched on the edge of the bed staring at the curtains. They mimicked real silk brocade but were mere clever forgeries. I needed a shower. I could do with some sleep, too, but the world hung black and miserable all around me. Everything seemed false and cruel with nothing worth the effort of doing. People stole, murdered, tortured, and abused one another, and otherwise decent people became twisted. Such a warped, warped world.

What can we do but keep on moving? I plucked the Foxy phone from the bed, and dialed. The phone rang imperiously in my ear until someone picked up the call.

"Eva Friedrich here. Who has the unmitigated gall to call at this hour?"

"Me, Phoebe. Does the offer to go with you to Cappadocia still stand?"

Five seconds' hesitation. I counted the beats. "Certainly."

"Good. Can you be ready to leave within the hour?"

🎐 22 🎐

Istanbul felt surreal in the early dawn, quiet but active with the occasional car whizzing by and men pouring into the mosque across the street.

The five o'clock adhan sounded just as I turned the corner, a haunting demarcation of the breaking day. I might have prayed myself if I knew how to with conviction. All my childhood attempts had sounded like pleading and today wouldn't be much different. *I need to get away and find Toby and Noel. Please help me. Amen.*

Pressing against the wall, I waited. Moments later, a little gray car pulled to the curb and the passenger door clicked open. Eva leaned towards me. "Phoebe, are you all right?"

I hauled my luggage to the curb and bent towards her. "Interpol wants me gone," I said.

"Did you steal something?"

"Absolutely not."

"Get in."

"But I am withholding evidence, just so you know. Technically what I'm doing is illegal. I'm probably the last person you should be connected with right now."

"I could say the same applies to me. We'll form a perfect pair."

I tossed my bags into the back seat and climbed in beside her. After taking a quick check in the rear view mirror, I fixed my gaze on the streets ahead, watching the city awaken on this early October morning. "Someone stole the kilim, Eva. It's gone."

I heard her sharp intake of breath. "Who do you think would do such a thing?"

"I have no idea but I'm thinking Maggie, possibly Noel, but that doesn't make sense because he's still tight with my brother, and it was Toby who sent it to me. Maggie admitted that much. It's incredible how strongly I feel its absence, like someone ripped the rug out from under me, literally. Maggie wants it destroyed. She seemed to know my whereabouts—who I saw, what I did. Maybe she found my hotel information and had her goons break into my room? Oh, God, what have I done?"

Eva gripped the steering wheel. "Who is this Maggie to you?"

"My nemesis, though she'd think that implied I was her equal, which she clearly doesn't believe. She's vicious and dangerous, and why the hell didn't I realize that sooner? Though, I feel a little dangerous myself right now."

"Phoebe, try to calm down. Why do you believe it was Maggie?"

I squeezed my eyes shut against the brilliant sunrise. "Who else could it be? The kilim is a key to the missing site, isn't it? She's after it, too. She knows the site lies in Cappadocia. She's probably imagining another Troy."

Eva remained silent. I turned to check behind us again. We'd have a good lead on Foxy, at least. "How will we know if someone's following us?"

"You mean Interpol?"

"Anybody. I have quite an entourage."

"If you can't identify anyone in particular, I'd say it will be difficult to determine, but we'll be thoroughly evasive, never fear."

"Where else could I have hidden the kilim to keep it safe?"

"With me, as I asked. If a dark energy knows you are in possession of it, then keeping it in a hotel safe was a mistake."

I looked at her. "A dark energy?" Hell, were we talking voodoo and Darth Vader types here? I really wasn't in the mood.

As if she sensed my thoughts, she added: "Think with your spirit, Phoebe. I mean dark against the light, the contrasts that keep the universe in check. Balance is everything. Whoever wishes to destroy the kilim is an agent of darkness."

I sighed and rubbed my eyes. "My friend, Nancy, would get your drift in a nanosecond, but my mind's too filled with concrete traumas like knifing a Russian sailor to think about that stuff now."

"Knifing a Russian sailor? Phoebe, you truly are in shock."

"I probably am but I really did, knife someone, I mean."

"You must tell me everything that happened once we're safely away from Istanbul. The Goddess made me delay my excursion longer than I expected—I meant to leave yesterday—and now I know why."

I stared straight ahead. If Eva was unhinged, as I was beginning to fear, what was I doing in the car with her? "Is there time to pick up a coffee?"

"Definitely not."

"Interpol wants me on a plane back to London this morning but I can't leave. I'm still in the best position to find Toby and Noel, especially now. Besides, Maggie knows roughly where this place is located, too. She's after the same thing you are." I paused. "What is that, exactly?"

Eva took a corner onto one of the main arteries. "Details later. When do they expect you on that plane?"

"The flight leaves at 11:00 a.m., but Walker is picking me up at 8:00. We have to avoid planes. As soon as they know I'm gone, they'll be watching the airports. No worries about Maggie, though. She thinks I'm on the Black Sea readying for a career in the sex trade."

"Great Mother of Goddesses! The sex trade?" Eva abruptly signaled onto a side street and headed in the opposite direction. "No airport, then. Alternate routes required."

"I should have told Interpol about the kilim. Maybe if I had, it would be safe, but maybe not. What do I know? But I do know I don't want police intervention. Toby needs to see me as much as I him, only for different reasons. He wants absolution and I want retribution. How do you factor justice into all that? I never could. I mean, I can't. There's a reason why I left the law. I've got to build up stronger stuff, be able to defend myself, not let people victimize me, ever. And Noel tried to contact me last night at the gala. That must mean something. I didn't know I had it in me to knife Sergei. On, hell, I knifed a man! I knifed Sergei." And then I started crying, bawling, really.

Eva kept her eyes on the road. "Phoebe, keep it together long enough to remove my phone from my bag and engage the speaker. Hold it up while I make a few calls. I need to organize our escape."

I did as she bid, remaining silent while she made several calls, speaking rapidly in Turkish to three men and one women.

"You know a lot of people here," I commented, wiping my eyes on my sleeve. I'd ditched the trench and put my freshly showered self back into my own clothes—skinny jeans, boots, my leather jacket.

"When you marry a Turk you inherit his family, and his friends, plus a network of former colleagues all over the country. This is my brother-in-law's car, one of them anyway."

"How long ago did Borek pass?"

"Ten years and two months ago." She kept her eyes on the road, hands fused to the steering wheel. "Time for personal histories later. Now I must concentrate on getting out of Istanbul."

Eva drove through the tributaries of city traffic, pushing on through the huge metropolis until the buildings clustered into apartments followed by a gray spread of factories and industrial spaces.

"Where are we going?"

"We'll catch the ferry across the Marmara then drive cross country to the Aegean. My nephew will convey us down the coast in his fishing boat. We'll dock some place where we'll less likely attract attention. From there, another nephew is lending us a car and we'll drive across country. Have you had any sleep in the last 24 hours?"

"Not unless being chloroformed counts."

"By the Goddess, Phoebe! Once we're on the ferry, you must sleep."

And sleep I did. After bundling myself from the car to the passenger deck of a ferry where all the windows looked out over a sea streaked with tankers, I turned my back, rested against my carpet bag, and slept until Eva roused me.

Soon, we were back in the car driving once again. I glimpsed long stretches of farmland, more industrial buildings, mosques, and tiny villages in between sleeps, only rousing when Eva shook me awake to have lunch in a little cafe. She ordered me something she referred to as "Turkish pizza" and strong, hot tea. I drank and ate as if in a daze, only dimly aware of people talking and laughing around me.

My throat felt scratchy and raw, my head ached with a relentless thud. Eva felt my forehead. "You're sick. Little wonder after what you've been through. Here, take these."

I watched her shake two red pills into my palm.

"Standard issue ibuprofen. Take two."

I swallowed the pills before climbing back into the car and falling into a deep, fast sleep. The world slipped beneath and around me in perpetual motion with hills, valleys, pavement, and briefly glimpsed farmlands flying by.

When Eva roused me again, it was dark.

"We'll stay here at my niece's for the night. You'll have Pinar's bed and I'll take the couch."

I don't recall much about the young woman who opened her house to us except she was petite, very pretty, and smiled broadly. I went straight to bed and slept so deeply, it was if I tumbled off the edge of a velvet cliff.

When I awoke, the sun was slicing sharp and bright through the curtains, and I heard people talking outside the door. Feeling restored, I dressed quickly and stepped into the small living area.

Eva, in a long cotton gown with her hands waving, was in an intense discussion with a young man, all conversation ending abruptly at the sight of me. "Phoebe, this is my nephew, Deniz. He'll be taking us down the coast today."

The young man smiled and nodded, saying something quickly to Eva in Turkish before dashing out the door.

"Are you feeling better?"

"I'm feeling much better, thanks. You look nothing like yourself. Does it bother you to don the traditional Muslim dress?"

"Why ever would it?"

"Because you're not Muslim. Do you feel like a fraud?"

"Phoebe, it's a disguise, not a mockery. Besides, I hold Islam in the highest regard. It is a beautiful and noble religion, the exact opposite of how these extremists and terrorists corrupt it for their purposes. In any event, Pinar had to go to work but sends us best wishes on our journey. We'll have some breakfast and then meet Deniz at the dock."

"Where are we?"

"Dikili but we'll head down the coast to Kusadasi which, as a tourist destination, should grant us sufficient anonymity to get lost in the crowd. Once there, another nephew—Borek had five brothers who all have children—Ege, is meeting us with another car. In any event, here's your disguise. Pinar found it for you. Try it on." She held out a patterned silk scarf accompanied by a long plain cotton dress, both predominantly an unflattering mauve pink.

"It belonged to Pinar's mother, I believe. It's probably too big for you but it will do."

I dropped the dress over my head. It fell from my shoulders like a sack, the sleeves dangling to my fingertips. At least that feature disguised my bandaged wrists, but otherwise, I felt like a kid going trick-or-treating in a grape-stained bed sheet. Eva wrapped the scarf around my head in quick, efficient motions.

"You've done this before," I commented.

"Many times."

"So you could fit in with Borek's family?"

"As a sign of respect, yes, but I was always an anomaly."

We grabbed our bags and hurried off in the borrowed car across bare, dusty hills until at last the Aegean came into view as a haze of blue against an equally flawless sky. We turned onto a small two-lane road running parallel to the water and carried on for another couple of miles until the road curved up and away from the water and into a densely wooded area.

"Keep an eye out for signs."

"What signs?" I hoped she didn't mean Goddess signs like three birds flying in formation.

"He said to take a left-hand turn into the village but, for the life of me, I don't see a village anywhere let alone a sign," Eva said.

I looked behind us. A little green car could be seen in the distance, its roof glinting like a beetle's back in the sun. "I think we just passed a sign back there."

We turned around until we found the road again—one lane jutting straight up into the forest. The green car had disappeared. "This must be it," Eva muttered, carefully nosing the car onto the lane, "Though it doesn't look much like a fishing village to me." The road wound through the dense growth for at least another mile before white buildings began appearing amid the trees.

I rolled down the window. "I can smell the sea."

And soon I could see it, too, but only in glimpses through branches as the road abruptly plunged downward. The forest fell away as the road took a sharp turn against a cliff edge and razor-backed downward towards the shore. "By the Goddess!" I heard Eva exclaim, "Why don't they believe in guard rails?"

After a dizzying decline, the car leveled out in a little village where a crowd of white three-story buildings tumbled against the shore. Dories and boats of all sizes had been pulled up on wooden slats along the water's edge while a few larger boats rocked gently in the cove.

Eva parked the car under a tree, leaving the keys on the floor, and urged me out. "Deniz can make sure this gets back to Istanbul. Come along."

"But won't someone steal it?"

"Not here."

The curious stares of countless eyes followed us as we made our way along the shore. I could only imagine how we appeared to the villagers. Eva carried only a knapsack tossed easily over one shoulder. I followed behind her, hoisting my carpet bag over one shoulder while dragging my roller bag over the pebbles with my other hand until a man suddenly came up to us, smiling and nodding. He took my roller bag from my hand and Eva's backpack, exchanging a few words to Eva before dashing on ahead.

"He's offering to help us take our bags to the boat," Eva explained with a grin.

"Oh, that's wonderful," I said, plunging my hand into my carpet bag. "How much should we pay him?"

Eva shook her head sharply. "Tipping could offend him. Phoebe, he's doing it to be helpful and because helping people is just the way things are done here."

After that, I thought maybe it was best to watch and learn. Playing the follower wasn't easy but I didn't see an alternative just then.

Despite my aching wrists, I savored the calm sea with the little fishing boats rocking gently in the cove. Gone were the skyscrapers, the congested streets, the crazy schizophrenic beauty of Istanbul's cultural jumble and, in its stead, the peaceful glory of the Aegean Sea spreading a cool balm of blue and white. Cleopatra may have gazed out on a vista much like this.

We carried along the rocky shore until we caught sight of Deniz waving to us from the only wharf.

On instinct, I turned suddenly to look back the way we'd come just in time to spy a small green car parked beside ours under the tree. "Eva, I—" but she had already scrambled ahead, our volunteer porter loping ahead. Well, damn. I scuttled after her, catching up just as we reached the jetty, where several fishing boats were moored.

"Eva," I whispered, "I think we've been followed."

"Pardon?" She turned, staring at me with an affronted expression. "Impossible, well, at best, unlikely. You must be mistaken."

I turned back but couldn't see the tree from where we stood. "Let's get on with it."

A man shouted up to us. I could just see the top of Deniz's head three feet below on the deck of a small white fishing boat lashed to the wharf. Deniz and another man were hoisting the bags from our helper's hands into the bottom level of a three-deck pilot house.

Eva was already climbing down the ladder. I tossed my carpet bag to Deniz and followed after, negotiating my cumbersome robes as gracefully as I could, frustrated by the cocoon-like sense of being wrapped like a sack of groceries. Once on the deck, I gazed around at the mound of fishing gear secured under a blue tarpaulin and inhaled the scent of motor oil and fish offal, the perfume of my childhood.

"I don't suppose women work fishing boats much here, but I can help untie ropes, handle the anchor, anything," I said to Eva. "I practically grew up on a fishing boat."

Deniz didn't understand much English but apparently grasped enough to shake his head vigorously and point towards the lower cabin of a three-story pilot house. "Must stay inside," he said. "We drive boat."

Eva beckoned me towards the cabin. "Come, Phoebe. Today we make like the locals. We don't want to attract attention."

I looked up to wave goodbye to our kindly porter. "But I think we already have." A crowd was gathering on the wharf, as if some telepathic communication had spread through the village alerting them to the spectacle of two strange women in an unconvincing disguise about to sail away on a fishing boat.

Eva looked up and shook her head. "Oh, blast them!" She called out to Deniz while tugging me by the sleeve towards the cabin.

We bundled ourselves into the cramped lower cabin, a narrow space dominated by two long benches with a table fixed to the floor in between. Here the fishers would eat a hasty lunch, maybe swig a mug of tea, but not much else since the work took place on deck outside or one floor up in the pilot house. Regardless of the discomfort, being aboard a fishing boat again delivered such a memory punch that I fought back tears. Dad, Toby, me, and the sea. For the first time since arriving in Turkey, I felt truly home yet totally lost. I wanted to man the wheel, let the salt air tangle my hair while steering towards the blue horizon, straight back home.

Remembering where I'd been while longing to know where I was going left me nothing to cling to but the empty horizon.

"How long a ride is it?" I called out to Eva as the engine rumbled to life.

"Approximately six hours," she shouted back while unpacking a small feast from her knapsack. Bottles of water, waxed paper wrapped pastries, and a plastic container of what looked like slices of roasted eggplant were deposited on the table, along with forks and knives. We'd only just had breakfast a few hours ago, but Eva attacked the meal with gusto, nodding to me to join in. I tucked into the eggplant and drank a bottle of water, smiling at her companionably across the table. "Pinar made these for us."

"Oh."

"We're off to find the Goddess, Phoebe," she called to me like a child excited over a day at the fair.

I nodded. "And I'm off to find my brother. Let's hope the two are connected."

"They are."

All I knew was that this path to Anatolia pitched me in the same direction as the kilim, possibly Maggie and Noel, and by association, Toby. It was the only lead I had and, since remaining in Istanbul was no longer an option, I chose to be a fugitive hurling into the unknown. Hell if I knew where I'd land.

Real conversation was impossible over the throbbing engine, so I tried to knit. Just as I feared, my aching wrists made that challenging and very slow yet I persevered.

Out the grimy window where the crowded wharf had long shrunk into the distance, long stretches of bright blue sea soothed the eye. Green cars couldn't follow us here and a boat on our tail would be noticeable. Maybe I could relax. Well, maybe not relax exactly, but at least escape for a few moments of solitude.

I studied my knitting, gently combing the butterflies of colored yarn free. Intarsia required both halves of my brain, the left to adhere to patterns and color boundaries, the right to flow deeply into my unconscious where yarn wove in and around the human heart. Nothing painful touched me here. I glanced once at Eva, finding her slumped against her knapsack snoring heartily in a similar tempo as the engine.

I just knit. I'd add *Knitting in a Fishing Boat on the Aegean* to my list of extraordinary places, soon editing the title to *Knitting in a Fishing Boat on the Aegean While Escaping Interpol,* which added a certain panache. I took photos with my now-charged iPhone.

Hours later, I looked up to find the water surrounding us populated by numerous boats, including sailboats with their sheets unfurled with both wind and light and, to the left, a band of heat-smudged land rising ahead. We were cruising into port.

I shook Eva awake. One glance out the window put her into instant alert. She sprang into action, shouting up to Deniz who called back.

I carefully tucked my project back into the carpet bag and poked my head outside. The air felt warmer here with a balmy breeze tugging at my robes. The sight of so much activity ahead startled me. I had conjured images of a rocky coastline where Eva and I would stealthily disembark in a secluded cove and scramble into the undergrowth. Instead, we were navigating a crowded waterway crammed with speedboats and pleasure craft, with two huge cruise ships rising like apartment buildings away to our right.

"How is this safe?"

But she was already on deck calling orders to Deniz, who yelled back excitedly. The boat puttered into a marina populated by little fishing boats about half a mile from the port's epicenter, which I could see on the left.

A battlement or fortress of some description rose on a spit of land linked to the fishing marina on the right. Deniz and his companion called out to another boat owner, presumably for permission to tether next to another craft since there were no free berths available. It appeared we were to boat-hop to the jetty.

Eva pulled me inside. "Take your robe off. Kusadasi is filled with western tourists. We'll fit in better dressed as Westerners."

I happily tugged off the robe and hijab, leaving them on the bench as I followed Eva outside. A fisherman was helping Deniz lash our craft to his amid many pleasantries and what I took to be an offer of tea. Deniz laughed, nodding while indicating Eva and myself.

"He just told them that he took us out on a tour of the coast for a little authentic Turkish flavor but now we have to catch a ferry," Eva told me before launching into a stream of Turkish herself.

The man nodded with a broad smile. In minutes, the fishermen were passing our bags from one craft to the other while helping us leap from boat to boat towards the shore.

We landed on a sidewalk in the midst of yet another Turkey.

❧ 23 ❧

We stood on a long congested promenade among cruisers in shorts and sunglasses poking through the market stalls like flocks of festive parrots. My roller bag made us conspicuous, since most visitors didn't lug anything heavier than shopping bags.

Eva scanned the streets. "Where is Ege? I neglected to ask what color of car he'd be driving." Hand shielding her eyes, she peered down the promenade.

"This doesn't look like the main road, Eva. Maybe we have to get through all these restaurants and shopping arcades where he's probably waiting."

"Yes, spot on. Let's go."

I fought the rise of unexplained panic. We were hundreds of miles away from Istanbul and yet I still felt as though we were being watched.

"Madam, would you like to see my beautiful handbags? Many more inside," a shopkeeper called.

"No thanks." I indicated to Eva to hurry with a jerk of my head. She caught my alarm and picked up her speed.

"I should have had Ege define a meeting spot," she admonished herself. "How will we ever find him?"

"Is he familiar with the port? This place is so rambling."

"I don't know."

"I think someone is following us." Foxy and Evan would have just waved. This one felt more threatening. "We've got to shake him, whoever he is." A large cement complex lined with pottery and leather shops rose ahead. "Quickly, in there!"

We scrambled into the arcade, blocking offers of hopeful shopkeepers along the way. My roller bag had become a liability. Not only did my wrist hurt from dragging it, but the extra weight slowed us down. But how could I just leave it? On the other hand, what did I really need now that the kilim was gone? Bare necessities like my knitting, that was it.

I made a flash decision and slipped into a public washroom. There, I removed the two silk tunics, the amulet against the evil eye, toiletries, plus a change of clothes from the case and tried stuffing them into my capacious carpet bag. Not everything fit. With the remorse of an amputee, I transferred some of my yarn into the roller bag, zipped it closed, removed all identification, and left it against the sink. It would probably be destroyed as a possible bomb threat.

Back in the arcade, Eva had disappeared from her watch. Frantically, I scanned the plaza, catching the eye of one man seemingly leisurely investigating a shop window two stores down. I turned and sprinted down the mall, checking over my shoulder just long enough to see him on my heels. I was almost at the outside door when Eva beckoned to me from a side utility entrance. "In here!"

"I thought you'd left!" I said as she shoved me through and slammed the metal door shut.

"I spied a bloke watching us so I opted to find an escape hatch. I'm trying to strike a deal with Amhad here."

Amhad, a bony little man standing but a few feet away, gripped a cigarette between stained teeth and pointed towards an equally senior rickshaw bearing a tattered blue canvas awning. Around us a warehouse space soared in aluminum roofing with loading bays lining one wall.

"Amhad?" I asked, looking at the man quizzically.

"Amhad doesn't speak much English. He and his son operate a little tourist trap here. They pick up the unsuspecting from the cruise ships and offer to deliver them to the shops but actually divert them in here, where they insist they buy a leather jacket before leaving. See the racks over against that wall? That's Amhad's shop. The man waving at us is his son."

I waved back while Amhad beamed tobacco-stained teeth, nodding pleasantly.

"Extortion must be a crime in Turkey, too."

"Of course it's a crime, Phoebe, but the tourists never lay charges. Are you ready? Amhad is going to drive us out to the main street, for a price, of course. Do you have cash? He says 100 euro fee but that's robbery."

"Tell him we'll give him the 100 euros," I said as I climbed into the cart. "It's either that or we buy a jacket, which hardly seems preferable. Amhad doesn't look strong enough to haul us anywhere," I pointed out.

Eva climbed in beside me, plunking her utility bag on her lap. "Looks are deceptive. Those skinny types are all sinew and muscle like a goat. Did you leave your hijab behind?"

"I did."

"Most unfortunate," she said, tying hers back over her head. "Try to stay hidden."

Amhad lifted the rickshaw's handles and spun us towards the open bays. Soon he was loping down the drive in an easy gate like a geriatric hackney. No one looked in our direction as our driver trotted us along the long paved drive and out into a kind of cul-de-sac populated by seafood bars and pomegranate stands. Two streets converged, one jutting uphill and the other forming a road lining the cove.

"Isn't that bay where we docked?" I asked, peering behind us through a crack in the awning. I caught a glimpse of our tail standing by the arcade entrance studying the crowd.

Eva saw him, too. "By the Goddess, what does he want?"

"Who knows? We're obviously the target of competing interests. He could be in Maggie's corner."

Eva called out to Amhad, pointing down the road. The man protested, arguing vehemently with his hands waving around like an agitated chicken. "He wants another 50 euros."

"For taking us few hundred feet further? Is he nuts?"

Then Eva shot forward. "Wait, I think I see Ege up ahead. See that white car parked midway down on the other side of the road with the young man standing beside it?" She waved her hand to Amhad to get moving.

The rickshaw jerked its way down the road, keeping close to the sidewalk. We were only 500 or so feet away from our getaway car when I turned to check for the arcade stalker, skimming my gaze over a restaurant patio in the process. By chance, I caught sight of Agent Walker sipping coffee from a paper cup next to a restaurant stall. And he saw me. He jerked as if electrocuted, tossed away the cup, and lunged towards us.

I tugged Eva's arm. "Interpol! Run!"

Slinging our bags over our shoulders, we bolted from the rickshaw and sprinted towards Ege's car while Amhad launched into a string of Turkish at our back, dropped the rickshaw handles, and bolted after us. Sam Walker had cut half the distance between us, with Agent Karputz joining him from somewhere on the side. Eva was shouting at Ege, who spun around and jumped into the car. We reached the vehicle as it rolled towards us just seconds ahead of the infuriated Amhad.

"Drive!" Eva shouted at the kid as I threw our bags into the back seat and leaped in after them, each of us punching down the locks while we were at it. The car rolled forward with Amhad pounding on the window.

Sam Walker halted in the middle of the traffic, dead center of the road with a phone pressed to his ear, shouting at us and at whoever was on the phone simultaneously. Ege swerved to miss him, running up onto the sidewalk and smashing into a daily special sign. He gunned the accelerator, pulling off the curb and back on the road by forcing a car to jam on its brakes to let us in. Pieces of signage flapped from our grill. We could just see Walker leaping over the sidewalk debris towards us.

"Drive, Ege!" Eva shouted.

"Who is he?" the young man cried.

"Just get us away from here!"

But the traffic on either side was too thick to move.

"Hell, we're buggered," I muttered, resorting to a Maxism.

The phone rang from inside my bag. Pulling it out, I saw the caller ID of AGENT SAM WALKER and knew exactly how he'd traced me to Kusadasi. I powered my phone off and called to Eva to do the same. Why didn't I remember to turn it off when we left Istanbul?

Eva bellowed at Ege. "Drive, boy, drive!"

"But the traffic, Auntie!"

"Forget the traffic. Make like one of those getaway drivers you see in the American movies. Drive like James Bond with the bad guys chasing us."

"James Bond?"

Eva sighed in impatience. "James Bond, the master spy in his Porsche or whatever."

"But my Toyota is no Porsche, Auntie!"

"Don't be so literal, my boy. Use your imagination!"

Ege straightened his shoulders and made a masterful attempt at stunt driving, at least as far as swerving back over the sidewalk went. This sudden diversionary tactic, though causing pedestrians to scatter screaming, zipped us out of Walker's sight and across the grass into the driveway of a huge hotel parking lot. He drove around to the back of the building and hit the brakes behind a garage. "Now what?" he asked, wiping his forehead on his sleeve.

"We need another car and a route out of town."

"But, Auntie, this my only car."

"Do you know anyone with a spare car? Think, Ege, think."

"Soon everybody on the Aegean coast is going to know that two women are attempting to escape," I said, my anxiety rising. "They'll figure out we've left the road soon enough."

"I'll phone my friend. He may have extra car," the boy said, thumbing a number into his phone. "Will they arrest us? Will I be thrown in jail?"

"Nonsense," Eva said. "You're not a criminal."

The sound of approaching sirens screaming away to our right was unmistakable.

"But you are?" Ege asked. "Auntie, are you in trouble again?"

"Stop worrying."

"Again?" I asked.

"Stop worrying," she repeated.

"The police are coming," I said as calmly as possible.

Ege was talking rapidly into his phone, his young face brightening with relief. "My friend has extra car and will lend it to you for small price."

"What price?" Eva asked.

"It doesn't matter. We'll pay what it takes," I interjected.

"Nonsense," Eva scolded. "Here, you must bargain for everything."

Ege turned back to his conversation, adding in a moment: "500 euros per week."

"Robbery!" Eva exclaimed. "Tell him a 250 Turkish lira flat rate and not a penny more."

Ege said the amount to his friend and listened for a second, nodding to himself.

I checked behind us. If Walker rounded that corner, we'd have to bolt on foot and how far would that take us? And the sirens were now on the main road.

"No Turkish lira, he says. Only euros. He says 350 euros flat rate," Ege said. "He says final offer."

"250 euros, then," Eva insisted.

"We'll take it at 350!" I cried. "Tell him yes. Eva, we don't have time for this. Where will we meet him, Ege? It has to be some place Walker would least expect us to go. He'll think we're heading for the main highway, which means we can't hit the highways until he's far ahead of us."

"The House of the Virgin Mary," Eva said, clapping her hands together. "Perfect! Tell your friend to bring the car there in, what, twenty minutes?"

"House of the Virgin Mary?" I asked. "We're going to a Catholic shrine in a Muslim country?"

"The Turks call it 'Meryem Ana' or 'Meryem Ana Evi' but it's more than a Catholic shrine. The Muslims honor it, too. Ege, get us there."

"How?" I asked.

"It's located on Mt. Koressos about 5 miles away."

"I don't mean in terms of directions, I mean we're blocked in."

"I know where it is," the boy said.

"Of course you do. You're a good Muslim son," Eva remarked.

"Why do I not feel like a good Muslim son with the police chasing?" Ege wailed.

"Hush. You'll be fine. Now all we have to do is escape this blasted parking lot undetected."

I took out my Foxy phone knowing damn well I was about to give Sir Rupert my precise location. I considered that an insurance policy as I tapped the icon with trembling fingers. The pin found our current location and in seconds I was studying a satellite view of the surrounding streets.

"Look," I pointed. "There's a service drive at the corner of this building leading to a parallel street."

In moments his little Toyota was weaving through the parked cars to a narrow lane bastioned by dumpsters and overhung by fig trees. Soon we were merging into traffic, cutting up one of the vertical tributaries heading for the hills. Looking down, I could just see the road running beside the water below. Police lights flashed amid the congestion surrounding a tour bus that seemed to be blocking the route in both directions. We took the first right-hand turn off the highway and onto a side street packed with hotels and restaurants.

"I know a back way," Ege stated.

"Of course you do!" Eva exclaimed with an air of triumph.

"Will I be arrested?" he asked again.

Eva turned to me. "Phoebe, you are a former lawyer. Tell him."

"I never wrote my bar exam and wouldn't know Turkish law anyway but I doubt you'll be arrested, Ege. They're not interested in you and, frankly, don't have the time to put you through the legal finagling. They'll question you, that's all."

"You must not tell them that we've taken another car," Eva added. "You'll say you dropped us off in town."

"They won't torture me?"

"This is not the CIA, my boy!"

"No, it's Interpol," I said glumly.

"Interpol? That's bad, yes?" Ege asked.

"They're not into torturing people for information, as far as I know." But what did I know? A face like Sam Walker's looked torturous enough.

"We'll soon be long gone and you certainly cannot be held accountable for my misdeeds," Eva added.

"Ege, you are still taking a risk in helping us and thank you for that, but I really don't think they'll do anything to you."

Or so I desperately hoped. Though I didn't share Eva's cavalier attitude, I really didn't see Ege as a big enough player to catch anyone's attention. On the other hand, I couldn't deny that my desperation was driving me to use people.

The car had begun to climb more steeply. We traversed the town through small back streets that cut a modern line across the port town but now were on a two-lane road heading straight up the side of a deeply forested mountain. Far below, the Aegean Sea basked in a luxurious blue with distant marble columns spiking the shoreline zenith. I took a deep breath. "Ephesus!"

"Ah, yes," Eva sighed, "one of the most beautiful cities of the ancient world, yet what we seek far transcends the Greeks and Romans, Phoebe, though they embraced our Goddess in Artemis. How I wish I could take you to see Her temple, once one of the seven wonders of the ancient world, now reduced to rubble by the narrow perspective of long ago marauders. But today we visit another goddess."

"We do?"

"The Virgin Mary is the closest to a goddess we have in the present time. The Goddess has been with us through the eons, appearing in many guises and by many names, including in this life as Mary, Mother of God. We hunger for the Divine Feminine in any manifestation. She figures prominently in the Muslim faith where she is recognized as the mother of a great prophet."

"I didn't realize that Islam intersects anywhere near Christianity or Judaism."

"Of course you didn't. Religions rarely highlight their commonalities, but prefer to pound us over the head with their differences; there is only one Universal Spirit, one God, rising far beyond gender boundaries. Man has claimed Him in his image, while we women claim Her in ours. We are both right and yet not."

"And Mary reportedly came here at some point?"

"According to legend, Mary was delivered here by Joseph, where she lived until her Assumption. Though archaeology hasn't confirmed it as truth and Catholic tradition places her Dormition in Jerusalem, I have no doubt as to its authenticity."

"Why?"

"A real archaeologist must work with spirit as much as with investigative strategies. How else are we to understand the history and structures of human societies if we don't allow in our humanity? Only, I hold that the Virgin Mary is the modern manifestation of the Goddess, not just mother of God but a manifestation of God Herself. Everything we do here is in Her name."

"So it follows that we are breaking multiple laws, including breaking a bargain with a rickshaw driver plus a mass of other infractions, all in the name of the Virgin Mary? Somehow I doubt she approves."

"You are fixating on too small a picture, Phoebe. Consider the whole fabric."

In reality, I kept my attention fixating on the back window, keening for police cars and sirens, my mind only half on goddesses. This couldn't be me, the upholder of all things legal, climbing this hill to parts unknown on a quest to find a goddess by any name.

The higher we climbed, the thicker the forest on either side, until far up on what seemed the apex of the incline, a golden statue of the Virgin Mary glowed to the left. Tour buses parked on either side, the statue's base amassed by visitors. All I could do was look up and gasp.

I was not a religious person. I couldn't abide or condone the murderous tyranny inflicted on humanity in the name of any dogma, yet, for one brief instant, I felt the impact of faith in its purest form. It was not the statue itself but the power of light the statue invoked that touched me on some level I couldn't understand. No words existed for that moment of sudden illumination but the effect quickly dissipated.

"Are you Catholic?" I asked Eva as the car eased between buses and continued up the mountain.

"Certainly not. I embrace all religions yet follow none. More commonalities link the faiths than differences separate them, when all is said and done, so why pledge allegiance to only one? I am a child of the One. Power and politics blind us into believing that division and war are critical to protect one's secular view. Our Virgin, our Goddess, does not represent these things. She, like Jesus, Mohammed, Buddha, and most of the true prophets, speaks of peace and love. Only man corrupts that message to his own ends."

"Auntie, I'll park over there in the far corner, okay?"

We had pulled into a large parking area filled with tour busses, taxis, and other vehicles lined with more trinket booths and cafeterias than I'd seen outside of a city center. This is a holy sanctuary?

"Yes, fine. Phoebe and I will just take a brief jaunt up to the shrine while you wait for your friend. Phoebe, give him the money, if you please. I am distressingly low on funds until we find an ATM. Ege can pay for the car while we disappear for a few moments."

I dug around inside my bag.

"But, Auntie, shouldn't you be here to make the deal?"

"The deal has already been struck, my boy. Just give him the 250 euros and let him have your car to get back into town. You can wait for us here and take a cab home yourself. Phoebe will give you the fare."

I counted out the euros. "Phoebe's almost running out of euros at this point, just so Eva knows, but here's 350 euros, as agreed. Hopefully that works." I passed a rolled wad of bills to the young man. "Your aunt's right, though: it makes way more sense to keep your friend out of it to avoid another witness for the police to interrogate."

The word "interrogate" caused the young man to pale.

"It will be fine," said Eva patting her nephew's hand. "Just wait for your friend. By my estimate, we have at least ten minutes before he arrives. I do not see it as remotely likely that the police will follow us here, in any case. They'll expect us to be heading out of town."

"Unless someone caught sight of us," I said, but Eva was already marching towards a ticket booth on the other side of the parking lot. I scrambled after her, wading along with the crowd to a path leading between concession stands selling religious memorabilia, books, bottles of holy water, and refreshments.

The noise and bustle soon hushed into a leafy parkland threaded through by the upward-leading path. Sunlight filtered through the canopy, a butterfly danced in the sun motes, and I was suffused by a deep envelope of peace. People stopped speaking. I was only vaguely aware of Eva. Though she walked beside me, part of my destiny in some way not clearly understood, we remained separate.

The path led steadily upward, past the footprint of an ancient structure to the left and, though I expected my archaeologist companion to launch into a lecture, she continued past without a word. The sanctuary evoked a profound inward-seeking communion I had never experienced. Like being in a church without walls, even the air seemed holy. Words were not encouraged or necessary.

We arrived at a small tree-shaded stone church at the hill's crest. We pilgrims threaded through the building into a central chapel graced by a candle-lit altar holding a black Madonna. Some visitors cried, most prayed. I lit a small white candle to place before the altar, something I did every time I visited a place of worship, regardless of denomination. Whether it be a cathedral in Italy or a Buddhist shrine, I didn't care. Something within sought hallowed ground to honor my dead through a small light of remembrance.

Since we were gently encouraged to keep moving in a building that could only hold a few supplicants at a time, I moved into the smaller ante-room, which I later learned was an area of worship for Muslims. The sight of a handful of hijab-wearing women clustered at the shrine praying struck me as poignant.

Back outside in the sunlit glade, people either sat on the benches in silent prayer or continued down the other side of the hill following the path to the gate. I quickly caught up to Eva, who I found fixing a message onto a stone wall lining the right-hand side of the downward path, a wall bristling with feathery messages of frayed paper, tissue, photographs, and written prayers. Others were doing something similar, and still others filled bottles from the faucet of a nearby spring.

I watched in silence as supplicants approached the wishing wall. I remained still yet deeply moved. Words seemed superfluous for this communion.

"Phoebe," Eva roused me, returning from her supplication. "We had best get back to the car park."

I nodded, falling into step beside her. As we wove down the path, people around us resumed speaking. "Obviously it's been restored, but does that chapel truly date to Mary's time?" I asked.

"My former colleagues believe most of the building dates from the sixth or seventh century, but it has foundations that may date to the first century AD, which places it firmly in the apostolic period. It was a small domicile originally, which lends even more credence to the story, but perhaps the most fascinating aspect of all is that its existence came to light through nothing short of a documented miracle." Eva's face seemed rapt with wonder, though her professorial tone continued.

"A miracle?"

"Verifiably, or as much as any miracle is verifiable. In 1812 a German nun, one Sister Anne Catherine Emmerich, a bed-ridden woman who had not journeyed beyond her own front door, began manifesting stigmata and experiencing visions, including one describing the Virgin Mary and Apostle John traveling from Jerusalem to Ephesus. She described Mary's house in detail right down to the location and aspect, all of which was recorded at her bedside by a man named Brentano. Brentano scribed that Mary had lived in a house built by John for her sole use, a stone building with a fireplace and a rounded back wall. According to the report, the room currently assigned as a Muslim chapel was once Mary's bedroom and had a spring running through it—perhaps an early form of indoor plumbing—which is the same spring flowing through the wishing wall. Because it's true makes it no less extraordinary."

We pressed through the congestion around the concession stands and bypassed the hawkers on our way to the parking lot. At first, we couldn't see Ege, since the recognizable white Toyota had disappeared, but his agitated waving finally caught our attention. He stood beside what at first glance looked to be an ancient army vehicle. Painted a dead-bird green, the scarred little truck bore numerous battle scars along its battered sides.

"What in the name of the Goddess is that?" Eva demanded.

"It's a 1983 Series 3 Land Rover, Auntie," Ege said, clapping his hands together.

"It looks like it hails from World War Two."

"Mustapha says it is in very good condition for its age."

"I've heard the same thing about me and don't consider it remotely flattering."

"He says it is very reliable since he fixed it last. Four-wheel drive, nearly new tires for bumping over rocks. He say he would charge most much more to rent it but for you, he gives excellent deal. You must return it in same condition or he will charge more."

"Pha! It doesn't look worth 350 euros if we bought it outright." Eva surveyed the truck with suspicion. "It does rather look like it's bumped over quite a few rocks already. Where did he get it? Oh, never mind. Blast it, anyway. We must make haste. Pass me the keys, dear boy. Thank you for everything." She embraced her nephew heartily, patted his cheek, and bolted for the driver's seat. "Come, Phoebe."

I hugged Ege, too, and climbed up into the passenger side. Inside, a tree-shaped air fresher dangling from the rear view mirror emitted a piny scent that couldn't quite mask the reek of dirty socks. Otherwise, the truck appeared relatively clean despite the tattered upholstery.

Ege poked his head through the open window. "He says he keeps my car until this returned in same condition in one week."

Eva let out a bark of laughter. "It will take far longer than that for our business to conclude, tell him. Get your car back, Ege. That wasn't the deal. Tell him we'll get this returned when we can."

"Ege, here," I passed him my last 200 euro. "Please give whatever is left after your cab ride to the rickshaw driver working the pier where we came in. You saw him chasing us earlier? Tell him we owe him more, which I'll try to get to him as soon as I can. Will you do that for me?"

The young man nodded, pocketing the money.

"Phoebe, we must go." Eva turned the key, and the truck started with a cough and pitched forward, spewing black fumes as it went. Ege backed away with his mouth covered as we lurched our way towards the exit.

"The police should be well ahead of us by now," Eva said. "We'll cross the back routes. I know some tracks through the villages they'd never suspect we'd use. The manpower for these local police forces is minuscule, so as long as they don't call the army on us, we should be fine."

"Why would the army be involved?" I asked.

"Interpol often work with the Turkish army in the rural regions. They are usually much better manned in the outreaches, which is where we're heading. My point is that matters may get more challenging."

I threw up my hands. "What, you don't find this challenging enough?"

And then, as if determined to emphasize the moment, the truck sputtered to a halt.

24

The Rover coughed before chugging down the hill in fumy protest.

"Hopefully this heap will remain equal to the task. Pray that the Goddess will lead us to Cappadocia without issue."

"Does the Goddess do spark plugs?" I asked.

"Why do you ask?"

"Because this thing is suffering from serious oil issues. I used to tinker with my dad's boat engine. Burning oil this badly in something this vintage probably means clogged spark plugs."

"Then, to answer your question, yes, the Goddess does spark plugs. As soon as we get someplace safe, you can have a look under the hood in Her name. Meanwhile, we need a map."

"We've got to keep the phones turned off or they'll track us."

"Not your Google maps, Phoebe, real maps. A paper version is always preferable to gadgetry. Until we obtain such, I'll take the back routes. Borek and I used to journey from the coast to Cappadocia all the time. He loved this land. He was, indeed, a true Anatolian boy."

We cut up alternative roads threading through thick forests, along lanes climbing between orchards of figs and pomegranate, and into winding strings of concrete villages. We stopped in one tiny place, estimated population fifty or less, and dropped into an alcove serving as the community's general store.

Besides the map, my remaining funds bought water, juices, crackers, a hunk of thick white cheese, oranges, and two meat-filled pastries. It amazed me how much that closet-sized depot could stock.

For good measure, Eva filled the gas tank at the nearby garage while I checked the plugs. As I suspected, they were gummed to death. After wiping them clean, I replenished the oil, and bought a roll of paper towels.

"We'll just have to hope she'll get us to wherever we're going, which is where, by the way?" I hadn't asked earlier, but now that a map spread across my lap, the time had come.

"Goreme and environs."

I located the area on the map, an estimated 600 miles away. "It will take hours to get there."

"I'm estimating 12 hours without stopping except for gas, bathroom, and spark plug resuscitation. What else can we do? They'll be watching the airports and the main routes. Cutting across country is our best option."

Settling in for a long, bumpy ride, I tried to keep my eyes open for possible pursuers in a vehicle that had probably lost its suspension a decade ago. Every bone in my body rattled but I had to admit, those back routes, even if it meant taking us miles off course, probably kept pursuers off our tail. Besides, the truck definitely ran better with the pedal down, since pausing or stopping only invited vehicular petulance.

I passed Eva one of the meat pies and devoured the other along with an orange, the map serving as my place mat.

"All right, Eva, we're in no immediate danger, so tell me your story," I said, wiping my fingers on a slice of paper towel. "I want to know exactly why you were disgraced with the Turkish government and what you're after in Anatolia. It's time, no excuses. Once you tell me everything, and I mean everything, I'll tell you my story, okay?"

"I am agreeable to that, Phoebe," she said, biting into the pie, scattering crumbs onto her cargo pants. I passed her a piece of paper towel, which she ignored. After chewing for a moment, she added, "but I must ask that you not judge me. You'd think that, at my age, judgment would no longer matter but I fear it does. I do want you to trust me, no matter what."

"You ask me to trust you unconditionally?"

"I ask that you have faith."

"Faith in you?"

"Just faith, faith that things will work out as they are meant to, regardless of how it may disrupt our lives in the progress. Faith doesn't judge."

"Just talk, Eva."

"Very well. In 1979, Borek and I were noted authorities, published widely, excavating at renowned sites, and enjoying a certain international status as guest lecturers. We were oft called upon by Turkish authorities to provide provenance for important artifacts and regularly contributed expertise to museums. Indeed, it was such a heady time for us both. To be partnered in such significant endeavors with one's mate can be so inspiring. We never competed. Ours was a true partnership based on love and mutual respect."

"What happened?"

"Borek made a significant discovery. He had such a gift, that man. It was as if he had an instinct for locating tombs and hill fortifications, though he would claim that topographical maps and research combined with an astute ear for local legend led him to such finds. The fact remains that he located sites where others did not. More importantly, people would tell him things. Why would they not? He was well-known in Anatolia, one of their own made good in the world of academia, a star, if you will."

"He was already famous then?"

"Oh, among archaeologists, quite. In any case, on one occasion, he was traveling the region of Yalakinar Malalles, or so he claimed, though he never told me exactly where. I was away lecturing in London at the time. He loved to journey around this ancient land, meeting and talking with the locals, always keeping his ears open for local traditions that might indicate the existence of ancient settlements."

"And?"

"Don't be so impatient, Phoebe. Good stories take time. And one night, he was staying as a guest in a village, something he often did to further his research, when a young woman approached him after dark, claiming that her family had stumbled upon an ancient treasure hidden in an underground city they had been guarding for generations, maybe centuries."

"An entire underground city?"

"They are relatively common in central Turkey. An estimated 50 miles of tunnels and cave houses exist underground in Cappadocia alone."

"Okay, so go on. A young woman approached Borek one night..."

"Clearly she was fearful. She claimed that it was only the women who guarded this secret, afraid to reveal it to their menfolk in case they were exposed to the Turkish Antiquities authorities and the find ripped away from them or worse. More than anything, she feared the riches they secured would be leaked into the black market and the significance of the site lost forever."

"She was educated?"

"She was a university student returning home for a visit and understood the historical value of the find, yes. She spoke English fluently, but her mother and aunts saw the site as more religious than archaeological. It had a deep spiritual connection for them."

"So she showed the treasure to Borek?"

"Oh, indeed she did but not in a way that he could easily relocate or identify. She led him there in the early hours of the morning, part of the way blindfolded, not an easy maneuver considering that the route traversed rough terrain and involved caves and cliffs. You'll better understand the landscape once we reach Cappadocia. In any case, once inside an underground cave system, this young woman revealed a shrine buried deep within the cliffs, an amazing Bronze Age find that Borek dated as possibly from the time of Troy IV."

"Homer's Troy?"

"No, this civilization would have predated Homer by over a thousand years. Borek estimated 1200 BC, making it contemporary with Mycenae, but it needed much more thorough study. The young woman refused to let him photograph anything or even to make a return trip. He had just that night to record the findings, which he did through a series of hasty sketches by lamplight. I've studied those sketches—gold daggers, goddess statuary, necklaces, and gold cuffs. The overriding images in the shrine were of a female deity counterbalanced by a bull—male and female represented in primitive yet powerful symbolic form."

"Gold," I said, thinking of certain thieves.

"But, Phoebe, there was also wall art of incredible intricacy. Preserved in the dark for thousands of years were these motifs of an early version of Cybele, the Vulture Goddess, motifs almost exactly like the ones on your kilim. Don't you see? Borek had discovered a lost Goddess shrine protected through the centuries by Her very own daughters! Is that not extraordinary?"

I swallowed hard. "Oh, yes, but how could they keep that secret against all the village men?"

"Borek believed that some men may have been entrusted with the secret but had kept it safe in honor of the Goddess or, as I suggested, more likely for fear how such a find might impact the life of the village, inviting violence, treachery, and the like, as gold is wont to do. The other fear is that it might be absconded by the government, thus secreted away from the village, eventually resulting in some foreign-financed archaeological dig to disrupt their village life. This was before cable TV bristled on every roof, which is so often the case now. They were trying to preserve their lifestyle."

"I get that but what did Borek do with these sketches and the information?"

"Nothing. The young woman had only taken him to the site to verify its age and attribute it to a specific civilization, something the mothers had no interest in, but she made him promise not to reveal the village name or vicinity. He could publish his notes but nothing more."

"And he agreed to that?"

"Certainly. Borek was a man of integrity. His word was rock; thus he would never reveal the details of the location to another soul, even to me. I knew the rough area, but with miles of cave formations and many tiny villages, that told me little enough. Yet what Borek showed me was convincing as to the significance of the find."

"But, as an archaeologist, keeping such a find secret must have been terribly hard."

"Difficult for him, excruciating for me. It proved my thesis, you see, confirming my life's work. Still, we knew that, without tangible evidence, these notes were worth nothing in the scholarly world. To publish them, or even tell of this incredible discovery would only heap ridicule upon his head, possibly ruin him. And yet there it was, the extraordinary story of a generation of women guarding a secret of incredible cultural, social, spiritual, and archaeological value for centuries. If he published findings without proof, he'd be ruined."

The silence that followed was relieved only by the sound of the tires rumbling along the dirt road. "So you published them in your name," I said after a moment.

"He didn't want me to, tried to stop me, in fact, but I had to get the word out, let the world see those incredible images with their own eyes, see the Goddess's arms extended into the vortex of the sacred feminine, sacrosanct, perfect, timeless, in Her glory, as is Her right. I had to connect those images to the same motifs we find in Anatolian kilims today, proving our need for balance in the cosmic, female balanced with male, the bull and womb, the Polat energies in harmony, rather than this destructive dysfunction of presumed male superiority over female! I had to, Phoebe!"

"And you published those raw notes without proof?"

"I tidied them up but did not submit them to an archaeological journal but rather the *London Illustrated News* in my name. I wrote of how this proved that the ancients were far wiser than we in the balance of the universe, that the Goddess was still alive in the hearts of Her priestesses."

"That doesn't sound very archaeological."

"Well, no, that is not the spirit in which it was written. Nevertheless, Turkish authorities demanded to know why they had not been informed. The antiquities laws are very strict here, as they should be. If ever a citizen or visitor should stumble upon an ancient site, which happens fairly often, the authorities must be informed immediately or the finders arrested."

"But you couldn't reveal the site because you didn't know where it was."

"No, so I claimed that it was I who had made the promise to the village woman not reveal my source. The Turkish authorities demanded that I take them to the village but, of course, I couldn't. They responded by banishing me from Turkey, treating me as if I were a bad girl who wouldn't obey her superiors. The impact of that moment was excruciating. "

"You were banned?"

"My banishment was not as a man's would have been. Mine was humiliating as I was barraged with condescending diatribes best reserved for children caught raiding cookie jars. On the other hand, that same attitude probably kept me out of prison."

"And Borek just stood by while you were humiliated?"

"No, of course not. He protested loudly, stating that he believed me absolutely—which he did, of course—and even wrote an article countering the vilification I received at the hands of my colleagues."

"But didn't he stand up and explain?"

"I did it without his consent so, no, of course not. I wanted his reputation to remain unblemished, which it did, after I took the experience as being totally my own. The Turkish authorities banished me and I returned to England without Borek."

"He wouldn't even come with you?"

"Why should we both lose our careers and reputations? He stayed in Turkey but visited me in London sometimes."

"Did he forgive you?"

"Of course he did. He loved me."

"And you forgave him for choosing his career over his life with you?"

"It could be argued that I did the same."

"But his love for you should have put you first, and your commitment to your lives together should have done the same."

"Phoebe, you are a romantic. I consider myself an idealist but not a romantic. You, I fear, are both."

"You made a promise to one another, a contract which you both broke. Promise and commitment are part of marriage vows. That's not idealism, that's an issue of morality as well as legality."

"You are right. I failed him and he failed me but we loved one another, despite it all. As the person I was then, head-strong and driven, I did what I had to. What I regret most is that I was not with him when he died. Until that moment, I always believed we would be together again, even if only in our retirement. I believed we had time, which we didn't. As it was, he was here in Cappadocia trying to find the site and thus exonerate my name when he slipped from a cliff and fell to his death. We never have enough time. That's the one fact we must all grasp. Time is finite. Love is not."

"I'm so sorry, Eva. I can only imagine the heartbreak you've experienced."

"Heartbreak is part of being human. None of us escape unscathed. We all have dark amid the light."

I closed my eyes. "I like to think of a life as a complex weaving. There are patterns in the mix of light and dark—joy and sorrow, good and bad—but the balance determines the strength of the design. Do we have enough light to counterbalance the dark? What if we have so much dark amid the light that it leaves our weave warped beyond repair?"

"Dear Phoebe, no weave is warped beyond repair. It's all in how you see it and how you make it. You are still the weaver, remember. You may not have the whole picture but some of the design is in your jurisdiction. Blend your warp into the bigger pattern, move on, and on no account dwell on the flaws. Where there are holes, let in the light. That's where faith comes in."

"Are you about to bring up the Goddess?"

"Would it help if I said God?"

"I'm not religious."

"Neither am I in the true sense. It's enough to be truly awake."

We drove along in silence for a while, lost in our thoughts as the sun sank deeper, a glory of red-gold hues intensified by deep ultramarine riding overhead. I remained fixed on the luminescence pooling on the horizon as it seeped away into the twilight. There is no light without dark. The impact of that adage had never affected me so profoundly.

"Now I understand why and where we're going," I said, after a while. "You want to find that village and locate the secret cache to protect the find, maybe exonerate your name. You needed to see my kilim to confirm the location. And the Bronze Age gold?"

"Gold is not my interest. My overriding impetus is to prove the strength of Goddess worship across time and patriarchy."

"Gold is interesting to somebody, lots of somebodies. And don't the same considerations still apply? I mean, if you find the site, won't Borek's promise have been for nothing and the site will be exposed?"

"It's already been exposed. I neglected to tell you what might be the most important part. A young archaeologist friend informed me a few months back that certain ancient artifacts from the Anatolian region had begun appearing on the black market—daggers mostly, but very distinctive in design. He sent me a picture, and the artifacts exactly matched one of the designs in Borek's notebook. Somebody has infiltrated the cache and is leaking the pieces into the black market."

I leaned forward. "Ah, now I understand Noel's and Toby's interest in the site."

"Don't be so quick to judge, Phoebe."

"Judge what, who? You knew my connection all along. That's why you've never pressed me for details on my side of the story. You already know it."

"Not all of it, I don't. I know about the Bermuda heist, certainly. Every archaeologist knows that story. My point is that you may have incorrectly attributed the identity of criminals chasing the Goddess hoard."

"I know Maggie and Noel are after it."

"Perhaps not for the reason you suspect. Phoebe, I knew about your kilim long before I met you in Istanbul."

I took a deep steadying breath. "So our meeting was staged?"

"Our lives are interwoven. The meeting only served to forge our alliance."

"You knew who I was all along."

"I am a researcher, Phoebe, and I have many connections."

"Why didn't you say something?" I stared straight ahead, my fingers icy in my lap.

"When have we had the chance? We have been on the run from the moment we meant, and first I needed to establish trust between us. We will find this site together and you can confront your demons just as I must battle my own. Finding this site is our mutual salvation. I said I will help you and so I shall."

"By withholding the truth, by lying?"

"I never lied, though I withheld the truth, certainly. You have trust issues, so I realized I had to tread carefully. There is more that I have to say, but perhaps I've said enough for now."

I closed my eyes and took a deep breath. "I can't wait to learn the next segment but first, I need to pee. We've been driving for hours. Let's find a station. How far away are we?"

"Maybe another three-hour drive. We are somewhere near Mustafa-pasa. There will be gas stations there and restaurants but that means entering a busy town. On the other hand, I doubt even the police can cover every mile of this place."

"Let's take that chance. Oh, and I'll drive the next leg." I had so much to think about and plan. Right then, I yearned to be back of control of something, even if it was just that ancient Rover.

So far, the truck had bombed along without too many incidents, other than the occasional stall, but the engine was misfiring more frequently now. We had to enter a populated area and do what had to be done. Meanwhile, I had to think. Eva had misled me to what end? On the other hand, she could help me get to a site that drew Toby and the others.

Electric lights began appearing embedded in the midst of weird organic rock shapes ahead. Mushroom chimneys? Strange flood-lit turrets and irregular twisting pinnacles rose from the earth all around.

"Did Gaudi hit this place with a wicked sense of humor or is this landscaping via deranged djinn?"

Eva laughed. "Natural earth formations, the effect of rain and wind on the soft porous rock indigenous to the area. The terrain is riddled with cave systems, some natural, some man enhanced—entire subterranean cities—all once inhabited by ancient civilizations, including the Hittites, and even the Christians escaping the Romans."

A magnificent cave hotel soared in flood-lit fairy spires along a main street where we stopped at a gas station. While Eva filled the tank, I used the bathroom and splashed water on my face as if that would shock clear thoughts into my brain. I bought an orange juice and stood outside waiting, gulping in the high cold night air along with the liquid.

We were at a much higher altitude, far from the humidity of the ocean, making the starry sky so clear it penetrated the haze of town lights. My gaze climbed upward, brushing the stars, before diving down again to the cave hotel, staring up at the glowing terrarium-like rooms.

Each room was unique, each suspended in the darkness like pools of warmth and light. My gaze dropped further, landing by chance on the lobby directly across the street. A man stood outside the glass doorway shooting furtive glances in our direction while talking urgently into his cell phone.

"Eva," I whispered. She stood by the gas attendant watching him refill the oil. I jerked my head towards the hotel. "We've got to get out of here."

She turned to the attendant. "Never mind that. Do you take credit cards?"

I jumped into the driver's seat and tried the engine. Nothing. I checked the lobby again. Two men stood there now instead of one.

I watched as the new arrival, a tall bearded man dressed in a hat and scarf over a leather jacket yanked away the other's cell phone and smashed it against the cement doorstep, bringing the heel of his boot crashing down on the little flip-top.

The first man responded with a swinging punch which the tall man easily deflected following up with a jaw-cracking upswing of his own. The blow pitched the shorter man backward onto the tarmac, after which the victor flexed his hand and bounded across the road towards us.

"Oh, shit!" I cried, the moment I identified that long bearded face. I rolled down the window. "Go to hell!"

He climbed into the passenger side. "Hello to you, too, Phoebe. Where's Eva? How the hell did you two get the Turkish army after you?"

25

Eva dove into the back seat. "I wasn't expecting you so soon, Noel."

"Change of plans," he commented.

"I suppose this scum-bag bastard is the young colleague you referred to?" I said.

"Phoebe, I—" Eva began.

"Talk later," Noel ordered. "That man alerted the cavalry. Could you force this rust bucket to move, Phoebe?"

"Think I'm not trying, you thieving butt-head? The engine is fried, get it?" I kept turning the key in the ignition. "Eva, did you plan this all along?"

"Certainly not," Eva said. "It's not what you think. If things worked according to plan, we would have all connected in Istanbul."

"Where you had plenty of time to explain."

"Not so. I—"

"Let me drive." Noel interrupted, placing one hand on the gear shift.

"No!" I elbowed him away. I couldn't deal with either of them right then, being too intent on getting the engine started. Maybe having Noel in the front seat was preferable to being captured by the Turkish army but not by much.

Of course, the engine refused to catch. "Damn!" I whacked the steering wheel, glancing towards the hotel in time to see the wounded man limping into the lobby.

"They'll be here in minutes," Noel said, his voice smoothed down to honey and tonic. "Ease up on the accelerator. Don't flood the thing. Stay calm. What's wrong with your wrists?"

"Don't tell me to stay calm, shit-head."

"I bring out your best adjectives, don't I?"

Headlights barreled towards us.

"Do what he says, Phoebe. The Goddess is on our side," Eva said.

"I know well enough not to flood the damn engine!" I kept trying the ignition, shocked when the Rover finally bolted forward in a string of jerky lurches. Praying to the power of momentum alone, I shifted gears, jammed on the accelerator, and rolled onto the road just as an army truck squealed to a halt beside us.

"There's a hill ahead," Noel said. "Switchback turns, no guard rails, straight down for maybe two miles. Can you handle that?"

"Of course I can handle that."

The truck hitched forward for another 500 feet, reached the crest of the hill, and stalled with the wheels still rolling. Uniformed men were running towards us.

I released the clutch, switched to neutral, and allowed gravity to lead us downhill, thinking I'd worry about the bottom once we got there. Shots fired, bullets pinging against the fender and hitting the rear tires, first right then left. Rubber burst, sending the truck veering towards the cliff edge.

"They're firing at us!" I gripped the wheel and wrenched the truck back on the road as we careened around the bend grating on the back rims.

Noel whistled, his hands gripping the dashboard. "You're good!"

"I'm damn good," I said between my teeth. "Driving is my thing."

"There's the sign to Goreme!" Eva called.

Letters flashed white on green in our dying headlights as I took the turn with a peal worthy of the Formula 500. For a few giddy seconds, I thought we'd crash into the rocks but instead we ground to a halt half-way up the rise before gravity kicked in and we began scraping backwards.

"Run!" I shouted.

I slammed up the handbrake, turned off the lights, and left the keys in the ignition while flood-lit rock formations rose on either side. I snatched our belongings from the rear seat, throwing Eva's knapsack and my carpet bag onto the road while stuffing the last of our food supplies into my pockets. Noel slung our bags over his shoulders and bounded towards the rocks.

"I know a shortcut through the valley!" Eva called.

A glimpse of headlights below fueled my adrenalin. I ran towards illuminated rocks thrusting into the night sky like gigantic penises, a sight made weirder by our elongated shadows shrinking towards us. I bounded deeper between twisting spires, oblivious of anything but plunging forward.

The ground changed from grass-bristled sand to rock. The moment we broke away from the floodlights, the surrounding shadows thickened like glue on tar. I stumbled, righted myself, and kept running.

Visibility shrank. Eva and Noel appeared like distorted lumps two shades lighter than the background, but they kept disappearing around corners leaving me hissing at them for directions. Finally, Noel picked his way back to me and clasped my hand firmly in his, tugging me behind him. I shook him loose and struggled on.

Men's shouts trumpeted the air at our backs. I imagined flashlights sweeping the area while we stumbled along blindly. And it seemed endless, those tortured rock towers. Large and small, they clustered in all directions, as dense as trunks of giant stalagmites frozen in some ancient dance. Sometimes the formations briefly fell away into a moon-bleached expanse which we'd sprint across until safely undercover.

We ran for what seemed like hours until Eva slumped against a rock trying to catch her breath. As I leaned nearby, I realized I could no longer hear our pursuers.

"They'll give up the search for tonight," Noel commented, as if reading my thoughts. "Probably resume in the morning with helicopters."

"Why is the army after us again?" I panted.

"Because you count Interpol among your fans, obviously." Noel took a swig of water from a bottle he pulled from a bag slung across his body. "I suspect they've engaged the army to bring you two in. Eva, how are you holding up?"

"Fine, thank you. Don't you worry, I'll make it."

"How far away from the valley are we?" he asked.

"I have no idea," she said, sinking onto her haunches. "I lost my way some time back. I am so very tired."

"Best to keep moving," Noel urged, helping her to her feet. "If they tracked you this far, they may guess the general direction we're heading."

"That they may, young man, but I know this terrain in ways they don't," she said, steadying her breath. "If I can reach the valley, I know many hiding places. It's got to be near here somewhere."

"Hold on to me. There, that's it." Noel tucked her arm into his and smiled down at her. "We'll be all right."

"I shouldn't have dragged you into this," she said to him. "You've risked so much for me."

"I'm here willingly. Let's see this thing through."

"Have you two been in contact from the beginning?"

"I'm sorry, Phoebe," Eva said. "I asked Dr. Halloran to help me locate Borek's hidden site long ago and he promised to do so. The timing has become even more critical."

I wrapped my arms around myself to keep from shivering. I was thousands of miles from home being pursued by the police, army, and God knows who else, in the company of a black market thief and a disgraced professor. All I could do was go with the flow until I could figure something out.

"Keep moving," Noel urged.

"Give me my carpet bag, please. I can manage perfectly well handling my own stuff." I held out my hand.

"I'm sure you can," he replied smoothly, shifting the weight of the two bags on his considerably broader shoulders, "but it's easier for me."

"It's fine to accept a little help sometimes," Eva said. "I have learned that much over the years."

"So, as a man, he gets to play predatory bastard while I, the lowly weaker sex, am helpless by virtue of my feminine nature, is that it?" I couldn't stop spewing juvenile garbage.

Noel laughed. "For the record, you drive more like a trucker than an earth mother."

"Can we just stop this?" Eva gripped Noel's arm and pointed between two boulders opening ahead. "Head that way." Together they continued picking their way over the rocks with me following.

455

The temperatures fell alarmingly. We had begun our day amid balmy Aegean breezes and now stumbled about in this frigid moonscape.

I soon lost all track of time. One minute blended into the next with sequence after sequence of stark shadows juxtaposed against ghostly peaks. Above, the stars spangled over moon-silvered turrets, while at our feet, shadows clung so thickly I could be wading in pitch. Nothing but a slight wind in an otherwise supernatural stillness accompanied our ragged breathing. At one point the earth shook under our feet.

"Tremors," Noel remarked. "There's been a series of minor earthquakes happening in this area in the past few days."

"Great." Exhausted, I began stumbling more and Eva, too, even when the earth wasn't moving. Eva clung to Noel. At one point, they turned a corner and disappeared, leaving me to face multiple paths branching ahead with no idea which one to take. I plunged left, the earth vibrated, and the ground dropped sharply under my feet.

The stone walls fell away as I hit hard on my left shoulder before tumbling downhill. Flashes of moonlit cliffs flipped over images of scrubby bushes again and again, but nothing I did could stop my rolling trajectory.

26

A heavy weight landed on top of me, grinding me to a halt and walloping the breath from my lungs. I spent winded seconds on my back looking up into Noel's shadowed face. Only when he shifted his knees to straddle me, did I force the air back into my chest.

"Are you all right?" He shoved the hair from his eyes.

I inhaled sharply. "Get. Off. Me."

He slowly climbed to his feet and offered me his hand. I stood there, knees trembling, my hand firmly in his, recalibrating.

"Are you all right, Phoebe?" Eva called down.

"Bruised not broken," Noel shouted back. "Stay where you are. We're coming up."

I yanked away my hand. "Not so fast. Where's Toby?"

"Istanbul."

"Why not here?" I began toppling sideways, he caught me, and I endured him pressing me even closer.

"I'll tell you later."

"I'm sick of later. Tell me now. He sent me the kilim so I'd find him."

"Will you listen? I said we planned to meet you in Istanbul, but matters got complicated so we had to thwart that initiative."

"I need to see him."

"You will."

"When?"

"Not now, obviously. We're standing on the edge of a bloody cliff!"

Without thinking, I shoved him hard, too hard. For a terrifying moment, I watched him skidding downward towards the edge. In seconds he caught his balance and scrambled back up towards me.

"Do you want me dead, is that it?" his voice more pained than angry. "Would that make up for all I've done?"

"I didn't mean to push you so hard but, to answer your question, no, I don't want you dead. I want you in prison suffering for years and years, and just so you know, there's no way I'm going to let you get away with another theft. I don't care what I have to do."

"I'm not here to plunder, Phoebe. I'm here to help Eva."

"Do you expect me to believe that?"

Eva scrabbled down towards us in a flurry of pebbles. "What's taking you two so long?" she called. "I was up there looking out over that cliff and realized that's it, that's the valley I've been seeking right below us. All we need do is find our way down and be delivered to the perfect place for the night."

"We'd better start searching," Noel said, turning away.

It took at least another hour to find a suitable descent, which turned out to be no more than a gorge eroded into the side of the soft tufa by eons of rain and wind.

As a path, it was steep and pebbly but had enough small trees and bushes springing on either side to offer handholds along the way. Noel, taking the role of scout, proceeded first, followed by me, then Eva, each of us making cautious progress down the cliff. Only with my bandaged hand and sore shoulder, I barely inched along, always waiting for the next tremor.

"Everybody all right up there?" Noel shouted.

"Just wonderful," I replied.

"Coming along," Eva assured him. From her labored breath above, I knew she was in no better shape than I.

There were moments when I found myself clinging to a bush under the moonlight with my feet scrabbling beneath me, wondering why in hell I put myself into when I could be miles away safely tucked into a warm bed.

Only then I remembered I'd lost safety long ago and all I could do was forge ahead.

We arrived at the far end of a narrow valley where a stream threaded through a band of trees. Overhead the moon-limned cliffs soared, accenting arched openings.

"Caves," I whispered, collapsing cross-legged onto the sand, relieved to be on solid ground at last.

"Yes," Eva said, landing beside me with a grunt. "Fourth century, mostly. Anchorite communities began forming through the leadership of Saint Basil, who brought his brothers here to avoid persecution. There are cells and chapels carved throughout Cappadocia, too many to count, but none of these contain the Byzantine frescoes that made the area famous. Those you'll find in other valleys and, of course, in Goreme."

"No one deemed these important enough to properly excavate," Noel remarked.

"Borek and I excavated here one summer but the funding soon dried up."

"It still makes a perfect refuge," Noel commented.

"It's been a sanctuary of one kind or another for thousands of years." Eva stretched out on the stony ground. "I could just drift off to sleep here."

Noel offered her his hand. "But don't. We still need shelter."

I gazed up at grill-like formations. "Are those dovecotes?"

"They are," Eva said. "They once used doves as both messengers and food."

"And their excrement also served as fuel. Pigeon poop is surprisingly versatile," Noel added.

I climbed wearily to my feet. "Any place in particular you see us spending the night?"

Noel hoisted Eva to standing, tucking her arm into his. She pointed towards the nearest cliff wall. "Over there. If memory serves me, there's a range of small cells clustered near to the valley floor. I'm sure none of us feel like climbing any more tonight."

One glance at the ghostly openings far overhead and I swore I'd rather sleep impaled on rocks. As it was, my teeth chattered and all I wanted was a roof over my head and a fire. Food would help.

Eva trundled over to a ragged opening a few hundred feet further along. Inside, the soft tufa rock had been carved into a Spartan three-room domicile. Ledges and niches hewn into the rock encircled a small fire pit with a hole overhead to funnel out smoke, though exactly to where I couldn't tell.

Noel foraged for twigs while Eva and I worked to clear the sleeping niches of animal droppings and debris.

"He really is here to help me find the site and protect the remaining artifacts," she told me while using a leafy branch as a brush.

"I just can't believe anything either one of you says."

"Oh Phoebe," she sighed. "Open your mind and heart."

We continued without speaking until Noel returned with a bundle of branches and proceeded to build a fire. Once a blaze crackled away, we gathered around cross-legged or perched on makeshift seats trying to warm ourselves while downing most of our food and water.

Noel contributed two protein bars and another water bottle to the feast. We split everything three ways, with Noel carefully slicing cheese and oranges with his knife. After devouring our meals, we each portioned a little something for breakfast, in my case half an orange and a piece of protein bar.

I studied Noel furtively in the firelight. With his shaggy hair and the kaftan worn under the battered black jacket, he could pass as a cross between a Serbian rebel and a motorcycle dude. When I first met him, he was clean-shaven but the beard did nothing to diminish the fierce angles of his face or obscure the full mouth frowning down upon the orange he segmented with careful deliberation. With different clothes he could hail from Cappadocia or Pakistan or even downtown North America, as if his mixed heritage granted him a visa for half the world without offering a passport to a single country.

He sensed me watching and our eyes briefly touched across the fire.

"What's the plan tomorrow?" I asked, dropping my gaze.

"We'll proceed to a village through the cliffs at the end of the valley," Eva said. "I'm known there so I can find someone to shelter us until we can catch a lift to Goreme where I own a house. It will be easier to sink into the woodwork there."

"You own a house?"

"A small one, yes. Borek and I bought it when we were excavating in the region. It's relatively central. Oh, and I loved the view so much he wanted me to have it. We can use that as our base while we work to find the exact location of the site."

"And how will we do that exactly?" I asked. Noel studied me as if he sensed I had no intention of going along with their plan, whatever the hell it was. He'd be watching me as closely as I him.

"We must ask questions, Phoebe. As women, we may be in the best position to elicit trust among the womenfolk. If the community is the one I suspect, it will be most difficult. Somehow we must convince them to allow us to help before the last of their heritage trickles away into the hands of the unscrupulous. Thieves are already at work, no doubt assisted by some villagers."

"And these thieves must be watching every stranger who passes by." I looked pointedly at Noel. "Do you have any idea who's infiltrated the site?"

"Probably a local," Noel said, biting into an orange. "He or she is filtering artifacts out one by one, selling them to multiple buyers through an intermediary. It's the middleman who fences them on the black market."

"Could the middleman be a middle woman?"

"If you're thinking Maggie, I doubt she would have got this far yet, and besides, she'll still have to cooperate with the local contact." He was feeding twigs into the fire.

"She had a map of Anatolia spread out in her room. She's in this somewhere."

"Her ruthlessness is boundless."

"She had Jason Young killed to--"

His head shot up. "She killed Jason Young?"

"Not personally but had him killed, yeah. She told me as much. Jason was your man, wasn't he?"

"Yes, but—"

"And you had him crawling all over my gallery while I slept upstairs."

"He would never have harmed you. He was your bodyguard, instructed by Toby and me to keep you safe. We were trying to ensure you and Max had everything you needed and, yes, I see now how this only complicated your life further and I apologize for that. I would have explained all that if you hadn't pulled the alarm."

I rubbed my eyes. "So it's my fault?"

"I'm only trying to explain how things went wrong."

"And keep going wrong."

"And we are now charged with setting all to rights." Eva held up her hand. "The Goddess has brought us together so that we can protect Her history against the ravages of the greedy. Perhaps her gift to us will be to help heal our wounds along the way. That is all that matters."

I thumbed toward Noel. "Does he really look like Goddess material to you?"

Noel spit a mouthful of seeds into the fire. "The Goddess chooses strange bedfellows."

"We are all Goddess material, Phoebe," Eva told me sternly.

"Maybe the Goddess should choose her partners better. This one betrayed his own father while conniving with his father's girlfriend and my brother to steal a fortune of artifacts. If that's not the ravaging of the greedy, I don't know what is."

"You're the only one I wanted to ravage," said Noel mildly.

I shot him a foul look. "My point is you're a cheat, a thief, and a—"

"'Scum-bag bastard' is my favorite. There, you hit poetic stride while touching on the truth of things, since I am technically a bastard," he said. "'*I am bastard begot, bastard instructed, bastard in mind, bastard in valor, in everything illegitimate*'."

"Do you always need Shakespeare to express your feelings? And, just for the record, Max would have done right by your mother had he known she was pregnant."

"He told you that?"

"He did."

"And you believed him."

"Yes." I paused. "Why do you hate him so much?"

"I don't hate him; I hold him in contempt. There's a difference."

"But why? He didn't know that your mother was pregnant."

"I realize that. After all, he didn't know my mother, period. It wasn't uncommon for a white man to drive into an Aboriginal community and knock up some local girl for a spot of fun. Most of them just drove on, too. No, I hold him in contempt for how he treated me once he knew the truth, as if I should be grateful that he deigned to pluck me from my shabby little Aboriginal community and accept me as his son in the first place. Supposedly, I should spend my life groveling for affection and recognition from that day forward."

"He loves you!"

"How the hell do you know?"

"Because I'm the one watching him blubbering into his drink every night while going on and on about how he wasn't a good enough this or a good enough that. He even begged me not to turn you in. You are his son, he said, and that's all that matters."

"That's called guilt."

"Stop it, both of you," Eva interceded. "Fathers and sons can brew a complex relationship, especially with the divisiveness of misunderstanding. I don't know Max, except by reputation, but I'm sure he does love you, Noel, and must be proud of all you've achieved—"

"Like what a fabulous double-crossing crook he's become?" I remarked.

"Like father, like son," Noel countered.

"Only now he's come clean while you're just getting dirtier by the minute." I hated this miserable sniping but I couldn't stop myself.

"Maybe I'm defining my own version of justice."

"Are you back to that Robin Hood of archaeology shit again?"

Eva climbed to her feet. "I said stop! It's been a long day and, in my case, heaped upon an even longer life, and I'm weary of your arguing. Don't you see how you are poisoning yourselves? Grow up, both of you."

We both gazed up at her.

"Noel," she continued, "maybe your father doesn't know how to express his feelings—men don't always have the emotional vocabulary to articulate these matters. Perhaps you could give him another chance. And, Phoebe, you are so driven with bitterness, you can't see the light in the stars. Noel's as wounded as you are, only bears his scars in different places. Open your eyes, both of you. For now, we're all too tired and overwrought to think straight. We need sleep. Maybe forgiveness will come later."

I sighed, knowing the truth of her words though unable to process them in any way that mattered. True enough, I couldn't see the light in the stars. Nothing shone for me anywhere, any place.

Though I said goodnight and made to go to my sleeping niche, I ended back at the fire, still roiling with the desperate need to make something right, though I wasn't certain what.

Noel continued to feed sticks into the blaze with focused intensity.

"I meant what I said about Max," I said softly. "Whatever you did to him, he forgives you, even accepts what you did as his due. Try to forgive him, too."

His eyes met mine. "You speak of forgiveness as if you know it well."

"I have to relearn a lot of things I understood better when I was younger. Seems as though I've lost everything over the past year. I'm trying to mend the best I can. Maybe you are, too, but neither of us know how." I turned away towards one of the alcoves.

Eva had already claimed a niche and lay curled on her side under her army-green parka, her scarves wrapping her head like a colorful mummy. Of the three of us, she had come best prepared with her thick quilted jacket and multiple layers. I, on the other hand, didn't have a single useful fabric to keep me warm, unless my half-knit yarn counted, which it didn't. The irony wasn't lost on me.

I picked up my carpet bag and chose another niche, plumping up the bag into a makeshift pillow. Meanwhile, Noel stretched his long body into the bench opposite mine, the space so constricted, his legs hung over the edge sideways.

Even with the fire blazing, the cave remained tomb-chill and Eva's snoring did nothing to improve the comfort. I lay staring into space, my heart pounding, thoughts live-wire twitching. It felt as if all the lives and deaths that had passed in this ancient place had fractured the air itself. I couldn't breathe without inhaling pain. My teeth chattered miserably. I wrapped my arms around myself wondering how I'd ever survive the night.

I was in that cocoon-like state with my eyes closed when something like a bag of potato chips landed on my chest. I looked up to find Noel standing over me unpacking a silvery blanket thing from its pouch. "An emergency blanket," he said, as if discussing the weather. "One of the items I packed for just such nights as these. It will help keep you warm, though it won't feel very cozy."

I tried to sit up, nearly whacking my head on the alcove wall. "You use it. You're no better dressed for the elements than I am."

"I'm just doing the manly thing. Couldn't you just play along for once and pretend you're of the weaker sex?"

I laughed. "Well, thanks. I'll accept this token of your gallantry."

"You're welcome." He hesitated, making no move to return to his niche. "We could always share body heat."

"Considering the size of these alcoves, that would be logistically impossible, though probably worth a few good laughs."

"Good point. Try to get some sleep. We have a long way ahead of us tomorrow and have to leave before dawn." He turned and walked back to his niche alone.

✻ 27 ✻

The predawn traipse through the valley was a mute, frigid stumble along the narrow valley with companions as numb with hunger and cold as I.

We followed the stream to the end of the valley before climbing up a narrow path leading sharply upward. Eva, though groggy and stumbling even with Noel's help, knew the way with an unerring sense of direction. She led us to the crest of a stony hill and pointed to a cluster of cement houses below, smoke curling up from their chimneys and windows beaming squares of light into the chill dawn.

"They take great risk in harboring fugitives," Eva told us, "but I have yet to meet a Turk who will turn away someone in need."

"Is this village connected to my kilim?" Though I still felt its absence, at least I had my tattoo.

"No. That one is on the other side of the plain but these people may still know something."

We skidded down the steep incline until we reached a dirt road curving into the village. The community consisted of maybe twenty humble houses clustered around a tiny domed mosque, with the occasional battered car or truck parked haphazardly in the street.

The first call to prayer blared from the mosque's single minaret as we approached, prompting Noel to urge us deeper into the shadows of an outbuilding. Men began pouring from their houses to the mosque, some still wiping their faces from morning ablutions.

"Which house is your friend's?" Noel whispered while a donkey bayed from a paddock behind us.

"The big one across the street," Eva told him, nodding towards the boxy two-story building opposite. Other than size and the occasional portico, all the houses looked the same. "It is good that the men will be attending the mosque, since that will give me a chance to speak to Cari alone. She was the one I came to know best. Here they keep to the old ways."

We watched the men enter the mosque in single file accompanied by the melodic chant that seemed to suffuse the entire town. After a few minutes, Eva beckoned us to follow as she slipped out behind the building and hobbled across the road. For seconds we were exposed mid-street with the sun rising in a shimmering red-gold overhead. While darting past the open mosque door, I glimpsed thirty or so robed men bent over in prayer. Maybe I only imagined the roar of a far-off truck accompanied by the thump-thump of a helicopter, but the urge to dive for cover overwhelmed me.

Eva reached the door and knocked loudly, beckoning to Noel to turn away, which he did, keeping his gaze fixed towards the street. Several agonizing seconds passed without a response until, finally, the door inched open onto the startled face of an older woman wearing a long skirt and a headscarf.

She stared out at Eva without recognition while Eva spoke in rapid Turkish, waving her hands about and pointing to me and then Noel. The woman's gaze fixed on Noel's back for what seemed far too long before beckoning us in.

The woman spoke to Eva who translated. "Quickly. First remove your shoes and then we must descend to the kitchen. Cari's husband and sons will return soon. Noel, Phoebe and I will be in the kitchen but you must wait apart." Noel had already removed his battered boots, he being familiar enough with the customs to know one never wears shoes in a Muslim household. "It is not fitting for a strange man to be in the company of women in this community, so Cari wants you to wait in another room until the men arrive."

He nodded and kept his head down.

I caught impressions of brilliant rugs covering every bit of floor and wall space. We descended the stairs while the scent of wood smoke mingled with spices rode the air. Once on the bottom level, Cari kept her face averted while pointing through a door where Noel was instructed to wait as Eva and I continued into the next room.

Here, two women sat around a low flat grill where something fragrant sizzled. They turned startled faces towards us and then promptly burst into excited Turkish. I was bid to sit between them on the rugs as the women smiled and asked me questions I couldn't understand.

"This is Canan and Berna, Cari's daughter and daughter-in-law, respectively. They want to know if they can offer you tea and breakfast."

"Oh, yes, please." I smiled, wishing desperately I could speak the language. "And a toilet."

Eva informed me toilets here consisted of a hole in the ground in a shed outside. We followed Berna to a tiny outbuilding, scattering foraging chickens as we went.

Inside, it was dark and cold, not to mention incredibly small for maneuvering jean removal and squatting over a hole. Thankfully, Eva had prepared me with tissue, not that I knew where to deposit it afterward. Since it was socially impossible to question people on their toilet habits, I kept my maddening questions to myself and figured things out as best I could.

Back inside, Canan led me to a wash basin set against one wall so I could clean my face and hands. Eva stood nearby waiting her turn and translating the women's excited questions. "They are so delighted to see us. They don't meet many women from other worlds here and are asking a million queries which I can only begin to answer. They have never seen red hair like yours and want to know if you have used henna to honor the prophet. I have explained that you are not Muslim but respect their beliefs."

"True enough," I said wiping my face on the towel offered. "But I saw a satellite dish on the roof. Don't they see lots of different things on television?"

"I'm not sure which programs they watch here-maybe only the Turkish soap operas-and perhaps the television is viewed mostly by the men. I think it rude to ask since this is one of the more conservative communities. Best not to pry. It is bad enough that I am going to request that they illicitly transport us to another town sixty miles away."

I passed Berna my towel and she handed me a mug of hot, sweet tea. "Will they do it?"

"No community takes on the army's scrutiny lightly. Fortunately, they remain suspicious of the government on principal. I've told them the truth: that we aim to stop a robbery of an important archaeological site and that the government misunderstands our intent and wishes to block us. Governmental red tape will only halt our efforts, I said."

"Did you say Interpol is involved?"

"That would only complicate matters." She paused to catch her breath. "Whether they turn us over to the army will be for Erol, Cari's husband, to decide. Erol owns the truck parked outside as well as the biggest herd of sheep in these parts. The fact that many of these villages keep archaeological findings to themselves is in our favor. For now, we must wait. Besides, this gives me a chance to ask the women a few questions."

I settled into a warm spot on the floor beside the grill, watching in fascination as Berna flipped a flat pancake-like bread in front of me, dousing it in olive oil, and sprinkling cheese. The tension slipped from my neck and all I could do was continue smiling while extending my hands towards the warmth. When the offer came for breakfast, I gratefully accepted, devouring the warm pastry while the women prepared the men's.

"Usually women are to wait until the men have their meal before eating." Eva said between bites. "We are exceptions as guests."

Cari took off upstairs with a tray, leaving Eva and me alone with the other two. As soon as she'd disappeared, Eva launched a battery of questions at Berna. By the tone of her voice, I sensed she was attempting to keep her questions casual but casual wasn't Eva. Soon her voice tensed into something more clipped and demanding.

Canan brushed crumbs from the floor rug with a broom while Berna kept pressing more food on us with a smile fixed tightly in place.

"Eva, this isn't going anywhere. Lighten up a little."

"They know something and we're running out of time. Do you have a picture of the kilim?"

"On my phone but turning it on might send out a tracking blip."

"I doubt that there is much of a cell service here but we'll have to risk it. Pass it to me, please."

I pulled my carpet bag towards me, fished out the phone, and reluctantly turned it on, reminding myself I meant to pry out the SIM card but had forgotten.

"Can you hurry?"

"It needs to reboot. What's the rush?"

"I want to show them the photo before the men come down or call us up. If I guess correctly, a secret of this nature is kept safe among the women only."

The phone finally came to life and I thumbed through my photos until I found the portrait of my kilim. "I miss it," I remarked, passing the phone to Eva.

"She is always with us, Phoebe."

"I mean the kilim itself."

"I know what you meant."

She spoke in earnest tones to Canan and Berna as their two heads leaned together over the photo. A quick look passed between the women before Berna handed the phone back to me. They shook their heads in unison.

Berna rose to her feet, smoothed down her skirt, and began gathering the dishes. I offered to help, but Eva informed me that, as a guest, I was to sit.

Eva added. "They're making more tea."

"Guess we can always use more tea."

"They say they know nothing, yet I'm sure they do."

"So I gathered."

"They're hiding something."

"Of course they are, but why would they tell us?" Just before returning the phone back to my bag, I glanced at the icons. Not surprisingly, there was no cell service out here, but several messages had come in before I'd turned the phone off back in Kusadasi. Two were from Serena, one unknown with a London number, a string came from Sam's Interpol number, and one from Max.

My breakfast suddenly churned. Supposing something had happened to

Max? What if the gallery was broken into or Serena harmed? Nothing I could do about it anyway. I turned off the phone and returned it to my bag. Canan stood watching me. I smiled back.

"Eva, please ask them if there's a place where we can bathe."

She did as I asked, prompting a response from Canan that included pointing over her shoulder. Berna chimed in with more detail, part of which included some kind of negotiation with her sister-in-law.

"They say there's a small haman in town which the women use between 1 and 4 p.m. every day. The rest of the time, the haman is used by the men. They've agreed to take us with them later in the afternoon, if the men agree."

"Why do the men have to agree to everything?"

"A haman is a public bath. Other village women will be there, too, and the news of strangers in town will spread." Eva rubbed her eyes and sighed. "I don't care one way or the other. I'm well used to Spartan living conditions. I'd be happy just to rest for a few hours."

"I care. For me, cleanliness is next to goddessness. I haven't had a proper bath in days."

At that moment, Cari returned and beckoned both of us to follow her upstairs.

We were ushered into a large sunlit room hung with vibrant red-based textiles with ceramic plates nestled within the occasional bare spaces. Cushioned benches lined the walls with a low carpeted table surrounded by big kilim-covered cushions centering the floor. Three men sat around the table cross-legged, one of whom was Noel, who appeared to be enjoying the male company along with his breakfast.

Cari quickly cleared the table and bid us join the men before she hurried downstairs. I arranged my limbs lotus position but Eva found this more challenging. After seconds of awkward shifting, she finally settled. "My apologies."

Noel introduced a small man with crinkled brown skin and sharp darting eyes as Erol, the family patriarch, while the handsome younger man sitting across from him was Polat, his son. I smiled and nodded, which seemed the only kind of communication I could manage. More smiling and nodding followed until I thought my face would freeze and my neck bob off as the conversation continued in Turkish. Eva and Noel did most of the talking.

I sat in mute observation sipping tea and watching as something Eva said prompted Erol to shake his head vehemently.

Polat intervened as if attempting to counter his father's position. The two men erupted in excited debate until Noel said something in halting Turkish. They studied him in silence for a moment.

"What just happened?" I asked.

"We requested that they drive us to Goreme but Erol said it was too risky," Eva explained. "Polat is willing but father is not. Apparently the government has made some heavy-handed statements about citizens dealing with foreigners over protected archaeological sites."

"And?"

"And they're considering the prospect."

Noel extended a warning hand for Eva to stop talking as he further pitched our case. Erol spoke next in a series of brief sentences checked off on the fingers of one sun-browned hand.

"He has agreed to take us tonight after dark providing we stay hidden in the meantime," Noel said. "He doesn't want the other villagers to know we're here because at least one family has a son in the army."

"So, no bath," I remarked.

Noel raised an eyebrow in my direction. "Bath?"

"I was hoping to use the haman."

"It doesn't sound like that's going to happen."

The incomprehensible drone of voices stirring together with a big breakfast lulled me into an upright doze. Before I knew, Eva was nudging me awake. "Come along, Phoebe. We'll go to the sleeping quarters and rest for the day."

I blinked into an empty room. "Where have they gone?"

"Noel is resting in another building."

Though the cushioned benches in the main room looked tempting, we were ushered upstairs to Polat and Berna's quarters, to sleep on the floor by the fire.

I glimpsed a bed behind a curtain but the floor suited me fine. By that time, I had redefined comfort. Food in my belly and a safe, warm place to sleep rated right up there in my new luxury category.

Eva dropped to the floor, pulled a blanket over herself and fell into a deep sleep. I joined her on the rug and slept as though berthed in a 5-star hotel.

Hours later I awoke with a start. Flinging off the blanket, I sat upright, keening my senses. Eva snored away on the floor beside me, but otherwise the surrounding house seemed unnaturally still.

The unmistakable rattle of truck tires grinding the village dust outside must have kick-started me awake. I shuffled over to the tiny window and peered out onto the street. A green army truck had just pulled into the village center.

✣ 28 ✣

"Eva, wake up. Grab your things!" I shook her once, snatched my carpet bag, and scrambled downstairs calling for the others.

No one answered. The kitchen, main room, and every space between lay empty.

Wait, it was the woman's bathing time. My heart galloping, I checked out the window again. Six uniformed men were now spreading up the street knocking on every door.

Eva arrived downstairs moments later, rumpled and dazed.

"We have to get out of here before the army arrives." I tugged her out the back door towards the outbuildings. Huddled together amid the squawking chickens, I scanned for the safest hiding place. Two squeezed together in the toilet shed? No room. Hide with the goats in the animal pen? Too predictable. The soldiers were bound to check the outbuildings. And where was Noel and why did I even care? I couldn't worry about him right now.

We slinked between the sheds, ducking under a pomegranate tree into a neighbor's yard, passed a table set with a backgammon game in progress and an ashtray filled with burning cigarettes. Men's voices called from inside the house as we sprinted into the next yard. More fruit trees strung with laundry offered a bit of cover as we crouched behind a drying blanket and strained to see the street.

"They must be starting from the far end," I whispered. "Maybe they won't get here for a few more minutes. Where's the haman?"

"Haman?"

I turned to her. "Would male soldiers storm into a bath house during women's bath time?"

"Good thinking."

I waited until the street was free of soldiers before clutching Eva's hand and dashing across the road. Two elderly men sat on their doorsteps watching us. I put a finger to my lips as we scurried by, my destination a small elaborately tiled stone building beside the mosque.

In moments we were descending marble steps into a dark, moist sanctuary. At first I couldn't see much but heard the agitated voices of women coming from somewhere.

We stood in a little tiled vestibule. On the right a curtain, on the left steam wafting up from under a tiled door. I glimpsed two other doors down the hall but Eva was already leading me towards the right. "The dressing room must be this way."

We stepped into a large shelved room with coat hooks and alcoves where Berna plus four other women were hurriedly dressing. Their excited chatter stopped the moment we entered. Eva launched into some too-long explanation while waving her hands and pointing towards the door. One woman responded, then another, with Berna having the last word.

"They are cutting short their bath to return home but some refuse. Berna will remain with us."

"Eva."

"The short version is they have told me that 'women as women are safe.' I believe it's an idiomatic expression but—"

"But we get the gist. They'll help." I stepped further inside and accepted the towel Berna offered. Most of the women had finished dressing and stood in their head scarves and skirts studying us openly. Berna indicated for us to undress while she shed her clothes again. The other women just stood, waiting. I turned to Eva, who had already shimmied from her gear to stand naked like some ancient fertility goddess.

"Wouldn't it be better if we stayed dressed?"

"Whatever for?"

"Because we may have to make a run for it."

"We can't stay clothed while our hosts are naked." She pointed to my towel. "Get on with it, Phoebe."

"But they're watching." In fact, a couple of them had stepped forward to help me disrobe. I gently pushed them away.

"They're curious. They've never seen a redhead before, probably never a naked Westerner, for that matter. They'll soon discover our equipment is basically the same. Hurry, the sooner we're with the other women, the safer we will be."

I packed away my modesty along with my clothes, piling everything on top of my carpet bag in one of the niches. Aware of their scrutiny, I wrapped the towel around my middle bits before the inspection grew too intimate. My tattoos may as well be outlined in neon so I kept them shielded. Satisfied the show was over, the women shuffled away, chatting amongst themselves up the stairs.

Inside the steam room, various tasks of grooming and washing suspended as we entered. I sensed they were at least as surprised by my hair color as our sudden arrival. While Berna explained, I scanned the tiled room with its taps and porcelain basins, shelves and benches. Some women were in the midst of washing their hair while others rubbed oils into their skins or received a massage from maybe a friend or a relative. We had interrupted a pajama party minus the pajamas.

"Here women share their secrets," Eva whispered. "Isn't it marvelous?" She greeted Canan. "It's all about bonding and dates from long before the Romans when public bathing centered the community."

Berna pointed to a marble platform in the middle of the room.

"She says you are to lay on the marble and she will tend you while Canan tends me."

"Define 'tend'."

"Rough bliss is my best explanation." Eva climbed onto the slab and lay on her back, sighing in pleasure as Canan poured warm water over her body.

Reluctantly, I climbed on the platform beside her, the marble uncomfortably cold and slick under my skin as I lay face-down. Nothing so far aligned with my definition of bliss. Two women even came up and giggled over the mermaid tattoo on my butt.

"Eva, being naked while a bunch of heat-seeking soldiers tromp around outside and women study me like I'm a zoological specimen makes me feel as vulnerable as hell."

"Relax," she murmured. "You could never be anywhere safer than with women in a haman," she murmured. "We are enveloped within the Goddess's womb among sisters, mothers, and wives. They are only curious."

"Wish they wouldn't giggle."

"Enjoy every moment while it lasts. Ouch!" She said something to Canan who made soothing sounds as she kneaded Eva's shoulders.

I couldn't wait for it to end at first. Berna washed my hair with some herbal-scented shampoo—rosemary or maybe sage—which was pleasant enough, though a bit robust when her fingers dug into my scalp.

Otherwise, I felt splayed on a pedestal like a sacrificial lamb in the midst of some ritual I didn't understand. The impression intensified when Berna finished with the shampoo and began rubbing pumice over my skin as if intent on scraping off the first two layers of epidermis. I had to force myself not to yelp. After exfoliation so intense my skin tingled pink and tender, she poured a warm stream of lemon-scented oil over me and began to massage my aching muscles with firm strong hands.

Finally, my tension melted into fragrant pliancy. By the time I flipped on my back, thoughts of soldiers and kilims had retreated. I felt Berna pause and opened my eyes to find her studying my goddess tat. She nodded, and approached that still-tender area with considerable care while her hands soothed and comforted.

I'm not sure how long the bliss lasted, certainly not long enough. After the cocooning hot towels had begun to cool, Berna nudged us gently and spoke hurriedly to Eva.

"She reports that the soldiers are still here and a car drove into the village a short time ago with a damaged man—I'm not certain of the exact transla-tion—accompanied by another policeman not in uniform. She says they insist upon performing their own search and are cooperating with the soldiers."

"Interpol?" I bolted upright. "The 'damaged' bit must refer to Sam

Walker's facial scars. He wears them like a badge. Damn, I knew he'd catch up with me sooner or later."

"These agents are asking different questions, she says, and insist upon exploring the village themselves. The villagers are incensed by this since they show little respect for the customs the army have afforded them. The villagers are requesting the army protect them against this insult."

"What if they search here and find us?"

A short exchange followed between Berna and Eva. "None of the villagers have betrayed us, she says, at least to her knowledge, but they don't know where Noel is hiding. The soldiers have been informed that many women are choosing to remain in the haman rather than be subjected to watching strangers invade their homes. It appears the captain has accepted this even if the two Interpol agents haven't. The captain is holding firm."

"This isn't good."

"No, but we have no choice but to remain here for now."

"I think I'd rather dress and wait in the dressing room until dark. Are there other rooms?"

"I'll ask." Berna pointed towards the vestibule. "There's a cold room and a men's dressing area at the rear. They don't use the cold room often in the cooler months."

"All right, I'll wait in the dressing room. I can always knit."

"I'll remain here." Eva sank back down on the marble while I climbed cautiously to the floor.

I followed Berna towards the vestibule, both of us entering the dressing area to change. I dug around in my carpet bag for clean clothes. There wasn't much to choose from: a slightly less grubby pair of jeans and a black turtleneck. I couldn't very well wear one of the silk tunics. Everything else had gone the way of the roller bag.

Berna touched my shoulder and held out a deep maroon robe. I nodded and thanked her. In a moment, she was gone.

The single bulb dangling overhead gave such feeble light, knitting would be a challenge and after the steam room, I was cold. Even dressed, I shivered.

Leaving the robe with my bag for now, I followed the urge to move. I strolled down the hall towards the back rooms, wondering if the building had a rear entrance or at least a more comfortable sitting area.

The first door opened onto a dressing room much like the one I'd just exited, only previous occupants had left a robe hanging on a wall peg with a tumble of clothes shoved under a bench. I quickly closed that door and opened the one beside it, stepping inside a larger room alive with the sound of running water and brightened by a circle of windows high up in the domed ceiling.

For a moment, I simply focused upward, appreciating the effect of the reflecting water on the blue tiles until I sensed movement. My gaze dropped to the rear view of a magnificently naked man with a tattoo curving around his body, standing not more than a few feet away. Busy toweling himself down, he didn't see me at first until a quick glance over his shoulder froze him to the spot.

"You don't knock?"

"The haman is still for women only."

"It's past 4:00."

"The village are extending the women's hours while Interpol searches the houses again. At least now we know where you're hiding."

"Hell."

"It's not that bad. By the way, you look rather good from behind."

"Phoebe..."

"Yes?" I waited while he just stood there in a half-turn. "Oh, I get it: you're shy. You did promise once to show me your full Kangaroo Dreaming tattoo, remember?"

He slowly straightened and turned, letting the towel drop to his side so that he stood before me full frontal, watching me study him wearing nothing but a little smile and that incredible Aboriginal Kangaroo Dreaming tattoo curving around his entire body in ochers, rusts, and black dots. Not that I was focused on the art, exactly. "Is this what you want to see?"

I scrutinized him up and down, taking my time, admiring his tall, lean build. Perhaps he had grown a bit too thin over the months since Bermuda, maybe his ribs protruded too starkly against his skin, but his shoulders remained as broad as ever until they tapered down to his waist, all properly muscled and impressively male. I dragged my gaze to his face.

"Remember, that it's cold in here."

"I have an excellent imagination." He looked so damn good right then I may have licked my lips. "Is there a back door?"

"Pardon?"

"A back door, a way to escape if Interpol tries to search the haman?"

He breathed out slowly. "Oh, yes. Ah, there's a door at the back of the men's dressing room. I guess they use that during the changing of the guard. Mind if I get dressed now?"

"Sure, but you don't want to bump into any of the women still in the building. Stay here while I get your things. I presume that's your stuff in the dressing room?"

He nodded.

By the time I returned carrying his bag plus the boots and robe, he had wrapped the towel demurely around his waist. I stifled my disappointment while passing him the clothes. "They don't look like yours."

"Erol lent me a few things. You've had a bath yourself, I see. Your cheeks are pink and your hair all—". His hand waved as it trying to snare the right word.

"Bushy?"

"Joyfully uninhibited."

I laughed. "That sounds like wishful thinking. I'd better get back to the women's side. See you later, at least your public parts."

But I didn't see any of him until much later.

❦ 29 ❦

Eva and I escaped through the back door camouflaged in borrowed robes with instructions to wait for Erol across the field.

Noel had already disappeared.

By then it was so dark, we could barely see one foot ahead of ourselves but, luckily for us, neither could the army. We could hear them banging through the haman from where we huddled in the dark even though the village had shrunk to no more than lights clustered in the distance.

"Where did Berna say we were to wait exactly?" I whispered as we crouched behind a rock.

"In this direction is all she said. Erol will drive out to collect us once the army leaves, which I hope will be soon. My knees can't take much more of this."

"Here, sit on my bag. Yarn makes a perfect cushion." I shoved it under her bottom and urged her into sitting. "How's that?"

"Oh, much better, thank you."

"How about a piece of bread? Cari gave me some for later."

"She gave me some, too, but right now I just need rest."

I slumped against the boulder beside her, oblivious to the pebbles biting into my skin.

"Dear Phoebe, forgive me for keeping so much from you." She reached across the dark and took my hand.

I squeezed it back. "You didn't know how I'd react. I get that."

"When I received Noel's message about the artifacts hitting the black market, I had to find my way here, no matter who it affected. In truth, I have been incredibly selfish, but I see all the casualties along the way a necessary sacrifice."

I stared at the town lights without focusing. "A necessary sacrifice," I repeated.

"I just need to get there, Phoebe, for the sake of history, for the Goddess, for all women. Thanks to you and Noel, the Goddess's mission and my life's quest are about to reach fruition."

I steered the conversation onto less hallowed ground. "How long have you known Noel?"

"I met him while guest lecturing in Queensland when he was still a student and over the months we became friends. Perhaps he needed a mother and I needed a son, so we filled those roles for one another. I always believed the Goddess brought him into my life to ease my way after Borek died."

"You know him that well?"

"Oh yes. When in London, we'd often meet for dinners, and once or twice he'd even escort me to the theatre. Such a caring young man. He knew how much I needed to return to Turkey and find this shrine and, even though he is risking his life and freedom, he is here for me now."

"You believe he came to Turkey for you?"

"He's an archaeologist so, of course, he wants to protect what's left of the shrine, but, yes, he came to Cappadocia at my request and for you, too. He and your brother initially thought that Istanbul would be a reasonably safe place to rendezvous with you. They had no idea what forces had already been mobilized. Once that became clear, they conspired to keep you in London but it was already too late. All has aligned according to the Goddess's will."

I had so much I wanted to counter, to argue against, but I knew there was no point. Sometimes the best that two opposing views can manage is to coexist on common ground. "You think you can protect the shrine somehow?"

"We must. Noel believes there is little in the way of artifacts remaining but the shrine itself is the true treasure. Besides, if I can stand for one moment in that ancient site and feel the power of the Universe as our species first imagined Her thousands of years ago, I will consider my life a wondrous success, despite the sorrows. Noel believes the robbers may yet destroy the site after they've ravaged it. We need to get there before that happens."

"I wish you had told me this earlier."

"Would that have made a difference?"

"Maybe not but I still wouldn't have felt so betrayed."

"I know I used you and I'm sorry."

We didn't speak for a while. She broke the silence with: "I do wish Noel would appear."

I scanned the surrounding darkness. "Me, too."

It took over an hour more before Erol's truck rumbled across the field to meet us. A dark ride in a battered truck down more ruts than roads followed as we bounced across sheepherder tracks and over the hills towards Goreme. Nearly three hours later, he pulled to a stop at the edge of town, announcing to Eva that we must walk the rest of the way. I tried to argue against that, since I didn't think Eva had the stamina for another long trek, but she cut me short.

"Let us just go, Phoebe. Erol is afraid his truck will attract too much attention and he has risked enough."

She leaned on me as we scrambled along footpaths and over fences in the dark, the details of which blurred together in a fast-forward of images and exhaustion.

We finally reached the town and trudged through the shadows uphill towards Eva's house, a little three-story stone structure perched at the top of a road scattered with similar homes. My feet screamed with fresh blisters, but I was beyond caring about anything but sleep.

"I called ahead to request my friend Ela light the fire and fill the larder. She looks after the place and rents it out to tourists in the summer. With luck, no one else will even know we're here. You may take the top floor bedroom and I shall claim mine on the next level."

I hauled myself upstairs, tossed my carpet bag on the floor, and dropped onto the bed fully dressed. When I opened my eyes hours later, I found myself inside a dark room hazy red by sunshine pushing patterns through a kilim-covered window. Pulling back the rug curtain, I peered down at the street, empty except for a foraging dog.

Had I only dreamed the last few days? Nothing seemed quite real anymore.

The scent of coffee lured me down a narrow stairway to a landing, where I glimpsed Eva through a half-opened door. I tiptoed in and found her sleeping deeply.

I carried on down to the bottom level with its tiny kitchen living area crowded by a table, two chairs, and one counter. A cushioned bench hugged the wall nearest the stove. Otherwise, the room was empty, yet coffee warmed on a hot plate on one counter with space enough for a single basket of bread and a plate of dolmades covered in cloths. Her friend must have been and gone.

After food and jolts of caffeine prompted a swell of gratitude, I stood in the center of the room, brushed crumbs from my jacket, and finally had time to panic. We were in such trouble—Interpol was after us, thieves, the army. I wasted a few minutes spinning in adrenalin until my gaze landed on Eva's duffel bag. She had dumped it on the floor when we entered the house last night, but now it sat on one of the chairs like a rumpled gnome.

I thought I'd bring her coffee along with the bag to her room but, as I reached down to pick it up, the bag tipped, dumping the contents to the floor in an orderly pile.

Eva had organized her stuff with clothes and fabric on the bottom and smaller items neatly tucked along the sides. I was just about to upend the pile and replace it in the bag when something caught my eye—the frayed edges of the bottommost layer was so familiar. I unfolded the Goddess with Vultures kilim across the chair and stared.

Eva had stolen it?

I flashed back and forth between joy at the reunion and a wrenching sadness. Of all the things I expected of Eva, this wasn't one. For a moment, I thought I'd upchuck breakfast or, at least, burst into tears. She stole my kilim? She spouted faith and trust while ripping me off?

How sad, how horribly sad. What kind of inner conflict twists a person like that, what makes them say one thing and do another? How could she truly believe such an act was justified?

My legs buckled beneath me and I slumped into a chair with the kilim spread across my lap. For a moment, I gazed down at the goddess motifs, struck anew by the energy woven there. She needed to go to that shrine at all costs. Nothing and no one else mattered. She said as much.

It would be so easy to judge, to criticize, but for some reason, I couldn't stir the necessary anger. That didn't make my next decision any easier.

Returning the kilim lovingly to the duffel bag, I carefully reconstructed the contents roughly as I found them. Scarves, two plastic zip bags—one stuffed with soap and toothpaste, the other prescription bottles—our grease-stained map, extra shirts and undies, her wallet. Her wallet? Without so much as a pang of guilt, I unfolded the leather and investigated the contents. She had a wad of euros in there plus at least as many pounds sterling. So she lied about that, too. I stuffed the wallet back and returned the bag to the chair.

When I climbed the stairs moments later, it was to tiptoe past Eva's snoring form and carry soundlessly to my top floor room. Fishing my two phones from my bag, I powered on both. I needed someplace utterly private. I couldn't risk Eva overhearing.

It was then that I noticed the pull-down ladder propped against the wall opposite the bed. It had to be a ladder to the roof. After checking the thing for stability, I climbed upward, bumped open the trap door, and climbed out into a bright chilly vista.

I stood blinking at an amazing landscape of twisted dawn-cast castle mounds, dancing conical hats, and far away plains rimmed with more of the same as the sun pushed molten peach into the horizon.

Hot air balloons rose in the sky like some aerial ballet adding to an unready majestic landscape. Below spread the town with lazy swirls of smoke threading the still air. I pulled out my iPhone, relieved to find a strong signal, and pressed redial for the last Agent Walker call.

The routing was nearly instantaneous. "Phoebe McCabe?" His voice grated over the line as if he'd been ripping apart fenders with his bare teeth. I must have woken him up. "Where are you?"

"I don't have much time so please listen, Walker. Remember how you said I should try to find out information when the opportunity presents itself? Well, I hitched a ride hoping it would bring me closer to the truth. As I see it, opportunity is now presenting itself in 3D with a side of balloons."

"Are you serious? You're a fugitive and a co-conspirator with art thieves and now you're implying you planned this all along as an undercover move?"

"I'm not saying I planned anything. I'm an impulsive creature who wasn't ready to return to London with so much unfinished business hanging over my head. I took a risk that coming to Anatolia would bring me closer to Noel and Toby and, so far, I'm half-right."

"Stay where you are, we'll pick you up, and just possibly I can get your sentence reduced for turning yourself in."

"You're not listening. I said I'm about to discover the truth, as in the location of this Bronze Age site everybody's excited about. Do you really think you can find that without my help? The locals aren't talking to the government officials, which means they won't talk to you, either, especially not you."

Silence spoke volumes. "Are you listening now?" I prompted.

"I'm listening."

"Good, so I'm here with Eva Friedrich along with Noel Halloran, who is temporarily missing in action but can't be far away. Do you want me to lead the authorities to the site and help you apprehend Halloran or not, yes or no?"

A pause followed. I could almost hear him considering the limited alternatives. "If you try double-crossing me again, I swear you'll be in such deep trouble, no amount of finagling will set you free."

"First, I want both you and the army off my tail until I locate the site." More negotiations followed and I didn't agree with all his conditions nor he of mine, but we compromised.

Afterward, I pocketed my iPhone and picked up the Foxy phone, waiting for long seconds before he picked up. "Sir Rupert Fox here."

"Phoebe McCabe here. Are you ready to be friends?"

"Phoebe! Where are you?"

"The question is, where are you? I figure we might have lost you back in Kudesai. Am I right?"

"Partly, yes, but we since deduced that you are somewhere in Cappadocia, as am I, by the way. I am currently ensconced at a lovely cave hotel just outside of Goreme."

"Luck you. I'll contact you again later with where to meet."

❧ 30 ❧

Eva stared down at the map of Cappadocia anchored on top of the diminutive table. "This is the village near where I believe lies Her shrine. Those hills are riddled with unexplored tunnels, most of which we believe were originally Hittite retreats, though this one is far older. Borek often mentioned the region. When I think back, perhaps too often."

I cleared the breakfast dishes and refilled our coffee mugs. "Are you sure he didn't drop other clues?"

"No, I don't believe so but I don't remember. Why hadn't I paid closer attention?" She scraped one of the wooden chairs closer and collapsed into it, her gaze fixed on the floor. "I still miss him. I wish he were still here. There's so much I'd like to say. Everywhere I look, I see his face, remember his voice, especially here."

I slipped the fruit plate back on the table and laid my hand on her shoulder. "All these memories must just crowd in around you."

"Yes, they do. I had no idea it would be like this. I've been here before since he died, but this is different. Phoebe," she laid her hand on mine. "I told you that I had no regrets but that's not true. If I had my life to do over again, I would never have published that article or left his side. I would have found another way to reveal the shrine."

"I understand," was all I could think to say. "Is Goreme where the kilim hails from?"

"Not here but close. I'm convinced it's near Begüm, which is not far away."

"Would seeing the kilim again help at all?" It was only a desperate hope that she might yet confess her theft.

"No," she said. "I have gleaned all I can there."

"Oh." Even now she wouldn't tell me. "I guess what the Goddess giveth, the Goddess taketh away."

She shot me a quick look. "The Goddess works in mysterious ways, Phoebe. It's best not to mock. In any case, Begüm is not more than 5 miles away but may as well be 20 leagues without a car."

"I'm not mocking. As I see it, nobody really owns anything. We just keep something treasured for a while before it lands in someone else's care, either by design or circumstance." I removed my hand and tapped the map. "So, how do you plan on getting to Begüm?"

"Unfortunately, Borek has no relatives still in this region and it's too risky to rent a car in either of our names. Perhaps I could borrow one from Ela's brother."

"Or a motorcycle. I used to own one years ago," I offered."

"There's an idea Either way, I must find transportation without attracting suspicion. Maybe I could sweeten the pot with a few euros."

"I'd lend you some but my funds are gone, if you recall. I figure what 'the Goddess giveth the Goddess taketh away' applies to money most of all."

"I have a few euros in reserve, Phoebe, in the interest of expediency. And you're still mocking the Goddess."

"I am not. I'm only using humor to navigate treacherous waters. I figure the Goddess would get the joke, seeing as She makes plenty Herself, including lots at my expense."

Eva still wasn't about to tell me about her money stash, either, yet anger wasn't what ruled me. Anger, above all emotions, seemed so irrelevant now. "So a car may take care of the transportation problem, but once in the village, how do you propose to locate the shrine?"

"For that I must win the trust of the local women. I will need to devise a plan for that but first, the transportation issue. Perish the thought of having to use the local bus. Interpol would find us for certain. In any case, relax here and enjoy the respite while I proceed to my friend's house to see if borrowing a car is remotely possible."

"Don't exhaust yourself. I'll find a car while you rest."

"You don't know the language, Phoebe. It's better that I go alone to attract less attention. Stay here. Noel may yet make an appearance and it would be good to have one of us meet him."

"I'm sure he could manage by himself. I still think I should go with you."

"And I still think you should stay put."

I watched her throw on the same brown robe borrowed from Berna. She paused at the door. "Phoebe, thank you."

"For what?"

"For not hating me despite everything." And out the door she went, blinking out the bright slice of sun as the door closed behind her.

Well, she was right about that. I didn't hate her.

I waited only long enough to make sure she had a good head start before I scrambled upstairs and tossed on my own borrowed robe and hijab.

Up on the roof minutes later, I called Foxy and arranged for him to pick me up outside the one landmark I recalled from our flight the night before—a carpet shop anchoring the corner at the bottom of the hill where a footpath connected with the main street. Soon I had bolted out the door, keeping my head down.

Foxy arrived a little later than planned but so did I, since it took me much longer than expected to retrace the tangled steps taken the night before. By then, I'd become adept at traversing backyards and footpaths weaving behind public streets.

Sir Rupert and Evan sat idling in a white Rover outside the carpet shop. In a testament to my disguise, neither recognized me until I knocked on the window.

"My dear, do get in. I am very relieved to see you well, though admittedly you led us on a merry chase, indeed. Brown is a good color for you, may I say. Not everyone can carry it off."

I slid into the back seat, taking in Sir Rupert's exquisitely tailored cashmere long coat and yellow knitted scarf, a combo worn incongruously over a pair of knife-pressed jeans decked out with a brand new pair of hiking boots. "Good morning Rupert, Evan. Would you drive, please, preferably to the main highway heading east?"

Though today I wasn't concerned about either Interpol or the Turkish army, that didn't mean I felt totally safe, either. Maggie's men had to be in the area somewhere. I pulled out the map tucked into my carpet bag and passed it to Foxy. "We're going to the tiny village circled in pencil."

"And why is that?" Foxy flicked his wrist to Evan who pulled away from the curb heading out of town.

"I'm researching the location of a certain site I believe interests you, too, but it would have made things so much easier if you had shared what you know earlier."

"I could say the same thing to you, Phoebe, and besides which, you are assuming I knew the details earlier, which I did not."

"But you do now?"

"Not totally, no, but the pieces are coming together rather admirably. Once we understood you were traveling with Eva Friedrich, all the dots connected—isn't that a tiresome phrase? I shall banish it from my lexicon henceforth."

"We? You said 'we'."

"Oh, Evan and I. Anyway, as I was saying, Dr. Yilmaz is known to us. In fact, I knew her late husband, too, and the sorry tale of their parting heated up the scholarly world for a while. Now I understand what everyone is after and must say, I am thrilled with the prospects. The question is, why are you including me in the dance at this late hour?"

I smiled at him and meant it. "You extended the offer of assistance, any time, anyhow, so I'm taking you up on the offer."

"But why now and what exactly is the how?"

"The now is that I need help, specifically a ride to the village, which is the probable site of the final dot you're connecting. As for the rest of the picture that makes up the how, it's still unfolding. I mean, I'm hoping to convince someone to lead me to the shrine but, obviously, I don't want to do this alone."

"Why not with Dr. Friedrich?"

"I plan to take Eva along but not on this leg. She often alienates people rather than inspires their confidence and I have reason not to completely trust her."

"And yet you trust me?" He clapped his gloved hands together as if receiving a long-awaited gift.

"Up to a point. I figure you're openly devious. I know that's a contradiction but, as underhanded as you are, you haven't told me a single lie, as far as I know. It may seem simplistic but I appreciate that, which doesn't mean I'm willing to help you steal precious artifacts. You do get that, don't you?"

"I would expect no less of you but, in turn, it may surprise you to know that I am not in the business of stealing precious artifacts, period. I haven't the stomach for it. I have personally stolen nothing."

"But you're interested in dealing with artifacts once they're stolen, kind of like an ever-circling commercial vulture?"

He laughed, slapping his thigh in delight. "That is it exactly! And I do appreciate vultures for the manner in which they tidy things up after the predators, don't you agree?"

"Vultures have risen in my estimation but I'm still not willing to kill to feed one."

His laughter filled the car. "Never fear, Phoebe, my dear. We will both meet our ends without resorting to murder."

"That's the idea. But maybe the two of us will be at cross-purposes?"

"I don't see it that way at all. It's just that we seek the same things for different reasons."

"An interesting distinction. Did you knit your scarf?"

"I did. It's brioche stitch. Quite a pleasant experience, if you don't mind two-color knitting. How I wanted to add three or four more shades into the mix but the pattern didn't call for it."

"Maybe someday we can just talk knitting."

"That would be delightful? You could visit me at my estate in Wiltshire —lovely old pile, though a monster to sustain. Now, where exactly in Begüm are we to go?"

The road stretched ahead as a curve of pavement plunging around and among those tufa towers, the landscape bleached an ashy white. Finally we turned onto a paved road clearly frequented by tour busses and jutted upward across the hills. By the time we pulled into the village, it was nearly 2:15.

I had expected to find a gathering of humble houses, but the modern structures rising from either side of the tiny street took me by surprise. Freshly minted three-story homes marched on either side of a little gold-domed mosque along a tidy street featuring a single glass-fronted-carpet-cum-coffee shop that would look at home in downtown Istanbul.

"How very interesting," Rupert mused. "I would hazard a guess that this is indeed the correct village."

"And that the community has been benefiting from some source of income." I hauled the robe over my head and removed the scarf until I had peeled down to my jeans, jacket, and turtleneck.

"Well, well." Foxy tapped his chin and peered out the window. "Touristic efforts appear to be especially lucrative or, no doubt, that is what they wish everyone to believe. Look at the sign in the carpet shop window. It seems the village sits on an underground city to which the community offers limited tours."

"An underground economy."

While Evan remained with the rental, Rupert and I entered the shop, which turned out to be a multipurpose carpet store, tour-booking depot, and coffee shop presided over by a young man busy working an espresso machine and an older one unfurling a brilliant kilim at the feet of a seated couple in an expansive gallery area. The four tables that ran beside the long marble counter were occupied by a mix of people sipping coffee or eating pastries while studying guidebooks and maps. I walked up to the counter and picked up one of the brochures stacked by the cash register.

"Hello. Be right with you," the young man said over his shoulder as he zipped around the counter carrying a tiny cup of coffee to place in front of a lone man scanning his phone. So, good English was spoken here along with German, judging by the guy's passing comment to the two women hikers.

I handed the brochure to Rupert. "This looks fascinating. I'd love to visit an underground city, wouldn't you, uncle?"

Foxy unfolded the glossy pamphlet and beamed down at the photos of tunnels. "Oh, indeed I would. Looks terribly dark and cramped, though."

"Very sorry," the young man said, returning to his post. "One tour only per day. The next one is tomorrow at 10:15 in the morning. Do you want to book?"

"My, yes, dear boy, but we really only have today. We would be willing to pay extra for a private tour. Can that be arranged?"

The young man hesitated, taking in Foxy's expensive attire. "I am not sure that is possible. My sister leads the tours and she is not available."

"Could you ask her for us? We can wait, can't we dear?" Rupert said, turning to me.

"Sure."

"I will try to contact her but no promises. Very busy in cafe right now."

"Take your time, dear boy. Shall we investigate the carpets, Phoebe?" Foxy asked me.

We strolled around the gallery while I pointed out what kilims attracted me most and why. Though none were as old and venerable as my Goddess with Vultures kilim, several bore a modernized motif in rich reds against a cream background. The workmanship was still exquisite with crisp detailing at least 20-40 knots per inch.

"If I hadn't already blown my budget, I'd buy those two," I told him. Still, I was distracted and kept scanning the shop. "Maybe I'll just go across the street to the haman while we wait."

"Splendid," Sir Rupert said as he accompanied me back to the counter. "Dear boy," he hailed the cafe attendant. "I don't suppose you serve proper tea with milk?"

"Yes, see?" The young man pointed to a row of tin teapots beside a jar of mixed bags on the shelf behind him and grinned. "Any kind, even green."

"Green? No, my, that won't do it all. I prefer English breakfast but any tea served in such a manner would be deadly tepid. Tin is not meant to brew anything more notable than canned beans in some dreadful camping scenario. Do you have real china?"

I slipped away, leaving Rupert regaling the poor guy on the specifics of English tea preparation, and stepped into the sunshine. Evan, leaning against the hood of the car reading a paperback, nodded to me as I crossed the street.

The haman I spied midway down bore the same signs of prosperity as the rest of the village, only more noticeable by its size and marble exterior.

Two entrances, one for men, one for women, meant that both genders could enjoy their ablutions any time.

Inside, I paid the attendant the last of my change and descended into the women's side of the bath house. In a modern dressing room, I stripped, determined to banish modesty in the name of research, and entered the women's area with head up and chest out. It took time to adjust to the light in the steamy interior but I soon realized I was not the only Westerner there. Most of the locals shampooing and soaping down took little notice of me. The haman was busy with at least fifteen women in the main steam area alone.

I wasn't certain what I was looking for or even why I'd come, except on some hunch that the Goddess motif must hold power for the women of this community. Where better to feel it than naked?

Some bathers were clearly tourists, especially the young blond having a pedicure in an adjacent room, and no one seemed particularly interested in me, though a couple smiled in welcome.

I circled the round steam room as if looking for an ideal spot to land my naked rump when I noticed one woman staring at my chest. She paused in the midst of towel drying her hair, bent over seized in a state of apparent shock. Somewhere on either side of thirty and probably Turkish with a cloud of thick dark curls, she slowly straightened and waited until I approached. By then I knew my breasts weren't as fascinating as the goddess tattoo rising beneath. Our eyes locked. I strode over to stand directly in front of her.

"Are you a sister of the Goddess?" I don't know where that question came from, but it seemed to suit the gravitas of the moment—one naked woman regarding another in a steamy interior.

Without replying, she gathered her towels and steered me from the steam area into a nearby sauna, empty but for us. She turned on me the moment the door shut behind us. "Who are you and why are you wearing that mark so openly on your chest?"

"I'm Phoebe McCabe and I'm here on the Goddess's business." I actually said that and, more strangely, even meant it. "Who are you?"

"I am Nadira Sonar and you should not be here, a stranger wearing Her mark so openly." Her English was excellent. "What do you think you know?"

"I am here with Eva Yilmaz. Does that tell you anything?"

She lifted her hands and let them drop. "No Yilmaz is welcome here, especially not Eva."

"Why not? If you know the story, you also know Dr. Yilmaz kept his promise to the village."

"He did not." She emphasized "not" with a hammer's force, her lovely face fierce. "He returned many years later trying to locate the shrine, but already our men were suspicious, thanks to Eva Yilmaz. The women of this village had kept this secret for centuries, but as soon as she published that article, it came to light that we were hiding something. Then men watched and pestered their women trying to pry the secret free but no one talked. Then Dr. Yilmaz returned and sought out my mother again, and all our efforts were for nothing."

"Your mother was the mystery woman who first brought him to the shrine?"

"That was a mistake she lived with all her days. Dr. Yilmaz's arrival brought it all to light again. My uncle—her brother—followed her and Dr. Yilmaz to the shrine one night and discovered the truth. He killed them both on the spot."

"Your uncle killed your mother and Borek Yilmaz?"

"Ssh! Keep your voice down. Yes, that is what I'm saying. You understand now the danger?"

"But why, why would he kill his own sister?"

"You don't understand. A woman couldn't just creep away some place at night with a man who was neither her husband nor a family member. My mother was married and yet she was alone with another man."

"She didn't have intercourse with him, did she?"

"Certainly not, but in my uncle's eyes she still dishonored her family. Do you understand now?"

"Oh, God, they were killed together?" I buried my head in my hands. "But how did you find out?"

"I followed my mother that night. I saw it all."

"Oh, Nadira. How awful to carry around that burden. Your heart must be broken."

"Many hearts are broken in this village. Many necks, too. Mine is only one casualty. You must leave. My uncle controls the site now and the village. All of the treasures have long ago seeped into the town and to foreign buyers. He would stop at nothing to keep secret what he has done."

"Are you safe?"

"I am lucky he didn't kill me, too, but my uncle could not bring himself to murder a child. I am his servant now, as we all are. I run his tours to the underground city, my father and brother run the carpet shop across the street. We work, we live, we survive, like the rest of the village."

"But what about your mother?"

"She is lost to me now, and if I dare share what I know to anyone, he will have my father and brother killed. That is what he said and I believe him. Many have already died here. No, I am not safe but I am trying to impress on you that neither are you. Go now and take Eva Yilmaz with you."

"No, please." I grabbed her shoulders. "You can't remain a slave and allow your mother's murderer to get away with this. Maybe she did make a mistake, but does that mean they both should be punished with their lives? That's just barbaric. That's not what the Goddess stands for. You're Her daughter, too, aren't you?"

Nadira pushed me away. "Would you get us all killed?"

"We can end this once and for all. If the treasure's gone, turn the site over to the authorities. Let the Goddess speak. What do you have to lose?"

"My life, my father's, and brother's."

"I have a plan. Help me play it out."

31

Whenen I emerged from the haman an hour later, Evan stood outside the car in conversation with another man with no Rupert in sight. I strode over to them, shielding my eyes against the sun.

Evan smiled as I approached, holding a hand towards the older man, the same one who had been displaying carpets to the young couple earlier. "Ms. McCabe, meet Mr. Sonar. His family runs the carpet shop cafe."

"Hi," I greeted Nadira's father, a short rotund fellow with graying hair wisping around a high forehead. When he smiled, his face crinkled into a thousand lines. "Your uncle has bought many fine things today, many nice carpets."

"Has he?" I looked around. "And just where is Uncle Rupert now, still inside drinking tea?"

"He is with my brother-in-law, Sarp."

"Buying more things," Evan added with a knowing smile. More like a smirk, actually.

"Really? Where?"

"Just up the street. We're to wait until he returns."

"You come inside," Mr. Sonar insisted. "I give you tea or perhaps you prefer coffee?"

"Tea, thanks." I followed him into the shop, almost empty now but for the lone man still reading his phone. How could anybody read a Blackberry screen for so long?

I took a seat a few tables away and waited for my apple tea while keeping one eye on the man. His jacket looked more Sears than Turkish leather, so I pegged him as possibly American or Canadian. After a few moments, he rose and stepped outside to talk into his phone.

I watched him uneasily. Where was Foxy? We had things to do, places to go. At last, in he walked, his face rosy and beaming. "Hello, Phoebe, dear. Did you enjoy the haman? I must say, I had a most excellent afternoon."

"Did you? Are you ready to head back to the hotel?"

"Are we not to take a tour of the underground city?"

I got to my feet. "Not now. Let's go."

We said our goodbyes to the Sonars and climbed into the waiting car, the phone man still talking on the street outside.

"That man is definitely a spy for somebody," I said, the moment the doors closed.

"Indeed he is but, never mind, he is quite toothless by himself," Rupert said, settling down in his seat wearing something like a beatific smile.

"I'm glad you're so relaxed about it because I'm not. He could work for some black market syndicate."

"He's a scout for Maggie's syndicate, as it turns out. She knows we're here but what of it? There's nothing left for her to steal, as you said."

"Maggie has a syndicate?"

"A network of hired guns and contacts sounds quite like a syndicate by my definition. She's been here asking questions but to no avail, as far as I can tell."

I studied him closely. "You've been vulturing, haven't you? You look like what my mother would have called 'the cat who ate the canary'."

"Phoebe, I'm either a vulture or a cat. I can't be both. In any case, I have been actively doing business, yes, and have, in fact, just spent a fascinating hour in the company of one Sarp Onur, the veritable mayor of the village in charge of all things related to the underground city."

"Including keeping the community under his control and acting as the kingpin for black market interests? I know. He murdered both Dr. Borek Yilmaz and Mr. Sonar's wife ten years ago."

"Pardon me?"

"I met Mr. Sonar's daughter in the haman. She told me everything, like how her mother was murdered by her own brother in a kind of disgusting honor killing. He's got a stranglehold on this village and it has to end."

"Oh my."

"I'm coming back here tonight at 10:00 with Eva for a personalized conducted tour."

"Oh, dear. Is that wise, given what you have just disclosed?"

"It's necessary. Eva needs to see the shrine, which she will at last, and I'm bringing in reinforcements to set up a sting or whatever it's called. Evan, as soon as we're on a hill somewhere outside of town, stop please so I can make a call to Interpol."

"Interpol?" Rupert's alarm was almost comical.

"Interpol. Look, if the business you did with Sarp today is the tiniest bit illegal, I don't want to know about it. Don't even try disclosing the details."

"I always operate within the margins of the law, Phoebe."

"Margins being the operative word. Now, would you stop the car so I can make my call?"

Rupert nodded to Evan, who pulled off on a viewing area overlooking a breathtaking valley of caves and conical hills. I scrambled from the car and climbed a rock, trying to fix the strongest signal. It didn't matter who tracked me now. Everyone knew where I was and it suited my plan to have Interpol keep tabs on me. And Maggie, too, for that matter.

Walker answered the call after four rings. He actually sounded awake, if not necessarily pleased. "Phoebe?"

"I'm here outside Begüm. We need to speak in private. Can you meet me somewhere?"

After I'd arranged to meet him at the back of Eva's house within the hour, I took the opportunity to call the gallery, only soon realized it was past closing time. I left a chirpy voice message telling Serena I was in Cappadocia on a hunt for more kilims but should be back in London soon. Duty served, I returned to the car and grinned at Sir Rupert. "Fabulous scenery," I remarked.

"Glorious, indeed. Is all well?"

"So far. Could I ask you for another drive to Begüm tonight?"

"Yes, of course. Consider me at your disposal, but I am most anxious. What you are doing is excessively dangerous."

"I won't be alone, Rupert."

"Yes, I understand that, but what help can I be among murderous cutthroats? We shall bring Evan along, of course, but nevertheless, this is all very risky."

"Evan can't come inside the shrine and neither can you. I'm sorry, Rupert. Nadira believes her Uncle Sarp will agree only to taking Eva and me to the shrine and, even so, we're not sure she can convince him of that."

Rupert slapped a hand over his heart. "Surely you're not proposing to use yourself as bait?"

"If necessary."

"No, Phoebe. I must protest!"

I patted his knee. "I'll be fine, Rupert. Let Interpol handle this. You stay on the sidelines and try to maintain your innocent facade."

No amount of badgering could shake my resolve, and by the time he dropped me off at the bottom of the path leading to Eva's house, he had reluctantly agreed to pick me up at the same spot at 9:30 that evening.

I climbed the stony path in my robe and hijab with my head down. It didn't seem worth walking all the way up to Eva's house when I'd be meeting Walker nearby in a few minutes. Instead, I found a sheltered area under a tree halfway up the path and waited.

Though a few pedestrians passed, nodding as they trudged uphill, mostly the little byway remained empty. It would be supper time soon and people were already home for their evening meal. The scent of grilling meat spiced the air from the nearby houses as the sun poured liquid tangerine over the horizon. Sun juice, I thought idly. Yum.

My mind wandered to food and Noel with equal hunger, my appetite for all things enhanced. I kept picturing one in a glass and the other naked when I noticed a man in a long white robe approaching from the main road below. I recognized the authoritative gait at once.

Stopping only a few inches away, he took in my robe and nodded. "Finally, face to face at last. Make this good, Ms. McCabe." He'd darkened his skin in disguise, but the effect only enhanced his Most Wanted look.

"All right, I'm going to fill you in on everything that happened today, plus everything I now know. Listen carefully." I launched into a rapid description of Begüm's secret, of Sarp Onur's role in the murder of Dr. Yilmaz and Nadira's mother, of the noose that kept the village in a choke-hold of black market dealings.

Describing Foxy's role and how Noel fit in was a bit more challenging, but I could honestly share only what they claimed; one was here as a dealer, the other as Eva's former student and substitute son. By the time I'd finished, I may have only imagined the tinge of reluctant admiration warming Walker's expression. I preferred to believe it real.

"I propose to act as bait at the shrine tonight. I asked Nadira to inform her uncle of how much I know and, of course, he'll want to bump me off like he did her mother and Borek."

"That's madness. You've just turned yourself into an even bigger target."

"If you can think of some other way to entice that man to reveal the secret site he has been plundering for years, bring it on. While you're at it, figure out a way to get him to provide a guided tour for me and the wife of the man he murdered. This is the only way I can take Eva to the site she craves to see so much while preserving what remains of this ancient shrine. Besides, I'm hoping to have the cavalry on my side for once."

He held up a hand. "Are you referring to the army? This is going to be enormously challenging to organize and there's not much time. I'll need to involve the Turkish Antiquities divisions, not to mention my colleagues in Istanbul all, in what, four hours?"

"You'd better get busy."

"You'll be underground, I presume, with people who know every twist and turn in a labyrinth of tunnels. Where exactly do you expect your backup team to hide supposing we can find you in time?"

I hesitated. "Surely you guys can figure that part out?"

"You'll need to be fixed with a wire, presuming I can get the equipment here in time, and possibly we can use a kind of dye. If you sprinkle it along the way, we can then use an ultraviolet light to follow."

"Oh, like a techno Hansel and Gretel. That sounds good." I didn't even try keeping the relief from my voice. "Sir Rupert Fox is picking me up at 9:30 to drive me to back to Begüm. There's a stretch of road between the main highway and the village where we can pull over and wait for you at, let's say, 9:45ish?"

"We'll be there." He turned to leave, then hesitated. "Phoebe, stay vigilant between now and the time we meet. A lot can happen in four hours."

"I know," I said as I turned and marched up the hill.

32

I shrugged out of my borrowed robe and scanned the room. "Eva?"

The duffel bag dumped by the door told me she'd returned, but still no response met my call. Anxiety drove me to take the stairs two at a time up into her bedroom where I found her spread-eagled on the bed as if she'd collapsed.

"Eva?" Perching on the edge of the bed, I shook her gently until her eyes fluttered open.

"Oh, Phoebe, there you are. I was worried to find you gone. Have you seen Noel?"

"Not yet. I'm hoping he's hiding out somewhere safe and will show up soon."

"As do I. If anything should happen to him because of me, I could never forgive myself."

"How are you feeling?"

"Tired, and after all that, I still didn't manage to get a car. Nobody wants to get involved with me, and in truth, I don't blame them. My name is known in these parts but not as I'd hoped."

"Don't worry, I think I have part of the problem solved. I have so much to tell you, but the short story is that I've arranged for us to see the shrine tonight. Before you get too excited, there are lots of strings attached and maybe a couple of nooses."

Eva propped herself on her elbows. "Tell me! How the Goddess smoothes our paths! This is extraordinary news, Phoebe."

"It's also complex, convoluted even, and dangerous. I also discovered something that may cause you pain."

"Pain is a relative matter to me these days. Spare nothing."

"I'll explain as much as I can." And I did, finishing off with: "So you see, this Sarp Onur couldn't let Borek return to Istanbul to reveal the site's location and his black market operation, which is why he killed him. I'm sorry, Eva."

"Borek was murdered," she said, staring up at the ceiling. "I'd always suspected that he'd run into trouble on that last journey. Now I know. And you will bring me face to face with both his killer and the Goddess? I am almost too overwhelmed with gratitude."

"It's going to be a very dangerous trek, Eva, and exhausting. I have no idea how far we'll have to walk or even if Interpol can set up what has to be a complicated sting. The more I think about it, the more convinced I am that the whole thing is crazy."

"Nonsense. I care nothing about the danger and, if you will help, I'll walk as far as it takes. What's crazy about taking risks and forging forward with spirit? Thank you, Phoebe, for doing the Goddess's work so magnificently. No matter what happens tonight, She will ensure that all will turn out as it should. I am happy, will be happier still. That's all I can say. You have brought this to my worthy fruition."

"We haven't arrived yet, so hold the thanks. Get some rest. We still have a few hours before we have to leave." I got to my feet, about to head for the door when she clutched my hand.

"Wait, Phoebe, please. I must tell you something."

"If it's about the kilim, I know."

She gazed up at me in surprise. "You do?"

"I do. Let's not talk about that now. I still have a few things to get ready before we go out tonight. Can I fix you something to eat?"

"No, thank you, but about the kilim—"

"Later. Rest while you can."

"I took it to keep it safe, that's all, but you must take it back when this night is over. She wants you to have it."

"Get some rest."

❧

Upstairs in my bedroom, I perched on the edge of the bed running the details of the plan over in my head. Of course, I wouldn't have the full logistics until I met Walker later, but I knew enough to understand how unprepared we all were. None of us had enough information on the tunnels to make a decent plan. We were delving deep into uncharted territory.

How many things could go wrong? All the bravado I'd mustered leeched away.

Supposing the army refused to play or Sarp Onur didn't trust his niece, or worse still, Nadira didn't trust me and backed out at the last minute? Or maybe she had no intention of helping us from the beginning? Why should she disrupt her life because some stranger with a carpet tattoo implores her to set her people free? Just who did I think I was? After all, the community had prospered by draining antiquities into the black market over the years. Maybe Sarp was their hero. What did I know?

I was so busy biting down on reality pills that I didn't realized that a cool breeze was ruffling my hair. I brushed a tendril from my eyes and paused. Did I leave the trap door open? I must have, since a square of dusk-hued sky marked the ceiling overhead. Well, damn.

Cautiously, I climbed the ladder, reaching the top to poke my head out into the descending night. I had planned only to fasten the trap shut but the sky held me captive. All I could see were stars emerging a billion miles above. Billions and trillions of galaxies and worlds, a cosmos of mystery and possibility, all spinning with an energy so fierce, it pushed through time itself. Maybe energy was time? Stars died, collapsing into dark holes, to be born again in brilliant swirling nebulae light years away. Who could measure such magnificence or relegate it to mere science alone?

"Phoebe?"

I whipped around. "Noel?" He was sitting under what looked to be a mound of carpets, silhouetted against the luminescence like an island in a starry sea. "You're safe."

"I am."

"I was afraid Interpol picked you up and forgot to mention it. How long have you been here?

"Only a few hours. The house was empty when I arrived, and this seemed the perfect place to rest after spending last night dodging the army. I didn't want to risk making myself too comfortable downstairs. This is ideal."

He stood up and stretched. "It's secluded, and once you pull up the ladder like so..." I watched as he crossed the distance between us and offered his hand to help me topside. He kept my fingers laced in his while he hauled up the ladder and closed the trap door single-handedly. "The roof is private both inside and out."

"Privacy which you need right now because?"

He kept holding my hand and I didn't mind at all.

"In case Eva comes up and we lose a chance to talk."

"Eva's downstairs sleeping so deeply, she won't be going anywhere for a few hours. She finally told me the whole story, well, most of it."

He gently pulled me closer, wrapping one arm around my shoulders. I didn't mind that, either. "I've gone along with her obsession for years. She believes, Phoebe. She's convinced that a public and academic endorsement of the Goddess shrine will somehow make the world a better place."

"Do you believe that?"

"It can't make it worse. Everything is twisted out of balance at the moment, and we need a strong dose of the feminine to balance out the forces destroying our planet, destroying our humanity. Yes, I believe it."

I peered up at him, trying to see his face. "You surprise me. I'm taking her to the Goddess shrine tonight."

"How did you manage that?"

"It's a long story."

"We have time."

"Then I'll tell you that Interpol is helping."

"So you're back on friendly terms with the police?"

"More like a truce in the name of the higher good, the higher good being the capture of black market thieves, murderers, and assorted miscreants—including you—while preserving what's left of the Goddess shrine."

I could feel the warmth of his breath on my hair. "I knew I'd be lumped in the miscreant category."

"Actually, you qualify as a black market thief."

"I'm overqualified, then. Have you actually located the site?"

"Yes and no. Tonight at 10:00 I've arranged for a private tour for Eva and me. Sorry, but you're not invited." I couldn't tell him the details in case he tried to prevent us from going. Or followed us and Interpol captured him. "You have to stay away."

"I'll follow you anyway."

"Don't. Look, Noel, I've never hidden the fact that I intend to assist with your capture."

"And yet you're not calling Interpol right now to say where I am."

I shivered despite how close I stood to him. "That wasn't the agreement. Besides, you still haven't told me where to find Toby."

"I'll remedy that right now." He pulled something from his pocket, holding it palm up in his hand. I could just see a little fold of paper glowing ghostly in the starlight. "Take it. It's an address, instructions, really. You'll find specific information on how to find Toby in Istanbul. He wants to explain what happened in person, and it's only fair to you both that he gets that opportunity. Read it, memorize it, then burn it. I promise you, he's waiting."

I took the folded paper and shoved it deep into my jeans pocket. "Thanks."

"And yet you're still not calling Interpol. Does this mean I'm forgiven or that maybe you've come to recognize a few of my redeeming features?"

"I hope you're not referring to the redeeming features I glimpsed in the haman?"

He laughed. "Glad you appreciated something."

"I figure Interpol will capture you soon enough, so why rush the moment?" I gazed up, trying to see his face.

"Let's not rush a thing."

When he brought his lips to mine, I was waiting. His kiss was long and deep, both leisurely and urgent all at once. Fire breeds fire, energy explodes into possibilities. I pulled him tighter.

Soon, we were lying back against the rugs. Did I love him? I didn't know. I only knew I loved everything at that moment—the stars, the sea, the universe, especially the universe and everything within it. I couldn't have felt more alive and he was part of that life force at that moment.

Afterward, he held me tightly against the chill of the evening and we stayed locked together unwilling to break the spell for a long time. Too long, in fact.

"Noel, I have to go," I whispered, disentangling my limbs. "I have to wake up Eva and prepare for tonight. If I don't get to see you again after this, if Interpol brings you in, I promise to visit you wherever they imprison you." I kissed him one last time before climbing to my feet. He never saw my tears though one may have dropped on his chest.

"Phoebe, wait."

"No time left." My voice hitched. "Could you replace the ladder?"

"If you think I'm letting you do this fool thing alone, you don't know me."

I pulled on my clothes while he repositioned the ladder, the air chill against my skin. He was balancing on one leg climbing into his jeans when I lowered myself down the steps.

"Wait, I said I'm coming down with you." He hopped towards the hatch.

"And I said you can't." And I pulled down the trap door and secured the latch.

He pounded on the roof while I tidied up. His muffled shouting reverberated through the wood while I pocketed my phone and stuffed a bottle of water into my jacket pocket for later.

I could hear his anger and frustration as I opened up the little fold of paper with Toby's whereabouts. It was more a string of coordinates than an address, so I committed it to memory and swallowed the paper, forcing the pulpy wad down with a wash of water.

"Phoebe, let me out! What the hell are you doing?"

Minutes later I was down on Eva's level calling out for her to get ready. "Our ride will be here in fifteen minutes," I said, bursting into her room.

The rumpled bed was empty.

"Eva?" She must have gone downstairs to have a bite to eat. I called her name all the way down to the bottom level, stunned to find it dark. I flicked on the lights and scanned the room: chairs knocked over, her duffel where she dropped it, the door wide open. No Eva.

Something moved behind me but I turned too late.

❧ 33 ❧

My captors gagged and blindfolded me before tossing me face-down into what felt like the back of a van. Everything rattled. The gritty mix of gas fumes and dirt hurt my lungs. Panic surged uncontrollably until I reined my emotions into calm.

I struggled onto my back. Better. At least I could breathe. I lay there with all my senses stretching outward. We were traveling over a rough road very fast. Where were they taking me? What would they do once they got there? Why had I locked Noel away? Veering into panic again, I fought back the surging adrenalin, trying to breathe as deeply as possible. Several minutes passed in a jiggling, bumping state of suspended terror as I locked panic down.

Something groaned to my left. I wiggled over inch by inch until I felt warmth against my thigh. Eva! My relief spiked then nosedived when I realized that she'd be bound, too, only how could she endure this brutality? I tried to communicate through the gag, managing a muted hum at best. Eva made no response. I nudged her and she groaned again. I settled for inching as close to her as I could go, hoping she'd sense the warmth of a friend nearby.

We bumped along for at least another hour, the van hitting potholes and rumbling over gravel. Suddenly, it squealed to a halt. Voices speaking

Turkish, two, maybe three men. The doors slid open and someone dragged me out by the feet. Fresh air hit my face as I was slung over a shoulder and bounced along in a loping jog. I went limp. Let them think I was unconscious like Eva. Eva! Surely they'd have the decency to carry her properly?

My carrier slowed his pace. A woman's voice now, sharp and angry. Men arguing back. Yet another voice barking authoritatively, which seemed to prompt my carrier to continue. Steps going down now, many, many steps, my head lolling like a rag doll over this guy's shoulder. I felt sick but I couldn't afford to vomit. I'd suffocate.

Then without warning, I was dropped backwards against a wall. Someone ripped off my blindfold and peeled off the utility tape sealing my mouth. I blinked into an earthen room strung with electric lights. Many people stood around, some in shadows where I couldn't see their faces, but I recognized Nadira crouching, shaking Eva on the ground nearby.

I roused myself. "What are you doing to her?"

Before Nadira could answer, the man hovering over me spewed verbal vitriol launched in Turkish but quickly changed to English. "You think we are stupid?"

I looked up at him, this man in his middle-fifties wearing coveralls and a baseball cap. He held a pistol in one hand. "You think I let you trap me and come here with police? This is my home, my village. This site belongs to us, not government. It is our land. No one steals our secrets! Tonight you die. How we kill them, Nadira?" He stooped long enough to pull the young woman to her feet, holding her by the arm while she tried to shake loose. "You decide. Your mother and her friend were killed by falling, yes?"

"Maybe we should sacrifice them to the Goddess?" Maggie stepped from the shadows. "That would be a good end, don't you think?"

I groaned. "I should have known you'd be involved in this somewhere."

"You should have known lots of things, hon, but you're not real swift. I work with people, like Sarp here, see? You could have bought some useful friends for once." She shrugged, a vision in fashion perfection in total black leather. "Too late now."

"Buying friends is an oxymoron, Mags."

"You're the moron 'cause my way works. Isn't that right, Foxy?"

Rupert emerged from the shadows, his expression apologetic.

Damn. Damn. "Were you working with Maggie all along?"

"No, in fact, we only forged our collaboration this afternoon." He twisted his hands together and actually had the nerve to look guilty. No need. I was the fool here, not him.

I closed my eyes and leaned against the wall. "Please don't hurt Eva."

"As if we can let either of you go," Maggie said. "You two have to disappear—simple. Get that? I told you in Istanbul. You never listen. Besides, Mr. Onur here promised to silence you permanently."

"This must be hurried," Sarp interrupted, shoving Nadira away. "We shoot them now."

"Now, now, Mr. Onur, no need to be hasty." Foxy said, refusing to meet my eyes. "We agreed that all would be handled in a civilized fashion. No rough-housing, no unnecessary haranguing, and that taking the two ladies to the shrine would be a fitting end, dare I say poetic? Shall we proceed there now?"

"How is murder ever civilized, Foxy?" I asked.

"Too much time." Sarp cut the air with his hand. "We kill now."

"No, no," Rupert insisted, waving his hands. "No guns, didn't I say no guns? Yes, I did. This must look like an accident. They are to fall off a cliff, didn't we agree?"

"Great story: two women were strolling the Cappadocian hills at night...'

"Hush, Phoebe. You are not helping," Foxy said sternly.

"I have idea." Sarp beckoned to four men standing against a far wall. I recognized Evan and a man that could have been my pursuer in Istanbul. The others I registered as just men with guns. "No more arguments. Take them to shrine. Nadira leads the way."

One man yanked me to my feet while Evan rushed to scoop a limp Eva into his arms. All formed a single file behind Nadira, with me being pushed along directly behind her, Foxy behind me, followed by Evan with Eva, and the others in a ragged string behind them. Sarp brought up the rear.

"Where are we?" I asked.

"The underground city," Nadira said over her shoulder. "This part once served as the grain storage area. We will pass through a wine cellar next. A city of several hundred people lived here once. At least fifty miles of tunnels have never been explored."

It was a subterranean world of hewn stone with niches and vestibules, low ceilings, and multiple tunnels cutting off in all directions. I imagined hundreds of people living here long ago, forced underground by religious persecution or the expansion plan of warring empires. Now it became the warren of tourists and thieves.

We skirted three large amphorae set into the floor lit above by recess lights. "For olive oil," Nadira, ever the guide, told us. The path dipped steadily downward.

"Watch your step," she cautioned.

How ironic, I thought. We were to tread carefully only so our captors could kill us later. Nadira didn't seem happy. Had she told her uncle my plan or did Foxy? Foxy. I didn't feel betrayed as much as stupid. My character assessment needed serious recalibration.

The tunnels narrowed so low we had to duck in parts, with Evan proceeding sideways with Eva. So far underground and hemmed in by stone, claustrophobia threatened me at every step. I focused on the electric lights illuminating the ceiling, floors, and walls. I kept my eyes fixed on Nadira's slim form ahead. "Where's the air coming from?" I asked, feeling a breeze on my face.

"There are ventilation channels leading to the surface all through the city. Careful." She raised one hand. "The first door lies ahead."

"Door?"

"The inhabitants used boulders to block various sections against their enemies. They are designed to be secured from the inside only. They are impossible to dislodge from the other direction."

"How ingenious," I heard Foxy say.

We squatted through a portal past a gigantic round stone that must have taken many hands to roll into place. Foxy poked me in the back as I scrambled through. I turned and caught him winking at me in the half-light. What?

Soon everybody pressed in after us. We crammed into a kind of hewn vestibule. That gave me an opportunity to check on Eva. She had flung an arm over Evan's neck by now and sat half-raised looking alert. Evan must have offered her water, since she held a bottle in one hand. I touched her arm and she mouthed something at me, nodding to Evan. I didn't get it. A quick glance up at him unsettled me further when Evan shot me a friendly smile.

"Can you imagine living down here?" Maggie asked no one in particular. I fought back a smart-assed reply.

"From here, the people moved off in many directions to their homes. Many families lived in each cave carved in these walls."

"Nadira," Uncle Sarp snapped. "No guiding! We are not tourists. Go."

We re-formed our line and continued deeper and deeper into the earth. Nadira had stopped the commentary except for pausing long enough to point out a Plexiglas-sealed hole in the floor. "If enemies reach this far, hot oil would be poured on their heads."

"An old and time-honored strategy," said Eva, rousing. By now, I figured she must have assessed the situation.

Many twists and turns on uneven ground followed until the ceiling lights ended and Nadira flicked on a flashlight, as did Foxy and three others behind us. "The rest is not open to the public. Very dangerous."

Without the lights, I could barely stay upright and twice tumbled into Nadira. "Is this leading to the Goddess shrine?"

"Yes," she said. "The two sites are separated by walls of stone. An earthquake uncovered it decades ago and we discovered it by accident."

"Keep moving!" Sarp shouted.

We wove over loose rubble, some of which had been cleared into an uneven path I imagined trod by the feet of many local thieves. Sarp considered the site his because the village lay near it. Did proximity equal ownership? Not by any law I knew.

Earthquake damage stood out in fallen walls, mounds of earth.

"Why is there damage here but not back where we've come?"

"The tufa is more porous," Nadira said, "and many caves exist close together with little support between. The earth shakes, it crumbles."

Many dark and twisty paths followed; many slip-slides down scrabbled hills into narrow valleys followed that. It was dark, the air constricted around us. I began to heave oxygen into my lungs. At last Sarp yelled, "Halt".

Nadira turned around to wait. "I did not want this," she whispered in my ear.

"Then why?" I asked.

Sarp pushed his way through. "You and you stay here and watch," he said, indicating two of his minions. "You, too," he said to Maggie. "Sir Rupert, his man, and the two women only go to shrine."

"I'm going," Maggie said.

He pointed his gun at her. "You wait here, I said."

"Don't tell me what to do. I came a long way to see this place so I'm going, too."

"I said no."

"Play your macho bullshit somewhere else, buddy. I'm coming." Maggie never did temper tone to circumstance. "I've got a gun I can wag, too."

Sarp nodded to one of his dudes to restrain Maggie, which prompted her man to intervene. A brief scuffle erupted.

"Stop!" Foxy cried. "This is folly! Mr. Onur, permit her to come. What is the harm?"

Sarp muttered away in Turkish before jerking his head towards a ragged opening in the wall ahead. "Go." Maggie won again.

Nadira picked her way through, beckoning us to follow. We were inside another dark tunnel, wider than the others, which at first seemed to be more of the same, only soon even I could tell that the walls were hewn differently.

The blocks were more squarely cut, with few round pieces. The mark of another, far older civilization rose around us. Occasionally, the flashlight beams licked across bands of relief so startling they seemed to leap out from the wall—a procession of bulls, a bird. I heard Eva gasp, but we were shoved along relentlessly.

Finally, Nadira came to a halt. "We enter the Goddess shrine now. Do not touch anything."

Sarp squeezed his way to the front. "No matter if they touch. All gold is gone. Move."

We stepped inside a large square stone room decorated by relief chiseled deep into the rock. Multiple flashlights flicked over a carved life-sized goddess featuring pronounced breasts and enthroned with leopards. Her outstretched arms held carrion birds in each hand. Though chiseled bull heads also decorated the shrine, the Goddess reigned supreme, like birth triumphing over death, the bearer of life signaling hope in the internal cycle.

The earth trembled beneath your feat and was still.

"Phoebe, look!" Eva whispered. "Evan, set me down at once." He lowered her gently to her feet. "Phoebe, quickly! Take pictures."

My gaze flew to the wall opposite, where brilliant color danced in Nadira's light, a wall of Goddess with Vultures motifs similar to my kilim only larger, more detailed, and almost as electric with energy. I pulled out my phone, hit the camera icon, and began filming. Here the Goddess manifested symbolically in still-vibrant pigments—blue, red, white, ocher—dancing across time itself.

"Do not touch," Nadira warned, her voice choking emotion. "Already the colors fade. All our lamps and the fires they've burned here are destroying the paintings. She will disappear soon."

The closer I came, the more I focused on where flakes of color had slipped to the floor.

"My maternal ancestors guarded Her for years. We kept her secret safe. Now look."

"She was this Neolithic civilization's idea of universal deity, balanced with the male, a spirit merged in the great giver of life," Eva marveled.

"Ancient beyond ancient, older than even the Egyptians," I whispered.

"Far, far older. We worship Her still in the Virgin Mary but she is... God's compassionate side, the Divine Feminine in partnership with the male and, as God, She has many faces, of both genders."

"Oh, my, how remarkable," Foxy effused. "What an honor to be here."

"Blasphemy!" Sarp interrupted. "Nadira, all of you. Move away. This place is an abomination to Mohammed. No woman is to be above man. It is written in the Koran and your Bible."

"Both are freely interpreted by man and steeped in the cultural and social morass of the ages," Eva pointed out. "This is how it began, how it is supposed to be."

"Silence! I will not hear such blasphemy! This place is an affront to Allah and must be destroyed."

"Uncle, no!"

"This shrine is to Allah, only by another name," said Eva.

"Wait, wait," Maggie stepped forward, running her own light around the shrine's parameter. "These paintings are all very nice but where did you find the gold? I mean, let's get practical here."

Sarp jerked his head towards the empty niches centered above each bull's head. "All around this room, gold vessels and other things, all gone now."

"There were ritual daggers embedded in cabochons, necklaces and bracelets on the Goddess's arms and feet, a magnificent headdress fashioned with tiny gold leaves," Nadira explained.

"There was a friggin' headdress? Sarp, you didn't say anything about a headdress. Did you hear that, Foxy?"

Rupert, standing beside me, seemed distracted. He kept nudging me in the arm. "Pardon me?" he asked while I pocketed the phone.

"Sold long ago," Sarp said before he could answer. "The first piece sold gave us the haman."

"Well, damn. I mean the bracelets and dagger I bought are real stunners and all, but a headdress, wow. I would love to be photographed wearing that. I'll have to settle for a phone selfie. Foxy, will you take my picture sitting on the throne?"

And then another tremor shook the earth., "Earthquake," I called.

Before he could respond, one of the minions left behind leaped over the threshold, shouting Turkish to Sarp.

"What's happening?" Maggie asked, swinging around with her phone in one hand, flashlight in the other.

"Interpol," Eva lowered herself down to sitting. "He says there are men coming through the underground city, our rescuers, presumably. Sarp wants to proceed to the next plan."

"Evan!" Foxy called to his man while turning to me. "I was afraid they'd never get here," he whispered, shoving something into my hands. "Flashlight and map. There's another exit through the tunnels leading to the other side of the village. Nadira highlighted the route. Use it to find your way out should we get separated. Matters are about to get messy."

Maggie swung towards him. "What? You chubby little bastard! You're double-crossing me?"

But Sarp was shouting, Nadira screaming, Evan wrestling one of the minions. Flashlights fell, rolling to the ground. A gun went off, then another, bullets ricocheting off the ancient bull's heads, lodging into the walls. And another damn tremor! I grabbed Eva and pulled her into a far corner, whispering "We have to get out of here! Rupert, where are you?" I called.

"I must stay." Eva told me.

"Here, Phoebe! Run!" Foxy's voice.

The shrine plunged into darkness, but for one fallen flashlight beaming light against the far wall. More shouting, with Sarp's voice rising above the rest.

"Go!" Eva pushed my arm.

I fumbled with the flashlight Foxy gave me. "I'm not leaving you."

But the Goddess had had enough. First came an earth-ripping shudder and then the ceiling began to fall.

❧ 34 ❧

I shielded Eva with my body as the mountain tumbled around us. Shrapnel plummeted my back. Chunks of stone flew from the walls amid a horrendous rumbling that sounded like the earth being ripped apart. Something huge crashed nearby. I huddled, waiting for the final blow, fully expecting to die.

Then the earth stopped shaking. I risked lifting my head, finding the air thick with dust and blacker than black.

Eva shifted beneath me. "Phoebe, my leg," she gasped.

I pushed to my knees, coughing in the saturated air. My hands found the pillar that had landed on her calves crosswise and hefted it to one side.

"Can you stand?"

"No. My left leg is broken...I believe."

"Hello. Is anybody there?" My muffled call barely projected so I tried again. Nobody answered. I felt around nearby searching for the flashlight Foxy had offered but my fingers dug into nothing but rocks and dirt. "We have to get out of here," I told Eva, fumbling for her hand. "Here, lean on me."

"You go. I will only slow you down."

"Stop saying that. Get up. Here, hang on."

She grunted. Struggling to stand, she slung her arm over my shoulder. "Do you have the pictures?" she asked.

"Yes, and videos, too, but let's worry about that later."

"They...are more important than ever."

"Of course."

I stumbled, banging against what felt like walls of dirt, while Eva hobbled, gasping at my side. Totally disoriented, probably stunned, I had no idea which way to turn. Mounds of rock blocked every direction.

"There." Eva nudged me to look down to where a bleary glow penetrated the settling dust.

A flashlight. I dug the thing out and shook it off. Now, the full destruction of the ancient site jumped into view as the light revealed mounds of stone and tumbled walls.

I moaned at the severed head of the fallen goddess staring stone eyes up to a ceiling that no longer existed. Eva began to cry but I was too fixed on escape to mourn.

A gaping space overhead swallowed the beam I shone upward, hinting that one, maybe two, tunnel levels had collapsed during the quake. Where I thought may have been the direction of the entrance was now chocked with rubble. The light flashed on a ragged opening that had appeared in the far wall.

Clutching Eva's waist, I helped her over the mounds towards the opening. The light caught the edge of a hand so dusty I thought it was carved stone. Brushing away the dirt revealed a wrist below a frayed sleeve. Not Foxy, not Evan, but probably one of Sarp's men. I felt for a pulse. "Dead," I pronounced. "Rupert! Nadira!" I called out.

"They are gone, Phoebe. Sarp planned to blow the shrine. I heard them talking...while we traveled through the underground but the quake... helped. Fools didn't comprehend how...I know Turkish." She fought to catch her breath. Recovering, she continued. "He wanted to shoot us but your friend, Rupert Fox—I knew him in London—said no. Some agreement...previously struck."

"Sir Foxy was playing a double game. He's a player and he played them for our side. Are you in pain? Why am I asking? Of course you are. Come on. We have to get you to a hospital. Interpol is coming to our rescue. All we have to do is get to them." I pulled her with me towards the opening.

"Phoebe, Sarp set explosives...intending to bury us...while he escaped through an alternate route. We must assume the route we came is...destroyed...and possibly our rescuers with it."

"No! We can't assume anything. Sam Walker would have alerted the army. There are lots of people coming to rescue us. Why are you hesitating? We have to get out of here. Nothing is stable." The earth rumbled as we stood.

"All the more reason..." she began coughing, "for you to go without me. I will only slow you down. I will stay here with the Goddess. You must go and tell the world what you've seen. Publish the pictures. Tell my story."

"I said stop saying that!" I pulled her by the arm towards the opening, flashing the light into the dark beyond. At first, I couldn't grasp was I was seeing. The relief-walled corridor leading up to the shrine had collapsed, not into mounds of rubble like inside the shrine but simply gone, fallen away into the abyss.

I held the light out over the edge waiting for the beam to brush against something—a floor, a wall, anything, but it didn't. All light was swallowed by the subterranean maw.

Eva, standing behind me, touched my shoulder. "Phoebe, the floor is gone. Probably...many levels, many centuries of underground networks...fallen."

A cold fear trickled down my spine. I swept the beam closer to the opening, illuminating a sliding mountain of rock to the left and the abyss bordered by a narrow ledge no more than six inches wide disappearing into the darkness to the right. Maybe I could cling to that lip of stone and shuffle along to whatever lay beyond, but not Eva.

Leaning out, she saw it, too. "Go, Phoebe. Leave me, please. Let me die... where and how I want. Thanks to you...I have found the Goddess and she will hold me safe...for my next journey. In all the ways that matter...nothing will destroy Her or me."

I pulled back. "I'm not leaving you. We came to Anatolia together, linked in our fates, like you've been saying all along. If we're meant to die here together, then that's the way it has to be. We'll just wait until we're rescued."

"Phoebe, listen. Focus on my words...these tunnels were carved thousands of years...ago. Think, thousands of years. Their tenuous relationship with the earth has been... shattered. Publish the pictures. Tell the Goddess story. Go now, please. I am happy...and filled with joy. I cannot explain it. Just trust what I say."

"No." I fumbled in my pocket. "I brought water. You take a deep drink and you'll feel better. They know where we are. They'll find us soon. We'll just wait. Everything will be fine. I have pain killers, too, in my pocket." I pulled out the water bottle and a fold of paper fluttered to the ground. I picked it up. "Oh, the map Foxy gave us."

Eva eased herself down to perch on the edge of broken wall, her back to the bottomless darkness. Taking the map and flashlight from my hands, she tipped light down over the diagram.

"That way," she pointed over her shoulder towards the ledge, "is a tunnel leading to the surface. Original entrance to Her shrine, probably a...processional avenue. This is Sarp's... escape route and...yours." She passed the map back. I stuffed the page into my pocket and handed her the bottle, which she didn't take.

"Give me back the flashlight and take the water. Drink, Eva."

"Phoebe, you have so much to live for. Your brother...Noel told me...and Noel himself is such a good man. I know you two danced on the roof like Borek and I once did... before I left him. I have lived my life. It has been full and...though not perfect, the most wondrous weave. I am so very grateful and...I see you as a daughter-friend, a gift...and I thank you and Her for sending you to me. But I am tired and in pain...you must go now and let me fly."

She dropped the flashlight to the floor and while I bent down to pick it up, she pushed herself over the edge, and flew away into the darkness.

✺ 35 ✺

She made no sound. I never heard her body hit the bottom, wherever the bottom was but, I swear, gazing down into the blackness at that moment, I saw a light. Maybe I only imagined it, or maybe the glow was within me but it burned brightly nonetheless. Somehow in some way, the glow became a warmth wrapped in her voice pleading to me to let her fly and to keep on going all at the same time.

I thought my heart would crack in two and crumble like the earth around me, but I paused midway to despair and turned my heart towards the stars. I might not be able to see their shine but I knew they existed.

I took a swig of water and pocketed the bottle. Mustering every scrap of resolve, I turned off the flashlight and shoved it into my other pocket. Darkness pushed in around me like congealing nightmares. Then I swung my legs over the broken wall and stepped out onto the ledge.

Utterly blind, I needed both hands to feel for handholds while shuffling sideways along the narrow lip. I balanced on the balls of my feet, focused on nothing but remaining upright above the void. Closing my eyes or leaving them open made no difference. Either way, this was the darkest night. I needed every bright thing in my life to lead me forward.

I fixed on the unseen starlight, on beloved faces living and dead, thinking love survives everything. Love is metaphysical, the strongest energy of all. Should I die that night, the energy of everyone I loved and who loved me would keep swirling across the universe carrying me along.

But I wasn't ready to die. Eva wanted me to live, so I had to for her.

Nose to the rock, I scuttled two inches to the left.

Love was forever, maybe the only forever there is. It takes courage to love, more courage to lose the ones you love, but why else are we here? I couldn't think of a single thing more worth living for.

My feet moved three inches further. Once I coughed hard enough to almost lose my footing, forcing me to cling to the wall, drenched in sweat. Everything ached with strain but I recovered to continue, inch by inch.

Who said that every great effort must be done step by step? I shrunk everything down by inches and centimeters and fixed on that truth.

Finally, my foot slid across a smooth flat surface. Shifting my weight to standing, I beamed the light up a broad corridor where relief-carved walls marched a procession of bulls and goddesses. I scrambled beside the ancient supplicants until I detected a glow mingling with angry voices ahead. A bolt of caution shot my delirious relief to a standstill. I switched off my light and tiptoed towards a waft of fresh cool air.

The corridor rose at a sixty-degree angle before leveling off and plunging sharply downward. Just before the decline, the tunnel narrowed up to an opening where a huge boulder was wedged partway across.

I crouched, shielded by the rock, gazing down on dust-smeared figures huddled around an electric lamp in a small cave-like space. At least two men lay on the floor face down as if they'd been struck from behind or shot—Evan, maybe, and a minion? I couldn't tell—while two others sat backs to the wall, Foxy on one side, eyes closed, Nadira on the other, eyes glittering in the lamplight.

The two arguers were Maggie and Sarp, who stood over the others, jerking their guns at one another. Behind them, I could just make out a sliver of night sky.

One of the men on the ground slowly turned his head towards Maggie. His hair was shaggy and dark, his limbs long and lean. I recognized the boots. I slapped my hand over my mouth to keep from crying out.

"I said I'm not going to wait in this frigging hell-hole for the next twenty-four hours. Finish them off and let's ditch this place before the sun rises." Maggie punctuated her sentences by poking the air with her sleek little pistol.

"No, you listen. Police out there. If they find us, no good," and then he broke into furious Turkish.

"He says Interpol knows about the underground city," Nadira said in a weary tone, translating from her position next to the outer opening. "The army will be all over the area. They don't know this entrance, but we still have to wait until they leave or you'll all be captured, he says."

"That's nutzoid! There's a friggin' army after us! They're not going to just leave because the underground city is blocked. They'll bring in mining dudes and maybe all kinds of heavy equipment types. This place will be crawling with journalists and cops. We have to leave now, while we have the chance. We're wasting time. I have people waiting for us back on the main road. All we have to do is get there."

While Nadira translated, I scuttled far back into the tunnel to pull out my phone. Though probably impossible to fix a signal deep underground, I'd left it alive just in case. Maybe I could hit the sweet spot now but the glowing screen registered no bars. And then I had an idea, a crazy idea. It meant risking the photos I'd just taken but I couldn't afford to let that hold me back.

I turned the phone back on, and brought up the selfie recording me strolling around the gallery that first day. Before I hit PLAY, I called into the air: "Interpol? Phoebe McCabe here. I'm in trouble! Yeah, we're at the other entrance. Fix my coordinates!" Then, I turned the volume up, hit Play, placed the phone on the floor, and scrambled back to press my back against the boulder door.

Footsteps pounded up the incline. Sarp squeezed into the tunnel first followed by Maggie, both leading with their guns. Bracing myself against the rock, I pushed hard into Maggie's back, sending the gun flying and her into Sarp, jettisoning both into a headlong tumble downward. A gun fired. I could hear Maggie cursing as I squeezed through the opening.

Noel pulled me through by the arm, tugging me aside before he and Nadira applied their shoulders to the boulder door. There was room for only two at the narrow portal.

"Do it this way!" Nadira called, showing him the ideal positioning. Noel bent his shoulder to the stone with his eyes fixed on me. "I so damn happy to see you, Phoebe McCabe!"

I watched, stunned, as the boulder rocked but remained in place. "I'm glad to see you, too," I said, shocked by the impact of the understatement.

Evan heaved himself off the floor and lunged half-dazed towards the rock, blood dribbling from his forehead. "Let me help."

Nadira stepped back. Foxy arrived at my shoulder to touch my arm. "Phoebe, you are alive! I cannot fully express my deep-felt relief! Evan, do be careful. You received quite a blow to the head."

A gun fired through the opening, the bullet pinging against the far wall. I shoved Foxy and Nadira out of range. The men continued grunting against the rock. Blood stained the tunic under Noel's jacket.

"Is he hurt?" I asked.

"Maggie shot at him but I believe he feigned the extent of his wounds. Just a graze. He managed to wrest Maggie's bloke to submission before she fired," Foxy told me.

"Look, it's moving! Push more to the middle and it will pivot shut!" Nadira's jubilance was cut short when Maggie wedged her arm through the crack and waved the gun around, firing blindly shot after shot.

"I'll kill you, you bastard!" she shouted, "You and that useless girlfriend of yours!"

Noel knocked the pistol from her hand and kicked her arm until she pulled it back.

I sprang after the fallen gun, picking it up, and sticking the muzzle through the crack.

"Phoebe, don't!" Noel said.

"Why not?" And I pulled the trigger. Only the gun was empty. Just when I needed a stupid gun, it was useless! I threw it down in disgust. Foxy pulled me back as the boulder door finally grated closed.

We stood in silence for a few seconds listening to Maggie wail and curse behind the stone.

"We made it!" Nadira cried joyously. "We made it, we made it!"

Noel turned and gathered me into his arms. I buried myself in his chest and started to cry. "Eva's gone," I told him. "She jumped, Noel. She just jumped so I could carry on."

He stroked my dust-caked hair. "Consider that her gift."

I gazed up at his lovely, bearded, dust-streaked face. "How did you get here?"

"You mean after you locked me on the roof? Rupert came to my rescue." He grinned down at me.

"Yes, I did, Phoebe," Foxy said. "Sorry to see your faith in me waver even for so brief a time, but after you insisted I couldn't accompany you, I returned to the village where Sarp was already plotting your demise. I hastened to insist I could aid him to silence you forever."

"I didn't betray you, either," Nadira added. "Mr. Fox only pretended to and I joined the game."

"And most admirably, too, my dear. Oh, my, how your uncle knuckled on to the plan. Why wouldn't he trust me after I had just purchased so many of his lovely artifacts? I do so love being the double agent. Maggie was already with him, you know. She would insist upon fouling up the best-laid plans."

"It was her idea to kidnap you, Phoebe. After Mr. Fox left, she convinced Uncle that you would contact Interpol. He arranged to have you kidnapped, all very quickly," Nadira said.

"And I arrived at Eva's house intent on sharing the details of what I believed to be the plan when I found you gone and Noel pounding on the roof."

Noel hugged me closer. "I thought I'd lost you," he murmured into my hair.

"Me, too," I told him hugging him back.

"Well, of course, I alerted Interpol immediately," Rupert continued. "Thus I became the plant—is that the term? Very James Bond like, I must say. Noel insisted on joining in, of course, but we couldn't let Interpol know of his presence."

"He was to wait at this entrance," Nadira explained. "Uncle said he planned to bring you here and throw you off a cliff but he lied. He must have planned to blow up the shrine all along but wouldn't tell me." She choked back a sob, staring wide-eyed as if only just realizing what had just happened. "He is a murderous man."

Foxy patted her shoulder. "Yes, yes, such a nasty person, your uncle. Never mind, dear. There's a black sheep in every family. Mine is my cousin, Reginald. Quite the blackguard, I must say. Now," he turned to where Noel and I stood locked together as if we'd never let each other go. "As much as I hate to tear asunder this romantic reunion, Interpol will no doubt arrive shortly. I signaled them as instructed. They know where we are. You must leave, Noel, before you are apprehended."

"Do you want me to go or stay?" he asked me. "If I'm arrested, I might get parole for good behavior in four years. On the other hand, if I go we could connect in more interesting locales than a prison facility on visiting days."

"Are you asking me to carry on an illicit relationship with a known criminal?"

He grinned. "Definitely, with an emphasis on the illicit part."

"Noel, dear chap, I hear a truck below. You really must leave."

I pulled away. "You'd better go."

"I'll be in touch. You'll know the message is from me when you see it."

"Go."

He kissed me one last time, released me, and scrambled into the rocks.

❦ 36 ❦

gent Walker's tone was surprisingly gentle. "Assure me that you are leaving Istanbul as planned."

I stared down at the deep Prussian blue of the Bosporus with my Foxy phone pressed against my ear. "Of course I'm assuring you. Why would I want to stick around here any longer than necessary? Sir Rupert and I are booked on British Airways tomorrow at 11:00 a.m. Besides, Max will be released from detox soon and my assistant is going nuts with the hired help. I have to get back home."

"Good," he said.

"What about you?"

"I have a few matters to attend to regarding returning the remaining artifacts to the Turkish Antiquities division and will also assist with the preparing of the report before I can return."

"Busy man."

"Very, but when I return to London in a few weeks, you will still have a lot to answer for, Phoebe McCabe. Don't think you're off the hook."

"Really? You have Maggie in custody plus the local black market connection tied up plus you couldn't have broken this ring without Sir Rupert and me. Surely I'm no longer on your Person of Interest list?"

"We still haven't apprehended Noel Halloren or your brother, remember."

"I can't do everything for you."

He actually laughed. "My point is, we're not planning to take our eyes off you just yet, so expect a visit when I return."

"Just remember to bring my iPhone with you; that is, if Maggie didn't destroy it."

"It's safe and I replayed the recording of her admission of guilt, though I'm not sure how much weight it will hold in court."

"Glad I could be of assistance. Now, if you'll excuse me, I'm going to finish my shopping."

I clicked END and turned to Foxy, who stood beside his black rental car while Evan, sporting a rakish bandage over his left temple, leaned against the hood. Both appeared to be enjoying the view.

"Noel managed to escape Interpol," I said.

Rupert brushed the sleeve of his new leather coat. "Of course he did. All is as it should be, don't you agree? What is even more extraordinary is that you and I are heroes of sorts."

"I wouldn't take it that far."

"I would. In fact, I rather like that version. There is a certain panache to being an antiques dealer who is also known for being at the crux of a covert operation recovering priceless artifacts at an ancient site. Very Indiana Jones meets James Bond, don't you think?"

"Considering that even the shrine has been destroyed, we didn't exactly recover anything."

Foxy smiled. "Maybe not officially, but I assure you I will not be returning to London empty-handed."

"Foxy, surely you're not implying that you plan to smuggle artifacts out of Turkey? They'll throw you in jail for half-past forever."

"Calm down, Phoebe, and I do prefer Rupert to Foxy, as I have said before. I assure you, the pieces are on their way to London as we speak and no one will ever be the wiser. There are ways and means, my dear."

I made a show of covering my ears. "I know nothing and I'd rather keep it that way."

He rubbed his hands together. "Of course you do. I shall never sully your ears with the details, and let me assure you that Onur had plenty of amazing pieces left in his safe. What Interpol recovered from Maggie alone will grace some museum admirably. Even Noel should be satisfied with this outcome."

"All those artifacts should remain in Turkey for the same reason I donated the Goddess kilim to Tayla today. It hurt to let it go, it really did, but she's going to request that it enter the Islamic Museum of Art with Eva's name as the donor. She's the real hero, Rupert." Thoughts of Eva twisted a double-edged knife of both joy and sorrow. "I definitely have a story to tell but the best part will always be hers."

"The story is of utmost importance. I am rather surprised that you parted with the kilim, however. It would have fetched a smashing price with this story surrounding it. Nevertheless, I have sent your gallery all those carpets you pointed out to me in Bergun—my thanks to you for taking me on this most excellent adventure."

"I didn't take you, you followed me, but I can't accept your gift either way."

"Of course you can. Consider them a finder's fee. Besides, as soon as I return, I shall contact all my decorating friends and implore them to purchase their antique carpets from you alone. I shall quite turn your business around, Phoebe, dear, now that we are friends."

As tempting as it was to argue the whole friendship concept, this wasn't the time. "We'll carry this conversation along some other time. Right now, I'm on to unfinished business."

"Your elusive brother, of course."

"I could turn these coordinates over to the police and apprehend Toby in minutes."

"But you won't any more than you aided in Noel's capture. He knew you wouldn't."

"Maybe I'll surprise them both yet."

"Nonsense, Phoebe. You'll make the right choice once again." He stepped closer to me and peered over my shoulder at the phone screen. "Where is he?"

"When I key the coordinates, the pin drops directly into the Bosporus somewhere over there." I pointed across the congested strait just as a ferry coasted past.

"He is on the Asia Minor side?" Foxy marveled.

"I think so."

"We must proceed there directly."

"We? Rupert this is something I have to do alone."

He studied me from under his caterpillar brows. "Very well, but permit us to drive you to the other side, at least."

Moments later, we were back in the limo cruising over the bridge spanning the two continents, my fingers twisting the handles of my carpet bag.

We were following the car's GPS this time rather than my phone version, Evan taking every turn the automated voice demanded. Soon the car was sliding downhill towards the water, pulling to a halt beside a large marina of floating berths crisscrossed through a quivering forest of masts and radar antennae.

My heart was racing. "He's on a boat."

"So it seems."

We got out of the car and stared across at the watery parking lot. Similar marinas to this could be found in any port city around the world, only the craft here ranged from humble fisher craft to every imaginable form of sailboat and pleasure yacht.

I keyed the coordinates into my phone again, watching as the dropping pin formed a circle somewhere dead ahead. "Thanks for the drive, Rupert. I'll take it from here."

"Phoebe, let me stay with you just in case."

"No, but thanks. I'll see you tomorrow."

I strode through the chain link gates, nodding at two men who were lugging equipment to some waiting boat. The smell of brine mixed with motor oil pinged my memory receptors, taking me home in a bittersweet instant. Once I reached the steps leading down to the berths, I paused.

Toby loved boats better than any other vessel. He'd bought a sailboat with his first big software check and often spoke of buying another, bigger version, but somehow I couldn't picture my brother living on the run with a sailboat. The fact that he was on the run and would stay that way until the day of his capture, struck me hard.

The steps clattered under my heels as I descended. I had no choice but to stroll the walkways between every berth, hoping that a name might jump out at me or even Toby himself would flag me down.

As the gulls wheeled overhead, I walked the boards, recalling the games we'd play as kids, me the spunky little tomboy shadowing my bigger brother's heels. How I adored him. We'd dive together, gunkholing around our bay's tiny islands, swimming the beaches near our cottage, the two of us inseparable until time and tide peeled us away.

On the day of our father's eighty-third birthday party when Dad's biggest surprise didn't show up as planned, my life plunged into a spinning vortex, leaving a hole I still struggled to mend. Grief, loss, and betrayal warps the weave but, as Eva claimed, nothing is irreparable.

All the boats looked the same at first glance, just a fuse of white streaked with color. My tears blurred the specifics. I was so sick of hunting, worn to the bone with waiting, that these last few steps had become unbearable.

And then I realized someone stood at the end of one of the floating walkways. He looked familiar yet I didn't recognize him at first—short hair, close-trimmed beard, sunglasses. With a start, I realized I'd seen him in London multiple times in different guises. He stepped forward.

"Phoebe?"

"Yes."

"My name's Kevin. I work for Toby. Follow me, please. He's over this way."

"You were tailing me in London."

"Yes, sorry. I was one of your bodyguards of sorts." He turned and shook my hand. "Hope I didn't frighten you."

"Not really. You had too much competition in that department."

I said nothing more as I trailed behind him two berths over. At the end of the berth, a magnificent yacht bobbed in its mooring, one of those sleek millionaire-types the wealthy sometimes moor in Halifax during the summer, all luxury and seclusion.

I seized to a standstill, staring at the glorious painted bow. A mermaid curled her tail along the white sides in a kaleidoscope of rich turquoise and trailing seaweed greens, long tendrils of red hair tangling in the gilded currents. I gasped.

"Stunning, right? The male version is on the opposite side. Are you ready? He's waiting."

I ran up the gangplank, across the wooden deck, and through a door that whispered open automatically. He was just inside an expansive cabin, sitting in a pilot chair of some kind. I hardly noticed as I dove into his arms, remaining bent over since he hadn't time to get to his feet.

"You bastard!" I mumbled into his shoulder, feeling his big arms squeezing me tight. My brother. Finally. "Why did you do this to us?"

"Phoebe." He was sobbing, "I'm sorry beyond words."

I pulled back, wiping my eyes on my sleeve. "Sorry doesn't cut it. You'd better do better and fast."

He had grown stockier from when I'd seen him last and now sported a full auburn beard like some Viking prince in a green hoodie. Only my brother had tears in his eyes, too, and my prince seemed different in so many ways. Older. Sadder. Reduced. "Why aren't you standing? Stand up."

"I can't."

Then I realized the pilot seat was a kind of souped-up wheelchair. "What happened?"

"Maggie. She shot me in a pique when Noel and I ditched her in France —long story—but it's not your sympathy I'm after."

"Good, because you're not getting it."

"Noel told me you helped put Maggie away. Thanks for that."

"Don't bother thanking me since you might be next. Why, Toby?" I lowered myself onto a stool across from him, never taking my eyes from his face. "Why did you betray Adrian, desert Dad and me, become a criminal, why?"

"I didn't plan it that way. It all happened so quickly but, first, Adrian is not the noble victim he's played himself to be. I thought I loved him at first until I discovered he was using me for a bait-and-switch scheme. He asked me to have the forgeries made to keep as mementos, claimed he would donate the real treasures to the respective museums—all very up-front and legitimate. Only that wasn't his plan at all. He intended to sell the forgeries to private buyers as genuine artifacts, make a few million dollars on the side, while keeping the real treasure all along. He was using me. I was totally hoodwinked by a consummate actor."

"So, you decided to retaliate?"

"Not exactly. Noel and I devised a scheme to expose Wyndridge, but it ran aground when Maggie found out and threatened to tell Adrian and Max. Max was a wild card. We couldn't trust him not to mess up, so we hatched a plan to escape with the treasure and offer it to Interpol as a sign of our good intentions."

"But it wasn't that easy."

"No, it wasn't. Because I had a complete set of forgeries made, I looked as guilty as sin. It was my word against Adrian's, the famous author/historian and Bermuda's shining glory. And then there was Maggie ready to play witness to my supposed duplicity. It all went to hell really quickly. We escaped with our lives that night. There was a point when we realized the world was crashing down around our heads and we had to make a decision to jump or be beaten to a pulp by the law. We jumped and here we are."

"International criminals on the run."

Toby spread his hands. "More like on the roll, in my case." Then his green eyes held mine. "Forgive me, Phoebe. I made a hell of a mistake, messed up my life and Noel's, plus yours and Max's, maybe Dad's, too."

"It was you who came to the nursing home that day, wasn't it?"

"Yeah, it was me, the wayward son crying in my poor father's arms with him bawling, too. He understood something that day, Phoebe, I swear he did."

Tears streamed my cheeks. "Maybe pain breathes life into fading memories."

"And maybe love does, too."

"So now what? You could give yourself up, face the consequences. I know you have the rest of the treasure stashed somewhere. You could turn it over to Interpol."

"And spend ten or more years in jail? We're guilty one way or another, regardless, and there's no guarantee that Adrian won't make a strong enough case to make my sentence longer still."

"Noel thought four years, max."

"He's an optimist. He never expected any of this to go this far."

"So, instead, just let keep going to the point of no return?"

He smiled, a brief flash of his old merriment escaping lockdown. "Yeah, sure. The optimist is almost happy with his lot right now. He intends to continue his artifact do-gooding where he can. I think he's smitten by you."

"I never told him I was smitten back."

"You can't fool me, or him. In the few hurried calls I've had from him, he seems convinced."

I stood up, beginning to cry really hard, sobbing, really. "Toby, I need to process all this and I just can't right now. So much has happened." I wiped my eyes again, heading for the door. "I have to go."

"Wait! Phoebe, I don't know when I'll see you again."

I stopped and turned to face him, my beautiful, wounded brother looking like Neptune defrocked. "You're going to keep on running, aren't you? You'll continue living like this, both of you?"

"Yeah, I'll help Noel on his mission and try to build a life for myself along the way. I'd only die in prison, Phoebe, especially like this. You know I would."

"You made some horrible, horrible mistakes."

"I did."

"And I'm having a hard time processing it all."

"But you know I love you despite what an ass I've been."

"Ass is too mild a word."

"You never let me swear in front of you."

"Damn right. The F word is a lazy man's substitute for verbal effort."

"And I'm not a lazy man, whatever else I am. I've just run aground right now. Phoebe, you know I'll still be there for you wherever I am. I have the financial means to help you."

"I don't want your money, Toby. Please stop laundering your funds through my bank account."

"That's all money I've legally earned through my software sales, which I still keep going through multiple holding companies. It's not laundered money. I earned it the hard way and it's a gift from me to you. I have far more than I need. This was never about money, you must know that."

"I still don't want it. I need to make it on my own." I took another step towards the door, pausing as it whooshed open.

"Tell me I'm forgiven." He said behind me.

I turned towards him again. "I can't just yet but I will say I love you and maybe that's the same thing. Maybe when you love, the forgiveness follows. I love you, Toby." I stepped out into the late afternoon sun.

Brushing past Kevin who waited on the dock, I strode up the walkway.

The sun would set soon. It would dip a golden orb into the ocean, gilding the horizon a brilliant orange-red. The stars would sail up into the velvet darkness, spangling the depths with bright pulsing illumination. Even in the fog and rain, the world never is truly dark. Somewhere the sun shines, the moon spreads her silver sails, and a human heart pours light into the shadows.

All I needed was to pull back and imagine the full design to be content that nothing and no one is perfect and yet everything is.

BEAUTIFUL SURVIVOR

BEAUTIFUL SURVIVOR

VOLUME 3

Crime by Design Book 3

I

Blame Maggie. Anyone who thinks that suspending an open office over a public business is a good idea should be shot. Actually, she'd been imprisoned, which would just have to do for now. Thanks to my partner's ex-girlfriend and my pseudo ex-aunt, I couldn't concentrate on anything, least of all the stack of bills topping my to-do list.

I'd been instrumental in putting the woman, an international's art thief, away only months earlier but my brother and my potential love interest were still at large.

My gaze wandered to the latest postcard on my desk—a pic of Santorini's blue and white coastline. On the reverse it read: WISH I WAS THERE, addressed to me, not Baker & Mermaid Fine Textiles and Ethnography. No return address, as usual. That postcard added to everything else driving me crazy that morning.

In a fit of pique, I gathered all the accumulated postcards from my drawer and dumped them into the trash by my desk. Maybe out of sight, out of mind might actually work for me this time.

I turned as Serena's footsteps clink-clinked up the glass stairs.

"Hi, Rena. Everything's going well down there? It's noisy enough."

"Yes, very busy. They ask questions and yabber yabber. Buyers from new restaurant opening in Chelsea. They will call it Trattoria Venezia, but no Italian chefs. Is that Italian, I ask? Still I smile, always smiling."

I grinned. "'Trattoria Venezia' as in pasta served at exorbitant prices with Italian chef optional? We have only one Italian tapestry in the whole lot. Is the decorator okay with that?"

Rena rolled her eyes and shrugged. "This decorator, she has ideas. Sir Rupert Fox sent them."

"They're from Foxy? In that case, they're serious buyers."

"Very—how do you say—'top drawer.' Very big pockets, no?"

Rupert warned me to expect a large decorating contingent heading our way at his recommendation and, as far as shady dealers go, he was true to his word. A big sale could change everything. "Max doesn't need me, then?" This would be the first big sale my partner/godfather/ "uncle" had handled since graduating from detox.

"No, he is fine, but there is a lady asking to speak with you, one of the group, very lovely. She is from Umbria but, like me, she left Italy long ago. She says it's urgent."

"Urgent?" I'd take any excuse to escape accounting but urgent usually didn't apply to the rare textile business.

"She asks for you."

I landed on the showroom floor moments later and scanned the space. Max held court at the front of the gallery, his silver hair gleaming as he bent to lift the corner of a Tree Kazak rug. "At least 75 knots per inch, all silk, incredible workmanship." His Australian accent added a dash of outback to our Asian offerings, a little kangaroo to the Kalamazoo.

Two clients huddled around him murmuring in appreciation, a man and a woman. I recognized her chic assemble from a fashion layout—Prada, I guessed. "I love the intricacy of the design," she said in a North American accent, "but do you have something in blue?"

Max swung to the opposite wall without hesitation. "Blue! By the pricking of my thumbs, something blue this way comes."

That left a solitary woman standing midgallery before one of our prized acquisitions, the early sixteenth century Star Ushak carpet. Her severe gray suit, tailored to accentuate a toned body, contrasted with the textile framing her. Her face remained as intent as it was beautiful, studying the carpet as if it were a portrait gracing the walls of the Tate.

I joined her, gazing up at the masterpiece. "Magnificent, isn't it? Four hundred years old and it once occupied a place of honor in the drawing room of a pasha, smuggled out of Turkey during the Ottoman era. Imagine, trampled on by thousands and still beautiful."

"If only women could accomplish such a thing," she said, Italian still dancing in her accent.

I turned towards her. "But we can. We just need fortitude on one hand, and a little chemical conservation on the other, or so I'm told."

She smiled sadly. "If only it were so easy. I have had both, but still I am worn. But you are much too young to think of such things."

"I'll be embracing the honorably threadbare look soon enough. Nothing chemical or surgical for me, though. Let my wrinkles be signs of a cautionary tale." I grinned, then I figured I'd better get down to business. "I'm Phoebe McCabe, by the way. You asked for me?"

"Yes, Nicolina Boyd, but please call me Nicolina. I am the wife of the Trattoria Venezia's owner." She indicated the man standing with Max, the same man whose hand lightly touched the shoulder of the woman beside him, the much younger blond now studying a rare textile in blue.

"Happy to meet you. My assistant said it was urgent. Is it about your restaurant?" I'd always been told to let the customer spin out the necessary information, but I could never wait that long.

"Not my restaurant, my husband's. I am merely the silent partner." She stared pointedly at the pair with Max, the woman clearly taking the lead. "The decorator, Susan Rafuse, she stands with my husband, Geoffrey. She plans a Moorish touch to the fifteenth century Venetian decor."

Amazing what dynamics you can pick up in mere seconds. "As in the crossroads-of-the-trading-empire with arched windows and Persian rugs?"

"Yes, with a small canal going around the outdoor patio."

An image of putt-and-play miniature golf popped into my head. "Is there real estate in London large enough to accommodate even a little canal?"

Nicolina's hazel eyes twinkled. "It is destined to be very tiny. Ms. Rafuse imagines it encircling the diners like a small, hmm, stream, perhaps, or a gutter."

I shot her a quick look. "How interesting. I'm sure the food will be as innovative as the decor."

"One hopes so. I will leave all the details to them. My mind is occupied with more important matters. I only came today to see you. Sir Rupert Fox, he says you are the best."

The best what? With Sir Foxy, you never knew until too late. "Ah, yes, Sir Rupert. He knows we have one of the most extensive collections of rare textiles and related ethnographic art in London. This Star Ushak is one our prizes."

"I will purchase this Ushak, yes."

Just like that. "You will? Oh, wonderful." The carpet was listed at 145,000 pounds sterling and usually clients negotiated downward by a few thousand pounds. Though we weren't a souk, a little haggling was still expected.

"I will not argue the cost," she said, as if reading my thoughts. "This beautiful survivor, she deserves much better. She is worth her price. I will give her a place of honor on my study wall, and never permit one more foot to walk over her for as long as I live."

That nearly knocked me speechless. "Thank you. Um, would you like to go to my upstairs office while we work out the details?"

At that moment, Susan Rafuse swept over, Geoffrey Boyd and Max in tow. "I'll take that one," the decorator said, pointing a raspberry-red nail at the Ushak. "It's exactly what I'm looking for. The blue is the perfect shade for the drapes and will center the entranceway exactly how I envision. Why didn't you show me this one first, Mr. Baker?" She frowned at my partner.

Max kept his bonhomie secured. "I was working my way there. It is our loveliest specimen and would certainly be an asset to any decor."

"Only it's sold," I said.

Susan fixed me in cool surprise. "Really, to whom?"

"To me, Susan," Nicolina said, her lovely face expressionless.

The two women faced one another in rigid silence.

"Ah, Niki, darling, surely you could let Susan have it?" Geoffrey intercepted. "That is why we are here, after all." He bore the attractiveness of a man used to wielding power, but still found himself depleted in present company.

"That is not why I am here," Nicolina said. "No, I have fallen in love with this carpet. I will grant it the dignity it deserves. Choose something else blue for your clients to walk on, Susan."

"Allow me to show you other indigo specimens that will positively vibrate loveliness upon your floors," Max said, sweeping one hand towards the back of the gallery. "How about this one over here?"

Only after Max had successfully pried them away from our airspace did Nicolina's shoulders soften.

"Well," I said a bit too cheerfully, "why don't we head upstairs and work out the details?"

"No, thank you," Nicolina said, touching her forehead as if warding away a migraine. "I mean to say that I will write you a check now, but prefer to speak with you in private. Not here. It is very important."

"It is? Oh, of course." If there was one thing Max taught me, it was never miss a beat. If Nicolina Boyd felt the need to speak with me alone, why not? Maybe hubby didn't approve of his wife purchasing such an expensive item while he was busy dropping ten times that amount—maybe along with his pants—with the decorator. "My partner's upstairs office is very private."

"No, forgive me, not at this location. Please. This is too important to speak of here—life and death, it is true. This afternoon. Would you meet Rupert Fox and me at Carpe Diem at 2:00 P.M.? It is urgent."

⚜ 2 ⚜

"**R**upert, what's this meeting with Nicolina Boyd about?"

"And a very good morning to you, too, Phoebe. I must say how pleased I am that the air has crisped somewhat after the sweltering summer we've endured."

"Why does Nicolina insist on my presence?"

"And if you arrive a smidgen early, I can explain."

"Why not explain now?"

"The business with Nicolina all unfolded rather quickly. Oh, I am so sorry, but I must dash, Phoebe. A client awaits who is most interested in the mosaic I sourced last year. Remember the one I told you about, the lovely piece no museum wanted? It so perfectly suits this man's needs, since he desires a genuine Roman touch to his courtyard. How delighted I am to have just the thing."

"It wasn't so much that no museum wanted it but that you were asking too high a price."

"Roman artifacts don't come cheap, Phoebe. Evan will pick you up at 1:45 outside your shop. Until then." And the phone clicked off in my ear.

I dropped the cordless into its stand and glowered down at my desk. The voices below had slipped into the subdued murmur of deals closing, papers being signed, agreements made—all very hushed and sober compared to the heated flurry of the earlier wooing process. I sensed that substantial funds were passing into our coffers, maybe enough to set us back on our feet.

Nicolina Boyd, on the other hand, wasted no time on technical details. She merely dashed off a check in her lovely cursive hand and passed it to me with delivery instructions for the next day. I was to bring the carpet to her St. John's Wood address tomorrow afternoon, and personally supervise the installation according to her specifications.

Footsteps clinked on the glass stairway behind me. Jennifer, our part-time assistant, dashed up garbed in some kind of elfin jumpsuit worn under a fur-trimmed vest. The Gwyneth Paltrow lookalike took her fashion design studies seriously. "Hi, Phoeb. Max sent me up to empty the trash. Says he doesn't want me underfoot while money's passing hands, though it isn't exactly flying through the air or anything, is it? Still, may I empty your trash?"

"Go ahead." I watched while she up-ended my garbage pail into the plastic bag, wrinkling her nose at the container of leftover supper wafting day-old salad dressing. "Bad habit," I remarked. "One of these days, I'll actually dine in my flat instead of my desk."

"Prawn and avocado again?"

"The same."

"You should try the curry prawns sometime. They'd probably smell better on the second day. Curry masks everything brilliantly. Hey, what's this?" She held out my wad of disposed postcards.

"Nothing. Please put them back."

She flipped through them. "They're gorgeous. Oh, wow. Look at this place—Capri! Oh, I've always wanted to go to Capri—Jackie Onassis, all the beautiful people. Just brilliant. And Toulon. Isn't that in France? Yeah, I'm sure that's in France. Oh, yuck—salad oil all over Mykonos. Hope it's olive."

I got to my feet. "Return them to the trash, Jennifer."

Perfectly shaped eyebrows arched over storm-blue eyes. "Who are they from? I mean, they don't say very much, do they?"

"Put them back."

She shoved them down into the bag without unlocking her gaze from mine. "They're from him, aren't they—Noel, Max's hunky son?"

"How do you know he's hunky?"

" saw him once when he was working here. Sorry, don't mean to pry. I mean, it must be so hard to be away from someone you care about, isn't it? If I had to be separated from my boyfriend for any length of time, I swear I'd just shrivel, wouldn't I? I so feel your pain."

"He's not my boyfriend."

"Well, no. A boyfriend has to be here in the flesh, doesn't he? This is all very much of the long-distance-relationship type of thing."

"There is no relationship. End of topic, and whatever you do, don't go making statements about Noel anywhere outside these walls to anyone."

She held up her hands. "I know, I know. All very top secret. Don't want Interpol knowing you've been getting messages from the criminal set, do we?"

I pointed up the stairs. "Max's bin is stuffed. I can feel it overflowing from here."

"On my way."

The moment her feet pattered up the next flight, I heard the whoosh of the front door closing. I poked my head over the railing and gazed down into Max's upturned face. "Are they gone?"

Max stood, hands plunged into his pockets and legs slightly apart as if buttressing against a brisk wind. "Gone, Phoebe, darling, but Baker & Mermaid is forging ahead. I can't remember ever having a sale that grand."

I dashed downstairs. "No talk of selling the gallery again—not that I'd ever agree—but can we lay that ugly topic to rest at last?"

"We may, love. I promise those words will never escape my lips again. This ship's on even keel once more." Once a passionate yachtsman, Max loved nothing better than a good sailing metaphor. Or even a bad one.

"And we will never let anything sink her." And I was always happy to jump in.

"We bloody will not. With you as first mate, how can we run aground?"

"Actually, I'm co-captain," I laughed, "So let's edit that to say: 'with we two as captains, how can we run aground?'"

"Ah, Phoebe, my girl, a ship can only have one captain. It just doesn't work any other way. We need a little celebration, what do you say?"

"Let's do it." Power struggles could wait. Besides, it had been such an arduous journey to re-establish my godfather's self-esteem after Maggie and alcoholism, the least I could do is allow him to man the helm for a while. When a guy's girlfriend shafts him by stealing millions of dollars of treasure, plus most of his personal assets, and tops it off by running away with his son, serious recovery is in order.

"We'll keep it in-house," Max said. "How about tonight after closing, let's say 5:00 P.M.?"

"What about adding Sir Rupert to the guest list?"

Max's response was predictable. "Sir Rupert Fox is not bloody welcome in my gallery."

"*Our* gallery," I countered. "And let me remind you, he referred the very clients that brought in the sales, that made the purchases, that just changed our fortunes for the better. The least we owe him is a proper thank you."

"You can properly thank him all you want, but I'm bloody well not doing it." He turned on his heels and strode towards the storeroom, rubbing his hands together. "Don't spoil the day, Phoebe," he said over his shoulder. "Let's count our ackers and consider what purchases we need to fill in the holes. It just might be time to reopen negotiations with Erdogan Sevgi. He sent us those photos of that West Anatolian coupled-column prayer rug last week, plus a couple of Kum Kapis. Couldn't afford them then, but probably can now. Oh, and Rena, get Artcurial Paris on the phone for me, thanks. If they have an auction coming up with good pieces on the roster, maybe I should attend. We'll soon have empty walls to fill."

My eyes met Serena's. She knew that Max was advised not to leave London for at least another few months. His weekly counseling meetings, plus the AA sessions, all required that his attention remain close to home. Still, he had to reach those conclusions on his own. I followed after him into the storeroom.

"Max, what do you know about Nicolina and Geoffrey Boyd, besides that they practically bought out the gallery today?"

He poured himself a coffee from our brew depot—a rolling mini-refrigerator with an electric kettle and coffee pot on top. "Not much, except what I've heard. Geoffrey's name appears in the rags sometimes with some big deal he's brokered—ultimate wheeler and dealer in the commodities trade. Nicolina is an enigma. She doesn't like the public eye. Stays in the background, yet she's the real classy one of the pair. Her grandfather was some kind of Italian count, which may be dime a dozen in Italy, but is still as impressive as hell, if you go in for that kind of thing. Did you catch the way Geoff was carrying on with Susan Rafuse?"

I picked up one of the mugs, peering inside long enough to confirm my suspicions that Jen had yet to take her dish-washing chore to heart. "Yes, and so did Nicolina. She seems resigned, or maybe determined, to look the other way. I just don't get those kinds of relationships. You're either together or you're not." And in my case, I was not. I plunged my hand into the refrigerator and pulled out a sparkling elderberry water.

"It might be a contractual thing, you know the way those wealthy toffs marry to align their fortunes? Or maybe they loved one another once, and things just fell apart." He leaned against the shelving, holding his mug, eyes unfocused, staring out to a sea.

"I know that look. You're thinking of Maggie again. Forget her. She done us wrong, but is now safely ensconced in a Canadian prison awaiting trial. Leave her there."

He took a sip and shoved his free hand into his pocket. "Yes, she's gone, and good riddance, but things were good once."

"Were they? Was that before she fleeced you of every cent you had and tried shipping me off to the Baltic sex trade?"

"Look, the woman was poison, I know that, but I spent decades with her. I can't just erase the bloody memory banks. Besides, we don't choose who we love."

"Don't we?"

"No, we bloody well do not."

"Anyway, forget all that for now. Back to the Boyds. Nicolina has asked to meet with Rupert and me this afternoon."

Max jerked his head around. "Foxy's in this?"

I took a swig of sparkling juice. "Somewhere. He referred the sale, remember? And I guess he knows Nicolina pretty well."

"You're not getting involved, are you?"

"What do you mean 'getting involved'? I have no idea what this is about, only that she just purchased a heritage carpet, and asked if I'd join her at a meeting. Sounds simple enough."

"So does plowing through quicksand until you take the first step. Foxy's a weasel. You can't trust that shady little bugger as far as you can throw him."

I stared at him. "Max, listen to yourself. You two were in cahoots once, friends even. Are you taking the higher moral ground now that you've come clean?"

He turned to face me. "Hell, yes. If it weren't for Foxy, I would never have gone so damn crooked in the first place. He made it so easy for me, practically delivered opportunities on a silver platter. Yeah, I was a weak knucklehead for giving in, but he was relentless. I don't know how he does it. It's like he's got a mainline to priceless artifacts all over the world. He can source them out like nobody's business. Stay away from him, Phoebe. He's dangerous. I'm giving him a wide berth the way I do whiskey and beer, putting them all in the same category as my addictive toxins."

"I can take care of myself. Surely I've proved that much by now? I'm in no danger of slipping into the dark side just because I'm friends with Foxy. I've got his number but I still like the guy. He's been good to me."

"Yeah, just remember that it's all part of his long-range plan. Someday he'll ask for the return of a favor and you'll find yourself over a barrel with no place to turn."

"If I'm over a barrel, I should be able to roll either way."

He flashed a brief smile and shook his head. "That's what I thought, too."

"But you had Maggie egging you on."

"Maggie was only part of the problem."

"I said I can take care of myself."

"So you think. Stay away from him. Don't go this afternoon."

"Of course I'm going. At the very least, I will not deny an important client a request for a private meeting. Max, remember Foxy saved my neck, not to mention Noel's, and just put Baker & Mermaid back into the black. We owe him big-time."

"That's the way he does things, Phoebe. I'm warning you."

Serena appeared at the doorway, a sign that our voices had raised past the levels of propriety. "Max, I have Artcurial on the line for you." She held out the phone, which he took with a nod, and proceeded to stride the length of the gallery with the thing pressed to his ear.

I turned to Serena, who stood watching me. "It is a happy day, yes?" she asked softly.

"Very."

"We wait and wait for the winds to change only to see that it blows up a storm?"

I nodded. "Don't tell me you're picking up on the sailing metaphors, too?"

$$\text{Ҙ} \quad 3 \quad \text{Ҙ}$$

Evan, Sir Rupert's driver and bodyguard, picked me up outside the gallery in the black Bentley. I climbed in and settled down into the leather seats, sighing as the engineering sealed away the street noises.

I noted that Evan's brown hair had grown a few inches and now brushed the top of his collar. Rupert didn't insist on uniforms, so he wore his own leather jacket and turtleneck, a combo that only heightened his British good looks.

Why was I even thinking like that?

"Traffic's heavy today, madam. Mr. Rupert provided a thermos of tea and biscuits in the case next to you, in the event we get held up along the way."

"Thanks, Evan. How's your head these days?" Evan had been walloped on the forehead with the butt-end of a pistol while we were in Turkey last year, and for a while had sported a rakish bandage over his temple. It suited him.

"It's healed completely, madam," he told me, his green eyes meeting mine in the rear-view mirror. And they were beautiful green eyes, like moss married to agate, something else I hadn't noticed. "There's a bit of a scar, that's all. Nothing serious."

"I'm sure scars are like badges of honor in your line of work," I commented, hoping he'd meet my gaze again, but he remained fixed on the road. Just as well. "Women don't always feel the same."

"Do you have a scar or two, madam?"

"None that show. And, could you just call me Phoebe?" He never did, so I don't know why I kept asking.

We cut across Hyde Park, Evan changing routes according to whatever traffic obstructions hindered our path. As usual, I could have reached Foxy's faster if I'd taken the tube but not nearly as pleasantly.

I helped myself to a bourbon cream but saved the tea until I reached Carpe Diem. The minutes sailed away in moving images of the London streets—double-decker busses, glossy black cabs, and throngs of people, plus the occasional glance at the driver's strong hands on the steering wheel.

Rumor had it that Evan had been once part of MI6. Whether that was true or not, I'd come to appreciate the man's many talents. He did have that spy-worthy vibe going for him.

Finally, we slid up to the curb outside Carpe Diem's Knightsbridge location, and Evan leaped to open the door. I climbed out and smiled up at him and he smiled back. Damn stupid butterflies flitted in my stomach all the way to the door. This had to stop.

Once at the shop, Rutger, Sir Rupert's security guard on permanent loan from an elite company, met me. "Afternoon, Ms. Phoebe." He stepped aside to allow me admittance to Carpe Diem's rarefied ambiance. Sir Rupert Fox's establishment did not invite casual browsers. Potential clients called in advance or, when discretion demanded, Rupert made house calls, carrying his offerings accompanied by both Rutgers and Evan, a dual-exhaust SWAT team of brawn.

While my eyes acclimated to the shadowy lighting, Sir Rupert Fox hastened from one of the side salons. "Afternoon, Phoebe," he said, rubbing his hands together. "I must say, you look quite fetching today."

"I don't, but thanks anyway." Anticipating a day in my office, I hadn't put much thought into my sweater and pants combo, other than to toss on one of my knit wraps and insist that all the colors got along. Foxy, on the other hand, wore his immaculate silk gabardine suit with his usual aplomb, finishing off the toast-brown theme with an alarmingly green silk bow tie.

He held up his hand to halt my forward motion long enough to hitch up his pant leg to reveal his latest green and brown argyle sock triumph.

I smiled. "Brilliant, literally. Have you gone off yellow?"

"Jonquil, and I have not so much gone off jonquil as I have briefly deviated to neon green, in the interest of adding a touch of electricity to a potentially cloudy British autumn, you understand. I rather like the pop of unexpected color, don't you? I just finished these last night."

"Lovely. Why am I here?"

"I did so wish to talk privately before Nicolina arrived, but she already awaits in the salon." He opened his hands in a credible *what's a guy to do.* "Let's not keep the lady waiting. Tea, Phoebe?"

"Yes, thank you, Rupert. I know what you're up to, by the way, I just don't yet know why you're up to it."

"Oh, ye of little faith."

He ushered me into the second of his two client salons. Unlike his first, which reeked of a stuffy cigar-smoking men who hunted grouse and chased down innocent mammals, this wood-paneled enclave featured Flemish tapestries, which I had helped source. At my insistence, he had also added fine old landscape paintings, including one he claimed to be a Sargent, and stirred in the warmth of knitted throws along with Tiffany lamps—still traditional, definitely elite, but inviting. We agreed that this newly decorated environment excluded no human on the basis of gender or age, though income remained a factor.

Nicolina Boyd sat by the fire and rose to meet me as I stepped forward. The iron gray suit had been replaced by a long column of maroon dress worn over a pair of felt boots, her glossy hair swinging loose around her shoulders. "Phoebe, thank you so much for coming. I need your assistance so very much." She took both my hands in hers and smiled down at me.

Her beauty was of the sort that emanates both grace and warmth. "A pleasure to see you again, too, Nicolina, but I really don't understand how I can help you in anything other than carpets."

"Oh, I believe you can help me very much, but I will explain. Won't you sit down?"

I took the seat indicated, a plump deep blue velvet chair, while Rupert poured the tea from his prized Nippon china. "No sugar, is that correct, Phoebe?"

"You know it is." He always asked, the query forming part of some polite ritual that I found both annoying and oddly comforting. I leaned forward, holding out the delicate cup while he poured his perfectly steeped brew. Having tea on our knitting afternoons had become one of my favorite midweek treats. Sometimes I almost forgot how much I loved coffee. "So, why I am here?"

"Don't mind Phoebe," Rupert said mildly. "She tends to dispense with preamble."

"Preamble only delays the inevitable," I said before taking my first sip.

"I will waste no time, then. My grandfather has passed and—"

"Oh, I'm so sorry, Nicolina," I said, lifting my gaze from the cup.

Her hand rose in an elegant flutter. "No sympathies necessary. My grandfather, Conte Giovanni Vanvitelli, was a difficult man. We had many disagreements, so that I had not seen him for years—a long story—but the circumstances of his estate are complicated, also."

"Any death in the family sends things reeling," I said.

"This is true. I did not attend his funeral two months ago. A very long story, as I say, but I try to shorten the version, yes? My eldest brother has inherited his estates near Naples and Campania—the lands, the winery, the castillo, the palazzo, all of it—but under the terms of my grandmother's will, I am to receive the villa near Amalfi upon my grandfather's death. My grandmother and I were very close. She insisted I inherit her estates in Umbria also but those were sold long ago. This only remains, and she protected it against my grandfather's, ah, how do I say it?" She turned to Rupert.

"I would suggest patriarchal maneuvering."

"That is very good—patriarchal maneuvering. So, she protected it for me, as I said. Now I must return to settle the estate, which is full of her tapestries and her collections."

"You don't want to keep the villa?" I asked.

She lifted her manicured hand from her lap and let it drop. A tiny gold ring gleamed on the middle finger of her right hand, but her left was bare. "Ah, but no. Too many memories. It will be so difficult, and I am overwhelmed, but must accomplish this with some speed. I need to return to London quickly, where also much is happening that requires my attention. Most items will be turned over to an auction house, but I hoped that you and Sir Rupert would accompany me for a first assessment, to help decide which pieces to keep, which pieces to go, and advise me as needed. Please say yes. I will be happy to pay whatever you request."

I looked from Nicolina to Rupert, whose eyes now glittered like a ravenous ferret. I swallowed a sip of tea and set my cup down. "Well," I began. "I know Rupert is a specialist on various rare collectibles but I wouldn't say I am when it comes to European textiles. I have some knowledge, I admit, but I am actually more of a generalist in art history."

Rupert cleared his throat noisily, lowered his cup, and stood. "Nicolina, would you excuse Phoebe and me for a moment? We have need for a bit of a promenade around the gallery, you understand. Exercise is so critical to one's well-being. We won't be long."

She gazed up at him in surprise. "Why, of course."

I stood up also. "No need for promenading. Nicolina should hear everything so she knows exactly who she's dealing with."

"But I do know who I'm dealing with, Phoebe," Nicolina smiled up at me.

"Indeed she does. Nevertheless, let us converse briefly in private. Pardon us, Nicolina."

He linked his arm in mine and steered me out the door into the gallery. The moment the door clicked behind us, he turned to me. "Phoebe, why are you attempting to sabotage this most marvelous opportunity? I hold Nicolina in the highest regard, and would do absolutely nothing to harm her. But besides that, you are being offered an all-expenses paid trip to Italy to spend time in a grand villa on the Amalfi Coast, sorting through rare valuables with your dear friend, Sir Rupert. Why do you hesitate?"

"What are you up to? You know damn well I'm not a European textile expert. I don't want that beleaguered woman to believe she's dealing with expertise I don't have. That's criminal."

"Don't be melodramatic, Phoebe, and don't be bandying about words like 'criminal' with too much abandon. Aren't you the co-owner of a foremost London textile gallery? You must do what we all do in this business: Learn what you need, when you need to know it. Take whatever profitable and interesting job that arises and thus build your repertoire. Besides, haven't you just helped shatter a black market operative in Turkey with the assistance of yours truly? Who could come with a better resumé than that?"

"Wait." I raised my hand. "In what way does our past involvement with the black market qualify us to help with Nicolina's estate? How are these two things in any way connected?"

"Such a suspicious mind." He shook his head, his expression pained. "I only said that to illustrate our growing acclaim. Nicolina's family are a bit challenging. She needs the support of those who will have her back against the tyrant embedded at the family's breast, so to speak. If we can handle a few gun-toting cutthroats, we can handle brother Lucca, not that he will likely take much interest in Nicolina's lesser estate with the rest of Italy to play with. In any case, our presence will not only be of a professional nature, but we will lend an additional measure of moral support. I consider myself to be highly morally supportive in ways that matter, as are you."

"Morality which, in your case, does not apply to legalities."

"I said in 'ways that matter'. Do pay attention, Phoebe. My point is that Nicolina is woefully isolated these days, what with that useless husband romping away with the hired help."

"A famous decorator is hardly the hired help but, yes, I get it. I feel for her."

"So you will accompany me?"

My gaze landed on the nearest display pedestal, with its bowl of glass encasing an intricate tiara composed of delicate gold leaves. "Oh, my god—a classical laurel wreath? You've got to be kidding!"

"Greek, third century BC. They found another cache recently north of Athens. Those golden laurels are becoming a dime a dozen these days. I picked that up for a song."

"Oh sure. Soon they'll be popping up in dollar stores the world over. How did you find that? Oh, wait—I keep forgetting—I don't want to know. One of these days Interpol is going to nail you."

"Nonsense. One can't nail a swimming fish, and it's you they are most interested in at the moment. I do believe that Walker chap has taken a shine to you. So, will you accompany me to Italy, yes or no?"

"Where are her parents in all this?"

"Deceased. They died in a tragic accident along the Amalfi Coast a few years back—drove right off a precipice, I understand. All very devastating.

Poor, dear Nicolina. She has seen so much tragedy and, indeed, it appears more lies ahead with the possible dissolution of her marriage. Will you help her, or must I approach some tedious old fart to assist me?"

"You know I'll go, but I'd appreciate the whole story first."

"The best stories unfold in due time. You already know everything you need for now. It's just that the family machinations are a bit complicated. These wealthy Italians can convolute even the simplest things in a most alarming manner. But none of that need worry us. Our job is to fly to Amalfi, spend a couple of delightful weeks sorting through her treasures, and no doubt purchasing a few pieces for our respective galleries in the ultimate right of first refusal. I must show you all my favorite places. Did I mention that I have a little hideaway in Italy? Oh, indeed I do. Mable and I purchased it as a retreat, but we had so little time to visit together before she took ill. I really must check on it while we are there. I—"

The door opened and out stepped Nicolina. "I do not wish you to be rushed but I must leave. So much to do. I fly to Naples very soon. Have you made your decision, Phoebe? Rutger, would you be so kind as to retrieve my coat?"

"Oh, we do apologize, Niki, my dear. Phoebe was just chattering away as she tends to do," Rupert said.

As the guard took off towards the coat closet, I stepped forward to take Nicolina's chill hands in mine. "Of course, I want to help however I can, as long as you understand exactly where my skills lay."

Her smile was brief and luminous. "Of course I do understand that, and I am so relieved! Now I have the foremost pair of rare antiques sleuths assisting me. How can I fail?" She slipped into her coat and swept out the door.

I turned to Rupert. "Fail what?"

4

The sun hung low in the sky by the time Evan dropped me off outside the gallery. Serena waited by the front door, the CLOSED sign glowing red on the glass window above her right shoulder. We locked the doors at 5:00 but it was only 4:45.

"Rena, what's he up to now?"

"Walker." She locked the door behind me and turned with her hands clasped over her Pucci print chest, a vintage market find. "This time he thinks he finds something."

"Impossible. There's nothing to find. I thought we were finished with all this foolishness."

Lights glowed at the back of the gallery, while the foreground brushed long shadows across the floor.

"He found something in the trash."

"In our garbage bins, you mean?"

She nodded. "In the alley."

"Agent Walker was rooting in our garbage tins in the back alley?"

She rolled her eyes. "He showed them to Max, who I thought would—how do you say?—hit the ceiling. We were preparing for our celebration and in he comes, but Max goes quiet."

"Max quiet?" I keened my ears towards the back of the gallery. Besides a low murmur coming from the storeroom, I heard nothing. His anger management must be working. "Where are they?"

"Upstairs in the office."

I nodded, straightened my shoulders, and headed for the stairs. Jennifer, slipping out from the storeroom, her phone in hand, met me before I reached the first step. "Phoebe, I'm sorry. I didn't know, did I? You said to toss them out, so I did. How did I know the cop would find them in the refuse bin?"

Oh, shit. The postcards. I took the steps two at a time, hung a right, and burst into Max's office, where my godfather sat in his chair, glowering down at the fan of colored photos spread across his desk.

"Phoebe McCabe, I knew you were hiding something."

I swung to Agent Sam Walker, standing there with his hitched-up eyebrow and that damn shiny head. He looked like some kind of damned skinhead, as if he could slit your throat without blinking an eye. "I hear you've been digging around in our trash. That's low even for you."

"Don't get defensive, Phoebe. You're the one with the explaining to do."

"Explain why I threw out a bunch of postcards?"

He pointed at the desk. "Those," he pointed to the postal array before Max, "are no ordinary postcards. They indicate what I've suspected all along: that you are in touch with the two fugitives under our investigation."

I plucked up one card—an aerial view of some little pastel-hued fishing village. "Yes, receiving unsigned postcards is highly suspicious. Would that be a misdemeanor or a felony? I keep forgetting. Let's see." I made a play at scrutinizing the back of the card. "No signature, or distinguishing features, either. Another crime."

"Look, Phoebe, those are from either your brother or Noel Halloran, so let's dispense with the games, shall we?"

"How wrong you are, Agent. Turns out, these are from an ex who has difficulty exiting. He thinks he can win me back with a travel log of all the things I'm missing while not in his company, not that it's any of your business, of course."

I gathered the cards up in a couple of clumsy sweeps and deposited them in the trash. Again. "I threw them away for a reason, and I object to you coming here and scrounging around, upsetting my staff, and essentially harassing us. This has to end."

Walker retrieved one card from the trash and held it between his fingers. "I'll just take one of these for interest, shall I?"

I snatched it back just as Max lifted the wastebasket out of Walker's reach to the other side of the desk. "You will not. You'll leave immediately. And the next time you grub around in our property, you'd better bring a warrant."

His surprise was almost comical, especially since his scar already shot one eyebrow into a permanently hike. "You've always cooperated with Interpol in the past."

"And look where that got me? You still don't extend me the courtesy I deserve." I glimpsed Max out of the corner of my eye. He was sitting back in his chair, enjoying the show. "I've already helped you bring one of the fugitives to justice, which should prove my legal commitment. Now, leave. I'll show you out the door, in case you take any unauthorized detours."

I stepped into the hall, Walker following behind.

"I know the way out," Walker said under his breath.

"And in and around and under, apparently. Remember, bring a search warrant next time."

The agent hesitated, fixing me with those bleached-blue eyes, the corners of his mouth quirking slightly as if he were repressing a mix of emotions. "Ask yourself whether this new manner is wise, Ms. McCabe."

"And ask yourself whether harassing us will help the cause, Agent Walker."

He turned abruptly and dashed downstairs, his feet pounding on the glass steps. Once I heard the front door open and close seconds later, I returned to the office and collapsed into the rolling chair opposite Max, elbows on the desk. "So, now I suppose we look guiltier than ever."

Max tapped a pencil on the desk but said nothing.

"I'm just sick to death of having him snooping around every week, looking for evidence that we're hiding something," I continued.

"Especially when it turns out we are," Max said.

Our eyes met. "I didn't want you to know about the postcards."

"Obviously, but why? Do you think I'd blow a gasket at the sight of

Corfu?" Surprisingly, there was no anger there. Either that or he was reining it in as part of the Max Rehabilitation Plan.

"That was actually Mykonos. Look, I didn't want you grilling me about my feelings for Noel again. I thought by telling you only that they were cruising around on Toby's yacht somewhere in southern Europe, that would be enough. Who needs the port-by-port exposé anyway? It's not like the cards say anything. Besides, I didn't want to rehash the details every time one arrived."

"We're talking about my son, here. Don't you think I have a right to know the details?"

"There are no details, that's the point. They're sending us these cards to let us know they're alive."

"Including the one that says *You're in my heart always?*"

"Okay, so that was personal, but, look, every time I mention Noel, you spin into this fantasy that we're going to end up happily ever after. That isn't going to happen. It can't."

He leaned forward. "What are you on about? You told me you and Noel had a thing back in Turkey."

I gazed past him out the little dormer window, staring unfocused at branches of the plane tree shifting patterns on the wall. "We did but a thing is not permanent."

"I thought you cared about him."

"I do—sort of." The bleary sun had snagged in the branches like some disintegrating balloon.

"I don't understand. Help me." He was running his fingers through his thick wavy hair.

"What Noel and I experienced in Turkey was mostly physical, but how can it ever become something more with him on the run? I want some-body here and now, not someday and maybe. I go upstairs every night to my empty apartment, wondering what would it be like to share all those common, insignificant, ordinary things that make up a life. I'm 34. I need to make a future. Even if they apprehend him, he'll spend the next decade in prison. I don't want a relationship in absentia."

He sat back hands clasped over his stomach, looking down at the desk. "Yeah, Phoebe darling, I get it."

"You do?"

JANE THORNLEY

"You're the closest I'll ever have to a daughter, and all I've ever wanted is for you to be happy. Sure, I'd love to see you with Noel, but I know how tough that would be. Loneliness is bloody crippling. Even the rooms ache when you go into them and find yourself looking for a face that isn't there, somebody you can't be with for one reason or another. The pain gets you by the short and curlies. I don't want that for you. Find yourself some nice bloke who lives in London and works a proper nine-to-five job, somebody who comes home to you every night."

I smiled. "In other words, somebody boring."

" Safe. Noel can never be that for you. He craves excitement and risk. You can never tie him down to some boring pedestrian life."

"I don't exactly want a boring pedestrian life."

"Can't have it both ways, darling."

But that's exactly what I want. "So, what about you?"

"I want what I can't have, too, always have."

I reached across the desk for his hand. His fingers laced with mine. "I know how hard it is for you getting over Maggie. You'll find another woman, Max, somebody worthy of you." Neither one of us could easily forget what Maggie did. At least I had the consolation of putting her away.

"Unlike you at the ripe age of 34, I'm 72 and no longer rich. I'm not such a good catch any more."

"Not every woman fishes for a mate by the size of his bank account. Anyway, enough talk. Let's go downstairs and celebrate, okay?"

"You go, darling. I'm just going to stay up here for a while. I'm not in a partying mood."

I shoved the chair back and got to my feet. "You're going to flip through those postcards, aren't you?"

"Maybe."

"When you're finished, give them to me, and I'll burn them in the grate."

"Just remember, you can't choose who you love. It's not as easy as turning off a switch."

So maybe I needed behavior management for my emotions.

I strolled down the hall to my flat and stepped into my light and textile-filled space. I scanned the room, my gaze brushing over cubbyholes of yarn, the art nouveau tiles along the mantle, my latest knitting project, plus all those extra chairs for people who never sat in them. I strolled into the kitchen, stared at the table with room for four that rarely ever sat more than one, since Max and I ate out when we shared a meal.

And then came the bedroom with its queen-size bed. Rolling over to the other side at night felt like a plunge into the ice age, so I always slept curled into an embryo with my back to the wasteland.

Before I plunged too deep into self-pity, I turned and left the flat, heading back down the hall towards Max's office. He was still staring at the postcards when I paused by the doorway. "I forgot to tell you that I'm going to Italy to help Nicolina Boyd dismantle her grandmother's villa. Apparently, it's filled with antiques and collectibles."

He looked up at me over his reading glasses. "Foxy's idea?"

"He recommended that the two of us do the job together, yes."

"That doesn't sound any alarms for you?"

"Look, Max, we're going to Italy to assess a villa full of rare textiles and collectibles. I'll be selecting prime pieces for the gallery before the rest goes to auction—in other words, doing my job. Besides, it's Italy; there are antique textiles. Of course I'm going."

He sat back. "I'd just hoped that your experience in Turkey would have taught you something."

"Oh, it did. It taught me not to trust Rupert Fox but to stay in contact with him where it's beneficial. We're flying out tomorrow night. You'll be fine without me?"

"I should go with you."

"Absolutely not. You need to stay in London. Besides, you're not invited, remember? You can't ostracize Rupert on one hand and expect him to invite you to the party on the other. I'll only be gone for ten days, maybe two weeks at the most. See you downstairs?"

"Maybe later." He returned to the postcards.

$$\text{卐} \quad 5 \quad \text{卐}$$

T he next afternoon, Jake, our delivery guy, and I drove through the leafy enclaves of St. John's Wood to deliver Nicolina's carpet. The Boyds' residence, a Georgian brick mansion with white-trimmed windows and multiple wings, sat tucked into a parkland behind a wrought iron fence. Jake and I were used to delivering expensive carpets to expensive houses, but this one trumped everything.

"Blimey, that's a corker." Jake tapped his hand on the steering wheel in appreciation. He had long ago anglicized his East Indian name in the interest of convenience. Though Indian by parentage, he was so English, he elevated soccer to an art form.

"Yes, very nice. So, how do we get in?"

"There's a blinking buzzer on the wall." He pointed.

"So there is, and it's literally blinking." I climbed out of the van and pressed down into the flashing button, waiting beside the cement post until someone answered.

"Yes?" came a man's voice.

"Phoebe McCabe from Baker & Mermaid here to deliver Mrs. Boyd's carpet."

The reply took a long time coming. I stared up into the camera hoping my face registered the picture of reliability. "Mrs. Boyd's expecting us," I said after a moment. I turned to look at Jake, who stood with his hands in his pockets studying his sneakers.

After a moment, the intercom crackled again. "I regret to inform you that Mrs. Boyd is not at home." The vowels came so highly polished, I could probably check my reflection in them.

I cleared my throat. "And you are, if you don't mind my asking?"

"I am Harris, the house assistant."

House assistant? "Well, Mr. Harris, may we leave the piece inside rather than make a return trip?"

I watched a leaf scuttle across the pavement while I kicked a pebble away with my toe. Finally, the gate swished open and we cruised into the circular driveway. A man decked out in a green button-down vest, white shirt, and black trousers—the house assistant, I presumed—pointed around to the back of the house.

"Uniformed, too," I said under my breath. "Who has uniformed assistants in this day and age?"

"The toffs," Jake remarked.

Seconds later, we parked in an area that reminded me of the back of some country spa, with a garage large enough to house at least ten cars or fifteen thoroughbreds. Mr. Harris, a slight man with an expression of perpetual forbearance, stepped forward to meet us. "Good afternoon. Please follow me."

Jake slid the bubble-wrapped carpet from the back of the van, hefted it over his shoulder, and grabbed his toolkit. Following behind Harris, we traipsed into what appeared to be a mudroom, or at least a repository of outdoor gear, including bicycles and raincoats, all relatively new, and in adult sizes.

"You may leave it there." The man pointed to a corner beside a stack of umbrellas sprouting from a brass stand.

"Ah, Mr. Harris is it? If I told you I was delivering a roll of gold leaf, would you suggest I stick it in a corner?"

"Certainly not, but didn't I hear you say it was a rug?"

"A carpet, yes, a very old and venerable carpet, and not to be too crass about it, very valuable. I'm certain Mrs. Boyd would not want it left back here."

"Very well," he sighed. "Step inside."

We followed him into a long white and black checkerboard-tiled hallway where everything was spotless, shiny and minimal. The only furniture consisted of dark wood tables and a long padded bench against one wall, though a crystal chandelier suspended overhead like a glorious remnant from another century. "You may leave the rug there."

I glanced at the long wooded seat. "I have instructions to supervise an installation. We have applied the fittings in advance so I can personally ensure it is properly mounted, as per Mrs. Boyd's instructions."

"I have no such information regarding such instructions. Please leave the rug where indicated. I will ensure Mrs. Boyd knows of its arrival. Perhaps she will contact you when she returns and arrange another time."

"Unfortunately, I'm leaving town tonight." *And so is she.*

Jake slid one end of the Star Ushak onto the floor and stood holding the roll.

"That is unfortunate, indeed, however—"

One of the mahogany doors to our right flung open and out stepped Susan Rafuse in jeans and a white shirt, an expression of annoyance darkening her attractive features. Her hay-gold hair had been scraped back into a ponytail, as if all irritants, including stray hairs, had better stay out of her face. "Harris, what's going on?"

I refused to register surprise. Catching sight of me, she emitted a chill smile. "Oh, you're the girl from Mermaid & Baker, aren't you? We spoke yesterday. Are you delivering the rugs? We left instructions for them to be dropped off at the restaurant the day after tomorrow."

"I'm delivering the Star Ushak carpet for Mrs. Boyd. She's expecting me."

Susan flashed a tight smile. "Nicolina's not here. That's the blue one, isn't it?"

"I wouldn't call it blue, exactly. It's more indigo." I was just making a point.

Harris stood by, eyes fixed down the hall.

Susan shook her head. "Indigo is blue."

"Yes, but not the ordinary variety. This one is overdyed to create a rich, saturated effect."

"I approve of saturated, and certainly approve of rich. I still need that one. It's the perfect rug for the entryway. I can't imagine why Niki would buy a rug without letting me have first option. Undo the top corner and let me take a look to see if it matches my paint chips. They're here in my pocket."

"Actually," I said. "Mrs. Boyd entrusted me with this carpet, was very specific about how she wanted it handled, and swore no one would ever walk on it again."

"How amusing. What are rugs for if not to be walked on? Just open the wrapping an inch so I can assure myself it's the color I want."

When I didn't budge, she flicked a penknife from her pocket and reached for the roll. Jake turned ninety degrees, shielding the rug with his body—my kind of guy.

"Are you kidding me? I'm not going to stab it to death." She laughed, though no humor reached her eyes. "This is ridiculous. Maybe I should phone Max."

"If you want." I pulled my phone from my pocket. "Use my phone. I have him on speed-dial."

She eyed my phone but made no move to take it. "I believe you misunderstand."

"The only misunderstanding here is that this carpet has been purchased by Mrs. Boyd for her personal space. I can't turn it over to anybody else, even for a minor inspection. It's an insurance matter," I lied.

Brisk footsteps marched down the hall and I turned, grateful for any interruption. A small dark-haired woman dressed in the same uniform as Harris strode forward.

"Excuse me, are you Ms. McCabe?" she asked.

"I am."

"Mrs. Boyd's personal assistant, Maria. I did not know you were here, or I would have come sooner." She looked pointedly at Harris, who failed to meet her eyes, and then to Susan Rafuse, who merely stiffened. "Mrs. Boyd has left instructions for the carpet to be hung in her office. Follow me, please."

Jake hefted the roll onto his shoulder and loped after Maria while Harris darted off down the hall in the opposite direction. Before I could move, Susan insinuated herself in front of me, forcing me to bring up the rear.

I studied the decor all the way up the curving staircase, noting the modernistic art, what looked to be a genuine Picasso sketch, and a Jeff Koons balloon sculpture on the next landing.

"Who's the art collector?" I asked.

"Geoffrey, of course," Susan remarked. "He's the one with the exquisite taste."

That cinched the deal: I now officially detested Susan Rafuse.

Maria unlocked the third door down and switched on the lights. We stepped into a large room with floor-to-ceiling books on three sides, a tall bow window in which nestled a cozy reading chair with a backdrop of drawn gold brocade curtains. Recessed lighting cast a warming glow over small collectibles encased in table stands or suspended on wall niches among the books. I wanted to linger over everything, study the smallest detail.

"Mrs. Boyd would like the carpet hung here." Maria indicated a bare space near an eighteenth century desk pulled away from the wall.

"The perfect spot," I remarked.

Maria smiled. "Mrs. Boyd wishes to gaze upon it as she writes."

"She's a writer?"

"An author of many books, yes," Maria nodded.

"History books about Italian villas, mostly," Susan commented in a tone a renowned chef might reserve for a sandwich-maker. "She really hasn't published anything new for years."

"Is there anything you need?" Maria asked me.

"No, thanks. We came prepared."

While Jake undid the wrapping and I measured the wall, Maria stood nearby, hands clasped in front of her.

"No need for you to stay, Maria," Susan said, while roaming the room investigating Nicolina's collections.

"I will remain," the assistant said, never taking her eyes from the decorator.

I focused on the installation, relieved not to be the center of Susan's attention. Once Jake was busy securing the carpet to its new home, I backed away to ensure it was level. "Looks good, Jake," I said, giving him the thumbs-up.

Only when I was about to complete the final adjustments did I see the portrait on the far wall. Like nothing I had seen before, the style appeared to be some meld of ancient and modern. "Oh." I stepped closer.

"Striking, yes?" Maria said.

"It is. At first I thought it was an Etruscan fresco, but the subject is more modern."

The profile of a young woman bore the archaic features of an Etruscan tomb painting—the kind I'd seen countless times in ancient art tomes—only instead of the headdresses, tiaras, or wreaths that completed an Etruscan woman's ritual apparel, this girl wore a kind of cloche, easily mistaken as a helmet at first glance. One small feature remained true to the original: the golden earring dangling just below her hat, a delicate confection of tiny dots and riposte so expertly rendered, it could be in real-life 3D. "Is it painted on stone?"

"Plaster," Maria corrected. "The Signora modeled it after the old frescoes."

"The Signora?"

"Madam's grandmother."

"Oh." Nicolina's grandmother was an artist? Well. I studied the painting more closely. The background appeared weathered, as if plucked from the wall of some moss-addled place, yet the mood emanated hope, akin to the Etruscan art it paid homage to.

This civilization danced with color and light, their tombs expressing a joy so effervescent, it's as if they dared death to douse their spirit even for a second. Of all the ancient peoples, I identified with the Etruscans most. "She was very talented," I said at last.

"She was," Maria agreed.

"That rug needs to be brought down by about one-half inch," Susan announced from across the room.

I glanced up. She was standing before the Star Ushak making a frame with her hands.

"No, it doesn't. I measured it and re-measured it," I said, joining her. "It's an optical illusion caused by the slightly diagonal weave. We think she suffered a trauma of some sort a few centuries ago."

"She?" Susan said. "You call her she? How amusing. If it were me mounting it, I'd compensate by setting it in a blue border to mask the unevenness."

I was about to make a snippy remark but thought better of it. I'd battled enough with this woman for one day.

"It looks perfect," Maria said. "May I tidy up now?"

"Oh, Jake and I will do that. We usually clean up messes we are responsible for."

"Not necessary. I know how madam prefer things," the assistant smiled, her eyes locking mine. *She wants us out of here so Susan Rafuse would have no excuse to stay.*

"Sure," I said brightly. "Jake and I will just head off now. Ah, Ms. Rafuse, you wouldn't happen to have the restaurant plans you could show me? I'm keen to see how you plan to lay the carpets."

Susan hesitated. "I really don't have time. Why don't you drop by the Venezia when Max delivers the rugs so you can see for yourself?"

"Perhaps I will." As if I could bear to see my beautiful carpets splayed on the floor like sacrificial lambs.

On that friendly note, Jake and I hastily packed up our tools and left the room, Susan trailing behind. I couldn't wait to escape that house.

Halfway to the van, I took out my phone, and called Rupert on his private line.

"Rupert here."

"And Phoebe here. I just installed a carpet for Nicolina, but she wasn't home. She told me she'd meet me here yesterday. You don't happen to know what's up, do you?"

"As it turns out, Nicolina contacted me last night and explained that she must fly to Italy rather sooner than expected—paperwork to sign or some such thing. She mentioned visiting her lawyer in Rome before joining us at the villa. We're to proceed to Amalfi as planned. Someone will meet us at the airport and drive us to her grandmother's villa where we will ensconce ourselves until Nicolina joins us."

"Okay, good. I was worried. The tension in that house is like wading in viscous fluid. Susan Rafuse was there, minus the wayward husband. Imagine having your husband's presumed-mistress holed up in your home? I mean, how humiliating is that? I needed to do battle just to install the carpet. Anyway, are we all set for tonight? You've made all the arrangements?"

"Indeed I have. Suffice to say that the tickets have been purchased and you need do nothing but meet Evan outside the gallery at the appointed time."

"I still need to pack."

"No need for that, either, except for personal items, of course. I took the liberty of purchasing a few items in your size that I thought would look particularly fetching in this nation of style."

"You bought me clothes?"

"Just a few things."

"No. The last person to buy me clothes was Maggie, which was hardly a pleasant experience. Besides, you and I have different tastes, as if that hasn't occurred to you already. Why would you do something like that without consulting me?"

"Now, calm down, Phoebe. The vintage apparel look might be best left to Kate Moss and other sylphs here in London, but might seem highly unsuitable in Italy. Italy is a nation of designers, as you've oft said yourself."

"Are you saying I don't dress appropriately?"

"Don't be defensive."

"I'm not defensive, I'm intensely irritated."

"My apologies. I assure you that I didn't mean to offend. No, I merely selected a few choice outfits which you can choose to wear or not, entirely upon your whim. Just trying to be helpful, you know."

"Thank you but no thank you," I said.

"Oh, my, must go. My business line is ringing. We will see you at the appointed time." And then he clicked off.

I stood glowering at a potted rose bush while still holding the phone when it rang in my hand. Max.

"Phoebe, where are you?"

"At the Boyd residence staring at a rose. What's wrong?"

"Nothing. I just wondered if you want to meet for lunch?"

"Sure. We're heading back to the shop now. We just installed the Star Ushak, though Nicolina didn't show."

"Didn't show, as in missing?"

"Didn't show, as in not here. She led me to believe she'd meet me, but apparently left early for Italy."

"She didn't just disappear, then."

I stopped, my gaze landing on another late September rose, a sweetheart variety with deep pink blossoms. "Of course she didn't just disappear. What are you getting at, Max?"

"It's just that so many rather sudden, dramatic things happen in that family, nothing would surprise me."

"I know about her parents' accident, about Nicolina's miserable relationship with her grandfather, and now what could turn into a messy divorce—what else?"

"Her grandmother went missing decades ago. Just upped and disappeared. Never seen again. Foxy didn't tell you?"

🙙 6 🙚

I stretched out my legs, unaccustomed to executive-class flying where it's possible to knit and drink a beverage without mishap. Rupert sat in the seat across from mine, head down over his latest sock project. "Why didn't you mention that Nicolina's grandmother disappeared?"

"Why ever would I mention it, Phoebe?" he said without looking up. "It was all very long ago, besides which, it hardly seemed relevant to our previous discussions. Oh, look at this: the dye is pooling the most hideous splotches just where I'm working an interconnecting line. This is most distressing. It simply does not pay to purchase inferior yarn."

"What happened to the countess?"

"As I recall, she simply disappeared one day, as in vanished. Apparently she was visiting her villa, no doubt for a bit of respite from the Count, and when the maid delivered her breakfast one morning, she was gone. The bed had been slept in, but no countess. It was quite the tabloid fodder in Italy for a while, I must say. Massive hunts ensued; the count issued a hefty reward, but all for naught."

"How long ago was this?"

"Must be nearly 20 years ago now."

"Was foul play suspected?'

"No such determination followed. There were no signs of foul play. The case went cold, all tangled in supposition and conjecture. The dear lady, so gracious and elegant, was prone to depression, as I understand, though at the time such things were never discussed. One theory posed was that she went wandering out onto the terrace one night and possibly stumbled over the wall onto the rocks below."

"Was she a sleepwalker?"

"I have no idea. I used to sleepwalk in my younger years after I'd tippled a bit too much but I certainly never left the house. Even in my sleeping state, I retained rather a heightened sense of self-preservation. Apparently, I'd walk into walls and such, but was not inclined to attempt a marathon."

I waited until he took a breath. "And the countess?"

"No body was never retrieved."

"How old was Nicolina when her grandmother disappeared?"

"Let's see, hmm, twenty, I believe. Yes, twenty. Shortly after the countess's disappearance, Nicolina had a huge argument with her grandfather and exited Italy to London, where she's lived ever since. I gather family relations remain a tad frosty."

"How well do you know her?"

"Oh, well enough. Mable and I attended her wedding to Geoffrey eight years ago, though Mable most definitely did not approve of her choice of husbands, nor did I. She thought Boyd terribly crass, but then, she believed all entrepreneurs suspect on principle. Luckily, she considered me more of a hobbyist than a businessman, though she must have had suspicions. In any case, Mable predicted the union would not be a happy one and she was correct, as always. Mable had an uncanny sixth sense, you know. She—"

"And how did you come to know Nicolina?"

"I met her many years ago when traveling to Italy with my father and, again, later through her grandfather. Count Vanvitelli was quite the collector, you see, with a keen interest in Etruscan art. I had the fortune to source many items for him over the years. He had a penchant for Etruscan jewelry, in particular, though he wouldn't turn down a fine piece of Greek or Roman embellishment. This is one of the many reasons why I am eager to assess the Countess's villa. Perhaps she was the recipient of her husband's exquisite taste, though I am certain the Count kept the gold elsewhere."

"And Nicolina's parents?"

"My word, I feel as though I'm being grilled, Phoebe. They were not collectors, unfortunately. Lucca senior was more of a financier, adept at keeping the family coffers well-greased, a businessman by nature, and his wife, Gordana, loved jewelry but not of the ancient variety. She was more a Bulgari type of girl. I did sell her a lovely pair of Roman earrings once. Quite ironic don't you think, to purchase something in England only to have it return to Italy?"

"You're just keeping up the tradition." I sipped my apple juice and picked up my knitting, selecting a shiny green ribbon to add to the mix.

"Don't be unkind, Phoebe. It doesn't suit you."

"I'm not being unkind, only referencing the pillaging of the ancient world by roving British explorers, archaeologists, and ..." I paused, trawling for the right word. "More recently, entrepreneurs."

The cabin attendant began rolling the refreshment cart down the aisle again. "I could get used to first-class service, but I'm going to excuse myself from the next round. They just announced that we'll be landing in Naples within the hour."

On my way to the toilet, I passed Evan, also traveling first class at his employer's insistence. He lay with his long legs stretched the length of his reclining bed, eyes closed, ears attached to earphones. He was an enigma, that man, but having him around had proved life-saving in the recent past. Who knew when six foot-three inches of well-built male might come in handy?

My imagination swerved to thoughts of Noel—another tall, good-looking man, though much leaner, who certainly came in handy when he was handy. Which he never was.

We landed in Naples an hour later. By the time we stood at the luggage carousel, it was nearly ten o'clock. I yawned as Evan hefted one, two, ten pieces of Louis Vuitton luggage onto a baggage trolley. I sidled up to Rupert. "You do understand that we're only going for maybe two weeks at the most?"

"Two of those are yours. As for the others, a man must be prepared."

"Mine?" I had completely forgotten Foxy's insistence on improving my style. Shit.

A man holding a sign reading RUPERT FOX waited for us in the arrivals area. He shot a worried glance at both the luggage trolley Evan steered as well as at the accompanying overloaded porter he'd commandeered.

"You are from Nicolina Boyd, I presume?" Rupert asked.

"Si, Signora Vanvitelli. Follow me, please."

We followed him across the arrivals level to a multistory garage and a tiny yellow Fiat.

"A Fiat? Surely you jest?" Rupert protested. "Ms. Boyd would never have me transported in such a minuscule vehicle." He surveyed the compact car with disdain. "This just won't do at all."

"At least it's your favorite color," I remarked.

The driver, a lean man of middle height and age, browned by sun, and sporting the thickest, darkest eyebrows I've ever seen, shrugged. "Signora Vanvitelli has not arrived," he said. "We use the Fiats always. Best for our small roads. Please, you get in."

"I will not," Rupert said. "Why, I am quite certain that four bodies plus luggage cannot possibly squeeze into so small a space. What do you think, Evan?"

Evan straightened from loading the luggage and glanced at the car. "It will be a challenge, sir, but I believe we can manage."

The driver flashed a grin. "Yes, see. It works, yes?"

Rupert shook his head. "No, it does not work. You must fetch something else—a nice Mercedes SUV, perhaps. This is an airport, for mercy's sake. They have rental depots here."

"But it is late, Signor Fox. No time. Please, get in."

"I will not."

"Rupert," I said, "It will take at least an hour to rent a car, maybe longer. I'm exhausted. Let's just get on with it, please."

"Oh, very well, but I am not happy, just so you know," he said.

We squeezed into the back seat. Evan took the front passenger side after helping the driver fill every available inch with luggage. Buttressed into position, I could see out the front window only by craning my neck between Rupert's shoulder and his hat box.

"What's your name?" I asked the driver once the car began to slide out of the garage. I gave up trying to catch his eye in the rear view mirror.

"I am Ricardo Di Cappo," he replied.

"Hello, Ricardo. I'm Phoebe McCabe. Call me Phoebe."

"To meet you is very nice, Phoebe."

Nobody had much to say after that.

"I would very much like a cup of tea right now," Rupert said before leaning back and closing his eyes. I peered out the side window at the darkened streets, hungry for a glimpse of this gorgeous country.

I had been to Italy many times when younger but always on guided tours and one back-packing excursion. Even so visits had only been to Florence and Venice. The sight of florescent-limned industrial spaces and chain-linked fences jarred against my vision of Naples. To me, Naples told a color story, some tale of warm-baked yellow set against a blue sky with pastel houses clustered against distant cliffs. Nothing about this nocturnal landscape fit. Eventually, I turned away and dozed.

Later, I jerked awake and stared, confused. The car was slowing down. Beyond the windows, the night spread inky with strings of lights far into the distance. We seemed to be driving right over the edge of a cliff.

Ricardo brought the car to a halt. "We are here. You go. Luggage comes after."

"Go?" I looked around. Behind me a narrow road, ahead a low white wall and darkness. "Go where?"

Rupert sat up and stared. "Oh, we're here, and have not expired in the process. Very good. Well, do wake up, Phoebe. Come along. My legs have cramped horribly."

Evan opened the door and I stepped out into what appeared to be an open-air garage occupied by one other small car—another Fiat—with room for maybe one other vehicle.

Except for a roof of vines and a kind of caged enclosure, it was open to the elements. A low wall ahead separated the parking area from what I assumed to be a drop into the blackness beyond. I could hear the sea crashing below as a warm, humid breeze tugged my hair. I shivered despite the warmth and stepped away, scanning all around seeking the villa.

"I believe the villa must be down, Phoebe, not up, and there is probably no other way to reach it except by a rather horrid set of stairs. Am I correct, Ricardo?"

The driver turned, his arms loaded with luggage. "Stairs, si. Stairs there." He indicated a gate opening on the far end of the parking area.

"As I feared—the Italians and their stairs. They can invent the most amazing things, yet still retain the most primitive means for getting up and down these blasted cliffs." Rupert touched my arm. "Through there, Phoebe."

I reached for my roller bag, but Evan snatched it from my grasp. "Go ahead, madam. Ricardo and I will attend the luggage."

Narrow stairs plunged downward, the only light provided by lamps set into the concrete. Negotiating each irregular step took so much concentration, I couldn't imagine being burdened with baggage, too.

Rupert huffed and muttered while I kept one hand on the wall, my eyes fixed downward. I glanced up only once, surprised to find enormous lemons dangling on the branches overhead.

"This is intolerable," Rupert muttered, stepping over squashed and rotting fruit. "Who is responsible for maintenance around here?" he said loudly.

Ricardo, burdened with luggage and panting heavily, made no comment. He probably lacked the breath.

At last, the steps leveled out and a grand building loomed ahead. Wrapped in shadows, scabs of terracotta paint peeling from its massive sides.

"Oh," I said.

"Yes, exactly." Rupert stood staring.

"Have you been here before?" I asked.

"Never," he said. "I visited one of the Count's other properties in Naples once long ago, but never here. My word, but it's rather rundown, isn't it?"

"It looks ... abandoned," I said.

"You go ... in, please," Ricardo managed to say while nodding toward the front door. "My wife and I, we live in back. Signora Vanvitelli asked that we take care of you. You are ready, yes?"

A sweep of stairs curved up from either side of a small flagstone terrace. I clutched my carpet bag closer and trudged forward, taking the marble steps with my eyes fixed on the lighted door. Behind me, Rupert followed, then Evan and Ricardo.

The moment we stepped into the hall, the men dropped the luggage in the entry and Evan exited for another load. I leaned over to Rupert. "You may be personally responsible for two hernias tonight."

"Nonsense, Evan works out until his muscles are quite formidable."

We gazed around the central hall, my eyes lifting upward to where a high painted ceiling featured nymphs and cherubs cavorting amid yellowing clouds. A tired chandelier pushed bleary light across the scene, illuminating one cherub directly above whose privates appeared to have had flaked away.

"Neutered by time," I whispered.

Rupert glanced up. "Oh, dear, yes. Poor lad won't be chasing nymphs any time soon, will he? What sorry signs of neglect I see all around. We shall have our work cut out for us."

"Please follow," Ricardo urged from halfway up a central staircase. "Your rooms this way."

"What, no refreshment?" Rupert asked, but the man had already disappeared up the stairs.

"Let's just get settled in," I said, heading for the steps. "Forget the tea."

"It appears I have little choice."

Up we went, with no time to do more than glimpse into the two darkened rooms opening on either side of the hall, the furniture in both huddled under white cloths like a crowd of ghosts.

Ricardo led us to the third of three floors and bowed before the first two doors opening along the central hallway. I stepped into the first, a spacious, high-ceilinged brown-painted room with a four-poster bed, minus its canopy. Two lamps glowed on the nightstands.

I was just about to toss my carpet bag on the bench at the foot of the bed when Ricardo poked his head in. "No, very sorry. This gentleman's room. Next door yours."

I turned to Rupert, who only sighed, saying, "Well, brown is more manly, I suppose."

"As if you care." I turned and entered the second room, finding exactly the same arrangement only in a pale blue.

Rupert followed me. "The rooms are quite lovely—Frette bed linen, which is the least one can expect—but I can't abide that fustiness. Rather makes me think I'm encased in a cigar box. The housekeeping leaves much to be desired."

"All I care about is a bed and bath. It all looks very clean," I commented, fingering the antique silk velvet bed hangings, complete with moth holes and few patches. The bedding had been turned down, revealing fine linen sheets wafting the scent of lavender.

"Hmmph." Rupert watched as I found my way to a little table holding bags of mixed nuts, chocolate, mints, and bottles of water. "I have one much like it in my room," he said. "It appears that hotels in the area may have been divested of their minibar offerings. Really, this is not good form."

I popped a handful of peanuts into my mouth and munched without comment. "'Night, Rupert."

"Oh, good. I hear Evan arriving with the rest of our luggage. Until later, Phoebe."

After he'd gone, I strolled to the window to study the faded blue silk drapes sweeping all the way to the ceiling. I stretched my hand through the folds to feel the glass door beyond—a balcony.

"You are comfortable, Signorina?"

I turned to find Ricardo behind me. "Yes, thanks. Would you mind opening the door for me?"

"The door? But the wind, it arrives very fast here. We keep doors closed at night. There are the bugs, yes? Always there are bugs."

"Still, if you wouldn't mind?"

"As you wish." I watched as he swept aside the curtains, unfastened the brass latch, and flung the doors open to the night. He stood back and smiled as the sound of crickets and crashing waves blew in on a briny breeze. "This is good, yes?"

"Very good, thank you."

"We make these rooms ready for you and very much hope you will be comfortable. The bagno, ah, bath, is down the hall to the left, and the toilet beside it. My wife gives breakfast downstairs when you wish."

Rupert appeared in the doorway. "I chose eight o'clock. I trust that is fine by you, Phoebe?"

"Fine by me."

"Very well. I will excuse myself." Ricardo bowed and slipped away.

I followed Rupert out into the hall. "Where is Evan staying?"

"Downstairs, unfortunately. In Italy, they always shove the servants in back rooms, which is quite unacceptable, in Evan's case. I want him on this floor with us, and will make the necessary arrangements tomorrow. In the meantime, Phoebe, isn't this exciting, to be here in this magnificent villa surrounded by all manner of rare and arcane treasures awaiting discovery?" He rubbed his hands together.

"So far, I haven't seen much in the way of valuables, rare or otherwise."

"We have only just arrived. Nicolina will join us soon enough and, in the meantime, we have much work to do. Do you fancy a little knitting before bed? It's not even midnight yet. The lights don't look nearly strong enough but I'm sure we can manage."

"Sorry, but I'm exhausted."

"Very well. I shall save my linen stitch instruction for another evening. Sleep tight, Phoebe. Our rooms are adjoining, by the way. Feel free to latch your side, should you entertain such concerns."

I never worried on that account. Rupert Fox had proved to be as safe a companion as any girlfriend, maybe more so since he'd never want to borrow my clothes.

"Our bathrooms and toilet facilities are opposite one another at the end of the hall," he continued. "I have chosen the suite on the right, though both are exactly alike. I just preferred colored towels to white. Thankfully the plumbing doesn't seem too argumentative. Night-night." And with that, he entered his bronze room and shut the door.

I returned to my chambers, uneasy at the sight of the curtains billowing in the breeze. They subsided once I shut the door to the hall. Breathing deeply, I gazed around at blue walls, stained and blotched in places. Somehow everything old and rundown still manages to look glorious in Italy, as if in tribute to stylish neglect.

Two seascapes hung on either side of the bed, while a huge wardrobe anchored the opposite wall. I strode over and pulled open the door, finding a freshly laundered bathrobe hanging in its cedar lining. I looped the robe over my arm and walked across to the refreshment table to nab a bottle of water and an orange. The little cache also included biscuits, plus a bottle of wine accompanied by two glasses—got to love the Italians.

Sometime when my back was turned, Evan must have placed my roller bag on the bench beside the two matching pieces of Vuitton and flipped open all the lids. My suitcase yawned open on a riot of mismatched colors with yarn stuffing the edges and side pockets. Rupert's designer bags, on the other hand, revealed depressingly tidy piles encased in clear pouches. I slammed their lids shut and dug around in my own bag.

Once I had changed into my comfy plaid tee, I padded to the door in my bare feet clutching my toiletry bag. A lamp glowed midway down the corridor. Good. I did not feel like navigating this house in the dark. When I was halfway down the hall, Rupert stepped out dressed in a navy paisley silk bathrobe and velvet slippers. We both halted, staring at one another.

"Have you even looked inside the luggage I provided?" he asked.

"No. I prefer my own clothes." I marched off down the hall and entered the bathroom with the white towels, when I remembered that I'd forgotten my toothbrush. Back to my room I went. By the time I returned, I could hear the water sloshing behind the door of Rupert's bathroom.

It took nearly 45 minutes to fill the tub sufficiently to cover more than three inches of my person. The whole time the pipes sounded as if a small animal might be fighting for life between the walls. I lay partially submerged, imagining the water flowing down from the Italian Alps along some ancient Roman aqueduct. It must take at least a century for every drop to arrive.

An hour later, I climbed into bed, exhausted and chilled. I lay with the light on, staring up at another painted ceiling, this one depicting an Arcadian landscape of rivers and streams with some distant ruin visible in the shadows on the far side of the room.

A crack ran diagonally across the sky from the ruin to the scene's only two occupants hovering directly overhead: a naked Zephyr and his lady nymph flying hand in hand amid the clouds. The nymph, full-figured and porcelain-skinned, smiled over at her handsome beau, seeming not to notice that his man parts had flaked clean away.

7

The next morning, Rupert stood outside my bedroom door swathed in his paisley robe looking pleased with himself. "I have proper tea. Do join me in my room for a nice brew before we descend to what will surely be a measly cup of brutish espresso."

"How did you come by tea?" I asked, pulling on my terry house robe and following him next door.

"Evan, of course. He set forth to find boiling water, and, naturally, brought all the necessary fixings."

"Naturally."

He swept a hand to one of the little lamp tables, now covered in crisp linen, and serving as a dining table on the balcony. "Always be prepared, Phoebe. I may not have been anything as banal as a Boy Scout but it's a fine adage for any occasion."

I stepped onto the balcony and stared. Ahead, down, and across spread the most stunning vista of earth and sea I had yet to witness—all deep green headlands rising above an azure expanse with little pastel buildings tucked into the hills.

The villa perched high on a cliff with nothing below but a sharp plunge of earth and trees, the surf shrouded from view by the tops of cypress and pine. Directly below the balcony lay a marble terrace lined with potted cypress.

"I love Italy," I said, taking a seat opposite Rupert, "and now I believe I really am on the Amalfi Coast."

"Yes, indeed. We must try to enjoy a little of its glory while here, though certainly not today. Milk, Phoebe?"

"Yes, please." I picked up the delicate Nippon cup. "You even brought your own china?"

"Most certainly. The Italians do not grasp the fine art of tea, though admittedly they do rather well in most culinary areas, excluding breakfast. To pour tea into some diminutive cup designed for lesser brews or—perish the thought—a mug, is just unacceptable."

"Won't Mrs. Di Cappo be expecting us down for breakfast?"

"No doubt. Evan has already done reconnaissance and reported that breakfast is to be no more than the usual European fare of rolls, bread, cheese, and cold meats—no butter, and with oranges only for fruit. Disheartening. I require eggs and bacon to keep constitution sufficiently fortified."

Sipping my tea, I studied him. "Let me guess: You're going to request that Mrs. Di Cappo cook you eggs and bacon?"

Rupert lowered his cup and flicked a fallen leaf from the table with his napkin. "Her name is Sophia, as it turns out, and to answer your question, not unless necessary. First, Evan will source sausages and bacon in town, after which he will endeavor to assume the breakfast duties, if that does not cause too much offense. If that appears to be too great a challenge, he will teach this Sophia the proper manner of cooking these items to my specifications. I will also require fried tomatoes and mushrooms, produce I know is available in abundance in this country. It should all work out rather well."

"For you. So Evan will teach an Italian how to cook?"

Rupert dabbed his mouth with the napkin before folding it on the table beside his silver teaspoon. "Evan is a Cordon Bleu chef, Phoebe."

"Your bodyguard is a chef?" Really, nothing should surprise me with either of them.

"He's not my bodyguard, but my driver and assistant. I only employ the most talented, as you surely know." He paused for a moment, smiling to himself as he topped up his tea. "He also happens to have been a Formula One racing driver. He will be up directly to clear the table."

"And a waiter. Is it true that he was once with Her Majesty's Secret Service?"

"Possibly. A man of many talents. As I was about to say, following that, we will descend to the dreary breakfast offerings."

Suddenly aware of how my hair erupted from my head like Medusa's last stand, I decided to dress before Evan arrived. "Excuse me," I said, climbing to my feet. "I'll meet you down there. Thanks for the tea."

On my way out, I scanned the ceiling, gazing up at another mythical scene. A satyr chased a nymph, who turned around to smile at this master of all things hairy and horny, while other nude maidens frolicked on the sidelines. The satyr kept his parts well-hidden so I couldn't check to see if he remained intact.

Back in my room, I set Rupert's two uber expensive pieces of luggage against the wall, and dug through my own roller, removing the jeans and olive green tee-shirt that Rena had given me, a shirt she insisted hugged my curves. Since we were working that day, I considered this practical.

When I tried to drag a comb through my hair, I realized had I left all my antifrizz concoctions and smoothing elixirs in London. Here in sleek, tanned Italy, I was destined to be pale, freckled, and bushy. In desperation, I clamped my curls into a kind of bun.

Downstairs, the morning light cast a somber glow on the fading paint, cracks, and stains, while revealing a grand old villa in the Baroque style. I strolled down the travertine corridor towards the sound of voices until I entered a large dining area where glass doors had been thrown open to the terrace. Rupert sat outside under a grape-entwined colonnade, deep in conversation with Evan. Both men turned to me as I approached.

"Phoebe, I neglected to mention earlier that I have heard from Nicolina and she requests that we carry on with our task until she arrives tomorrow evening."

"Fine." I took the seat Evan scraped back for me and allowed him to adjust the snowy napkin on my lap. Before me sat a basket of rolls, a plate of sliced cheese, cold meats, and quartered oranges. "Looks good," I remarked reaching for a bun. "Is Ricardo's wife around?"

Rupert cleared his throat. Today he had donned a navy twill smoking jacket with a jonquil ascot tied at his neck. He did not appear outfitted for a day poking around dusty old things, but then, I knew Evan got dirty so Rupert didn't have to. "Sophia will no doubt join us directly. I'm afraid she's rather piqued at the moment."

Several minutes passed before Sophia marched out bearing a pot of steaming coffee and a fixed smile. "Buon giorno, madam," she greeted while refilling both my and Rupert's mug. Evan had retreated.

"Thank you for the buns. Did you make them?" I asked smiling up at the woman's tense face.

Sophia shrugged by way of saying she did not speak English, which prompted Rupert to translate along with his own editorial. "She did not make the buns, Phoebe, but purchased them at a local bakery: hence they are not fresh, quite dry, in truth. Can you imagine? Purchasing buns in Italy when you are entertaining esteemed guests at a former countess's villa? Quite unacceptable. Evan can whip up a batch with his eyes closed and he hails from east Wiltshire."

A brief but lively exchange erupted between Sophia and Rupert, which I sensed had nothing to do with buns. Sophia turned on her heels and marched back into the house.

"I gather that educating Italians to British mores is not going well." I speared a piece of cheese with my fork.

"Not so much British mores as the proper care of guests. When the owner of an estate has allowed staff to grow flaccid, service sags Try the oranges, Phoebe. At least they are fresh."

The remainder of breakfast passed with more of Rupert's disgruntled mutterings, while I tried to block out his griping and savor the view.

An hour later, we got to work in the first of the two major salons, Evan and Ricardo standing by to assist. Apparently, Nicolina had instructed us to focus on the lower floor's two salons until she arrived.

We would gather the objects, room by room, and compile them by category—art, textiles, china, objects of interest. Anything not worthy of our attention, such as ashtrays and coasters, would be piled in one corner, not that I could see any ashtrays or coasters. The room had obviously not entertained anybody for many years.

I looked around. "It doesn't look like there's much here." The room held the minimum of furniture and decorative objects, much as one might expect in a hotel that had been packed away for the season. Yet, with its baroque plasterwork and painted ceiling, it managed to look lush. Several paintings hung on the walls. A Venetian mirror in an ornate gilt frame hung over the marble fireplace, with one tapestry hanging opposite the Palladium windows. Otherwise, the ornate marble-topped tables held lamps and vases.

"Possibly the more valuable objects are stored elsewhere," Rupert said, frowning.

"What were you expecting?"

"At the very least, I thought I might find a fine painting or two."

"The place has been vacant for years, perhaps decades, so it's not surprising it's been stripped. But from the way Nicolina spoke ... " I turned to Ricardo. "Ricardo, have other family members removed some items, to your knowledge?"

"I am most sorry, but Sophia and I have been only here five years. Other caretakers before."

"Maybe everything's been plucked," I said to Rupert.

"I certainly hope not, for Nicolina's sake. Do let us begin," Rupert said, raising his hands like a conductor signaling his orchestra. "Evan, please be so kind as to bring that painting over to the light. Yes, that's the one. Though it looks much like a neoclassical piece, I suspect it may be considerably later. Yes, the others, too."

Rupert lowered his head over the paintings, muttering to himself all the while. Meanwhile, Ricardo removed all the drop-cloths in both salons, and assisted Evan with taking down the artwork and the two tapestries.

Approximately an hour later, Rupert raised his head, eying Ricardo.

"Ricardo, do tell me what else you have by way of vehicles should I wish to take Phoebe for a bit of touring?"

"The Fiats, Signor. No others."

"The Fiats," Rupert repeated. "A Fiat is not what I had in mind." Moments later, he sent Ricardo and Evan off to rent a car. "Get something suitable, whatever your choice," Rupert told Evan. "We'll need it for touring. You know my preferences."

"Yes, sir."

After they left, Rupert busied himself investigating the paintings, one by one. I focused on one of the two wall-mounted tapestries which Evan had placed on the floor before leaving. The textile featured a woman in eighteenth century clothing strolling beside the Grand Canal, accompanied by her servants and a dog, the Rialto bridge visible in the background. I scrutinized the weaving, witnessing the damage up close, mourning the biggest holes.

On my knees, I scanned every inch with a magnifying glass, pausing long enough to take photos of each segment. The threads were wool on silk, the tapestry delicate, and I estimated at least 250 years old. It was time-consuming work, but absorbed me totally, right up until voices outside broke my concentration.

I looked up. Rupert was staring towards the windows. "Whatever is that?" he asked.

"Company," I said. "But isn't Nicolina only arriving tomorrow?"

"So she said, and Evan couldn't have returned so soon."

"Then who comes a-calling?" I asked.

We dusted ourselves off and went to the Palladium windows. A white convertible sat parked in the driveway with two black sedans pulled up behind. A man with a high forehead and receding hairline stood by the driver's side, peeling off a pair of leather gloves. His deep tan contrasted with his cream linen suit, the whole package a study in relaxed Mediterranean insouciance.

Two others, dressed similarly, though not as impeccably, strolled up to stand beside him. The first man turned to study the house. Instinctively, we stepped back from the window.

"It can't be," said Rupert. "This won't do at all."

"Who are they?" But before Rupert could answer, the door swung open and the men stepped into the hallway.

We hurried to meet them. The driver of the convertible spied us at once, and said something in Italian.

Rupert stiffened and stepped forward, his hand extended. "Count Vanvitelli, what an unexpected pleasure. I am Sir Rupert Fox. You may remember me. I was acquainted with your grandfather. We met many years ago."

Count Vanvitelli shook Rupert's hand but withdrew it quickly. "Rupert Fox," he said, changing to perfect English. "Forgive me, the name seems familiar yet I cannot place it."

"I have done a little business with your late grandfather in the past, as I mentioned. My sincere condolences."

"Yes, indeed, but my grandfather was of an age." And then he flicked a cool gaze over me and issued a thin smile. "And this must be your assistant."

I stepped forward. "No, I own another firm specializing in rare textiles, but Sir Rupert Fox and I are working together at your sister's request." We shook hands, though nothing in my hand-shaking experience had ever been quite like that. He merely squeezed my three middle fingers and held them for a few seconds along with my gaze, before abruptly dropping both.

"And where is Nicolina?" He swung around as if half-expecting to find her hiding behind a door.

"She is not here at present," Rupert explained. "She expects to arrive tomorrow night."

He turned to Rupert. "And what is your business exactly?"

Rupert cleared his throat. "Nicolina has requested that we do a first assessment of the villa's contents in preparation for sale."

The Count's aquiline features darkened. "For sale, you say? I am certain you misunderstand." He gazed down the hall before snapping his fingers at his companions. Both men darted off, one upstairs, the other down the hall, while Vanvitelli strolled into the first salon, hands plunged into his trousers.

Rupert and I hastened after him.

"What can we do to assist you, Signor Vanvitelli?" Rupert asked.

The Count nodded. "Nothing, in fact. Our family has very reputable assessors and auctioneers on retainer who are familiar with Italian antiquities. What is your background and experience?"

Rupert launched into his boilerplate resumé, which included the names of several references of notable European collectors and art aficionados. Nothing appeared to impress Vanvitelli. I didn't even warrant consideration, apparently, which suited me. After several minutes of continued scrutiny, the count wandered across the hall to the next salon, and continued his investigation.

Rupert tried several times to engage him in conversation but the man barely acknowledged his existence. Soon, one of the men returned to the salon and addressed his employer in Italian. They exchanged a few sentences while Rupert listened intently and dabbed his brow with his hankie. Following the return of the second man, the Count nodded to Rupert. "I will depart now. Please inform my sister that I will return." And with that, he swept from the house, his men following behind.

"What just happened?" I asked Rupert once the door clicked shut behind them.

"We have just encountered the bully who Nicolina had hoped would stay far away. It seems we will not be so lucky."

"I admit that he's the first count I've ever met, but he struck me as a bit off. What's with the two dudes he sent to search the house? Did he think Nicolina might be hiding under the bed, or was he looking for something else?"

Rupert dabbed his forehead again. "I have no idea, Phoebe. Do stop with the questions. Let us proceed with our tasks until Evan returns and we can go forth some place suitable for lunch. No doubt Sophia will only toss a desiccated sandwich in our direction, if she deigns to feed us at all."

Halfway into the first salon he halted. "I forgot that I told Evan to fetch some food stores before returning. Now we will waste away while waiting for a suitable repast."

I brushed past him. "If you hadn't turned your nose up at breakfast, you might be better fortified now. Let's get to work. That will take your mind off your stomach." Judging from Rupert's girth, I doubted he was in much danger from fainting.

An hour or so later we were still hard at work. Rupert mumbled over a set of vases while I turned my attention to the second tapestry, a fifteenth century Flemish piece of deer leaping through a flower-strewn forest. It was exquisite, the mille fleurs spreading a carpet of flowers against a rich forest-green background. The quality of the mordants coupled with the expert weaving had left this piece much less damaged than the first, despite its age. Even so, the backing had begun to disintegrate and I knew the piece needed a strong dose of preventive medicine.

"This needs reconstructive surgery by a qualified textile restorer," I said, scrutinizing the silk velvet backing. "I know conservationists in England, not here. Still, this is valuable. I ..." I looked up, my words fading away. The room was empty. "Rupert?" I stood up.

The salon across the hall was also empty. Returning to the corridor, I strode towards the dining room and kitchen areas, passing several doors that opened into a library, a den, a storage room, and a cloak closet, respectively, all vacant. Even the kitchen, a large room with a massive stove and fridge, smelling faintly of disinfectant, sat still.

My feet echoing on the tiles brought the full impact of being alone in this painted vault of a house. Overhead, a slipstream of bucolic cupids grinned down, that one male missing his key anatomical piece.

What was going on here, what *had* gone on here?

I called out to Rupert all the way up the grand staircase. On the second floor landing, I paused. The hall hung in shadows, but for the light shining through the balcony door at the far end. Faint sounds rustled midway down.

Removing my sandals, I padded down the corridor, the marble cool on my bare feet, until I reached a half-open door. Poking my head in, I was greeted by the back-end of Sir Rupert Fox on hands and knees rifling through a kind of storage cubbyhole, one hand holding a flashlight.

"Looking for something in particular?" I asked.

He backed out and hefted himself upright, red-faced, and perspiring. "Phoebe."

"Rupert."

"Have you completed your task so soon?" He pulled a hankie from his pocket and mopped his forehead.

"Have you?" I leaned against the door jamb.

"Certainly. I was just assisting Nicolina by searching for more valuable objects than the paltry items downstairs."

I glanced down at the brass padlock on the floor. "By breaking into her cupboards?"

"I did not break in, Phoebe, I merely removed a particularly troublesome hindrance which I shall henceforth reapply."

"And did you find anything?"

"No, I did not." He stooped to pick up the lock, slammed the cupboard door shut, and clicked the device in place.

"What are you looking for?"

"Valuables, rare items that may rescue Nicolina from her increasingly dire circumstances. Back up, Phoebe."

I stepped back into the hall. "Maybe it's time you told me what's really going on."

"I had hoped Nicolina herself might disclose the details, as I'm sure she will when she arrives, but for now suffice to say that things have grown rather worse for her of late."

"How so?"

"Nicolina filed for divorce the day she left for Italy. She had reason to believe this villa would be her financial salvation, given that she signed a most unfortunate prenuptial agreement with Geoffrey. However, last night she called to say her lawyer has dropped a bomb that shatters that assessment: her grandfather did not deed this villa to his late wife without strings. In fact, it is destined to remain as part of the Vanvitelli holdings. Nicolina may live here until she passes, and even sell the contents, but not the villa. If we don't find significant assets, she will be destitute."

❧ 8 ❧

I followed Rupert downstairs. "I don't understand prenuptial agreements."

"That is because you are not wealthy. Prenuptial contracts ensure that whatever assets go into a marriage remain with the original parties in the event of a divorce."

"I understand them in the legal sense—I studied law, remember. What I meant is, I don't get why two people who supposedly love each other would even agree to such a contract."

"And so I return to my original utterance: because you are not wealthy. When Nicolina married Geoffrey, he was by far the wealthier of the pair, while Nicolina had reason to believe she might eventually inherit at least a portion of her grandparents' multitudinous estates. Neither party wished to lose their assets in the event of a divorce—divorce hardly being a rare occurrence these days—hence the prenuptial."

"So, love wasn't the focus of that marriage contract but preserving assets was?"

"Phoebe, to the very wealthy, marriage is often about maintaining power and resources, and forging family alliances. To many, love is either a lucky happenstance or an emotional nuisance. Not all embrace the more romantic view."

"All right then, humor me: Nicolina married Geoffrey thinking she had something worth protecting but now learns she owns nothing outright?"

"Under the terms of the will, it has been revealed that only the contents fully belong to Nicolina. She has been granted the right to stay here as long as she lives, after which the property returns to the original Vanvitelli trust, of which she has been excluded."

"But now we see the contents may have been stripped."

"So it appears."

We arrived at the bottom hallway. Rupert swatted the dust from his navy twill sleeves.

"But I thought Nicolina's grandmother protected the estate for her?" I persisted.

"As did Nicolina but the fine print says otherwise. Most distressing. The late Count Vanvitelli had purchased the villa as a wedding present for his bride while never intending for her to own it outright. He was a man who preferred to keep all assets under the family name."

"And married females were not apt to retain the family name."

"And married females living in London, even less so. Count Vanvitelli had no intention of dispersing the estate equally between the two grand-children, either. Indeed, everything goes to Lucca, the eldest, the male, and henceforth the new Count Vanvitelli, as is the tradition."

"Even now, in the twenty-first century."

"Phoebe, look around. You are in Italy, the most artfully designed, brilliantly modern bastion of tradition in existence—after Britain, of course."

"But surely her parents ensured she inherited directly from them?"

"Her father was to be the next Count Vanvitelli, so he was essentially awaiting his inheritance, also. What monies they had in their own names were dispersed between both children, true, but that was over a decade ago. I understand the largess received made for a comfortable buffer rather than a handsome inheritance. In Nicolina's case, it is all but gone, used by her husband for his various investments."

"Wouldn't Nicolina's brother ensure that she's well-provided for? Oh, hell—forget I said that. I just made her sound like a spinster aunt from a Victorian novel."

Rupert's small blue eyes glittered fiercely. "Rather. I have no idea what her brother's intentions are, but why should she be placed in such an untenable position? Either way, it is an appalling situation, and one we must help rectify."

"How? Nothing I've seen inside this villa can possibly provide a living for anyone."

"Exactly."

"So," I took a deep breath. "What are you looking for, Rupert?"

"I just told you."

"No you didn't. You have your eye out for something very valuable, something specific. Tell me what it is so I can help you find it."

A speck of dirt on Rupert's right sleeve demanded his immediate attention. "I continue to seek anything that might help improve the sum total of her assets."

"What aren't you telling me?"

He continued to pick delicately at that stain. "We have always had an agreement between us, Phoebe. I tell you what you need to know, when you need to know it. All else falls into the best-you-stay-out-of-it category. How many times have you told me how you don't want to know the details of my interests?"

"What does that have to do with us being here? Here your interests are Nicolina's interests, right?"

His eyes met mine at last. "Exactly so."

"But?"

"But what?"

"Rupert, you insisted I come here with you and here I am. At least you could tell me what you're hiding."

He pressed his hands together. "I apologize, Phoebe, truly, but I assured Nicolina that her secrets are safe with me. You must ask her the details when she arrives."

Sophia did not make an appearance again that day and, when Evan had not returned by 1:00, Rupert called him and discovered that he had driven the new rental up the coast in search of the choicest offerings for breakfast.

"Select something for supper tonight, also, my good man," I heard Rupert say. "Sophia has quite disappeared, so I shall have you cook supper tonight. I had planned on taking us all out to dine but, under the circumstances, believe it best we remain on the premises until Nicolina arrives."

Once Rupert clicked off, he turned to me as I gathered the bread and cheese for lunch. The refrigerator was all but bare. "You should not have to do this, Phoebe."

"Making lunch is no problem. Unlike you, I do it all the time. Why do you think it's best we stay around 'under the circumstances.' What circumstances?"

"Nothing of import. It's just that the house feels rather in an uproar and you fixing lunch is simply unacceptable," Rupert said, following me outside. "That's what we have servants for. We need tea."

"I plugged in the kettle. Cordon Bleu training is not necessary to boil water, either," I said. "I could teach you, if you want."

"Don't be facetious, Phoebe."

"I wasn't."

But even after I made the tea according to his specifications, using his teapot with the tea warmed perfectly with the tea cozy provided, he still complained all the way through lunch. Finally, I picked up my cheese and bread, grabbed my mug, and strolled along the terrace.

"That's very rude, Phoebe," Rupert called after me. "One should never leave a dining companion, let alone eat while walking."

"I'm strolling," I said over my shoulder. "Consider this the ultimate in slow food movement. I'm sure you'll be fine on your own for a few minutes."

The sun beat down upon the terrace, hot and bright. This time of year, the weather cooled at night but burned warm and brilliant during the day. I scuffed my sandals over the stones, imagining the grand parties that might have swirled on this terrace once. Now grass sprouted between cracked and broken flagstones.

Over the marble balustrade and far away, the sea plunged a deep shining blue speckled with white and the occasional fishing boat. Every part of me longed for that water, to swim, to sail, to just be. My brother and I had grown up by the ocean and I wondered where Toby was now. Sailing somewhere on the Mediterranean, I guessed, probably with Noel, his only companion. Though I longed for both in different ways, I needed to forge a life for myself without either. That left all my empty places aching, but I saw no other way.

I sipped my tea and gazed out towards the horizon. Finishing up the last of my sandwich, I left plate and mug on the marble balustrade and carried on.

The back of the villa claimed the earth and sea as its yard, so I guessed a stairway down to the shore must be tucked away somewhere. I found it at the far edge of the property, in an overgrown copse of cedar and untidy rosebushes. A marble stairway sprouting grass and weeds curved downward and disappeared from view.

Slipping in and out of the sun, I dove down through the cedars and cypress on steps scummed with moss. It was a long way down. I counted two hundred and ninety-five steps, with terraces of lemon and olive trees along the way, each level offering a landing with a marble bench flanked by statues of a Roman god and goddess, one on each side.

I passed Athena and Apollo, Mars and Venus, Janus and Vesta. My childhood ancient mythology obsession helped me recognize each deity. Mars carried a shield, Venus a myrtle crown. The statues were reproductions of original Roman sculptures and probably the same age as the villa.

At the bottom, the steps morphed into a narrow stone path curving against the cliff edged by a rusty railing. I carried along, ducking beneath the overhanging vines, until I rounded a corner to arrive at a small stone jetty. Metal stumps sticking out from the crumbling concrete indicated this must have been a swimming platform once, but the waves crashing against the edges weren't welcoming, even for me. I turned and followed the path back to where Neptune gazed out to sea at the base of the stairs.

Unlike the other gods, the lord of the ocean stood alone, a broken trident grasped in his mighty hand. A goddess companion wasn't the only thing he was missing. Someone had smashed away his man-barnacles. And this was no accidental maiming. Nothing else had been damaged, and the exposed marble shone white under the breakage. The deed had been done recently and with force. It would take an ax or a hammer to smash away thick marble like that.

None of this made sense.

Minutes later, I trudged my way back up, stopping at the first landing, this one opening onto a narrow olive grove. Jupiter and Minerva stood guard here. Minerva held a vase of mangy weeds, too pitiful for such a brainy goddess but better off than what the top god, Jupiter, endured. He'd had his nuts knocked off, too. In fact, as I investigated every landing, every statue, on my way back up, I discovered that no god remained intact.

I trudged upwards. What the hell was going on here? Had some man-hating Amazon broken in and mutilated everything male in the villa?

When I reached the terrace, Rupert was waiting. "Phoebe, please don't just take off like that. I worry so."

I leaned against the balustrade, panting. "Why? You knew I wouldn't have gone far. But listen, I've discovered the most amazing ... things, or absence of ... things"

"What did you find down there? Something of interest, perhaps?"

I narrowed my eyes. "Like what?"

"Oh, you know, anything—maybe a tomb or something of that ilk?"

"Why would you expect to find the family crypt on the family's holiday villa? Unless you're more specific, I can't help you. I saw lots of things—waves, moss, crumbling stairs, missing genitalia."

"Phoebe, you can be incorrigible sometimes." He turned and marched back towards the kitchen, me following behind. "Try not to wander off again."

"I did see something interesting."

He turned.

"All the male statues have their bits smashed off," I said. "Off as in deliberately castrated. Have you noticed that every male painting or sculpture on this property is missing his critical elements?"

"Such as that unfortunate flying eunuch in the hallway?"

"Him, plus every one of his fellows. Try looking up. I've yet to see a nude male left intact. Haven't you noticed?"

Rupert's bristly eyebrows meshed. "I never look up, if I can help it. A rather nasty mishap on a motorcycle years ago left me with a permanent neck injury so, no, I have not noticed. How extraordinary. Who would do such a thing?"

"A very angry woman, or maybe two very angry women."

We were standing eye to eye. "What would make a woman that angry?" he asked.

"Oh, I can think of dozens of things—betrayal or adultery, for a start, but the real question is who did it, and when? Who felt such rage that she would vandalize art?"

"Maybe it was just that—a vandal."

"Inside the villa, on a stepladder, targeting only males?"

"Nevertheless, that doesn't sound like something a woman would do, especially not a countess, if that's what you're implying."

"What does being a countess have to do with it? Passion is passion, and are you inferring women can't climb ladders or wield sledge hammers?"

"Well, no, of course not, but how likely is that in such a place?"

"As likely as any other, once we know the story behind it."

"Surely you are not considering the late countess as being capable of such an act?"

"Why not? But there's been somebody else also, somebody more recent. Those gods on the steps were parted with their jewels relatively recently."

"That is preposterous. Nobody's lived here for many years, and Nicolina has only made periodic visits. Why would she deface her own property?"

"But it's not hers, is it? How long has she really known that this estate doesn't fully belong to her? Anything fixed to the walls or part of the property belongs to the Vanvitelli estate—that means frescoes, even statues—so she wouldn't be defacing her own property, would she?"

"Really, Phoebe, I do not appreciate this line of inquiry one iota. We are here to help Nicolina, not accuse her of some preposterous crime. Come, I hear voices from the kitchen. I believe Evan has returned and possibly Sophia, also. Enough of this." And with that, he swung around and darted away.

9

Sophia's voice rose from the kitchen, shrilling above Evan's whose tone remained calm and matter-of-fact—in Italian. The man spoke Italian, too. Hell.

Since I couldn't understand, I didn't linger, and neither did Rupert. Both of us veered away from the kitchen, with him muttering something about his presence being "an unfair advantage," as if that ever worried him before.

I resolved to resume work on the second tapestry, only it occurred to me, as I gazed down at the Flemish masterpiece minutes later, that I was nearly finished. Two hours' work max and my job at the villa would be complete, unless Nicolina pointed me in another direction. Whatever textile collection her grandmother may have once owned had long gone.

I wandered out into the central hallway and saw Rupert in the first salon holding a large blue and white vase. He caught my eye and sighed. "It pretends to be Ming," he commented.

"A forgery?"

"A reproduction, no doubt replacing the authentic item that once resided within these walls."

"I'll leave you to it, then." I continued strolling through the villa, my gaze on the ceilings. Most of the murals on the bottom floor were landscapes, the cupid slipstream in the hall being the only place with nude males. Even then, all but one wore strategically placed wisps of fabric, or were orientated in such a way that the critical bits were shielded. Only that one little guy over the entrance let it all hang out and look where that got him.

At last, I escaped the glowering house, stepped down the front steps and onto the tiny front patio. There, Ricardo was busy washing down the flagstones. I greeted him and strode under a lemon tree to pull out my phone. In seconds I was connected to London. "Max?"

"Phoebe! How's it going down there?"

"Fine, but a little slow. I mean, there's not much here in the way of textiles, so I'll be done with my part soon. How are things at the gallery?"

"Good, I'd say. I delivered the carpets to the restaurant. Susan Rafuse had the gall to question the price on one of the pieces, though I negotiated with Geoffrey Boyd, not her. Irked me, I tell you."

"Did you get hold of Geoffrey to clarify things?"

"I tried, but he's out of the country."

"He's got a cell number, doesn't he?"

"No one's willing to give it to me. Not to worry, I'll handle it. I have the paperwork. So, tell me, what has old Foxy been up to?'

"Mostly complaining but I'm almost getting used to that."

"He can be such a pain in the butt sometimes."

We chatted for a while longer, Max passing me on to Rena, who rattled off a hundred questions on my first impressions of Amalfi, which I couldn't provide, since I hadn't left the villa. In the end, I hung up feeling fortified after a little inoculation of home.

Back at the villa, Ricardo was busy sweeping the front terrace. Pocketing my phone, I strode towards him. "Ricardo, do you have a ladder?"

"A ladder?" he asked, looking up.

I finger-mimed climbing a stepladder. "Something to climb up so I can investigate the top of the curtains?" That sounded lame even to me, but I guessed Ricardo had long ago given up questioning odd requests.

"You wish to climb up to look at curtains?" Well, maybe he hadn't.

"I must decide whether they are salvageable."

He opened his mouth as if to say something, but closed it abruptly and walked away, one finger raised in the wait-a-minute signal. He returned shortly with an aluminum stepladder balanced over his shoulder.

"Sorry, that's too short."

"Too short?"

"The windows reach up to the ceiling. You must have a very tall stepladder designed for reaching the tops of the windows, or even the ceiling?"

"Of course. One momento." He dashed away again, returning moments later with a much longer, much older, wooden version.

"That looks like it's been around awhile."

Ricardo nodded. "Yes, very old, but still safe. I check."

"Oh, great." I pointed up the stairs. "Upstairs in my bedroom, please. I'll take the other end."

"Si," he said and together we maneuvered up the stairs.

On the way up, I asked him, "Which room belonged to the late Countess?"

"Yours, Signorina. Mrs. Boyd want you there."

Interesting. So, I was staying in the same room where the lady had mysteriously disappeared years ago? Now I'd sleep soundly for sure.

"Please put it over there." I indicated the window and watched as he propped open the contraption's legs, shook it briefly, and indicated it was ready to use.

"I climb up and take curtains down for you, yes?"

"No, but thanks."

He stood watching. "I stay for your safety."

"No, go please. This will take a while, and I prefer to work alone."

"But you climb. Not safe to climb alone. I stay, yes?"

"Go. Please."

Finally, I shooed him out. The moment he disappeared, I locked the door before scraping the ladder inch-by-inch to below the two lovers flying overhead. I gave the ladder a few forceful shakes, having good reason to distrust climbing apparatus on principle. Paint speckled its legs and the bolt holes were rusty but it still seemed sturdy enough.

I began to climb up, a long way up. Though sunshine pushed through the windows, the higher I got, the less light reached the ceiling, yet still the mural glowed. When I reached the final step, the ceiling remained two feet overhead. About three feet to the right, directly over the bed, the lovers flew in a muted explosion of blues, cream, and greens. Though the clouds had sallowed to yellow, and the sky dipped to a saddened blue, I imagined their original glory.

It was a fresco. The artist had applied the pigment directly onto the wet plaster, aka Michelangelo and the Renaissance masters, a method that didn't require binders, since the drying plaster became the fixative. I had tried the technique long ago in art classes, and always appreciated the speed and confidence an artist needed to execute this style.

I stared up at the painting, struck by the delicate rendering of the faces —a nymph whose eyes sparkled and whose flushed cheeks glowed above a tiny irregular birthmark on her chin. Did nymphs have birthmarks? Elemental creatures born from river and stream, earth and sky, were supposed to be perfect. On the other hand, the villa dated from the late eighteenth century when beauty spots became a fashionable affectation. But this was more splotch than spot. Still...

My attention slid across to Zephyr, her beau, distinctive by the wind that tangled his long shoulder-length hair and his slightly blue body tinge, as if he shivered in his own cool. His face, however, warmed in health and appreciation of his lady, the look in his eyes luminous with love and desire.

He was as handsome as she was beautiful, but why such an extraordinary nose? These two, though attractive, bore human flaws. I stared at Zephyr's finely formed lips curving into a smile as he locked eyes with his lady-love. Lucca's nose was similar, as was his mouth, only when I saw him yesterday, his had lips curved down with disdain.

Well, damn, these were portraits! I was gazing up at the late Count and Countess Vanvitelli flying in nude youth and love, though the surrounding sky must have been painted centuries earlier. Even the range of flesh tones and the clarity of the color hinted of a different artist, a different time. Who had painted over the original faces in this tribute to love fresh and flying free if not Nicolina's grandmother, herself an artist?

Finally, my eyes skimmed down Zephyr's naked torso to his missing gonads. Whether Count Vanvitelli's likeness had extended to all aspects, I'd never know. Fishing my iPhone from my pocket, I took several photos before turning my attention to the long diagonal crack that erupted between the lovers and extended all the way across the ceiling to just above the wardrobe. I expected it to be a natural fissure, the result of the house settling, or even an earthquake, but not this. Like the angry castration, the fissure had been gouged deep into the plaster, so deep in places that the wood showed through.

I climbed down and inched the ladder over by the wardrobe where the fissure ended in what looked to be a ruin on a hill. Once I reached the top of the ladder, I needed the phone light to see the artwork. Definitely a ruin, but not one I would expect in a classic fresco. Instead of the usual crumbling white columns, this looked more like a castle with a medieval bell tower and an unusually long drawbridge. Why a castle in a classic mythological scene?

After taking more photos, I climbed down, landing just as somebody knocked on my door.

Rupert stood in the hallway. "Phoebe, what are you up to? Ricardo said you were looking at the tops of the drapery, which I knew could not be correct."

"I was investigating the ceiling and, just as I thought, somebody has chiseled into the fresco. Rupert, someone personalized the faces of Zephyr and a nymph, too, but neutered Zephyr. It must have been the missing countess, who was also an artist. There are other inconsistencies. Look, I'll show you."

"Why is that even important? Phoebe, do not allow yourself to be sidetracked. I came to inform you that something fortifying awaits us on the terrace—tea, well and proper—and that Evan will be creating a magnificent meal for us tonight. Care to join me?"

❧ 10 ❧

We dined under the pergola overlooking the sea, the table set with fine china and a crisp linen tablecloth so new, I suspected it had been purchased that very day. Evan's cooking exceeded my expectations and the wine even more so. Sophia and Ricardo vacated the scene while he prepared our feast, which was probably a good thing. With bruschetta, insalata mista, a primi of seafood pasta, and a secondi of grilled fish with vegetables, dining stretched well into the evening.

Rupert leaned towards me, bottle in hand, about to tip the last of the vintage white into my glass. "Phoebe, do drink up. That's a fine Orvieto selected to pair perfectly with the dish."

I held up my hand. "No, thanks. If I'm not careful, I'll be asleep within the hour. Is there coffee?"

"Coffee?" Rupert asked.

I may as well requested nitroglycerin.

"Yes, coffee. I could really do with a cup."

"Would you prefer espresso or Americano, madam?" Evan asked, appearing at my elbow like Zephyr blown in on a breeze.

I gazed up at him. The man looked so damn good in an apron. "Americano, please."

He bowed and dashed inside, my eyes fixed on him until he disappeared.

"Phoebe."

I swung back to Rupert. "Yes?"

"You are not listening."

"Sorry. What did you say?"

"I said that Nicolina will be arriving the day after tomorrow. She called to alert me to the fact that she's been held up again, and wishes us to carry on without her."

"Carry on with what? There are no textiles other than the two tapestries, and it doesn't look as you have much more to do on your end, either. What about the other floors?"

"The second floor is all bedrooms, much like our own, whereas the third floor appears to be stock full of a myriad of dreary household items of little worth."

"So what are we to carry on with?"

"I am certain she has other places unknown to us which she wishes us to search."

"Search?"

"I meant to say, survey, of course. Certainly Nicolina indicated that the villa contained items of worth."

"I'll be interested to know where they're stored."

The coffee arrived. I smiled up at Evan and added sugar to my mug. "As well as why the women of this household took axes and chisels to every exposed man parts. If I were you, I'd keep my legs crossed." I was looking at Evan.

"That would be most difficult to move, Madam," he smiled. Such a great smile, too.

"Really, Phoebe," Rupert interrupted, sounding annoyed. "The state of the fixed objects is not our concern. Consider that a private matter best ignored while we are guests."

"Excuse me?" I turned back to him. "Cupid's flying right over the doorway, making his damage hard to ignore."

"Nevertheless, we don't wish to cause Nicolina undue distress by bringing up these distasteful things. We have been brought here for a specific task. Let us stay focused, shall we?"

I gave up on engaging him on the topic and savored my coffee and the view, at least until Evan retreated and I had to gaze at the Amalfi. Later, we retired to Rupert's room for a knitting session.

We sat companionably together straining our eyes beside the little lamp—he working on his linen-stitch scarf, me on my free-flow wrap. He insisted the doors remain open in case somebody somewhere thought we were up to no good. Apparently knitting is perceived to be the epitome of innocence and open doors proved we were at it.

"I neglected to request that Evan purchase decent lamps," Rupert said.

The man himself could probably hear us from across the hall, if he was listening, and I suspected he always listened. Somehow he managed to clean the dishes in record time. Sophia had finally agreed to make up the room for him earlier in the day, and Rupert's right-hand man now sat with his laptop.

I tried not to steal too many glances, but he piqued my curiosity. What was he studying, with his legs stretched out in the ultimate man-spread and those wire-rimmed glasses on his fine, straight nose? Why did I even care? Noel would have looked just as gorgeous in that position, not that I'd ever seen him in any setting quite so domestic. Not that I'd ever seen him in any domestic position, period, though I'd readily recalled a few carnal ones.

"Phoebe, is the wine affecting you? You are quite flushed." Rupert studied me over the top of his glasses.

"That must be it—you know me and wine—but supper was delicious, wasn't it? I love the way Evan seasoned that fish with fresh lemons and that bruschetta—magnifico!"

Rupert peered at me sharply. I dropped my eyes, trying to focus on my wrap, but my gaze soon slid off again, landing on a framed picture Rupert had propped on his nightstand. The head and shoulders of two young people beamed out at the camera—a girl with big Twiggy-like eyes and a guy with long hair and sideburns. "Is that you and Mable?"

"Yes, it is—taken during the week we first met, as it turns out. We were on Carnaby Street at the time."

"That's so sweet—you carrying it around with you. You were so young."

"Are you implying that I am so very old now?" he said, lips tugging into a smile. "In truth, we were young. That was in 1979, after all."

I picked up the photo, shocked to look down at that young, hip version of Rupert. By the looks of that paisley jacket and those exaggerated sideburns, he was a dandy even then.

"Isn't she beautiful?" he asked.

I studied Mable, with long trying-to-be-straight hair and the renegade bangs curling where she probably wished they wouldn't, a prominent overbite, and a glorious smile. I grinned down into her joy, those sparkling eyes, that infectious youth. And then I fought the sudden urge to cry. Wine can also make me emotional. "She was," I managed. "I wish I had met her."

"Oh, and how she would have loved you, and you her. She taught me how to knit, you know."

"Yes, you mentioned that, but you never said she was a redhead."

"Did I not? How surprising. Oh, yes, my love had such flaming red hair, complete with a veritable feast of freckles. She was beauty personified, though, of course, she couldn't see that. How I miss her," he sighed. "Never a day passes when I don't think of her. We would have been married 45 years next week."

"Next week would be your anniversary?"

"Yes, that is why I thought to visit our little retreat in Orvieto while we're here. That's where we honeymooned, you know. Oh, that reminds me, I have a present for you. Wait just a moment."

After tidying his knitting by the chair, he left his seat, returning moments later to pass me a set of keys.

I studied them in my hand—four keys on a silver wine bottle key holder. "What's this for?"

"Those are the keys to my nest in Orvieto, Phoebe. I made a few extra sets, and have given them to those I hold in the greatest esteem, anyone in fact who might benefit from an occasional escape for an enchanted moment of exulted repose."

I gazed up at him. "I'm touched, but Rupert, I can't accept these."

"Why ever not?"

"Well, I just don't exult in my repose. that much. I mean, I don't..." I trailed away.

"Exactly as I thought. You have just such a need of this place. Someday, when you are in London, and the world gets too much for you, fly to Italy for a week or weekend, whatever you can manage, and visit my little nest.

It's just an hour or so north of Rome. Quite manageable, all considered, and so lovely. Though there are tourists certainly, the city does not attract the same multitudes as the towns in Tuscany, for example. Breathe, recharge, permit the tension to ease from your life—that's what I go for, when I can get away, which is pitifully seldom."

My fingers wrapped around the keys, a lump in my throat. "Thank you, Rupert. I don't know when I could ever use these but just knowing ..." I couldn't find the words.

"That you have options?"

"Yes, exactly." Actually, *just knowing you care that much to give me such a gift* would have been closer to the truth, but it was probably better that he finished my sentence for me.

"Well, I do hope to have time to take you there before we fly home, if only for a day. It would be about six hours drive from here but well worth the trip. I'm far up in the oldest part of the city, up on the walls with the most commanding views."

I said nothing, thinking of how I really should get back to Max as soon as I finished here—not that he needed me exactly, but maybe he might. And then there was a gallery with all my plans and goals. Don't we all need to feel needed by something or someone?

"Please do let me know in advance when you are going, however, so I can ensure the fridge is properly stocked, and that nobody else is in residence," Rupert continued.

"Do you have many guests there?" I snugged the keys deep into the inside pocket of my carpet bag. A tear in the lining offered an extra-secure spot for keys, credit cards, and spare cash. "Who else has keys?"

"Oh, just a few—a very few—special friends," he said, settling down with his project again. "I must say, I do love this stitch. Do let me show you how to manage it. I can only imagine what you'd come up with all those colors you favor."

"Sure," I said, only half-listening. He considered me a most trusted friend? "Aren't the Vanvitelli estates near Orvieto?"

"Not Vanvitelli, but Nicolina's grandmother's parents, and their properties were in Umbria and environs, yes. Why do you ask?"

"Just wondering."

We settled in to knit and I even managed a few rows of linen stitch without my attention straying down carnal paths.

"Have you heard from Noel lately, Phoebe?" he asked after a bit.

My fingers tightened. "Noel?"

"Yes, you know—that dashing young chap you got along with so famously in Turkey last year?"

I studied the length of amber-hued silk strung amid my fingers, holding it to the light to test the color.

"You remember, the tall archaeologist who declared himself off to save priceless antiquities from the hands of unsavory sorts, even if it meant that he became a wanted man in the process?"

"Rupe, enough. I know who you mean but just don't know how to answer the question."

"Easily, I would think. A simple yes or no will suffice."

I rested my knitting on my lap. "I received a postcard only this week—a single postcard, one of many I've had from either Toby or Noel since we parted ways in Turkey."

"Splendid. Then you remain fresh in his heart."

"Oh, come on now. I mean, from Toby, yes—he's my brother and I'll take what I can get—but from Noel? How can I consider this a relationship, or anything lasting, or even vaguely fulfilling, when I can't be with him, or see him regularly, or even get to know him?"

"Oh, dear." He fell silent. "I thought you might wait for him," he said after a moment.

"Like a lady in a tower doing her needlework while her knight gallops off to war? Forget that. Life is now. These moments are the only ones we're sure of, and waiting until I'm 40 for a possible reunion just won't cut it. A lot of what I felt for Noel in Turkey was probably physical anyway, and now I just don't know if we had anything more sustaining. I probably never will know, at this rate."

"Perhaps it's too soon to make such a decision?" Rupert suggested.

"Or, maybe I should have made it last year before we, you know, explored anything." Noel and I had done quite a lot of exploring. "He's a criminal. That's a fact, regardless of whether he stole that treasure for the right reasons or not." I laughed, caught myself, sobered, and added:

"Stealing for the right reasons—I get that. Both he and Toby made an error in judgment, but you can believe that Agent Walker and his ilk don't care about that. Am I supposed to wait until after he is caught and serves his time in maybe 10 years?"

"I do grasp your dilemma." Rupert paused his knitting, gazing at me. "But I had hoped that you had found your soul mate."

"But I'm really after a soulmate who will be my roommate. As far as I'm concerned, it was a fling."

"How will you let him know?"

"Let him know what? I can't very well send him a *Dear John* postcard, anyway."

"No, you certainly cannot. You must see him in person."

I locked my gaze with his. "You're in touch with him, aren't you?"

"Not directly, for that would be entirely too dangerous for us both. We have a system of intermediaries who contact me when Noel has a piece that might of interest."

"You mean, like a Greek gold laurel wreath or a spare golden votive?"

"Really, Phoebe, I do not appreciate your tone. Noel ensures that museum-worthy pieces end up where they belong, whereas I receive only the leftovers for my clients. But back to the issue at hand: I do not speak with him directly but have had some success getting messages to him through intermediaries."

"How, and through whom?"

"You know I can't tell you that. Let us just say that he asks about you in nearly every message I receive."

My gaze dropped. "Damn. Why didn't you say something before?"

"Phoebe, did you or did you not insist that you did not want to know about certain aspects of my business, and that I was to shield your ears from the particulars?"

"Just because I don't want to know the details of your black market dealings doesn't mean I don't want to hear personal news about Noel and Toby."

"There is no personal news, Phoebe. My connections with Noel are hardly of the cozy variety, but I must continue to stress that the kind of message you wish to send to him now need be of the personal variety."

"I agree there, but it's not likely to happen without risking all of us, is it?"

We stopped talking after that, except for Rupert's instructions on how to manage linen stitch in multiple colors, something I decided to attempt in a moment of weakness.

Meanwhile, the night thickened around us. After another hour, Rupert yawned behind his hand. "My, my, but it must be getting late."

I glanced at my phone. "It's only 10:15."

"Indeed, and soon it will be quite past my bedtime." He stood, laying his knitting in a tidy pile of navy and jonquil on the table.

"Since when?"

"Phoebe, do you mind terribly if we say goodnight?"

"Sorry, of course not. I was just enjoying the company." I stuffed my pile of multicolored yarns into my carpet bag and got to my feet. "I'll see you in the morning."

"Over eggs and bacon, as is only proper."

Evan looked up and smiled as I walked by. "Good night, madam."

"'Night, Evan." He had a lovely smile, or maybe it was the way his eyes crinkled in the corners that got me. I realized with a stab of guilt that I wouldn't mind tucking him into bed as long as sleeping wasn't on the agenda. What an unworthy thought. Would I really shift from one unsuitable romance to another so quickly? Was I nothing but a ticking bomb of hormones?

I paused at the doorway of my room, realizing how much I'd rather not spend the night there. Thoughts of the missing countess, of the castrated lover flying overhead, seemed too ominous. Yet, what choice did I have? The other rooms were dusty, the beds unmade.

Refusing to be daunted by my own imagination, I took my toiletry bag and resigned myself to an icy bath, only this time the water poured hot and steamy. Whoever gets to the bath first wins the heat. Rupert would be very testy tomorrow morning.

Both men's doors were shut when I walked passed afterward, so I had no opportunity to warn Rupert of his pending icy plunge.

Back in my room, the coffee kept me wired enough to work further on my linen stitch, though my rectangle was emerging nothing like Rupert's.

Finally, I yawned. Rising from my chair, I stretched my arms overhead and stepped onto the balcony.

Every bedroom had a private veranda in the Italianate style. So civilized, I thought. Leaning over my balustrade, I could see lights stringing along the headland while below, the terrace and hillside lay thick with shadow. On the other hand, Rupert's lamp washed pale light through his closed drapes next door. So much for his bedtime.

Leaving the door ajar, I retreated inside, yawning all the way. I climbed into bed, lying there with the covers pulled up to my chin, staring overhead at the lovers flying hand-in-hand amid the shadows. Zephyr's severed parts glowed a blotchy gray in the lamplight.

Zephyr, spirit of the wind, sometimes gentle as a breeze, sometimes howling wild and furious, was the perfect spirit for this room, buffeted as it was by winds blowing in from the Tyrrhenian sea. Had the late count been like this mercurial lover? Had he driven his wife to some pitch of fury intense enough to make her, an artist, deface his likeness? Yawning again, I turned off the light, closed my eyes, and drifted away.

The room was still dark when I awoke. I sat up. Something had nudged me from sleep—a noise, maybe. My phone read 1:45 A.M.

Climbing from bed, I tiptoed over to the balcony door and peered out. The half moon rose low in the sky, washing silvery light across the terrace. Leaves rustled in the breeze and the air felt chill on my bare legs. About to pull the door shut, I paused, listening. I thought I heard whispering. Yes, distinctly human voices mingled among the leaves.

Crouching low, I ducked to gaze through the railings. Two flashlight beams wove through the bushes below. Burglars? I pulled back, returned to my room, and quickly pulled on my clothes.

I'd rouse Rupert and Evan, find Ricardo, sound the alarm.

In the hall moments later, I stared at Rupert and Evan's now opened doors. What the hell? A quick check revealed the beds hadn't been slept in and both men gone. They were outside searching for whatever?

I grabbed my phone, slipped on my sandals, and dashed downstairs. In moments, I was opening the kitchen door onto the terrace, pausing for mere seconds when I found the bolt locked, but too annoyed to care. I slid it open and ran down the length of terrace to the stairs, slowing down only at the first step.

I'd sneak up on the pair of weasels, catch them in the act of whatever the hell they were acting on, and join the hunt.

On the first landing, I paused. No flashlights now, and the path ahead was so dark, only a few bars of moonlight penetrated the gloom. I had no choice but to turn on my phone and hope they wouldn't see me coming.

Aiming the light towards the stairs, I carried on down two more flights and reached a landing before someone jumped me.

❧ 11 ❧

He grabbed me from behind, pinning my arms so I couldn't move them, while lifting me up until my feet left the ground. I kicked out, but he kept me swinging around so my feet couldn't hit anything. My sandals flew off, followed by the phone toppling two steps below. Someone called out in Italian. My captor replied, the only phrase I caught being *È quella ragazza di inglese*, whatever the hell that meant—something about an English rag, maybe.

When I screamed, my captor squeezed so hard, I thought he'd break my arms. "Zittisca!" his voice grated in my ear. "Zittisca!"

"Okay, okay. Let me go!" I gasped.

The other man was bounding up the steps, his black-on-black shape slipping in and out of the moonlight. Once he reached me, things would get a whole lot worse. I had to do something. I stilled, thinking I'd shove him down the stairs as soon as he came close, only my target hesitated, as if guessing my intention.

I got a good look at his build—stocky, muscular—but no facial features. He wore a ski mask.

I had to do the unexpected. While he inched up the stairs on the left, I shot my legs to the right, my feet landing on a statue. I pushed so hard, my captor lurched backwards, and the statue slipped off its pedestal.

622

The god tipped, my captor grunted, and the man below ducked as Apollo came in for a crash landing.

My captor fell back against the balustrade, taking me with him, but the impact loosened his grip long enough for me to wrench away, turn, and knee him in the groin.

The second man still fought to heave Apollo off his back, so I dashed down those two stairs to snatch up my cell phone. Bad move. Once I had the phone, he struck out and clutched my ankle, throwing me off balance.

I teetered on the edge, expecting to go hurling down those marble steps and break into a million pieces, when somebody shouted in English from the above. My attackers whispered in raspy Italian.

The guy released my ankle as the other helped heave away the statue. I fell against the railing, steadied myself, and fumbled with my phone to bring up the camera app.

Both men were now upright. My fingers trembled as I held up my phone, flashing multiple takes at my two assailants. Guy No. 2, one arm hanging limp, reached for his belt with his other hand. With a shock, I saw he packed a handgun. His companion pointed up the stairs where two men were now dashing towards us.

"Io l'ucciderò, cagna," one guy hissed at me before they both leapt over the balustrade into the bushes below.

"Phoebe, are you all right?" Evan asked, arriving seconds later, Ricardo close behind.

"Yes. They went that way." I pointed over the railing.

Evan hurled himself after them, Ricardo following with less enthusiasm. I slumped down on the stair, trying to steady my heart, while trying to remember the dial code for the Italian police. Did I need a 40 or a 04? I could hear crashing in bushes, Evan shouting, and after a moment, a single gunshot cracked the night. I froze, staring into the darkness, heart hammering.

"Phoebe? Phoebe where are you?" Rupert called from above.

I looked up to see him hurrying down the stairs. "I'm here. What's the number for the police?"

He arrived, panting heavily. "No police. Evan has it all in hand."

"Somebody just fired a gun. We need the police."

"We do not." He thumped down on the step beside me, pulled a hankie from his pocket, and began wiping his face. "Have you been harmed?"

"I'm fine. Why no police?"

"Because I'm quite certain Nicolina would not like them involved in such a matter."

"What matter? What the hell is going on?"

"Phoebe, the police are not always the good guys in these situations. Let us talk inside. I could use a nice cup of tea."

I'd never get anywhere until I agreed. I retrieved my sandals and linked my arm in his as we climbed back up the stairs and into the kitchen. Sophia, waiting by the table with a tray of wine and biscotti, rushed to my side to check for damages.

"I'm fine, Sophia, really."

"Vino, acqua?" she asked hurriedly.

"I'm certain the lady would prefer tea," Rupert said before repeating himself in Italian with considerably more embellishment.

"I'm certain I wouldn't." I sat down and poured a glass of the wine into the little glasses provided. "I'm happy with wine, Rupert. Leave her alone." To Sophia I added, "This is perfecto, grazie. Biscotti?" I held up a biscuit.

"Cantucci," she responded, nodding. "Gradirebbe dell'acqua?"

I caught the "acqua" part and guessed the gist. I smiled. "Si, grazie."

"Prego," she said, darting to the refrigerator.

I took a sip of the sweet wine while eying Rupert, who fussed around the tea kettle as if resigned to boiling his own water. Sophia shooed him away and plugged in the kettle. He returned to sit down opposite me, hands folded on the table in front of him.

"Phoebe, you quite gave us a shock tonight."

"Imagine mine when I found you gone from your bedroom."

"We heard something in the garden and hastily rushed to search the grounds."

"Dressed conveniently in total black? Stop lying." Sensing Sophia listening in, or attempting to, I added, "We'll finish this discussion later." I sipped the wine and waited.

After 20 minutes, in which time Sophia served Foxy a weak, but apparently decent, cup of tea, Evan and Ricardo returned, their arms and faces scratched.

Evan caught Rupert's eye and shrugged. "They got clean away, Sir," he said. "We chased them all the way up to the road."

"Who fired that shot?" I asked.

"One of the burglars, madam. The bullet didn't come close."

Ricardo looked at him in surprise. "The shot, it came too close—maybe a foot near. We chased the men to road but they escape in Alpha Romero."

"An Alpha Romero? My, what well-heeled burglars," I remarked and crunched into a cantucci, tasting almond.

Rupert got to his feet. "Well, no harm done, either way. We must be off to bed, catch up on our beauty sleep, as they say. Thank you, Ricardo. You have been most helpful. We will provide a full report to the signora when she arrives later today."

Ricardo shot back the last of his wine, nodded to Sophia, and the two of them exited, locking the terrace door behind them.

The moment the latch clicked, I leapt up and slammed shut the door leading from the kitchen into the hall. "What the hell is going on? Do you know who those men were?" I asked, turning to Rupert.

"However would I know? Two local boys expecting to break into what they believed to be an abandoned villa is my guess," he said.

"In an Alpha Romero?"

"Maybe they borrowed their father's car."

"Stop it." I pulled out my phone. "I took pictures of my assailants. One wore a ski mask, one didn't. Imagine my shock when I recognized one of Count Vanvitelli's men? You're going to tell me what's going or you won't be getting your beauty rest tonight, Foxy."

I was prepared to block the door bodily, if I had to. To make a point, I leaned against the hall door, arms outstretched. I stared at Evan, daring him to move me, which I knew he'd do without a moment's hesitation and enjoy every second. His gray-green eyes locked on mine, a tiny smile lifting his lips. My, what big biceps he had. I shook my attention back on point. "Speak, Foxy."

"Phoebe, there's no need for that. Oh, very well. The count is no doubt seeking the same thing we are—approximately two hundred thousand pounds of Etruscan gold. Now may we go to bed?"

"I s this the late count's Etruscan gold collection we're talking about?"

Rupert sighed. "I had quite forgotten mentioning that but, yes, that is the one. It went missing some time ago. I believe Lucca expected to find it stashed among his grandfather's effects and properties, with specific information relating to its safe-keeping. It appears that isn't the case. Perhaps the late Vanvitelli secured it away in a vault somewhere, but nobody can locate such a vault and, really, why would he stash such a hoard and not inform his heirs?"

"And that's what you're really here to find?"

"Yes, in part."

"The largest part, I'm sure. Why does the current count think it's here?"

Rupert glanced longingly at the electric kettle as if craving his sedative of choice. "It must be somewhere, mustn't it? Nicolina requested that we search everywhere."

"But why here?"

"Because, Phoebe, part of that hoard, if you don't mind me calling it that, though I admit it's rather a distasteful term, belongs to her late grandmother and, according to her will, to Nicolina."

"Wait," I held up one hand. "Didn't you say that everything belongs to the Vanvitelli estate?"

"It does, but these were personal effects, pieces Countess Augustina found on her own family estate in Orvieto, and which she willed to Nicolina. As such, they belong to Nicolina wholly, though even if she locates them, she will be unable to remove them from Italy due to Italian antiquities laws—a tedious detail."

"So the collection was never declared to the Italian government and nobody owns them legally, including any Vanvitelli."

"Yes, yes, very well, but there are ways of encouraging the government to look the other way."

"It's called bribery."

Rupert cleared his throat. "In any case, if Nicolina could only retrieve her share, she could sell it, and thus regain some measure of her missing inheritance."

"And I'm sure you would be willing to transport some of that loot to London and negotiate the sale, since that's one of your specialties. I'm finally getting the picture."

"I don't appreciate your tone."

"Let me get this straight: You have been searching the house for this missing hoard and apparently the count sent his men to do the same tonight?"

"So it appears. Whatever occurs, we must ensure that Lucca does not find the gold before we do, or it will be lost to Nicolina forever."

"Now that I understand why you're really here," I stepped away from the door, "why did you bring me?"

"I thought it would be fun, Phoebe. I thought what a grand time we would have on the Amalfi Coast while assessing a villa filled with lovely old things and knitting in between. You know how much I adore our knitting sessions. Besides, I want us to hone our skills as antiquities sleuths. I knew how much you would enjoy it. How was I to know the place would be so ravaged, or the count so involved?"

"Yes, how could you possibly know that?" I doubted he would acknowledge my irony.

"This has just grown immensely more complicated than I expected. I believed Nicolina would share the whole sorry tale with you before now, and elicit your help accordingly, but she is delayed. In the meantime, I thought we would have such a wonderful time together, as we did in Turkey."

I opened the door. "In Turkey I was kidnapped, shot at, nearly killed multiple times, and gained a good friend only to lose her again under harrowing circumstances. If that's your idea of fun, leave me out of it. I'm going to bed." And with that I left them standing there and headed for my room.

"Wait, Phoebe, surely you will not traipse off to London, will you?"

"I don't know what I'm going to do."

Events in Turkey nailed me straight through the heart and Foxy's notion of us becoming some a pair of antiquities sleuths, simply ridiculous. His motives were hardly altruistic. Sir Rupert Fox did nothing without ulterior motives, something I knew but chose to overlook again and again. Max was right.

I climbed back into bed, my brain live-wired with questions. Do I stay or do I go? Was I really up to yet another escapade involving men with guns? At least in Turkey, my quest had been personal. I'd been seeking three key people in my life, one of whom screwed my godfather—literally and figuratively—plus seeking my brother, and a man I might have loved. Or love. Or could love. Maybe. *Damn.*

As if life wasn't complicated enough. Why would I become involved in this mess on top of it all? The Vanvitelli squabble had nothing to do with me, and the stakes were intensifying by the moment.

After tossing and turning, I finally fell into a fitful sleep, waking as tired as if I'd never rested at all. The day glowed bright and clear through the windows as I padded downstairs for breakfast.

The scent of frying bacon suffused the house. Halfway down the hall, I found Sophia glowering into a vase of flowers she was arranging while Ricardo focused on mopping the floor. I responded to their tense buon giornos and carried on into the kitchen.

"Morning madam," greeted Evan from his place by the stove. He smiled over his shoulder before turning to continue forking the sizzling meat. "Sir Rupert will join us directly. Fresh coffee is in the pot and I'll be making tea directly."

"Thanks." I poured myself a mug while trying not to steal glances at the man in his crisp white apron with the biceps incongruously bulging in his black tee shirt. A girl needs a muscled chef to keep bacon in its place, that's for sure. Taking my mug, I strolled onto the terrace and breathed the fresh morning air.

Moments later, I hung a left to an area I'd yet to explore. Away from the porticoed terrace, I glimpsed a cottage tucked into the cedars—Sophia and Ricardo's house. For the first time, I noticed a flagstone path weaving through the trees nearby. I followed it, discovering another terrace jutting into a kind of patio-cum-look-out extension overlooking the Amalfi.

The view took my breath away. I stood staring, coffee untouched. I approached the chest-high railing and leaned over, stunned to find a 200-foot drop straight over the cliff to the rocks below. The sea surged in a mighty wash, as menacing as it was beautiful.

This made the perfect location for the late countess to tumble to her death, if such a thing even happened. I agreed with Foxy that sleepwalking, though credible in itself, was challenging where it required hoisting a leg over a three-foot wall. Unless she had help, which changed everything. I backed away, snatched my mug from the wall, and returned to the kitchen.

Foxy was waiting for me on the terrace.

"Phoebe! What a delightful morn. Come join me for eggs and bacon, with the very best pot of tea man can find anywhere in Italy."

The table had been positioned to maximize the view. Evan slid out my chair. "How would you prefer your eggs, madam?" he asked.

"Poached medium hard," I told him, "and my bacon crisp, thanks."

"Bacon is always most flavorful with just a touch of moist fat adhering to the edges, rather than overdone as the Colonialists are wont to do," Rupert said. "The Americans fry their meat to within an inch of its life."

"Because it's supposed to be dead before we eat it. I'll take my bacon crisp, please, Evan. Thanks."

Evan slipped back to the kitchen.

"You know I meant American as in North American," Rupert said. "You being Canadian, of course."

I turned to him. "I know what you meant. I also know you're trying to deflect last night's incident as well as the fact that you dragged me into this without providing the critical details. If you think pandering to me now will alter my decision to return to London, you're wrong." Actually, I hadn't made up my mind one way or the other, but he didn't need to know that.

"Phoebe, I am most sorry for urging you to accompany me without providing all the details, but Nicolina requested that she have the opportunity to tell her story herself. What could I do, betray her confidence? She will arrive today. What harm is there in at least waiting until her arrival before making any hasty decisions? Please do allow me to make it up to you by treating you to a tour of this glorious location. Let us drive along the Amalfi Coast this morning and enjoy the day while we await Nicolina's arrival? I propose a visit to Ravello, followed by lunch at one of my favorite restaurants in Positano. What do you say?"

I sipped my tea. Positano, Ravello, a drive along one of the most stunning drives anywhere. "Why not?"

"Splendid! We shall have a simply wondrous day."

After breakfast, we met downstairs, me dressed in what I considered relaxed holiday attire in a pair of black capris, a striped tee-shirt, and sandals. Rupert, however, turned up decked out in a cream linen suit, straw hat, and a pair of woven leather shoes. His one gesture to casual wear consisted of a black tee shirt worn with a little animal print silk scarf knotted at his neck.

"Did you even look inside the suitcases I provided?" he asked, scrutinizing me.

"Nope. Let's go."

We climbed up the stairs to the parking area, Evan dashing ahead. When we arrived at the top, my shirt was already damp as the intense humidity glommed onto my skin and Rupert resorted to dabbing his forehead with his hankie.

I forgot everything when I saw the very sleek, very red car Evan stood beside. "A sports car?" I said.

"A GranCabrio MC," Evan hastened to explain. "A Maserati."

"You rented a Maserati?"

"Indeed, isn't it marvelous?" Rupert clapped his hands together. "Evan did attempt to secure the convertible options, but I fear we were too late and must settle for the sunroof. Nevertheless, we shall have the honor of driving an automobile with a noble sporting pedigree, noted the world over for its feisty speed and aerodynamic performance, a worthy ride."

In other words, better than a Fiat. Why we needed a sporting pedigree and feisty speed for a road notorious for death-defying feats of driving, I had no idea, but resolved to enjoy the ride. At least we were in the hands of a competent driver.

"Is it true that all roads lead to Rome?" I asked no one in particular.

"It is, indeed," Rupert replied. "For in fact, this very road is called the Roma Road, as pedestrian as that may seem, for it will take you to Rome via Naples in one direction, and to Rome via Salerno, on the other. Do get in, Phoebe, dear—the front seat, that is. I will claim the rear to ensure you have the most picturesque of rides today."

I slipped down into the front seat as Evan shut the door, marveling at the sensation of being strapped into a low-lying bullet with a panoramic view. As the car purred onto the narrow road, my attention swerved up to the soaring cliffs, to the straight-down plunges onto surf-slashed rocks below. We'd dart briefly through shadowy tunnels only to burst out seconds later into blinding sunshine. Evan would flash-speed on the rare straight stretches, only to slow back down to restrained power as the circumstances warranted, his muscled arms commanding the steering wheel.

"Do the heights and hairpin turns disturb you, Madam?" Evan asked, his eyes on the road.

I laughed. "Never!" Actually, I'd hang over the side if I could, just to buzz myself up on glimpses of those cliff plunges.

Rupert sat far back in his seat, his gaze glued straight ahead. Every time we veered near a particularly vertiginous edge, he'd lean over to the opposite direction.

Oncoming busses honked at the knife-edge turns as larger vehicles had no choice but to use both sides of the road. At least once, we slowed down to allow a donkey train loaded with saddle bags of stone to plod down a steep incline onto the road. Pastel buildings pressed in around us at every town. We stop-started many times to accommodate narrow streets crammed with people and vehicles followed by dazzling coastline supernaturally enhanced by sun, sea, and nature, all in high relief.

At the city of Amalfi, we took a sharp turn up the mountainside towards Ravello.

"You will adore Ravello," Rupert said from the back seat. "It was one of Mable's favorite places."

As the road climbed, Rupert fell silent while I flashed photos out the window with my phone camera—more dramatic plunges, a monastery perched on a wooded peak, flash-glimpses of broken towers, and everywhere orchards, vineyards, and olive groves.

As I sat back in my seat after one photography session, I happened to catch Evan checking the rear-view mirror. I turned to see a car behind us. "Is everything all right?"

"Everything is excellent, madam."

Moments later, we parked in the parking area overlooking the sea and walked through a tunnel to the town's magnificent central courtyard, where a ruined castle loomed amid the trees on one side and the plaza spread out under spreading umbrella pines ahead. Ravello charmed in every way.

After strolling through the tiny streets, investigating ceramic shops and sampling wine, Rupert and I sat in a cafe on the piazza sipping cappuccino while Evan took off down one of the alleyways.

I watched him disappear around a magnificent ruined arch, thinking that even he must require time out but, before we'd finished our drinks, he was back in view. He strolled in a leisurely fashion behind two black-garbed men. Clearly they weren't tourists. The younger wore tight black pants and a longer-cut jacket, fashionable but too warm for the day. The other, a gray-haired guy, carried his leather jacket over one arm and puffed away at a cigarette while engaging his companion in lively dialog. When they took a seat at the cafe across from ours, Evan claimed one several tables away.

"Something's up," I said to Rupert.

"Yes, indeed. It appears we are being followed."

"Lucca's men?"

"Most likely. Perhaps he wishes to keep an eye on us, for whatever reason. Let us press on to lunch. They will have a difficult time of it if they expect to tail us there."

Rupert tossed a twenty euro note onto the table and together we rose to walk back to the car. Despite our head start, Evan managed to arrive at the car before us. I looked up at him as I climbed into the passenger seat. "I'm not even going to ask."

"I beg your pardon, madam?"

"Never mind."

I saw no sign of a tail as we wound our way back down the mountain, nor did they appear as we curved along the coast. But then, the highway was so tortuous and the towns so congested, it would have been a challenge keeping us in sight. We were on our way to Positano, past Nicolina's villa, and back the way we'd traveled from the airport.

And the Amalfi Coast's poster town didn't disappoint. If possible, the road curling down towards the sea was higher, more dramatic, and more beautiful than all the others. Hotels, restaurants, and boutiques clung to the cliffs all the way down the mountain, and every vista spun away over terraces of pastel houses stacked one on top of the other as if worshiping sun and sea. While I'd hoped we'd weave all the way down to the beach for lunch, Evan pulled into a tiny parking area wedged beside hotel steps about halfway down.

"The Hotel Poseidon," Rupert announced. "Today, you are my guest, Phoebe McCabe."

A valet took the keys while we dashed up the marble stairs and into the lobby. A gentleman stepped forward to shake Rupert's hand. "Dear Signore Fox, it is such a pleasure to see you again after so long a time."

"It is my deepest pleasure to return, Stefano," Rupert assured him.

"Ah, yes. Your table awaits."

He ushered us through to the back where flower and vine-covered porticoes framed more stunning vistas. We strolled by multiple pools and sitting areas, past cozy nooks washed with sunlight and shadow, down to the restaurant level where another terrace edged the vista under pergolas of vines and flaming-red bougainvillea.

"Oh," I sighed, sitting down at what had to be the best table, affording the choicest view. I couldn't take my eyes from the bay below, hiving with little pleasure boats and tour cruises, the layers of terraced houses, the colors, the light. I smiled up at the waiter delivering our menus, noting that Evan had not taken a seat.

"Where'd Evan go?" I asked Rupert after the waiter took our wine order.

"He's keeping his eyes on the perimeters, Phoebe—doing his job, in other words."

"Doesn't he get to have lunch?"

"Assuredly he does," Rupert said, twitching his caterpillar brows. "But he will dine in the kitchen, as do the other drivers and tour operators, where he can best forage for information. It is a truth little known by employers that the staff know more about what's truly going on than they. Evan, the good lad, keeps one ear to the ground at all times. I recommend the scampi, by the way. Truly a specialty of the house. Shall I order the wine?"

Of course he ordered the wine. If left to me, I would have chosen the house wine, not being a connoisseur. Rupert, on the other hand, took his wine seriously. After the waiter poured a little into his glass, he held it to the light, savored its scent, and turned the liquid delicately in the glass. "Excellent, and fine legs it has, too."

Wine with legs was a first for me, but Rupert explained the difference between thin wines and those which dribble prettily on the inside of the glass, something I understood to be preferable somehow. I only cared that it tasted wonderful and enhanced everything I ate.

The scampi served with multiple dishes of fresh pasta, a salad, perfectly married with the wine, Rupert explained. The food was delicious, my companion at his most entertaining, and the setting unparalleled.

Rupert didn't seem at all concerned with the possibility of being tailed by Count Vanvitelli's men, and soon, neither did I. The wine played a role. If one glass smoothed away rough edges of life, then the second positively polished it up.

By the time we rose to leave, the world glowed. I waited with Rupert as the valet brought around the Maserati, and sighed in pleasure as I slid into the seat. Had we been anywhere else in the world, I might have napped on the way to the villa, but this was the Amalfi Coast and I wasn't going to miss a thing.

Even in my semi-stupor, I noticed the black car pull out from the parking area across the street, sliding in close behind us.

Evan's gaze shot to the rear-view mirror.

"It's them, isn't it?" I asked. "I can see the Hugo Boss dude behind the wheel."

"Who, madam?"

"I know we're being followed by Lucca's men." I turned towards the back seat, expecting to see Rupert looking mildly interested but instead he was snoring.

I turned back to Evan. "Are you going to try losing them?"

"I'm afraid that's nearly impossible on this road."

"Why do you think they're tailing us?"

"I wouldn't like to say, madam."

"Which is more honest than saying you don't know. Hoping we'll deliver them to the missing Etruscan gold in broad daylight, maybe?"

"Perhaps, madam."

"Will you stop calling me that?"

But he remained focused straight ahead, though "straight" hardly fit the setting. We meandered our way up the mountain towards the coastal highway, the black sedan remaining no more than a few cars behind. Once, snagged in traffic in the town of Arienzo, we were close enough that I could see the driver clearly. It was the younger of the two, with his artfully short hair, high cheekbones, and jaw clenched in resolution.

"I'll just add that nothing about the driver's expression seems friendly. In fact, if I had to coin a term, I'd say 'murderous.' I don't recognize him from last night, either."

The moment the traffic thinned on the two-lane highway, the sedan fell behind, blocked by a tour bus and a little white truck with a fish painted on its side.

I tried to relax, telling myself that it made no sense for Lucca to harm us. Who were we but the lowly help rooting through his grandmother's crumbling villa? Unless he thought we knew more about the gold than we did. But how did that fit with the Count's impervious dismissal yesterday? He clearly thought we were beneath his notice, though the episode in the garden last night opened up other questions. Oh, hell. Wine did not improve my cognitive abilities.

My gaze flew to the first stretch of straight road we'd hit since Positano, a park-like swerve of sky and sea shadowed by the sheer rise of cliffs on our right. We now drove on the inside lane on a highway the width of a bread stick. A gaggle of yellow-uniformed racing bikers pumped their muscular legs ahead of us, but otherwise, the road lay clear.

Evan swerved to pass them, jolting the Maserati into a speed-spurt that left the bikers behind just as the black sedan came into view around a corner behind us.

"They're picking up speed," I said, as if Evan wasn't accelerating to compensate. I could have said something stupid like *you're crazy to be trying to outrun that lot here,* but words failed me when the sedan rammed into our rear. The Maserati leaped for the edge, Evan swerving it back in an instant, gunning the car down the center of the road directly in line with an oncoming bus rounding the next turn ahead.

"My word," Rupert mumbled, rousing from his nap. "What is happening?"

"All in hand, Sir," Evan said through clenched jaws.

Rupert said nothing, gaze fixed on the windshield. We were picking up speed. Evan planned to broad-side the bus? I sat rigid right up until Evan masterfully swerved the Maserati to the extreme right, squeezing through the narrow space between the bus and the cliff with nothing to spare.

I glanced up into driver's terrified face as we scraped past. The bus slammed on its brakes, leaving it angled diagonally across the road. The sedan jetted into the opening after us, only to smash the bus's left head-light and grind to a halt.

Smiling, Evan relaxed at the wheel, flexing his gloved hands while easing the car back down to cruising altitude.

I fell back against the seat. "You guessed there might be enough room for a sports car but not the sedan."

"A strategic guess, madam," Evan responded.

My mouth was dry. "Sure."

"Evan is such a remarkable driver," remarked Rupert, recovering his voice from the rear.

We traveled the rest of the way back to the villa without incident. As we approached our caged parking area, I chanced to note a car parked halfway up a narrow lane across the street, the same one I'd noticed when we left that morning. Then the driver had been leaning against the hood, reading a map, seeming innocent enough. This time he sat behind the wheel, talking on his phone.

"We're being watched here, too," I remarked.

"Forget that for a moment, Phoebe," Rupert interrupted. "I do believe Nicolina has arrived."

13

The guy across the street no longer tried to hide the fact that he was still watching us. "We're being staked," I said.

"Yes, yes, I know," said Rupert. "Tiresome."

The moment the Maserati inched to a stop, I flicked off my seatbelt and bolted out the door.

"Do let the dear woman settle in from her travels first, Phoebe," Rupert called to my retreating back. "It appears that she has only just arrived."

I pretended not to hear as I dashed down the stairs towards the villa, noticing that the steps had been washed and the rotting lemons removed. Inside the front hall, the scent of wax and cleaning solvents assaulted me as I searched the ground floor for Nicolina. I found her in the kitchen, deep in conversation with Sophia.

Both women shot around when I burst into the kitchen.

"Phoebe," Nicolina approached with her hands outstretched, taking mine in hers. "Did you have a lovely day? I hear you went to Ravello and Positano. Did you enjoy the jewels of the Amalfi Coast?"

"Yes, all very lovely," I said gazing up at her. Strain bruised the skin beneath her eyes and her smile seemed forced yet nothing dispelled her beauty. I squeezed her hands, finding them soft and warm in mine. "Nicolina, I know how difficult all this upheaval must be for you and I'd like to help, but I can't without answers. I need to know what's really going on. Apparently, there are a few things you need to tell me personally?"

"Now, now, Phoebe," Rupert said, puffing into the kitchen behind me. He paused for a moment to dab his forehead. "Let us sit down someplace private and discuss everything properly over refreshments. How lovely to see you again, Nicolina, dear. I trust you had a pleasant journey?"

I tightened my grip on Nicolina's hands. "Refreshments can wait, I can't. Your brother's men jumped me in the garden last night and today they apparently tried to run us off the road. I was hoping you'd finally tell me what's really going on?"

"Run you off the road?" She tugged away her fingers and brought one hand to her throat. "But that cannot be. You must be mistaken."

"Definitely not," I said.

"I mean, an accident, perhaps? Those drivers on the coast—so reckless."

"No accident. A couple of dudes bumped the back of our car deliberately at a critical moment rounding a bend."

"Phoebe, let's not be alarmist," Rupert interrupted. "I'm sure those lads were only tailing us a little enthusiastically and—"

I shot him a look. "Enough, Rupert." Turning back to Nicolina, I repeated myself. "Who were those men, Nicolina? Who's staking out the villa across the street—is it your brother, Lucca?"

"Yes, Lucca," she said, finally. "My brother thinks to protect me, that is all."

"By running us off the road?"

"No, no, you do not understand."

"Then, help me."

"Yes, we will talk now." Nicolina turned to Sophia, speaking Italian. To me, she added, "Sophia, will provide tea and wine in the yellow salon. We will meet there in twenty minutes. I wish only to change first."

"Thank you." I watched as she strode from the room, Sophia hurrying after, leaving Rupert and me alone.

He took a deep breath. "I trust you are satisfied? To alarm the lady like that when she has already endured so much—"

"Stop right there, Rupert. Nicolina's not made out of china. I have a feeling she's far stronger than you give her credit for. See you in twenty," and I left him standing there.

We all convened at the appointed time in the yellow salon. Nicolina had changed from her black-suited travel clothes into a cream linen pleated dress, whereas Rupert had donned a silk smoking jacket over perfectly pressed trousers—the two of them a walking testament to meticulous ironing. I had pulled on my wrinkle-resistant top printed in an all-over pattern of scrolling vines—my nod to historical references-and resigned myself to winning the Most Shabby award.

Ricardo and Sophia turned the salon into a seating area by hauling over a little marble table to hold wine and tea, plus a couch and two chairs. After Nicolina requested the curtains drawn, she asked her two attendants to leave, so we could speak in private. Evan was allowed to remain, but he sat back in a corner as silent as sphinx.

"As I thought," Rupert commented once the servants left. "Your employees have not been apprised of the circumstances."

"Neither have I," I said, unable to resist.

Nicolina smoothed her skirt as she took a seat. "They know all that is needed."

"Please tell me what I need, then. I deserve that much."

"Yes, you do and I am sorry. It is a very long story," Nicolina said, pressing her palms from her thighs to her knees. "I did not think it would come to this." She glanced at Rupert. "How much do you tell her?"

"Nothing," I replied.

"I attempted to avoid the specifics, as you requested, but Phoebe is quite insistent," Rupert said.

"I only expect what's fair," I pointed out. "You asked me to help assess your estate, only there's nothing here worth assessing. Now I discover that there's a hidden agenda all along and it looks as though your brother has something to do with it."

She turned to me. "I am sorry, please believe this, but I was—am— desperate. I had thought to tell you details in London, but then matters— how do I say it?" She turned to Rupert.

"Accelerated."

"Yes, accelerated. First, I heard from my lawyer of new difficulties with the estate, and then Lucca phones. My elder brother, the new count, is very much a bully, like our grandfather, and sees things differently—so controlling."

"What things? Tell me the whole story," I said.

"Lucca thinks something important is hidden here at the villa."

I was not a patient person, and dragging out answers was killing me. "Something important being the Etruscan gold?"

"You know of the gold?"

"Yes, so be honest. If you want me to help—not that I believe I can do anything under the circumstances—you must tell me everything. Please start from the beginning, like with your grandmother."

"My grandmother? Where do I begin? Yes, my grandmother was a very talented woman, a painter. Before she married, she would paint many portraits of local people living around Orvieto. Do you know Orvieto?"

"I know of a very fine white wine and a famous cathedral," I said, admitting my ignorance.

"Yes, but more, so much more. It is very old, built over Etruscan cities that came long before. Old and beautiful, and my grandmother, she loved the people, the land, everything. They were her people. She knew in her heart," Nicolina placed one hand over her chest, "that we trace a maternal line from our noble ancestors, the Etruscans. Her portraits captured the true heart, our spirit back through time, you understand?"

I nodded. "Yes, I think so. It's comforting to ground your family in a noble lineage, and from what I know of the Etruscans, they were an amazing people."

"They were, yes," Nicolina said, brightening. "They loved to dance and sing, were great artists and designers."

"The Romans learned much from the Etruscans," Rupert added. "They copied their engineering feats and admired them even while inevitably crushing them under the long imperial arm. We herald the Romans for their brilliance, which in truth they were in countless ways, yet so much of what we see today as Roman is truly Greek and Etruscan. They were a civilization of borrowers and—"

"And your grandmother admired the Etruscans so much that she infused some of the Etruscan style into her portraits," I said before Rupert gathered too much momentum. "I remember that painting in your study."

"It is beautiful, yes? It is my favorite. Many more once hung here but have now disappeared." Her eyes briefly raked the bare walls and dropped to her hands. "As I say, she was very talented and independent, also, but she fell in love with the handsome count from Naples that was my grandfather. Napoli men are very dashing, yes? Dark and handsome, passionate men, not like the northerners who have cooler heads." She smiled at no one in particular, her gaze fixed on some far point across the room. "Swept away by love, she told me once."

"That's common enough between men and women," I said, thinking of Noel, also dark and handsome. We were also swept away by something, lust perhaps.

"It was not so common then for the south to fall in love with the north," Nicolina continued. "For Italy, it is like two countries, each very different. My great-grandfather in Napoli expected his son to marry a local girl, one from Naples, but no, he falls for the beautiful northern girl. My grandmother told me how he wooed her, like a prince in a fairy tale. He would bring gifts and arrange fetes in her honor. Once he gave her a studio he had built just for her on the grounds of his Naples villa. She was not so rich, my grandmother. Her family owned vineyards and properties, yes, but more humble, not like my grandfather with his title and many lands. But for a short time, they were happy."

"It must have seemed very Cinderella-like in the beginning," I remarked.

She gazed away, eyes still unfocused. "They did not live happily ever after, as in the story. In the beginning, all was perfect, yes? So many things are perfect at the start." She spread her hands.

"She painted their portraits over the original art in her bedroom, didn't she, in honor of their love?" I gazed overhead. "The faces of Zephyr and the nymph are portraits."

"You noticed? Oh, of course you did. That is why you are here, to notice things," she said, turning to me. "I knew that you would see differently. It is true, early in their marriage, this villa was their nest, very romantic."

"How extraordinary," Rupert mused.

"Yes, they were very much in love then. They shared many things at first—a love of Etruscan art, especially. My grandfather, he loved art and beautiful things, but for my grandmother, the Etruscans were like her blood. These interests kept them together for a time, I think. My grandfather collected many Etruscan pieces for my grandmother, and she had Etruscan necropolis on her vineyard, which they both explored together."

"She had Etruscan tombs on her property?" I asked.

"Oh, many. They are deep into the hillside of my great-grandparents' vineyard. It is not uncommon to find such tombs in the north, but much rarer to find them untouched. Is that the correct term?"

"Pristine, perhaps, unplundered?" Rupert offered.

"Pristine, yes." Nicolina studied her hands. "My grandmother found such a place on her vineyard, a tomb of a very rich couple, husband and wife, with jewelry and gold, many fine sculptures and potteries. Such a find was rare. The funerary sculpture showed the man and wife looking at one another in love and respect." Her eyes met mine. "Etruscan women were equal to the men. They were honored and owned property."

"Yes," I said. "I remember reading about that. They sat as equals with the men during feasts."

Nicolina smiled sadly. "The Romans thought this a scandal before they conquered them. Always the same: The strong overtake the weak and, so many times, more is lost than gained."

"So, they found this tomb on your grandmother's vineyard ..." I prompted.

"Yes, I continue my story: My grandmother wished to inform the government and bring in archaeologists. She wished to turn the site into a museum, as is done all over Italy, but my grandfather refused. This is where the troubles began. The economy turned bad and my grandfather struggled. Now it seemed he was not so rich. He wanted to sell off part of the gold and lands, my grandmother's lands. He knew my grandmother would refuse."

Rupert cleared his throat. "As reprehensible as that may sound, wealth requires great resources to maintain itself."

"Sympathy for the devil, Rupert?" I asked him mildly. He frowned and looked away. "Sorry, Nicolina. Please go on. So, things were going poorly economically and your grandfather wanted to sell the Etruscan treasure?"

Her palms remain pressed into her thighs. "My grandfather, it seems he was doing many things which my grandmother did not approve. The Etruscan gold was only part. One day she came home and found him in bed with another woman. An old story, is it not?" She turned to me, her eyes welling. "A tired old story."

I reached over and placed my hand over hers. "A very old, very painful, story. Your grandmother must have been deeply hurt and also furious."

She nodded. "Furious, yes. It was, as they say, the last straw. She did a very foolish thing—I say foolish, but who is to say what one will do when all is lost and the heart broken? Who is to judge? Some say foolish, but to her, it was all she could do. She took the Etruscan gold and as many of the artifacts she and her servants could pile into a van. She took only the pieces that were hers or given to her, but those were the richest ones."

"My word, you mean that she stole the gold? Your grandfather didn't just hide it in a vault as is the speculation? I had no idea!" Rupert said.

"She did not steal the gold," Nicolina cut the air with her index finger. "She took what was hers."

"I understand what you're saying," I said, "but I'm guessing that no one saw it that way. Whatever the laws were at the time, the find was never declared to the authorities."

"This is true, and my grandfather was a powerful man known for his art collections."

"So your grandmother would look guilty, no matter what the circumstances," I said.

"Yes. It is all very complicated. Why must everything be so complicated? My grandmother hid the treasure. Here is another problem: The gold had already been sold by grandfather to a very powerful man, but not delivered. This man, also a collector, was very angry and demanded the gold."

"But nobody knew where it was?" Rupert said.

"No, no one," Nicolina shook her head.

"What happened to your grandmother after that?" I asked.

"She refused to tell my grandfather where she hid the gold. My grandfather, he did everything in his power to force her to tell, including keeping her away from her children and grandchildren. He brought her here. She lived like a prisoner here. It must have been so terrible. I can't bear to think of how she suffered. These walls have seen such pain. All this was years ago, and Italy is a very old country, you understand. Women were not powerful like men, and the old ways ruled. Her own parents were gone and her husband a very powerful man. Do you see?"

"Yes," Rupert and I said in unison.

A single tear rolled down her cheek. "This place holds much sorrow. I could not live here."

I offered her a refill of the sweet wine, but she shook her head while pulling a tissue from her skirt pocket.

"And then she disappeared," I said, "but left the villa to you in her will?" I said.

"The will she changed before all this happened." She dabbed her eyes with the tissue with such delicacy. I could never cry with such finesse. "She wrote a will, witnessed by my mother and the three servants. It said that all the gold jewelry from her estate was to go to her grandchildren. We were all still so young then. I was to receive all her jewelry, including the Etruscan pieces, and the other artifacts would be divided between my brother and myself. The properties in Orvieto were to go to my mother and then to me, but that would not happen. They were sold by my grandfather long ago, when money grew scarce. When my grandfather married my grandmother, her land became his. She knew that only Lucca would receive the title and the other Naples properties, as tradition. She tried to give the women something of our own, but no. We thought that this would be safe but we were wrong."

"Why did your grandfather treat you that way?" I asked.

She balled the tissue in her lap. "Once, we all came here on holiday before all the horror began. It was still a happy time. We were still a family —so much love, you understand? Things were not so good between my grandparents, but this I only sensed. My grandfather arrived and he was as imperious—a good word, I think—as always, but kind to me. He loved me, yes, but a year later, all was torn apart."

"Why did your grandfather excise you from his will, Nicolina?" I asked softly.

Nicolina took a deep breath, still focused on the wall beyond. "Because I discovered things and I could not be silent, the same things grandmother discovered. My brother and parents all said no, do not accuse him, but I would not listen. I named such ugly things and only some of them were true."

"What things?" I asked.

She shook her head. "I accused him of making my grandmother's—all our lives—hell."

Rupert inhaled sharply. "You accused him to his face?"

"I did. He is responsible for turning our noble family into something cheap."

"Cheap how?"

She waved away the question with one elegant hand. "By putting gold over love."

"Because he sold your grandmother's properties and tried to sell the Etruscan gold?" I asked.

"Yes," she sniffed.

"And then, because you accused him," I prodded, "not only did your grandfather embed some caveat into the deed of this villa, but he removed you from his will?"

"Yes."

"And did your parents protest this before their tragic accident?" Rupert asked.

Nicolina dropped her head into her hands. "My parents were murdered before they could protest."

"Murdered?" Rupert exclaimed. "But, Nicolina, this is a serious charge! Who would have killed them, surely not your grandfather?"

"No, of course not!" Nicolina got to her feet, turning first to Rupert, then to me. "My grandfather was not a good man, but a murderer, no! He would not kill his own son, or his heirs—his family, no, never! I know this now. If not for love, then pride. He caused my grandmother—all of us—great pain, yes, but he did not kill her. Forgive me, I should not have asked you here. It is too dangerous. You must leave tomorrow." She strode for the door, Evan leaping up to open it for her.

"Wait, Nicolina, please," Rupert called. "Let us help you."

She paused in the hallway and swung around, her voice lowering to a harsh whisper. "You must not get involved further. I thank you for all you have done. Rupert, you have been a great friend, but I was wrong to ask you here. I am wrong to think that I can free myself and this family from this curse. It will not be, and I should not drag more people into the fire."

"But we are here to help you, my dear. Please! I have resources of my own," Rupert implored, but Nicolina's footsteps clattering on the marble stairs were the only response.

❧ 14 ❧

I awoke very early the next morning by loud voices arguing in Italian. My iPhone read 8:15 A.M. Leaping from bed, I threw on the terry robe and ran into the hall.

Rupert and Evan were already there, keening their ears at the top of the stairs.

"What's going on?" I asked.

"I believe Lucca has arrived," Rupert said.

"At this time in the morning?"

"Apparently the count is an early riser," Rupert remarked.

The battle in the main hall was escalating. "Maybe we should go down and give Nicolina moral support?"

"She seems to be doing rather well on her own," Rupert said. "However, should she falter we will certainly intervene."

"'We' meaning Evan," I glanced up at the driver, embarrassed to find him gazing down at me. He looked damn good, as usual, in the house terry robe, whereas I probably resembled something round and vaguely fluffy. I looked quickly away, relieved that Nicolina seemed to be dominating the argument.

That woman could scream. Something crashed against a wall.

"I believe that's the non-Ming vase," Rupert remarked. "Pottery creates such a distinctive sound when it shatters."

"What's she saying?" I asked.

"They are both speaking so quickly, I can hardly keep up. She has just called the Count a number of very unflattering things and told him to get out of her house."

Lucca's voice bellowed.

"Now Lucca says it his house and she is only permitted to stay there temporarily. He is insisting that she allow a few of his men to stay inside for her, ah, protection." Rupert tilted his head. "Oh, and nothing in this place is worth anything of note, he says, so why does she insist upon having these useless—oh my, I do object to that term. I am not certain how to translate that."

"I believe 'twits' would be appropriate, sir," Evan remarked, gazing straight ahead.

"Such an insult! Never mind, Phoebe," Rupert said, patting my arm. "We shall rise above it. Now he adds that 'hanging around when grandfather cleaned everything out long ago.' Oh," Rupert caught his breath. "He's insisting that somebody named Butano thinks she knows where the Etruscan artifacts are hidden, and that, if that's true, she must tell him before it is too late. He says that this Butano will watch their every move until he locates it, so she had best not be keeping anything secret. That name does sound familiar but whatever does he mean by that?"

Nicolina's response was shrill, Lucca's retort like a string of baritone blows.

"Perhaps I should go down and break this up?" Evan asked.

"Good idea," I said. "I'll go, too."

"Wait," Rupert touched my arm. "The count will have his henchmen in tow. Let us not provoke a scene until we are certain that he won't leave on his own accord."

Then a single gunshot ripped the air. We sprang down the stairs at once, me taking the lead. At the bottom step, Evan firmly pushed me aside and stepped ahead.

In the middle of the corridor, Nicolina and her brother stood facing each other about four yards apart, both deadly still. Nicolina, white-faced and disheveled in her silk robe, pointed a pistol at her brother, who stood rigid with shock. Pottery shards lay strewn on the tiles between them, and I guessed a bullet was lodged in the wall somewhere.

Three men burst through the front door behind us and lurched to a halt, taking in the scene. Lucca barked at them and they hastily backed out the door. "And you," he said, turning to Rupert, speaking English, "you must take your friends and leave this house at once! This is family business and no concern of yours. My sister is not well."

"Do not dare to suggest that I am not sound in the brain, Lucca," Nicolina said in a steely voice. "Once that worked for grandfather, but not now, never now. My friends stay as long as I wish. It is you who must go. Leave before I shoot closer."

"You are dangerous with a gun, dear sister. Do not be so ridiculous," he said.

Nicolina aimed the pistol towards the ceiling and shot the neutered cupid right between the eyes. "See how I am dangerous? My aim is perfect, brother. Do not think that I miss you by accident. Now leave!" The final word was delivered with such fury, Lucca backed away.

"I will go, but you know this will never end until our family rights the wrongs of our grandmother. The longer you wait, the more you risk us all. We have lost our parents. Is that not enough for you?" he said. "Butano is out there waiting now."

"I said *lasciare*! And take your men with you! I do not need their protection."

Once Lucca slammed the door behind him, Nicolina sank onto a stool and leaned against the wall, the gun hanging limp in her hand. Rupert made to take it from her, but she held it away, engaged the safety catch, and plunged it into her pocket. "No. I must have a gun always. You must, too, if you are to stay." She looked at him, her expression half-pleading. "It is very dangerous to be friends with me."

Rupert straightened, clearing his throat. "And yet I am, and will remain so. Of course we will stay, but why would your own brother harm you, let alone us? His men quite gave Phoebe a fright yesterday."

"That was not them on the road, but in the garden, yes." Nicolina turned to me. "Lucca keeps two or three watching the villa and me at all times. I have no say. They come and search for the gold whenever they wish, always looking, but never finding. They would not have harmed you but they are bullies, like my brother."

"One of them fired a gun," I said. "I felt like they would have harmed me if they could."

"Like animals, when you kick them, they bite back. Lucca would not let them harm me or you. He blusters, that is all, and tries to protect, in his fashion. He fears for me as much as himself but I cannot talk to him. You see how it is. I cannot stand that he blames grandmother for everything. Grandfather is to blame."

"Why does who is to blame matter?" I asked.

"You are right. It is all the same. We are doomed either way." She closed her eyes.

I stepped forward. "Who is Butano? What aren't you telling us?"

Her eyes flew open. "My brother keeps bodyguards because he is afraid."

"Of what?" I said, wanting to scream with frustration.

"Butano is the powerful man who bought the gold from my grandfather."

"And he is Camorra," Evan remarked.

"Camorra?" I may have croaked out that word. "Camorra, as in the murderous crime society? They say they're as bad as the Mafia."

Nicolina nodded. "In the south, yes, but they operate worldwide. Vicenzo Butano was head of a very powerful Camorra clan when grandfather sold the gold to repay his debt. But he did not deliver. Butano was furious. He blamed my grandfather, our family. It was an insult, à blow to the honor, and also the failure to meet the contract. A deal had been struck, a contract made."

"That Butano?" Rupert croaked.

"He is why my grandfather locked my grandmother here—for her safety, as well as to make her say where she hid the gold. My grandmother, she did not weaken. That gold was her heritage and her husband betrayed her. Then she disappeared and my parents were killed. Butano thought murdering my parents would force my grandfather to talk, but he did not know where the gold was hidden. The Camorra are very powerful here. They own Campania; they run the government; they rule us all."

"Oh, my God." My hand flew to my mouth. "The Camorra drove your parents off the road."

"Yes. Now you understand." Nicolina climbed to her feet. "I want you to stay but that is selfish. Of course, you must go. It is too dangerous."

Rupert had paled but Evan's mask stayed true. "We cannot leave you, Nicolina," Rupert said. "We must find this blasted gold."

"If a miracle happens and we do find it," I began, "what will you do— pass the gold over to the crime lords? Butano must be very old now."

"He is dead but his spawn carries on his name," Nicolina said. "You would really stay?"

I said nothing. I was terrified. It was crazy, this whole thing was crazy. How could we win against the Camorra and why should I get involved? "Are they really still holding a grudge against the Vanvitellis after all these years?"

Nicolina shrugged. "In Italy, no one forgets. People in Siena still complain that the Florentines won a war five hundred years ago. Yes, the Butanos hold a grudge. They will never forget. It is not money, though my grandfather sold land to repay the debt. It is honor. The Butanos will not stop until they receive what they say is theirs. For a time, things were quiet but, when my grandfather died, it begins again." She paused, searching our faces. "You must think, talk together. Do not jump too quickly to say you will help. I cannot bear to have you harmed because of this. Lucca is right: It is the Vanvitellis' problem. We will talk again later."

Nicolina left us to dress, the three of us climbing upstairs behind her. As her door closed at the end of the hall, I stopped at my bedroom door. "Rupert, there's no way in hell I'm comfortable being involved in the Camorra."

"Phoebe, believe me when I say that I am as alarmed as you are. I certainly understand if you decide to leave, but I refuse to desert her. Let us talk further after breakfast, shall we?"

Nodding, I entered my room and shut the door, my heart racing. What had I gotten myself into? What I had done in the past was fueled by equal parts extraordinary circumstances and pure adrenalin—oh, and maybe a dose of rage. Had I known in advance where I would end up in Turkey— imprisoned, kidnapped—I probably would have cowered in my bed. Still, here I was again, only this time with a decision to make.

A few minutes later, while attempting to push a comb through my hair, Nicolina knocked at my door. "May I come in?" she asked.

"Of course." I stepped aside, watching as she strolled into the room. She looked more composed now, dressed in her navy sweater and wide-legged pants, but her pale face remained tight with emotion.

"You have seen these paintings, yes?"

I dropped my comb on the bedside table and joined her as she gazed up at the ceiling. "The artwork is hard to ignore, even if all the males weren't missing their genitalia. Am I right in thinking that was your grandmother's doing?"

She sighed. "This she did when imprisoned here."

"She must have been enraged."

"Very, yes."

"So much so that not only did she hide the gold, but she climbed up to the ceilings all over the villa to castrate every single male?"

"Yes." She flashed a smile. "She had much time on her hands, si? She once painted those faces, also—my grandfather as Zephyr, she Amalfi, the nymph. That was for love, but look how love ends? She is dead and so are my parents. Maybe soon, all Vanvitellis will be gone. We wish for a happy ending but look how it goes?"

"I am sorry, sorry for your family and anxious for you. You must be very angry yourself. You castrated the gods on the stairs to the sea, didn't you? Those were recent," I said.

She pressed one hand over her mouth. "Childish of me, yes? Foolish. I flew here one weekend when I discovered my husband in bed with another." Her hand dropped and with it any trace of levity. "As if my grandmother's pain and mine were the same. I took a hammer and I banged off everything male, thinking of my grandfather, my husband, the Butanos, maybe even my brother. Like my grandmother, I felt the same." She shrugged. "No happy ending for the women in my family, you see. Like my grandmother, I blame the men. I blame them all."

"Maybe you can find your happy ending without a man, find it in yourself first?" I sounded like a self-help article but meant it. "There are happier endings that aren't necessarily the happily-ever-after kind with marriages and children."

Nicolina frowned. "I believe that, but why should men win and we lose always? Not for me, not now, maybe never. The Butanos will torture this family until we are gone. It is the way. Lucca has two children. I fear for them, I fear for us all." She turned to me suddenly and gripped both my shoulders. "Forgive me for asking you to come. It was wrong. Now you must go."

"No, as in absolutely not." Did I really say that? I stepped back.

Her hands dropped to her sides. "But you must. You see how dangerous it is. Rupert, he has a bodyguard, but you are a woman and—"

I raised my hand. "Don't say it, don't say 'you are a woman and more vulnerable,' or anything even close."

"But, it is true," she protested. "We are made to be helpless."

"No. We have brains, don't we? Do you seriously believe that our sex has to live with that—that restriction?" I almost said *shit*.

She opened her mouth as if to counter, but changed her mind. "No," she said, after a moment. "You are right. The women in this family, we have lived too long under our men. It is time to take charge."

"The women in this world have lived too long under men, period. I am not leaving," I repeated. *Oh my god, I am not leaving! The Camorra are following our every move but I'm not leaving!*

"You are so brave. How can I ever thank you?" She clutched me in a brief hug and then released me. "Here, you must take this. I have another." My gaze dropped to the pistol she turned butt-end towards me. "Take it," she urged.

My hand reached out and clutched the pistol, thinking how a year ago I would have resisted. Not now. I took a deep breath. "We'd better find this gold."

❧ 15 ☙

For two days, we searched every inch of the villa, including the dusty, mouse-ridden attic. We shoved around furniture and thumped walls looking for hollows, and even went so far as to sledgehammer away the plaster in places, all to no avail.

"It is no use," Nicolina said late on the second afternoon. "It has all been searched again and again by many people. It is not here." She sank onto the chair in the salon and buried her head in her hands.

"We simply have to explore other possibilities," Rupert remarked.

"Right." I wiped my face on my sleeve, trying to remove the dust after the attic episode. "Maybe your grandmother thought hiding it here was too obvious. Maybe she found a less likely location. Where was she the night she took the gold?"

Nicolina locked eyes with mine. "She found my grandfather in bed with a maid at one of his palazzos in Napoli. It is there he kept the collection in a locked case in a safe, but the timeline? That I do not know. She returned with her servants later—maybe one night, maybe two—and removed the gold."

"They drove a van up to a palazzo and just loaded up the gold and left?" I asked. "It sounds like one of those heist movies."

Nicolina smiled. "The palazzo overlooks the sea with a single road through the gate. My grandmother, she had keys to all the properties. It was not so difficult. My grandfather was not home. My father, he told me that grandfather had driven here to the villa to win her back, but while she went to the palazzo to take the gold, they crossed paths without seeing each other, you know?"

"Okay, then." I began strolling around the couch and chairs, now grouped like an island in a bare expanse of floor. "Could she have hidden the gold in one of the other estates?"

"Allora, but all have been searched. Nothing my grandfather owned would be safe. He looked everywhere many times." Nicolina clasped her hands in her lap.

"What about your grandmother's vineyard in Orvieto?" I asked.

"All searched and searched again," Nicolina said. "Even the casks for storing wine. Those properties are sold now."

Rupert sighed gustily. "Ah, the vino—the region is known for its exquisite whites."

"And the necropoli?"

"They now belong to the city of Orvieto. My grandmother would be happy for that, at least."

I turned to her, exasperated. "We need a map. Nicolina, do you have one?"

"Yes, somewhere. I will find. Excusi," she exited the room, leaving Rupert and I alone.

"There's something we're missing here," I told him.

"No doubt, but what besides gold?"

"I don't know," I said, "but I feel like it's right there in front of us, but we just can't see it."

Nicolina returned minutes later and spread a map across the couch. "I have circled all of my grandparents' properties. You see there and there?" she pointed three red-penciled circles in and about the coast of Naples, plus four along the Amalfi Coast, including the villa. "Those are places my grandfather sold." she indicated properties circled in ink, "and here are the Vanvitelli properties now."

I nodded, staring down at impressive real estate. "And the Orvieto properties?"

Her finger traced a line from just above Italy's booted ankle up to a region approximately upper-shin. "In pencil I circled them here and here. They belonged to my grandmother's family—all sold." Nicolina and Rupert exchanged glances.

"All gone," Rupert said.

"He sold your grandmother's estates but not his own?" I asked.

Nicolina nodded. "He would say that the south is superior, better climate, better wine—the old rivalries."

I stared at the map, prodding my mind to see hidden patterns.

Rupert, stared at the map without speaking.

"Surely your grandfather demanded answers from those servants?" I asked.

Nicolina brushed hair from her forehead. "They were killed only weeks after the gold disappeared—an accident, it is said."

"Another murder?" I asked.

"A boat off the coast, it capsized. They were taking my grandmother's things from Napoli here to the villa and hired a boat instead of driving—the road is treacherous, yes? Butano's work but nothing could be proved."

"Surely they didn't sail all the way down and around the coast?" I asked.

"No, no," said Nicolina. "They drove part way and hired a boat from Sorrento there," she indicated a spot just across the bay from Naples.

"In the day or at night?" I asked.

"At night."

"Why would anybody sail the coast at night unless they were up to something? Maybe they transported the gold somewhere else before heading to the villa?" I said. My gaze shifted further left on the map to knobs of land jutting into the sea close to Naples. One tiny spot appeared to have been circled in pencil but erased out. "Your grandparents owned an island?"

Nicolina caught her breath. "Yes, just off Procida—very small, just a cottage, but—" she paused, "but it still remains in our family. I thought it not important."

"The least likely place may be the likeliest," I pointed out.

She looked at me. "You are thinking the gold may be there?"

Rupert clapped his hands together. "Phoebe, I catch your drift. You are thinking that perhaps they stashed the gold on the island and were sailing back when ambushed by Butano—good thinking, certainly worth investigating."

"Yes." I studied the tiny nub of land. "And it's close enough for a boat ride to and from this coast. We should go immediately."

"It is no more than a few buildings and everyone walks. There are only two houses, ours and the caretaker's," Nicolina said. "It is not used, very run-down. But, if you go, I should stay so Butano will not be suspicious."

"They will be suspicious in any case," Rupert said. "They'll be sure to follow us, so we will require diversionary tactics." He turned to Evan, who stood by listening intently. "We are prepared for diversionary tactics, aren't we, old boy?"

"Absolutely, Sir," Evan said with a nod. "Diversionary tactics are our specialty."

"But we cannot leave you alone," Rupert said to Nicolina.

"I will be fine," Nicolina said. "I have a gun and Lucca's men outside."

"But will that be enough protection?" Rupert asked.

"I think, yes. If I stay without more protection, it will appear less suspicious," she said.

"Excellent. We shall charter a boat and proceed this afternoon. Evan, do be so kind as to search your laptop for boat rentals."

"Will you be wanting something very fast, Sir?" Evan asked.

"Of course," his employer responded, "in case Butano gives chase. Besides, we like fast things don't we?"

"We do indeed," Evan said with a smile.

"So do I. Wait," I held up my hand. "Are you thinking some boat equivalent of a Maserati? Fishing boats are less obvious. What they lose in speed, they'll gain in invisibility. No one will give them a second glance."

"A fishing boat?" Rupert straightened. "Certainly not—foul-smelling things—I can't abide them. Besides, Phoebe, on this coast there are so many flashy boats, we're sure to blend."

"People only have to look at you once to assume you wouldn't be caught dead on a fishing boat," I said.

"Because I would not."

"She may have a point, Sir," Evan added.

"Of course, I do. Look, I can captain a fishing boat in all conditions, just as long as I have a nautical map," I said.

Evan, bent down to speak quietly in my ear. "I believe Sir Rupert intends for me to man the helm, madam."

"But I have extensive experience with watercraft, Evan. I'm the best woman to 'man the helm,' as you call it."

Evan gave a little nod. "I'm am sure you are very skillful, madam."

"You may be the best woman, Phoebe, my dear, but Evan here is the best man. His experience with sea maneuvers is extensive. It is he who must man the craft. I must insist."

Nicolina and I exchanged glances. *And so it goes.* I gazed up at Evan, deciding not to fight this one. "Is there anything you can't do?"

He thought for a moment, perhaps too long a moment. "I can't knit, madam."

"I'd teach you how if you'd drop the 'madam'."

Evan flashed a smile, holding my gaze seconds longer than necessary.

"Phoebe," Rupert placed a firm hand on my arm. "You must remain with Nicolina."

I exhaled slowly. "Since you obviously don't need me, I will, of course."

"Nobody needs to stay with me," Nicolina insisted. "I am not such a shrinking rose, and I have a gun."

"A gun will be little enough protection should Butano's men attempt to penetrate the villa. At least your brother's men are still guarding you," Rupert said.

"They are more like prison guards," Nicolina protested, "big bullies, like my brother. I have told him I do not want them here."

"Surely not?" Rupert turned to her. "You must request that he repost them immediately. They may be all that's keeping Butano from entering the estate."

Nicolina flicked her hand. "No matter, he did not listen to me. He never listens. They are still there—Lucca's men on this side of the road, Butano's spread all over."

"Oh, perfect." Rupert dabbed his forehead with what appeared to be a crisp new hankie. He must have brought a suitcase full. "Nevertheless, I believe that it is probably not Butano's intention to penetrate the villa just yet. He will watch and wait for you to make a move, thinking that you will lead him to the treasure, eventually. I suspect his impatience will mount."

"Meanwhile, we'll stick together, you and I," I told Nicolina.

She reached out and squeezed my hand. "Thank you, Phoebe. You are a friend, both of you," she added, including Rupert, "but what you do is very dangerous. Still, I stay."

"Good, we'll stay together," I said, sounding braver than I felt. "We'll defend the fort, so to speak."

"Oh, dear." Rupert fanned himself with the map. "I do hope that won't be necessary. We must move quickly and return as soon as possible, but first to plot a diversionary plan. It is so blasted hot here. For once, I long for England." He glanced at Evan. "Evan, a plan, old chap."

"I'm on it, Sir." Evan excused himself and exited.

"What do you have on hand by way of automobiles?" Rupert asked Nicolina.

She shook her head. "I am very sorry, only the two Fiats, one I keep for driving here—the keys I keep on a hook in the kitchen—and Sophia and Ricardo use the older one. That is it besides your Maserati."

"Best we use the newer Fiat and leave the Maserati here, lest Butano's men recognize me and give chase, as they did previously. I'm certain they'll follow us in any event, but hopefully will remain none the wiser."

"Yes, but would you not want to go very fast in the Maserati?" she asked.

"If matters proceed as I envision, speed will not be the key so much as stealth. Evan and I will simply amble our way down to the nearest boating facility in your little Fiat and appear to take a joyride as harmless tourists."

"At night?" I asked.

"Phoebe, look at the sky," he swept his hand towards the curtained window, where we could only imagine the canopy in question. "By my estimate, sunset will be upon us in another two hours. My driver is merely transporting me on a leisurely sunset cruise, much like other pleasure seekers plying the Tyrrhenian Sea as we speak. I shall look the picture of touristic innocence. I even have the perfect outfit. Now, if you will excuse me, I had best prepare myself." And with that, he left the room.

"But wouldn't the Butanos think it odd you're not using the Maserati?" I called after him. He didn't respond.

"You do not agree with his plans?" Nicolina asked.

I turned back to her. "We don't always agree on the specifics. Excuse me, I'll just see what he has up his sleeve."

"Yes, and I will go to see Sophia and Ricardo. They must have enough food for two days."

"You won't tell them what's going on, will you?" I asked, as she reached the hall.

"Allora, I am not such a fool!" she assured me.

Moments later, I found Rupert and Evan, heads together, in Evan's room. They glanced up as I pushed through the half-opened door.

"You need to tell me what your plans are step-by-step," I said. "Nicolina and I are going to feel like sitting ducks while you go off on your joyride."

Rupert straightened. "Phoebe, this is hardly a joyride."

"Figure of speech."

"Of course, I will share all the necessary details. We are seeking a suitable watercraft and will proceed as if off to join the merry boaters plying the waves beyond Naples. We will appear to be sailing towards the lovely isle of Procida." He rubbed his hands together, the picture of glee. "I shall wear my Italian linen suit with the coordinating brogues and possibly a straw hat. Did I bring my hat, Evan?"

"You did, Sir," the driver said without lifting his eyes from the laptop. "Two of them." Beside him on the desk, I couldn't help noticing a large tome entitled *The History of the Etruscans*.

"Very good," Rupert turned to me and smiled.

"Rupert, stop imagining yourself as Agent 007 zooming across the sea in a cigarette boat, circa 1959, even if your driver was a former spy. This is serious. There are all kinds of cross-currents at work here, none of them are of the oceanic variety."

"Whatever are you talking about? I am perfectly aware of the dangers." He steepled his fingers and paced the room. "We will proceed directly to the marina at Sorrento to best approximate the path taken the evening of the servants' watery departure. If all works according to plan, we will be back here by the day after tomorrow, hopefully with new insights as to where Grandmother Vanvitelli secreted a fortune in Etruscan artifacts, if not in actual possession of the gold. You see," he paused, spreading his hands, "it is all falling together brilliantly."

"The only brilliance I see is the glitter of ancient gold in your eyes. Don't forget why we're here."

He slapped a hand over his heart. "Phoebe, you wound me. I remain focused on ending this untenable situation for Nicolina and, indeed, the Vanvitellis."

"While keeping an eye out for any profitable opportunities that might appear along the way— 'vulturing,' in other words."

"Sir, the boat's booked," Evan said, looking up.

"Very well, I shall go change. Pack me a bag, dear chap," he called to his man as he scuttled from the room, me at his heels.

"Already done, Sir," Evan called behind him.

"This whole thing makes me squirrelly," I said, following Rupert into his room.

"Phoebe, you are merely nervous about staying here without benefit of my protection, but fear not, for Lucca's men are at hand."

"It's not that."

"Then, perhaps you regret missing out on our little escapade? I know I've provided only the merest taste of the Amalfi region but—"

"It's not that, either."

"What then?" he asked turning to face me.

"Something's off around here but I can't put a finger on it."

"Of course, something is off: the Camorra have us surrounded while attempting to squeeze out Etruscan gold, which we don't possess! How 'off' can one get?"

"Besides the obvious, I mean." I lifted my eyes towards the ceiling. "It's this house, it's Nicolina, it's everything."

"Pull yourself together, Phoebe. You do have an active imagination. I am most certain that is all that affects you now. Remember, my success rate in these matters is rather high, as is yours, I might add. I think of every contingency and have multiple alternative plans in the offing. Now do leave me to change. Time is of the essence."

I withdrew to my room. Piles of rubble by the wardrobe marked where we'd knocked through the wall earlier. All we'd gained from that episode was a few gaping holes showcasing old wood and patches of dry rot. I gazed around and sighed. Moments later, I picked up my knitting, perched on a chair, and furiously worked a few teal-on-green linen stitches, trying to steady my nerves.

Soon Rupert appeared at my door. "Phoebe? Have you the phone I gave you?" he asked.

I didn't look up. "My Foxy phone? Of course."

"Please ensure that it remains engaged at all times. I will text you with information as to our progress, and do keep me informed as to what goes on here likewise, which is hopefully nothing," he said, stepping towards me. He now wore a navy double-breasted linen sport jacket, white pants, and a polo shirt with a coordinating paisley ascot knotted at his neck.

"Sure." I stood up, fished out the Foxy phone from my pocket, and turned it on. "I don't want to spoil the mood, but you look more like the Duke of Windsor than Double-Oh-Seven."

"Phoebe, don't talk such nonsense. I am merely dressing the tourista part."

"Since when do tourists dress in other than shorts and a fanny pack?"

"When they choose not to look like run-of-the-mill buffoons. Is the phone in working order?"

"As far as I know. Now I'm back to two phones, one tracking my every move. Why do I feel like the more technologically connected I am, the less I know what's going on?"

"You worry far too much."

"For good reason."

"One more thing," he held out the keys for the Maserati. "Just in case you and Nicolina need beat a hasty retreat."

I took the keys. "Well, there's a comforting thought—the two of us zooming along the Amalfi Coast chased by a crime gang."

"Don't be so melodramatic. Perhaps you need a gun, too."

"Nicolina has lent me one."

"Very well, then. Now, do excuse me, for we must be off," and he turned and exited the room.

Minutes later, Nicolina and I stood together watching Rupert and Evan climb into the diminutive bee-yellow car. In any other circumstances, I might have laughed, but tonight nothing struck me as funny.

As the car pulled up beside us, Nicolina stepped up to the passenger side. "The Maserati, have you left the keys?" she asked Rupert through the open window.

"Phoebe has them, but I trust you aren't planning any evening excursions?" Rupert said.

She laughed. "But no, I ask in case we must leave quickly."

"My thinking exactly. Hopefully that will not be necessary. Until later, then," and Rupert buzzed up the window as the car drove away.

Nicolina and I watched as the rear lights disappeared around the corner. "Well," she said, turning to me. "What shall we do to keep busy, Phoebe? Do you play backgammon?"

I didn't, actually, but she taught me the rules on the terrace until the sun pooled hot pink into the sea. As it grew dark and chillier, we moved into the salon and continued to play while the aroma of cooking permeated the villa. The quality of Sophia's meals had improved significantly since Nicolina's arrival and dinner was the one thing I really looked forward to on that long evening.

"Do you have a lover?" Nicolina casually asked over our eighth full round of backgammon. By then, I was winning at least half our games.

"Um, no," I said, keeping my eyes on the tiles.

"No? But I am surprised. You are so young and lovely. I thought there would be many men."

"One is enough, providing I find the right person."

"Me, I have tried and failed," she said quietly. "I wish you more success."

I met her eyes then. "I'm sorry about your husband, Nicolina. I can just imagine how much that betrayal hurts."

She shrugged. "I am to blame, I think. I was too eager to find safety, and Geoffrey, he is very rich and powerful, and offered me what I thought I

***

needed—protection, money, escape from Lucca. I think sometimes that I am very much my grandmother's girl."

"In what way?"

She lifted her hands to the ceiling. "I try to escape our history, but can we ever? It follows us everywhere. Another person cannot break that chain for you. Now I am done."

"Done what?"

She jerked to her feet. "Done playing by men's rules. Supper must be ready now. I will go check with Sophia so soon we will eat."

I watched her sweep from the room before pulling my Foxy phone from up my sleeve and checking for messages. As I'd hoped, Rupert had texted: *All's well. Had a lovely ride to the island. Cottage is splendid, though in need of much care. Did not notice any giving chase. Will text again tomorrow. R.E.F.*

Smiling, I slipped the phone back up my sleeve and pulled my iPhone from my jacket pocket to message Max: *Work almost done. Will have lots to tell you when I return. Love Phoebe XXX.* If I told him the truth, he'd fly to Italy in a microsecond, and possibly risk all the hard work he'd put into his rehabilitation.

By the time I'd put the cell away, Nicolina had reappeared.

"Sophia is ready for us now. She has prepared a favorite of mine, a dish from Oliveto—ravioli di funghi. Do you know it? The porcini mushrooms are very fresh this time of year."

"Wonderful." And it was, though I suspected culinary experiences in Italy usually spelled delicious. That night we dined under the portico while the terrace fireplace burned warmly in the grate. As comforting as it was, it didn't dispel the chill of my misgiving. I kept checking my Foxy phone on my lap shielded by the tablecloth.

Nicolina missed nothing. "Is Rupert all right?"

"Yes, so far," I said with a smile, as I tucked my phone up my sleeve for what I told myself must be the last time that night, and picked up my fork. "This is incredible."

We dined and chatted as if the Camorra weren't outside our gates, as if I was an honored guest rather than an employee of sorts. The night drew on, as did the dinner. Italians did not believe in rushing meals.

Sophia appeared at my elbow, about to refill my wine goblet for the second time.

"Thank you, but one glass is enough for me," I said, waving her away. She stepped back with a brief smile.

"In Italy, we drink much wine," Nicolina remarked.

"Oh, yes, I know. It's just that too much makes me sleepy."

"But why not? It is night. You will relax."

"No thanks, really." My past experiences with drinking in heightened circumstances had not ended well. I needed to maintain all my faculties, which was challenging enough after a big carb-fest. The first course, a salad, was hardly small, and the second pasta course would have sufficed most people under normal circumstances. Along with bread and the ravioli came the main course of grilled fish. Dessert was the best tiramasu I'd ever tasted, but instead of coffee, Sophia served that sweet after-dinner wine along with a silver plate of almond cookies—more sugar, more alcohol.

"Oh, I can't," I insisted, but she poured me a tiny glass of port-like wine as if she hadn't heard me.

"Try to relax," Nicolina said. "In Italy, wine and conversation are the best dinner companions, you see. This is Vin Santo, my favorite. As a child, I was permitted a small glass with sweets. It was such a treat. It's a lovely conclusion to a fine meal."

I couldn't be rude, so I sipped, tasting bitter with the sweet. I smiled at my hostess, who watched me across the table. "Tasty. I can see why you loved it as a child."

"As an adult, too. It comforts me before bed. Try to drink more."

I nodded, pretending to sip while doing a lip-press against the glass. As expected, the combination of sugar, carbs, and alcohol had already delivered a knock-out punch to my bloodstream. I stifled a yawn.

Nicolina continued to chat while the candles flickered in the breeze before the dying fire. I heard her ask Ricardo to add fresh wood, or was I only imagining that since it was in Italian? I was so sleepy, I could hardly keep my eyes open.

"What terrible company I am," I said. "The wine has made me tired. I should head for bed."

"But you have not finished," she said, getting to her feet. "Excuse me one momento. Please finish your Vin Santo."

The moment she slipped through the terrace doors, I poured what remained in my glass into the nearest potted vine. *Sweet dreams, trumpet vine.* By the time Nicolina returned, my glass sat empty.

"Oh, good. Now you will sleep well."

To prove her point, I crushed another yawn into my napkin. "I'm sure that's true. I'll just head to bed now. I'm a terrible guest," I said, standing up.

"Not true," Nicolina assured me, rising also. "You are the perfect guest, but me, I am not so good a hostess. I should have offered coffee."

"Not too late," I said, brightening. "I'd like an espresso."

"So sorry, I apologize. No espresso. We ran out."

I was certain Evan had bought extra stores on his shopping expedition but it wasn't worth arguing about, and sleep seemed preferable, anyway.

Arm in arm, Nicolina walked me down the darkened hall beneath the neutered cupid while I wondered idly why somebody didn't turn on the lights. Up the stairs we went.

"I will retire, too," my companion said. "It has been such a long day, yes?"

"It has," I agreed, pausing at my door. Nicolina turned to wave at me from the end of the hall. I returned her wave and headed straight for bed.

❧ 16 ❧

I awoke fully clothed. My bed lamp was on, and my brain felt gummed and woozy. I sat at the edge of the bed, struggling to think.

Must clean my teeth and wash my face. Going to bed without doing either was against my manifesto. How did I let that happen?

I yawned, trying not to drop back to sleep. As I climbed to my feet, the room tipped and swayed. My knees buckled, and I sat back down.

My mouth tasted like a mouse had camped out on my tongue.

Something wrong here, something very wrong.

I stared at my carpet bag, which sat upended on the floor, its innards tossed into a sad little colored nest of tangled yarn. Slowly, I lifted my gaze and scanned the room. Both my suitcases and Foxy's yawned open, the contents scattered around the floor. *Oh my god, I've been robbed!* I struggled to stand, gripping the bed for support. But wait, I didn't have anything of value. Butano must have broken into the villa and searched for the gold, but why here, why in my room, in my suitcases?

Nicolina! They must have Nicolina! I lurched to the door and tried to yank it open, but it held fast. I stared at the doorknob in disbelief. My heart thudded, my head spun. *They locked me in!*

Stay calm, I warned myself. I leaned against the door, forcing my brain to function, my heart to settle.

Butano must have kidnapped Nicolina. Nothing else made sense. I needed to call for help, maybe contact Lucca, certainly Rupert, but where were Sophia and Ricardo? Maybe they had them, too, or worse, those two had been working for Butano the whole time.

That had to be it. The Santo had tasted off. Sophia poured me a glass against my wishes. She tried to drug me. I pressed my eyes shut. She *had* drugged me, and whatever was in that stuff, it was strong enough to knock my lights out after only one gulp.

Oh, god. I pressed my hands to my face. Nicolina had drunk two glasses. She might be near-death right now, or worse. I had to find her, get help.

I stumbled back across the room, banging into the wall and knocking a painting to the floor. The crash ricocheted in my skull. Someone had to have heard that. I stilled, listening, but the house felt dead the way old buildings do when no living thing walks the halls.

I needed my brain back. I needed coffee. My gaze landed on the basket on the nightstand. Did I imagine seeing a package of chocolate-covered espresso beans? I lunged to the stand, gripping the marble top while rifling through the basket. In minutes, I found the packet, had it ripped open, and was chewing the beans, swallowing them one after the other, washed down with water.

Caffeine jolted the first clear thought into my head moments later.

Okay, so Butano had Nicolina, which might mean Butano's men had subdued Lucca's gang in the process.

Where were my phones? I rummaged through the tossed carpet bag pile, finding my iPad, but no iPhone. Whoever locked me in didn't want me calling reinforcements.

No, wait—I'd put my iPhone in my jacket pocket. I slapped my hand over the pocket to confirm it missing. The Foxy cell, which I'd slipped up my sleeve at dinner, remained.

I glanced down, shocked to realize the state of my clothes—jacket pockets inside out, sweater yanked up to my bra, jeans only half-zipped. I'd been searched.

I pulled out my Foxy phone, texting an urgent message to Rupert: *Locked in my room. They have Nicolina. Sophia drugged me.*

I didn't have Lucca's number but Rupert must. If he didn't get back to me ASAP, I'd call him directly, followed by the police. I didn't care about all this fear of the cops thing, but I needed to get out of this room quietly, and I needed whoever locked me in to think I was still knocked out. I couldn't risk speaking out loud into a phone.

It was still only 12:34 A.M.

Stealth mattered. I crept to the balcony door, still ajar. If Butano thought I wouldn't shimmy down the balcony on a tied bedsheet, he was right—or, at least, not as my first option. The bedsheet thing probably worked better in movies than in reality, anyway.

The terrace hung deep in shadows and the wind rustled the trees, but I couldn't hear footsteps or voices. On the far perimeter, the lights from Sophia and Ricardo's cottage glowed. *Bastards.* I retreated into the room and scrambled to the door.

The lock appeared original to the house—an eighteenth century brass mechanism worked by a three-inch key which, I noted, had disappeared from my bedside table. Fine, underestimate my intelligence, why don't you? Any reader of Victorian novels knows that many domestic antique doors might be unlocked with a straight implement, such as a hairpin, which I didn't have, or a knitting needle, of which I had plenty.

As it turned out, it didn't take long, and a tapestry needle worked best. After five minutes of wiggling, the lock clicked open.

I returned to the room long enough to stuff necessities into my carpet bag. The Maserati and Orvieto keys remained tucked within the ripped lining. I'd take those, plus the clothes on my back, and nothing more, though somehow my tangled knitting project ended back in the bag, too. As for the gun Nicolina had lent me, I was not surprised to find it gone from the drawer where I'd shoved it.

Moments later, I eased open the door and scrambled down the hall to Nicolina's room. The room lay open, the bed still made. Butano must have nabbed her shortly after we said goodnight.

I stepped into the darkened hall and fumbled-felt my way down the stairs. In the main corridor, I followed a glimmer of light emanating from the back of the villa.

Still no sign of life. Pressing against the wall, I inched along until I reached the kitchen, peered through the half-opened door, and found the empty room blazing with lights. Three espresso cups sat on the kitchen table, along with a pack of cigarettes. The unwashed supper dishes remained stacked on the counters.

Scuttling out through the terrace doors, I dove into the dense shadows of the shrubbery edging the patio. The night was cool with a breeze shifting light through the cypress. Voices reached my ears in snatches, riding the wind from the di Cappo cottage.

I scampered across the pavers towards the cottage, and dove into the sanctuary of the bushes. Voices rang more clearly now, arguing in Italian—Ricardo's and Sophia's—agitated, querulous. Edging my way through the bougainvillea, I heard a second female voice exclaiming in frustration. I slipped to the half-open window, slowly raising my head to eye level.

The sight nearly knocked the breath out of me: Sophia and Ricardo standing in a kitchen opposite Nicolina—a very spry, upright Nicolina, who paced the floor, her hands slicing the air. She pointed to something, demanding answers from Sophia, who only shrugged. Ricardo stood by with his eyes on the floor.

What the hell was going on? I crouched back down, my relief at seeing Nicolina alive plunging into a stunned free-fall. She had drugged me? She had body-searched me? What other explanation was there, since she obviously wasn't suffering from ill effects of the Santo? The drug had been for me. She wanted to immobilized *me*, but why?

Fishing out my Foxy phone, I ensured the MUTE was engaged, and checked the screen. No response. He had to be asleep. Slowly, I raised myself just far enough to peer through the window again. Nicolina was still pacing, one ear pressed against a phone. She said "si, si" and "no, no" followed by a string of sharp-honed words that didn't sound happy. Suddenly, she swung around and threw a set of keys onto the table. Ricardo jumped like he'd been electrocuted, swiped up the keys, and made for the door.

I ducked back down. A door slammed in the villa and then another, followed by the sound of footsteps beating up the outer stairs to the road. A car engine sputtered and stalled. The ignition ground again and this time the car rumbled to life.

I slid deeper into the bushes seconds before two other sets of footsteps followed after the first. Nicolina and her two servants were taking off in one of the cars?

I scrambled after them, taking two stairs at a time.

I was almost at the top when I heard Nicolina cry "Pronto!" followed by tire squeals. By the time I sprung up the last few steps and reached the garage, the car had gone, disappearing around one of the two corners that twisted before the villa.

Shit, shit, shit! I needed to phone Foxy, the cops, somebody, but I couldn't let them get away. I dug the Maserati keys from my carpet bag and ran towards the sports car. Damned if I would let Nicolina get away with this.

Halfway there, I froze. I had no idea which way they'd gone, left or right. I hadn't a clue where they were heading, either. Driving the Amalfi Coast at night didn't seem the smartest move, either.

Swinging around, I bolted back downstairs, through the villa to the cottage, speed-dialing Rupert in the process. The phone was still ringing in my ear when I entered the kitchen where the three had been moments before. I scanned the top of the table seeing cigarettes, a map, coffee mugs, my iPhone! I shoved the phone into my jacket pocket as Rupert's voice reached my ears.

"Phoebe!"

"Rupert, Nicolina drugged me, not Butano! She just drove off with Ricardo and Sophia."

"Calm down."

"I am calm! She got away and I have no idea which way to head, left or right. I—"

"I said calm down."

I caught my breath, staring straight ahead at the wall clock created from an painted pottery tile. I breathed in and out, focusing on the blue glazed flowers twining amid the green leaves, the same kind of pottery I saw in Ravello.

"Listen carefully," Rupert continued. "Get as far away from the villa as you can go, immediately. As soon as you are positive no one is following you, pull over and call me back. I will explain more then. Go right, head towards Amalfi, and follow the signs to Salerno, understand? Not left towards Naples. I will explain later. I have reason to believe Butano's men may come after you. Phoebe, are you listening?"

"I'm listening. Where am I going?"

"To my place in Orvieto. I will explain later. I beg your pardon?" I heard him say to someone. "Surely not?"

"Rupert, what's going on?"

"Phoebe, are you in the car yet? We're running out of time."

I scrambled from the cottage, through the house, and up the stairs, phone pressed to my ear. "Maybe she was searching for the Maserati keys. Why is she doing this?"

"I don't have time to talk, I said. Must hang up now."

"Are you coming—" but he'd clicked off.

I swore a hundred shades of fury as I popped the lock, tossed in my bag, and climbed into the sleek, low car. So what if this was a sports car? I'd driven many fast things before, including an old boyfriend's motorcycle, ancient Land Rovers, Jeeps, fishing trawlers, speedboats, and even sailboats. Surely, I could manage a million-dollar road-jet humming with pent-up speed and technology?

The thing hummed as I backed onto the road. I ignored the backup camera—too distracting—and swung the car to the right, retracing our path from earlier in the day. That would be earlier in the day when, in broad daylight and in the care of a professional driver, we had been nearly run off the cliff by dudes from a crime lord. So what if I was alone on one of the world's most deadly drives—at night, at frickin night, in a frickin Maserati?

The car cruised down the narrow road like skin on silk, my hands gripping the wheel as I tried to focus on the narrow deserted road ahead. Forget about what lies below, I told myself. Don't focus on the spin-away gulf of empty air beyond those flimsy guard rails, or how deep the drop, how torturous the turns.

At least the road was almost empty, maybe because no one with half a brain would dare take on this road at night.

A flash of headlights zoomed up behind me. I had a half-brainless companion, after all.

ℜ I 7 ℜ

Whoever kept me company on the Roma Road that night stayed a respectable distance behind. Good thing, since restraining a warp-speed car to a donkey-train pace took concentration enough. Every time I touched the accelerator, the Maserati leapt forward like a cheetah escaping captivity.

"Not like that, buddy," I said aloud. "Here we go slow and take every turn with exquisite care."

Driving at night, with the reflective signs catching the headlights, seemed easier than driving in the daytime with the panoramic distractions. I could focus on the road while still keeping one eye on the car behind.

Or, that's what I told myself.

If that was Butano's man behind me, he was missing out on a prime opportunity to run me off the cliff. Who would think twice if a tourist hurled to her death in a Maserati at the dead of night on the Amalfi Coast? They'd only need to check my blood-alcohol level to make a reasonable conclusion.

But when the driver still made no move after miles and miles of opportunistic locations that included knife-back turns and clear stretchers of eerily empty road, I relaxed. He had to be some innocent driver, after all.

Why would Butano want me, anyway? Surely those bad boys would have taken off after Nicolina first? Or Foxy? Could they really expect me to know where the gold was hidden?

I might even worry about Nicolina if she hadn't shafted me. As it was, I knew nothing, absolutely nothing, not even where I was going, no thanks to her.

And hadn't I bought into her signora in distress ruse? She played me.

Unconsciously, I slammed my foot on the accelerator, sending the Maserati bolting ahead but managed to hard-turn the wheel just seconds before we would have gone flying through a guard rail.

Enough. Calm down. I needed to call Rupert, but where on this minuscule road could I do that? I had no choice but to keep on driving, part of my brain numbed down to road-fixed tunnel vision.

Eventually I drove through the sleepy streets of Amalfi, following the signs to Salerno, almost giddy with relief. I had made it that far.

The car behind me was soon swallowed by sporadic traffic disgorging from bars and clubs. There would be no better place to pull over and make a call so I dashed up a side street, double-backed on a tiny road curling upward through the city, and pulled into a public parking lot before a magnificent cathedral.

I cut the engine and flicked off the lights. It was 2:34 A.M. and I was still alive. Slowly I exhaled, picked up my Foxy phone, and speed-dialed Rupert. I counted twelve beats before he answered.

"Phoebe!"

"Rupert! I—"

"Why are you in Amalfi? You should be heading towards Salerno, and then to the autostrada to catch the highway straight towards Rome, and on to Orvieto."

"You're tracking me? Oh, of course you are. I don't think I'm being followed. Look, I've lost Nicolina totally. I have no idea—"

"We're tracking her, too. Phoebe, do listen. Someone scuttled our boat and all power to the island has been cut. I am unsure how long the batteries will last. Pardon? Oh, Evan thinks possibly 5 minutes."

"What? You're still on the island? But—"

"Hush! We're on red already. You must get to my house in Orvieto at once. Use the car's navigation system. You have the keys?"

"Yes."

"Good. I shall have assistance waiting and I have just sent you an email giving precise instructions. And, trust me, you are being followed. Butano has all of us followed, expecting one of us to take him to the gold. You must lose him. If he tracks you down and learns that you know nothing, he may kill you for spite. The Camorra are ruthless."

"But—"

"I said plug in 42 Via Pecorelli, Orvieto, into your GPS and drive like the furies!"

"But what about Nicolina?"

"Forget Nicolina. It appears she's heading towards Rome. For now, just drive. Pardon? Must go."

"No, wait!"

"Things are alarming here!" And he clicked off.

I sat gripping the steering wheel. Things are alarming here, too. Fear percolated back into my bloodstream—anxiety for me, anxiety for Rupert, and plain fury at Nicolina. Nonstop adrenalin pumping into my system would burn me out too soon, and I still had a long way to go.

Pushing down the window, I inhaled the night. Around me, the town lights glowed, the stepped tops of the architecture silhouetted against a luminous starry sky.

I was alone, thrust into another untenable situation for all the right reasons gone wrong. And I had to get moving. Again.

Tapping the dashboard screen, a map appeared, showing my position as somewhere in Amalfi city. The system appeared intuitive. Fine. I chose the country, which conveniently listed options for Italian cities beginning with "O," and tapped Orvieto, and added the street name, watching as the system glommed onto my destination. Up popped a blue line that snaked a route across country—a long way across country—an estimated 5-hour drive, shooting right past Rome. All roads lead to Rome, all right.

A woman's voice instructed me which turn to take.

"Well, thanks for that," I said, taking comfort in befriending something vaguely human. Glowing dials, warmly colored indicator lights, a disembodied voice—what else did I have?

The gas indicator dropped to one bar. Slowly, I backed up onto the road and cruised down the hill, keeping an eye out for an all-nighter station, which I found near the port at the bottom. Self-service wasn't an option here, but the attendant insisted on admiring the car while muttering over the damaged bumper as if holding me responsible.

"Camorra," I said with a shrug. His alarm might have been comical some other time, some other place. "Pronto, pronto," I added to hurry him up. That worked, too.

Armed with vending machine espresso, I resumed my journey minutes later, back on the last stretch of Amalfi coastal road following the route prescribed by the navigation system. I'd dubbed her "Delphi," in honor of oracles everywhere. She told me where to go and I told her where to go— simple as that. Talking helped.

The crazy things we do when trying to stay sane.

The Maserati and I curved up and around hills on the twisty road in a surreal landscape, heading for Salerno, which came upon me suddenly in an expanse of crisscrossing ramps leaping over a huge port with parks and modern buildings. Fluorescent lamps washed everything in a cool, impersonal glow.

"You could have warned me," I said aloud.

"Turn left onto the Via Irno," Delphi responded.

"Go to hell."

Signs to the autostrada appeared. Edgy with caffeine and exhaustion, everything jarred and jabbed. Not until I swerved onto the on-ramp heading for the A2 to Naples did I note the car picking up speed behind me.

Positive it was the same car that tailed me along the Almafi, I hit the accelerator, and bolted down the road. Surely the Maserati could out-drive anything, and I didn't care if the police flagged me down. If a speed limit existed, I flew past it. My only goal was to gain distance between me and my tail.

Eighteen-wheelers gunning for Naples dominated the road as I wove in and out of the lanes, the black car keeping pace. Impossible to doubt he was following me now and, I realized with a jolt, his car had no trouble keeping up. If this continued, I'd reach Orvieto with unwanted company. I had to shake the bastard.

Possibilities flicked in and out of my brain as the miles flew by. Finally a decent idea took hold. I eased into a lightening cruise of about 90 miles per hour, noting that my tail matched my speed accordingly. Keeping a steady speed, I wove in and out of traffic as if unaware of being followed, still on a fast trajectory towards my destination.

The turn-off for Naples came and went as I continued north on the A1 towards Rome. After about two hours, what I'd been waiting for finally aligned: four or more tractor trailers in a row on the right-hand side approaching an exit to a place called Tivoli. Hoping that the tractors shielded me from view, I zipped between two of them and darted down the ramp, deep into a little town.

Nobody followed.

Delphi went crazy, telling me where to rejoin the autostrada. I told her to shut up while I followed the secondary road signs towards Rome, so exhausted my eyes tried to scratch their way through my lids.

Up and down, around and back again, the Italian country roads totally stymied me. I swore I drove into the same village twice. After twenty minutes, Delphi recalibrated and was back to telling me where to go, this time indicating back roads. At a place called Guidonia Montecelio, I allowed her to guide me back onto the A1, where I proceeded to bypass Rome, thinking I'd shaken Butano's boys at last. By rights, they should be somewhere far ahead, mistaking somebody else's taillights for mine.

An hour and a half later, I picked up the first signs for Orvieto. By then, both my gas tank and I were almost drained. With only a few miles left, we should make it.

The sanctuary Rupert promised glowed in my mind. I'd find a safe haven, maybe food, and certainly a bed. It wasn't until Orvieto rose like an otherworldly land against the predawn sky, that I checked my rear-view mirror. Headlights were bearing down on me.

Shit! I gunned the car up and around the curving road heading up the plateau. Two choices ahead—left or right. I slammed my foot on the gas heading right.

Seconds later, I was zipping into a long, treed boulevard ending at a square with a ruined castle to the left. Delphi was telling me to take a right-hand turn through the gates up a medieval street narrowing the higher it went. Instinct told me to slow down, but adrenalin powered me faster.

I hung a hard right, the boys sticking to me so close, I could almost feel their breath down my neck. Delphi was droning on and on, repeating the words *Proceed by foot, proceed by foot* until I fired my finger at the mute button.

Fear-blind, I negotiated maddening tiny lanes, winding higher and higher up the ancient town.

Soon I'd have nowhere to go. Two more turns followed by a flash decision to hang left brought me to a dead end. I slammed on the brakes. Out of road. The lane swerved through a narrow arch crammed up the throat of two buildings, leaving me no way back and no way ahead.

Behind me, my pursuers screeched to a halt and jumped from the car—two men, pistols pulled.

Panic spiked. I hit the gas, jolting the Maserati under the arch and up the tapering lane, tires bouncing over cobbles.

Foot down full, I ground the car against the walls, cringing against the sound of screeching metal, the crunch of side mirrors and door handles smashing off.

Seconds later, the Maserati crushed to a halt, impossibly wedged, engine whining.

Men shouted behind me. I popped the trunk open while pushing the sunroof button, hitched my bag over my shoulder, and crawled out onto the roof to slide down the hood.

In seconds, my feet hit the cobbles and I was powering up the dark lane.

18

No way to go but up. Rupert said his house was at the top, and since I couldn't find street signs, or slow down long enough to key the address into my phone, up would have to do.

Stone buildings along medieval lanes crowded in on top me. I ran blindly upward, hoping that my pursuers couldn't easily track me among these ancient arteries. Orvieto lay in Umbria, not Campania—not Camorra territory, so maybe they didn't know this city. Maybe they'd stumble around in this maze of streets, wasting time like I was.

But I still had to find Via Pecorelli before they found me.

Sirens wailed somewhere far behind. A wedged-in Maserati with its keys still in the ignition was bound to attract attention. Did the bully boys hide their own car in case somebody traced the license plates? Would anything slow them down?

I needed to find Rupert's house. He said help would be waiting. God knows what he considered to be help, but even if it was a gun, I'd take it.

The sun was just cracking between the buildings ahead when, exhausted and panting, I leaned against a wall to catch my breath. I was almost there, almost at the top. When I raised my head seconds later, the silhouette of a man etched into the light through an archway ahead. Fear jolted.

I turned and ran back, got as far as maybe 50 feet, and nearly smacked into a second man.

"No," I said, backing away. "I don't know anything. Leave me alone."

He stepped forward, a young man in tight jeans and a bomber jacket. Smiling, he placed a finger to his lips. "You come quietly—no noise—and you not get hurt."

"Like I believe that. What do you want with me?"

"You come, meet my cousin."

While he spoke, me stepping backwards all the while, I snaked a hand into my bag and clutched my iPad. When the other man arrived seconds later, I flung the tablet at him, and tried to lunge past him up the lane. One tackled me from behind, slapping a gloved hand over my mouth.

Now they had me pinned, one on either side. I muffled screams, kicked out at their legs, and tried shoving them off-balance. One dragged me into a doorway, whacked my head against the door again and again, then slapped my face so hard, my ears rang.

After that, I could hardly stand. My head hurled shards of pain. My legs sagged as the men dragged me downhill. Voices and sirens erupted all around. I struggled to look up and speak, but couldn't manage either.

Cobblestones, the scuff of fallen leaves, and chestnuts streamed in my line of sight at my feet.

A woman's concerned voice asking my captors something. One of them replied, me picking out the words "mia sorella malata."

"No," I gasped, trying to lift my head, but the men rushed me on, one muttering what seemed like endearments for the benefit of passersby. I let my legs go, falling to my knees. "Help!" I cried.

They yanked me up and tried to shove me towards a car. My brain cleared enough to see we were in a plaza—flashing lights and a crowd gathering on the far side of the square. I recognized the gate where I'd first driven in. They found the car! I tried to scream but a hand crushed against my mouth as something sharp dug into my ribs.

A voice rasped in my ear. "You speak, I shoot."

Did it matter? They'd kill me anyway.

Then, like a dream sequence from a Hollywood movie, I saw a helmeted motorcyclist bearing down on us from across the plaza at full speed.

It all happened so quickly, yet I experienced it in weird slow-mo—the motorcycle side-swiping the guy to my left, knocking him to the ground, pivoting, and zooming back towards the second man.

Guy number two, still gripping me in one arm with his gun in the other, raised his hand to shoot. I shoved him to the right, sending his shot wild, and kicking myself free in the process.

As I fell back against a parked car, the cyclist bounded off his bike, wrenched the gun from the guy's hand, and brought it butt-down across his temple before kicking him to a heap on the cobbles.

Now, the first guy was back on his feet lunging towards me. He only made it about a yard before the cyclist hit him from behind, knocked him to the ground, and shot him in the head point-blank with the pistol.

Shot him in the head point-blank!

I slumped against the car, stunned. I had to escape this murderous bastard, didn't care whose side he was on. When I spun around to run, he caught me in his arms. "Phoebe, are you hurt?"

I stared up at him, dumbfounded. I couldn't see his face, but I knew that voice. "Noel?"

He touched the side of my face gently. "What did those bastards to do you? I'd kill them all if I could. Hop on. We've got to leave pronto."

He looped one arm over my shoulders and steered me towards the man moaning in the grass, dropping the gun nearby. "Let them think these two got in some kind of street fight. Wouldn't be the first time."

While I swayed on my legs, he hefted his bike upright, straddled the seat, and held out his hand.

I hesitated.

"That crowd will soon lose interest in the million-dollar car you demolished and find us equally fascinating. Jump on."

"You shot him"

"And he'd do the same to me."

"You shot hi, point-blank!"

"Get one the bike, Phoebe."

So, I climbed on. "My iPad. I ... threw it at him. It's on the street ... up there somewhere."

"Found it. Your carpet bag's in my saddle bag. Hang on."

I clutched his waist as we ducked in and out of lanes snaking through the ancient town. Everything passed in a haze. After multiple twists and turns, I felt the bike plunge downward into a dark place smelling of earth. We bumped along for maybe minutes or days, I couldn't tell anymore. The darkness seemed to twist back on itself like a giant's entrails. Flashes of other arteries flew by in the headlights until the bike screeched to a halt beside an earthen wall.

The moment he cut the engine and kicked the stand in place, I slid off the seat onto the ground.

❧ 19 ❧

As dreams go, this had to be the best: waking up in Italy to a gorgeous man gazing down at me with concern in his deep-set eyes.

"Phoebe?"

But reality delivered the sucker punch. "Shit!" I lurched onto my elbows. "Noel!" I touched my cheek and moaned.

He gently lowered me back into the pillows. "Easy now. Those bastards gave you quite a wallop. Rest." He pressed a cool cloth against my cheek. "The swelling's down, but you aren't ready to dash anywhere soon."

I took a deep breath, not taking my eyes off him—clean-shaven now, more damn handsome than ever. "You shot a man in the head."

"I had to. The Rachiti brothers are dual murder powerhouses known for killing innocent Campanian citizens. There's no way in hell I was going to let them add you to the list. I have to say, though, you do have a way with enticing the worst specimens to chase you."

"You included."

He laughed. "I guess I qualify, depending on who you ask."

"Ask me. I saw you shoot a man in the head point-blank."

"Those weren't soldiers, Phoebe. We're not waging some honorable war here, if there even is such a thing. These are cold-hearted killers. Do you think shooting somebody is easy for me?" His expression had darkened, the facial angles cutting hard and deep.

"You made it look that way."

"When you've witnessed what I have, and know what you're up against, you do what's necessary. Shooting one bastard probably saved twenty or so lives, including yours."

"So they were Camorra?"

"Cousins to the Butanos. Here, swallow these—ibuprofen."

I lifted my head, my eyes locked on his.

He said softly: "I'd have done anything to keep you safe, Phoebe." One arm scooped me up to sitting while the other held a glass to my lips.

Oh, God. *He'd do anything to keep me safe. He shot a man for me, too, and that makes it all right?* Yeah, probably. I swallowed, the pill lodged in my throat. I started coughing. He patted my back until my breathing steadied, rubbing me the way you might soothe a child. "Steady, lady. You're safe now. Here, take another drink."

I lifted my head long enough to take a deep draw before leaning forward against his one arm, letting the other do its magic on my back. He smelled of some woodsy aftershave and faraway places ... warm, strong, and deadly safe ... *deadly safe.*

"As it was, I needed to keep one alive to talk to the police," he continued, his hand slipping up under my shirt, so warm on my skin. "I left the youngest breathing in a faint hope he might be reformed—as if. Now the local police will get involved, questions will be asked, assumptions made as to why a damaged Maserati and a pair of Camorra killers ended up in the lovely little city of Orvieto."

"You've thought this all out."

"Yes. Felix Rachiti will try to lie his way out of it, but the police will suspect he killed his brother, as he almost did a few years back. Meanwhile, the lovely redheaded Maserati destroyer may not even arise in conversation. Should keep the authorities busy until we figure out our next move. God, I've missed you, Phoebe, but you are hell on cars." He hugged me and kissed my bare back. I could die a thousand deaths just then, savoring every one as long as he kept holding me—Noel, archaeologist, murderer, thief.

"You're the assistance Rupert said would be waiting." I whispered. I tried pulling away but he nudged me back to resume the gentle massage. That man was hellishly good with his hands.

"I am. I hope you're a bit happy to see me. Actually, I've been here for a few days, ever since Rupert sent word that you were on your way to Italy." His voice took on the same gentle warmth as his touch.

I lifted my head. "Is he all right?"

"The last I heard, he'd just discovered his boat sinking off the Vanvitellis' island. He sounded a bit frazzled for Foxy, which usually means Boy Friday can't rescue him in an instant."

"Boy Friday being Evan?"

"The same."

"And Toby?"

"So, Toby was cruising around Capri when the call came that Foxy'd been hijacked off Procida. Toby's on his way to him now."

I jerked up again. "But Toby can't take on the Camorra by himself!"

"Relax," he lowered me back. "He's not by himself. We've taken on some comrades-in-arms since I last saw you last—a few well-trained hired guns who can help us out in a pinch. Besides, Fox is never without an ace up his sleeve, though I think this took even him shirtless."

"You wouldn't say that if you saw what he was wearing. I'm still going to kill him when I see him. He knew more than he told me." I pulled away and lay back on the pillows before Noel's hand left me too weak to resist.

"You may have to stand in line. Foxy has equal parts enemies and friends, despite his best efforts to teeter away on the fence."

"I keep thinking he's my friend and he cares for me, but then he drags me into this muck-up with a crime gang."

"He is your friend, and he does care for you, but that doesn't mean he won't drag you into a vortex. Friendship and danger aren't mutually exclusive to Foxy's way of thinking. He thinks this is a spot of enjoyable stimulation and that Bit Friday of his lives for this stuff." He added that last part with a credible British accent.

"How much did he really know about the Vanvitellis?"

He leaned back in his chair, crossed his arms, and regarded me seriously. "I have no idea how much he knows about the Vanvitellis, but I suspect plenty. He knew the former Count well. They did business

685

together and go way back to when he was a boy traveling with his father in Venice. Apparently the count was listing a friend in Venice when they first met. Later, Foxy sourced Roman and Etruscan artifacts and aided the count in selling off parts of his collection."

"That much he told me, but where do the Camorra come in?"

"The late Count Vanvitelli had been in cahoots with the Butanos for decades—paying for certain favors to grease his business dealings, which is common in Naples. The elder Butano had an interest in antiquities, too, which is, I believe, how it started. Butano was a discerning collector, as was Vanvitelli."

"So, when Foxy told me he didn't know the Butanos were involved, he was lying."

Noel leaned forward so that his long fingers rested on his thighs. "His Foxiness is a master of the fine art of strategic avoidance. It's what he isn't saying that you have to watch for."

"I fall for it every time."

"Maybe you want to."

"What's that supposed to mean?"

"You're here, aren't you? I think you love the thrill. Still, in Foxy's defense—and I can't believe I'm saying this—he was probably blind-sided by the Camorra's involvement here—or, maybe I should say, he underestimated it. He told me that he was coming to the villa to assist Nicolina in finding some part of the hidden stash of the count's missing Etruscan gold. He knew about the Butano-Vanvitelli feud, of course—everybody with an ear to the ground does—but he believed it over and done with. The debt had been paid, and it has been at least a decade or more ago—old news, in other words. Meanwhile, it seems the vendetta is very much alive."

"He forgot this was Italy."

"He forgot this was Italy and involved a crime family."

"And Nicolina?"

"Now, her I can't fathom. What in hell is she up to?"

"That's what we have to find out."

He grinned, one of those heart-stopping smiles that temporarily numbs all my gray cells and behaves wickedly with my baser desires. "What?" I managed to say.

"You said 'we,' as in the two of us. I like the sound of that, Phoebe. It might mean you haven't eliminated me as a contender for your heart just yet." He stood up. "Now, I'm going to retreat into the kitchen and whip up a little dinner. You must be starving. Rest up and I'll nudge you awake when it's ready."

❦ 20 ❦

I slept the day away. When I finally awoke, I stepped onto the tiles and padded over to part the brocade curtains. We were high on a top floor. Below, a cobbled lane wound past a low wall over which spread faraway lights. My head pounded, but not as viciously, and I was starving.

In the adjoining bathroom—narrow, painted blue, paintings stacked artfully one on top of the other—a pile of fluffy lime-colored towels sat next to unopened packages of herbal bath oils and a claw-foot tub. I avoided the glass shower—water pounding on my skull hurt just thinking about. Instead, I poured honeysuckle emulsion into hot steamy water and sunk my aching body deep into the suds, sighing with pleasure.

My thoughts wandered to Noel, grew a little too heated, and quickly cooled down with thoughts of Max. He'd be worried that I hadn't called that day, but if he knew the truth, he'd fly to Italy in a shot. That couldn't happen.

I soaped up my arms in slow, languid motions, wondering if Noel had heard from Foxy, or if Nicolina was yet on the move. Suppose things were afoot while I lay around in bed or steeped myself in fragrance? Dropping the sponge, I pulled the plug, and dragged my body up to standing. Enough. Like I had time to relax.

Emerging pink and fragrant, I realized my clothes had been laundered and folded on a stool by the door. Good. Facing Noel decked out in some-thing as body-accessible as a bathrobe was riskier than driving a Maserati around the Amalfi. I pulled on my jeans and sweater, let my hair do its unruly thing, and stepped into the hall.

As I expected, the house bore Foxy's DNA in every detail, from the mix of art and antiques lining the stucco walls, to the color scheme of manly neutrals punched up by shots of bold color. I followed the scent of something delicious down the stairs, pausing in the hall to admire a painting of Orvieto. Maybe I was buying time, delaying the inevitable shock of seeing Noel again, this time with me upright and cognizant.

Noel. How could I tell him that whatever we had between us just couldn't continue, that is, if it had even really started?

I found him in a candlelit room, setting a marble pedestal table with linen napkins and silverware. He didn't see me at first, so I studied him, fighting the impossible attraction he exerted on me. He wore his hair shorter now, still curly but styled, and he had dressed in tailored slim black pants with a sweater that showed off his lean build. With his dark hair and swarthy complexion, he could pull off local as well in Italy as he did in Turkey, but the Italian finesse suited him.

Without turning, he said: "Are you going to just stand there watching me?"

"Sure, why not? You've changed."

"I have?"

"You're more stylish now, almost Italian-looking."

"A man on the run has to blend. The last time you saw me, I was a ragged nomad dodging bullets in Cappadocia, borrowing clothes where I could find them. I don't think I'd bathed in days."

"I saw you once after you'd just emerged from the haman and you looked pretty damn, ah, clean ..." *Why did I say that?* My face burned.

He turned to me then, a smile spreading, slow and sensual. *Damn, damn, damn.* "And now?" he asked softly.

I shrugged, striving for equilibrium. "And now you're still on the run, but obviously more stylishly. What's for supper?"

He lowered his gaze. "Beef Burgundy, only the Burgundy had been swapped out for Chianti. It won't be ready for another twenty minutes.

Sorry for not going Italian, but this is the only dish I can reliably cook, besides toast and eggs."

"Chianti's Italian enough for me. Are those potatoes I smell roasting? How can you go wrong with that combination—savory and tender?" Ah, hell. I needed to just shut up. "Wow, I'm so thirsty."

"How about a glass of water or juice?"

"Oh, yes. I drank everything you left by my bedside."

"I'd offer you wine but that's hardly wise, considering you probably have a mild concussion. How about tea, if that doesn't sound too Foxified?"

"You couldn't possibly Foxify yourself that much but, sure, tea would be great."

"Hang on and I'll switch on the kettle, but first take a seat." He swung out a chair as if realizing my legs were about to give out, his eyes on my face.

I sat down with my usual lack of grace and pondered the situation. The last time Noel and I had shared tea, we were in Bermuda, and he wore nothing but a fluffy pink bathrobe. It was a good look on him—masculine juxtaposed with feminine. What was wrong with me? I had to be made of firmer stuff than this.

When he returned moments later, I tried a more neutral topic, trying to keep my thoughts in line. "I see Foxy retains his favorite colors here," I said, indicating the linen napkins, the profuse bouquet of chrysanthemums on the side table, and the touches of art glass everywhere.

"You mean yellow?"

"*Jonquil*, please."

We laughed. Our eyes touched, mine sliding quickly away. "Have you heard anymore from him or Toby?"

"Nothing. I didn't expect to just yet," he said pulling out a chair for himself. "Toby will only reach Procida in about another hour and Foxy's still offline. By now Foxy and Evan may have already deployed some of their impressive network of favors."

"He has friends everywhere, doesn't he?"

"And enemies. His Foxiness works on a system of mutual assistance: he helps someone in times of need in expectation that they will return the favor, which they usually do." He crossed a leg over his knee, the fingers of one hand drumming his thigh.

"But how can he contact his network without phone or laptop?"

"Through me. He sent an email earlier with a list of contacts he referred to as 'The Italiano File.' Consider me on his 'favors owed' list. I shot the messages out as per his instructions, so I can only hope help is on its way—besides Toby and crew, that is. Try not to worry about either of them—easier said than done, I know."

"I want to talk to Toby."

"Of course you do. I'll make that happen, but for now, he's got his hands full, and so do I keeping you safe. Let's focus on the Camorra fan club you've established."

"May I remind you that you shot one of their dudes."

"I was hardly on their Christmas list to begin with. Toby and I have had prior run-ins with the bastards, but why you, that's what I want to know?" He leaned forward, clasping his hands between his knees. "I think you'd better fill me in. Foxy's information was rushed and probably only half-true, anyway."

"I don't get why me, either. I'm only the lowly textile expert apparently called in to assess pieces that no longer exist."

"Did Foxy ask for you or did Nicolina?"

"Both. I'm a pawn, but I'm not sure whose."

"Why did Foxy say he wanted you to go to Amalfi with him, besides putting the two of us together?"

I hesitated, realizing the truth of that for the first time—Foxy as matchmaker, an unsettling thought. "He insisted that he saw us as two gallery owners developing into some kind of artifact sleuths—maybe a hybrid between Indiana Jones and his beloved James Bond with a dash of the Old Curiosity Shop thrown in. You know how much he loves the 007 stuff."

"You'd be dynamite at that."

"I would not. I can't see myself as some gun-toting antiques avenger. Besides, I'm a coward."

"You are not. When mad enough, you really kick butt."

"I do?"

"Don't tell me you haven't noticed? Anyway, you could learn new skills, take up martial arts, prepare yourself."

"Are you kidding me? What part of danger and disaster do you think I crave?"

"All of it, or you wouldn't end up to your ears in it again and again. Admit it, Phoebe, you love the stimulation."

I stared at him. What if he was right? But I couldn't deal with that just then. I took a deep breath. "The Turkey episode might be fun to Foxy and may have greased his fantasy, but it just left me reeling. He's forgotten about Eva."

"He didn't know Eva," Noel said softly. "We did."

We gazed at one another without speaking.

"And what did Nicolina say?" he asked after a moment.

"That she needed my help, but I'm realizing now that what she required had nothing to do with assessing antiquities. I'm not sure what her game is yet, but she has one."

"Sure she does, and I don't believe even Foxy knows the details. I just checked her location—still in Rome." He caught my unspoken question. "One of the other favors Foxy asked was for me to track Nicolina Boyd from a device he'd planted in her purse. He connected me to a website where he's been monitoring her movements, which I've been instructed to take over while he's offline."

"I think she knows where the Etruscan hoard is buried. That's the real reason Foxy came to Amalfi. Maybe he was part of her scheme to retrieve it all along but didn't realize that she's already found it. She's been playing him, too, just not on as many chords. Lucca was right about his sister's duplicity."

"Count Lucca?" Noel leaned back and crossed his arms. "Phoebe, the new Count Vanvitelli inherited the legacy of the old. The Camorra's liaisons don't wither away when a business associate dies. The relationship gets passed on. But, as I understand it, Lucca is trying to break loose."

I stared at him. "You mean Lucca is Camorra, too?"

"By association. He's done business with them."

"And where does Nicolina fit into the Camorra side of things?"

"I'm not sure. From what I understand, the women in the family have strongly objected to their family's crime involvement."

"That fits with Nicolina's comments about being tired of playing by the rules of men. She's breaking free, or trying to."

"Good luck with that, considering there's a fortune's worth of priceless Etruscan gold at stake."

"Gold that Nicolina believes is hers, and never belonged to her grandfather to give away to the Camorra."

"More like he tried to use it to pay his debts. The late count was up to his ears in creditors."

"You know a lot about this."

"Once Foxy told me who was involved, I did my homework. We've been developing connections all through Italy."

"What did your connections unearth about Nicolina?"

He stroked his chin. "Not much. I just can't get a fix on her. I know her grandfather sold off her grandmother's properties, including all the ones here in Umbria, and that she married some wealthy businessman, and bolted for London, but that's it."

"Classic escape-the-family move. She wants that gold because she's sick of men sucking her assets dry. Do you know that every single male statue and fresco in that villa has had his gonads either chopped or scraped off?"

"Ouch."

"Some of the castration was performed by her granny years ago, but Nicolina's responsible for the most recent desecration."

"Sounds like seriously angry women."

"Angry women are dangerous, remember that."

"Do you think I could forget that? You shot me in Bermuda."

"That was an accident, but my aim is much better now, just so you know. I might have shot Maggie in Turkey if I hadn't run out of bullets." To think I came that close. "Anyway, I think Nicolina needed a ruse to deflect her true intentions—to hide the gold someplace safe—and that both Rupert and I served the purpose. The stash can't be all that big, size-wise,—mostly jewelry, she said. She could transport something like that in a suitcase. Why is she in Rome?"

"Her husband has an apartment there, so maybe that's just a stop-off for somewhere else. She's been there for hours."

"She's divorcing Geoffrey. Anyway, we have to go to Rome and check it out."

"In your condition—half-concussed with the Camorra on your heels? They're murderers, Phoebe. Killing is part of their honor code. To prove his worthiness to enter the network, a youngster must kill somebody. You'd make a perfect first kill."

"Thanks for that, but we can't just stay here."

"We can for now. It's the safest place."

"How safe?"

"Consider it a foxhole. Orvieto is built on top of a system of ancient tunnels, some of which date back to Etruscan times. Foxy bought this house because its cantina opens up into that underground system, and designed for strategic escapes."

"A cantina?"

"Cellar."

"Oh, hell. I forgot about that ride early this morning. He thinks of everything."

"More than you'd expect. He had an elaborate security system installed, too. Evan is a master of technology gizmos, apparently. You can see anyone approach from multiple directions. Besides the cantina entrance, there's the front door, plus a fire escape. Both have steel doors, and are rigged with booby traps. He didn't just renovate this place as a retreat, he designed it as a refuge."

"Sounds like you know it well."

"I've been here before."

"Alone?" I could slap myself sometimes. "Anyway," I hurried on, "no matter how secure it is, we can't just stay here."

"We need to remain at least until you're fit enough to travel, and then we'll jet on over to Rome and see what Nicolina's up to."

"By jet you mean motorcycle?"

He shrugged. "You destroyed the Maserati. Anyway," he got to his feet. "I'm trying not to mourn. How about supper before my potatoes turn Pompeian?"

And so we ate at that intimate little table designed for a couple rather than a crowd, with the candlelight casting a romantic glow on a mood I was determined to keep all business. I kept my gaze on my plate, avoiding Noel's dark eyes, or from studying too closely the way his mouth quirked when an idea hit.

"Do you think she intended the Camorra to harm Rupert and me? No, wait," I asked while slicing the tender beef. "I'm guessing she didn't. I bet she sent Foxy on a wild goose chase to deflect the Camorra's attention from herself, and maybe tried to drug me for the same reason—either that or she didn't think I was worth taking seriously."

"Many a fool's made that mistake," he remarked.

I studied my plate. "Are you referring to yourself?"

"Just an observation. Some mistake your easygoing manner as inertia, without realizing you're stirring up a firestorm under the surface. I suspect Nicolina's guilty of the same error."

For a moment I couldn't quite pull my words together. "She used me," I said carefully. "But I don't think she really means me harm. She's driven and angry, and doesn't care who gets hurt. I want to catch her but I admire her, too."

"Why?" I glanced up and found him regarding me steadily.

"Because she's a fighter. I admire fighters, anyone who doesn't just accept the status quo. I don't want her to lose this war she's waging, but she will if this murderous feud continues, Noel. If Nicolina has the Etruscan gold—which the Camorra believe is theirs by right—she's on their hit list indefinitely. Plus, that treasure will stay underground forever, either in her hands or theirs. The only way to end this is to get that gold to the authorities, safely away from both Butano and the Vanvitellis. Then, not only does it get into the treasury of the Italian domain, but both sides will finally end their hunt."

"Sounds very tidily legal. As if life provides such tidy endings in Italy," came his wry response.

"Better a messy ending than no ending at all." We studied one another for a moment. "What do you want out of this, Noel?"

"You don't know?" he asked.

"You want to see the treasure safely tucked into a museum, for the people and of the people, and if a tiny bit of it manages to lubricate your coffers enough to keep you and Toby going, all the better."

"Ha," he said, gaze dropping to his plate. "That's the only reason you think I'm in Orvieto, is it? Well, why not? Would you like more beef?"

I passed my plate, watching him scoop up the tender portions, plus a spoonful of mixed vegetables.

"I'll help you find Nicolina and the Etruscan gold," he said, not looking at me.

"Thank you. I really need your help, and I know Foxy's after a little side business, too." I longed to say more, so much more, but couldn't. "For some reason, I still care about him. I mean, besides his obvious irritating charm—but the man's a crook and a—" I stopped midsentence. I could be describing Noel, plus half my family. Our eyes met.

He smiled the tiniest smile. "I'm not a crook, Phoebe."

"Maybe not a crook, exactly, but a criminal by definition. You steal, no matter what your reasons. That's a crime in legal terms. Now it seems you kill, too."

"I do what I must to help myself and those I care about. I survive. That's the lesson I've learned over the last year: Do what it takes. Am I nothing but a thief and a murderer to you?"

I hesitated. "You know my feelings are more complicated than that."

"How complicated?"

"Very. I know you and Toby leapt into this mess with mostly good intentions, that everything went spinning out of control very fast, but you still have it in your power to stop it."

"You mean, go to prison—I did the crime, so serve the time?"

"It's an option."

"Not any more, Phoebe—not for me, not for Toby—never for Toby. Can you imagine prison for a paraplegic? In Turkey I said I'd go to prison if you'd wait for me, but a lot has happened since then."

"Because you've stolen more, killed people?"

"Life on the run can be deadly but it's either do the dirty deed or die."

The remains of supper had begun to congeal on the plate. I studied the bits of meat glistening in the candlelight. My appetite had vacated. I took a deep breath. "Do you ever think of Max?" I had to ask. "He's still your father. You must care."

"Of course I care. Unfortunately, caring and acting on it are two different things for me at the moment." He got to his feet. "How about dessert? Gelato from the shop down the hill. They claim it's the best in Italy, as do about 40 others. I have pistachio and dolce leche."

"Dolce, please." Even gelato didn't tempt me, really.

"I'll be right back."

So, we were going to avoid talking about Max while completely side-stepping our own nonrelationship? My fault. I'd forced this frigid friendliness. Noel may not understand the walls I'd erected, but he knew they were there.

After dessert, which I stirred around in my dish while it melted, he led me to his office in the kitchen—a laptop on a table spread with papers and maps. "There's Nicolina. Still not budging from Rome."

A fixed dot blinked on the screen. "Her husband's apartment?"

"Looks that way."

I pressed my finger on the bridge of my nose. My head had launched another pounding campaign. "But why Rome?"

"Perhaps it's neutral territory, since she apparently no longer owns land in Italy."

"Noel, we have to go. We can't wait."

"We must wait. The police are all over Orvieto now and the Camorra, too. I wouldn't be surprised if some official somewhere paid off somebody else to look the other way. We can't count on the police for help."

"How do you know the Camorra are here?"

"While you slept, I took a stroll."

"Don't the Camorra know you?"

"Only by name. You, on the other hand, they know by sight, which brings up another matter."

I looked up at him. "Which is?"

"Your disguise. First thing tomorrow, I've arranged for you to look considerably less like yourself."

✿ 21 ✿

"**I** need to run a few errands this morning, so rest up while I'm gone, all right?"

I gazed at Noel over my coffee mug. Resting up was the last thing I intended to do. "Sure. How long will you be gone?"

"Just a few hours. This place is the securest safe house you can imagine. Just don't answer the door."

"Like I would. I plan to stare at Nicolina's flashing tracking signal all morning."

"Exhilarating. Right then, see you later." And he was gone, shopping bag in his hand in some vision of sexy domestication.

The moment the door clicked shut and I heard the bolt slide into place, I was on my feet, prowling the three floors. At first, I was only distracting myself by admiring Rupert's decor, but returned again and again to the kitchen laptop. Nicolina still hadn't moved.

I fished out my cell phone and iPad from my carpet bag, found them near dead, and plugged them in to recharge. It occurred to me then that I was way behind in keeping Max apprised with what was going on. Maybe by the time my devices recharged, I'd figure out what not to tell him.

I strolled into Noel's room two doors from my own. Just being in the presence of his things—the boots neatly paired under the window, the sweater folded on the brocade stool, the leather jacket tossed on the made-up bed—caused erratic behavior in my vulnerable bits. What was it about this man that even the sight of his sweater knocked me sideways?

I wrenched my eyes away and studied the books stacked on his bedside table. Not a tablet or e-reader guy, Noel preferred real books, the kind he could have and hold. Maybe he liked his women the same way. Maybe he had some girl in a Mediterranean port somewhere ready to share his berth.

Stop! I hated the way my mind worked sometimes.

Tomes on Etruscan history appeared to be his reading topic of choice, hardly surprising given vocation and location. He shared similar reading tastes to Evan—touching. I lifted the top volume and flicked through the pages, pausing over the flyleaf, staring down at an inscription in Italian. It was addressed not to Noel, or even to Rupert, but to Alexandria Vanvitelli, date 1982. I almost dropped the book. Why would Noel have a book belonging to Nicolina's grandmother here in Rupert's house?

I heard the front door unlock, followed by the sound of his footsteps in the hall below. I scrambled down the stairs, book in hand, and almost ambushed him in the kitchen.

"Whoah!" he said, holding up his hands.

"Look what I found?" I indicated the book.

He dropped the shopping bag on the chair. "From my nightstand. How interesting. How did that get into your hands?"

I flipped the pages open to the inscription. "Look at the inscription."

He picked up the book and read: "My Italian isn't great but I believe it reads: *To my darling Alexandria. Together in the past as in the present. Your loving husband.*" He raised his eyes to mine. "I didn't read this. I tend to bypass personal inscriptions unless they're at least a few centuries old—my code of ethics. I borrowed these from Foxy's shelves. What were you doing in my room?"

"Why would Foxy have a book inscribed to Nicolina's grandmother?"

"Presumably because they were left in the house when he bought it. The count was in a hurry to offload these properties at the time, if I understand correctly," he said, laying the book back on the table.

My face must have registered shock.

Noel rubbed his chin. "Well, hell, you didn't know that Foxy bought this place from Count Vanvitelli, either?"

"How could I when the damn bastard failed to mention it?"

"What did I say? Always worry about what Foxy's not telling you."

"What else am I missing?"

"That will take much longer to untangle, but to begin with, it's my understanding that he bought more than one property from the Count. This is the only one I know about officially—oh, and not because he told me, by the way, but because my network hunted the details for me."

I wanted to scream. "You'd think Foxy would mention that, considering we were in Nicolina's villa when he offered me the keys. Nicolina isn't mention it, either."

"There's a chance Nicolina didn't know."

"And here I was so touched that he gave the keys to me, thinking he was being so generous, so considerate. He said I needed a little refuge, and that I was to consider this mine."

"Phoebe," Noel extended his hands as if to take my shoulders but let them drop. "Even though he deliberately neglects to tell you critical details, doesn't mean what he does say isn't the truth."

I rubbed my temples. "Well, how paradoxical is that?"

"Paradox is Foxiness's particular gift." He stood there, arms crossed, looking down at me.

"I still want to throttle him." I mimed choking a neck with my hands.

"You might want to wait to see if he's still alive first. He's still not answering my calls."

My eyes met his—all humor gone. I caught my breath. "Do you think he's all right?"

"Who knows? For now, I'm more focused on keeping you alive and maybe me, too." He strode across the kitchen and flicked closed a gap in the curtains. "The Camorra are crawling all over this town." Turning back to me, "I repeat, why were you in my room?"

"Curiosity—what difference does it make now?"

"It matters to me. Curiosity or suspicion? After all we've been through, do you still not trust me? Is that why you poked around my things? Is that why there's this distance between us?"

I gazed at him, stunned. "Why would I trust you, Noel? Why would I trust anyone?"

"What then?" At that moment, somebody rang the doorbell. "Great timing. We'll get back to topic later. Stay here," he warned as he dashed off down the hall.

I slipped out of view of the doorway and collapsed down at the kitchen table. Moments later, I heard Noel's deep baritone alternating with a woman's alto approaching the kitchen. I turned as a little woman in a burlap-colored brown jacket, knee-length woolen skirt, and headscarf walked into the kitchen carrying what looked to be a battered black doctor's bag.

We nodded and smiled at one another.

"Phoebe, meet Maria. She's going to be your makeup artist," Noel introduced us with a sweep of his hand.

I got to my feet. "My makeup artist?"

Maria asked Noel something in Italian. Noel responded with a tilt of his head, a lift of his hands, and an expression of pained resignation.

"What did she say?"

In response, Maria dropped her bag on a chair and walked over to fluff my hair with her hands. "No, no, no," she murmured, turning me around. She shot a couple of questions to Noel who only nodded and said, "Si, si, si."

"Would you mind telling me what's going on?" I asked.

"She says that it is a shame to cut and color those glorious red locks, and I agree with her completely but it has to be done."

"What?" You may as well have poked me with a cattle prod. I backed against the counter. "Cut my hair? Who said anything about cutting my hair?"

"Phoebe," Noel's tone deepened. "Do you want to get out of here alive or not?"

"Of course."

Maria stood looking from one of us to the other, hands clasped loosely over her stomach.

"Then let Maria work her magic. She may not look like an expert, but she has been working in the costume department of the local opera house for decades and can transform anyone. I've asked her to change your looks so you can't be recognized."

Maria interrupted Noel with a quick question, her finger wagging. "She says that she works best if given a character sketch, or at least I think that's what she means. She wants to know what character you want to be."

I gazed at Maria who gazed back. "What character? You mean like as in Brunhilde or Carmen?"

"I think it's safe to say she means as in books or films, not opera. You running around in a horned helmet and a breastplate isn't going to up your incognito factor."

I shrugged. "I really have no clue. If you'd asked me when I was a kid, I'd have told you to make me into a mermaid, or maybe Superwoman, but these days, it's enough sometimes just to be myself."

"I can't imagine you hanging on to the backseat of a bike dressed like a tuna or in yellow tights, though I might enjoy that last version. Come on, Phoebe, name a character."

"Oh, I don't know. Transform me into somebody kick-ass. You choose."

"Fine, leave it to me. In the interests of time, we've got to get this show on the road." He provided Maria with instructions that involved significant hand mannerisms, motorcycle sounds, and something that looked like a kung fu chop.

Like that eased my mind. Maria nodded her assent, opened up her bag, and pointed to the chair.

"Feels like an execution," I said, taking a seat.

"Never mind," Noel assured me. "Phoebe is about to end in appearance only. A totally kick-ass version will arise from the ashes. By the way," he added, crouching briefly in front of me, "I truly love the original look but a man has to make sacrifices." He sprung up and shifted behind me. "Now, try to relax. No glancing into a mirror or anything so devious until after the process is complete."

"What am I supposed to do in the meantime?"

"Sit," Noel said between his teeth.

"Fine, but at least give me my iPad so I can keep occupied."

While Noel dashed off to retrieve my tablet, Maria stepped towards me holding a pair of shears. "No," I protested weakly.

"Si," she replied with vigor. In seconds, the first auburn lock landed on my shoulder. Noel returned in time to witness the second and the third, frowning as more hair drifted to the floor.

"I hope you're enjoying this," I said.

"Do I look like I am? I love your hair, but at least it's a renewable resource, whereas you definitely are not." He passed me the iPad. "Suck it up, McCabe."

I frowned up at him and returned to my tablet. For a while, I focused on sending emails while trying not to think about what was happening above my ears. I fired off a couple of quick messages to Max and Serena, saying that the work had become more complicated, but that it was coming along—not a lie, exactly, but definitely a foxyism.

God, I missed them both. A vision of all of us together—father, son, friend, boyfriend-lover—here in Italy as real tourists hit me hard. Shaking away the notion, I tapped off a message to a law school friend specializing in real estate law for British citizens.

Periodically, Maria would nudge my head up and force me to stare straight ahead, intent on some exacting maneuver. When she reached the lump on my skull, she muttered strings of Italian and demanded an explanation from Noel, who now leaned against a counter, watching. He responded in halting Italian.

"What was that about?"

"She wanted to know how you got that lump on your head."

"And you told her what?" I asked.

"I hope I said you hit your head on a beam, but I couldn't recall the exact word for 'beam,' so I may have said something totally incongruous," he shrugged, "like perhaps you hit your head on a bedpost."

I sighed, returning to my iPad. Still nothing from Foxy. When I looked up later, I found Noel behind the laptop. Our eyes met over the screen, mine with a question. He shook his head and frowned. Nicolina still hadn't budged.

When I had no hair left worth mentioning, Maria stirred up a concoction in a plastic bowl and proceeded to dab the goop onto my scalp. I closed my eyes and prayed she'd turn me into a blond, something colorful and glamorous. After a blow dry followed up by strenuous straightening with a flatiron, Maria finally stepped back to admire her work.

Noel slowly climbed to his feet, whistling. "My god. I wouldn't know you if I saw you on the street."

I bolted for the bathroom, switched on the light, and stared at my reflection. Phoebe McCabe had vanished. In her place, some wicked elfin face stared out at me from under a crop of straight black hair swept asymmetrically over one eye. I swore.

Noel appeared behind me. "Dynamite."

"I'm like the Girl with the Goddess Tattoo."

"I saw that tattoo, along with another, if I remember correctly—a mermaid and a goddess? I think that's what they were. It was very dark and I was very preoccupied at the time."

22

After Maria left, Noel and I settled in around the kitchen table with our maps and technology, plates of crusty bread, cheese, and fruit. We were staring down at the map I'd snatched from Sophia's and Ricardo's kitchen.

"What do you think it means?" I asked Noel, who munched reflectively on a pear. "Obviously she's circled all the properties currently still owned by the Vanvitellis, and penned in those that once belonged to her grandmother's family, like this one."

"Interesting that all the properties sold lay in Etruscan territory, and that Foxy bought at least one."

"That reminds me," I said, picking up my cell. "I wonder if Alyssa got back to me. I asked if she'd ask her paralegal to dig around and see if we could find if Sir Fox bought anything else while he was at it." I scrolled through my messages, most of which were from Max and Rena that I'd read later. My thumb landed on the name of my old law school buddy. Clicking on the message, I read aloud, skipping the *Long time no hear! When are we going to get together for lunch?* stuff.

"*...so, we discovered that Fox did purchase two properties in Italy between the years of 1998-2002, both from the same vendor. It's difficult to tell since in both cases the intermediary was a real estate company who shielded their client's names. I could* *contact a colleague in Italy to do a deed search, if you want, but I'll probably have to pay somebody somewhere. LOL. Do you need to know which? All were located north of Rome, one in Orvieto, the other a few miles away in a place called Bagnoregio. If you need more detail, let me know, and we'll dig deeper. Cheers, Alyssa."*

I looked up at Noel. "Where's Bagnoregio?"

"Over yonder," he thumbed over his shoulder, "A few kilometers in that direction, as the crow flies, and you can believe the roads will not follow a route even half as direct as said crow. I believe it's in another province."

"Not Umbria?"

"In Lazio, which is right next door."

"Lazio," I mused. "What's the chances of the late Countess's family having property in both provinces?"

"Why not? The provinces were only officially formed in the 1940's and the ruling classes had land stakes long before that, even if all their feudal status had been stripped by then. It's reasonable to assume that a long-established family might end up with properties in more than one province by the time the regions were divvied up. What are you doing?"

"Asking Alyssa to track down the names of the buyers or buyer for me. I'll pay. I take it she means somebody somewhere might need to be bribed to release confidential stuff. If Foxy purchased two properties, I need to know from whom." I fired off the message before placing the phone back on the table and leaning over the map. "Do you see Bagnoregio circled here, or am I just missing it?"

Noel leaned forward, brushing my arm in the process. "You're not missing it. There's Bagnoregio," he placed his index on a tiny spot, "but not circled."

"So Nicolina deliberately left it off. Is Bagnoregio in Etruscan territory?"

"All this region," he swept a broad arch through central Italy, "is in the original Etruria region—Tuscany, Umbria, and Lazio. Looks like we need to find out where that other property is."

"Yeah, we do. Since neither Foxy nor Nicolina mentioned this mysterious second place, though Foxy apparently owns it." I pulled back, placing a little distance between us by leaning against the counter instead. "I know you must have combed every inch of this place but what's the chances there's something hidden here?"

"Highly unlikely. If gold was stashed here, Foxy wouldn't have given us the keys. Besides, I'm not above exploring every crevice."

I remembered. "What about in the tunnels below? What if this is all part of some convoluted plan to lure us here? Orvieto sits on a warren of Etruscan tunnels, right?"

"Etruscan, Roman, medieval. There must be over 1,000 cisterns, caves, secret passages, and the like riddled through here, enough to worry engineers that the whole thing may collapse one day. Despite that, there are countless entrances to the system from private homes and the main walls. Hiding something here makes zero sense, but allow me to escort you on a proper tour to ease your mind."

Sir Rupert Fox by way of Evan, as Noel revealed, had wired his little retreat for every possibility, including, it seems, a siege. I surveyed the entrance to the tunnel through a four-foot tall door behind the refrigerator. Shelves on either side of the downward stairs held every imaginable jar and bottle of foodstuffs, including rare vintages of wine and jars of caviar. I stared down the tunnel's throat. "Why do we always end up in a tunnel or a cave?" I mused.

"Because that's where our species have hidden things of importance for time immemorial. We bury what we don't want found."

"And you and I always seem to end up looking for them."

"Being an archaeologist is my excuse. What's yours?" I heard the smile in his tone.

"I figure it's the company I keep—friends and relatives included."

"What about lovers?"

I paused before moving briskly forward. "So, you park your bike down there, too?"

"There are several entrances to this warren all around Orvieto. I use whichever one is handiest. Let me show you Foxy's study next."

We traipsed upstairs to a little room overlooking the front street. I'd glimpsed inside earlier but other than a set of stunning needlepoint cushion covers, and what I thought might be a genuine piece of mounted Roman mosaic, nothing had caught my interest.

Noel carefully lifted the framed mosaic from the wall and placed it on the chair, revealing a brass toggle which, when flicked, activated a sliding wall behind us.

I stared in disbelief. "Did Foxy tell you about this?"

"Of course not. I spent a leisurely few days exploring every inch of the place. True to character, I knew he'd have something hidden somewhere. Foxy always surprises. Voila!"

I stepped into the hidden room, scanning across a sophisticated-looking surveillance system, plus a shelf of various electronic objects, my gaze landing on the painting over the desk—an oil of a castle perched on a crest of land with an impossibly long drawbridge threading through the mist. "That's it!"

"What?"

I fished out my iPhone and tapped my photo library, passing Noel the photo of the ceiling art. "I saw this on the ceiling next to the wardrobe in Nicolina's villa, half-hidden in the shadows. Everything else in the mural is classic Roman-nymphs-romping-in-Arcadia except this, which struck me as more fantasy than mythology."

Noel studied the photo and then the painting. "It's definitely the same image of some jumble of styles, mostly medieval."

"So why did Nicolina's grandmother paint it on her ceiling and why does Foxy have a painting of the same castle?"

"It's not a castle." Noel squinted at the photo. "More of a village or hamlet, with a central watch tower over the gate, but it does seem incongruous next to the nymphs."

Stepping closer, I studied the painting, in particular the signature, a distinctive ornate "A" followed by a curlicue of tangled letters. "Alexandria painted this, too." I couldn't suppress my excitement. "Noel, everything on that ceiling, from the severed lovers to the castle, is a message. Nicolina's grandmother painted a subtle indicator as to where she hid the gold, intending only one grandchild to understand the imagery."

We stared at one another. "You mean the gold is hidden wherever that hamlet is?" he asked.

"Exactly, and Nicolina knew where it was all along. Only now that her divorce is pending has she decided to claim it. Everything else, including the villa and Orvieto, is a red herring."

"So, it's not in Rome?"

"No, and I have a feeling that neither is Nicolina. We have to find that hamlet. That's where she is. Is that Bagnoregio?"

"I've never seen anything exactly like that. I understood Bagnoregio to be a relatively ordinary-looking stone town with nothing specific to recommend it, but I'm no expert in Italian geography or archeology and, really, there's nothing ordinary about anything Italian, in my opinion. I'll just do a quick Google search." He pulled out his smart phone and brought up a short piece on Bagnoregio featuring a town square centered by a dreary statue.

"Still, it's the only lead we have right now, so let's start there. If we find that hamlet, we'll find Nicolina and the gold. Didn't you say Rupert claimed the tracking device was put on her purse?

"I'm sure he said that."

"Nicolina changes outfits at least twice a day. A woman with her sense of style would change purses, too. The one with the tracker is still in Rome."

His eyes widened. "I never thought of that."

"Men never would. So, let's leave for Bagnoregio now. I'm properly disguised."

"We'll leave tomorrow morning, first thing. You need at least one more good night's sleep to recuperate before hurling across country to parts unknown on the back of a motorcycle. Besides, we're not going to find anything driving around in the dark when we don't know what we're looking for."

I thrummed with impatience but had to admit that made sense.

"In the meantime," he continued, "I bought a few wardrobe additions to complete the new you." He held out a plastic bag. "Why not change and we'll go to supper to see how effective your transformation is? My favorite eatery is just across from the cathedral. You'll love it."

I eyed the bag and then him. "You actually want me to walk the streets as the Girl with the Mermaid Tattoo?"

"You'll find the assemble more chic than punk. Besides, you and I will be masquerading as lovers, so I figured we'd best look like a pair."

"No nose ring?"

"No nose ring."

I took the bag, heading for my bedroom to change.

23

"Salute," Noel and I toasted one another over glasses of an exquisite Brunello inside a bistro walled in rare wines and beers. If possible, the second glass slid down more smoothly than the first, and the crostini di funghi and bruschetta reduced me to monosyllables of delight. The girl with the kick-ass black hair didn't avoid a glass or two of exquisite wine with a man she found wildly attractive, especially in Italy. She took action first, worried about the repercussions later. In fact, typical of her response to wine, she didn't worry about repercussions at all.

Later was so yesterday.

To say I did not feel myself was an understatement. The fact that I was trying to behave like this man's girlfriend didn't help. Even my familiar tapestry bag had been left behind in lieu of a sleek, little cross-body number that went with the bomber jacket and tall leather boots. Besides, Orvieto was magic that night, making transformations all the more fitting. The streets lilted with music and laughter pouring out from the restaurants and bars. Halfway down one of the central arteries near the teatro, a band rocked the streets with an energetic rendition of Jimi Hendrix's *All Along the Watch Tower*.

Noel and I leaned against a wall, listening, as if we had nothing better to do than be relaxed and happy. When we peeled ourselves away to continue strolling, Noel's arms around my shoulders, he whispered something in my ear—I don't remember what—and I laughed. When I reached up to whisper something back, his lips met mine halfway and all conversation melted away. Forget pretending to be lovers. By the time the cathedral gonged eleven o'clock, we were lovers by intent, if not action.

Whatever we were doing or pretending to do, I was enjoying it so much that I almost strolled right by Agent Walker. Reality tripped me up. Nobody else looked like him. What was he doing leaning against a potted olive tree sipping beer in Orvieto?

I tightened my grip on Noel's arm. "Keep walking," I hissed.

"What else would I do, kiss you again?"

"Good idea." I tugged him up a boutique-lined lane and into the closed shop's doorway. "Kiss me like you mean it."

"I do mean it. I thought you got that part." In seconds I was in his arms again, plunged into a deep, stirring act of camouflage. It was all I could do to remember Walker existed, let alone worry what he was up to. When we broke away, the agent had disappeared, or so I hoped, since I couldn't risk more than a glance at where he'd been standing. At least he wasn't the first thing I saw at the bar across the street.

"Walker," I managed to say, steadying myself against Noel. "Here. I mean, there. In Orvieto."

"What's he doing here?" Noel asked, still holding me close.

"Following me. Stop doing that with your hand. The bastard doesn't let me go anywhere without ... tagging behind. Let go of me for a moment so I can think." I stepped back. "He thinks I'll lead him to you and Toby, and he's right. I just don't know why he followed me here. Even I thought this trip was innocent. We'd better get back to the house."

"Good idea." Noel looped his arm around my shoulders again and we kept our heads down as we exited the alley and followed the street back uphill. "He'd never recognize you, or me, either, but I just saw one of the Camorra who might recognize me, at least."

"I thought you said they didn't know your face?"

"They don't, except for one. I don't know if she saw me or not."

"She?"

"Yes, she. Don't be sexist, Phoebe. Criminals come in both genders."

"So we have Interpol and the Camorra after us?"

"Apparently Interpol is interested in you, as well as both Foxy and his ex-MI6 operative Boy Friday, and we already know how popular I am with everyone."

I stumbled. "How did a former Secret Service agent get to work for Foxy?"

"Fox hired him after he'd supposedly retired from Her Majesty's Secret Service."

"Well," I mused, "that explains why his stellar skills extend way past breakfast."

"Breakfast?"

"Yes, breakfast. He's good with bacon. Are you jealous?"

"Any fool can cook bacon."

"Yeah, but not any fool can look like him doing it."

We wove up through the streets, taking quieter lanes away from the Friday night crowd, until we found ourselves alone in a cobbled lane. "That's where I killed a Maserati up ahead." They'd already towed away the remains.

"Yes. I can't bear to ponder the destruction. Let's take another route back."

I stopped, listening.

Noel tensed beside me. "You hear it too?"

"The footsteps stop when we stop, move when we move," I whispered. "We're being followed."

He pulled me tighter and shoved something jingly into my pocket. "If anything happens, if we're separated, take the bike and head for Bagnoregio. Do you know how to rode a bike?"

"I owned one once, though not this powerhouse kind."

"It's like riding a bike. I'll meet you there. Get back to the house. The keys are in your pocket."

"Wait, we're not going to be separated. We—" but I didn't finish my sentence before a motorcycle gunned up the lane.

"Straight ahead, turn right at the cafe, two doors down, turn left. The door behind the trash bin. Left, right, and right again. Push the button to unlock. I'm going to play decoy. Run!"

He shoved me to the right while he bolted left. I saw the bike zooming after us and sprang to the side just as three men burst into the junction.

Two of them plus the bike took after Noel, while I jetted up the street, tossing anything I could lay my hands on to slow the third one down. He banged into a sandwich board I'd flung, giving me the seconds I needed to dart into a lane beside a tiny cafe closed for the night.

Two doors down, I dove to my hands and knees behind a refuse bin, spied the little wooden door and yanked it open by its ringed handle.

Clutching it still, I listened for footsteps, hearing a man's footfall in the lane slowing down while he sensed for movement.

My heart pounded in my ears. *Move on. Nobody here.* He hesitated, took another step, followed by another. In agonizingly slow moments, he passed me and turned a corner. In seconds, I was on my stomach pushing myself backward into a tunnel. Tugging the door shut behind me, I realized I'd just shoved myself into the dark.

❦ 24 ❦

Did Noel say right, right, right again and straight ahead or left, right, right again and straight ahead? As I beamed my phone light onto the narrow tunnel, I knew how much it mattered.

Behind me, rattling trash bins signaled that my pursuers had found the door.

I jolted down ahead, hesitating at the junction of left and right, but turning right. God help me if I got that wrong. On I ran, listening for footsteps behind me while trying to stay upright on the uneven surface.

After twenty feet, I shut off my phone and flattened myself against the wall. I heard them stop, whispering urgently while deciding which route to take—two of them now, one giving commands. He ordered the second man in one direction, while he carried on towards me, his flashlight blazing ahead.

If I stayed, he'd see me. If I moved, he'd see me. I sprang to the right and bolted down the tunnel, taking another right and another, him close behind.

Shit.shit.shit. There were lights ahead. I could be leading him right to Foxy's house.

I broke out into a wide, lit corridor. A tour guide was describing the underground features to a knot of tourists. I scattered them like a bowling ball, my "sorry" aborted when somebody tackled me from behind. I fell hard, knocking the wind from my lungs. My pursuer tried wrenching my hands behind my back but somebody pulled him off. Three men were wrestling with him as I lurched to my feet, waved a thank you, and took off. I never saw their faces.

Panic seared as my feet thudded on the earth. The risk of becoming lost in this twisting warren hit hard. My cell phone wouldn't work, and I'd taken so many turns already, I knew I was lost.

Then, like a gift from the dark, I recognized features from that bike ride the night before—more illuminated sections, part of an ancient well, and an arched corridor. Noel had warned me of an upcoming sharp left-hand turn, and I thought I recognized one just like it. I dashed left down an unlit tunnel, switching the phone back on as I ran.

Suddenly, footsteps joined mine in the dark. I saw the chrome of Noel's bike glinting ahead the exact instant a gunshot cracked the air. For a panicked second, I thought I'd been hit, but the bullet flew wide.

I pulled out Noel's keys and pressed the fob. Something grated like nails on sandpaper. A gunshot blasted, the bullet pinging on stone near my right shin.

I ducked, leaping past the bike and squeezing into a dark opening to press up against solid rock. I swung around and pressed the fob again and again while sliding to the ground, back to the wall. I stared in horror as the door closed with aching slowness.

My attacker's silhouette rose no more than twenty feet away, heading towards me. A gunshot blasted from nowhere and he fell to his knees with a yelp.

Footsteps beat from somewhere to the left while the door clicked shut on the final two inches. Someone pounded on the hidden wall—not calling out, just testing. I listened, heard something flick against the exterior—a penknife, a key?—then stop. After several minutes, everything stilled.

I expelled breath I didn't know I'd held. Who shot the Camorra dude —friend or foe? I couldn't assume an enemy of Camorra necessarily meant a friend to me. Noel would have called out my name. Whoever shot that guy must want me, too.

My legs quivered when I stood. I'd been unconscious the night I arrived, so missed exploring Foxy's idea of a vestibule—a gray concrete space with nothing but a mounted security monitor and an impressively stocked gun case. A light automatically blazed cool fluorescence into the space.

I studied the monitor's grainy image of a now-empty tunnel. The night-vision camera could be toggled up/down/left/right, but revealed nothing except the bike's taillight jutting into the far right-hand view. Whoever shot the Camorra guy had disappeared.

If the Camorra had Noel, they'd kill him.

I turned to the gun case—locked with no keyhole. Glass separated me from a nice little handgun I suddenly needed badly. I wasn't above smashing the glass, but first I began pressing each of the fob's five electronic buttons until a mechanism clicked and the cabinet glass slid open.

I removed the handgun and gazed at it glinting in my hand. These things made me twitchy. I hated them on principle, but nothing else seemed as effective for my present situation. Foxy kept this one fully loaded, and I took it with me as I headed upstairs.

By the time I reached the main floor, the doorbell was ringing relentlessly. I hadn't reached the secret room before I heard pounding somewhere at the rear of the house. The bastards thought they could break their way inside. I thanked Foxy for his bastion of a house before remembering how I got here, and reverted to cursing him.

The full scope of his fortress's security central didn't hit me until I stood again in the secret room. The two monitors zoned in on the front street from different angles, while the fire escape and tunnel entrance were similarly covered.

My heart rammed in my chest as I watched one man trying to jimmy the lock up front, while another took a hatchet to the fire escape door. Metal on metal reverberated through the speaker system. They were both crazy. And deadly. And coming after me.

My smartphone pinged a text alert. I glanced at the screen long enough to read Alyssa's message: *Sir Rupert Fox bought both properties from a Vanvitelli, kept one and sold one at 8 Via Medina in Civet di Bagnoregio to an Amalfia Solfio.*

Civita di Bagnoregio? Amalfia Solfio? I flash-Googled Civita di Bagnoregio, pulling up a photo so much like the paintings, I gasped. Bagnoregio had two towns, one of them this otherworldly outcrop? And

Amalfia, as in the nymph Amalfi on the villa ceiling? That couldn't be a coincidence.

A reverberating thud vibrated the speakers so loudly, I almost dropped the phone. My back-door visitor had upped his efforts.

I saw icon buttons below each screen—a flame and a spray symbol—which I was sure indicated some Bond-worthy defense maneuvers of Evan's devising. I pressed the spray button, watching in amazement as it ejaculated a toxic puff into the face of the front-door intruder, sending him screaming backwards. Mace? Pepper spray?

My finger hovered over the flame button, repelled by the thought of the damage that might inflict. Wait, why did I care? These guys wanted to kill me. Down came my finger, triggering a fire stream like an oxyacetylene blast. The back-door guy's clothes ignited in a whoosh. He pounded down the metal steps screaming.

I fell back into a chair, stunned. Okay, so what else did Foxy have here?

Mostly objects I didn't recognize lined the shelves. I'd seen enough spy films to guess what the watches and pens might do, but the rest were inscrutable. I tested one pen with a retractable knife along with something that looked to be a single-bullet cigarette lighter, plus a stick of spearmint gum. Evan obviously had ingenuity plus more time on his hands than he knew what to do with.

I was studying an innocent-looking package of toothpicks when Foxy's house phone rang. I stared at the cordless device on the desk. That could be Foxy calling. I dove for the phone, picking it up on the third ring.

"Yes?"

"You must listen if you want to keep boyfriend alive, Phoebe McCabe." A man's voice.

I swallowed hard. "Who's this?"

"No mind. You go out back door now or I kill him. No tricks."

"How do I know you won't kill him regardless, or if I know you even have him?" I stammered.

Muffled noises followed before Noel's voice came across harsh and pained: "Don't listen to them, Phoebe. Stay—" The sickening thud that followed turned my stomach.

"Don't hurt him. I'll do what you want."

❦ 25 ❦

I stood inside Foxy's security depot, running through possible outcomes. Obeying the Camorra ended the same way as not obeying them: Noel died, I died. All options were equally hideous, but none worse than me staying safe while they had Noel.

Back at the shelves, I began shoving odd things into my pockets—a pack of toothpicks, another ballpoint pen, that stick of chewing gum —really?

If it was small enough to fit into my pocket, in it went. The gun was probably useless. That would be the first thing they'd take. I'd hide the carpet bag along with the gun, and just take the shoulder sling thing with my pockets full of spy-wear accessories.

Hoisting my bag over my shoulder, I headed from the room, pausing long enough to flick the wall switch and replace the mosaic cover.

My phone rang in my bag before I reached the hall door. The Foxy phone! "Rupert, is that you?"

His voice rasped. "Phoebe, you must proceed ... at once to ... Sorrento ... the pier. Toby is ... waiting. Go now."

"Where are you?" I wailed.

"No ... time ... they are coming. Save yourself." And then the phone clicked off.

Save myself? Was he kidding me? I tried the redial function but the phone rang unanswered.

I hurled downstairs. When I reached the main floor, the house phone rang again. I picked up an extension on my way to the kitchen.

"Hello?" By then I was almost at the cantina door.

"Phoebe, why you take so long? You want friend to die, yes?"

I spoke calmly from a place I didn't know I had. "Leave him alone, I said. I'm coming."

"You take too long," he snarled, but I was already in the basement, flicking open the tunnel door. The cell reception blinked in and out.

It took maybe ten seconds to stuff my carpet bag under the motorcycle seat, relock it, and press the door's CLOSE button, another minute to find a hiding place for the keys—deep into a crevice in the opposite wall—and a few seconds more to dive back into the cantina before the door inched shut.

I scrambled back upstairs, crying into the phone: "I'm out here waiting for you. Where are you?"

More noises in the phone. The guy barked: "What you say? My man waits."

"I'm out front." And by then, I was. The door slammed behind me as I collapsed onto the step, looking as if I'd been waiting for minutes, except for the panting.

"I said fire escape!" yelled the man in my ear.

"You did not!" I closed my eyes and dropped the phone. God, they were going to hit me, bang my head against the wall, whatever. How could I help Noel if knocked senseless? And Foxy and Evan, where the hell were they? Shot somewhere, in danger, maybe dying. I wanted to scream.

Seconds later, two men bounded up the street. One man's eyes nearly swollen shut, the other's singed jacket barely covered patches of scorched skin. I lurched to my feet, holding up my hands. "Don't hurt me. I'll go with you."

The eye guy whispered into a cell phone, while the burn guy flung me against the wall and searched me. While his hands slammed against my legs, unzipped my boots, whacked my pockets, I stared straight ahead at the wall of old stone houses. *Must be the same kind of rock they'd quarried in these parts for centuries. The Etruscans must have used the same stone. What was the time? Must be around 1:00 A.M. Everybody up this residential end was asleep and obviously refused to rouse for a pack of street rowdies.*

The acrid scent of the guy's singed hair turned my stomach. I knew he had to be suffering, knew I was responsible, and felt sorry for him, as foolish as that sounds. I avoided meeting his eyes.

Moments later, he flung me around, pushing me downhill while I tried putting my clothes back together. He'd taken the lighter but left the chewing gum, toothpicks, and pen. Fool.

We kept heading down, burn guy shoving me hard, though I made no move to resist. I thought we'd go to a car but no. Instead we turned several corners, winding deeper into the maze of medieval streets until we reached a tall flat-fronted building.

Eye guy knocked, the door opened, and someone shoved me into a hall-way. I stood squinting under a beautiful stained glass chandelier illuminating a semi-demolished hallway. A glowering man stood before me, jerking his head towards a stairway.

"Upstairs!" eye guy barked.

I stumbled upward, past a wall stripped to the boards, until we reached the next level littered with toolboxes and reeking of fresh paint.

Four men watched as eye guy shoved me down the hall and into a big room pulsing with monitors placed on makeshift stands all around the room.

Burn guy flung me to the floor. "Stay!" He said something in Italian to a guy manning the monitors, who jumped up to stand before me, pistol in hand.

"Where's Noel?" I cried.

"Shut up," burn guy snarled. He kicked me hard in the leg. "You wait. No move or my friend, he shoots!" and then he exited the room, leaving me with this guard—a soft-eyed, floppy-haired kid of maybe nineteen who tried to look menacing.

He reminded me of a cocker spaniel puppy with a pistol. What was with this world where kids point guns at innocent people, where life is worth so little?

I sat there nursing my leg, struggling not to cry, and failing miserably. By the time I heard footsteps clattering on the tiles, I was sobbing uncontrollably.

"Hi, Ms. McCabe, so we meet again," said a woman's voice.
I looked straight up into the eyes of Susan Rafuse.

❧ 2 6 ❧

"**Y**ou give 'you look a fright' a whole new meaning, Phoebe."

I blinked up at the impossible sight of Geoffrey Boyd's New York decorator standing in a sleek tanned leather jacket.

"Susan Rafuse?" I gasped.

"Susan Butano Rafuse, but what's in a name?" She indicated for Puppy Face to bring her a chair, which he did, sliding a plastic-covered seat from the wall.

Not until settled comfortably did she speak again. "Do you like it?" she asked, one hand indicating the room, or maybe the house. "I've been engaged by my client to restore it to its former glory with a modern edge. I admit, I'm planning more edge than glory, but it's been serving its current purpose rather well, in the meantime."

"You're a Butano?" I said, hitching a sob. "And a decorator?"

"So, I run the family US division while exercising my decorating chops, along with several other family holdings—what of it? But look, no time for chats. Tell me where Nicolina is."

"How the hell do I know? Tell me where Noel is."

"We're not trading information here. It doesn't work that way." A cell phone rang in her pocket. She slipped it out and pressed it to her ear.

"Really, both of them? Good. Do what's necessary when you get there," she told the caller.

Returning the phone to one pocket, she pulled a pistol from the other and pointed it at me. "Okay, so we have your friends—Sir Rupert and the other fellow, plus you and your boyfriend. Now all we need is Nicolina and the gold. Where are they?"

"I don't know anything, I said. What about Geoffrey?"

"What about him? I said that pairing him to Nicolina wouldn't solve anything, but my late father thought Geoff could bring her to heel, and so did Geoff, so I agreed. It was a sacrifice to watch him pander to her all these years, when we were meant for one another. Well, I'm tired of pandering, and tired of waiting. Nicolina's been nothing but trouble from day one, and it's time to put an end to it. Where is she? Tell me before I finish off your lover."

"Just stop with this senseless killing and hurting people! What's with you people, anyway?" I lurched to my feet. "Where's Noel? Take me to him right now!"

Susan sprang up and whacked me in the jaw with her pistol butt so fast, I never saw it coming. I slumped back against the marble mantle, holding my cheek.

"That's for trying to keep that blue rug from me, and for harming my men. Lucky for you I didn't set them loose on you, but I may yet. You don't get to give lectures or orders here, Phoebe McCabe. You're in our realm now. Get that through your head while you still have one. Tell me where Niki is before I lose my patience. I'm getting tired of chasing that bitch down. She's got that gold somewhere in this town and I mean to find it."

I struggled not to start bawling again. Hell, I think she loosened a molar. "I honestly don't know. You can beat me all you want, but I still can't tell you what I don't know. She brought me here to assess her villa's antiques, only there weren't any. Then everybody took off and left me in the villa like I was chicken shit. What's with that? Don't I matter? So I took the Maserati and came here to be with Noel. I didn't even know about the gold until a couple of days ago." My sniveling was no act but I was playing it up for my audience. She thought me a weakling so I was playing pathetic to full advantage.

She studied me, pistol steady. "You may actually be telling the truth.

What a pleasant change, since nobody else does. You should have heard that hunk of yours talking on and on about nothing, none of it true. Look where that got him? Still, if you don't know where she's at and neither does he, you're both useless to me. Anyway, we still have Rupert Fox and his henchman so I plan to go ask him myself."

In seconds, she was back on her cell phone, barking at someone in Italian. She dropped the phone into her pocket and rattled something to puppy face, who jumped from his chair and nearly wrenched my arm from my socket in order to prove what a bad boy he was.

She pointed to the door as he yanked me from the room. "Can't get blood on the walls," she murmured, following us out. "Paint covers only so much."

"What are you going to do to me?"

"Take you to your boyfriend, naturally. It's the least I can do."

Puppy face flung me into a dark room. I fell to my knees, trying to adjust my eyes. When the overhead light flicked on, there was Noel crumpled and bloodied on the floor.

"There he is. A bit roughed up, but we left him alive in case you needed more incentive. Looks like that's no longer necessary," Susan said from the door.

I scrambled over to him, moaning at the sight of all the blood, his mangled arm, all the blood. "What have you done to him, you murdering bitch!" I cried.

"You two take a few minutes to say your final farewells, while I go off to meet Sir Rupert. Bet he knows where Niki is. You won't have long. I'm sending Enrico and Gio up to finish you off. Good boys deserve their treats."

The door slammed shut, leaving me alone with Noel.

"Phoebe," he whispered.

I couldn't bear to see him like this, bruised and bloodied, with one arm twisted at an odd angle behind his back, and that beautiful face swollen ... all for me. "What did they do to you? God, I'll kill them for this!"

"Kind of ... not going to happen, girl," he said through swollen lips.

I tried to hoist him to sitting.

"Ah, leave me!" he hissed. "They broke my bloody arm."

"I can make a sling."

"Leave it, I said. They're coming back for us both soon."

I lowered him gently back to the floor. "Noel, I'm sorry."

"You should be. I told you to stay put. You'd be...safe now."

"I don't do safe any better than you." I was crying all over him. I glanced quickly at the door and back to his face, trying to find an unwounded inch I could stroke. "I need to ask you something."

"Like last words?"

"Not if I can help it. Help me figure out how to use these things so we can get out of here."

"You have ... a gun?"

"I have something better—toothpicks, a pen, and a stick of chewing gum."

"Im ... pressive."

"From Evan."

"Show me." He groaned, trying to sit up. I helped him lean against the side of a huge fireplace.

"What do they do?" I asked.

"Not what ... they seem."

"I figured that much. What can I do with the gum?"

"Careful," Noel warned.

The door flew open as I was pulling the gum from my jacket pocket. Enrico and Gio—burn guy and eye guy, now bandaged—stood in the entry looking murderous.

"Hi," I said. "I was just going to enjoy a little chew—spearmint, I think. Do you mind?"

Burn guy pulled his lips back into a sort of smile—he was having trouble moving his scorched lips—and sauntered forward to whip the stick from my fingers.

"Be careful with that," I warned. Why was I warning him? Who was trying to kill whom here?

He offered the stick to eye guy, like the nice dude he was.

"Wait, I'm serious. Don't take my gum," I said.

"Phoebe," Noel hissed. "Let them have it."

"No!" and I meant it. Suddenly, I didn't want to kill anybody. "Leave it alone!"

Meanwhile, eye guy was shaking his head, so Gio—or maybe it was Enrico—popped it in his mouth and chewed with exaggerated satisfaction.

Noel grabbed my arm, shoving me inside the walk-in marble fireplace, using his body to shield mine. We huddled for mere seconds before the explosion rocked the house.

🏶 27 🏶

hat had I done?

"The chimney's going to give! Move!" Noel rasped, shoving me into the room.

I couldn't see. Darkness and dust choked my lungs. I took two steps, one foot diving into nothingness before he hoisted me back with his good arm. "Stay behind me," he hissed.

"You're in worse … shape than … me," I coughed.

He was pushing me and I was stumbling. Pandemonium exploded around us. Men screamed, somebody called out. Noel kept pushing, I kept stumbling. I tripped once, recovered, and lunged on, gripping his hand. Together we half-climbed, half-slid, down the stairs until we reached the door.

The chandelier was rocking violently as I turned to see a man on the stairs behind us. He raised his gun just as the ceiling cracked open and the floor crashed on top of him in a roiling wave of dust.

Noel flung me onto the street and fell to his knees beside me. We watched, stunned, as the house collapsed in on itself, and a fire ignited somewhere deep in the chaos.

"All that for a stick of gum?"

Beside me Noel bent his head to the ground. The explosion must have hurt him even more. "Oh, Noel. Come on, we can't stay here!"

I urged him back to his feet. He was such a mess, yet he'd come this far. He lurched forward, me helping. I kept thinking how, even with the Camorra, he kept protecting me with everything he had. "We've got to get back to Foxy's place through the tunnels. Can't risk the street. Which way?"

"Here."

No one saw the two bloodied plaster-smeared survivors lurching up the street. We would have looked like something out of a horror movie had anyone noticed, but the sirens and shouting tore all interest in another direction.

We kept to the back lanes. Noel sagged multiple times, and once fell so hard to his knees, I didn't think I could get him back up.

"Just a bit farther," I urged. "We'll get to Foxy's house, I'll get a doctor-"

"No ... doctor," he growled, heaving himself up and moving again. One arm dangled limp, his face so swollen he could barely see without tipping his head up to peer through his eyes.

"You've got to get a doctor!"

"Over ... here," he whispered.

It was nothing but a boarded-up door sized for minipeople tucked into an alley wall.

"We can't get through that."

He didn't answer, just kicked the planks until they cracked open, and then forced me to my knees and through. I stopped trying to talk after that. The rest of the way was nothing but blind stumbling through the blackest dark while wheezing in stale air.

And yet, he knew which direction to take, plunging into each dark tributary with an unerring sense of direction, sometimes nudging me forward if I hesitated.

We broke into a wider corridor I felt rather than saw, and still he stumbled on.

"This way," he croaked.

After a few minutes, he turned right, lumbered along for a few moments more, and fell to his knees. "Up ahead. You have the ... keys?"

"I've hidden them, but I can't find them in the dark," I hissed.

Noel shook his head. "Think ... I'm done."

"No, get up!"

Lights flooded the corridor across from us. I turned, listening to the faint sounds of motorcycles echoing against the stone somewhere deep in the warren.

"Someone's coming," I whispered. I scrambled across the tunnel using the light to help locate my hidey-hole. I poked out the keys and pressed the door opener.

When I returned, Noel was on his back. I shook him, but his head just lolled side to side.

"Get up!"

The wall was scraping open, the bikes growing closer, and I was still trying to hoist a full-grown man to his feet.

Finally I got him upright and moving. I used his parked bike to prop him up until the door opened far enough to shove him through. By then a man was shouting and another answering in the tunnel beyond. The bikes —more than one—roared closer.

I was trying to force the door shut before it had fully opened. *Hell, Foxy, you've got to fix this thing!* Oh, God, I just hoped he'd be in good enough shape to fix something.

Only when the wall reached its full open position would it deign to begin closing. I pressed hard on the fob, as if that helped. All I needed was for those guys to see us, and the game would be over.

The wall continued to inch across. The bikes roared closer. I heard men's voices over the roar of the engines, snatches of English. I chewed on my bottom lip and kept pressing the fob.

"Here."

I turned. Noel was pointing to a wall switch I'd missed. "Faster."

I flicked the switch and the door efficiently slid shut. "Well, damn." I shuddered. So close, too close. "Noel, we've got to get you upstairs."

I turned to see him propped against the wall, out cold. On the opposite wall, the monitor showed shadow figures running past the camera.

"We made it." I crouched beside him, trying to nudge him awake. "Noel, wake up. I think I know where Nicolina went."

He opened one eye, or at least tried to. "Where?"

"Civita di Bagnoregio. I saw the promontory on Google. It matches the paintings."

He nodded. "Go."

"And leave you? Wait here." I leapt up the stairs, returning with water, bandages, bread, and cheese, plus a cloth wrapped in a baggie of ice cubes.

He was out again.

"Noel," I whispered. "Wake up." I gently sponged the dirt and blood from his face. He groaned, tried to squeeze his eyes open. "Drink this." I made him swallow a couple of painkillers with water. "I'm going to call a doctor, then I've got to get help for the others. Susan Rafuse, the decorator, is Camorra, and Nicolina's husband is in this somewhere, too. They've got Foxy and Evan! Come, let's get you upstairs. Can you hear me?"

"No time," he gasped, pushing away. "Go. Help them."

"But I can't just leave you, I said."

"Leave ... me!" He coughed.

"No!"

"For Christ's ... sake ... Phoebe ..."

"But I can't do anything!" I wailed.

"Yes ... you ... can."

"You need help."

"Call Toby. My phone ... and bike keys ... kitchen ..."

I ran back upstairs, retrieved his phone, plucked up the keys from the table, and returned, shutting the kitchen/basement door behind me.

When I got back downstairs, Noel was coughing up blood. "Noel!" I fell to my knees beside him. He held out his hand. I dropped the phone into it and watched him unlock the password.

"Toby's 'Neptune,'" he managed, the phone sliding from his grip.

I picked the thing up, scrolling through until I could speed-dial for Neptune. A mechanical answering machine told me to leave a message. "Toby, Phoebe here. Noel's hurt badly. We're here at Foxy's, in Orvieto. Noel's bleeding everywhere! Oh, god! Send help. I love you!"

Bawling like a baby, I leaned over Noel, trying to sponge his face.

"Stop. Phoebe ...." he murmured.

"Yes?"

"Go .... help ... them."

"No!" I almost shouted the word.

Then he slid to one side, eyes closed. I tried to rouse him again and again, but this time he stayed under. I couldn't leave him but what if I could do something to help Foxy and Nicolina? Then again, what if leaving this man meant letting him die? Toby was hundreds of kilometers away on a bloody boat. So, stay with this man, who was wounded and needed me, or risk the deaths of three people I probably couldn't save anyway?

Finally, I stood up. "I'm going, then. I'll take your bike."

Noel didn't respond and his breathing was becoming more labored.

I kept on talking. And crying. "You stay in the cantina, okay? In case someone manages to breech the house's defenses. Can you hear me?"

He clearly didn't. I placed the phone in his lap, checked the monitor to see the tunnels empty, and flicked the door open.

I was straddling the bike while the door slid shut, thinking I needed to discover how to work the other Foxy tricks I'd pocketed—were they all explosives? Tips on driving a big powerful motorcycle would help, too, but at least I knew the basics.

And then a man barked: "Stop right there!"

❦ 28 ❧

Something dug into my back. "Get off the bike, nice and slow, and turn around." English accent. I couldn't believe it!

Another man spoke in Italian-laced English somewhere behind me. "You are under arrest for criminal activities in the country of Italy regarding murder, extortion, and the acquisition of stolen antiquities." He proceeded to translate in Italian.

"You've got to be kidding me!" I cut him off. "I'm not Camorra!" I turned to the man with the gun, squinting into the flashlight. "I don't have time for this, Walker. It'll take maybe twenty minutes to get across to Civita di Bagnoregio before the Camorra kill Sir Rupert Fox , Evan, and Nicolina Boyd—oh, and take the Etruscan gold. Are you going to help me or not?"

The hand dropped. "Phoebe McCabe?"

"Yes, me. I know I don't look like myself, but I can explain later." With me under the helmet, he couldn't see the worst of it.

"You've got blood all over you", he said, angling down the flashlight over my hands.

The sight of Noel's blood broke me up all over again. "More people will die—if we don't get going," I sobbed.

"Open up the door," the Italian agent ordered, stepping forward. "We will apprehend your companion, Noel Halloren."

"Noel Halloren—really? We don't have time for this, I said." I couldn't the men's faces through their helmets but I sensed Walker calculating.

"The Camorra are after Rupert Fox and Nicolina Boyd," I said through my sobs. "I just blew up a Camorra stronghold back there, but there's more of them on their way to Civita. There's like a swarm of them. Are you just going to stand there? Let's go!"

I prayed to the gods and goddesses that everything I'd done would not be for nothing, but every wasted minute dragged me closer to futile.

"You're responsible for that explosion?" Walker asked in disbelief.

"Yeah, but I didn't expect a little wad of gum to make such a mess. Could we just go?"

Walker turned to his companion. "Luigi, I know her. She's a boatload of trouble, but she's probably telling the truth—mostly. Let's follow her to this Civita."

The Italian agent nodded. "We will go to Civita. Lead the way, Signorina."

"You lead the way, agent. I haven't a clue how to get there, and we need the fastest route. I was planning on winging it anyway. No time to read a map. Let's go!" I revved the engine in emphasis.

Seconds later, we were zooming through the underground tunnels on our motorcycles—Luigi first, then me, with Walker bringing up the rear.

Driving a road hog motorcycle is not like driving a lesser model, I soon realized, especially in a tunnel. It's more like clinging to a powerful wobbly horse throbbing between your legs. What I lacked in finesse, I made up in determination because at least I knew how to work the gears and drive fast.

Bad enough I was leaving Noel behind, at least I had to make it count.

The Italian agent knew his way through the tunnels and rode that bike with expert precision. Not me. I prayed I could get onto the road and out into fresh air in one piece.

Thoughts of Noel stabbed all my vulnerable places, so I tried fixing on the goal, instead: Get to Foxy, Evan, and Nicolina; keep the Camorra from inflicting more damage. Forget about how. How could come later, but at least now I had help.

We broke out into the night, zipping down the streets of Orvieto, past firetrucks and police cars, the air screaming with sirens. I wove in and around the onlookers, trying to keep up with the agent ahead, catching glimpses of the billowing smoke illuminated in the city lights. God, I was responsible for that? I just killed and wounded human beings—bad human beings, maybe, but humans still. Maybe I did what I had to do, but it felt like death and destruction.

The road curved through the city, out the gates, and down the plateau towards the valley. Agent Luigi gunned his bike, taking every corner like a pro, while I gritted my teeth and mimicked his actions. Soon we were weaving through the countryside, following tiny roads twisting among fields and vineyards tangled in mist with a half moon hanging in the sky above. The motorcycle and I became one.

Would Foxy even be alive when we reached Civita? What if I'd miscalculated and that wasn't Nicolina's hideout? What if they were already dead and the Camorra had the gold? Was this my fault? Could I have stopped this somehow if I'd been smarter, braver, more in tune? And what if Noel died from his wounds because I left him?

And what if Noel died?

God, I couldn't keep doing this. I had to shut that head-voice up.

After maybe twenty minutes, we picked up a sign for the Commune of Bagnoregio. Soon after, headlights appeared behind us, rapidly gaining. It could have been anyone, friend or foe, but when Walker hung back to check, someone fired a gun, which settled the question.

I nearly lurched off the bike when the second blast cracked. We were so exposed! Where in hell could we hide?

Walker raced up beside me. "Cut across the field ahead! Follow the other agent!" he yelled.

"What about you?"

"Forget me." He was talking into a mike, in touch with the other agent by radio. "Do as I say!" he barked before hanging back. Did he think he could delay that car by himself—one exposed cyclist taking on a car of armed bastards? Couldn't think about that, either.

Hands slick on the handlebars, I fixed on Luigi's shrinking taillight, cringing every time a shot ripped the air. By the time he plunged off the road into a field, the headlights had dropped out of sight.

We bounced and lurched between the narrow plantings, cutting along ruts so narrow, leaves and vines whipped against us as we hurled past. Once, the helmet slipped over my eyes, nearly sending me flying. I shoved it back and powered on, fear like bile freezing in my chest. Wisps of mist tangled among the vines, spooky and otherworldly.

When we burst onto the road again and began climbing upward, I thought we'd made it, that we'd shaken the bastards, and were on the final stretch. Then a car careened around the corner behind us. Luigi slowed down, signaling me to pass him as he took on the approaching car. I zoomed on. They were cops. They knew what they were doing.

I, on the other hand, did not.

I drove like a madwoman because I was.

Where the hell was Civita? Nothing ahead but this sleeping gray-stone town. I gunned it straight, rounding a bend, nearly yipping in relief when I saw a sign pointing ahead. The bike in full throttle, I hurled down a walled avenue funneling towards some unknown destination.

Shots fired far over the hills. I hoped to God the agents were all right, but I couldn't go there. I broke into a paved lot with five erratically parked cars abandoned beside a stone building. Two Fiats sat nose-in next to the wall. Where the hell was Civita? Not that hulk of stone that said BAR above two stone gateposts? The place looked dead.

I zoomed between the posts, thinking that at least the car couldn't follow me here. A shadowy sea of mist rose from the valley floor. I had arrived on a plateau but where was the town?

When I heard car doors slamming behind me, I knew they'd caught up. A man shouted. They were on foot now chasing me in. I spun the bike around, desperate for a path, a sign. Nothing but picnic tables clustered on a patio in a small park—no tower, no village. I bit back a scream of frustration. Terror gripped my chest as footfalls pounded on the path behind me.

Something far off in the distance caught my attention—a ghost ship sailing the fog? I zipped the bike straight ahead, only to screech to a halt at a dead-end look-off. The ghost ship reappeared briefly, then quickly concealed again in a cloud of fog. Spinning around, I zoomed back, realizing I was heading right towards the men, but stymied as to where else to go.

I didn't look at them, couldn't look at them, but a flash glance registered three figures running forward. I veered away, heading towards a wooded fringe just as a bullet ricocheted off the fender. The second shot blasted the front tire, sending me hurling. I grabbed a tree branch just before the bike crashed.

In seconds, I had dropped to my feet and was lunging towards the whirring machine, the men's footsteps pounding closer.

The bike's front wheel had crumpled, and it took me too many seconds to disentangle my carpet bag from the wreckage. But I needed it. I flung the bag over my shoulder just as the men reached the woods. The mist had thickened enough that they couldn't see me, and I prayed they'd be drawn to the bike's headlights first.

Hobbling now, I stumbled through the fog-fused thicket, blind. The margin of trees hugged a cliff but I could see nothing beyond.

I nearly fell into a deep stairwell. Hesitating only seconds, I tossed down the carpet bag and jumped, trying to land on my good leg. I hit the bag with my knee, my hand grazing the concrete, with one ankle twisting beneath me. Shit.shit.shit! Hoisting myself up, I lurched down the steps.

Men shouted overhead. They'd found me. They called out for me to stop in two languages.

At the bottom of the stairs, I turned left, and hobbled on and on, blocking out the sound of shouting men, the pain, the ache in my heart. With the fog intensifying, I lost all sense of direction.

The footbridge came on me so suddenly, I faltered. The ancient town floated before me on its misty sea while the footbridge plunged down, disappearing into the fog before materializing again on the other side. Signs rose all around me; one in particular said CONSTRUCTION in a string of languages.

I turned. Three figures were approaching. One yelled "Halt!"

I plunged down into the gray-black sea and was swallowed whole. Seconds later, I was lost.

❧ 29 ❧

A ghostly soup swirled around me.

The bridge was fixed, the road paved like a narrow lane. Thank god nothing swayed. I knew they'd track me down in a matter of minutes. I had no place to run, no place to hide. I plunged my hand in my bag, grabbing the gun I couldn't see to aim.

Footsteps told me they were gaining on me fast, while I limped down the center of the path like easy prey. I couldn't out-hop them. *So stop. They can hear you, too.*

I slowed to a painful limp, as silent as I could manage, and sneaked over to the guard rail where lamps pushed smudges of light into the dark.

Better to go stealth. Using the railing to lessen my weight, I hitched myself along as the span plunged steadily down. I hopped as silently as possible, my trackers scanning every inch with their flashlights behind me.

Twice I crouched behind a barrel as someone ran past me—a locater scout—and twice he ran back to his companions, muttering in Italian.

The fog and darkness offered some protection, but it couldn't last. Soon, they'd find me. They walked three abreast, thinking to sweep me out, clever bastards but not clever enough. I hopped faster, hoisting myself up in jerky motions as the bridge began angling upward.

I'd never make it, couldn't make it. What about those Foxy items in my pockets? What if I could make another explosion, blow the bridge up, and them with it? No, no good. I'd blow myself up, too. Once was enough.

I didn't see the object until I whammed into it—something hard and metallic, another barrel. A barrel? They appeared every so many yards, a part of the repair work, maybe.

Oh, god, a barrel! Why didn't I notice before? Heart whamming inside my chest, I pushed the thing onto its side and kicked it down the incline.

It bump-bumped down the bridge and walloped at least two of the guys, by the sound of their grunts. Two feet further up, I found another barrel, and another, as if workers had marked off a repair section. Well, thank you, guys, because those barrels maybe saved my life, maybe even broke a knee cap or two.

With my pursuers immobilized and disoriented, I hopped faster, hitching myself towards an ancient gate rising in the mist. I hobbled under an arch into a town slumbering in time. The occasional thinning fog swirled in wisps around the corners of the old building, but nothing else moved.

Those guys would soon recover and come after to me.

I pressed myself into the shadows and risked looking back. Nobody following. Taking a deep breath, I struggled on, limping up a little medieval street flanked by high stone walls, everything carved into rock. My sneakers barely made a sound, yet I felt as though my every move could awaken the dead.

The road opened into a little piazza where houses clustered around a church centuries old. At that moment, stone seemed the coldest, most heartless substance in the universe, and even the fog-wisped lights did nothing to dispel the illusion. And here was I, cocking a pistol like an interloper planning to shoot at phantoms.

Signs pointed to a museum, a soap shop, an olive oil seller, and a couple of trattorias around corners and up tiny lanes. A blue and white tile set into a wall read Via Medina. Via Medina!

I limped straight down a lane pitching downward to the left, the occasional lamp casting a misty light across the cobbles. Past a sign to an Etruscan olive press cave, a deteriorating fountain, and a closed shop, I hobbled on until I reached a corner twisting even deeper down.

The houses here appeared restored, with artful embellishments like potted vines crawling up either side of glossy doors. A lamp shone on the terracotta plaque of 8 Via Medina set into a half-open wrought-iron gate.

The gate squeaked as I stepped inside. Two motorcycles sat parked in the narrow walkway ending at a low wall. Stone steps led up to a flaking turquoise door. Voices drifted down from inside—a man and a woman.

Fear makes a weighty companion. The gun felt too heavy, awkward, and deadly, but I needed it, needed everything I could get.

I slipped past the steps to the back wall, suddenly out of courage. What the hell was I doing? I couldn't just barge in there, a lone woman in a nest of vipers.

I wavered, I trembled. All the pent-up fear and adrenaline pounding over me, reducing me to nothing but bruises and strains and trauma. I couldn't do this, I couldn't!

But I must.

Over my shoulder, the edges of the world dropped into nothingness. The wall, the house, and village itself, clung to the very edge ... like me.

I fixed on the door, inhaled deeply, and took one step forward, then another and another. I dropped my carpet bag on the flagstones and took only the gun, holding it up as if it were a beacon, something to steady me, as if anything could.

At the top of the steps, I paused. The door was ajar, meaning whoever was inside had entered in a hurry, and remained confident no one would follow—or didn't care. The door, a heavy arched thing with brass hinges, barely squeaked when I pulled it open and stepped inside.

I stood a full minute listening. Stairs reached up into the darkness and light washed over the uppermost steps beneath another open door.

I heard nothing. The gun felt slick in my hand. My heart pounded in my ears. I took one step after the other, with my eyes focused on the door. At the top, I held my breath and poked my head around the corner.

A large empty room opened up—scattered rugs over a stone floor, a couch and chairs, a sink and stove, a huge smoldering fireplace. Light poured out from another room to the right.

Slowly, I stepped down into the space, keeping to the wall as I edged towards the light. A table had been knocked over, a painting lay facedown on the floor. There'd been a struggle; someone had fought back hard.

I almost stepped into a puddle of blood. *They've killed somebody!* My hands started shaking so violently, I could barely hold the gun. Voices again, two sets—one from the room down the hall, the other from some-place further away, rumbling and shrilling—beneath my feet. A basement? God, how could I tackle one room of killers, let alone two?

Somebody moaned from the open door ahead. I limped on, gripping the gun with both hands. I reached the door, saw a man bent over with his back to me, saw Rupert slumped against the wall with his eyes closed, saw a body lying facedown on the floor, and knew it was Evan.

"Back away from him or I'll shoot," I said.

❧ 30 ☙

The man swung around. He'd been striking Rupert. He'd been *beating* Rupert!

"B-back against the wall," I ordered.

He didn't move. No gun. His only weapon was his blood-smeared hand.

Evan lay still. *Oh, my god—had he killed him?* Rupert, slumped unconscious, blood dribbling into his eyes.

My mouth went dry. "I said, back *up!*"

The man smiled then, if you could call it that—more like a jerk on one side of his mouth. "You want to kill me, then shoot," he said.

"You think I won't? You think I *can't?*" He must have noticed my hand shaking, but a slow fury began taking over, cooling my nerves. The gun lifted as if on its own, and the words that came next didn't sound like mine. "I could kill you right where you stand, you brutal bastard, and not think twice. Don't tempt me. Move against the wall, back to me, I said."

He hesitated, but stepped over Evan to lean against the other wall, still smirking.

"I told you, *face the wall!*"

Something moved behind me. I whipped around. Two figures hurled forward. I fired. Somebody jerked sideways, the second kept coming. The guy at my back wrestled me from behind, while I fired wild shots at the ceiling, the wall. My pistol flew from my hand.

A woman's voice barked in Italian as the man threw me face-first to the floor. He wrenched my wrists behind my back, as I stared at Evan's battered face. He was still breathing.

"So you knew where it was all along?" I heard Susan Rafuse say overhead.

I tried to turn towards her but the henchman kept me in his grips. "I figured it out," I gasped, wincing as bullyboy tightened the ropes on my wrists. I tried to buck him off but that was pointless. "I guessed."

"Have you guessed also where the gold is hidden?"

I paused. "It's not here?"

"Don't play games, Phoebe. We're running out of time. Flip her over, Gio."

Gio rolled me over. I glanced from his handsome face to Susan's, taking small pleasure in how frayed she looked—dirty face, strain-darkened eyes. "I'm not ... playing ... games." I bit down on the words. Lying on my bound arms hurt like hell.

"You were there when my client's house blew up. What happened?"

"How the hell do I know? One minute your bullyboys are about to beat me senseless, then *kaboom*. Did your idiot henchmen leave too many explosives lying around?"

"Shut up! You have no idea what goes into running an organization like this."

Bingo for that lucky guess. I *knew* that wad of gum couldn't account for all that mess in Orvieto, but must have triggered a larger explosion. "Don't have a clue what it takes to run a bunch of murderers and extortionists, you mean."

"The least you could have done is died in the explosion, and saved me the trouble," she snapped. "Where's the goddamn gold!" She kicked me hard in my leg.

"I don't know, I said. Do I look like I know where gold is? What have you done to them?" I nodded to Rupert and Evan. "Where's Nicolina?"

She laughed. "Look around. What do you think I've done with them? The same thing I'm going to do to you."

"Rupert!" I called. No answer.

Another man entered the room speaking urgent Italian. Susan swung towards him, firing a round of questions, which he answered quickly. As he withdrew, she turned back to me. "If only I had time to do to you what I'd like."

"But you don't. Interpol will be all over this town soon enough."

"Ah, but you'll be dead and we'll be gone. Take her to the basement. Come back for the others."

Gio wrenched me to my feet and hoisted me out the door. He steered me through the house towards the front entrance, then abruptly swung right towards a set of stairs heading down.

I briefly balanced at the top of those steps, witnessing how two tracks gouged into the stone on either side—old, very old—before Gio jerked me forward. He played at flinging me down head first but pulled me back just in time, laughing at his vicious little joke.

"You're just a fun guy, aren't you, Gio?" I said, as he began kicking me downward.

My feet hardly propped me up but the fingers digging into one arm held fast. He released me on the final three steps, sending me hurling, scrambling to keep from smashing face first onto the stone. But I had to land somewhere—if not on my face, then my knees.

I slammed the floor in a brutal kneel.

Seconds ground away as I bent over, waiting for the pain to crash into me. When it hit, Gio had me back on my feet, steering me across some large light-filled cavern, where he flung me against a wall. I glimpsed a windows, easels, and an urn before my face crashed against the stone. I slid back to my knees with a moan.

Footsteps retreated as I fought tears, my head leaning against the rock. My nose bled. Pain blinded me.

"Phoebe, is that you?" A woman's voice.

Lifting my head, I slowly looked around. A cave of some kind, no, a basement, or a studio. Or a mausoleum. A huge stone platform lay ahead, the circular top decorated by a row of marble chests carved with ancient figures—funerary chests, maybe. Propped between urns, portraits of faces, both modern and ancient, peered out. Stone figures reclined atop of sarcophagi, staring into space, some holding paintings in their marble hands. Etruscan hands, modern paintings. I took a deep breath. Must have hit my head hard.

"Phoebe. Here." The voice continued speaking in Italian.

"Nicolina?"

I struggled to stand, couldn't, and fell back down. Cursing, I fought my way back up, stood swaying, and finally stumbled towards the shadows.

Nicolina sat deep in a wall alcove amongst the statuary, hands bound in her lap, beside another, much older, woman. Both sat so still, they could be marble like the ancients surrounding them.

I lurched forward until I could prop myself up at the back of the sarcophagus and stare. "Your grandmother?" I whispered, gazing at the lady beside her. At least ninety, her beauty remained vivid in the blue of her eyes. She sat with her bound hands resting in Nicolina's lap and smiled. I smiled back.

"Alexandria?" I whispered.

"You guessed!" Nicolina said. "I knew you would."

"I only just did." I stared at Alexandria in wonder. Tears glistened in her eyes, but the strength in her bones was unmistakable. "You have lived here all this time?" I asked the older woman.

Nicolina replied. "Yes, this Etruscan olive press is her studio and her home. She escaped my grandfather long ago, to come here. Rupert helped. He bought this house from my grandfather and arranged for her to live here under a false name. My parents knew. My father tried to protect us but ... he could not protect even himself." She struggled to remain composed.

"Rupert bought this place for your grandmother?" I was having trouble grasping this.

Alexandria spoke softly in Italian, Nicolina listening intently. When Nicolina's gaze returned to mine, tears rolled down her cheeks. "She does not understand so much these days, my nona. Much of her memory is gone, but she wants you to know she is happy here all these years. Sir Rupert helped gather all these pieces, her companions. They are Etruscan, many from the necropolis near her home. Beautiful, yes? Their faces are of those passed. So realistic, so filled with love. Time can not erase such love, not even the centuries." She glanced towards the statuary. " The 'faces of ages', she called them. I cannot translate well from the Italian, but they have watched over her while she painted. They are her friends, these beautiful survivors."

Her grandmother spoke again and Nicolina nodded. "She repeats so much. They survived the Romans, the Greeks, and all those that came after. She once told me it has been an honor to be in their company. She has painted among them, and lived among them, and been happy here in this crumbling village. But her mind, like the village, now erodes."

"She hid the gold in the villa and you found it," I said.

Nicolina shook her head vehemently. "There is no gold. I found nothing. You must believe that. My grandmother destroyed it long ago."

And yet I didn't quite believe her. "You brought Rupert and me to the villa for what then?"

"Rupert insisted that we try to find it. He hoped nona might remember, but Susan was tracking me down. I had no idea she wanted the gold and Geoffrey, but he is not worth keeping."

"You married him to appease the Camorra?"

"I thought it would help, yes. He is in very deep with them, but I could not play by their rules."

"Yes, I get that," I said softly.

"You must forgive Rupert, even if you cannot me. He did not know of the Camorra's renewed ... interests. I sent him to the island to keep him safe, and drugged you for the same. It did not work, but please forgive me."

"But all you wanted was to protect your grandmother?"

"Yes! Look how she has survived? How could I let them hurt her, but they will now!" She began sobbing in earnest.

"And where is Sophia and Ricardo?"

"I sent them back to the villa to help you. I did not know you would follow me here."

Her grandmother added something. Nicolina nodded, smiling sadly. "She wants to thank you for coming. She does not understand what is happening."

"Perhaps you shouldn't tell her." My tears rolled unchecked.

"And now you all will die."

I swung around, gripping an Etruscan arm for support. Susan Rafuse stood beside Geoffrey. Behind them, two men lugged the limp bodies of

Rupert and Evan across the open floor to a bare wall. "What are you going to do to us?" I asked.

"We have enough explosives left over from the Orvieto fiasco to make a kitchen gas leak look like an accident," Susan said. "Old women can be so careless."

I tried to laugh. "With bodies in the basement?"

"What's left of you will be scattered somewhere down on the valley floor." She looked past me to the two women. "It doesn't have to be this way, Nicolina. If you told us where the gold is, this will all be over."

"You think I'm stupid?" Nicolina said, tensing against the ropes. "Do you think I don't know that you will kill us anyway? That's what the Camorra do, they kill. The gold is gone, I told you."

"And I don't believe you!" Susan burst out. "End this once and for all! Tell me where it is!"

Alexandria said something terse in Italian.

Susan clenched her fists. "Stop saying that!" she cried. "Do you really expect me to believe you *destroyed* the gold to end this war, you crazy old bag? What kind of fool melts down millions of dollars of ancient gold and then sells it for *food?*"

Alexandria spoke, Nicolina followed. "The kind who wants no more bloodshed, no more deaths. Your family killed my parents. You forced us to live like your slaves for decades. It must end. My grandmother sacrificed the gold to end this war."

"Nicolina, please," Geoffrey stepped forward between the statuary, finally finding his voice. "Don't let it end this way. Tell us where the gold is, and I promise, you will all be released. Your brother and his family will live on safe. I can offer you ..." He lifted one gloved hand as if orchestrating a boardroom deal, but stopped as if it suddenly occurred to him that all his collateral had vanished.

Nicolina hitched a laugh. "Geoffrey, do not take me for a fool! You are bound to this shrew. Has she taken your balls as well as your brains? You are the same as the rest!"

I stopped listening. My attention fixed on the activity behind Susan and Geoffrey. The henchmen had propped Evan and Rupert against the far wall, and one now fiddled with a black box. I'd seen enough movies to recognize detonators and bombs, though I wasn't certain which was which. The black box had blinking lights. Must be a bomb.

One man was heading upstairs. Would he turn on the gas while this one detonated the bomb? The explosion caused by gas and the bomb combined could blow up the whole town.

The man crouched, calling to Susan.

"Enough." Susan cut Geoffrey off mid-sentence. "We have to go. Say goodbye to your soon-to-be-widow, and let's get out of here. Put them against the wall with the others."

Henchman grabbed me first, shoving me across the room to land butt first on the floor beside Evan. While the bullyboy collected Nicolina and Alexandria, I glanced down at Evan. He was badly beaten but unbound. One eye glittered at me through swollen lids. *Playing possum.* I leaned towards him. "I have the toothpicks and a pen from Orvieto in my pocket. What can I do with the toothpicks?" I whispered.

"Impact." His voice scraped.

Impact. "Small or large?"

"Like a ... land mine."

Land mines blew up people and I needed to blow up bullyboy, but I also needed to do something about that bomb. The two were hardly compatible. *Worry about that later. Need to get my hands free.* "Can you get the pen and the toothpicks from my pocket, undo my hands? Left-hand side."

I glanced up. Susan and Geoffrey had gone. Nicolina struggled against the thug trying to drag her away from her grandmother. Her eyes met mine over bullyboy's shoulder. She was creating a diversion. Alexandra inched her way past me, heading for the bomb. *Heading for the bomb!*

I leaned forward far enough for Evan to stick his fingers—two of them broken—into my pocket and fish out the pen and toothpicks. Five inno-cent-looking wood shards and a stupid ballpoint pen. He picked up the pen, clicked up its blade, and sawed at my bindings.

Across the room, Nicolina battled the dude, scratching, kicking.

The knife fell twice. Evan picked up and resumed the sawing.

Nicolina shoved the thug against a funerary urn and he lunged back with a growl.

My gaze shifted left. Alexandria was lifting the bomb in her bound hands and shuffling across the room with it.

"No! Alexandria!" My wrists broke free just as the henchman whacked Nicolina across the face and flung her in the middle of the room.

I sprang forward, tossing the toothpicks across bullyboy's path as he pushed through the statuary towards me. Split-second decision to put my shoulder against an Etruscan nobleman and tip him to the floor. I dove behind a sarcophagus.

The explosion muffled beneath the statue but the floor rumbled. Chunks of marble flew into the air. I prayed the circle of Etruscans took the brunt of the explosion.

After seconds, everything stilled. I crawled out from behind the sarcophagus to see bullyboy's feet sticking out from beneath the rubble and Evan slicing away Nicolina's ropes. Rupert moaned from against the wall, but no one had been hurt further except a few Etruscans, standing with missing appendages and a few shattered urns.

I hoisted myself up and hobbled along, calling for Alexandria.

At first I couldn't see her, couldn't find her, but then the dust cleared, and I saw her standing by an open door. I lurched to her side just as she tossed something beyond. We stood together, the breeze blowing onto our faces as the box hurled down toward the valley, now clear of mist in the rising sun. The explosion that followed rocked the floor.

"Brava!" I said.

"Si, brava!" the countess replied with a nod and a smile. "Buon giorno," she said.

"Buon giorno," I agreed.

We turned as footsteps pounded down the steps—Agent Walker and uniformed policemen, along with Lucca and one of his dudes.

"Nona!" Lucca said, shocked still at the sight of his long-lost grandmother.

"Phoebe!" Walker said, springing towards me, almost as if he wanted to take me in his arms. He stopped. "My god, you look a fright!"

"Thanks. Did you catch them?" I asked.

"Who, the woman and her gang? Yes—we have them in custody, and are rounding up the others now."

"Did you turn off the gas upstairs? They planned to blow the house."

"Hang on," Walker said something to one of the policemen, who dashed back upstairs. He turned back to me. "You're bloody amazing. I heard an explosion down here, too. What happened?"

"An ancient Etruscan sacrificed himself for this lady. Mind if I tell you the rest later? Got to check on a friend." I stumbled across to Rupert, slumping down beside him as the police fanned across the room. I squeezed his hand, so relieved when he squeezed back that I almost started crying all over again.

"Phoebe. Is ... all well?" he whispered.

"I think so. How about you?"

"Yes, you know. I hope I have ... a scar."

"Badge of honor?"

"Yes ... exactly." He forced his head around to look at me and gasped. "My word ... Phoebe, what have you done ... to your hair?"

❧ 31 ❧

Neither Rupert nor Evan suffered lasting physical damage, but both required a few weeks' hospital stay in Rome before being permitted to fly home. Other than bruised kneecaps, a sprained ankle, and an alarming makeover, I emerged relatively unscathed, at least on the outside.

I visited both men every day in the most gorgeous hospital I had ever seen, perched as it was on an isle in the middle of the Tiber river, compliments of Rupert's considerable connections.

Evan, always a man of few words, said very little other than to give my hand a quick squeeze on my first visit. I may have only imagined that his way of looking at me had changed. Maybe he really didn't fix his eyes on me in a significant way. Perhaps that was just a trick of the light, or a result of swelling. In any case, I pretended not to notice. The man always interested me in unsettling ways.

Foxy, however, had plenty to say. "As much as I hate to reiterate, I do not like this look on you at all," Rupert said on the first day he began feeling truly himself. Surrounded by designer arrangements from Europe's foremost floral ateliers, he sat up in bed as if enthroned in accolades. I could just imagine how he publicized our recent adventures.

"It's supposed to be a disguise, Rupert. It was rather stunning initially

—before it got singed in Orvieto. Anyway, it will grow out." Noel's words kept rolling through my head: *Hair is a renewable resource but you are not.* Noel. I left too many things unsaid and now every unspoken thing ached more deeply than all my surface wounds.

"Yes, well, I suppose that's some consolation, but I must say, the combination of that singed black hair and your bruises is all very shocking."

It's true, I did not blend into this stylish city. A Mediterranean pine stood framed in the window across his private room—all deep green curving sweeps—reminding me that even the trees in Italy pulled off a more artistic coif than I could manage on even a good hair day. "I'm avoiding mirrors in the meantime. How are you doing today?"

"You asked me that already, Phoebe. I am improving markedly, as I assured you the first time, and just as I surmised, the doctors think it likely a small scar from the bullet wound will be visible on my arm. Isn't that splendid?"

I couldn't suppress my smile. "You always wanted one of those."

"I had hoped for something slightly more visible that could be borne proudly in testament to my heroic achievements."

"Your modesty will no doubt be advertisement enough."

"But have we not had a thrilling adventure together, and saved two beautiful ladies from a desperate fate? Yes, it is true that I did not reveal the critical details to you, but at least now you understand why."

"Do I? Well, yes I do, and no I don't, but let's not get into all that again. I will say that you actually are a hero in my books—buying that house for Alexandria, helping her live safely and comfortably away from the Count for all those years. That is far more altruistic than I ever gave you credit for. You're not even too miserable over the missing gold, either. This must be the first time you've returned home without any spoils. You are a man of many surprises."

"And you are a woman of amazing determination and resourcefulness. They shall herald your feats throughout the antiquities world, my dear."

"Don't think of heralding anything. These recent events aren't bringing me one step closer to joining you in some kind of antiquities sleuthdom, so don't start scheming. It's not happening."

"'Sleuthdom'? Phoebe, that is not even a word."

"You know what I mean. I adore you, Foxy—though you drive me crazy

—but I'm still trying to play it legal. Working with you means slipping across that line in ways I can't live with."

"Only you've already slipped," he said softly.

I tried brushing the hair from my face, but there wasn't enough left up there to brush. My hand dropped to my lap. "That's not fair. Just because I won't turn people I care about over to the police doesn't mean I'm not on the right side. And, by the way, I still haven't heard from Toby or Noel."

"Keep your voice down, Phoebe—in our line of work, one never knows who's listening—but I have it on good authority that you will be hearing from Toby soon."

"Noel's all right?"

"I told you yesterday that he is recuperating somewhere safe. Nothing has changed, except possibly today he is measurably more recuperated. Now, do calm down and leave this all to me."

"Why don't they contact me themselves? Why can't I have my own brother on speed-dial?"

"Because to do so is ill-advised and will risk you all, you know that. Your Walker monitors everything. My word Phoebe, we've had this discussion again and again. You do sound so plaintive when you carry on like this. It quite causes my wound to ache horribly. Now hush, someone comes."

We looked to the door as Nicolina stepped into the room, a vision of her own innate elegance in a deep claret-toned cashmere dress. Even her bruises seemed artful somehow. It was that Italian thing again. I stood up to greet her.

"Phoebe," she said, holding out her arms to me. "Many times I have hoped to see you here. Our phone conversations have not been enough." She enveloped me in an embrace scented of sun-warmed gardenias, kissing the air on either cheek. "Oh, your poor dear hair. So sad! I owe you so much. I am so very sorry." Pulling away, she kept hold of my hands and peered deeply into my eyes. "You have forgiven me, yes?"

"Of course, Nicolina, really. I do understand."

"And have you thought about my offer to join Lucca, Nonna, and me for a few days on the Amalfi? He wishes to apologize properly for his poor behavior, and so do I. You must see our family at its best, see how we are happy again, happy thanks to you. And my nonna, I know she so would love to have you with us."

"Thank you, Nicolina. I would enjoy that, but I don't want to impose on you now that you are finally together as a family. It's enough that you've opened your apartment to me here in Rome. Besides, I really need to return to London. Max is badgering me for details and I've told him he has to wait only a few days longer."

"Oh, but slightly more than a few days," Rupert interrupted from his floral throne. "Did you not tell me that that tiresome agent of yours insists that you fly back together?"

"Yes, he says I'll never get anywhere as long as I look nothing like my passport photo. Still, he's expecting to leave no later than Sunday, after he finishes up whatever paperwork is necessary to extradite Geoffrey and Susan."

"And today is only Wednesday, so truly you do, indeed, have sufficient time for a respite on the Amalfi," Rupert pointed out. "How special would it be to enjoy that exalted coast in such esteemed company. And there is the little matter of my luggage. I hesitated to bring it up earlier—well, in truth, I wasn't in any condition to bring up anything—but Phoebe, all my luggage remains in Nicolina's villa, and though I can have it shipped, it would be best if you could accompany it back to London. I will pay all associated costs, of course, but I would rather it arrive in your care than be entrusted to some oaf in a shipping company."

"I'm sure you have very reliable oafs on call for your shipping needs, Rupe, but, yes, I'll handle that for you." Really, that was the least I could do.

Nicolina smiled down at me. "See, it is settled. We will fly to Naples this evening and you will be my proper guest."

And so we did. What followed turned into the vacation any woman would crave—relaxing days spent on one of the world's most beautiful coasts, a guest in not one, but two gorgeous villas, both Lucca's own, and now also Nicolina's, since the Count had offered to share the family properties. The Count was all graciousness, and Nicolina her warm, engaging self. I enjoyed Alexandria's company and ate far too much.

For a few days, I allowed the sun to warm my skin, the hours to heal my trauma, and some tiny bit of the ache inside my heart to lessen, though I knew I'd carry the worst of it back home.

On the day my respite ended and I was due to return to the neglected villa and collect the luggage before flying on to London, Alexandria, Nicol-ina, and I waited in the driveway as the car pulled up to deliver us further along the coast.

"This may be my last visit to the villa, too," Nicolina said. "We have no desire to return to a place that represents so many broken dreams. We will sell it now. That is best. Allora, let us go."

I nodded, gave her grandmother a farewell hug, and climbed into the car. Minutes later, we were sailing through Naples toward the vivid Amalfi Coast, both Nicolina and me in the back seat, lost in our thoughts. The miles were sailing by when a text message pinged on my phone. I fished out my iPhone and read: *Where Neptune gazes out to sea.*

I read the words over and over again, hardly daring to believe their meaning. Toby and Noel were waiting for me on the villa's jetty? They knew I was heading there and they were waiting! My excitement bubbled like a pent-up geyser. This had to be Foxy's doing, Foxy who made things happen for me as much as to me.

When the car had finally come to a halt, I restrained myself from running down those lemon-garlanded stairs straight to the water's edge. Nicolina might not know of the assignation, though I suspected she knew everything. Still, I couldn't risk exposing her to even more police scrutiny. In the event the police questioned her about my connections, I wanted her to say truthfully that she knew nothing, because she didn't. It was chal-lenging enough that she had Camorra entanglements, let alone add in my black market relations. So far, we'd all emerged from potential legal wran-gling rather well.

Ricardo met us at the steps and we went together to the upstairs rooms to supervised loading the luggage. I made sure that my roller bag, plus the two Foxy had given me, was added to Rupert's substantial pile, before making my excuses to retreat for a bit of air. Nicolina insisted I take my time, that I still had at least a couple of hours before I had to meet Sam Walker at the Naples airport.

Once out of sight, I hobbled down the steps between the sentry of gods and goddesses towards the sea, breathing in the salt air, reveling in anticipation. Noel, this time I'd tell him what he needed to hear, what I needed to say.

The moment I reached the bottom, I saw the boat bobbing out in the cove.

"Phoebe McCabe?"

I swung around. A tall blond guy stood in the shadows. "I'm Bruce Cox, friend of your brother's. He's waiting for you on board. Here, I'll take you over."

We zipped in a Zodiac across the waves to Toby's expansive yacht. It was all I could do not to try leaping up those metal stairs regardless of my ankle. Still, I managed to reach topside and lunge into my brother's arms in record time.

"Phoebe!"

I squeezed him hard, luxuriating in one of those priceless moments when siblings are finally together, and have the good sense to celebrate it. I wanted that hug to last forever, commit to memory every detail—the feel of his love, the azure glow of the sea over his shoulder, the bristles of his beard against my cheek. "Toby!"

I pulled away, my tears dampening my bruised cheek. "I needed to see you so badly." I gazed at him. His skin, a mass of freckles around his full beard, had assumed a burnished glow. He'd filled out since I saw him last year, as if my big brawny brother had ripened in the sun, his wheelchair shrinking correspondingly under the force of his presence.

"Life on the run suits you," I said.

"It's life on the sail. I'm at sea, doing work I love, and if it weren't for the fact that I'm a criminal and can't see my sister on a regular basis, life would be mighty fine."

"They won't stop looking for you."

"I know, I know." He stoked my head, oblivious of my ravished hair. "Lord, girl, I can't believe what you've done—kicked a dent in the Camorra, helped save the day."

"It's not like we ended the Camorra forever more. There are still plenty left, but at least we broke the kneecaps of one branch. Susan Rafuse and Nicolina's husband are on their way to jail, though both Italy and the US want to try Susan."

I sat beside Toby's captain's chair, holding his hand, trying to keep from scanning the cabin for signs of Noel, or asking for him too soon. He must be below deck in one of the cabins. "I couldn't have done any of it without

Noel's help. He saved my neck multiple times. You got the message I sent from Orvieto?"

"Yes, it came through, but we already had a couple of guys heading there by then. We broke into Foxy's hole through the tunnel door—well, I didn't naturally, but my men did. It wasn't easy. Noel was in pretty bad shape by then, but still alive, but—"

"But how is he now? Where is he?" I didn't even last a full minute.

"He's safe and in good hands."

I stared. "You mean ... he's not here?"

"No, Phoebe," Toby said, taking my hand again. "He needed more care than we could give him on board. He's in a medical facility on an island, tucked far enough away that Interpol can't trace him. Did you think he'd be with me?"

"Well, I'd hoped. It's just that I needed to tell him something ..." I let the rest of my words hang, not daring to speak further. Toby sat there, reading my face.

"Is there something you want me to tell him?" he asked after a moment.

I shook my head. This was one message that required a personal delivery, though I didn't know how or when.

After that, I tried focusing on Toby alone, shoving thoughts of Noel as far back in my heart as I could manage. Our visit was brief enough—only twenty minutes—so maybe it was best that Noel hadn't been there.

But I didn't believe that.

Later, I met Sam Walker at the Naples airport. By then I was tired of the interrogation he and the Italian police had put me through over the days since Civita, and I only wanted time to think. I didn't encourage conversation, and he took the hint. He did cock an already overcocked eyebrow in the direction of substantial luggage retinue, however.

"They're not mine," I said. "Since Rupert and his assistant are both in hospital, I agreed to supervise the return of his luggage to London. The man changes clothes every few hours."

Walker whistled. "Unbelievable."

He was too deep into conversations with uniformed custom and immigration officials to pay much attention after that. We were cleared through a special section, the Italian officials whisking us away from the tourist lines, and through some kind of expedited clearance. Arrivals in England followed a similar route. Here, Walker fast-tracked us through the hoards at customs. It paid to have a well-known Interpol agent in attendance.

Max was waiting as I steered the mounds of luggage through the doors into Heathrow's arrival hall. At first, he didn't recognize me, and I could have probably walked right past him, the poor little charred punkster with the mound of designer luggage.

"Max?"

"Bloody hell!" His gaze flew from me to the baggage and back again.

"It's not mine, but Foxy's," I explained.

Two men approached. I recognized Rutger, Foxy's security guard. "Evening Ms. McCabe. Sir Rupert requested I manage the transport of his baggage back into the city."

"Go ahead. I'm happy to get it off my hands."

I linked arms with Max and proceeded to answer most of his questions on the way to the parking lot. He had plenty, and the more I responded, the more intense they became. In fact, they continued all the way from the airport to London, into the gallery, and up the steps to my apartment.

"I can't bloody believe you put yourself at risk like that," he said for the fifth time.

"Okay, okay, Max, enough. These were extenuating circumstances, and I just got dragged deeper and deeper. Can we just let the thing drop until tomorrow?"

"But what about Noel, what about my son?"

"He agreed to see you. He did, Max. That's something, isn't it?"

The front buzzer rang. We looked at one another. "Who'd be ringing the bell this time of night?" he asked. "Stay here. I'll go check."

While he dashed downstairs, I ran my bath, and stared at myself in the mirror. First thing the next day, I had to go to a salon and see if somebody could lessen the disaster happening on my scalp.

"It's just the rest of your bags," I heard Max call from the living room.

"What bags?" I asked, joining him.

Foxy's two designer rollers looked incongruous perched on my scatter rug beside baskets of overflowing yarn. "Those aren't mine, they're Foxy's. I don't know why Rutger dropped them off here."

"They have your name on them," Max pointed out. "Do you mean, they really aren't yours?"

"No. Rupert selected some clothes for me to wear on the Amalfi Coast but I refused."

"Did you pack these bags yourself?"

I laughed. "You sound like a ticket agent: 'Did you pack your bags yourself?' Of course not, they're from Foxy, I said. What are you doing?"

"What's it look like?"

It looked like he was breaking open the brass lock mechanism and tossing the couture duds onto the floor. It looked like he was slicing open the bottom of the suitcase with his Swiss army knife, and revealing some kind of false bottom.

He lifted five velvet pouches and gently plucked a pair of gold earrings from one. "They are magnificent—Etruscan, maybe fifth century B.C."

"Oh, my god," I whispered, slapping my hand to my mouth. "I just smuggled a fortune of Etruscan gold into Britain!"

"I warned you about Foxy. Welcome to the dark side, Phoebe."

ABOUT THE AUTHOR

JANE THORNLEY is a Canadian author of mystery and suspense who lives in Nova Scotia. Though both a writer and a designer, Jane has lived many lives including teacher, school principal, software consultant, superintendent of schools, and librarian. She also has also lead tour groups around the world, including Italy, Turkey, and Morocco.

When she's not traveling, Jane lives a very dull life. Luckily her imagination makes for it.

Join her newsletter to keep up with new releases, prizes, books, gifts, and deleted scenes. Join here: www.janethornley.com

And please leave a review. Reviews are very appreciated always!

Made in the USA
Coppell, TX
07 July 2021